THE OUTLAWS OF THE MARSH
VOLUME 2

SHI NAI'AN AND LUO GUANZHONG

TRANSLATED BY SIDNEY SHAPIRO

ADAPTED AND REVISED
BY
COLLINSON FAIR

The Outlaws of the Marsh, v2

Luo Guanzhong

Translated by Sidney Shapiro

Adapted and Revised by Collinson Fair

Copyright 2007 Silk Pagoda

ISBN: 1-59654-376-0

Silk Pagoda is an imprint of Disruptive Publishing.

CHAPTER 51

WINGED TIGER BRAINS BAI XIUYING WITH HIS RACK

BEAUTIFUL BEARD LOSES THE PREFECT'S LITTLE SON

"A band of travellers were passing the forest along the highway when our men stopped them," said the messenger. "One is Constable Lei Heng from Yuncheng Town. Chieftain Zhu Gui has invited him to the inn, where he is now being wined and dined. I was sent to report."

Chao Gai and Song Jiang were overjoyed. Together with Wu Yong, they went down the mountain. Zhu Gui had already ferried their guest to the Shore of Golden Sands. Song Jiang hastily kowtowed.

"It's been a long time since we parted," he said. "I've thought of you often. What brings you to our humble abode?"

Lei Heng returned the courtesy. "I was sent on official business by my local county to the prefecture of Dongchang. On the way back, I was stopped at the crossroads by bandits who demanded passage money. When I mentioned my name, brother Zhu Gui insisted that I stay with him for a while."

"A Heaven-sent good fortune!"

Song Jiang invited Lei Heng to the fortress, introduced him to the leaders, and feted him with wine. For five days, they met and chatted every day. Chao Gai inquired after Zhu Tong.

"He's now the warden of our county jail," said Lei Heng. "The new magistrate is very fond of him."

Song Jiang brought the conversation around to Lei Heng joining the band. But the constable said: "My mother is very old. I can't abandon her. I'll join you after she's lived out her final years."

He kowtowed and bid them farewell. Try as he might, Song Jiang could not persuade him to remain. The other leaders presented him with precious gifts, as did, of course, Song Jiang and Chao Gai.

Lei Heng went down the mountain with a large bundle of gold and silver. The leaders saw him off to the foot of the road. There he was ferried across to the highway and returned to Yuncheng. Of that no more need be said.

As to Chao Gai and Song Jiang, on coming back to Fraternity Hall they requested Wu Yong, military advisor of the stronghold, to determine the assignments of the various leaders. Wu Yong consulted with Song Jiang and, the following day, all were summoned to hear the dispositions. The first were those in the inns on the outer perimeter.

"Sun Xin and Mistress Gu were tavern-keepers originally," said Song Jiang. "We're instructing them to replace Tong Wei and Tong Meng, for whom we have another use. Shi Qian shall help Shi Yong, Yue Ho shall help Zhu Gui, Zheng Tianshou shall help LiLi. Thus, we will have taverns to the north, east, south and west, each selling wine and meat, and each with two chieftains, to receive bold fellows from all over. Ten Feet of Steel and Stumpy Tiger Wang shall hold the lower part of the rear mountain and look after the horses. The small fort at the Shore of Golden Sands shall be commanded by the brothers Tong Wei and Tong Meng. The small fort at Duck's Bill Shore shall be held by uncle and nephew Zou Yuan and Zou Run. The road in front of the mountain shall be guarded by a troop of cavalry under Huang Xin and Yan Shun. Xie Zhen and Xie Bao shall hold the first pass in the front of the mountain, Du Qian and Song Wan the second, Liu Tang and Mu Hong the third. The three Ruan brothers shall guard the water fortifications on the south side. Meng Kang shall continue to be in charge of boat building. Li Ying, Du Xing and Jiang Jing shall supervise all money, grain, and gold. Tao Zongwang and Xue Yong shall control building and repair of rampart walls and terraces. Hou Jian shall govern the making of clothes, armor, banners and military garments. Zhu Fu and Song Qing shall arrange the feasts. Mu Chun and Li Yun shall build the housing and the palisades. Xiao Ran and Jin Dajian shall deal with all correspondence and documents regarding guests. Pei Xuan shall head the legal department, and dispense rewards and punishments. Lu Fang, Guo Sheng, Sun Li, Ou Peng, Ma Lin, Deng Fei, Yang Lin and Bai Sheng shall control the stronghold's various hostels. Chao Gai, Song Jiang and Wu Yong will live on the summit in the center, Hua Rung and Qing Ming will live to the left, Lin Chong and Dai Zong will live to the right—all within the fortress. Li Jun and Li Kui will live on the front of the mountain, Zhang Heng and Zhang Shun on the rear. Yang Xiong and Shi Xiu will protect both sides of Fraternity Hall."

The assignments having been made, one chieftain, was feasted each successive day. The organization of the mountain fortress was now tight and efficient.

After leaving Liangshan Marsh, Lei Heng, shouldering his pack and carrying his halberd, made tracks for Yuncheng. At home he saw his mother and changed his clothes. Taking the official reply, he called on the magistrate in the county office, reported verbally, and handed over the various documents and endorsements. Then he returned home to rest.

As usual he signed in and checked out at the county office every day, while awaiting a new assignment. He was walking down a street one day when a voice hailed him from behind.

"When did you get back, Constable?"

Lei Heng turned around. It was an idler known as Li the Second.

"Only a couple of days ago."

"You were gone for quite a while. Maybe you haven't heard. A travelling singer has come from the Eastern Capital. She's beautiful and talented. Her name is Bai Xiuying. The wench called to see you but you were out on a mission. She's performing at the theater now. She sings all kinds of ditties. They put on a variety show every day there —dancing, music, and singing. The place is jammed. Why don't you go and have a look? She's a delicious little actress."

Lei Heng, having nothing better to do, went to the theater with Li the Second.

Placards in letters of gold had been put up all around the entrance, and from a flagpole a vertical banner hung down almost to the ground. They went in and took the first seats on the left. A preliminary-act comedian was performing on stage. Li left Lei Heng in the crowd and slipped out for a drink.

After the comedian finished an old man came out. He wore a bandanna covering his forehead, a tea-colored silk gown bound by a black waist sash, and carried a fan.

"Bai Yuqiao from the Eastern Capital, that's me. I rely in my old age on my daughter Xiuying, who sings and dances and plays musical instruments. We travel all over and entertain."

A gong crashed and the girl came on stage. She bowed in each direction. She plied her stick against the gong with such rapidity that it sounded like scattering peas. Then she cut it short with one sharp blow and recited:

Twittering fledglings soar as old birds return,
Gaunt grow the old sheep while lambkins wax fat,
Men struggle a lifetime for clothing and food,
But lovebirds fly freely to where pleasure is at.

Lei Heng shouted his applause.

"Next on my program," said the girl, "is a romantic story called: 'A Love Pursues in Yuzhang City.'" She spoke a few words and began to sing, alternately talking and singing while the audience in the mat-awning-covered courtyard roared approvingly.

Just as Xiuying reached the climax of the tale, the old man interrupted.

"'Though not such a skill as earns horses and gold, it moves men of intelligence,'" he averred. "You gentlemen have applauded. Now, daughter, come down. The next act is rattling the drum with money..."

The girl took up a platter, pointed at it, and chanted: *I'll go to the rich, halt where there's gain, pass when I'm lucky, and head for prosperity.* When I place this before you, don't let it go away empty."

"Walk among them, daughter. Which one of you gentlemen will start us off?"

Holding the platter, the girl approached Lei Heng. The constable groped in his purse. He hadn't a penny.

"I forgot my money today. I'll bring you some tomorrow."

Xiuying laughed. "'If the first brew of vinegar isn't strong, the second is sure to be even flatter.' Sitting in a front seat, you ought to set a good example."

Lei Heng reddened. "I didn't bring any money. It's not that I'm unwilling."

"You remembered to come to hear me sing, sir. Why didn't you remember your money?"

"I could give you four or five ounces of silver. It means nothing to me. Unfortunately I forgot to bring any."

"You haven't a penny in your pocket, and you talk grandly of four or five pieces of silver! Do you expect me to 'Slake my thirst looking at a sour plum' or 'Assuage my hunger with a drawing of a muffin'?"

"Have you no eyes, daughter?" Bai Yuqiao called. "Can't you tell the difference between a city man and a rube? Don't waste your time on him. Ask some kind gentlemen who has a little sense to start us off."

"Are you saying I haven't any sense?" Lei Heng demanded.

"If you know how a polished scholar should act, a dog's head can sprout horns!" the old man retorted.

A noisy stir ran through the audience. Lei Heng grew angry.

"You cheap lackey! How dare you insult me!"

"Does it matter what I say to a cowherd like you?"

Someone in the audience recognized Lei Heng, and he cried: "Stop talking like that. He's our county's Constable Lei."

"Did you say 'constable' or 'constipated'?" Yuqiao sneered.

Lei Heng couldn't contain himself. He leaped from his chair onto the stage and seized the old man. With one punch and one kick he puffed up his lips and knocked out a couple of teeth. The attack was fierce, and others rushed to separate them. Lei Heng was persuaded to go home, and the audience hastily departed.

Now it happened that the singer had been intimate with the new magistrate when he was still in the Eastern Capital, and this was one of the reasons she had brought her show to Yuncheng. After Lei Heng gave here father such a drubbing, she called a sedan-chair and went directly to the magistrate.

"Lei Heng beat up my father and drove out my audience. He's deliberately abusing me."

"Draw up a complaint, immediately," the magistrate heatedly exclaimed, in a clear demonstration of the influence of "pillow power." He also examined the old man's injuries and had these noted as evidence.

Lei Heng had friends in the county office, and they tried to intercede for him. But they couldn't prevail against the girl. She refused to leave, and pouted and flounced until the magistrate had to give in. Lei Heng was arrested, brought before the court, beaten till he confessed, collared with a rack, and an order issued that he be paraded in the streets. At the girl's insistence, the magistrate instructed that Lei Heng be put on display at the theater door.

The next day, when Xiuying went to perform, Lei Heng stood by the entrance way. The guards were public servants like Lei Heng himself, and they were reluctant to strip him, as this type of punishment required. The girl thought: "I've already come out against him openly. Why fear to infuriate him further?"

She went to a nearby tea-house, sat down, and called the guards over. "You're all closely connected, so you go easy on him," she said. "The magistrate ordered you to display Lei Heng, bound and stripped, but you're too full of sympathy. Just wait till I tell the magistrate! We'll see whether I can cope with you or not!"

"Don't lost your temper, madam. If we have to, we'll strip him."

"In that case, I'll reward you."

The guards had no choice but to remove Lei Heng's clothes there on the street. "We can't help ourselves, brother," they said apologetically.

During this turmoil, Lei Heng's mother arrived, bringing him food. She saw him standing there, naked, and she started to cry.

"You work in the magistrate's office, just like my son," she berated the guards. "Is it worth the money she gave you to act like this? You might get into trouble yourself, some day."

"Listen, old mother, we wanted to do the right thing. But the complainant came to see the 'bound and stripped' sentence enforced, and we couldn't refuse. She threatened to make things hot for us with the magistrate. So we couldn't save face for Lei Heng."

"Who ever heard of a complainant seeing to it in person that a sentence is carried out?"

A guard lowered his voice. "She's very close to the magistrate, old mother. One word from her and we're sent up. That's why we're in such a fix."

The old woman began opening Lei Heng's bonds. "That slut knows how to use her connections. I'm going to untie this rope. Let's see what she can do about it."

Xiuying, in the tea-house, heard all this. She walked over. "What did you just say, old baggage?"

Lei Heng's mother pointed at her angrily. "You've been mounted and pressed by thousands, you screw for any man who comes along, you bitch! What right have you to swear at me?"

Xiuying's willow tendril eyebrows contracted, her starry eyes glared. "Old bawd," she screamed. "Beggar woman! How dare a low person like you curse me?"

"What are you going to do about it? You're not the magistrate of Yuncheng!"

The actress rushed up and with one push sent the old woman staggering. Before she could steady herself, Xiuying closed in and slapped her left and right.

Lei Heng, a filial son, was enraged. He raised his rack and brought it down on Xiuying's head. A corner of it struck her squarely and split open her skull. She collapsed to the ground, her brain matter flowing, her eyes bulging, absolutely motionless. Plainly, she was dead.

The others at once brought Lei Heng to the magistrate and reported. The magistrate directed that Lei Heng be taken to the scene under guard, together with county officials, the district chief and witnesses, and that an examination of the body be conducted. This done, all returned to the court, where Lei Heng freely confessed. His mother, under surety to appear, was ordered to return home and await further instructions. Lei Heng, a rack around his neck, was committed to prison.

The warden of the prison was Zhu Tong the Beautiful Beard. When Lei Heng was delivered, he couldn't do much for him. But he treated him to wine and food, and instructed a guard to sweep out and prepare a clean cell. Not long after, Lei Heng's mother also brought food.

Weeping, she said to Zhu Tong: "I'm over sixty, and this child is everything to me. You two have been such friends. Have pity and look after him."

"Don't worry, old mother. You needn't bring him food any more. I'll take care of everything. If I can find the chance, I'll save him."

"Do that and you'll be like my parents reborn! If anything should happen to him, it would be the end of me!"

"I'll remember. You can rest assured."

The old woman thanked him and left.

Zhu Tong tried to think of a way to rescue Lei Heng, but in vain. He asked someone to intercede with the magistrate, and spread bribes among high and low. The magistrate was very fond of Zhu Tong, but he hated Lei Heng for having killed his paramour, and was deaf to all pleas. What's more, the old scoundrel Bai Yuqiao flooded the magistracy with petitions that Lei Heng pay for his daughter's life with his own. And so, after sixty days of detention, Lei Heng was ordered committed to the prison in Jizhou Prefecture. The record scribe was sent on ahead with the relevant documents, and Zhu Tong was directed to deliver the prisoner there under armed escort.

Zhu Tong selected a dozen guards and left Yuncheng with Lei Heng. After marching ten *li* they came to a tavern.

"Let's have a few bowls of wine," Zhu Tong suggested.

Everyone went into the tavern and drank. Zhu Tong took Lei Heng out in the back, as if they were going to relieve themselves. In a secluded spot, he opened the rack and freed him.

"Go home, brother, quickly, and get your mother. Travel all night, find refuge. I'll take the consequences."

"I don't mind fleeing, but you'll be implicated."

"Brother, you don't know. The magistrate is furious that you've killed his doxy. You're under sentence of death. If you went to the prefecture, they'd surely execute you. Letting you go isn't a capital offense. I have no parents to worry about. It doesn't matter if all my property is confiscated in recompense. Go as far as you can, and quickly."

Lei Heng kowtowed his thanks. He hurried home along a path from the rear door. He gathered his valuables and departed with his mother. They travelled through the night to Liangshan Marsh, where he joined the band. Of that no more need be said.

Zhu Tong buried the rack in the deep grass. He emerged and shouted: "Lei Heng has escaped'. This is terrible!"

"We'll chase him to his home and bring him back," exclaimed the guards.

Zhu Tong delayed them to give Lei Heng time to go a long distance, then returned to the county office.

"I was careless," he confessed. "The prisoner got away on the road. We searched without success. I'm willing to accept any punishment."

The magistrate liked Zhu Tong very much. He would have preferred to let him off. But Bai Yuqiao threatened to go to a higher court and accuse Zhu Tong of deliberately letting Lei Heng escape. The magistrate had no choice but to report the matter to the prefecture of Jizhou. Zhu Tong's family immediately sent someone there who spread bribes around liberally. When the constable was remanded to Jizhou the prefect knew all about it. He imposed a sentence of twenty blows, and ordered that Zhu Tong be committed to the prison in the prefecture of Cangzhou.

Zhu Tong, a rack for travelling around his neck, set out with two guards carrying the relevant documents. Members of his family gave him clothing and money, after tipping the guards. On leaving Yuncheng, the party followed a winding road to Henghai County in Cangzhou Prefecture. The trip was uneventful.

The prefect was holding court when the guards delivered the documents and their prisoner. He could see that Zhu Tong, with his ruddy face and handsome beard extending down past his middle, was no ordinary person. Favorably impressed, the prefect said: "Don't take this man to prison. I want him here in the prefecture as my attendant."

The rack was removed, a reply was written, and the two guards took their leave and returned to Yuncheng.

From then on Zhu Tong served in the prefectural office. He dispensed a certain amount of largesse among the sheriffs, captains, keepers of the gates, messengers, jailors and guards. Since he had an amiable disposition as well, he was liked by all.

One day the prefect was sitting in his court. Zhu Tong stood below in attendance. Summoning him forward, the prefect asked: "Why did you let Lei Heng go and end up here?"

"I would never have dared to do that. It's just that I was careless, and he escaped."

"Did you really deserve such a severe punishment?"

"The complainant in the original case insisted that I confess to having released him. So the sentence had to be severe."

"Why did Lei Heng kill that singer?"

Zhu Tong explained the circumstances in detail.

"Then you considered him filial and thought letting him go was the only chivalrous thing to do?"

"Would I have had the temerity to deceive the authorities?"

Just then, from behind a screen, the prefect's little son came out. Only four years old, he was a pretty child, and the prefect loved him better than gold or jade.

The boy went directly to Zhu Tong and asked to be picked up. Zhu Tong held him in his arms, and the child grabbed his long beard.

"I want this bearded fellow to carry me. No one else," piped the little boy.

"Let go of him," said the prefect. "Behave yourself."

"I want him to carry me. I want him to take me out to play."

"I'll take him outside for a stroll," Zhu Tong suggested. "We'll be back soon."

"All right," said the prefect. "Since that's what he wants."

Zhu Tong carried the child to the street and bought him some good sweets. After a short while, he brought him back.

"Where did you go?" the prefect asked the little boy.

"This bearded fellow took me on the street to play. And he bought me sweets and fruit."

"You shouldn't have spent your own money," the prefect said to Zhu Tong politely.

"Only a small token of my esteem," said Zhu Tong. "It's not worth mentioning."

The prefect ordered wine for the constable. A serving girl brought a silver pitcher and platter and poured Zhu Tong three large beakers of wine in succession.

"Any time the child wants you to take him to play, you can carry him out for a walk."

"Your wish is my command, Excellency."

Thereafter, Zhu Tong took the little boy for a stroll every day. He had money in his purse and he wanted the prefect to be pleased, so he spent it on the child freely.

Half a month went by, and it was the fifteenth day of the seventh month— the Driving Out of Devils Festival. Glowing lanterns were set afloat upon the river, and people prayed and did good deeds. That evening, the nursemaid spoke to Zhu Tong.

"The child wants to see the river lanterns, Constable. Madam, his mother, says you can take him."

Zhu Tong promised he would. The little boy was dressed in a green silk robe, and short strings of beads were tied to the two tufts of hair sticking up like horns on the top of his head. Zhu Tong carried him on his shoulder as they left the gate of the prefectural compound and walked towards the temple. Lighted lanterns were sailing upon the water.

It was early evening. Zhu Tong strolled around the temple grounds with the little boy. People were earning blessings by setting live fish free in a special pool. The child climbed on a railing overlooking the river and watched happily as the lanterns floated by. A man behind Zhu Tong tugged him by the sleeve.

"Brother, would you come away a moment so we can talk?"

Zhu Tong looked around. To his surprise, there was Lei Heng.

"Get off that railing and sit here," Zhu Tong said to the child. "I'm going to buy you some candy. Don't leave this spot."

"Come back quickly. I want to watch the river lanterns from the bridge."

"I'll only be a minute." He turned and went off with Lei Heng.

"What are you doing here?" Zhu Tong asked.

Lei Heng pulled him into a secluded corner and said: "After you saved me, I had HO Other place to go with my old mother, so I joined Song Jiang's band in Liangshan Marsh. I told them of your benevolence, and Song recalled your kindness to him in previous days. Chao Gai and the other leaders were extremely moved. They sent me and Military Advisor Wu Yong to see you."

"Where is Teacher Wu?"

A man stepped out from behind him. "Wu Yong is here." He kowtowed.

Zhu Tong hastily returned the courtesy. "It's been a long time, Teacher," he said. "I trust all has been well with you?"

"Our stronghold leaders send their respects. They've deputed Constable Lei Heng and me to invite you up our mountain to join our righteous assembly. Though many days have passed, we haven't dared to approach you. Tonight, we meet at last. Please come with us to our fortress and satisfy the wish of our highest chieftains, Chao Gai and Song Jiang."

For some time Zhu Tong was unable to answer. Finally, he said: "Teacher, you're making a mistake. You mustn't ask me that. Suppose we were overheard? Brother Lei Heng committed a death-penalty crime. Out of chivalry I allowed him to escape. He could no longer let himself be seen, so he went up the mountain and joined your band. Because of him, I've been exiled here. But if Heaven is merciful, in another year or so I'll be able to go home and become a respectable citizen again. Why should I do the sort of thing you propose? Please go back, both of you. Staying here, you may cause misunderstanding."

"But, brother, you're only an attendant, here," Lei Heng argued. "That's no job for a real man. It's not only me who wants you to join us. Our highest chieftains have both been hoping to see you for a long time. What will they think if you delay?"

"Brother, what are you saying? You haven't thought. I let you escape because your mother was old and your family poor. Now you suggest I'm lacking in chivalry."

Wu Yong interceded. "Since the constable doesn't want to go, we shall bid farewell and leave."

"Please give my humble regards to the chieftains," said Zhu Tong. They walked together towards the bridge.

There was no sign of the little boy. Zhu Tong groaned. He searched high and low. Lei Heng grasped his arm.

"Don't bother looking, brother. Probably the two men who came with us, when they heard you say you wouldn't go, took the child away. We'll go find them, together."

"This is no time for jokes. That little boy is the prefect's very life. I'm responsible for him."

"Brother, just come with me."

Zhu Tong, Lei Heng and Wu Yong left the temple and went outside the city. Zhu Tong was quite upset.

"Where have they gone with the child?" he demanded.

"We'll go to my place, brother," said Lei Heng. "I'll return him to you."

"The prefect will be angry if I get back late."

"Those two who came with us are ignorant fellows," said Wu Yong. "They must have taken him to where we're living."

"What's their names?" asked Zhu Tong.

"I don't know them," said Lei Heng. "I heard one of them being called Black Whirlwind."

Zhu Tong was shocked. "Not the fellow who killed those people in Jiangzhou?"

"That's the man," said Wu Yong.

Zhu Tong stamped his feet in anguish and groaned, then hurried on. When they were about twenty *li* from the city, they saw Li Kui the Black Whirlwind ahead.

"Here I am," called the big fellow.

Zhu Tong hastened up to him. "Where is the prefect's son?"

Li Kui hailed him respectfully. "Greetings, brother Warden. The child is here."

"Bring him out, then, and give him to me."

Li Kui pointed to his own hair. "I'm wearing his bead decorations."

Zhu Tong looked, and demanded in alarm: "Where is he now?"

"I put a drug in his mouth and carried him from the city. He's sleeping in that grove. Please see for yourself."

It was a bright moonlit night, and Zhu Tong plunged in among the trees. He saw the little boy lying dead on the ground.

Zhu Tong rushed out the grove, enraged. The three men were gone. He peered in every direction. Then he saw Black Whirlwind standing in the distance. The big man smote his battle-axes.

"Come on. Come on," he cried.

Wild with fury, Zhu Tong hitched up his robe and tore after him. Li Kui continued retreating, with Zhu Tong in pursuit. But what chance had he to catch up with the experienced mountain traveller? Soon he was gasping for breath.

Ahead of him, Li Kui called again: "Come on. Come on."

The seething Zhu Tong wanted to swallow him down in one gulp. But he couldn't get near him. The chase dragged on through the night. Gradually, the sky brightened. Li Kui moved faster when Zhu Tong speeded up, slower when he lagged, and not at all when he halted. Zhu Tong saw him enter a large manor.

"The rogue has gone to ground at last," thought the constable. "Now I can have it out with him."

He hurried into the courtyard and halted in front of a large hall. In racks on either side were many weapons. "This must be some big official's residence," he thought. He called: "Is anyone at home?"

A man emerged from behind a screen. And who was it? None other than Chai Jin the Small Whirlwind.

"Who are you?" Chai Jin enquired.

When Zhu Tong saw this handsome and graceful lord, he bowed and replied: "My name is Zhu Tong. I was warden of the Yucheng prison. But I committed a crime and was exiled here. Last night I took the little son of the prefect to watch the lantern floating on the river, and Black Whirlwind killed him. He's here now in your manor. May I trouble you to help me seize him and turn him over to the authorities?"

"Since you are Beautiful Beard, please be seated."

"May I beg to ask your name, my lord?"

"I'm Chai Jin, and am called the Small Whirlwind."

"I've long known of your great name." Zhu Tong kowtowed. "I didn't expect to have the honor of meeting you today."

"Your name has also been long known to me, sir. Please come into the rear hall where we can talk."

As he followed Lord Chai inside Zhu Tong asked: "How does that scoundrel Black Whirlwind dare to hide in your manor?"

"That's easy. I have always welcomed bold men of the gallant fraternity. An ancestor of mine gave up the throne, and because of that the first Song emperor bestowed on my ancestors the Wrought Iron Pledge. When a wrongdoer takes refuge with us, no searchers dare enter. A dear friend of mine knows you well. He's one of the leaders in Liangshan Marsh—Song Jiang, called the Timely Rain. He wrote a secret letter instructing Wu Yong, Lei Heng and Black Whirlwind to stay here at my place and invite you to go with them up the mountain and join the band. Since you couldn't be persuaded, Song ordered Li Kui to kill the prefect's son, to cut off any chance of you returning to the city, and thus compelling you to go to the stronghold and assume a chair of leadership. Teacher Wu, brother Lei, aren't you coming out to apologize?"

The two men emerged from an anteroom and kowtowed before Zhu Tong. "Forgive us, brother," they said. "We were acting on brother Song Jiang's orders. If you go with us to the fortress, you'll understand."

"I know you brothers meant well, but your methods were too cruel!"

Chai Jin murmured soothing words.

"I'll go if I have to, but I want to see Black Whirlwind first!"

"Brother Li," the lord called. "Come out and apologize."

Li Kui walked from a side room and voiced loudly a respectful greeting. The sight of him sent flames spurting thirty thousand feet high in Zhu Tong's heart.

He couldn't control his rage. He rushed towards Li Kui murderously. It took the combined efforts of Chai Jin, Lei Heng and Wu Yong to restrain him.

"I'll go up the mountain," said Zhu Tong. "But first you have to promise me one thing."

"Not one but scores, if you so desire," said Wu Yong. "What is it you wish?"

And because of Zhu Tong's request, there was turmoil in Gaotang Prefecture and strife in the Liangshan Marsh stronghold. A noble patron of learning fell into the clutches of the law, a hospitable relative of the emperor was cast into a dungeon.

What was the demand which Zhu Tong made? Read our next chapter if you would know.

CHAPTER 52

LI KUI BEATS TO DEATH YIN TIANXI

CHAI JIN IS TRAPPED IN GAOTANG PREFECTURE

"If you want me to go up the mountain," said Zhu Tong, "you must kill Black Whirlwind to appease my rage! Then I'll go."

"You can eat my prick," roared Li Kui. "I was carrying out the orders of brothers Chao and Song! It hadn't a tooting fart to do with me!"

Zhu Tong moved to throw himself on Li Kui. The other three restrained him. "If Black Whirlwind is there, I'll never go up that mountain," Zhou Tong vowed.

"That's easy," said Chai Jin. "I'll keep him here with me. You three go on to the stronghold and satisfy the wishes of Chao and Song."

"The prefect is sure to send a warrant for my arrest to Yuncheng County. They'll take my wife and children. How can we deal with that?"

"Don't worry," said Wu Yong. "Song Jiang has probably brought your family into the fortress by now."

Only then did Zhu Tong relax. Chai Jin treated his guests to wine, and the same day saw them off. They left towards evening. Lord Chai provided them with three riding horses and an escort of vassals. He accompanied them to the outside of the pass. At the final parting, Wu Yong gave *f-* Li Kui some words of advice.

"Behave with care. Stay a while in the lord's manor. Don't stir up any trouble and get him involved. In a few months or half a year, after Zhu Tong has cooled down, we'll bring you back to the fortress. We'll probably invite Lord Chai to join us, too."

The three mounted and departed. Chai Jin and Li Kui returned to the manor. Zhu Tong went with Wu Yong and Lei Heng to become a member of the band in Liangshan Marsh. When they came to the end of Cangzhou Prefecture, the vassals rode the horses back, and the three continued on foot.

The journey was uneventful, and they soon reached the tavern ran by Zhu Gui. He sent word to the stronghold of their arrival. Chao Gai and Song Jiang, accompanied by greater and lesser chieftains, were waiting to greet them on the Shore of Golden Sands, to the beat of drums and the shrilling of flutes. All got on their horses and climbed to the fortress, where they dismounted and went to Fraternity Hall. They talked for a while of old times together. Then Zhu Tong voiced his apprehension.

"You've called me to the mountain, but the prefect of Cangzhou is certain to notify Yuncheng County to seize my wife and children. What can I do?"

Song Jiang laughed. "Set your mind at ease, brother. We sent men to fetch them several days ago."

"Where are they now?"

"They're resting at the place of my father the squire. Why not go and see for yourself?"

Zhu Tong was delighted. Song Jiang led him to his father's villa. Zhu Tong was reunited with his family. He observed that they had brought all their valuables.

"A man came with a letter the other day saying you had already joined the mountain band," his wife related. "So we packed our belongings and travelled through the night to get here."

Zhu Tong kowtowed and thanked the brigand leaders. Song Jiang asked both him and Lei Heng to make their homes on the mountain summit. For successive days he gave feasts in their honor, as new chieftains. Of that no more need be said.

The prefect of Cangzhou, when it began getting late and Zhu Tong didn't return with his son, sent people out to look for them. They searched half the night. The next day, someone found the body in the grove, and notified the prefectural office. Shocked, the prefect went to the grove. He wept as though his heart would break. He had the body encoffined, and cremated it.

Summoning court the following morning, he issued notices for the arrest of Zhu Tong to all the surrounding areas. Yuncheng County reported that Zhu Tong's wife and family had fled to places unknown. Rewards for Zhu Tong's apprehension were offered in the various prefectures and counties. Of that we'll say no more.

When Li Kui had been with Lord Chai for over a month, a messenger delivered an urgent letter to the manor. Chai Jin accepted and read it. He was astonished.

"In that case I'll have to go," he exclaimed.

"What's the trouble, Excellency?" asked Li Kui.

"I have an uncle, Chai Huangcheng, who lives in Gaotang Prefecture. That rogue Yin Tianxi, brother-in-law of the prefect, Gao Lian, has taken over his garden. My uncle is so infuriated that he's fallen ill, and he may not live. He must have some dying words he wants to impart. My uncle has no children. I'll have to hurry to his side."

"Would you like me to keep you company?"

"I'd be glad if you're willing to go."

Chai Jin packed some luggage, selected a dozen good horses, and told a number of vassals to get ready. The next day at dawn Lord Chai, Li Kui and their company climbed into their saddles, left the manor and headed for Gaotang.

They arrived in less than a day and dismounted in front of the residence of Chai Huangcheng. Chai Jin left Li Kui and the others in the outer hall and went to his uncle's bedroom. Seated beside Huangcheng's bed, he wept. The lady his uncle had married after the death of his first wife came in.

"You've had a tiring ride," she said. "You mustn't upset yourself."

Chai Jin greeted her courteously and asked what had happened.

"The new prefect, Gao Lian, is also the military commander here," she said. "Because Marshal Gao in the Eastern Capital is his cousin, he feels he can do anything he pleases. He brought with him his brother-in-law Yin Tianxi. Everybody calls him Counsellor Yin. Although quite young, Yin knows he has the prefect's backing, and he hurts people with his outrageous behavior. One of his toadies told him that we have a pretty rear garden with a pavilion overlooking a pool. He broke in with twenty or thirty scamps one day, examined the garden, and wanted to drive us out of our home and move in himself.

"Your uncle Huangcheng said to him: 'Our family is of noble origin. An earlier emperor bestowed a Wrought Iron Pledge on our family that no one may oppress us. How dare you seize my home? Where is my wife and family supposed to go?'

"The knave wouldn't listen. He insisted that we leave. Your uncle tried to push him away, and was beaten for his pains. He's been in bed ever since. He can't get up and he can't eat. Medicine doesn't seem to do any good. Heaven may be far but the grave for him is near, I'd say. Fortunately, you've come to take charge. So even if the worst should happen, we won't have to worry."

"Don't despair, aunt. We'll get a good doctor to treat him. If there's any dispute about this, I'll send a man back to Cangzhou to get the Wrought Iron Pledge, and show that to Yin. If we have to go before the authorities, or even the emperor himself, we have nothing to fear."

"Huangcheng failed in all his efforts," said his wife. "But I'm sure, in your hands, we'll get results."

Chai Jin stayed a while with his uncle, then came out and told Li Kui and the others about the dispute. Li Kui jumped to his feet.

"That unreasonable varlet! I'll give him a couple of licks with my axes first, then we can start discussions'."

"Calm yourself, brother Li. You can't get rough with him without any provocation. Besides, although he may have powerful backing, our family is protected by the Pledge. If he won't listen to reason here, in the capital there are persons just as influential as he, and the law is clear. We'll fight him in court."

"The law, the law! If everyone obeyed the law, everything would be serene! I'm in favor of hitting him first and talking afterwards. If he complains to the court, I'll hack him and the friggin judge together!"

Chai Jin laughed. "No wonder Zhu Tong wanted to fight you. You're both such hotheads. This is an imperial city, not your mountain stronghold where you can act as you like."

"So what? Jiangzhou and Wuweijun are also imperial cities. Didn't I kill men there too?"

"Wait till I've seen how the land lies. When the need arises, I'll ask your help, brother. Until that happens, please remain here quietly."

At that moment a servant hurried out to request Lord Chai to go to his uncle. Chai Jin went quickly to the bedside. His uncle spoke to him with tears in his eyes.

"You're a man of high principle, nephew, a credit to our ancestors. I die today because of the humiliation imposed on me by Yin Tianxi. You owe it to me as one of the same flesh and blood to write a complaint to the emperor and obtain redress. From beneath the Nine Springs of the Nether World I will thank you. Take care of yourself. I have no other bequests."

Having spoken, Huangcheng died. Chai Jin wept bitterly. His aunt feared he would faint. "Restrain your grief," she urged. "We must talk about the funeral arrangements."

"The Wrought Iron Pledge is in my home. I haven't brought it. But I'll send a man for it immediately. If necessary, I'll file a complaint in the Eastern Capital. But uncle has passed away. First we must proceed with the encoffining and dress in mourning. We'll confer about other things later."

Chai Jin ordered that inner and outer coffins be prepared in the official manner, and that a memorial tablet be set up in keeping with the rites. The whole family dressed in deep mourning, and young and old lamented. Li Kui, outside, heard their weeping. Angrily, he ground a fist into the palm of his hand. But when he asked the servants what was going on, no one would tell him. Monks were invited to conduct the prayers.

Two days went by. Riding a spirited horse, Yin Tianxi and twenty or thirty cronies had been carousing outside the city, amusing themselves with slingshots, crossbows, blowpipes, inflated balls, stick branches for catching birds, and musical instruments. Now, pretending to be drunker than they actually were, they staggered up to the residence of Chai Huangcheng. Yin reined in his horse and shouted a demand to see the person in charge.

Chai Jin, wearing mourning, hastily emerged. Yin addressed him from his saddle.

"What part of the family are you?"

"I'm Chai Jin, the nephew."

"I gave orders the other day that they were to move out. Why haven't I been obeyed?"

"Uncle was sick in bed. We couldn't disturb him. He died in the night. We'll move when the forty-nine day mourning period is over."

"Farts! I give you three days more. If you're not out by then, I'll put a rack around your neck and let you taste a hundred blows of my staff!"

"You mustn't persecute us like this, Counsellor. We're descendants of a royal family, and protected by an old imperial Wrought Iron Pledge. It must be respected."

"Take it out and let me see it," Yin shouted.

"It's in my home in Cangzhou. I've already sent for it."

"The rascal's lying," Yin said angrily. "Even if there is such an edict, it doesn't scare me. Men, give this fellow a drubbing!"

The gang started toward Chai Jin. Li Kui, the Black Whirlwind, had been watching and listening through a crack in the door of the house. Now he pushed it open, dashed up to Yin with a roar, dragged him from his horse, and with one punch knocked him sprawling. The thirty ruffians rushed to Yin's aid. Li Kui promptly flattened half a dozen. Yelling, they all turned and fled.

Li Kui picked Yin up and pummelled him with fist and foot. Chai Jin couldn't restrain him. It wasn't long before Yin was lying dead on the ground.

Chai Jin groaned. He led Li Kui to the rear hall and said: "They'll be sending men here very soon! You can't stay! I'll deal with the prosecution. You've got to go back to Liangshan Marsh, quickly."

"I can go, but you'll be implicated."

"The imperial Pledge will protect me. You must go at once. There's no time to lose."

Li Kui gathered his battle-axes, took some travel money, left through the rear gate, and set out for the mountain fortress.

Not long after, more than two hundred men, armed with swords, spears and staves, surrounded the residence. Chai Jin came out and said: "I'll go with you to the authorities and explain."

They bound his arms and went in to look for the culprit, a big swarthy fellow. He was gone. They took Chai Jin to the prefecture court, where he knelt in the center of the hall. Gao Lian, the prefect, had ground his teeth in venomous rage when he heard that his brother-in-law had been beaten to death, and had been waiting for the assailant to be brought in. Now, Chai Jin was flung down at the foot of the prefect's dais.

"How dare you kill my Yin Tianxi?" Gao shouted.

"I am a direct descendant of Emperor Shi Zong. My family has a Wrought Iron Pledge of imperial protection from Tai Zu, the first emperor of Song. It's in my home in Cangzhou," Chai Jin replied. "I called to visit my uncle Chai Huangcheng, who was gravely ill. Unfortunately, he died, and we are now in mourning at his residence. Counsellor Yin came with thirty men and wanted to drive us out. He wouldn't listen to my explanations and ordered his men to beat me. One of my vassals, Big Li, while defending me, killed him in the heat of battle."

"Where is Big Li?"

"He panicked and ran away."

"He's your vassal. Would he have dared kill a man without orders from you? You deliberately let him escape, and now you try to delude this court. Rascals like you never confess unless they are beaten. Take him, guards, and give it to him hard!"

"To save his master my vassal Big Li accidentally killed a man. It's not my fault. We have Emperor Tai Zu's Pledge. Am I to be beaten like a common criminal?"

"Where is the Pledge?"

"In Cangzhou. I've already sent for it."

"The scoundrel is opposing this court," Gao Lian raged. "Beat him, guards, with all your strength!"

They pounded Chai Jin till his flesh was a pulp and his blood streamed in rivulets. He was forced to confess: "I ordered my vassal Big Li to kill Yin Tianxi." A twenty-five-catty rack for the condemned was placed around his neck, and he was cast into prison. Yin's body, after inspection by the medical examiner, was put into a coffin and buried. Of that no more need be said.

Yin's sister wanted vengeance. She had her prefect husband confiscate the property of Chai Huangcheng, arrest the members of his family, and take over for themselves the house and gardens of the residence. Chai Jin languished in jail.

Li Kui travelled through the night to get back to Liangshan Marsh. On arriving at the fortress he reported to the leaders. Zhu Tong was filled with rage the moment he saw him. He rushed at Li Kui with his halberd. Black Whirlwind, brandishing his axes, clashed with him in combat. Chao Gai, Song Jiang and the others exhorted them to stop. Song apologized to Zhu Tong.

"Killing the prefect's little boy wasn't Li Kui's idea. Military Advisor Wu Yong thought of this device when you wouldn't agree to joining us. Now that you are here, forget it. Let's all strive together in harmony and loyalty. We don't want outsiders to laugh at us."

Song Jiang turned to Li Kui. "Tell sir Beautiful Beard you're sorry."

Li Kui glared. "A fine business. I've done plenty for this stronghold. He hasn't done a thing. Why should I tell him I'm sorry?"

"Although it was the Military Advisor's order, you did kill the prefect's son. From the point of view of age, Zhu Tong is your older brother. Kowtow to him, for my sake. Then I'll kowtow to you, and that'll be the end of it."

Li Kui couldn't very well refuse. To Zhu Tong he said: "I'm not afraid of you, but brother Song Jiang insists. I can't help myself. I apologize." He threw his axes aside and kowtowed, twice.

Only then was Zhu Tong appeased. Chao Gai ordered that a feast be laid to cement the reconciliation.

"Lord Chai went to Gaotang because his uncle, Chai Huangcheng, was ill. The prefect's brother-in-law, Yin Tianxi, wanted to take over the house and gardens, and cursed Chai Jin. I knocked the lout around and killed him," said Li Kui.

"You escaped, but they're sure to prosecute Lord Chai," Song Jiang cried in alarm.

"Calm yourself, brother," said Wu Yong. "We'll know more about it when Dai Zong returns."

"Where has brother Dai Zong gone?" asked Li Kui.

"I thought you'd only stir up trouble, hanging around Lord Chai's manor," said Wu Yong, "and I sent Dai Zong to bring you back. If he found you were gone, he'd surely follow you to Gaotang."

Before the words were out of his mouth, a scout entered and announced: "Superintendent Dai has returned."

Song Jiang went forward to welcome him. After Dai came into the hall and was seated, he was asked for news of Lord Chai.

"I went to his manor and learned that he and Li Kui had left for Gaotang. I hurried after them. In Gaotang, the whole city was agog. Everyone said:' Yin Tianxi tried to seize the residence of Chai Huangcheng, and a big dark fellow beat him to death. Lord Chai was implicated, and tied up and cast into prison. All the property of Chai Huangcheng's family has been confiscated. There's no guarantee that Lord Chai's life will be preserved."

"That swarthy rogue has done it again," said Chao Gai. "Wherever he goes, there's turmoil."

"Chai Huangcheng was beaten by Yin, and he died of rage. Then Yin came to take over his residence and ordered his men to beat Lord Chai. Even if he were a living Buddha, I wouldn't let him get away with it!" Li Kui retorted.

"Lord Chai has always been benevolent to our fortress," said Chao Gai. "Today, he's in danger. We must rescue him. I'll go personally."

"You're the highest leader here, brother, you shouldn't make a move lightly," said Song Jiang. "I've long been indebted to Lord Chai. Let me go on your behalf."

"Although Gaotang is a small city, it's densely populated, has a large military force, and plenty of grain. We mustn't underestimate it," said Wu Yong. "I propose that we ask twelve chieftains to lead a vanguard of five thousand men, with a supporting force of three thousand under ten chieftains."

The twenty-two chieftains bid farewell to Chao Gai and the others and left the mountain stronghold for Gaotang.

By the time the vanguard force reached the edge of the prefecture, Gao Lian had already been informed by his scouts. "I'd been intending to clean out that lair of shabby bandits in Liangshan Marsh," he sneered, "and now they present themselves to be tied. A Heaven-blessed chance." He directed his aides: "Transmit my order immediately to muster our army, go forth from the city, and engage the enemy. Let the citizenry man the walls."

On horseback Gao was military commandant, afoot he was the prefect. As soon as his order was issued, all his officers, from generals to sergeants, assembled their units and inspected them on the drill fields, then marched out of the city against the foe. Gao Lian had a personal contingent of three hundred crack troops known as the "Flying Miracles," who came from Shandong, Hebei, Jiangxi, Hunan, north and south of the Huai, and east and west of the Zhejiang River. Shouting, banners waving, drums pounding, gongs crashing, they waited only their adversaries' approach.

With the arrival of the five thousand men under Lin Chong, Hua Rong and Qin Ming, the two hosts confronted each other, drams and banners plainly visible, each temporarily halted by powerful flights of arrows. Trumpets blared, and the big battle drums throbbed.

Hua Rong, Qin Ming and the ten other chieftains reined in their horses at the most advanced position. Lin Chong, his serpent lance at the ready, spurred his mount forward.

"Gao the thief," he yelled. "Come out, quickly!"

Gao Lian gave his animal its head. With thirty officers he rode to the arch of pennants. There, they halted. Gao pointed at Lin Chong.

"Death-deserving rebel brigands! Dare you disturb our city?"

"People-harming crook," shouted Lin Chong. "One of these days I'm going to the Eastern Capital and pulverize your scoundrelly relative Gao Qiu, that thievish minister who deceives the emperor! I won't rest until I do!"

Gao Lian turned fuming to his cohorts. "Who will ride out and seize this robber?"

From among the officers emerged a captain named Yu Zhi. He clapped his steed and advanced brandishing his sabre. Lin Chong galloped towards him. They had fought less than five rounds when Lin Chong ran his serpent lance through the man's chest and brought him tumbling to the ground.

Gao was startled. "Who will get our revenge?"

Another captain, Wen Wenbao, holding a long lance, astride a sleek brown horse with equipage of tinkling bells and clinking jade, was already racing towards Lin Chong, his animal's hoofs churning a cloud of dust.

"Rest a while, brother," cried Qin Ming. "Watch me cut this varlet down."

Lin Chong reined his mount, retracted his steel lance, and allowed Qin Ming to go ahead. The two battled more than ten rounds. Qin Ming deliberately left himself open. As Wen lunged and missed, Qin swung his mace and stove in the captain's skull. Wen collapsed at his horse's hoofs, and the frightened animal scampered back to the defenders' position. From both sides rose a mighty roar.

Gao Lian, having lost two of his officers, drew from its sheath upon his back his precious Dragon Sword. He muttered an incantation, then shouted: "Speed." And from the midst of his army a black mist rolled. Soon it covered half the sky. Sand flew, stones rolled, the earth quaked, the heavens shook. A weird gale swept across the field against the brigands. Lin Chong, Qin Ming, Hua Rong and the others couldn't see. Terrified horses whinnied and bolted. The fighters turned and fled.

Gao Lian waved his sword. His three hundred Miracle soldiers charged, followed by his entire army. Lin Chong's forces scattered in disorder, exclaiming piteously. Of the five thousand, more than a thousand were destroyed. For fifty *li* they retreated, and finally made camp. The rout complete, Gao Lian returned with his army to the city.

When Song Jiang's contingent reached the camp, Lin Chong and the others told them what had happened. Song Jiang and Wu Yong were shocked.

"What magic can it be," they wondered, "that is so potent?"

"Probably some evil spell," Wu Yong averred. "If we knew how to turn back the wind and fire, we could defeat them."

Song Jiang opened his Heavenly Books. In the third volume he found the necessary formula. Delighted, he memorized the words of the incantation. Then he reorganized his ranks. At the fifth watch they breakfasted. Banners flying, drums pounding, they marched rapidly towards the city.

This was reported to Gao Lian, who again mustered his victorious troops and his three hundred Miracle soldiers. He opened the gates, let down the drawbridge and deployed his men in battle positions.

Song Jiang, sword in hand, rode to the front. He could see a bevy of black pennants in the midst of Gao Lian's army.

"Those soldiers are his so-called 'Spellbinders'," said Wu Yong. "He's probably going to work some magic again. How are you going to cope with him?"

"Don't worry. I have an antidote. Let none of you have any fear or doubt. Just concentrate on plunging into the fray."

Gao Lian, to his officers, said: "Avoid clashes and combat. But when I bang on my shield, rush together in strength and grab Song Jiang. I will reward you well, personally."

He hung on his saddle a bronze shield emblazoned with heraldic emblems of dragon and phoenix. Shouts rose from the opposing armies, as he rode forward, holding his sword. Song Jiang pointed his finger at him.

"I couldn't get here last night and my brothers carelessly took some casualties. Today I'm going to wipe all of you out, completely!"

"Dismount, you rebellious brigands, and let yourselves be bound," Gao shouted back. "I don't want to have to soil my hands with your blood!"

He waved his sword, whispered a few word under his breath, then yelled: "Speed!"

A dark miasma appeared, and was driven by a strange wind towards Song Jiang and his forces. Before it could reach them, Song muttered an incantation and twisted the fingers of his left hand into a cabalistic sign. With his right hand he pointed his sword.

"Speed!" he shouted.

The wind reversed itself and blew back towards Gao's position. Song Jiang was about to order his men to charge. Gao quickly raised his bronze shield and beat on it with his sword. His Miracle soldiers were at once concealed in a Swirling cloud of yellow sand. From his army hordes of monstrous animals and poisonous serpents poured forth.

Song Jiang and his men were scared stiff. Throwing away his sword, Song pulled his horse around and fled. His officers crowded together and ran for their lives. His troops rushed away, every man for himself.

Again Gao Lian brandished his sword. With his Miracle soldiers in the lead, and followed by the rest of his forces, his entire army launched a murderous assault. Song Jiang's men were severely defeated. Gao Lian chased them for more than twenty *li.* Then gongs were beaten as a signal for his soldiers to re-assemble, and they returned to the city.

At a hillock Song Jiang reined in his horse and pitched camp. Although his men had suffered heavy losses, fortunately all of his chieftains survived. When his forces were settled he conferred with Military Advisor Wu Yong.

"We've been vanquished twice in our attack on Gaotang. We can't seem to break his Miracle soldiers. What are we going to do?"

"Since the rogue can work spells, he's sure to raid our camp tonight," said Wu Yong. "We must plan our defense. We'll leave a small contingent here, and the rest of us will go back to our original encampment."

Song Jiang ordered that only Yang Lin and Bai Sheng and certain men remain. The others returned to the old camp and rested.

Yang and Bai led their fighters half a ft behind the hillock and hid themselves in the deep grass. At the first watch a gale rose and thunder crashed. From their place of concealment Yang and Bai and their three hundred men saw Gao Lian advancing on foot, followed by his three hundred Miracle soldiers. Howling and whistling, they rushed savagely into the camp. They found it was empty, and started to leave.

Yang and Bai let out a yell. Gao and his Miracle soldiers, fearing a trap, scattered and ran. The brigands winged random volleys after them with their bows. An arrow struck Gao Lian in the left shoulder. The fighters spread out and pursued, killing as they raced through a pouring rain.

By then Gao Lian and his Miracle soldiers were far away. Yang and Bai had only a limited contingent. They dared not go any deeper into enemy territory. Abruptly, the rain stopped, the clouds vanished and the stars came out. In the light of the moon, the brigands collected twenty enemy wounded, who had been felled before the hillock by blade and arrow, and led them to Song Jiang's camp. They told of the strange thunderstorm.

Song Jiang and Wu Yong listened in consternation. "That was only five *li* away, but we didn't have any wind or rain here," they said.

Everyone discussed it. "Truly magic," they agreed. "It rained only in the place, and from a height of just three or four hundred feet. The clouds must have picked up water from nearby ponds."

"Gao Lian charged into our camp carrying a sword and with hair unbound," Yang Lin related. "I hit him with an arrow, and he returned to the city. I didn't go after him because we hadn't enough men."

Song Jiang rewarded Yang Lin and Bai Sheng. He had the wounded prisoners executed. He set up seven or eight small strong points around the main camp and assigned a chieftain to each, as a precaution against an enemy raid. He also sent a messenger back to the mountain fortress for reinforcements.

Gao Lian, in the city, nursed his wound. "Defend the city," he instructed his army. "Be constantly on the alert. But don't get involved in any battles. When I've recovered there will be time enough to capture Song Jiang."

After the defeat inflicted upon him, Song Jiang brooded. He said to Wu Yong: "We can't seem to lick Gao Lian. Suppose he gets more troops from somewhere and they attack in force. How will we be able to withstand them?"

"There's only one way to counter his magic," said Wu Yong. He spoke softly in Song's ear. "If we don't get that person to help, we may not be able to save Lord Chai, and we'll never take the city."

Truly, to dispel the magic clouds and mists a person had to be found who understood the secrets of Heaven and Earth. Who, then, was the man Wu Yong proposed? Read our next chapter if you would know.

CHAPTER 53

DAI ZONG SEEKS GONGSUN SHENG A SECOND TIME

LI KUI SPLITS THE SKULL OF LUO THE SAGE

"If we are to break Gao Lian's spells," Wu Yong said to Song Jiang, "we must send a man immediately to fetch Gongsun Sheng."

"The last time Dai Zong went, he spent many days, but all his inquiries failed," said Song Jiang. "Where can he look for him now?"

"The prefecture of Jizhou has numerous counties, towns and villages under its jurisdiction. He'd never find him in such places. It seems to me that since Gongsun is a Taoist, he's more likely to live on some famous mountain where there are Taoist caves and retreats. We'll ask Dai Zong to search in the mountainous regions of Jizhou. He'll surely find him." Song Jiang summoned Dai Zong and explained what was wanted.

"I'll go," said Dai. "But it would be better if I had a companion."

"When you use your magic travel method, who can keep up with you?" said Wu Yong.

"I'll put some charms on his legs too, and he'll be able march swiftly."

"Let me be your companion," Li Kui requested.

"If you want to travel with me, you must eat only vegetarian dishes on the road and obey my commands."

"No problem. I'll do whatever you say."

"Behave yourself and don't cause any rows," Song and Wu cautioned him. "Return quickly, once you've found Gongsun."

"Because I killed Yin Tianxi, Lord Chai is being prosecuted. Don't I want to save him? I wouldn't stir up any trouble."

The two emissaries concealed weapons on their persons, tied their luggage, bid a respectful farewell to Song Jiang and the others, left Gaotang and set out for Jizhou. When they had walked about thirty *li,* Black Whirlwind halted.

"Let's have a bowl of wine before going on, brother."

"You can only have vegetables with your drink during the magic travel.."

"What difference would a little meat make?" Li Kui said, laughing.

"There you go again. It's getting late. We'll find an inn for the night, and continue on in the morning."

They walked another thirty *li,* until it was dusk, and put up at an inn. They made a fire, cooked rice and bought some wine. Li Kui carried a bowl of vegetables and another bowl of vegetable soup into the room, where he joined Dai Zong.

"Why aren't you having any rice?" Dai asked.

"I don't feel like it."

Dai Zong thought: "That rogue must be fooling me and eating meat behind my back." He finished his own vegetable dish and went softly to the rear. There was Li Kui with two measures of wine, wolfing down a platter of beef. "I knew it," Dai said to himself. "I won't say anything, but tomorrow I'll have a little fun with him." He went back to their room and slept.

Li Kui finished off the meat and wine. Afraid that Dai might question him, he returned quietly and went to bed.

At dawn Dai awakened and told Li to light a fire. They cooked a few vegetables for breakfast, then put their luggage on their backs, paid the bill and left the inn.

Before they had gone twenty *li,* Dai said: "We didn't use our magic method yesterday, but today we have to make time. Tie your bundles on tight. I'm going to work the magic on you. We'll be covering eight hundred *li* before we rest."

He attached four charms to Li Kui's legs and said: "Wait for me at the tavern up ahead." He muttered an incantation and blew on Li's legs. Black Whirlwind strode off. He flew as if he were riding a cloud. Dai Zong laughed. "I'll keep him hungry all day." He affixed charms to his own legs, and followed.

Li Kui didn't understand this magic, and he walked as usual with a free stride. At once the sound in his ears was like the rush of wind and rain, the houses and trees on either side seemed to fall backwards as he passed, his feet felt propelled by cloud and mist. He grew frightened and tried to stop several times. But his legs refused to halt. It was as if someone were pushing them. They moved without touching the ground. Taverns selling meat and wine continued to fly towards his rear. He couldn't buy anything.

"My old grandpa," he swore. "Let me stop a minute!"

Soon the red sun was level in the west. Li Kui was hungry and thirsty. But he still was unable to halt. Drenched in a foul sweat, he panted for breath. Dai Zong narrowed the gap between them.

"Brother Li," he called, "why don't you buy a snack to eat?"

"Save me brother," Li Kui bawled. "I'm dying of hunger!"

Dai Zong pulled a few wheat cakes out of his tunic and commenced to munch.

"I can't stop. How can I buy anything?" Li Kui yelled. "Give me a couple of cakes to take the edge off my appetite."

"I will, if you'll only stand still."

Li Kui extended his hand back, but his reach was short by about ten feet. "Good brother," he cried. "Let's stop!"

"It's very peculiar today. I can't halt my legs either."

"Aiya. My friggin legs won't listen to me. They just keep running. If they get me mad I'll take my big ax and cut them off!"

"That's a good idea. Otherwise even by next New Year's day you'll still be running."

"Good brother, you're making fun of me. If I chop my legs off, how will I be able to get back?"

"You probably didn't obey me last night. Now even I can't halt. Well, you can just keep going."

"My lord and master, forgive me and let me stop!"

"With my magic you can't eat meat, especially beef. If you eat one slice of beef, you have to run until you die."

"That's terrible! I deceived you last night, brother. I secretly bought six or seven catties of beef and ate them all! What am I going to do?"

"No wonder even my legs can't be halted. You're going to be the death of me."

Li Kui bawled his laments to the heavens. Dai Zong laughed.

"Promise me one thing and I'll remove the spell."

"Ask me quickly, master, you'll see how I obey!"

"Will you deceive me and eat any more meat?"

"If I do, may a boil as big as a bowl grow on my tongue! I saw you sticking to vegetables, but I thought that would be too much of a nuisance, so I tried to fool you. I'll never do it again!"

"In that case, I'll forgive you."

Dai Zong caught up, and brushed Li Kui's legs with his sleeve. "Stand," he cried. Li Kui immediately halted. "I'm going on ahead," said Dai. "You can follow slowly."

But when Li Kui attempted to step out, he couldn't lift his feet. They felt like cast iron. "Another calamity," he yelled. "Save me again, brother!"

Dai Zong looked back and laughed. "Did you mean what you just vowed?"

"I respect you like my own father! Would I dare go against your commands?"

"You'll really obey me?" Dai encircled Li Kui's wrist with his hand. "Start," he ordered. The two easily walked on.

"Have mercy, brother," Li Kui begged. "Let's rest."

They found an inn, and entered. When they got to their room, Dai removed the charms and burned a few sheaves of sacrificial money.

"How are you now?" he asked.

Li Kui kneaded his limbs and sighed. "These legs feel like they belong to me again at last."

Dai told him to order wine and a vegetable meal, and set water on to boil for washing their feet. Afterwards, they retired and slept until dawn. They got up, performed their ablutions and had breakfast. They paid the bill and set forth. When they had gone about thirty *li,* Dai produced the charms.

"I'm only giving you two, today," he said to Li Kui. "You won't go quite so fast."

"My honored father, I don't want them!"

"You promised to listen to me. We're on an important mission. I won't play any tricks. But if you don't obey me, I'll immobilize you like I did last night. You'll have to stand right here until I go into Jizhou, find Gongsun, and come back.'*

"Tie them on, tie them on," Li Kui said hastily.

Dai and Li attached to their legs only two charms each. Dai Zong then spoke the incantation. He held onto Li as they continued their journey. Using this magic, Dai could stop or go whenever he pleased. Li Kui dared not disobey. On the road they consumed nothing but wine and vegetable dishes, resuming their march immediately after.

But we mustn't be too wordy. Travelling by magic means, in less than ten days they were resting at an inn in the outskirts of Jizhou. The following day they entered the city, with Li Kui disguised as Dai Zong's servant. They inquired all day, but could find no one who knew Gongsun Sheng. They returned to the inn and retired.

The next day they explored the small streets and narrow lanes of the city, again without success. Li Kui fumed irritably.

"That beggarly Taoist! What friggin place is he hiding in? When I see him, I'll drag him off by the head to brother Song Jiang!"

Dai Zong frowned. "There you go again. Don't you remember what you suffered last time?"

Li Kui laughed apologetically. "I wouldn't, actually. I was only kidding."

Dai again berated him. Li dared not reply.

They spent another night at the inn. They rose early the next morning, and searched the villages and towns on the city's perimeter. Whenever they met an old man, Dai greeted him respectfully and asked the whereabouts of Taoist teacher Gongsun Sheng. But none of them knew him, though Dai made dozens of inquiries.

By noon both men were hungry. They went into a noodle shop by the side of the road to buy something to eat. The place was full and all the tables were occupied. The two stood waiting in the aisle.

"If you gentlemen would like some noodles," a waiter said, "you can sit with that old man."

Dai Zong saw an old fellow seated alone at a large table. He hailed him respectfully and bowed, then he and Li Kui sat down opposite, side by side. Dai told the waiter to bring four bowls of noodles.

"One for me and three for you," he said to Li Kui. "That should be enough."

"Hardly. I could do six without any trouble."

The waiter grinned. Time passed, and there was no sign of the noodles. Li Kui saw steaming bowls being carried into an inner room, and he began to lose patience. The waiter placed a bowl of hot noodles down before the old man, who tucked in without any ado, bending low over the table to sip.

"Waiter," the impetuous Li Kui cried angrily, "you're keeping me waiting." He slammed his fist on the table, bouncing hot soup out of the bowl into the old man's face and spilling the noodles.

Annoyed, the old man grabbed Li Kui. "What right have you to overturn my noodles?" he shouted.

Li Kui clenched his fists and was going to hit him. Dai Zong yelled at him to behave, and apologized on his behalf.

"Don't quarrel with this fellow, old gentleman. I'll buy you another bowl."

"You don't understand, sir. I've a long way to go. I wanted to have some noodles and get home early to hear a sermon. Delaying my breakfast delays my journey."

"Where are you from, and who are you going to hear?"

"I'm from Two Fairies Mountain in Jiugong County, which is part of Jizhou Prefecture. I came into town to buy some good incense. I'm on my way back to the mountain to hear Luo the Sage. He's lecturing on 'How to Live Forever'."

Dai Zong thought: "Could Gongsun Sheng be there, too?" And he asked: "Old gentleman, do you have a Gongsun Sheng in your village?"

"If you asked someone else, sir, you probably wouldn't get any answer. Most people don't know him by that name. He's a neighbor of mine, and he lives alone with his old mother. For a time he was away from home on religious wanderings, and he was called Gongsun the Pure. Now, he's given up his family name altogether, and he's known simply as the Pure Taoist. No one calls him Gongsun Sheng. That was his secular name. They wouldn't know who you meant."

"This is really a case of 'Wearing out iron shoes seeking in vain, then finding a solution with the greatest of ease'! Old gentleman, how far is Two Fairies Mountain from here? Is the Pure Taoist at home?"

"It's only about forty-five *li* from this county. Pure Taoist is the leading disciple of Luo the Sage. His master would never let him leave."

Dai was delighted. He urged the waiter to hurry with the noodles, then he ate with the old man. Dai paid the bill, and they left the shop together.

After asking the old man for directions, Dai said: "You go on ahead, old gentleman. I'll join you later. I want to buy some incense and paper money first."

The old man bid him farewell and departed.

Dai Zong and Li Kui returned to their inn, collected their luggage and bundles, attached the charms, left the inn and set out for Two Fairies Mountain. Using the magic travel method, they covered the forty-five *li* in no time. They asked the way to the mountain on arrival at the county town of Jiugong.

"Go east from here," their informant said. "It's only five *li.*"

The two followed directions and, sure enough, in less that five *li* they reached the foot of Two Fairies Mountain. There, they met a woodcutter. Dai bowed courteously.

"Could you tell us where the Pure Taoist lives?"

The woodcutter pointed. "Through that mountain pass. There's a little stone bridge right outside his gate."

The two traversed the pass and saw a dozen thatched buildings surrounded by a low wall. Outside there was a small stone bridge. As they approached it they met a peasant girl coming from the enclosure carrying a basket of fruit. Dai Zong bowed.

"I see you're from the Pure Taoist's home. Is he in, do you know?"

"He's in back, refining cinnabar pills."

Pleased, Dai softly instructed Li Kui: "Conceal yourself in that thicket. After I've seen him I'll call you."

Dai Zong went in and looked around. A reed curtain hung in front of the door of a three-room thatched cottage. Dai coughed, and a white-haired old woman emerged. He bowed politely.

"I would like to see the Pure Taoist, old mother."

"What is your name, sir?"

"Dai Zong, from Shandong Province."

"My son is away on a religious journey. He hasn't returned yet."

"We're old friends. I have something important to tell him. Please let me see him."

"He's not home. You can leave a message, if you wish. You can see him when he comes back."

"I'll drop in again."

Dai bid the old woman farewell and returned to Li Kui outside the gate.

"I'll have to use you today. His mother says he's not at home. Go in and ask to see him. If she tells you he's away, start smashing things but don't hurt her. I'll rush in and stop you."

Li Kui took his pair of axes from his bundle, tucked them in his waist sash, and entered the gate. "Send someone out," he shouted.

The old woman hastily emerged. "Who is it?" she called. She became frightened when she saw Li Kui glaring at her, and said: "What is it you want, brother?"

"I'm Black Whirlwind from Liangshan Marsh. I'm under orders to invite Gongsun Sheng. Tell him to come out, so we can meet face to face. If he refuses, I'll set this friggin place on fire and burn your home to the ground!" And he shouted: "I want him to come right out!"

"Don't be like that, bold fellow. This isn't Gongsun Sheng's house. My son is called the Pure Taoist."

"Just tell him to come out. I'll know when I see his friggin face."

"He's on a religious trip and hasn't returned."

Li Kui pulled out his big axes and knocked down a wall. The old woman moved forward to stop him.

"If you don't call your son, I'll kill you," cried Li Kui. He raised his axes.

The old woman collapsed to the ground in terror. Gongsun Sheng emerged from the house, running.

"Don't you dare," he yelled.

At the same time Dai Zong shouted: "Iron Ox, how can you frighten this old mother?" He helped her to her feet.

Li Kui tossed his axes aside and hailed Gongsun respectfully. "Brother, forgive me. This was the only way to get you out."

Gongsun first supported his mother into the house, then returned and invited his two visitors into a quiet room and asked them to be seated. "How fortunate you've tracked me down," he said.

"After you left the mountain, brother," said Dai Zong. "I sought you in Jizhou, but was unable to discover where you'd gone. So I gathered a band of brothers and went back to the stronghold. Brother Song Jiang recently tried to rescue Lord Chai in Gaotang, but was twice defeated because of magic used by the prefect Gao Lian. He can't cope with it, and has sent me and Li Kui to request your assistance. We searched all Jizhou for you without success. Fortunately, we ran into an old gentleman in a noodle shop who told us where to find you. A village girl said you were at home refining cinnabar, but your old mother insisted you were away. So I asked Li Kui to arouse you into coming out. It was a crude method, and I beg your pardon. But to brother Song Jiang at Gaotang, every day is like a year. We urge that you go with us and demonstrate your unflagging chivalry."

"I have drifted about since childhood, and have become acquainted with many gallant men. Though I left Liangshan Marsh and returned home, I haven't forgotten you. But my mother is old and has no one to look after her, and my teacher, Luo the Sage, wants me by his side. I was afraid the stronghold would send people looking for me. That's why I changed my name to the Pure Taoist and hid myself here."

"Song Jiang is in danger. Have mercy, brother. You must make this trip."

"My mother has no one to take care of her, and my teacher never would let me go. It's really out of the question."

Dai Zong kowtowed and pleaded. Gongsun raised him to his feet. "We can talk about this later," he said. He served his guests wine and vegetable dishes in the quiet room, and the three ate.

"If you refuse to go, brother," said Dai Zong, "Song Jiang will surely be captured by Gao Lian. The chivalry of our mountain fortress will be ended."

"Let me ask my teacher," said Gongsun. "If he agrees, I'll go with you."

"We'll go to him at once."

"Relax and spend the night here. We can start the first thing in the morning."

"For Song Jiang in his present position each day is like a year. Please, brother, let's go now."

Gongsun led Dai and Li along a road to the Two Fairies Mountain. It was the end of autumn and the beginning of winter. The days were short, the nights long, and it grew dark early. By the time they were halfway up the slope, the red sun was sinking in the west. They followed a path through the dimness of a pine grove to the temple presided over by Luo the Sage. On a vermilion plaque over the gate inscribed in letters of gold were the words: "Temple of the Purple Void."

The three straightened their clothes in the Garments Pavilion, then proceeded along a covered walk to the Hall of Pines and Cranes. Two boy novices informed the Sage of their arrival. He ordered that they be invited in. They entered. Luo had just finished his prayers and was seated on a cloud-decorated dais. Gongsun advanced and greeted him, then stood and waited, body bent respectfully. Dai Zong hastily kowtowed. Li Kui only stared.

"Who are these two gentlemen?" Luo asked.

"Brothers of former days I've told you about, Teacher, gallant friends from Shandong. Gao Lian, prefect of Gaotang, has been using magic. Brother Song Jiang has sent these two brothers to ask my help. I wouldn't venture to decide on my own. I've come to ask Teacher's permission."

"You've escaped the fiery pit of human frailty, you've learned to make longevity pills. Why go back to that life?"

Dai Zong again kowtowed, "Please allow Teacher Gongsun to go with us," he requested. "After he's broken Gao Lian's spell, we shall escort him back."

"You two gentlemen don't understand," said Luo the Sage. "This is not a matter of concern to religious persons. Leave here. Make other plans."

Gongsun could only lead them away. They left the Hall of Pines and Cranes and went down the mountain the same night.

"What did that old mystic teacher say?" asked Li Kui.

"Why didn't you listen?" said Dai Zong.

"I couldn't understand his gibberish."

"He said Gongsun couldn't go."

"We travel all this distance, I'm given a hard time, and we finally find him," shouted Li Kui, "and all we get is parts! That old thief had better not make me lose my temper or I'll crush his hat with one hand, grab him by the waist with the other, and fling him down the mountain!"

Dai-Zong frowned. "Do you want to be rooted to the spot again?"

Li Kui smiled abashedly. "No, no. I was only joking."

When they reached Gongsun's home the Taoist prepared some food. He and Dai Zong ate, but Li Kui sat wrapped in thought and didn't touch a morsel.

"Rest here tonight," said Gongsun, "and tomorrow I'll plead with my teacher again. If he agrees, I'll go with you."

Dai Zong bid him good night, put his luggage in order, and retired to the quiet room with Li Kui. But Black Whirlwind couldn't sleep. He endured his wakefulness till around the fifth watch, then got up softly. He listened to his companion. Dai Zong was snoring peacefully.

"Are you a friggin craven?" Li Kui mentally addressed Gongsun. "That old man is full of crap! You used to be a member of our stronghold. Why do you need permission from that friggin teacher? Suppose he doesn't agree? Won't that harm brother Song Jiang? I won't stand for it! I'll kill the old rogue! Then Gongsun will have no one to ask, and he'll have to go with us!"

Li Kui groped for his two axes, quietly opened the house door and, step by step in the moonlight, made his way up the mountain. The double portals of the Temple of Purple Void were shut, but the fence around the compound was not high, and he cleared it in a leap. After opening the portals in readiness for a retreat, he crept into the grounds till he came to the Hall of Pines and Cranes. He heard someone within chanting scriptures. He crawled closer and poked a hole through the paper window. Luo the Sage was seated alone on his dais. Two smoking candles on a table before him shed a bright light.

"That wretched Taoist," thought Li Kui. "He deserves to die." Stealthily, he crept to the latticed door and, with one push, swung it creaking open. He charged in, raised his axes and brought them down on the Sage's forehead. Luo collapsed on his dais. His flowing blood was white. Li Kui laughed.

"The varlet must have been a virgin. He's still got all his male essence. He hasn't used any of it! There's not a drop of red blood in him!" Li Kui took a close look at his handiwork. His ax had cleaved the Sage's hat and split his head right down to his neck.

"Today, I've removed a trouble-maker," Black Whirlwind observed with satisfaction. "We won't have to worry about Gongsun not going."

Turning, he left the Hall of Pines and Cranes and hurried along the corridor. A young black-clad novice blocked his way.

"You killed our teacher," the boy yelled. "Don't think you can escape!"

"Little knave," cried Li Kui. "Have a taste of my axes!"

He chopped, and the boy's head rolled to the foot of the terrace. Li Kui laughed.

"I'd better get out of here."

He left the temple portals and flew down the mountain. At Gongsun's house he slipped in and closed the door behind him. Once more he listened in the quiet room. Dai Zong was still asleep. Softly, Li Kui returned to bed and slept.

Gongsun rose at daylight and laid out some breakfast. He and Dai Zong ate.

"Please take us up the mountain again so that we may plead with your teacher," said Dai.

Li Kui bit his lips to keep from laughing.

The three followed the same path and climbed the slope. At the Hall of Pines and Cranes inside the Temple of Purple Void they were met by two novices.

"Is the Sage within?" asked Gongsun.

"He's meditating on his cloud dais," the boys replied.

Li Kui was astonished. He stuck his tongue so far out in consternation, for a long time he couldn't pull it back. They pushed aside the door curtain and entered. Sure enough, there seated on the dais was Luo the Sage.

"Could I have killed the wrong man last night?" Li Kui wondered. "What brings you three here again?" Luo queried. "We wish to beg your permission for Gongsun our teacher to rescue mercifully many people in distress," said Dai Zong.

"Who is that big swarthy fellow?"

"A brother in chivalry of mine, Li Kui."

The Sage laughed. "I was going to refuse Gongsun. But for that dark fellow's sake I'll let him take this one trip."

Dai Zong kowtowed, and relayed the information to Black Whirlwind.

Li Kui thought: "The rascal knows I wanted to kill him. Why does he make such friggin remarks?"

"I'll send you three immediately to Gaotang," said Luo. "How will that be?"

They thanked him, and Dai Zong said to himself: "This Sage has much stronger magic than my Miraculous Travel Method."

Luo directed his novices to bring three handkerchiefs.

Dai asked him: "How are you going to get us to Gaotang so quickly? Please explain."

The Sage stood up. "Come with me."

They left the hall and followed him to the top of a bluff. A red kerchief was spread upon the ground.

"Purity, stand on that."

Gongsun placed both feet on the kerchief. With an upward sweep of his wide sleeve, Luo cried: "Rise!"

The kerchief turned into a red cloud and carried Gongsun high into the air till it was two hundred feet above the mountain.

"Stop," shouted Luo the Sage, and the red cloud hung suspended.

Next, a blue handkerchief was spread, and Dai Zong was told to stand upon it. At the command, "Rise," it changed into a blue cloud and soared up till it was at a level with the red. Each the size of a large sleeping mat, the two clouds circled in the heavens. Li Kui stared, open-mouthed.

Luo then had a white kerchief spread upon the bluff top, and he instructed Li Kui to step on.

"This is no joke," the Black Whirlwind grinned. "If a man fell off he could raise quite a bump on the head!"

"You see those other two, don't you?" said Luo.

Li Kui stood on the kerchief and the Sage shouted: "Rise!" The kerchief changed into a white cloud and started upwards.

"Aiya," yelled Li Kui, "mine is unsteady! Let me down!"

Luo waved his right hand, and the red and blue clouds smoothly returned to earth. Dai kowtowed his thanks, and stood on Luo's right. Gongsun stood on his left. Above, Li Kui was shouting.

"I have to piss and shit like everyone else! If you don't bring me down, I'll pour it on your head from up here!"

"I'm one who has given up the material world. I've never harmed you. Why did you come over the wall at night and hack me with your axes?" Luo asked.

"If I weren't possessed of virtue, you'd have killed me. And you murdered my novice."

"It wasn't me! You're mistaking me for somebody else!"

The Sage laughed. "Although all you did was chop off a couple of gourds, your intentions were bad. I'm going to make you suffer a bit for that." He waved his hand. "Go!"

An ugly wind blew Li Kui into the clouds. Two warriors, wearing head kerchiefs of imperial yellow, escorted him under guard. The wind and rain howled in Li Kui's ears. He looked down. Houses and trees seemed to be falling backwards as he passed. His feet felt as if they were being hastened by clouds and mists.

He had no idea how far he had gone. He was scared out of his wits, and was trembling all over. Suddenly, he heard a scraping sound, and found himself rolling down the roof of the main hall of the prefecture of Jizhou.

The magistrate, Ma Shihong, was holding court. Arrayed outside the building were many police and functionaries. When they saw a big swarthy fellow tumbling down from the sky they were very startled.

"Bring that rogue here," shouted Ma.

A dozen jailors and guards hustled Li Kui forward.

"Where are you from, rascally sorcerer?" demanded the magistrate. "Why have you dropped from the heavens?"

Li Kui, in his fall, had banged his head and split his brow. He was too stunned to speak.

"He must be a wizard," Ma affirmed. He directed that punishment implements be brought.

Guards and jailors tied Li Kui up and dragged him to the grassy sward before the hall. A captain poured dog's blood on his cranium. Another tipped a bucket of urine and turds and drenched him from head to toe. Li Kui's mouth and ears were full of the stuff.

"I'm not a wizard," he bawled. "I'm an attendant of Luo the Sage!"

Everyone in Jizhou knew that Luo the Sage was a living spirit on earth. They were reluctant to harm Li Kui any further. They pushed him before the magistrate.

"Luo the Sage is famed for having attained virtue and becoming a living god," said a functionary. "If this is one of his followers, we mustn't punish him."

The magistrate laughed. "I've read a thousand books and know ancient and modern history, but I've never heard of a living god who had a disciple like this! He's just an evil sorcerer. Guards, give him a good drubbing!"

They had no choice but to turn him over and beat him till he was more dead than alive.

"Admit you're a wizard, knave," shouted the magistrate, "and we'll stop."

Li Kui had no choice but to confess that he was "Wizard Li the Second." A big rack was nailed around his neck and he was cast into prison. He was put into the section for the condemned.

"I am a spirit general and officer of the day," he asserted loudly. "How dare you place a rack on me? I'm going to wipe every one of you out in Jizhou Town!"

The guards and warden all knew that the virtue of Luo the Sage was of the highest purity, and they admired him greatly.

"Who are you, really?" they asked Li Kui.

"Officer of the day, spirit general, and intimate of Luo the Sage! I made a mistake and annoyed him, so he flung me here that I might suffer a bit. But he'll be sending for me in two or three days. If you don't serve me meat and wine I'll slaughter you and your whole families!"

The guards and warden were frightened. They bought wine and meat and invited Li Kui to dine. Seeing this, he grew wilder in his speech, which scared his listeners still more. They brought hot water for him to bathe in, and clean clothing.

"If you stint on wine and meat, I'll fly away," he threatened. "I'll make you suffer!"

The guards and jailors apologized and entreated. Needless to say, he I remained in the Jizhou prison.

All of this Luo the Sage related to Dai Zong, who pleaded that he spare Li Kui. Luo kept Dai as his guest in the hall and questioned him about activities in the mountain fortress. Dai said that Chao Gai and Song Jiang were chivalrous and charitable, doing only what was morally right, never harming faithful officers of the emperor, noble-hearted men, filial sons, righteous husbands or chaste wives. He told of their many virtues.

Luo was very pleased.

Dai stayed with him for five days, and each day he kowtowed and begged the Sage to save Li Kui.

"Men like that can only be driven away," said Luo. "Don't take him back with you."

"You don't understand," replied Dai. "Li Kui is stupid, he doesn't know the rites, but he has his good points. First of all he's absolutely straight. He'll rarely ask anyone for anything. Secondly, he doesn't flatter people, but when he's loyal it's to the death. Third, he's not lecherous, greedy or treacherous, but brave and bold. For these reasons, Song Jiang loves Li Kui. I wouldn't be able to face brother Song if I went back without him."

Luo laughed. "I've known for some time that he is one of the stars of Heavenly Spirits. Because many people on earth behave too wickedly, as a punishment to them and him he was sent down to kill them. Would I dare go against the will of Heaven and harm a man like that? I only want to rough him up a little, then you can have him back."

Dai thanked the Sage, and Luo called: "Are any warriors around?" A wind rose outside the Hall of Pines and Cranes, and when it passed a warrior in a turban of imperial yellow stepped forward and bowed. "What are your orders, Teacher?"

"Bring that man back you escorted to the Jizhou prison. He's paid for his crime. Go and return quickly."

The warrior respectfully assented. In about half a watch, he dropped Li Kui down from the air. Dai hastily helped him to his feet.

"Where have you been these last couple of days, brother?" he asked.

Li Kui saw Luo the Sage and fervently kowtowed. "My own father, I'll never dare to offend again!"

"You must curb your temper from now on," said Luo. "Concentrate on serving Song Jiang. Shun all wicked thoughts."

Li Kui again kowtowed. "You are like my own father! Would I dare disobey your commands?"

"Where did you go these last few days?" Dai pressed him.

"The wind that day blew me to the Jizhou magistrate's office and rolled me down the roof. They all grabbed me and that friggin magistrate said I was a wizard. He had me knocked down and tied up and told his prison guards to pour dog's blood and piss and shit all over me and beat me till my legs were jelly. Then they put a rack on me and threw me into prison.

"'What spirit general are you to come down from heaven like that?' they asked me. 'Personal attendant to Luo the Sage and officer of the day spirit general,' I told them. 'Because I've made some mistakes I have to suffer a bit. But I'll be called for in a couple of days.' Though I was beaten, I got some good food and wine out of it. Those rogues were afraid of the Sage, so they let me bathe and gave me a change of clothes.

"They were wining and dining me just now in a pavilion, when that yellow turbaned warrior jumped down from the sky. He opened my rack and told me to close my eyes. It was like a dream, till I landed back here."

"The Teacher has over a thousand such warriors," said Gongsun. "They're all his personal attendants."

"Living Buddha," cried Li Kui. "Why didn't you tell me before and save me from making that stupid error?" Again he kowtowed to the Sage.

Dai Zong also kowtowed. "I've been here indeed a long time," he said. "The military situation at Gaotang is desperate. Please be merciful and let teacher Gongsun go with us and rescue brother Song Jiang. After we've smashed Gao Lian we'll escort him back."

"I was opposed to letting him go, originally. But because of your lofty loyalty I shall permit him to make the trip. I have something to impart first which you must remember."

Gongsun came forward and knelt before the Sage to receive his instructions.

Truly, he was filled with desire to save the world and bring tranquility to the land, a man destined for high rank and prestigious position.

What, then, did Luo the Sage say to Gongsun Sheng? Read our next chapter if you would know.

CHAPTER 54

DRAGON IN THE CLOUDS DEFEATS GAO LIAN BY MAGIC

BLACK WHIRLWIND GOES DOWN A WELL AND RESCUES CHAI JIN

"Younger brother," said the Luo the Sage, "the magic you've learned is the same as Gao Lian's. But now I'm going to teach you the Divine Method for Summoning the Five Thunderbolts. With this you can save Song Jiang, defend the country, preserve peace for the people, and act righteously on Heaven's behalf. I will see to it that your old mother is looked after. You may rest assured. You are one of the stars of Heavenly Spirits. For that reason, I permit you to help Song Jiang. Retain the virtues you have learned. Let no mundane desires lead you astray, lest you be deflected from your important cause."

Gongsun Sheng knelt and received the Method. Then, with Dai Zong and Li Kui, he took leave of the Sage and his Taoist colleagues, went down the mountain and returned home. Collecting his twin swords, his iron helmet, and Taoist cloak, he bid farewell to his mother, and set forth along the road out of the mountains.

When they had travelled thirty or forty *li,* Dai Zong said to Gongsun: "I'll go on ahead and report to Song Jiang. You and Li Kui follow the highway. I'll come back and pick you up."

"Good, you do that," said Gongsun. "We'll move as fast as possible."

"Take care of the Teacher," Dai admonished Li Kui. "If anything goes wrong, I'll make you suffer for it."

"He knows the same magic as Luo the Sage," Black Whirlwind replied. "I wouldn't dare neglect him!"

Dai Zong affixed his charms and, invoking his marvellous travel means, swiftly departed.

Leaving Two Fairies Mountain and Jiugong County behind them, Gongsun and Li Kui pushed on along the main road, resting in inns at nightfall. Black Whirlwind was afraid of the Luo the Sage's magic. He treated Gongsun with the greatest solicitude and kept his impetuosity tightly in check.

On the third day of their journey, they came to a town called Wugang, a populous, busy place.

"These last couple of days have been tiring. Let's have some wine and noodles before going on," Gongsun suggested.

"Fine," said Li Kui.

They saw a small tavern beside the post road and went in. Gongsun sat down at the head of the table. Li Kui undid the pack around his waist and seated himself opposite. They ordered wine and vegetable tidbits.

"Have you any meatless pastries?" Gongsun asked the waiter.

"No, we've only meat and wine here," said the man. "But there's a shop at the town entrance that sells date cakes."

"I'll go and buy you some," Li Kui volunteered. He took copper coins from his purse, headed into town and bought the cakes. Starting back, he heard people in a crowd by the side of the road cry admiringly: "What strength!"

Li Kui looked. They were surrounding a big fellow, watching him manipulate a large ribbed iron mallet. He was tall, his face was pitted with smallpox scars, and there was a large groove in his nose. Li Kui estimated the mallet to weigh about thirty catties. The man swung it and smashed a paving block to bits with a single blow. The crowd cheered. This was more than Li Kui could bear. He shoved the packet of date cakes inside his tunic and reached for the big hammer.

"Who the hell are you, that you dare take my mallet," the man shouted.

"That's some friggin farce you put on, trying to win applause! It hurts my eyes," said Li Kui. "I'll show these people how it should be done!"

"Go on, take the hammer. But if you can't wield it, I'll punch your neck!"

Li Kui picked up the mallet and flipped it about as if it were a child's slingshot. He toyed with it for a few minutes, then set it down lightly. He was neither red in the face nor panting, and his heart did not beat fast.

The man dropped to his knees and kowtowed. "I would know your name, big brother."

"Do you live around here?"

"Just up ahead." The man led Li Kui to a house and unlocked the door. He invited Li Kui in and asked him to be seated.

Li Kui noted an anvil, hammers, a forge, pincers, awls and pokers. "Must be a blacksmith," he thought. "We need a man like this in the fortress. Why don't I ask him to join?"

"What's your name?" he queried.

"I'm called Tang Long. My father was a garrison officer in the prefecture of Yanan. Because he was good ironsmith, he served directly under Old General Zhong. He died a few years, ago. I'm mad about gambling, and I've knocked about a lot. I'm here as a blacksmith temporarily only to earn my keep. My real love is play with weapons. Since I'm marked all over with smallpox scars, people call me the Gold-Coin Spotted Leopard. May I ask, brother, what your name is?"

"Li Kui, Black Whirlwind of Liangshan Marsh."

Tang Long kowtowed twice. "I've heard so much about you. Who'd have thought we'd meet today!"

"You'll never prosper hanging around this place. Come with me to Liangshan and join us. We'll make you a chieftain."

"If you don't despise me and are willing to take me along, I'll gladly serve as your groom." He pledged himself to be Li Kui's younger brother, and Black Whirlwind accepted him.

"I have no family to entertain you here," said Tang Long, "but I can treat you to three cups of simple wine in town to mark our brotherhood. Rest here tonight, and we'll set out tomorrow."

"There's a teacher in the tavern ahead, waiting for some date cakes I've bought. We have to go as soon as he's eaten. We must leave immediately."

"What's the hurry?"

"Our brother Song Jiang is involved in a fierce battle on the edge of Gaotang Prefecture. Only this teacher can save him."

"Who is he?"

"Don't ask. Just get your things together and come."

Tang Long hastily packed a bag, took silver for travelling expenses, put on a broad-brimmed felt hat, hung a dagger at his waist, and grabbed a halberd. He left his dilapidated home and crude furnishings, and followed Li Kui to Gongsun Sheng in the tavern.

"Where have you been all this time?" the Taoist demanded reproachfully. "I'd have gone back if you kept me waiting much longer."

Li Kui was afraid to reply. Instead, he introduced Tang Long, and told of their pledge of brotherhood. Gongsun was pleased to learn that he was a blacksmith. Li Kui produced the date cakes and instructed the waiter have them heated. The three downed several cups of wine together, ate the cakes, and paid the bill.

Tang Long and Li Kui shouldered the packs. With Gongsun, they left the town and made their way along a winding road towards Gaotang.

By the time they had covered two thirds of their journey, Dai Zong returned to meet them. Gongsun was delighted.

"How's the battle going?" he asked.

"Gao Lian has recovered from his arrow wound. He marches out with soldiers and challenges us every day. But brother Song Jiang is afraid to engage them. He's waiting for you."

"It will be easy."

Li Kui introduced Tang Long to Dai Zong and related what had transpired. The four men hurried on to Gaotang. About five *li* from the brigands' camp they were met by Lu Fang and Guo Sheng leading a hundred cavalrymen. The four mounted and proceeded to the camp.

Song Jiang and Wu Yong were waiting to greet them. Obeisances were exchanged, the travellers were offered wine, politely questioned about their journey, and invited into the headquarters tent. All the chieftains came to congratulate them on bringing Gongsun, Li Kui introduced Tang Long. When the courtesies were completed, a celebration feast was laid.

The next day Song Jiang, Wu Yong and Gongsun conferred in the tent on how to smash Gao Lian. "Give the order to attack the city," Gongsun said to Song Jiang. "We'll see what the enemy reaction is. I have a plan."

Song Jiang transmitted the command to the leaders of each encampment. These led their men to the moat around Gaotang, where they again made camp. At dawn, everyone rose and had breakfast, and the warriors donned their armor. Song Jiang, Wu Yong and Gongsun rode to the fore.

Mid waving banners the men shouted, while the thunder of drums and the bray of gongs beat against the city walls.

During the night an officer had reported to Gao Lian, the prefect, now recovered from his arrow wound, that Song Jiang's forces had arrived. In the morning Gao put on his armor, opened the city gate, lowered the drawbridge, and rode forth with his three hundred Miracle soldiers, plus officers high and low.

When the two armies were in sight of each other's drums and pennants, they spread out in battle position. Intricately carved drums thundered. Beribboned, embroidered banners waved. From Song Jiang's position a V-formation of ten horsemen trotted up. The left wing consisted of Hua Rong, Qin Ming, Zhu Tong, Ou Peng and Lu Fang. In the right wing were Lin Chong, Sun Li, Deng Fei, Ma Lin and Guo Sheng. The three commanding generals rode between them.

On the opposite side, golden drums pounded, and a front row of banners parted to permit the forward passage of Gao Lian, prefect of Gaotang, surrounded by twenty or thirty of his officers. He halted before the banners and hurled imprecations.

"Swamp bandits! Since it's a fight you want, we'll fight you to the death! Whoever runs is no real man!"

"Who will ride forth for me and cut this scoundrel down?" Song Jiang demanded.

Hua Rong, lance raised, kicked his horse and cantered to the center of the clearing.

"Who will take this rogue for me?" Gao Lian called.

A captain named Xue Yuanhui, wielding a pair of sabres, galloped forward on a spirited mount. The two men battled several rounds. Hua Rong turned his Steed and rode towards his original position. Brandishing his sabres, Xue raced in pursuit. Hua Rong slowed his horse slightly, fitted an arrow to his bow, twisted around suddenly in his saddle, and let fly. Xue tumbled head first to the ground. Both sides roared.

Angrily, Gao Lian clanged his sword three times on the animal-embossed bronze shield hanging from the pommel of his saddle. A yellow dust storm rose from the midst of the Miracle soldiers, dimming the sun and darkening the earth and sky. The men yelled, as from the yellow cloud there emerged savage beasts and weird serpents. Song Jiang's forces began retreating in alarm.

But then Gongsun pulled out an ancient sword with a pine tree pattern. He pointed it at the enemy, muttered an incantation, and shouted: "Speed!"

A golden ray shot into the yellow cloud and zapped every serpent and beast. As they fell they were seen to be only white paper cutouts, and the haze of yellow dust disintegrated.

Song Jiang pointed with his whip. All three contingents charged, mowing down men and horses of the foe. Their drums and banners were scattered in disarray. Gao Lian fled to the city with his Miracle soldiers. Song Jiang's forces chased them to the foot of the walls. But the drawbridge was hurriedly raised and the gates slammed shut. Logs and ballista stones rained down on the attackers.

At Song Jiang's command, gongs were beaten as a signal for his forces to make camp and be counted. They had won a stunning victory. Song Jiang summoned Gongsun to his tent and thanked him for his marvellous Taoist sorcery. Then he rewarded the army's three contingents. The next day they divided and assaulted the city vigorously from all sides. To Song Jiang and Wu Yong, Gongsun said: "Although we destroyed more than half the enemy effectives last night, the three hundred Miracle soldiers got safely into the city. We must pound them hard, for tonight that villain is sure to raid our camp. We'll pull out in the dark of night, first erecting false palisades, and lie in ambush all around. Tell our men when they hear the sound of thunder and see flames rising in the camp to rush in and attack."

Orders were so given. Early in the afternoon they withdrew from the city and returned to camp, where they drank and loudly made merry. When darkness fell, all quietly slipped away and took up ambush positions on the camp's perimeter.

Song Jiang, Wu Yong, Gongsun, Hua Rong, Qin Ming, Lu Fang and Guo Sheng waited on a rise. Sure enough, in the middle of the night Gao Lian mustered his three hundred Miracle soldiers. Each man carried on his back an iron gourd containing sulphur, nitrate, and other gunpowder material. Each held a hooked blade and an iron whisk, and bore in his mouth a reed whistle. Around the second watch the city gate was opened, and the drawbridge lowered, and they marched forth with Gao Lian at their head and followed by thirty cavalry.

As they neared the brigands' camp Gao Lian performed a secret spell. A black mist erupted heavenward. A wild wind howled, driving before it sand and stones, ripping up earth and soil. With their fire-making equipment, the three hundred Miracle soldiers ignited the contents of their gourds, and blew together on their whistles. In the inky darkness, the flames illuminated their bodies as they surged into the camp, brandishing sabres and axes.

On the bluff, Gongsun grasped his sword and murmured an incantation. A thunderbolt burst in the empty camp, setting it ablaze. The frightened Miracle soldiers tried to run, but they were engulfed by flames, which reddened earth and sky. There was nowhere they could flee.

The fighters lying in ambush now closed in on the palisades. They could see very clearly from the outer darkness. Not one of the three hundred Miracle soldiers was allowed to escape. All were slaughtered, to the last man.

Gao Lian hastened towards the city with his thirty remaining cavalry. A pursuing battle steed was rapidly closing the gap between them. Its rider was Panther Head Lin Chong. He had almost caught up when Gao Lian yelled for the drawbridge to be lowered, and clattered into the city with eight or nine of his escort. Lin Chong captured the rest.

Once inside, Gao Lian ordered the citizens to man the ramparts. Song Jiang and Lin Chong had annihilated virtually his entire army as well as all his Miracle soldiers.

The next day, Song Jiang's forces again surrounded the city. "Who'd have thought he'd foil the magic I studied for years," Gao Lian said to himself. "What can I do?" He would have to dispatch men to neighboring prefectures to plead for aid.

Hastily, he penned notes to Dongchang and Kouzhou. "They're not far," he thought, "and the prefects in both received their appointments through my cousin. I'll request them to send reinforcements immediately." He dispatched two senior staff officers with the missives, letting them out through the west gates. They travelled west along the road at top speed.

The brigand leaders wanted to pursue them, but Wu Yong said: "Let them go. We'll use their own plan against them."

"What do you mean?" Song Jiang queried.

"They're very weak in the city in both officers and men, and they're begging for aid. We can have two of our columns pretend to be reinforcements and stage a mock battle with us on the road. Gao Lian will surely open the gates and come out to help them. That will be our chance to take the city. Meanwhile, we'll lure Gao Lian off onto a small path, and there we'll capture him."

Very pleased, Song Jiang directed Dai Zong to return to Mount Liangshan and fetch two columns of men and horses and have them approach the city separately.

Every night Gao Lian burned huge fires in the center of the city as a beacon and watched eagerly from the ramparts for his reinforcements. After several days, defenders on the walls observed a turmoil among Song Jiang's troops, though they didn't seem to be attacking. When this was reported to Gao Lian he quickly donned his armor and mounted the ramparts. He saw two columns of men and horses, their dust obscuring the sun, their shouts shaking the heavens, advancing rapidly. The brigand forces surrounding the city scattered at their approach.

Convinced that rescuers had arrived, Gao Lian mustered his forces. He opened the gates, and all charged out, dividing to join the fray.

When Gao Lian reached Song Jiang's position he saw the brigand leader, together with Hua Rong and Qin Ming galloping off along a path. Gao Lian and his men chased after them hotly. Suddenly, he heard cannon fire on the other side of the hill, and he grew suspicious. He and his unit turned around and started back. Gongs crashed on both sides of the path, and down the right slope came Lu Fang, and down the left slope came Guo Sheng, each leading five hundred men.

Gao Lian fled hurriedly, most of his escort already wiped out. When he got to the outskirts of the city he saw the banners of the men of Liangshan flying from its walls. No reinforcements were visible anywhere. Gao Lian ran with his broken remnants towards the mountains.

Before they had gone ten *li,* a body of men and horses surged out from around a bend, headed by Sun Li, and blocked their road. "I've been waiting for you," Sun shouted. "Dismount and be bound!"

Gao Lian turned to go back. But from behind another unit appeared, with Zhu Tong in the lead. Both sides began closing in. With all roads cut, Gao Lian could only abandon his horse and scramble into the mountains on foot. His soldiers ran with him.

Frantically, Gao Lian mumbled an incantation and shouted: "Rise!" On a black cloud he floated as high as the hilltops. Then Gongsun rounded the slope and saw this. From his horse, he gazed towards the sky and uttered a few phrases. "Speed!" he cried, pointing his sword upwards.

Gao Lian plummeted to earth from his cloud. Lei Heng sped forward from the side. With one sweep of his halberd, he cut him in two.

Lei Heng carried Gao Lian's head as all went down the mountain. A messenger was dispatched to report the news to Song Jiang swiftly. Song Jiang pulled back his outlying troops and entered Gaotang. He ordered that the citizenry were not to be harmed, and had proclamations posted assuring them that their lives and property were safe.

Next, he went to release Lord Chai from prison. The warden, jailors and guards had all left. Only the prisoners themselves, about fifty in number, remained. Their fetters were removed.

But Lord Chai was not among them. Song Jiang was worried and puzzled. In one of the buildings he found the family of Chai Jin's uncle, in another the family of Chai Jin himself. They had been arrested in Cangzhou and imprisoned here together. Because of the continuous fighting, they had not been questioned.

Only Lord Chai could not be found. Wu Yong directed that the jailors and guards be summoned. One of them said: "I am Lin Ren, the warden of this prison. Prefect Gao Lian instructed me to keep Lord Chai in a separate cell and make sure he didn't escape. 'If luck goes against us,' Gao Lian said, 'finish him off.' Three days ago he ordered me to take Lord Chai out and kill him. I could see that he was a good man. I didn't have the heart. So I stalled. 'He's very ill,' I said. 'He's eight tenths gone already. There's no need to do anything.' But then they really put the pressure on me, so I said: 'Chai Jin's dead.' The prefect was busy fighting every day, and he had no time. But I was afraid he'd send people to check up. If they found Chai Jin, I'd be in for it. So yesterday I took him to a dry well in the rear courtyard, removed his fetters, and pushed him in to hide there. I don't know whether he's alive or dead."

Song Jiang hastily had Lin Ren lead him to the well. He peered down into its black maw, unable to fathom its depth. He called, but no one answered. A rope was lowered. It extended about ninety feet before touching bottom.

"He doesn't seem to be there," said Song Jiang, and tears rolled from his eyes.

"Don't upset yourself, Commander-in-Chief," urged Wu Yong. "We won't know until we send someone down to see."

Before the words were out of his mouth, Li Kui the Black Whirlwind pressed forward and shouted: "Let me go."

"Good," said Song Jiang. "You're the one who put him in his predicament. It's only right that you should repay."

Li Kui laughed. "I'm not afraid to go down. Just don't cut the rope."

"Don't be funny," said Wu Yong.

A long rope was tied to a large basket, a frame placed over the well mouth, and the rope slung over the frame. Li Kui stripped to the buff, grasped his battle axes, and sat in the basket, which was lowered into the well. Two copper bells were affixed to the upper portion of the rope. * Gradually, the basket reached bottom. Li Kui crawled out and felt around. He touched a heap of bones.

"Father and mother," he cried. "What friggin thing is this?"

He continued groping. The well bottom was damp. There wasn't a dry place to set foot. Li Kui put his axes in the basket and felt around with both hands. The area was quite wide. Finally he touched a man, crouched in a puddle.

"Lord Chai," he exclaimed.

But the man didn't move. Li Kui put a hand in front of the man's face. Only faint breath was coming from his mouth.

"Thank Heaven and Earth," Li Kui said. "He can still be saved!"

He climbed into the basket and shook the bells. The others hauled him up. He emerged alone and told what he had found.

"Go down again and put Lord Chai in the basket," directed Song Jiang. "After we've got him out, we'll send the basket down for you."

"I had two tricks played on me at Jizhou, brother. I don't want this to be a third."

Song Jiang laughed. "Would I fool you? Go down, quickly."

Once more Li Kui got into the basket and descended into the well. On reaching bottom, he crawled out, carried Lord Chai over, put him in the basket, and rang the bells. Those above began pulling immediately. When the basket reached the top, everyone was delighted to see Lord Chai.

Song Jiang examined him. He had a gash on his forehead, the flesh on both legs had been beaten to a pulp, and his eyes were half open and half closed. He was a sorry sight. A doctor was called to treat him.

Li Kui was bellowing at the bottom of the well. Song Jiang ordered that basket be lowered and that he be pulled up. Li Kui was very angry when he reached the surface.

"You're no good, any of you," he raged. "Why didn't you send the basket down for me?"

"We were so worried about Lord Chai, we forgot," Song Jiang explained. "Please forgive us."

He ordered a cart for Chai Jin to lie on, and more than twenty others for the lord's family and that of his uncle, together with their valuables. He instructed Li Kui and Lei Heng to escort them to the Liangshan stronghold. He also directed that Gao Lian's entire household of thirty or forty, good and bad alike, be executed in the marketplace. The warden Lin Ren was rewarded. As much as possible of the riches in the prefecture's treasury and the grain in its granary, as well as Gao Lian's private property, were packed and carried off to the mountain fortress.

The brigand officers, high and low, left Gaotang and returned to Liangshan Marsh, troubling none of the prefectures and counties they passed through on the way. After several days, they reached the stronghold. In spite of his illness, Chai Jin got up and thanked Chao Gai, Song Jiang and the other leaders. Chao Gai ordered that a house be built near Song Jiang's residence on the summit for Lord Chai and his family.

All of the leaders were very pleased, for they had acquired two more commanders—Chai Jin and Tang Long. They banqueted in celebration. Of that we'll say no more.

By then Dongchang and Kouzhou had heard that Gao Lian, prefect of Gaotang had been killed and that the city had fallen. They immediately dispatched written reports to the emperor. Officials who had escaped from Gaotang also brought news of this to the capital. Marshal Gao Qiu thus learned that his cousin had been slain.

At the fifth watch the next day he went to the imperial ante-hall and waited for the morning bell. Hundreds of officials in ceremonial robes thronged the inner hall, waiting to attend the audience. At the third section of the fifth watch, the emperor entered the imperial chamber. Three times the ceremonial staff tapped, and civil and military officials formed in separate ranks as the emperor seated himself on the throne.

"Let those with business present their petitions," intoned the chief of ceremonies.

Marshal Gao stepped forward and spoke: "Of late Chao Gai and Song Jiang, leaders of the bandits in Liangshan Marsh in Jizhou Prefecture, have committed a series of terrible crimes, plundering cities and robbing government granaries. In savage hordes they slaughtered government troops in Jizhou and ran riot in Jiangzhou and Wuweijun. Most recently, they wiped out the entire city of Gaotang and walked off with everything in the granary and treasury. They are like a canker in our vitals. If we don't quell them quickly they will grow so strong that we shall be unable to control them. I beseech Your Majesty to act."

The emperor was shocked. He ordered Gao to assemble an army, arrest the culprits, thoroughly purge the Marsh, and kill all such persons.

"We don't need a large army to deal with those petty outlaws. If Your Majesty will grant me a certain man, he will take care of them," said Gao.

"If you consider him so useful, he must be good. Have him go at once. Let us hear news of victory soon and we shall raise him in rank and reward him well. He will be given a high and important post."

"He is the direct descendant of Huyan Zan, the general from Hedong who won fame at the start of the dynasty. His name is Huyan Zhuo. He wields two steel rods and is a man of peerless courage. At present he is garrison commander of Runing Shire, and has under him many crack soldiers and brave officers. With the services of this man we can restore order to Liangshan Marsh. If given good officers and skilled troops and placed at their head, he will swiftly clean out the lair and return victorious."

The emperor directed the Council of Military Affairs to send an emissary to Runing immediately to fetch Huyan Zhuo. When the imperial court was concluded, Gao personally selected an official from the Council to serve as the emissary. He was sent forth that same day, and a time limit set for his return.

Huyan was conducting business in his military headquarters in Runing when an officer at the city gate entered and announced: "An emissary has come with an imperial edict ordering you, General, to the capital for a special mission."

With several prefectural officials Huyan went to the gate and conducted the emissary to military headquarters. Huyan read the edict and had a feast laid for the emissary. Then he donned his helmet and armor, saddled his horse and gathered his weapons, and left Runing with an escort of thirty or forty. They travelled through the night and soon reached the capital after an uneventful journey. Huyan Zhuo dismounted before the Chancellery of Imperial Defense and went in to see Marshal Gao.

Gao Qiu was holding court. The gate-keeper announced: "Huyan Zhuo, summoned from Runing, is at the gate." Very pleased, Gao directed that he be brought in. After asking Huyan solicitously about himself, Gao rewarded him.

Early the next day, Gao presented Huyan to their sovereign. The emperor could see that he was no ordinary man, and the imperial countenance smiled. He presented Huyan with a fine horse known as the Ebony Steed Which Treads in Snow. Pitch black in color except for snowy white hoofs, it could cover a thousand *li* in a single day. This beast was given to Huyan as his mount.

After thanking the emperor, Huyan Zhuo returned with Gao Qiu to the chancellery, where they discussed how to take Liangshan Marsh.

"I've spied out that place, Your Excellency," said Huyan. "They've many officers and men, and they're well equipped with fine horses and weapons. An adversary not to be despised. But I have two men I can guarantee to lead my vanguard, while I follow with our main force. We definitely will win a great victory."

Gao was delighted. "Who are these men?" he asked.

And because of the two Huyan guaranteed, the mountain citadel added fresh wings, and the fighters of Liangshan Marsh smashed the government hosts.

Truly, though their names were never inscribed in the Imperial Commendation Records, they were registered in the rolls of Fraternity Hall.

Who were the men Huyan proposed? Read our next chapter if you would know.

CHAPTER 55

MARSHAL GAO RAISES A THREE-COLUMN ARMY

HUYAN ZHUO DEPLOYS AN ARMORED CAVALRY

"I have in mind a district garrison commander in Chenzhou, a man named Han Tao," said Huyan. "Originally he's from the Eastern Capital. He's passed the Second Degree Military Examination and wields a datewood lance eighteen feet long. Everyone calls him the Ever-Victorious General. He can lead the vanguard. The other man I want is a district garrison commander in Yingzhou. His name is Peng Qi, and he also hails from the Eastern Capital. His family have been military people for generations. He uses a three-pointed two-edged lance. His skill with weapons is extraordinary, and he's known as the Eyes of Heaven General. This man can be second in command."

Marshal Gao was very pleased. "With Han and Peng in the van, we need have no fears about those impudent bandits," he exclaimed.

He wrote out two summonses and directed the Chancellery of Imperial Defense to dispatch messengers from the Council of Military Affairs with them immediately to Chenzhou and Yingzhou to fetch Han and Peng. In less than ten days the garrison commanders arrived in the capital. They went directly to the chancellery and presented themselves to Gao and Huyan.

The next day Gao and his entourage went to the training ground and watched imperial troops practicing and drilling. Then Gao returned to the Chancellery and conferred with the Council of Military Affairs on important matters of military strategy.

He asked Huyan and Han and Peng: "How many men have the three of you together?"

"About five thousand cavalry," said Huyan. "Ten thousand, if you include the infantry."

"Go back to your respective cities and pick three thousand of your best cavalry and five thousand foot soldiers. Assemble, set forth, and clean out Liangshan Marsh."

"Our cavalry and infantry are crack troops," said Huyan. "Both men and horses are in fine fettle. Your Excellency need have no worry about them. But we're short of clothing and armor. We don't want to cause delay and inconvenience, but we must request more time to prepare."

"If that's the case, go to the capital armory and pick out as much as you need in the way of clothing, armor, helmets and weapons. I'll issue the order now. We want your forces well equipped so that they can cope with the enemy. The day you're ready to march I'll send officials to check you over."

Huyan took the order and went with some of his people to the armory. There he selected three thousand sets of steel armor, five thousand sets of horsehide armor, three thousand bronze and iron helmets, two thousand pikes, one thousand swords, countless bows and arrows, and over five hundred cannon, and loaded them all onto carts. The day the three men were leaving the capital Gao issued them three thousand battle chargers and all the grain their forces would require, and gave them personal gifts of gold and silver, silks and satins.

Huyan, Han Tao and Peng Qi submitted written guarantees of victory, and took their leave of Marshal Gao and officials from the Council of Military Affairs.
'

They mounted their horses and rode back to Runing. The journey was uneventful. When they arrived, Huyan directed Han Tao and Peng Qi to return to their respective cities, raise their armies and bring them to Runing.

In less than half a month the three columns were complete. Huyan issued the equipment he had drawn from the imperial armory—clothing, armor, helmets, swords, pikes and saddles. He also had chainmail made, plus various other items of military ware, and distributed these as well among the three columns.

They were ready to go. Gao sent two officials from his chancellery to review them. The officials handsomely rewarded the three commanders, and Huyan marched forth with his three columns. Han Tao led the van, Huyan commanded the main force in the middle, Peng Qi and his men brought up the rear. The three columns of infantry and cavalry were a splendid sight as they hastened grimly towards Liangshan Marsh.

To the mountain stronghold came a far-posted scout with a report of the approaching troops. Chao Gai and Song Jiang, together with Military Advisor Wu Yong, magic expert Gongsun Sheng, and the various other chieftains had been feasting daily in celebration with Chai Jin. When they heard that Two Rods Huyan Zhuo of Runing was leading an army of infantry and cavalry to attack, they conferred on strategy.

"I've heard of him," said Wu Yong. "He's a direct descendant of Huyan Zan, the general from Hedong who helped establish the dynasty. His skill with weapons is superb. When he wields those two steel rods of his no one can come near him. We must use our most competent and courageous officers. To capture him we'll have to apply first force and second guile."

Before the words were out of his mouth, Black Whirlwind Li Kui spoke up. "I'll nab the wretch for you!"

"You'd never do it," said Song Jiang. "I have a plan of my own. We'll ask Qin Ming the Thunderbolt to fight the first bout, Panther Head Lin Chong the second, Hua Rong the third, Ten Feet of Steel the fourth, and Sickly General Sun Li the fifth. These bouts must come one right after the next, like the spokes of a spinning wheel. I myself will head ten brothers who will command our main divisions. On the left will be Zhu Tong, Lei Heng, Mu Hong, Huang Xin and Lu Fang. On the right will be Yang Xiong, Shi Xiu, Ou Peng, Ma Lin and Guo Sheng. Our water approaches will be defended by boats under the command of Li Jun, Zhang Heng, Zhang Shun and the three Ruan brothers. Li Kui and Yang Lin will lead two columns of infantry and lie in ambush as reinforcements."

Shortly thereafter, Qin Ming went down the mountain with a unit of men and horses. They set up a battle position on a broad plain.

Although it was already winter, the weather was pleasantly warm. The next day, they saw in the distance the approaching government troops. The van, led by Ever-Victorious General Han Tao, made camp and built surrounding palisades. There was no fighting that night.

The two armies faced each other at dawn the following day. Horns blared, and the thunder of drums shook the heavens. On Song Jiang's side Qin Ming the Thunderbolt rode forth from the arch of pennants, his wolf-toothed mace athwart his mount. On the opposite side at the arch of pennants appeared Han Tao, leader of the van. Holding his lance crosswise, he gave his horse rein and shouted at his foe.

"We heavenly hosts have arrived! But instead of surrendering, you dare to resist! You're asking to die! I'll fill in your Marsh and pulverise your Mount Liangshan! I'll capture you rebellious bandits, take you to the capital, and have you smashed to bits!"

Qin Ming was a hot tempered man. Without a word, he clapped his steed, and rode straight at Han Tao, flourishing his mace. Han Tao kicked up his horse, levelled his lance, and galloped to meet him. They fought over twenty rounds, and Han Tao began to weaken. He turned to go. From behind him came Huyan Zhuo, commander of the main contingent. He saw that Han Tao was being bested, and he charged forth on the snowy-hoofed black steed the emperor had given him, roaring and waving his steel rods.

Qin Ming recognized him, and prepared to do battle. But Lin Chong the Panther Head cantered up, calling: "Rest a while, commander. Let me go three hundred rounds with this fellow, then we'll see."

Lin Chong levelled his serpent-decorated lance and charged Huyan. Qin Ming wheeled his mount to the left and rode out of sight behind a bend. The new adversaries were evenly matched. The lance and rods interwove in flowery patterns for more than fifty rounds, but neither man could vanquish the other.

Hua Rong appeared for the third bout. At the entrance to the field of combat he called: "Rest a while, General Lin Chong. Watch me capture the lout."

Panther Head turned his horse and departed. Huyan had seen enough of his high-powered use of weapons. He let him go and returned to his own position, while Lin Chong disappeared around a bend with his men. Huyan was already among his rear column when Hua Rong emerged with lance at the level. Peng Qi the Eyes of Heaven General, astride a glossy brown piebald that could run a thousand *li* in a day, rode towards Hua Rong. Holding crosswise his three-pointed, two edged, four-holed, eight-ringed weapon, Peng shouted: "Traitorous robber! You're devoid of all morality! Let's fight this one to a finish!"

Hua Rong was furious. Without a word, he clashed with Peng Qi.

More than twenty rounds they battled. Huyan could see that Peng was weakening. He gave his horse rein and engaged Hua Rong.

Before they had fought three rounds, the girl warrior Ten Feet of Steel rode out for the fourth round. "Rest a while, General Hua Rong," she cried. "Watch me take this oaf!"

Hua Rong led his contingent off to the right and departed round a bend. Even before the battle between Peng Qi and Ten Feet of Steel approached a decisive stage, Sun Li the Sickly General, who would fight the fifth bout, had already arrived. He had reined his horse at the edge of the field of combat and was watching the two contestants.

They fought in a cloud of dust with murderous intensity, one with a long-handled sabre, the other with a pair of swords. For over twenty rounds they battled. Then the girl separated her blades and rode off. Peng Qi, eager for glory, gave chase. Ten Feet of Steel hung her swords on the pommel of her saddle. From inside her robe she pulled out a red lariat bearing twenty-four gold hooks. She let Peng Qi draw near, then suddenly twisted around and flung the rope. The noose landed squarely on him before he could ward it off, and he was dragged from his horse. Sun Li yelled a command, and his men rushed forward and grabbed the fallen rider.

Huyan, enraged, galloped to the rescue. Ten Feet of Steel clapped her steed and met him. The seething Huyan would have swallowed her down in one gulp, if he could. They battled more than ten rounds, Huyan increasingly frantic because he couldn't defeat the girl.

"What a spitfire," he fretted. "After all this fighting, she's still so tough!"

Impatiently, he feinted and let her close in, then raised his steel rods and started to bring them down. The swords were still in their resting place when the rod in Huyan's right hand was only a hair away from the girl's forehead. But Ten Feet of Steel was clear of eye and swift of hand. A sword sprang into her right fist, flew up and warded off the blow with a clang of metal and a shower of sparks.

The girl galloped back towards her own position. Huyan raced in pursuit. Sun Li promptly levelled his lance, intercepted Huyan and engaged him in fierce combat. Song Jiang moved up with his ten divisions and deployed them in battle formation. Ten Feet of Steel and her contingent, meanwhile, had ridden away down the slope.

Song Jiang was very pleased that Peng Qi the Eyes of Heaven General had been taken. He rode to the front to watch Sun Li and Huyan do battle. Sun Li sheathed his lance and went at Huyan with the steel rod ribbed like bamboo, which had been hanging from his wrist. Now, both were wielding rods of steel. Even their style of dress was similar. Sun Li wore a five cornered iron helmet bound in place by a red silk band around his forehead, a white-flowered black silk robe flecked with jade green, and darkly gleaming gold embossed armor. He rode a black stallion, and wielded a bamboo-shaped steel rod with dragon's eyes. Truly, a bolder picture than Yuchi Gong, that hero of old.

As to Huyan Zhuo, he wore a high pointed five-cornered helmet bound round the forehead by gold-flecked yellow silk, a black robe with sequins of seven stars, and darkly gleaming armor of over-lapping leaf. He rode the snowy-hoofed black stallion given him by the emperor, and wielded two octagonal steel rods polished bright as water. The one in his left hand weighed twelve catties, the one in his right thirteen. He indeed resembled his ancestor Huyan Zan.

Left and right over the field of combat they fought for more than thirty rounds, with neither man the victor.

When Han Tao saw Peng Qi captured, he quickly gathered the rear column and led them forward in a headlong rush. Song Jiang, afraid that they would break through, pointed his whip, and his ten commanders moved their divisions up to meet them, the last two spreading out in an enveloping pincers. Huyan hurriedly wheeled his columns around and each engaged their adversaries.

Why didn't the Liangshan warriors win total victory? Because of Huyan's "Armored Cavalry." Both horses and men wore chainmail. The battle steeds were draped to their hoofs, the soldiers protected to the eyes. Although Song Jiang's animals were equipped with some cover, this consisted mainly of red-tasseled net masks, copper bells, and plumes. The arrows sped by his archers were easily deflected by the chainmail. And all three thousand of Huyan's cavalry were armed with bows. They spewed flights of arrows which discouraged the men of Liangshan from coming any closet.

Song Jiang hastily had the horns sound the call to withdraw. Huyan also pulled his forces back twenty *li,* where they made camp.

The Song Jiang army encamped west of the mountain and settled their horses. At Song Jiang's command, his swordsmen hustled Peng Qi forward. Shouting for them to fall back, Song Jiang rose and untied his captive's bonds, then escorted him into the headquarters tent. He seated Peng Qi as a guest and kowtowed. Peng Qi at once returned the courtesy.

"I am your prisoner. By rights I should be killed. Why are you treating me with such courtesy, General?"

"Most of us are hunted men who have taken temporary shelter in the Marsh. The imperial court has sent you, General, here to arrest us. The proper thing for me would be to submit and be bound. But I fear for my life. And so I've criminally clashed with you. I beg your forgiveness for my presumptuousness."

"I have long known of your fraternal devotion and righteousness, of your aid to the endangered and your succor to the needy. But I never expected such chivalry! If you will spare my miserable life, I will serve you with every breath in my body!"

That day Song Jiang had the Eyes of Heaven General Peng Qi escorted to the mountain fortress to be introduced to Chao Gai and given refuge there. After rewarding his three armies, he conferred with his commanders on the military situation.

Meanwhile, Huyan Zhuo discussed with Han Tao how to vanquish Liangshan Marsh.

"Today, those louts moved forward in a quick covering action when they saw us coming at them," said Han Tao. "Tomorrow, we ought to hit them with our entire cavalry. That way, a big victory will be guaranteed."

"Exactly what I had in mind. I just wanted to make sure you agreed."

Huyan then ordered that all three thousand of the cavalry be stretched out in a single line, divided into troops of thirty, and that all the horses in each troop be connected together by chains. On nearing the foe, the men were to use arrows at a distance and their lances when they got close, and drive relentlessly ahead. The three thousand armored cavalry would become one hundred platoons, each locked in solid formation. Five thousand infantry would follow as support.

"Don't challenge them in person, tomorrow," Huyan admonished Han Tao. "You and I will stay behind with the reinforcements. When the fighting starts, we'll rush them from three sides."

It was decided they would go into action the next day at dawn. The following day Song Jiang set five troops of cavalry to the fore, backed by the ten divisions, with two contingents to left and right lying in ambush.

Qin Ming rode forth and challenged Huyan. But the imperial troops only shouted, and no one appeared. The five Liangshan cavalry units spread out in a line. Qin Ming was in the center, Lin Chong and Ten Feet of Steel were on the left, Hua Rong and Sun Li were on the right. The ten divisions under Song Jiang stood to the rear, a dense mass of men and horses. About a thousand imperial foot soldiers were arrayed opposite. Although they beat their drums and yelled, not a single man rode out to joust Song Jiang grew suspicious. He quietly gave the order for his rear forces to withdraw, then rode up to Hua Rong's contingent to look. Suddenly, a volley of cannon fire erupted from the opposite side. The thousand imperial foot soldiers separated into two sections and platoons of linked cavalry poured through in an enveloping three-sided phalanx. Arrows winged from both flanks. The middle bristled with long lances.

Startled, Song Jiang ordered his archers to reply. But how could they withstand this assault? Every animal in the thirty-horse platoons galloped together, unable to hold back even if it wanted to. From all over the hills and plains the linked cavalry charged.

Song Jiang's forward five cavalry units were thrown into a panic. They couldn't stem the tide. The rear divisions, also unable to make a stand, broke and ran. Song Jiang raced away on his horse, guarded by his ten commanders.

A platoon of imperial linked cavalry closed in after them. Li Kui, Yang Lin and their men rose out of their ambush in the reeds and drove them off. Song Jiang fled to the water's edge. Li Jun, Zhang Heng, Zhang Shun and the three Ruan brothers were waiting with war boats. Song Jiang hurriedly boarded one of craft and ordered them to rescue the chieftains and get them into the boats, quickly.

A platoon of linked cavalry rode right up to the river and showered the craft with arrows, but shields blocked the arrows and no one was hurt.

The boats were rowed hastily to Duck's Bill Shore, where everyone disembarked. In the fort there a count was made. They had lost more than half their effectives. Fortunately all of the chieftains had been saved, although several of their mounts had been killed.

Shortly thereafter, Shi Yong, Shi Qian, Sun Xin and Mistress Gu arrived. "The imperial infantry swarmed all over us," they reported. "They levelled our inns and houses. If our boats hadn't rescued us, we would have been captured."

Song Jiang consoled them and took stock of his commanders. Six had arrow wounds—Lin Chong, Lei Heng, Li Kui, Shi Xiu, Sun Xin and Huang Xin. Innumerable lesser chieftains had also been struck by arrows or otherwise wounded.

When Chao Gai learned of this, he came down the mountain with Wu Yong and Gongsun Sheng. They found Song Jiang frowning and depressed.

"Don't fret, brother," Wu Yong said soothingly. "Both victory and defeat are common fare for the soldier. Why worry? We'll work out a good plan to deal with that linked cavalry."

Chao Gai ordered the naval forces to strengthen the shore stockades, repair the boats, and guard the beaches day and night. He urged Song Jiang to return to the mountain stronghold and rest. But Song insisted on remaining at the fort on Duck's Bill Shore. He agreed only that the wounded commanders should go up and recuperate.

Huyan Zhuo went back to camp after his tremendous victory and had the linked horses unchained. Warriors came forward, one by one, to claim their commendations. They had slain countless numbers of the foe. More than five hundred prisoners had been taken, and over three hundred battle chargers. Huyan sent a messenger to the capital to report the glad tidings, and he richly rewarded his three columns.

Marshal Gao was holding court in his chancellery when word came from the gatehouse: "Huyan Zhuo has won a victory in his campaign against Liangshan Marsh. A messenger has brought the news."

The marshal was so delighted that he went to the imperial court early the next morning and, without waiting his turn, relayed the information. Extremely pleased, the emperor presented him with ten bottles of vintage wine bearing the imperial yellow seal, and a fine brocaded robe. He directed that an official deliver one hundred thousand strings of cash to Huyan's army. Bearing the imperial order, Gao returned to his chancellery and dispatched an official with the money.

On learning that an imperial emissary was coming, Huyan and Han Tao went twenty *li* to meet him. They brought him to the camp, accepted the emperor's reward with thanks, and served wine and entertained the emissary. He suggested that the rewards be distributed among the troops at once. He said he would wait until they had captured the brigand leaders, and then he would take them, in addition to the five hundred prisoners already rounded up, to the capital, where they would be paraded through the streets and punished.

"I don't see Peng Qi around," the emissary noted.

"In his eagerness to take Song Jiang, he plunged deep into enemy terrain and was captured," Huyan explained. "Those villains won't dare attack again, but we're going after them. We must eradicate their mountain fortress, sweep clean the marsh, capture the brigands and destroy their lair. Unfortunately, they're surrounded by water, and there are no roads leading in. We can see their forts in the distance, but the only way we can hit them is with long-range cannon. I have heard that in the Eastern Capital there's a cannon expert named Ling Zhen. He's known as Heaven-Shaking Thunder. He makes pieces with a range of fourteen to fifteen *li.* When his stone cannon balls land, the earth and sky quake, mountains tumble and cliffs split asunder. If we can get him, we'll smash the bandits' lair. Ling Zhen is also very skilled with weapons. His archery and horsemanship are splendid. I wish you'd go back to the capital and speak to the Marshal about this. Ask him to rush Ling Zhen out here, and we'll take the brigands' stronghold."

The emissary agreed, and set out the next day. Nothing happened on the road. On reaching the capital he went to see Gao and told him that Huyan requested cannoneer Ling Zhen so that he could perform a great deed. Gao issued a summons for Ling Zhen, who was assistant custodian of the imperial armory. Ling's ancestral home was in Yanling. In the Song Dynasty, he was the best cannoneer in the country, which was why he was known as Heaven-Shaking Thunder. Moreover, he was an excellent fighter with all kinds of weapons.

Ling Zhen reported to Marshal Gao, who commissioned him a commander of the army in the field and instructed him to ready his horse and arms and depart. Ling gathered the powder and explosives he needed, plus various types of cannon, stone balls and mountings, and loaded them on carts. Taking his armor, helmet, sabre and luggage, he left the Eastern Capital with thirty or forty soldiers and headed for Liangshan Marsh.

When he reached the camp he called first on Huyan, the commanding general, then on the leader of the van Han Tao. He inquired about the roads and paths distant and near the brigands' shore fort and the state of the cliffs guarding their mountain stronghold. Ling Zhen prepared three types of cannon—Fireball, Golden Wheel, and Mother and Sons. He had his soldiers assemble the mountings, brought his guns to the river bank, and primed them for action.

Song Jiang, in the Duck's Bill Shore fort, conferred with Wu Yong on how to achieve a break-through on the battlefield. But they could not think of anything.

A spy entered and reported: "The Eastern Capital has sent a cannoneer, Ling Zhen, Heaven-Shaking Thunder. He's set up guns near the river and he's getting ready to bombard our forts."

"It doesn't matter," said Wu Yong. "Our mountain stronghold is surrounded by a marsh which is full of creeks and ponds. It's a long way from the river. Even if he has guns that can reach the sky, he'll never hit it. We'll just abandon this fort on Duck's Bill Shore and let him shoot. Then we'll talk some more."

Song Jiang left the fort and returned to the mountain stronghold. Chao Gai and Gongsun Sheng escorted him to Fraternity Hall.

"How are we going to crack the enemy?" they asked.

Almost before the words were out of their mouths, they heard the boom of artillery at the foot of the mountain. Three cannon balls were fired. Two landed in the river. A third scored a direct hit on the Duck's Bill Shore fort.

Song Jiang watched glumly. The other leaders blanched.

"If Ling Zhen could be inveigled to the river we could nab him," said Wu Yong. "Then we could discuss what to do about the enemy."

"We'll send Li Jun, Zhang Heng, Zhang Shun and the three Ruan brothers in charge of six boats. Zhu Tong and Lei Heng will be on the opposite shore," said Chao Gai. And he told what each would do.

The six naval leaders received their orders and divided into two units. Li Jun and Zhang Heng took forty or fifty good swimmers in two fast craft and slipped across through the reeds. Backing them were Zhang Shun and the three Ruan brothers with another forty or so men in a fleet of small boats. On reaching the shore, Li Jun and Zhang Heng and their men, shouting and yelling, charged up to the cannon mountings and knocked them over.

Soldiers hurriedly reported this to Ling Zhen, who at once took two Fireball cannon and his lance, mounted his horse, and hastened to the scene with a thousand soldiers. Only then did Li Jun and Zhang Heng and their men leave. Ling Zhen chased them as far as the reedy shore, where a line of forty small craft, manned by a hundred or more sailors, were moored.

Li and Zhang went aboard, but didn't cast off. When Ling Zhen and his force came in sight, everyone on the boats shouted and jumped into the water.

Ling Zhen's men seized the boats. Zhu Tong and Lei Heng, on the opposite shore, began yelling and pounding drums. Ling Zhen ordered his soldiers to board the craft and go across and get them.

When the boats reached the middle of the river, Zhu Tong and Lei Heng struck a gong loudly. Forty or fifty swimmers rose from beneath the waves and pulled the plugs from sterns. Water flooded the craft. Strong hands capsized many of the boats, dumping the soldiers into the river.

Ling Zhen made haste to go back, but his craft's rudder had already been removed under water. Two of the chieftains clambered aboard. With one quick rock, they turned it bottom up. Ling Zhen landed in the water. He was grabbed by Ruan the Second from below and dragged ashore. There, other chieftains who were waiting had him bound and; taken up the mountain.

Over two hundred soldiers were captured. More than half of the remainder had been drowned. The few who escaped with their lives reported to Huyan Zhuo. He hastily mustered his forces and galloped to the rescue. But the boats had already crossed to Duck's Bill Shore. It was too far for arrows. Besides, the raiders were gone.

All Huyan's fuming was to no avail. He could only return to his camp, seething with rage.

When word reached the stronghold that Heaven-Shaking Thunder Ling Zhen had been captured, Song Jiang and all the leaders went down to the second gate to meet him. Song Jiang personally untied his bonds.

"I told you to invite the commander courteously to call at our fortress," he said to his men reprovingly. "How could you behave so rudely?"

Ling Zhen kowtowed and thanked the leaders for not killing him. Song Jiang poured him a libation cup. Then, he took Ling Zhen by the hand and led him up to the fortress. Ling Zhen saw that Peng Qi had been made one of the chieftains. The cannoneer sealed his lips and said not a word. Peng Qi offered him some advice.

"Leaders Chao Gai and Song Jiang act righteously for Heaven, receiving bold fellows from all over. They are waiting only for an amnesty and acceptance into the emperor's forces so that they may serve the country. Since you and I are here, we should take their orders."

Song Jiang added a few courteous apologetic phrases.

"I can remain easily enough," said Ling Zhen. "My only concern is that my wife and mother are still in the Eastern Capital. When it's known about me, they're sure to be put to death. What can I do?"

"Rest easy in your mind," said Song Jiang. "In a few days we'll bring them here."

Ling Zhen thanked him. "You are too considerate. When I die I'll be able to close my eyes."

"Let a feast be laid in celebration," Chao Gai directed.

The next day there was a meeting of the leaders in Fraternity Hall. As they drank Song Jiang discussed with them the problem of the linked cavalry. No one could think of how to cope with it. Finally, Gold-Coin Spotted Leopard Tang Long rose to his feet.

"Though I have no talent, I'd like to suggest a plan," he said. "But we need a certain weapon and a cousin of mine."

"What kind of weapon, and who is this cousin?" asked Wu Yong.

Calmly, Tang Long clasped his hands together, stepped forward and replied.

And truly, from the capital of jade and gold, a man fabulous as a unicorn and bold as a lion was lured to captivity.

What was the weapon, who was the man? Read our next chapter if you would know.

CHAPTER 56

WU YONG SENDS SHI QIAN TO STEAL ARMOR

TANG LONG LURES XU NING UP THE MOUNTAIN

"My ancestors have always been armorers," Tang Long said to the chieftains. "Because of this skill my father was raised by Border Area Governor Old General Zhong to be head of the Yanan garrison. The linked cavalry method won victories for the previous emperor. The only way you can beat it is with barbed lances. I have a drawing of such a lance, passed down to me by my family, which can serve as a likeness. I can make one for you, but I don't know how to use it. Only my cousin, an arms instructor, knows. The art has been handed down from generation to generation. They never teach it to any outsider. My cousin can ply the lance ahorse or on foot. When he goes into action, he's like nothing human."

"You don't mean Xu Ning, Arms Instructor of the Metal Lancers?" Lin Chong interrupted.

"The very man."

"I'd forgotten until you mentioned him. His skill with metal and barbed lances is indeed unique. We met many times when I was in the capital and tested our military arts against one another. We developed a deep mutual respect and affection. But how can you get him to come up here?"

"Xu Ning has a matchless ancestral treasure. It protects his family from evil spirits. I often saw it when I went with my father to visit Xu Ning's mother in the Eastern Capital. It's a suit of goose-feather armor hooped in metal. Known as 'lion's fur', it's light and snug-fitting, and no blade or arrow can pierce it. Many high officials have begged to see it, but Xu Ning always refuses. He cherishes it like his life. He keeps it in a leather box which he hangs on the central beam of his bedroom. If we can get hold of that armor, he'll have to come whether he wants to or not."

"No problem at all," said Wu Yong. "We'll ask our talented brother Shi Qian, Flea on a Drum, to attend to it."

"If it's there, I'll get it, by hook or crook," Shi Qian avowed.

"Do that, and I guarantee to bring Xu Ning up the mountain," said Tang Long.

"How?" Song Jiang demanded.

Tang Long leaned close and whispered in his ear. Song Jiang laughed. "Very shrewd."

"You'll need three men to go with you to the Eastern Capital," Wu Yong said. "One to buy the gunpowder and other ingredients for the cannons, and two to fetch Commander Ling Zhen's family."

Peng Qi rose and said: "If someone could go to Yingzhou and fetch my family as well, I would consider it a blessing."

"Have no fears, Commander," said Song Jiang. "Write notes, both of you, please. I'll have people see to it." And he directed: "Yang Lin, take some money and the letter, and go with men to Yingzhou and bring Commander Peng Qi's family. Xue Yong go to the Eastern Capital in the guise of a medicine pedlar who gives exhibitions of weapons skill and fetch the family of Commander Ling Zhen. Li Yun dress as a merchant and buy the gunpowder and other ingredients. Yue Ho and Tang Long accompany Xue Yong."

After Shi Qian went off down the mountain, Song Jiang had Tang Long make a sample barbed lance, under the supervision of Lei Heng who came from a family of blacksmiths. Once this was done, he directed the stronghold's armorers, with Lei Heng in charge, to copy the model in large numbers. Of this we'll say no more.

A send-off feast was laid for Yang Lin, Xue Yong, Li Yun, Yue Ho and Tang Long, and they went down the mountain. The next day Dai Zong also departed to inquire carefully into the situation. It would be hard to tell all the details in a few words.

Shi Qian concealed on his person certain tools and implements as he left Liangshan Marsh. He followed a winding road until he reached the capital. He spent the night at an inn and the next day quietly entered the city. He inquired where he might find Arms Instructor Xu Ning.

"Go through the gate of the battalion compound," a man instructed, pointing. "He lives in the fifth house. It has a black gate in the corner of the wall."

Flea on a Drum entered the compound and looked first at Xu Ning's front gate, then walked around and examined the rear. The house and courtyard were enclosed in a high wall, but he could see a cute two-storey building, and beside it a tall decorated pole. He studied the layout a while, then called at the house of a neighbor.

"Do you know whether Arms Instructor Xu is at home?"

"He doesn't get back till evening. He leaves again at the fifth watch for guard duty in the palace."

Shi Qian thanked the man politely and returned to the inn. He got his tools and hid them on his person.

"I'm going out and probably won't be back tonight," he said to the attendant. "Look after the things in my room."

"No need to worry. This is the imperial city. We don't have any thieves around here," the attendant replied.

Shi Qian went into the city, had some dinner, then quietly approached the home of Xu Ning in the compound of the Metal Lancers Battalion. He looked around but couldn't find any suitable place to hide. Night was falling, and he took up a position inside the compound gateway. Soon it was dark. There was no moon in the winter sky.

He noted a big poplar behind an Earth God Temple. He shinnied up, sat astride a limb, and watched silently. Xu Ning returned and went into his house. Two people with lanterns closed and locked the compound gate, then went back to their homes. In a drum tower the beat of the first watch sounded. Through the chill overcast the stars appeared lustreless. Dew turned to frost. All was still.

Shi Qian slid down from his tree, stole to Xu Ning's rear gate, and effortlessly scaled the courtyard wall. He crossed a small garden to the kitchen and peered in. Two serving girls were still cleaning up in the light of a lamp. Up the decorative pole he went, and over to the upcurved eave of a corner of the roof. Lying in this concealment, he looked into the window of the upper storey. Xu Ning and his wife were seated beside a stove. The woman held a child of six or seven in her arms.

It was their bedroom. Sure enough, there was a big leather box tied to the beam. Near the door hung a bow and arrows and a dagger. On a clothes rack were garments of various colors.

"Plum Fragrance," Xu Ning called, "fold these clothes for me."

One of the serving girls came up the stairs. On a long sideboard table she folded a purple embroidered robe, an official tunic with a green lining trimmed at the bottom by multi-hued embroidered flounces, a colored silk neckerchief, a red and green belt sash, and several handkerchiefs. These, plus a yellow kerchief packet containing a golden sash decorated with a lichee design and from which two otter tails dangled, were all wrapped in a cloth and placed to warm on a fender above the stove. Shi Qian's eyes didn't miss a thing.

Some time after the second watch Xu Ning went to bed.

"Are you on duty tomorrow?" the wife asked.

"The emperor is going to the Auspicious Dragon Hall. I must get up early and go at the fifth watch to attend him."

The wife said to Plum Fragrance: "Your master is on guard duty tomorrow at the fifth watch. You girls get up at the fourth, heat water and prepare something to eat."

"Obviously, that leather box on the beam has the armor in it," thought Shi Qian. "It would be best if I could take it during the night. But I must do it without alarming them, or tomorrow I'll never get out of the city, and that would ruin our whole operation. I'll wait till the fifth watch. There'll be time enough."

When both husband and wife were in bed, the two serving girls lay down on pallets outside the bedroom door. A night lamp had been lit upon the table. Soon the four were asleep. The girls had worked hard all day, and were exhausted. They snored lustily.

Flea on a Drum crept over, produced a long hollow reed, poked it through a hole in the window, and puffed. The lamp went out.

Around the fourth watch Xu Ning rose and called to the girls to fetch hot water. Awakening, they noticed that the lamp was extinguished.

"*Aiya!*" they exclaimed. "You've got no light."

"Go to the back and get another one. What are you waiting for?"

Plum Fragrance and the other girl opened the door at the head of the stairs and went down. As soon as he heard the stairs creak, Flea on a Drum slid down the pole and hid in the darkness beside the rear door. The girls opened this, came out and went to open the gate in the courtyard wall. Shi Qian darted into the kitchen and hid under the table. Plum Fragrance returned with a lighted lamp, closed the door and started the stove. The other girl went upstairs with a burning charcoal brazier. Before long, the water was boiling, and Plum Fragrance took that up, too.

Xu Ning washed, rinsed his mouth, and called for some heated wine. The girls laid out meat and buns. When Xu Ning finished, he instructed them to feed his orderly who was waiting outside. Shi Qian heard him descend the stairs and tell his orderly to eat. Then Xu Ning shouldered his pack, took his metal lance and came out. The girls lit a lantern and saw him to the gate.

Flea on a Drum emerged from beneath the table, mounted the stairs, climbed the lattice wall to the beam and crouched upon it. After closing the house door, the girls blew out the lantern, came up the stairs, undressed, and threw themselves down on their pallets.

When he was sure they were asleep, Shi Qian on the beam extended his long reed and again puffed out the lamp. Softly, he untied the leather box. He was about to come down when the wife, hearing a noise, awakened.

"What's that sound up on the beam?" she called to Plum Fragrance.

Shi Qian promptly squeaked like a rat.

"Can't you hear, mistress?" said the girl. "Those are rats, fighting."

Shi Qian emitted a series of squeaks like a whole battle, slipped down, stealthily opened the door at the head of the stairs, agilely swung the box to his back, went down the stairs, opened the house door, and stepped out. The various guards were departing, and the battalion compound gate was open, it having been unlocked at the fourth watch. He mingled with the crowd and left swiftly, not stopping until he reached his inn outside the city.

It was still not yet light. He knocked on the door and went to his room to get his luggage. He tied this and the box to a carrying pole, paid his bill, left the inn and headed east. Only after covering more than forty *li* did he stop at an eating house and make himself some food.

Suddenly a man came in. Shi Qian looked up. It was none other than Dai Zong the Marvellous Traveller. Dai observed that Shi Qian had got what he had gone for. The two conversed in low tones.

"I'll take the armor to our mountain fortress," Dai Zong said. "You follow slowly with Tang Long."

Shi Qian opened the leather box, took out the metal-bound goose feather armor and wrapped it in a bundle, which Dai Zong tied to his body. The Marvellous Traveller left the inn, performed his magic rites, and sped off to Liangshan Marsh.

Shi Qian tied the empty leather box openly to one end of his carrying pole. He finished eating, paid the bill, shouldered the pole, and set out. When he had gone about twenty *li,* he met Tang Long. They went into a tavern to confer.

"I want you to follow me along this road," Tang Long said. "Whenever you see a tavern, eating house or inn with a white chalk circle on the door you can go in and buy meat and wine. At those inns you can rest. Put the leather box where everyone can see it. Wait for me one stage from here."

Tang Long slowly drank his wine, then proceeded to the Eastern Capital.

In Xu Ning's house, the two serving girls rose at daybreak. They observed that not only was the door at the head of the stairs open, but the inner door and house door below as well. They made a hasty check. Nothing seemed to be missing. They went upstairs and reported to their mistress.

"We can't understand it. All the doors are open, but nothing is gone."

"At the fifth watch, I heard a noise on the beam. You said it was rats, fighting. Better take a look and see whether that leather box is all right."

The girls did so, and screamed. "It's disappeared!"

Hurriedly, the wife got out of bed. "Ask someone to go to the Auspicious Dragon Hall at once and notify the master. Tell him to come home as soon as possible."

Plum Fragrance and her companion hastily sent three or four men, one after another, with the message, but all returned with the same reply: "The Metal Lancers have accompanied the emperor to the Inner Palace Gardens. The Gardens are surrounded by his personal guard. Nobody can get in. You'll just have to wait for Xu Ning to come home."

The wife and girls were like ants on a hot griddle. But there was nothing they could do. They fluttered about anxiously, unable to eat or drink.

Only at dusk did Xu Ning remove his official robe. He gave it to his orderly. Carrying his metal lance, Xu slowly returned. At the gateway of the battalion compound, a neighbor spoke to him.

"Your house has been robbed! Your wife has been waiting for you all day!"

Startled, Xu Ning hurried home. The serving girls met him at the door.

"The thief must have slipped in when you left at the fifth watch," they said. "All he took was that leather box on the beam."

Cries of anguish burst through Xu Ning's lips from the depths of his vitals.

"Who knows when that thief crept into our room," exclaimed his wife.

"Anything else wouldn't have mattered," said Xu Ning. "But that goose feather armor has been a family heirloom for four generations! It's never been lost. Marshal Wang the dilettante offered me thirty thousand strings of cash, but I hadn't the heart to sell it. I thought I might need it in battle again. Because I was afraid that something might happen to it, I tied it on the beam. Many people asked to see it, but I said it was gone. If I raise a hue and cry about it, they'll surely laugh at me. Now it really is gone. What can I do?"

That night he couldn't sleep. "Who could have stolen it?" he wondered. "It must have been someone who knew I had the armor."

His wife thought a while and said: "The thief must have already been in the house when the lamp went out. Someone who became enamored of it and tried to buy it from you probably sent a high-class housebreaker to steal it when you wouldn't sell. Get people to ask around quietly and find out where it is. Then we'll decide what to do. Don't 'disturb the grass and alert the snake'."

Xu Ning listened in silence. He rose the next morning at dawn and sat brooding in the house.

At breakfast time, there was a knock at the courtyard gate. The orderly went to see who it was. He returned and announced: "Tang Long, son of the head of the Yanan garrison, is calling to pay his respects."

Xu Ning directed that he be invited in. On seeing Xu Ning, Tang Long kowtowed.

"I trust all has been well with you, cousin," he said.

"I heard my uncle had returned to Heaven," Xu Ning replied. "I was tied down by official duties and your home is far away, so I never went to offer my condolences. I haven't had any news of you, either, cousin. Where have you been? What brings you here?"

"It's a long story. I've had bad luck since my father died, and wandered to many places. Today, I've come directly from Shandong to the capital to see you."

"Cousin, stay a while," said Xu Ning. He ordered that wine and food be brought for his guest.

Tang Long took from his pack two, long thin gold bars like scallion leaves, weighing twenty ounces, and presented them to Xu Ning.

"Before he died, my father asked me to give you these as a remembrance. There wasn't anybody I could trust to deliver them, so I've come today to hand them to you myself."

"How very kind of uncle to think of me. I've done absolutely nothing to show my esteem. I'll never be able to express my gratitude."

"Don't talk like that, cousin. Father was a great admirer of your skill with arms. He was sorry we lived so far apart and couldn't see each other. That's why he's left you these momentous."

Xu Ning thanked Tang Long and accepted the gold bars. He had wine served and entertained him. But his brows were knit and he looked glum all the while they were drinking.

Finally, Tang Long rose and said: "You don't seem very happy, cousin. Is something troubling you?"

Xu Ning sighed. "Of course you don't know. It's a long story. Last night we were robbed."

"Did you lose much?"

"Only the goose-feather metal-hooped armor known as 'lion's fur', left to me by my ancestors. But it's a remarkable suit, and last night it was taken. I'm very upset."

"I've seen that armor. It really is beyond compare. My late father often praised it to the skies. Where were you keeping it?"

"In a leather box tied to the main beam in the bedroom. I can't imagine when the thief slipped in and got away with it."

"What's the leather box like?"

"It's of red sheepskin, and the armor inside is wrapped in fragrant silk quilting."

"A red sheepskin box?" Tang Long appeared startled. "Does it have cloud head sceptres stitched in white thread on the surface, with a lion playing with an embroidered ball in the middle?"

"Cousin, where have you seen it?"

"Last night I was drinking wine in a village tavern about forty *li* from the city. I saw a sharp-eyed thin swarthy fellow carrying it on a shoulder pole. I wondered what was in it. As I was leaving the tavern I asked him: 'What's that box for?' He said: 'Originally it held armor. But now it's only got a few garments.' That must be your man. He evidently has hurt his leg, because he walks with a limp. Why don't we go after him and catch him?"

"If we can do that, it will be a blessing from Heaven!"

"Let's not delay then. We'll go at once."

Xu Ning quickly changed into hemp sandals, fastened his dagger, took his halberd, and left the city with Tang Long through the east gate. They strode swiftly along the winding road. Ahead they saw a tavern with a white circle on its wall.

"Let's have a bowl of wine," Tang Long suggested. "We can inquire here."

They went in and sat down. Tang Long asked the host: "Has a sharp-eyed dark thin fellow carrying a red sheepskin box passed this way?"

"There was a man like that last night. He seemed to have a bad leg, and was limping."

"Did you hear that, cousin?" Tang Long exclaimed.

Xu Ning was beyond speech. The two paid for their wine and hurried through the door. Further on, they came to an inn. A white circle marked its wall. Tang Long halted.

"I can't go another step," he said. "Why not spend the night here, and continue the chase early tomorrow morning?"

"I have official duties. If I'm not there for roll call I'll surely be reprimanded. What can I do?"

"You needn't worry about that, cousin. Your wife will explain, of course."

At the inn that night they again made inquiries. The attendant told them: "Last night a thin swarthy fellow put up here. He slept late and didn't leave till mid-morning. He asked about the road to Shandong."

"That means we can catch him," said Tang Long.

The two men rested at the inn and departed before dawn, continuing along the winding road. Whenever they saw a white chalk circle on a wall, Tang Long called a halt for food and wine, and to ask the way. At each place they were told the same thing. Xu Ning was anxious to retrieve his armor, and he hastened along with Tang Long.

As daylight again began to wane, they saw ahead an ancient temple. In front of it, Shi Qian had rested his load and was sitting under a tree.

"Good," exclaimed Tang Long. "There, cousin, beneath that tree, isn't that your red sheepskin box?"

Xu Ning looked, then rushed forward and seized Shi Qian. "Impudent scoundrel," he roared. "How dare you steal my armor!"

"Stop, stop. Quit your yelling. Yes, I took your armor. What are you going to do about it?"

"Vulgar beast! You have the nerve to ask me that!"

"See if there's any armor in that box."

Tang Long opened the container. It was empty.

"What have you done with my armor, rogue?" Xu Ning demanded.

"Now listen to me. My name is Zhang. I'm an eldest son and I come from Tai'an Prefecture. A wealthy man in our prefecture knows Old General Zhong of the Border Garrison and learned from him about your goose feather armor and that you don't want to sell. So he hired me and another man called Li the Third to steal it. He's paying us ten thousand strings of cash. When I jumped from that pole in your yard I sprained my leg and I can't walk fast. So I've let Li go on ahead with the armor and have kept only the box. If you pressure me and take me before the court, I won't say a word even if I'm beaten to death. But if you forgive me, I'll go with you and get it back."

Xu Ning hesitated for several moments, unable to decide.

"There's no danger of him flying away, cousin," said Tang Long. "Let's go with him and recover your armor. If he doesn't produce it, you can always state your case to the local magistrate."

"That's quite true, cousin," Xu Ning agreed.

The three men continued along the road and spent the night at an inn. Xu Ning and Tang Long kept an eye on Shi Qian. But Flea on a Drum had bandaged one leg as if it were sprained, and Xu Ning, thinking he couldn't walk very fast, wasn't especially watchful. The following morning they rose and went on. Shi Qian frequently bought them food and drink, by way of apology. They travelled all day.

The next morning Xu Ning was growing increasingly anxious. Was Shi Qian really leading them to the armor? During their march they came upon three or four horses hitched to an empty cart by the side of the road. Behind it stood the driver. A merchant stood to one side. When he saw Tang Long, he dropped to his knees and kowtowed.

"What are you doing here, brother?" Tang Long queried.

"I had some business in Zhengzhou," the merchant replied. "I'm on my way back to Tai'an."

"Excellent. We three would like a ride. We're going to Tai'an, too."

"I wouldn't mind even if there were more of you, to say nothing of only three."

Very pleased, Tang Long brought him over to Xu Ning.

"Who is this?" Xu Ning asked.

"I met him last year when I went to a temple in Tai'an to burn incense. His name is Li Rong and he's a righteous man."

"Since Zhang can hardly walk, I suppose we'd better ride." Xu Ning told the driver to start, and the four men got in the cart.

"Tell me the name of your rich patron," Xu Ning demanded of Shi Qian.

Flea on a Drum stalled for a few minutes, then said: "He's called Lord Guo."

"Do you have a Lord Guo in Tai'an?" Xu Ning asked Li Rong.

"Yes. He's a very wealthy man who hobnobs with big officials," Li Rong replied. "He supports a whole bevy of hangers-on."

Xu Ning said to himself: "Since there is such a person, I needn't be suspicious.

Li Rong chatted about play with weapons, and sang a few songs. The day passed quickly and pleasantly.

Soon they were only little more than two stages from Liangshan Marsh. Li Rong had the driver take the gourd and buy some wine and meat for his three passengers. Li filled a ladle and offered it to Xu Ning, who drained it at one go. Li called for more. The driver, pretending that his hand slipped, let the gourd drop, spilling its contents on the ground. Li shouted at him and ordered him to buy more wine.

Suddenly, Xu Ning began to drool from the corners of his mouth, and fell headlong in the cart. Who was Li Rong? Actually, he was Yue Ho the Iron Throat. He and the other two jumped down and hurried the horses on. They went directly to the tavern of Zhu Gui, the Dry-Land Crocodile, where they all carried Xu Ning to a boat and ferried him across to the Shore of Golden Sands. Song Jiang had already been informed, and had come down the mountain and was waiting with the other leaders.

Xu Ning by then awakened from the drug, and he was given an antidote. When he opened his eyes and saw the men standing around him, he was astonished.

"Cousin," he said to Tang Long, "why have you duped me into coming here?"

"Listen to me, cousin," said Tang Long. "I had heard that Song Jiang accepted bold men from all over. And so in Wugang Town I pledged myself a blood brother to Li Kui the Black Whirlwind and joined the forces in the stronghold. Now Huyan Zhuo is using linked cavalry against us on the battlefield and he's got us stymied. I proposed barbed lances, but you're the only one who knows how to wield them. So I thought of this scheme: Shi Qian was sent to steal your armor, and I tricked you to take to the road. Then Yue Ho, disguised as Li Rong, put a drug in your wine when we were crossing a hill. Please come up to our mountain stronghold and become one of our leaders."

"Cousin, you've ruined me!"

Song Jiang advanced, wine cup in hand, and said apologetically: "I'm here in this marsh only temporarily, just waiting for an imperial amnesty so that I can repay our country with my utmost loyalty and strength. I'm not covetous, I don't like killing, and I never perform unrighteous or un-chivalrous deeds. I devoutly hope you will sympathize with me, Inspector, and join me in acting in Heaven's behalf."

Lin Chong also sought to mollify him. Cup in hand, he said: "I'm here, too, brother. Please don't refuse."

"You duped me into coming," Xu Ning said to Tang Long. "The authorities are sure to arrest my wife. What can I do?"

"Don't let that worry you, Inspector," said Song Jiang. "I personally guarantee her safety. In a few days you will be reunited."

Chao Gai, Wu Yong and Gongsun Sheng all apologized to Xu Ning, and a feast was laid in his honor. The most agile of the young brigands were selected to learn the use of the barbed lance. Dai Zong and Tang Long were dispatched to the Eastern Capital at all possible speed to fetch Xu Ning's family.

Within ten days Yang Lin brought Peng Qi's family from Yinzhou, Xue Yong brought Ling Zhen's family from the Eastern Capital, and Li Yun returned with five cartloads of gunpowder and explosives. A few days later Dai Zong and Tang Long led Xu Ning's family up the mountain. Amazed, Xu Ning asked how they had come.

"After you left and were unable to report for roll call, I dispensed a little money and jewelry as bribes," his wife related, "and said that you were sick in bed. So there wasn't any fuss. Then suddenly cousin Tang Long arrived with the goose feather armor. 'We got it back,' he said, 'but cousin fell ill on the road, and he's lying in an inn at death's door. He wants to see you and the children.' I believed him, and we got into the cart. I don't know where we went, but we twisted and turned and ended up here."

"Everything else is fine," Xu Ning said to Tang Long. "It's just too bad my armor had to be left at home."

Tang Long laughed. "You'll be glad to hear, cousin, that after sister got in the cart, I went back into the house and got it. I also inveigled your serving girls into wrapping up all your valuables. I put them and your armor on a carrying pole and brought the whole lot."

"It looks as though we'll never be able to return to the Eastern Capital."

"There's one more thing I must tell you. We ran into a party of merchants on the way. I dressed in your armor and smeared my face. Using your name, I robbed them. By now the Eastern Capital must have sent out notices for your arrest."

"You've harmed me grievously, cousin!"

Chao Gai and Song Jiang offered words of apology. "If we hadn't done that, Inspector, would you have been willing to remain with us?" They allotted a house to Xu Ning and his family.

The leaders met to discuss how to deal with the linked cavalry of the enemy. By then the barbed lances manufactured under the supervision of Lei Heng were ready. Song Jiang and Wu Yong requested Xu Ning to teach their men how to use them.

"I'll gladly reveal all my secrets. I'll train your junior officers," said Xu Ning. "Let me have the most stalwart."

In Fraternity Hall the leaders watched Xu Ning select men to learn the use of the barbed lance.

And as a result, a force of three thousand armored horses was smashed, and a hero was taken within a designated time.

How then did Xu Ning teach the barbed lance arts? Read our next chapter if you would know.

CHAPTER 57

XU NING TEACHES HOW TO USE THE BARBED LANCE

SONG JIANG BREAKS THE LINKED-UP CAVALRY

In Fraternity Hall, the chieftains requested Xu Ning to demonstrate the barbed lance. He was a fine figure of a man. Tall, broad-shouldered and thick at the middle, he had a round fair face adorned by a mustache and goatee. After selecting his trainees, he went outside the Hall, picked up a barbed lance and showed how it was done. The spectators cheered.

"If you're using this weapon on horseback," he said, "you must swing from the waist. Advance in seven moves—three hooks and four parries. Then, one stab and one cleave. A total of nine changes. If you're on foot, the best way is to advance eight steps and parry four times. This will open the door. At the twelfth step, change. At the sixteenth, turn completely around, alternately hooking and stabbing. At the twenty-fourth, push your opponent's weapon up, then down. Hook to the east and parry to the west. At the thirty-sixth, making sure that you're well covered, seize the tough and fight the strong. This is the correct method of using the barbed lance. We have a jingle that goes:

Four parries, three hooks, seven in all,
Nine changes in total weave a magic spell,
At step twenty-four parry forward and back,
At step sixteen do a big turn as well."

As Xu Ning demonstrated, stage by stage, the chieftains watched. The fighters were delighted by the way he plied the lance. From then on, he taught the deftest of them day and night. He also showed infantry how to hide in brush and grass and snag the legs of horses, instructing them in three secret methods.

In less than half a month, he had taught five to seven hundred men. Song Jiang and the other leaders were extremely pleased. They made preparations to break the foe.

Huyan Zhuo, since the capture of Peng Qi and Ling Zhen, had been riding forth with his cavalry every day to the edge of the river and hurling challenges. But the brigand leaders near the shore only continued holding the various beach heads and installing sharp stakes under the water. Huyan was able to send scouts along the roads west and north of the mountain, but he had no way of getting to the stronghold.

Inside the brigand fortress Ling Zhen was directed to manufacture several types of cannon, and a day was set for the attack against the enemy. The men who had been learning the use of the barbed lance were by now quite adept.

"I'm neither clever nor far-sighted," Song Jiang said to the other chieftains. "I wonder whether my idea will meet with your approval."

"We'd like to hear it," said Wu Yong.

"Tomorrow we won't use our cavalry, but will fight entirely on foot. The military tactics of Sun and Wu are very suited to wooded and watery areas. We'll take the infantry down, divide them into ten units and lure on the enemy. When they charge with their cavalry, we'll withdraw into the reeds and brush. Our men with the barbed lances will already be there lying in ambush. For every ten of these will be an equal number with big hooked poles. The lances will bring down the horses, the poles will snag the riders. We'll prepare similar ambushes on the open plain and in the narrow defiles. How does that plan strike you?"

"I think that's how we ought to do it," said Wu Yong. "Conceal our soldiers and seize their officers."

"Barbed lances and hooked poles together. Exactly the way," said Xu Ning.

Song Jiang then formed ten infantry units, with two leaders in command of each to go down the mountain and lure the foe. Naval craft to serve as reinforcements were put under the command of nine chieftains. Six cavalry units were also dispatched under six chieftains. Their function was to shout challenges at the enemy from the side of the mountain. Ling Zhen and Du Xing were to have charge of the cannons.

Xu Ning and Tang Long were given leadership of the men with the barbed lances. The main army was under Song Jiang, Wu Yong, Gongsun Sheng, Dai Zong, Lu Fang and Guo Sheng. They issued all general orders and commands. The remaining chieftains were to defend the various forts.

That night at the third watch the barbed lancers crossed the river, spread out and went into ambush. At the fourth watch the ten infantry units moved across. Ling Zhen and Du Xing took with them Fiery Wind cannon and mountings, and set them up on a height. Xu Ning and Tang Long, as they crossed to the opposite shore, each carried a trumpet in a bag.

Dawn found Song Jiang and the main army lined up along the river. They beat drums, shouted and waved their banners.

When news of this reached Huyan Zhuo in the headquarters tent of his central army, he directed Han Tao of his vanguard to go out and scout. Then he ordered that the horses of his armored cavalry be linked together. He put on his armor, mounted his snowy-hoofed black steed, took up his double rods, and rode forth towards Liangshan Marsh with his men and horses.

He saw Song Jiang with a large force on the other side of the river and spread his troops out in battle formation. He conferred with Han Tao, who said: "They have a detachment of infantry, I don't know how large, due south of here."

"Who cares how large! Charge them with our linked cavalry!"

Han Tao galloped forth with five hundred horsemen. But to the southeast another force of infantry appeared. Han Tao was about to send part of his cavalry against them, when to the southwest he saw still another detachment, waving pennants and shouting. He pulled his entire unit back.

"There are three bandit detachments to the south," he told Huyan. "They've all got Liangshan Marsh banners."

"For a long time those rascals have refused to come out and fight," Huyan mused. "They must be up to something."

Before the words were out of his mouth, to the north was heard the boom of cannon. Huyan swore. "Ling Zhen has gone over to the bandits! They've got him to bombard us!"

While they were all watching south, three more units welled up in the north. "Those bandits surely are hatching some scheme," Huyan said to Han Tao. "We'll divide our army in two. I'll fight north with one column, you fight south with the other."

They were about to do this when four more enemy units appeared to the west. Huyan began to grow panicky. Northwards, a volley of cannon fire erupted, and projectiles landed upon the bluffs. They were shot from one large and forty-nine smaller cannons, which is why the battery was called Mother and Sons. The shells burst with an overpowering roar. Huyan's soldiers, confused before the combat even started, dashed wildly amid the cavalry and troops led by Han Tao.

The ten brigand infantry units ran east when chased east, and west when chased west. Huyan was furious. He advanced north with his army. Song Jiang's men plunged into the reeds. Huyan came tearing after them with a large contingent of linked cavalry. The armored steeds, galloping in tandem, could not be checked. They crashed in among the dry reeds, tall grass and tangled thickets. A shrill whistle rent the air, and barbed lances on both ends of the linked lines snagged the horses' legs and brought them tumbling to the ground. The animals in the middle whinnied in fright. Long poles snaked out of the reeds and hooked the riders.

Huyan, realizing he had been tricked, gave his horse free rein and raced back south after Han Tao. To the north behind him Fiery Wind cannon thundered. Here, there, all over the hills and plain, brigand infantry gave chase. Linked armored cavalry rolled and fell everywhere amid the reeds and grasses, and everywhere were caught.

Han Tao and Huyan knew they had been duped. They rode madly about after their mounted men, seeking an escape route. But every path was thick as flax with the banners of Liangshan Marsh. No path was safe, and they headed northwest.

Before they had gone five or six *li* they were confronted by a strong unit with two bold fellows in the lead—Mu Hong the Unrestrained and Mu Chun the Slightly Restrained. Both carried halberds, and they shouted: "Defeated generals, stand where you are!"

Huyan, enraged, charged the two, brandishing his rods. They fought four or five rounds, then Mu Chun withdrew. Fearing a trap, Huyan did not pursue, but rode due north along the road.

Another powerful band came down the slope and blocked his way. It was led by Two-Headed Snake Xie Zhen and Twin-Tailed Scorpion Xie Bao. They raced towards him, each gripping a steel fork. Flourishing his rods, Huyan clashed with them in combat. They fought six or seven rounds, and the two brothers retreated. Huyan chased them less than half a *li* when from both sides suddenly twenty-four men with barbed lances surged forth. Huyan had no more heart for battle. He turned his mount and hurried off, northeast.

Again he was stopped, this time by Stumpy Tiger and Ten Feet of Steel, husband and wife. The road clearly was perilous, but the thorns and brambles on all sides were even worse. He kicked up his steed, brandished his rods, and charged through his interceptors. Stumpy Tiger and Ten Feet of Steel were unable to catch him. He rode pell-mell northeast, his army in ruins, his men scattered like raindrops and stars.

Song Jiang's trumpets sounded a return to the mountain, where each warrior came forward to claim his reward. Of the three thousand linked armored steeds, a troop and a half—brought down by the barbed lances —had their hoofs damaged. These were stripped of their armor and kept for eating purposes. But the mounts of more than two troops were in fine condition. These were led up the mountain to be fed and cared for and used as brigand mounts. All the armor-bedecked cavalrymen were captured alive and taken to the stronghold.

Five thousand imperial infantry, pressed fiercely on three sides, tried to flee back into the midst of their main army, but were all brought down by the barbed lances and caught. Those who ran to the river were rounded up by the naval chieftains, put on boats, ferried across, and escorted up the mountain under guard. The men and horses previously captured by the imperial forces were recovered and returned to the fortress. Huyan's palisades were dismantled and new forts were built along the banks. Two inns were again erected to serve as eyes for the brigands, and as before Sun Xin, Mistress Gu, Shi Yong and Shi Qian were put in charge.

Liu Tang and Du Qian brought Han Tao to the stronghold, a bound captive. Song Jiang personally untied him and invited him into the Hall. He apologized and had a feast laid in his honor. Peng Qi and Ling Zhen, at Song's behest, urged him to join them. Han Tao, who originally was one of the stars of Earthly Fiends, was naturally of the same persuasion, and he promptly became a chieftain of Liangshan Marsh. Song Jiang had him write a letter to his family, then dispatched men to Chenzhou to bring them to the fortress, where they and Han Tao were reunited.

Song Jiang rejoiced. He had broken the linked cavalry, captured many men and horses, and collected large quantities of armor and weapons. Every day he and his cohorts feasted in celebration. But as usual they guarded all approaches against possible attack by imperial soldiers. Of that we'll say no more.

Huyan, having lost so much of his imperial army, dared not return to the capital. He rode alone on his black steed with the snowy hoofs, his armor hanging over the pommel as he hastened from the scene of his disaster. Without money, he had to take the gold belt from around his waist and sell it for silver.

"It happened so suddenly," he said to himself. "Who can I look to for refuge?" Then he remembered. "Murong, the prefect of Qingzhou is an old friend.

Why not go to him? His sister is an imperial concubine. If, through her influence, I can be given another army, I may still get my revenge."

Towards evening of his second day on the road, he was hungry and thirsty. He dismounted at a village inn by the roadside and tied his horse to a tree near the front door. He went in, placed his rods on a table, sat down and told the host to bring wine and meat.

"We've only wine here," said the host. "But they just slaughtered a sheep in the village. If you want meat, I'll buy you some."

Huyan opened the ration bag at his waist and took out some of the silver he had exchanged for his gold belt. He gave his to the host.

"Get a leg of mutton and boil it for me. And mix some fodder and feed my horse. I'll spend the night here. Tomorrow, I'm going on to Qingzhou."

"There's nothing against staying here, sir. But we don't have a good bed."

"I'm a military man. Any place I can rest will do."

The host took the silver and went off to purchase the mutton. Huyan removed his armor from his horse's back and loosened its girth straps, then sat down outside the door. He waited a long time. At last the host returned with the sheep leg. Huyan told him to boil it, knead three measures of flour for griddle-cakes, and draw two drams of wine.

While the meat was cooking and the griddlecakes were on the pan, the host heated water for Huyan to wash his feet and led the horse to a shed in the rear. The host chopped grass and boiled fodder. Huyan warmed some wine and imbibed a while. Soon the meat was ready, and Huyan invited the host to eat and drink with him.

"I'm an officer of the imperial army," Huyan said. "Because I've had a set-back in arresting the bandits of Liangshan Marsh, I'm going to join Prefect Murong of Qingzhou. Take good care of my horse. It was given to me by the emperor, and is called the Ebony Steed Which Treads in Snow. I'll reward you handsomely later on."

"Thank you, Excellency. But there is something I must tell you. Not far from here is Peach Blossom Mountain. On it is a band of robbers. Their leader is Li Zhong the Tiger-Fighting General. Second in command is Zhou Tong the Little King. There are about six or seven hundred of them, and they rob and pillage. Sometimes they raid this village. The authorities have sent soldiers to capture them time and again, but always without success. You must sleep lightly during the night, sir."

"I'm a man of matchless courage. Even if those knaves came in full force it wouldn't matter to me. Just make sure to feed my horse well."

He dined on meat and wine and griddlecakes. Then the host spread a pallet and Huyan lay down to sleep.

Because he had been depressed for several days, and because he had drunk a few cups of wine too many, Huyan reclined without taking his clothes off.

Around the third watch he awakened. He heard the host, to the rear of the house, lamenting. Huyan jumped up, seized his twin rods and went into the back yard.

"What's the trouble?" he demanded.

"I went out to add some hay and I found that the fence had been knocked down. Someone has stolen Your Excellency's horse! Look, there —torch light three or four *li* off in the distance. They must be heading for that place."

"What place are you talking about?"

"The robbers you see on that road are bandits from Peach Blossom Mountain!"

Huyan was startled. He ordered the host to lead the way, and they gave chase for two or three *li* along the edges of the fields. But the torches had vanished. There was no telling where they had gone.

"This is terrible," said Huyan. "I've lost the emperor's gift horse!"

"Go into the prefecture tomorrow and report the theft," advised the host. "They'll send soldiers to catch the robbers. That's the only way you'll get the animal back."

Sunk in gloom, Huyan sat until daybreak. Then he set out for Qingzhou, instructing the host to carry his armor. It was dark by the time they reached the city, and they put up at an inn for the night. Early the following morning Huyan presented himself at the prefectural court and kowtowed before Murong.

The prefect was astonished. "I heard that you had gone to catch the bandits in Liangshan Marsh, General," he said. "What are you doing here?"

Huyan related what had transpired.

"Although you lost many men and horses, it was not through lack of diligence," said Murong. "The bandits tricked you. It wasn't your fault. The area under my administration has often been raided by them. Now that you're here you can first clean out Peach Blossom Mountain and retake the steed presented you by the emperor. Then you can capture the robbers on Two-Dragon Mountain and White Tiger in one fell swoop. I'll report your exploits to the emperor, and you'll again be given command of an army and can get your revenge. How will that be?"

Huyan again kowtowed. "I'm deeply grateful for your concern. If you'll be kind enough to do this, I'll repay you with my life."

Murong invited him to accept temporary quarters in a guestroom, where he could change his clothes, eat and rest. The prefect told the host who had been carrying Huyan's armor to return home.

Three days passed. Huyan, anxious to retrieve the imperial gift horse, entreated Murong to give him soldiers. The prefect mustered two thousand infantry and cavalry, which he put under Huyan's leadership, and presented him with a black-maned charger. Huyan thanked him, donned his armor, mounted, and marched off with his men to recapture his horse, heading straight for Peach Blossom Mountain.

On the mountain Li Zhong the Tiger-Fighting General and Zhou Tong the Little King, having obtained the Ebony Steed Which Treads in Snow, feasted and celebrated every day. A scout who watched the road reported: "Soldiers and horses from Qingzhou heading this way."

Zhou Tong rose and said to Li Zhong: "Brother, hold the fort. I'll go and drive back the government forces."

He mustered a hundred brigands, took his lance, mounted, and rode down to meet the foe.

Huyan Zhuo approached the mountain with two thousand infantry and cavalry and spread out in battle position. Riding forth, he shouted: "Robbers, come and be bound!"

Zhou Tong the Little King deployed his men in a single line and cantered out with levelled lance. Huyan gave his mount rein and advanced to do battle. Zhou Tong spurred his animal. Soon the two horses drew together.

The riders fought six or seven rounds. Zhou Tong wasn't strong enough. He pulled his steed around and headed up the slope. Huyan chased him a while. But he was afraid of being tricked. He rode hastily down the mountain and set up a camp. There he waited for the next opportunity to fight.

Zhou Tong returned to his stronghold. "Huyan Zhuo is a highly skilled warrior," he told Li Zhong. "I couldn't stop him. I had no choice but to come back. If he pursues right to our fort, what can we do?"

"I hear that Sagacious Lu the Tattooed Monk is in the Precious Pearl Monastery on Two-Dragon Mountain with a large band of men. With him, what's more, is some fellow called Yang Zhi the Blue-Faced Beast, and a newly arrived pilgrim Wu Song. They're all formidable fighters. I'll send a letter requesting their aid. If we get out of this danger thanks to their efforts, I'll be glad to pay them tribute every month."

"I've known about those brave fellows for some time. I'm just afraid that monk still remembers the first time we met, and won't want to help."

Li Zhong laughed. "Never mind. He's a good man, very forthright. When he learns of the fix we're in, he'll sure come with warriors to the rescue."

"Yes, that's true."

The letter was written and two competent brigands were picked to deliver it. They rolled down the rear slope and struck out for Two-Dragon Mountain. They reached the foot of it in only two days. The brigands on guard there questioned them closely on the nature of their business.

Three chieftains sat in the main hall of the Precious Pearl Monastery. Sagacious Lu the Tattooed Monk was first in command. Yang Zhi the Blue-Faced Beast was second. Third was Wu Song the Pilgrim.

In the building at the entry gate were four lesser chiefs. One was Shi En the Golden-Eyed Tiger Cub. The son of the warden of Mengzhou Prison at the time Wu Song killed General Zhang and his entire family, he and his father had been made responsible for apprehending the culprit. Rather than do this, Shi En had abandoned his home and fled. For some time he was a wanderer. Later, his parents died, and he heard that Wu Song was on Two-Dragon Mountain. He had hurried to join him.

Another lesser chief was Cao Zheng the Demon Carver. He had been with Sagacious Lu and Yang Zhi when they took Precious Pearl Monastery and killed Deng Long. He too subsequently joined the band.

The third was Zhang Qing the Vegetable Gardener. The fourth was Sun the Witch. These two, husband and wife, had sold dumplings stuffed with human flesh at Crossroads Rise on the Mengzhou Road. They had joined in response to repeated letters from Sagacious Lu and Wu Song.

Cao Zheng, hearing that there was a letter from Peach Blossom Mountain, carefully questioned the messengers, then went up to the hall and reported to the three chieftains.

"When I left Mount Wutai I put up in Peach Blossom Village, and there I gave that prick Zhou Tong a good drubbing," Lu recalled. "Then Li Zhong came and recognized me. He invited me up to their mountain for a day of drinking. He pledged me his blood brother and wanted me to stay and be their chieftain. But the stinginess of those two annoyed me. I collected some of their gold and silver drinking vessels and left. Now they send messengers pleading for aid. Let them come up. We'll hear what they have to say."

Cao Zheng soon returned with the two emissaries. They hailed the chieftains respectfully and said: "Murong, prefect of Qingzhou, has recently been entertaining Two Rods Huyan Zhuo, who failed in an attack on Liangshan Marsh. The prefect has sent him to clean out our mountain strongholds on Peach Blossom, Two-Dragon and White Tiger, so that he may be given another army and take Liangshan and get his revenge. Our leaders beseech you great chieftains to come with armed forces and save us. When all this is over, we will be glad to pay tribute."

"We defend our own mountain and fortress. As a rule we don't go to anyone's rescue," Yang Zhi said to Wu Song and the Tattooed Monk. "But if we don't help, we'll damage the prestige of the gallant fraternity, for one thing. For another, if we let that lout capture Peach Blossom Mountain, he'll look on us with contempt. Let's leave Zhang Qing, Sun the Witch, Shi En and Cao Zheng to hold the fort. Then we three can take a little trip."

He mustered five hundred foot soldiers and sixty cavalrymen. Each donned his armor and equipment, and all headed for Peach Blossom Mountain.

When Li Zhong heard the news from Two-Dragon Mountain, he led three hundred brigands down as reinforcements. Huyan Zhuo rushed his entire complement to block their path. He deployed his men and, brandishing his rods, rode out against Li Zhong.

Li was from Dingyuan in Haozhou Prefecture, where his family, for generations, had earned their livelihood by their skill at arms. Because of his stalwart physique, he was known as the Tiger-Fighting General. But in his clash with

Huyan he discovered he had met his match. After ten rounds or so, he could see it was going badly. He parried his adversary's weapons and fled.

Huyan, with a low opinion of Li's fighting ability, chased him up the mountain. Zhou Tong the Little King was at mid-point on the slope. He promptly threw down stones like goose eggs. Huyan hurriedly turned his mount and returned to the foot of the mountain. He found his government soldiers shouting in alarm.

"What are you yelling about?" he demanded.

"There, in the distance. A body of men and horses racing this way!" exclaimed the rear guard.

Huyan looked beyond them. A big fat monk on a white horse was leading a contingent, trailed by a rising cloud of dust. It was Sagacious Lu the Tattooed Monk.

"Where is that prick who was beaten at Liangshan Marsh?" he was roaring. "How dare you come here and bluster?"

"I'm going to kill you first, bald donkey," Huyan responded, "to work off the rage inside me!"

Lu twirled his iron Buddhist staff, Huyan waved his rods, the horses met, the opposing forces shouted. The two men fought forty or fifty rounds with neither emerging the victor.

"This monk is fantastic," Huyan marvelled to himself.

On both sides trumpets blared and the contestants withdrew to rest. But after a short interval, Huyan grew impatient. Again he rode his steed into the arena. "Come out, thief of a monk," he cried. "Let's fight to a finish!"

Lu was about to meet the challenge when Yang Zhi said: "Rest a bit longer, brother. Watch me nab this oaf!"

Waving his sabre, he rode forth and clashed with Huyan. Forty or fifty rounds they fought with neither vanquishing the other.

Huyan was filled with admiration. "Where did they get two like these?" he wondered. "Truly remarkable. They never learned such jousting in the greenwood!"

Impressed by Huyan's superb skill with arms, Yang Zhi broke off the engagement, turned his horse and galloped back to his position. Huyan didn't give chase, but also turned his mount around. Both sides withdrew their forces.

"This is our first venture here," Sagacious Lu said to Yang Zhi. "We'd better not camp too close to them. Let's pull back another twenty *li*. We'll come out and fight again tomorrow."

With their men, they crossed to a nearby hollow and there set up a camp.

Huyan brooded in his tent. "I expected taking this gang of cheap robbers would be as easy as snapping bamboo," he thought. "Who knew I'd ran into such adversaries. What rotten luck!"

He could see no way out of his dilemma. Just then a messenger arrived from Prefect Murong.

"The General is ordered to return at once with his soldiers and defend the city," the man said. "Bandits from White Tiger Mountain under Kong Ming and Kong Liang are on their way to raid the prison. To prevent anything from happening to the prefectural government, the General is requested to hurry back with his forces."

This was just the excuse Huyan was looking for. He set out for Qingzhou with his infantry and cavalry that very night.

The next day Sagacious Lu, Yang Zhi and Wu Song led their brigands, waving banners and yelling, down the mountain. To their astonishment, there was not a sign of their foe. Li Zhong and Zhou Tong came down with men from their own mountain and invited the three chieftains to their stronghold. There, they slaughtered sheep and horses and spread a feast in their honor. At the same time they dispatched scouts to find out what was happening on the road beyond.

As Huyan was leading his contingent back to the city he saw a body of men and horses already on the outskirts of Qingzhou. At their head were Kong Ming the Comet and Kong Liang the Flaming Star—sons of Squire Kong who lived at the foot of White Tiger Mountain. In a quarrel with a local rich man, they had slaughtered him and his entire household. Next, they gathered six or seven hundred men, occupied White Tiger Mountain, and took to pillage and plunder. Prefect Murong arrested their uncle Kong Bin, who lived in the city and threw him into jail. They had been heading for Qingzhou to get him out. Now, they found themselves confronted by Huyan Zhuo and his contingent.

The two sides spread out and engaged in battle. Huyan rode to the front of his position. Prefect Murong, watching from a tower on the city wall, saw Kong Ming, with levelled lance astride a charger, attack Huyan. They met and fought over twenty rounds. Huyan wanted to display his prowess before the prefect. He noted that Kong Ming, whose skill with arms was not exceptional, was now entirely on the defensive. Huyan drove in close and snatched him off his horse.

Kong Liang and his men turned and fled. Murong, from the tower, shouted for Huyan to go after them. The government soldiers pressed hard and captured more than a hundred of the foe. Badly defeated, Kong Liang and the rest of his forces ran in all directions. Towards evening, they put up in an ancient temple.

After capturing Kong Ming, Huyan led him into the city and presented himself before the prefect. Murong was delighted. He directed that a rack be placed around the prisoner's neck, and that he be confined in the same jail as his uncle Kong Bin. The prefect rewarded the troops and entertained Huyan. He asked about the brigands on Peach Blossom Mountain.

"I thought I had only to stretch out my hand and take them, as easily as catching turtles in a jug," said Huyan. "But unexpectedly a band of robbers came to their rescue. Among them was a monk and a big blue-faced fellow. I fought them both, but couldn't defeat either. Their skill is out of the ordinary. It's not the usual style of robbers in the greenwood. So I was prevented from capturing the bandits."

"That monk," said Murong, "is Lu Da, who was an major under Governor-General Zhong of the Yanan border region. Later, he shaved off his hair and became a monk, and he's now known as Sagacious Lu the Tattooed Monk. The big fellow with blue tinged complexion was once an aide in the palace in the Eastern Capital. He's called Yang Zhi the Blue-Faced Beast. Their third leader is Wu Song, known as the Pilgrim. He's the Constable Wu who killed the tiger on Jingyang Ridge.

"These three occupy Two-Dragon Mountain, from where they rob and plunder. We've sent troops to catch them several times, but they killed four or five of our officers. We haven't caught one of them to this day!"

"Their skill is superb. So that's who they are—Palace Aide Yang and Major Lu. They certainly deserve their reputation! But don't worry, Excellency. You have me here. I'll nab every one of them and turn them over!"

The prefect was very pleased. He gave a feast in Huyan's honor, then invited him to rest in a guest-house. Of that we'll say no more.

Kong Liang was leading the remnants of his beaten unit along the road. Suddenly, a band of men and horses emerged from among the trees. The bold fellow at their head was Wu Song the Pilgrim. Kong Liang rolled from his saddle and kowtowed.

"I trust all has gone well with you, sir warrior!"

Wu Song hastily returned the salutation. He raised Kong Liang to his feet.

"I heard you two brothers had occupied White Tiger Mountain and formed a righteous gathering," he said. "Several times I intended to pay my respects. But I wasn't able leave our stronghold, and the road to your place is difficult, so I couldn't get to see you. What brings you here today?"

Kong Liang told how his brother was captured while trying to rescue their uncle Kong Bin.

"Don't be upset, friend," said Wu Song. "I have six or seven brothers with me in our band on Two-Dragon Mountain. The other day Li Zhong and Zhou Tong on Peach Blossom Mountain were strongly attacked by government troops from Qingzhou, and they asked for our assistance. Lu and Yang went with some of our forces and fought Huyan Zhuo all day. For some reason, he and his men suddenly left in the night. The Peach Blossom Mountain people feasted Lu and Yang and me and presented us with a snowy hoofed steed. I'm taking our first contingent back to our stronghold. Lu and Yang are following and will soon be here. I'll tell them to raid Qingzhou and save your uncle and brother. How will that be?"

Kong Liang thanked Wu Song. After a considerable wait, Sagacious Lu and Yang Zhi arrived with their cavalry. Wu Song introduced Kong Liang.

"I once met Song Jiang in his manor and put him to a lot of trouble," Wu said. "Today, for the sake of chivalry, we can combine the forces of the three mountain strongholds, attack Qingzhou, kill the prefect, capture Huyan Zhuo, and divide the money and grain in the storehouses for the use of our various bands. What do you say?"

"Just what I was thinking," asserted Sagacious Lu. "Let's notify Peach Blossom Mountain, and ask Li Zhong and Zhou Tong to bring their men. The three bands can strike Qingzhou together."

"It's a sturdily built city, its armed forces are strong, and Huyan Zhuo is a courageous fellow," mused Yang Zhi. "I don't mean to disparage us, but if you want to succeed you'd better take my advice."

"Let's hear your strategy, brother," said Wu Song.

Yang Zhi spoke briefly, he wasted no words.

And as a result, smoke rose from the ruins of every house of the citizens of Qingzhou, and the heroes of the Marsh ground their fists into their palms as they advanced belligerently.

How did Yang Zhi propose to Wu Song that Qingzhou should be attacked? Read our next chapter if you would know.

CHAPTER 58

THREE MOUNTAIN BANDS ATTACK QINGZHOU

WARRIORS UNITED RETURN TO THE MARSH

"A large force is needed to take Qingzhou," said Yang Zhi. "We know that the famous Song Jiang, called the Timely Rain in the gallant fraternity, is in Liangshan Marsh. Huyan Zhuo is his enemy. Our Two-Dragon Mountain band will co-operate with the Kong brothers' band. We will wait here till the men from Peach Blossom Mountain arrive, and go with them to assault the town. Brother Kong Liang, you must travel at top speed to Mount Liangshan and beseech Song Jiang to join our attack. That is the best plan, because you and he are great friends. What do you brothers think?"

"Sounds all right to me," said Sagacious Lu. "I've heard a lot of good things about Song Jiang, though I'm sorry to say we've never met. People chatter about him so much they've nearly made me deaf. He must be quite a man, to be so famous. I went to see him when he was with Hua Rong in Fort Clear Winds. But by the time I got there, he was gone. Never mind. Kong Liang, you want to rescue your brother. You'd better hurry and ask Song Jiang's help. We'll stay here and start the battle against those pricks."

Kong Liang directed his men to remain with Sagacious Lu. He took only one companion. Disguised as a merchant, he set out swiftly for Liangshan Marsh.

Sagacious Lu, Yang Zhi and Wu Song went to their mountain strongholds and fetched Shi En and Cao Zheng and about two hundred fighters. On Peach Blossom Mountain when Li Zhong and Zhou Tong received the news they brought their entire force, except for forty or fifty left to hold the fort. All contingents converged outside the town and prepared for the assault. Of that we'll say no more.

On leaving Qingzhou, Kong Liang followed a winding road till he came to the tavern on the edge of Liangshan Marsh run by LiLi, who was called Hell's Summoner. There he stopped to buy some wine and ask the way. Kong Liang and his companion were strangers to Li. He invited them to be seated.

"Where are you from?" he queried.

"Qingzhou," said Kong Liang.

"Who is it you wish to see in the Marsh?"

"A friend of mine, on the mountain."

"Important chieftains live in that fortress on the mountain. How can you go there?"

"It's a chieftain I'm seeking—Song Jiang."

"In that case I have an obligation to you." LiLi ordered his attendants to serve wine.

"We've never met," said Kong Liang. "Why so courteous?"

"Anyone seeking a chieftain in the fortress is sure to be one of our kind, an old friend. He must be properly received and his arrival reported."

"I am Kong Liang, from a manor at the foot of White Tiger Mountain."

"I've heard brother Song Jiang mention you. We'll escort you to the stronghold today."

The two drank ceremonial cups of wine. LiLi opened a window overlooking the water and shot a whistling arrow. From the reeds on the opposite side of the cove a brigand propelled a boat. It stopped beside the tavern. LiLi invited Kong Liang on board. The craft was sculled to the Shore of Golden Sands, and the men began to climb.

Kong Liang was impressed by the bristling array of weapons at each of the three gates through which they had to pass. "I heard that the stronghold was well equipped," he said to himself, "but I never thought it was on such a scale!"

Brigands had gone ahead to report, and Song Jiang came down to greet him. Kong Liang hastily knelt and kowtowed.

"What brings you here, brother?" Song Jiang asked. Kong Liang burst into tears. Song Jiang said: "If you're in any danger or difficulty, don't hesitate to speak. We'll help you, no matter what it is. Brother, please rise."

"After we parted, my old father died. My brother Kong Ming quarreled with a well-to-do neighbor and killed him and his entire family. The authorities were hot on his trail, so we went up White Tiger Mountain and formed a band of six or seven hundred. We lived by robbery and pillage. Murong, the prefect of Qingzhou, arrested Kong Bin, our uncle whose home was in town, and threw him into prison with a heavy rack around his neck. My brother and I staged a raid to rescue him, but outside the walls we were met by Huyan Zhuo who wields two rods. Brother fought, and Huyan captured him. They took him into Qingzhou and put him in prison also. There's no guarantee they won't kill him.

"I was chased and had to run. The next day, I met Wu Song. He introduced me to his companions. One was Sagacious Lu the Tattooed Monk. The other was Yang Zhi the Blue-Faced Beast. We were like old friends the moment we met. We discussed the rescue of my brother. Wu Song said: 'We'll ask Lu and Yang to get Li Zhong and Zhou Tong from Peach Blossom Mountain, and join the forces from three strongholds in an attack on Qingzhou. You hurry to Mount Liangshan and request Song Jiang to help save your uncle and your brother.' That's why I'm here. I pray, for the sake of my departed father, that you rescue them. I'll be eternally grateful."

"It will be easy. Don't worry. Come pay your respects to our leader Chao Gai. We'll talk it over together."

Song Jiang presented Kong Liang to Chao Gai, Wu Yong, Gongsun Sheng, and the other chieftains. He related that Huyan Zhuo had gone to Qingzhou and cast his lot in with Prefect Murong and had recently captured Kong Ming, and that Kong Liang was seeking his rescue.

Chao Gai said: "Since the two brave brothers out of chivalry and righteousness, desire to rescue their uncle, and since you, brother Song, are their friend, we should indeed assist them. But you've ridden forth on expeditions many times, brother. This time you hold the fort and let me go."

"You're our highest leader. We mustn't lightly put you to any trouble," said Song Jiang. "This is a personal matter. Kong Liang has come all this distance to see me. He'd be embarrassed if I didn't go personally. I'd prefer to handle this alone with a few of our brothers."

Immediately, chieftains high and low pushed forward and volunteered. "We'll give our all," they cried. "Only take us along!"

Song Jiang was very pleased. That day a feast was given for Kong Liang, and Song Jiang direct Pei Xuan to muster men for the expedition and divide them into five contingents. The vanguard was to be led by Hua Rong, Qin Ming, Yan Shun and Stumpy Tiger Wang. The second unit was under Mu Hong, Yang Xiong, Xie Zhen and Xie Bao. The chief generals Song Jiang, Wu Yong, Lu Fang and Guo Sheng commanded the central force. The fourth contingent was headed by Zhu Tong, Chai Jin, Li Jun and Zhang Heng, while the unit bringing up the rear was under Sun Li, Yang Lin, Ou Peng and Ling Zhen.

When the five battalions were mustered they had fighters on horse and on foot totalling three thousand, under twenty commanders. The other chieftains remained with Chao Gai to hold the fortress. Song Jiang took his leave of Chao Gai and went down the mountain with Kong Liang and the brigand force.

Their march was uneventful, and they harmed none of the prefectures and counties along the way. They soon reached Qingzhou. Kong Liang went on ahead and informed Sagacious Lu. The Tattooed Monk and his companions prepared a welcome. When Song Jiang and his central battalion arrived, Wu Song led Sagacious Lu, Yang Zhi, Li Zhong, Zhou Tong, Shi En and Cao Zheng forward to greet him. Song asked Sagacious to be seated.

"I've long known of your fame, brother," said the monk, "but I never had the chance to pay my respects. I'm very happy to meet you today."

"I don't deserve such courtesy," Song Jiang protested. "In the gallant fraternity your virtue is well known, Reverend. To be able to look upon your benevolent face is the greatest joy of my life!"

Yang Zhi rose and bowed. "I passed through Liangshan Marsh earlier," he said, "and the chieftains were kind enough to ask me to stay. But I stupidly declined. Today, you call here within sight of our mountain lair. Nothing under Heaven could please me more!"

"Everyone in the gallant fraternity has heard of Yang Zhi. My only regret is that we hadn't met sooner!"

Sagacious Lu ordered that wine be served, and introductions were made all around.

The next day Song Jiang asked about the situation in the prefectural town.

"After Kong Liang left, we had four or five clashes, with no clear result," said Yang Zhi. "Qingzhou's mainstay is Huyan Zhuo. If we capture him, we can push into that town like hot water through snow."

Wu Yong laughed. "He can be taken, but by guile, not by force."

"How do you propose to do it?" Song Jiang asked.

Wu Yong softly outlined his plan. Song Jiang was delighted.

"Very shrewd!"

That day he issued his instructions, and the next morning they proceeded to the walls of Qingzhou. They surrounded the town, beat their drums, waved their pennants, shouted, and shook their weapons. Murong was informed, and he hurriedly summoned Huyan Zhuo.

"Those bandits have brought help from Liangshan Marsh. What are we going to do?" demanded the prefect.

"Don't worry, Your Excellency," said Huyan. "By coming here they've lost their favorable terrain. It's only in the marsh that they can act up. Now that they've left their lair, we can nab them as fast as they come. They've nowhere to deploy. Please go up on the ramparts, Prefect, and watch me slaughter those rogues!"

Huyan quickly donned his armor and mounted his charger. He shouted for the gates to be opened and the drawbridge to be lowered. He rode forth at the head of a thousand infantry and cavalry, and spread them out in battle formation. From Song Jiang's contingent a horseman emerged. He was carrying a wolf-toothed cudgel. In a stentorian voice he cursed the prefect.

"Grafter! People-injuring thief! You've destroyed my home, and today I'm going to get my revenge!"

Murong recognized Qin Ming. "You were an officer of the imperial court," he shouted. "The state treated you well. How dare you rebel! When I capture you I'll have you smashed into ten thousand pieces! Nab that outlaw for me, first!" he yelled to Huyan.

Flourishing his rods, Huyan rode towards his objective. Qin Ming gave his steed full rein and galloped to meet Huyan, waving his wolf-toothed cudgel. They were a well-matched pair, and they fought nearly fifty rounds with neither vanquishing the other.

Murong felt the contest was lasting too long. He was afraid Huyan would lose. Hurriedly, he had the gongs summon his troops back to the town. Qin Ming did not pursue the departing foe, but returned to his own position. Song Jiang instructed his commanders to withdraw fifteen *li* and make camp.

Inside the town, Huyan got off his horse and reported to the prefect. "I was about to take that Qin Ming," he said. "Why did you sound retreat, Your Excellency?"

"You'd fought many rounds. I feared you were tired, so I called our forces back to rest, temporarily. Before he and Hua Rong rebelled, Qin Ming was commanding general here. The knave is hot to be underestimated."

"I'll take that treacherous bandit, Your Excellency, rest assured. When I fought him just now he was getting clumsy with his rods. Next time, watch me smash him!"

"I know what a hero you are. But tomorrow, I want you to break open a gap in the enemy lines so that I can send out three men. I shall dispatch one to the

Eastern Capital to ask for assistance, and two to neighboring districts and prefectures to raise troops to help capture the bandits."

"Your Excellency is indeed far-sighted."

The prefect wrote out a request for assistance, selected three officers, and made the necessary arrangements.

Huyan returned to his quarters, removed his armor and rested. Before dawn the next day an officer entered and reported: "On a hill outside the north gate three horsemen are observing the town. The one in the middle is wearing a red gown and is riding a white steed. The man on the right is Hua Rong. We don't recognize the man on the left, but he's dressed as a Taoist."

"That man in red is Song Jiang. The Taoist must be his general, Wu Yong. Don't alert them. Muster a hundred cavalry and bag all three."

Huyan hastily put on his armor and mounted. Rods in hand, leading his hundred horsemen, he had the north gate quietly opened and the drawbridge lowered, and rode swiftly towards the hill. Song Jiang, Wu Yong and Hua Rong continued staring at the town. Huyan raced up the slope. Only then did the three turn their mounts and walk them slowly away.

Before a grove of withered trees they again reined in. In hot pursuit, Huyan had just raced to the edge of the grove when shouts rang out and horse and rider dropped into a concealed pit. From both sides fifty or sixty men snared Huyan with hooked poles, hauled him out, and tied him up. Others extracted his horse.

By then the rest of Huyan's troop came charging up. Calmly fitting arrows to his bow, Hua Rong brought down the first five or six. Those behind halted abruptly, yanked their steeds around and, yelling, galloped off.

Song Jiang returned to camp and took his seat. Knife-wearing attendants pushed Huyan Zhuo before him. Song immediately rose and ordered that his bonds be removed. He personally conducted Huyan to a chair and greeted him respectfully.

"Why are you doing this?" Huyan asked.

"Would I be ungrateful to the imperial court?" Song Jiang retorted. "I was hard pressed by corrupt officials and forced to commit a crime. I've had to seek refuge in this marsh while awaiting an imperial pardon. I never expected to stir into action so mighty a general, for whom I have such great admiration. It was very wrong of me, and I beg your forgiveness."

"I am your prisoner. Ten thousand deaths would be too light a punishment. Yet you treat me with such courtesy!"

"Never would I presume to harm you. Heaven is my witness."

"Is it your wish, respected brother, that I should go to the Eastern Capital and ask for a royal pardon to bring to your mountain?"

"You couldn't possibly do that, General! Marshal Gao is a narrow-hearted villain. He forgets a man's large accomplishments and remembers only his small failings. You've lost a lot of troops, money and grain. He'd surely hold you culpable. Han Tao, Peng Qi and Ling Zhen have all joined our band. If you don't scorn our mountain stronghold as too humble, I'd be happy to relinquish to you my place as chieftain. When the court has use for us and issues its imperial pardon, we can once again serve our country with our utmost efforts."

Huyan hesitated for several minutes. But, firstly, since he was one of the stars of Heavenly Spirits, he naturally was of the same chivalrous mentality. And, secondly, he was overwhelmed by Song Jiang's courtesy and reasonableness. With a sigh, he knelt.

"It's not that I lack loyalty to the government. But your exceeding gallantry leaves me no choice but to agree. I'll follow you faithfully. The situation being what it is, there's no alternative."

Song Jiang was very pleased. He introduced Huyan to the other chieftains and directed Li Zhong and Zhou Tong to return his mount the Ebony Steed Which Treads in Snow. Then the chieftains conferred on how to rescue Kong Ming.

Wu Yong said: "If Huyan can trick them into opening the gates, we'll take the town easily. It will also put an end to any thought he may have of rejoining them."

Song Jiang went to Huyan and said: "It's not loot I'm after, but Kong Ming and his uncle are imprisoned in Qingzhou. We can't save them unless you get the town to open the gates."

"Since you've been kind enough to accept me, of course I'll do my best."

That night ten chieftains disguised themselves as government troops and rode forth with Huyan at their head. At the town moat they halted.

"Open the gates," shouted the general. "I've escaped and returned!"

Soldiers on the wall recognized Huyan's voice and hastily reported to Murong. The prefect had been brooding over the loss of the general. Now, hearing that he had come back, Murong was delighted. He jumped on his horse and rode to the town wall. He saw Huyan with about a dozen mounted men. He couldn't make out their faces in the dark, but he knew the general's voice.

"How were you able to return?" Murong called.

"Those knaves trapped my horse and took me to their camp. Some of my commanders sneaked this mount to me, and we got away together."

Murong ordered his soldiers to open the gates and lower the drawbridge. As the chieftains entered the town, he came forward to greet them. With one blow of his cudgel, Qin Ming knocked the prefect from his saddle. The Xie brothers set the town to the torch. Ou Peng and Stumpy Tiger Wang dashed up the wall and killed or scattered the defenders.

Song Jiang and the main force, seeing that Qingzhou was on fire, surged in. He transmitted an urgent order that the townspeople were not to be harmed, but to empty the town's treasury and grain stores. Kong Ming and his uncle and Kong Bin's family were rescued from the prison. Song Jiang directed that the fires be extinguished. The prefect's entire family, young and old, were killed, and all their possessions distributed among the marauders.

At daybreak a count was made of those families whose homes had been damaged by the fires, and they were given grain as relief payments. The money and grain taken from government stores came to nearly six hundred cartloads. Over two hundred good horses were also captured. A great feast of celebration was held in the main hall of the prefectural government, and the leaders of the three mountain strongholds were invited to go together to the fortress on Mount Liangshan.

Li Zhong and Zhou Tong sent people to Peach Blossom Mountain with orders to collect men and horses, and as much money and grain as possible, and then set fire to the stronghold and abandon it. Sagacious Lu dispatched Shi En and Cao Zheng to Two-Dragon Mountain. There, with Zhang Qing and his wife Sun the Witch, they assembled the brigands, loaded their money and grain, and burned down their stronghold in Precious Pearl Monastery.

In a few days time, the forces from the three mountains completed their preparations, and the entire body, led by Song Jiang, set out for the Mount Liangshan fortress. Song put Hua Rong, Qin Ming, Huyan Zhuo and Zhu Tong in the van to clear the way. Not a single prefecture or county was harmed during the march. Villagers, carrying their babes and supporting their old folk, burned incense and kowtowed in greeting.

The cavalcade reached Liangshan Marsh several days later. Chieftains of the water forces met them with boats, and Chao Gai and the leaders of the infantry and cavalry were awaiting them when they landed on the Shore of Golden Sands. They climbed together to the big stronghold, entered Fraternity Hall and took their seats.

A big feast was laid to celebrate the addition of twelve new chieftains: Huyan Zhuo, Sagacious Lu, Yang Zhi, Wu Song, Shi En, Cao Zheng, Zhang Qing, Sun the Witch, Li Zhong, Zhou Tong, Kong Ming and Kong Liang. Lin Chong rose and thanked Sagacious Lu for his aid in the rescue.

"I've thought about you a lot after we parted in Cangzhou," said the monk. "Has there been any news of your wife?"

"After I took over from Wang Lun, I sent someone home to fetch her. He found that Marshal Gao's wicked son had kept after her so hard that she finally killed herself. Her father was very depressed, and took ill and died."

Yang Zhi related how he met with Lin Chong when Wang Lun was still in control of the lair. All agreed that this had been fated. It was no accident. Chao Gai told the story of the capture of the birthday gifts on Yellow Earth Ridge. Everyone laughed heartily.

More feasts were given for several successive days. Of that we'll say no more.

The fortress had been strengthened by many men and horses, and Song Jiang was exceedingly pleased. He ordered Tang Long to oversee all metalwork and manufacture many kinds of weapons and armor. Hou Jian, who he put in charge of banners and clothing, added flags and pennants of every size and shape, embroidered with dragons, tigers, bears and leopards, and decorated with golden standards, white tassels, crimson fringes and black covers. On all sides of the mountain broad glacis were constructed. On the western and southern roads two taverns were rebuilt, both to receive visiting gallants and to listen for and quickly report the approach of government troops. Zhang Qing and his wife Sun the Witch, who originally had been innkeepers, were given charge of the tavern on the west. The south side tavern remained under Sun Xin and his wife Mistress Gu. Zhu Gui and Yue Ho continued to run the tavern on the east side, and LiLi and Shi Qian the one on the north. More barricades were set up in each of the three passes, and chieftains assigned to their defense. All were abjured to perform strictly their defined duties.

One day the Tattooed Monk spoke to Song Jiang. "I have a friend, a pupil of Li Chong, called Nine Dragons Shi Jin," he said. "He's now on Mount Shaohua in Huayin County in the prefecture of Huazhou. With him, joined in brotherhood are Zhu Wu the Miraculous Strategist, Chen Da the Gorge-Leaping Tiger, and Yang Chun the White-Spotted Snake. I think of Shi Jin often. He saved my life in the Waguan Monastery, and I won't forget it. I'd like to go and see him, and bring him and the other three back to join us. How does that idea strike you?"

"I've heard of Shi Jin's fame. It would be fine if you could bring him here. But don't go alone. Take Wu Song. He's a pilgrim monk. He'll be an appropriate companion."

Wu Song expressed his willingness to go. Sagacious collected his luggage and put on his slanting hat and waist bag, as suited a meditation monk. Wu dressed as a pilgrim. The two bid farewell to the chieftains, left the mountain and crossed the Shore of Golden Sands. Starting early and resting late, they travelled many a day until they came to the border of Huayin County in the prefecture of Huazhou. They headed directly for Mount Shaohua.

Song Jiang was worried about them after they left. He directed Dai Zong the Marvellous Traveller to follow and keep an eye on them.

Sagacious Lu and Wu Song reached the foot of Mount Shaohua. Brigands in ambush stepped out and barred the road. "Where are you monks from?" they demanded.

"Is there an Excellency Shi Jin on this mountain?" countered Wu Song.

"You're asking for Chieftain Shi? Wait here a while. I'll report your arrival to our leaders and they'll come down and greet you."

"Just say Sagacious Lu is here."

The brigand wasn't gone long. He returned with Zhu Wu the Miraculous Strategist, Chen Da the Gorge-Leaping Tiger and Yang Chun the White-Spotted Snake, who welcomed the two callers. But Shi Jin was not among them.

"Where is His Excellency?" queried Sagacious. "Why isn't he here?"

Zhu Wu stepped forward. "Aren't you Major Lu Da from the district of Yanan?"

"I am. And this pilgrim is the Constable Wu Song who slew the tiger on Jingyang Ridge."

The three chieftains hastily bowed. "We've long known the fame of you both! We heard that you'd set up a stronghold on Two-Dragon Mountain. What brings you here today?"

"We're not there any longer," said Sagacious. "We've joined Song Jiang in the big fortress on Mount Liangshan. Today we've travelled specially to see Excellency Shi."

"Please come to our stronghold on the mountain, then," said Zhu Wu, "and I'll tell you all about him."

"If you've got anything to say, say it! Waiting is too much of a friggin nuisance!"

"The reverend is an impatient man," Wu Song explained. "Why not tell him now?"

"After Excellency Shi joined us three on this mountain, we prospered," said Zhu Wu. "Recently, he went down and met an artist, a man named Wang Yi, from the Northern Capital in Taming Prefect. Wang had been painting some murals he had promised the Emperor of Golden Heaven Temple on Mount Huashan in the Western Range. He'd gone there with his daughter Jade Branch. Ho, the prefect of Huazhou—a crooked grafter who harms the people, one of Premier Cai's clique—went to the temple one day to burn incense and was struck by the girl's beauty. He sent emissaries several times to ask for Jade Branch as his concubine. Wang Yi wouldn't agree, so he took her by force and ordered the father exiled to a distant military region. Wang Yi, while passing through here on the way to exile, met Shi Jin and told him the story.

"His Excellency rescued him and brought him up the mountain, killing his two escorts. Then he went to the prefectural office to destroy Ho. But he was discovered, seized, and thrown into prison. The prefect is also mustering a force to wipe us out. We've nowhere to go and no way to cope. Our situation is bitter!"

"That prick has no manners! How dare he act so tough!" cried Sagacious. "I'll finish him off for you!"

"Please come to our stronghold for a conference," said Zhu Wu.

Sagacious was unwilling, but Wu Song pointed and said: "Can't you see the sun is already settling on the treetops?"

The Tattooed Monk roared impatiently and blew out a gusty breath. Reluctantly he went with the others to the Mount Shaohua fort. The five sat down together. Wang Yi was introduced to Sagacious and Wu Song.

He told how Prefect Ho extorted decent people's money and seized their daughters. The three chieftains had cows and horses slaughtered and entertained the two visitors at a feast.

Sagacious refused to drink. He said: "Brother Shi isn't here, so I won't touch a drop. All I want is a good night's sleep. Tomorrow I'll go into town and kill that oaf!"

"Don't stir up any trouble, brother," Wu Song urged. "You and I can hurry back to Mount Liangshan and report. We'll request Song Jiang to lead a large force against Huazhou. In that way we'll rescue Excellency Shi Jin."

"By the time we get men from the fortress brother Shi Jin's life will have vanished!"

"Will you save him by killing Ho?" Wu Song was strongly opposed to the monk's going.

"Calm yourself, Reverend," said Zhu Wu placatingly. "Constable Wu Song is right."

"It's calm people like you who are going to be the death of brother Shi," cried Sagacious. "His life is in that fellow's hands and you sit here drinking and piddling over details!"

They finally persuaded him to drink a cup or two of wine. Lu went to bed with his clothes on. He rose at the fourth watch the next day, took his Buddhist staff and knife and set out swiftly for Huazhou.

"He wouldn't listen to me," said Wu Song. "He's sure to get into a jam!"

Zhu Wu instructed two discreet brigands to follow and keep track of the impetuous monk.

Sagacious rushed directly into town and asked where he could find the prefectural office.

"Across that bridge and to the east," he was told.

He had just reached the pontoon bridge when someone advised him: "Get out of the way, monk. His Excellency the prefect is coming!"

"I was looking for him, and here he drops right into my hands," Sagacious said to himself. "That lout is a dead man!"

The prefect's escort of honor passed in pairs. His enclosed sedan-chair was guarded on either side by ten captains carrying whips and spears and iron chains.

"It won't be easy to get at the wretch," thought Sagacious. "And if I try and fail, I'll be a laughing stock!"

The prefect looked through the window of his sedan-chair and saw Sagacious, who was obviously hesitating whether to approach him. Ho crossed the bridge and at the prefectural office got out of his chair and summoned two of his captains.

"Invite that big fat monk on the bridge to come to my residence for a vegetarian meal."

The captains went to the bridge and said to Sagacious: "The prefect invites you to a meatless repast."

"The knave is sure to die by my hand," thought Sagacious. "I wanted to strike him, but because I was afraid I couldn't get at him I let him pass. I'm still after him, and now he invites me!" He followed the captains to the prefectural compound.

Ho had already left instructions. When Sagacious arrived at the front of the hall he was told to leave his staff and knife and go to a rear building for his vegetarian meal. Sagacious demurred. Everyone berated him.

"For a monk you don't know very much! How can you carry weapons deep into the prefectural compound?"

Sagacious thought: "With my two fists alone I can crush that oaf's skull!" He left his staff and knife on the porch and followed the captains inside.

Prefect Ho was seated in a rear building. He shouted: "Seize that bald robber!"

Thirty or forty policemen poured out of closets on both sides and pounced on Sagacious. Even if he were Prince Nezha how could he avoid Earth's net and Heaven's snare? Indra himself couldn't escape from such a dragon's lair and tiger's den!

Truly, the moth destroys itself in the flame, the angry turtle must die when it swallows the baited hook.

How did Sagacious Lu save himself from the clutches of Prefect Ho? Read our next chapter if you would know.

CHAPTER 59

WU YONG BY A RUSE OBTAINS THE GOLDEN HANGING BELL

SONG JIANG FIGHTS ON MOUNT HUASHAN IN THE WEST

The policemen rushed Sagacious Lu to the foot of the prefect's platform.

"Where are you from, bald donkey?" shouted Ho.

"What crime have I committed?"

"Who sent you here to kill me? The truth, now!"

"I'm a monk, a man who's renounced the world. How can you ask me that?"

"I saw you waiting to attack my sedan-chair with your staff, but you didn't dare. Bald donkey, you'd better confess!"

"This bucko didn't try to kill you. Why have you arrested me? You're wronging a peaceful man."

"Since when does a monk call himself 'this bucko'? He's a plundering bandit from the fifth region West of the Pass, for sure, who's come to avenge Shi Jin! If we don't beat him, he won't admit it. Guards, give this bald donkey a good drubbing!"

"Don't you put a finger on me! Let me tell you something!" yelled Sagacious. "I'm Sagacious Lu the Tattooed Monk from Liangshan Marsh! It doesn't matter if you kill me! When my brother Song Jiang finds out and comes down from the mountain, you might just as well cut off your own donkey head and send it to him!"

Prefect Ho was furious. He had Sagacious Lu severely beaten, then ordered his underlings to fasten a big rack around the monk's neck and throw him into the jail for the condemned. At the same time he sent off a dispatch to the central authorities, requesting instructions. Lu's Buddhist staff and knife were locked away for safe-keeping.

This matter was soon the talk of the entire prefecture. Lesser brigands got wind of it and hastened up Mount Shaohua to report. Wu Song was shocked. "Two of us were sent to attend to something and one has already been captured," he thought. "How can I go back and face the chieftains?"

While he was pondering another bandit arrived from the foot of the mountain and announced: "A chieftain dispatched from Mount Liangshan. He's called Dai Zong the Marvellous Traveller, and he's waiting below."

Wu Song hastily went down, brought him up, and introduced him to Zhu Wu. They told Dai how Lu had refused to take advice and had fallen into a trap. Dai was startled.

"I can't stay here long," he exclaimed. "I must return to Mount Liangshan and let our brothers know, so that they can send forces to save him."

"I'll be waiting anxiously," said Wu Song. "I hope our brothers will hurry to the rescue."

Dai Zong ate a vegetable meal, then worked his magic travel formula and sped towards Liangshan Marsh. He reached the stronghold in three days. He related to Chao Gai and Song Jiang how Sagacious Lu had wanted to kill Prefect Ho in order to save Shi Jin, but had been snared himself, instead. Song Jiang was alarmed.

"Two of our brothers in difficulty," he said. "Of course we'll rescue them. We mustn't delay. We'll muster men and horses immediately and set out in three contingents."

In the van of the first unit were Hua Rong, Qin Ming, Lin Chong, Yang Zhi and Huyan Zhuo. They commanded a thousand armored cavalry and two thousand infantry and took the lead, pushing through mountains and spanning rivers.

The middle unit was headed by Song Jiang, with Wu Yong, Zhu Tong, Xu Ning, Xie Zhen and Xie Bao as his lieutenants. They led a mixed force of infantry and cavalry numbering two thousand.

Bringing up the rear with fodder and grain were Li Ying, Yang Xiong, Shi Xiu, Li Jun and Zhang Shun, leading also two thousand infantry and cavalry men. This brought the expedition to a total of seven thousand. They left the mountain fortress, a turbulent stream of spears and halberds, men and horses, moving like the wind, and headed for Huazhou.

After several days on the road, they passed the halfway point, and Dai Zong was sent to announce their coining to the stronghold on Mount Shaohua. Zhu Wu and the other two leaders prepared animals for slaughter and fine wines in anticipation of their guests.

Song Jiang and his three contingents then arrived at the foot of the mountain. Wu Song went down with Zhu Wu, Chen Da and Yang Chun to greet Song Jiang, Wu Yong and the other leaders and invite them to the stronghold. When all were seated Song Jiang asked about the situation in the town.

"Prefect Ho has imprisoned your two chieftains. He's only waiting for word from the imperial court before disposing of them," said Zhu Wu.

"What should our rescue plan be?" queried Song and Wu.

"It's a big town with a deep broad moat. A very difficult place to attack," said Zhu Wu. "Only by striking from within and without at the same time can you capture it."

"Tomorrow we'll go to the outskirts and take a look," said Wu Yong, "then we'll discuss our plan."

Song Jiang drank for some time. He longed for dawn so that he could start reconnoitering.

"They've got two of our big chieftains in their prison. They're sure to be prepared," said Wu Yong. "We can't go during daylight. But there will be a bright moon tonight. Let's start down late in the afternoon. At the first watch, we can reconnoiter."

When the sun was well past its meridian, Song Jiang, Wu Yong, Hua Rong, Qin Ming and Zhu Tong rode down the slope and advanced along a winding road.

At the first watch they neared the town of Huazhou. They dismounted and observed it from a bluff.

It was the middle of the second lunar month. The moonlight was bright as day. There Wasn't a cloud in the sky. They could see several gates in the strong high wall enclosing the town. The moat was deep and wide. For a long time they stared, noting also Mount Huashan, west in the distance. Truly a formidable well-guarded town! What was to be done? None of them could think of a plan.

"Let's return to the stronghold," said Wu Yong, "and talk there." The five rode back through the night to Mount Shaohua. Song Jiang was frowning. His face wore a troubled expression.

"We'll send a dozen or so clever young men down to keep an ear cocked for what's going on," Wu Yong decided.

Before three days had passed, one of the scouts returned and reported: "The emperor has dispatched a Marshal of the Council of Imperial Defense, bearing a set of imperial golden hanging bells, to bum incense on Mount Huashan. He's come from the Yellow River to the Weihe."

"Brother, our worries are over," Wu Yong told Song Jiang. "Our plan is here." To Li Jun and Zhang Shun he said: "I want you to do this and this..."

"The problem is we don't know the terrain," said Li Jun. "It would be best if we had someone to lead the way."

"How about me?" Yang Chun the White-Spotted Snake proposed.

Song Jiang was very pleased, and the three went down the mountain.

The following day, at Wu Yong's suggestion, Song Jiang, Li Ying, Zhu Tong, Huyan Zhuo, Hua Rong, Qin Ming, and Xu Ning followed quietly with five hundred men to a fording point on the Weihe River. There, Li Jun and Zhang Shun were waiting with more than ten large boats. Wu Yong told Hua Rong, Qin Ming, Xu Ning and Huyan Zhuo to lie in ambush upon the bank; Song Jiang, Wu Yong, Zhu Tong and Li Ying boarded the vessels; Li Jun, Zhang Shun and Yang Chun then concealed the boats along the shore. The party waited there through the night.

At daybreak, they heard the distant sound of gongs and drums, and three government craft hove into view. On a yellow banner was inscribed the words: *Marshal Su Who Burns Incense on Mount Huashan by Imperial Decree.*

On Song Jiang's boat, Zhu Tong and Li Ying, each holding a long spear, stood behind him. Wu Yong was on the prow. They blocked the government vessel with their own when it reached the cove. A captain wearing a purple robe and silver girdle emerged from the cabin with twenty men.

"What boat are you?" he shouted. "How dare you interfere with the passage of a high minister?"

Song Jiang, hands clasped before him, bowed and hailed the officer respectfully. Wu Yong, from the prow; replied.

"Song Jiang, a champion of the righteous, from Liangshan Marsh, awaits your gracious orders."

A chamberlain who was on board came forward and said: "A marshal of the imperial court is on his way to Mount Huashan to burn incense on orders of the emperor. Why do you robbers interfere?"

Song Jiang continued bowing.

"We are champions of the righteous," replied Wu Yong. "We want only to see the marshal's honored visage so that we may offer him our plea."

"Who do you think you are, requesting to see the marshal!" cried the chamberlain. And two captains who stood on either side barked: "Keep your voices down!"

Song Jiang still did not stir from his position.

"We are inviting the marshal to come ashore. We have something to discuss with him," said Wu Yong.

"You're mad!" exclaimed the chamberlain. "The marshal is an imperial official. How can he talk with the likes of you!"

"If the marshal is unwilling to meet us I'm afraid our boys may give him a shock," Song Jiang said, standing erect.

Zhu Tong waved the pennant that was attached to his spear, and Hua Rong, Qin Ming, Xu Ning and Huyan Zhuo suddenly emerged with their men from their places of concealment. Setting arrows to their bow-strings, they took up positions on the bank by the ford. The terrified boatmen plunged into the interiors of the government vessels.

Alarmed, the chamberlain hurried in to report. Marshal Su had no choice but to emerge and take a seat on the prow. Again Song Jiang bowed and hailed him respectfully.

"Why do you halt my boat?" the marshal demanded.

"We would not presume to behave improperly."

"Then why, sir champion, do you block our passage?"

"We wouldn't dare. We want only to beseech the marshal to come ashore. There is a matter we wish to discuss."

"I am under imperial orders to burn incense on Mount Huashan, champion. How can I confer with you? A minister of the imperial court is not so lightly to be called ashore!"

"If Marshal Su refuses," said Wu Yong from the prow, "I'm afraid our followers will be equally unyielding."

Li Ying waved his pennanted spear and Li Jun, Zhang Shun and Yang Chun came rowing up in a boat. While the startled Marshal Su watched, Li and Zhang, sharp gleaming knives in their hands, leaped onto the government vessel, and knocked two of the captains into the water.

"Stop that nonsense," Song Jiang shouted. "You're startling His Excellency!"

Li and Zhang promptly dived into the river and heaved the two captains back. Both Li and Zhang were as at home in the water as they were on dry land. Now they bounded smoothly onto the deck.

The marshal's soul seemed to have left his body. Again Song Jiang yelled at his men.

"You boys get out of here! Stop frightening the marshal! I'll persuade him to come ashore myself."

"If you have anything on your mind, champion, why not tell me about it here?" said Su.

"This is not the place to talk. Please come to our mountain stronghold. We have no wish to harm you. May the Spirit of Mount Huashan destroy me if I'm lying!"

Marshal Su no longer had any choice. He disembarked. He was given a horse, helped to mount, and led off by the outlaws.

Song Jiang and Wu Yong instructed Hua Rong and Qin Ming to accompany Su up the mountain. He himself swung into the saddle and followed, after ordering that the marshal's retinue plus the incense, sacrificial items and golden hanging bells all be brought along. He left only Li Jun, Zhang Shun and a hundred men to guard the boats. All the other chieftains returned to the stronghold.

There, Song Jiang dismounted and escorted Su into a large hall. He seated the marshal in the middle. The chieftains stood in lines on either side. Song Jiang kowtowed four times. He remained kneeling before Su.

"Originally I was a small functionary in Yuncheng County," he said. "A judicial proceeding compelled me to become an outlaw and take refuge in Liangshan Marsh. I am waiting for an imperial amnesty so that I may devote my services to our country.

"Two of my brothers, though blameless, have been framed by Prefect Ho and thrown into jail. We wish to borrow the imperial incense and accoutrements, plus the golden hanging bells, as a means of getting into Huazhou. When we've finished we'll return them. It will have nothing to do with you, Marshal. We pray that you consent."

"If you take the imperial incense and things and the matter becomes known, I will be implicated."

"Just blame everything on me when you get back to the capital, Marshal."

Su realized that men like these couldn't be refused. He therefore agreed. Song Jiang respectfully toasted him and laid a feast in thanks. He put the clothes of the entourage on his own men. From among the outlaws he selected a handsome, clean-shaven fellow and dressed him in the garments of the marshal, as an impersonation of Su Yuanjing. Song Jiang and Wu Yong were made up as chamberlains; Xie Zhen, Xie Bao, Yang Xiong and Shi Xiu as captains. Outlaws in purple robes and silver girdles carried pennants, banners, ceremonial equipment and symbols of office, and bore reverently the imperial incense, the sacrificial objects and the hanging golden bells. Hua Rong, Xu Ning, Zhu Tong and Li Ying dressed as guards. Zhu Wu, Chen Da and Yang Chun provided quarters for the marshal and his entourage, and wined and dined them.

Qin Ming and Huyan Zhuo were given command of one contingent of men and horses, and Lin Chong and Yang Zhi another, and were directed to advance in two columns towards the town. Wu Song was dispatched to the gate of the Mount Huashan Temple to wait for the trumpet's call, and then go into action. Dai Zong was sent on ahead to announce the coming of the "imperial mission."

To make a long story short, the procession left the mountain stronghold, descended to the fording point, got into the boats and embarked. Instead of calling on the prefect in Huazhou it went directly towards Mount Huashan Temple. Dai Zong announced its imminent arrival to the abbot of the Yuntai Monastery and the deacon of the temple. The clerics hurried to the shore to give welcome with flowers, candles and lanterns, banners and precious panoplies. The imperial incense was placed in a miniature pavilion, which the monks respectfully carried into the temple, along with the hanging golden bells.

The abbot approached the "marshal," and Wu Yong said: "He's been ill all through the journey. Get him a sedan-chair."

Attendants helped the "marshal" into the conveyance and he was carried to the temple's Hall for Officials and invited to rest. "Chamberlain" Wu Yong addressed himself to the abbot.

"The marshal is here under the emperor's decree with imperial incense and golden hanging bells to offer homage to the god. Why hasn't the local prefect appeared to welcome him?"

"We've already dispatched a messenger. I'm sure he'll be here shortly," replied the abbot.

Before the words were out of his mouth, the public prosecutor of the prefecture and sixty or so constables came as an advance party with wine and fruits to call on the "marshal." The outlaw who was disguised as this official, although resembling him somewhat, was unable to imitate his speech. Therefore he pretended to be ill and sat on a divan wrapped in a quilt. The public prosecutor, seeing the pennants, banners and serrated flags, all obviously imperial equipage from the Eastern Capital, was completely convinced of his authenticity.

The "chamberlain" went in twice, ostensibly to confer, then led the public prosecutor inside, where he knelt at the edge of the dais, a good distance from the "marshal," and kowtowed. The "marshal" pointed and mumbled something. Wu Yong led the public prosecutor forward, meanwhile berating him.

"The marshal is an important minister, very close to the emperor. He's come a long distance to this place under imperial decree to burn incense, and was ill on the road. Why didn't your prefectural officials go well forward to meet him?"

"We received notification that he was coming, but we had no idea he was so near. That's why we failed to greet him and he reached the temple ahead of us. The prefect was intending to come, but bandits on Mount Shaohua have joined forces with the outlaws in Liangshan Marsh to attack the town. We're on constant alert, and he doesn't dare leave. He sent me on ahead with wine of greeting. He'll be following soon to pay his respects."

"The marshal refuses to drink a drop until your prefect arrives and welcomes him with proper ceremony," announced Wu Yong.

The public prosecutor called for wine and drank with the "chamberlain" and the "retinue." Wu Yong again went inside and returned with a key. He led the prosecutor to see the pair of golden hanging bells. He opened the lock and, from their scented bag, removed the bells, showed them to the prosecutor, and suspended them from a bamboo frame. They were of matchless workmanship, having been made by the most skilful craftsmen in the imperial palace. Encrusted with pearls and precious jewels and with a red silk lantern suspended between them, they had hung in the center of the palace's Hall of the God. Only the special craftsmen of the imperial court could have created them.

After permitting the prosecutor to view the bells, Wu Yong returned them to their container and locked it. He then produced many documents from the Council of Administration and handed these to the prosecutor. He also requested the "marshal" to choose an auspicious day for conducting the sacrifice.

The prosecutor and his constables examined the documents, bid farewell to the "chamberlain," and returned to Huazhou to report to the prefect. Song Jiang thought with satisfaction: "Although that rogue of a prosecutor is crafty, we've got him completely buffaloed!"

By then Wu Song had taken up his position outside the temple gate. Wu Yong directed Shi Xiu to conceal a knife on his person and join him there. He also told Dai Zong to disguise himself as a captain.

The abbot of the Yuntai Monastery served a vegetarian meal, and ordered the overseer to have the temple tidied up. As Song Jiang strolled around the grounds he thought it a splendid place. The buildings were unusually fine. Huashan Temple was truly like heaven on earth.

Song Jiang then returned to the Hall for Officials. A gate-keeper reported: "Prefect Ho has arrived." Song summoned Hua Rong, Xu Ning, Zhu Tong and Li Ying—the four "guards," each bearing arms—and stationed them on either side. He positioned Xie Zhen, Xie Bao, Yang Xiong and Dai Zong—all with concealed weapons—to the left and right.

The prefect, who had come with more than three hundred men, dismounted before the temple and swarmed in with his party. "Chamberlains" Wu Yong and Song Jiang observed that all were armed with swords.

Wu Yong immediately shouted: "A marshal of the imperial court is within. Trivial persons keep back!"

The crowd halted, and only Prefect Ho advanced. "Chamberlain" Wu Yong said: "The marshal invites the prefect to enter." Prefect Ho walked into the Hall for Officials and kowtowed before the "marshal."

"Prefect," said Wu Yong, "do you acknowledge your misfeasance?"

"I didn't know the marshal had arrived. I beg forgiveness."

"The marshal has come to Mount Huashan in obedience to the emperor's decree to burn incense. Why didn't you go well forward to welcome him?"

"We didn't know his arrival was imminent, and so were remiss in our duty."

"Seize him!" Wu Yong shouted.

Xie Zhen and Xie Bao had already pulled out their daggers. With one kick they knocked Ho to the ground, then cut off his head.

"Into action, brothers!" shouted Song Jiang.

The prefect's three hundred followers were paralyzed with fright. Hua Rong and the others closed in and swept them down like abacus beads. Half of them scrambled to the temple gate. But there Wu Song and Shi Xiu, brandishing their knives, waded in while outlaws bent on slaughter attacked from all sides. Not a single man of the three hundred got away. Some came later to the temple, and these too were killed by Zhang Shun and Li Jun.

Song Jiang ordered that the imperial incense and the golden hanging bells be packed up, and all quickly boarded the vessels. Even before they reached Huazhou they saw two columns of smoke rising. They surged into the town and first freed Shi Jin and Sagacious Lu from the prison. Next, they broke open the storehouses, took everything of value, and loaded it on carts. Sagacious rushed to the rear hall and got back his knife and staff. Jade Branch had long since jumped into a well and committed suicide.

Leaving Huazhou, they got into the boats and returned to Mount Shaohua, where they restored to Marshal Su the imperial incense, the golden hanging bells, the pennants, banners and symbols of office, and respectfully expressed their thanks. Song Jiang presented him with gold and silver on a platter. All of his retinue were similarly rewarded, regardless of rank.

A farewell banquet was given for them in the stronghold and gratitude to the marshal was again expressed. The chieftains escorted them down the mountain to their boats at the river ford. Every vessel and every single possession were returned to their owners. Once more Song Jiang thanked Marshal Su.

Song returned to Mount Shaohua and conferred with the four gallant leaders. They removed all money and grain from the fortress and set it to the torch. Then the outlaws, with horses, grain and fodder, set out together for Liangshan Marsh.

As to Marshal Su, after embarking he sailed to Huazhou. There he learned that the Mount Liangshan brigands had slaughtered soldiers, plundered the storehouses of money and grain, killed over a hundred army officers, stole all of the horses, and annihilated hundreds in the Huashan Temple.

Su instructed the public prosecutor to send a written report to the Council of Administration for transmission to the emperor stating that "Song Jiang robbed the imperial incense and hanging bells en route, and was thereby able to lure the prefect to the temple and murder him."

The marshal burned the imperial incense at the Huashan Temple and entrusted the golden bells to the abbot of the Yuntai Monastery. He then hastened back to the capital, travelling day and night, and reported to the emperor what had transpired.

Song Jiang, after rescuing Shi Jin and Sagacious Lu, again divided his forces into three contingents and, accompanied by the four gallant fellows from Mount Shaohua, returned to Liangshan Marsh. They harmed no one in any of the prefectures and counties through which they travelled.

Dai Zong was sent on ahead to the fortress to report their coming. Chao Gai and the other chieftains descended the mountain to welcome them. Together they went up and entered Fraternity Hall. When greetings had been exchanged, all joined in a feast of celebration. The following day Shi Jin, Zhu Wu, Chen Da and Yang Chun, at their own expense, gave a banquet in thanks to Chao, Song, and the other leaders. Several more days passed.

To skip the minor details, one day Dry-Land Crocodile Zhu Gui suddenly arrived and reported: "On Mount Mangdang in Peixian County, Xuzhou Prefecture, there is a newly formed band of robbers, about three thousand in number. Their leader is a Taoist named Fan Rui. His nickname is Demon King Who Roils the World. He can summon the wind and rain, and he's a fantastic military tactician. He has two lieutenants: One is called Xiang Chong. His nickname is Eight-Armed Nezha. He carries a round shield pierced by twenty-four throwing knives. He can hit a man at a hundred paces and never miss. In his hand is an iron javelin. The other is called Li Gun. His nickname is the Flying Divinity and he also carries a round shield. Only his is pierced by twenty-four darts. These too are infallibly deadly at a hundred paces. He holds also a precious sword.

"These three sworn brothers occupy Mount Mangdang, and they rob and pillage. Now they have decided to come and swallow our fortress. I heard about this and had to report."

Song Jiang was furious. "How dare those crooks behave so rudely," he fumed. "I'll go down and deal with them!"

Nine Dragons Shi Jin stepped forward. "My three brothers and I have just come to the stronghold and haven't yet made the slightest contribution. We'd like to lead our own men and seize those robbers."

Song Jiang was delighted. Shi Jin mustered his contingents. Then he, Zhu Wu, Chen Da and Yang Chun donned their armor, bid farewell to Song Jiang and went down the mountain. They crossed the water in boats from the Shore of Golden Sands and hurried along the road directly towards Mount Mangdang. In three days they came within sight of it. Here it was in ancient times that the first Han emperor Gao Zu killed the snake.

The three units proceeded to the foot of the mountain. Hidden robber scouts had already gone up to report.

Shi Jin deployed his forces from Mount Shaohua in battle formation. Guarded completely in armor, astride a steed as red as a glowing coal, he rode at the head of his men, a three pointed two-edged blade in his hand.

The three leaders behind him were Zhu Wu, Chen Da and Yang Chun. Zhu Wu wielded two double-edged swords as he rode forward.

Reining in their steeds in front of their position, the four watched for some time. They saw a swarm of men come racing down the slope, preceded by two bold stalwarts. The first was Xiang Chong, of Peixian County, Xuzhou Prefecture. He carried a round shield in which twenty-four throwing knives were inserted. In his right hand he held a javelin. Attached to his back was an identifying pennant reading: *Eight-Armed Nezha.*

The second brave fellow, from Peixian County, was Li Gun. He bore a round shield pierced by twenty-four darts. The shield was in his left hand. In his right he grasped a sword. Attached to his back was a pennant inscribed: *Flying Divinity.*

When Xiang Chong and Li Gun saw Shi Jin, Zhu Wu, Chen Da and Yang Chun, astride their horses before the opposite position, they said not a word. Instead, while lesser robbers beat gongs and cymbals, the two charged, brandishing their shields. Shi Jin's force couldn't withstand them. While the rear guard withdrew, Shi Jin's forward unit resisted, but Zhu Wu's middle unit yelled and ran for their lives for twenty or thirty *li.* Shi Jin was nearly hit by a flying knife. Yang Chun dodged too slowly, and was wounded by one of them. His horse was injured, and he abandoned it and fled on foot.

Shi Jin counted his forces and found he had lost half. He conferred with Zhu Wu and the others. They were intending to send someone to Mount Liangshan for aid when a fighter came and reported: "There are some two thousand men and horses on that highway to the north where the dust is rising." Shi Jin and the others mounted and looked. They saw the banners of Liangshan Marsh. Riding at the head of the contingent were Hua Rong and Xu Ning. Shi Jin hastened to greet them. He related how Xiang Chong and Li Gun had attacked with their whirling shields and how his forces had been unable to withstand them.

"Brother Song Jiang has been worried about you. He was sorry he let you go. He's sent us two to help," said Hua Rong.

Shi Jin was very pleased. The two units combined and made camp.

At dawn the following day, as they were preparing to muster their men and go forth against the foe, a fighter arrived and reported: "More cavalry are approaching on the highway to the north." Hua Rong, Xu Ning and Shi Jin rode out to meet them and saw an army of three thousand men led by Song Jiang personally.

Shi Jin told him how formidable Xiang Chong and Li Gun were with their flying knives, darts and whirling shields, and that he had lost half his men. Song Jiang was greatly alarmed.

"Let's make camp first," Wu Yong suggested, "then we can talk this over."

The impatient Song Jiang wanted to muster their forces and drive directly for the foot of the mountain. But it was already growing dark, and on Mount Mangdang blue lanterns were visible.

Gongsun Sheng said: "Those people must know magic. The blue lanterns in their camp show that someone there is able to cast spells. We'd better fall back. Tomorrow I'll use a counterspell and we'll catch a couple of them."

Pleased, Song Jiang ordered his army to withdraw twenty *li* and make camp.

Early the next morning Gongsun worked his spell. And as a result, a demon king with clasped hands presented himself at Mount Liangshan, a miraculous general with full willingness surrendered in the Marsh.

What then was the spell Gongsun offered to Song Jiang? Read our next chapter if you would know.

CHAPTER 60

GONGSUN SHENG DEFEATS THE DEMON KING ON MOUNT MANGDANG

CHAO THE HEAVENLY KING IS HIT BY AN ARROW IN ZENGTOU VILLAGE

Gongsun told Song Jiang and Wu Yong his strategy.

"It's the same one used by Zhuge Liang when he positioned the boulders on the battlefield at the end of the Han Dynasty when the country split into three," said the Taoist. "We'll arrange our army into four groups and eight sections of eight companies each, totalling sixty-four, with the commander-in-chief in the middle. It will thus have four heads and eight tails, and be able to turn in any direction like the wind and clouds above the earth, as quickly as any wild beast, bird or reptile. When the enemy come down from the mountain and attack, we'll open into two and let them come in deep. As soon as our forces see our seven-starred banner wave, let them surround the enemy like a long serpent. I have a magic formula that will drive those three robber leaders to the center. Back or forward, left or right, they won't be able to get out. We'll dig a concealed pit and drive them into it. On either side we'll have men hidden with hooked poles, ready to take them."

Song Jiang was very pleased. He issued the appropriate orders, directing his officers to act accordingly. He deployed his positional forces under eight fierce commanders. These were: Huyan Zhuo, Zhu Tong, Hua Rong, Xu Ning, Mu Hong, Sun Li, Shi Jin and Huang Xin. He put Chai Jin, Lu Fang and Guo Sheng in charge of a central force. Song Jiang himself, plus Wu Yong and Gongsun, were in overall command, with Chen Da to transmit their orders by flag signals. Zhu Wu was directed to take five men to a nearby height, and from there observe the battlefield and report developments.

By mid-morning the army had neared the mountain and was spreading out in battle formation, banners waving and drums pounding provocatively. On Mount Mangdang twenty or thirty gongs thunderously crashed, shaking the earth. The three robber leaders proceeded down the slope, spreading out their force of over three thousand men. Fan Rui, their bold chieftain, rode in the van, with Xiang Chong and Li Gun to his left and right.

At the edge of the battlefield he reined in his horse. Fan Rui could work magic, but he knew little of military tactics. He watched while Song Jiang divided his army into four groups and eight sections. "Go on, deploy them," he said to himself with secret satisfaction. "That's exactly what I want you to do."

He turned to Xiang Chong and Li Gun. "When you see the wind rising, take five hundred knife twirlers and pitch in."

The two lieutenants, each grasping his shield, javelins and flying blades at the ready, waited for Fan Rui to start. His bronze comet hammer in his left hand, a two-edged sword in his right, the Demon King Who Roils the World muttered a few magic phrases, then shouted: "Speed!"

A wild gale rose on all sides, whipping up clouds of sand and stones that darkened the sky and obscured the sun. Shouting, Xiang Chong and Li Gun charged with their five hundred knife twirlers. Song Jiang's army separated into two, and the foe moved in. They were immediately beset by powerful bowmen from both sides. Only forty or fifty of the robber band were able to advance. The remainder withdrew to their original position.

Song Jiang, observing from high on a slope, saw that Xiang Chong and Li Gun were the midst of his forces. He directed Chen Da to wave the seven-starred banner. The outlaw army rolled and shifted into the form of a long snake.

Xiang Chong and Li Gun ran east and hurried west, turned left and wheeled right, but nowhere could they find an escape route. No matter in which direction they hastened, Zhu Wu pointed them out from his height with a small flag.

Gongsun also watched from a bluff. He unsheathed his ancient sword with its pine tree decorations, muttered an incantation, then shouted: "Speed!"

At once, a wind closely pursued Xiang Chong and Li Gun, whirling at their heels. The sky darkened, the sun lost its glow. They couldn't see a single man or horse. Everything was enveloped in a black fog. They completely lost sight of the men behind them. Panic-stricken, the two desperately sought a way back to their own forces, but in vain.

Suddenly there was a sound like a clap of thunder. The two cried out in consternation. Together they tripped and tumbled head over heels into a deep pit. From both sides men with long hooked poles hauled them out. They bound the captives with ropes and brought them to the mountain slope and requested rewards. Song Jiang pointed with his whip. His three contingents plunged into a murderous assault. Fan Rui's men fled towards Mount Mangdang. Many couldn't escape. More than half were killed.

Song Jiang recalled his troops. When he and his chieftains were seated outside his tent, fighters led in Xiang Chong and Li Gun, under guard, and delivered them beneath his standard. He quickly ordered that their bonds be removed, and he went forward personally, wine goblet in hand.

"Forgive me," he said. "In the course of hostilities, we couldn't do anything else. I, the humble Song Jiang, have long known of the great fame of you three warriors. I was hoping to invite you to our mountain to join our righteous cause, but I never could find a suitable opportunity. If you won't consider it beneath you, return with us to our stronghold now. Nothing could give me greater happiness."

The two fell to their knees and kowtowed. "We know the great name of the Timely Rain, as who doesn't?" they responded. "Unfortunately, we were never able to pay our respects before. We failed to recognize your vast integrity, and went against Heaven's will. Today you have captured us. No death would be too heavy, yet you treat us so courteously. If you decide to spare our lives, we swear to serve you faithfully to the end of our days. As to Fan Rui, he can't get along without us two. If you, righteous leader, will let one of us go back, we'll try to talk him into joining you. Does that seem all right?"

"No need to keep one of you here as hostage. Both of you can return to your stronghold. I'll wait for your good news."

"Truly a man of noble generosity! If Fan Rui doesn't agree, we'll seize him and present him beneath your standard."

Song Jiang was very pleased. He invited them into his headquarters, wined and dined them, gave them fresh suits of clothing, and presented them with two fine horses. He directed a few of the outlaws to return their shields and weapons, escort them down the mountain, and see them off. The two were extremely grateful.

When they reached the foot of Mount Mangdang, members of their band were astonished to see them, and escorted them up to Fan Rui. He asked them what had happened.

"We've gone against Heaven's will and deserve to die," they said.

"Why do you say that, brothers?" he demanded.

They told him how chivalrous Song Jiang had been.

"Since Song Jiang is so generous and gallant, we shouldn't go against the will of Heaven," said Fan Rui. "Let's all join him."

"We've come to propose that very thing."

That night they set the affairs of the stronghold in order. The following morning, they presented themselves to Song Jiang and kowtowed before him. He raised them to their feet and invited them into his tent and seated them. Impressed by his manifestation of complete trust, they spoke frankly and at length about their various backgrounds.

The three invited the chieftains to their fortress on Mount Mangdang, where they slaughtered steers and horses and feasted Song Jiang and his lieutenants. They also rewarded the men of his three contingents. After the banquet Fan Rui pledged himself as a pupil to Gongsun Sheng. Song Jiang directed the Taoist to teach Fan Rui his Divine Method for Summoning the Five Thunderbolts, much to the latter's delight.

In the next few days, the livestock was led away, the stronghold's money and grain was packed, and belongings were laden on pack animals. Men and horses were assembled and the fortress was put to the torch. All then went with Song Jiang and his chieftains back to Liangshan Marsh. The journey was uneventful.

Dai Zong flew up the mountain to report their arrival. As they were about to ford the river at the edge of the marsh, a big fellow on the road near the reeds saw Song Jiang and kowtowed. Song hastily dismounted and raised the man to his feet.

"What is your name, sir, and where are you from?"

"My family name is Duan, my given name Jingzhu. Because of my red hair and yellow beard, I'm called the Golden Dog. My family are from Zhuozhou

Prefecture, and I earn my living rustling horses in the north. This spring I stole a splendid animal north of the Spear Range. It's white as snow, without a single hair of a different color. From head to tail it's ten feet long, and stands eight feet high from hoofs to back. It can cover a thousand *li* in a day. It's famed throughout the north as the White Jade Lion That Glows in the Night. It belonged to a prince of the Tartars. When it was put out to graze at the foot of Spear Range, I nabbed it. In the gallant fraternity the Timely Rain is famous, but I never had a chance to meet you. I wanted to present you with the horse as a mark on my respect. But while passing through the village of Zengtou, southwest of the prefectural town of Lingzhou, it was seized from me by the fifth son of the Zeng family. I told him it belonged to Song Jiang of Liangshan Marsh, but the churl was very insulting, and I dared say no more. I got away as quickly as I could. I've come here specially to inform you."

Song Jiang took a liking to the thin rough-looking fellow. In spite of his odd appearance, he was clearly not an ordinary person.

"Come with us to the stronghold," he said. "We'll talk about it there." He took Duan in his boat and they crossed to the Shore of Golden Sands.

Chao Gai, the Heavenly King, and the other chieftains, escorted the returning leaders to Fraternity Hall. Song Jiang introduced Fan Rui, Xiang Chong and Li Gun to the chieftains. Duan and the three greeted them with respect. Drums beat clamorously, and a feast was held in celebration.

More and more men were joining the mountain citadel. Bold fellows from all over came like the wind. And so Song Jiang instructed Li Yun and Tao Zongwang to supervise the building of new dwellings, and to construct additional forts on every side.

Duan spoke again of the merits of the horse. Song Jiang sent Dai Zong the Marvellous Traveller to the village of Zengtou to inquire about it. In four or five days Dai returned.

"Zengtou has something over three thousand families," he told the chieftains. "One is known as the Zeng Family Establishment. It is headed by Zeng the Elder, who comes originally from the land of the Tartars. He has five sons, called the Five Tigers of the Zeng Family. Their names, in order of age, are: Tu, Mi, Suo, Kui and Sheng. Their instructor is Shi Wengong, and his assistant is Su Ding. The village is defended by six or seven thousand men and stockaded camps. They've built more than fifty cage carts, boasting there is no room on this earth for both us and them. They say they will capture all of our chieftains, that we are enemies.

"The thousand *li* horse known as the Jade Lion is ridden by the instructor Shi Wengong. Even more infuriating, the wretch has composed a rhyme which he's taught all the kids in the village. It goes like this:

When our horses' bridles jingle
God and demons with fear tingle.
Iron carts plus iron locks,

Prisoners nailed in iron stocks.
Liangshan Marsh we'll cleanly flush,
Chao Gai to the capital we'll rush,
And capture Timely Rain—that's Song,
And his war mentor Wu Yong.
Five Zeng tigers boldly stand,
Famed far and wide throughout the land.

Chao Gai was enraged. "How dare those animals be so unmannerly!" he fumed. "I'm going down there personally. If I don't capture those rogues I won't return!"

"You're the leader of our fortress, brother," said Song Jiang. "You mustn't lightly take action. Let me go."

"It's not that I want to steal your thunder," said Chao Gai, "but you've gone many times. You must be weary from combat. This time I'm going. Next time, brother, it will be your turn."

Song Jiang pleaded in vain. The furious Chao Gai selected five thousand men and twenty chieftains and set forth. The remainder stayed with Song Jiang to guard the stronghold. Chao divided his forces into three brigades and went down the mountain, ready to march on Zengtou Village.

Song Jiang, Wu Yong and Gongsun saw them to the Shore of Golden Sands. While they were drinking a sudden wind snapped the pole supporting Chao Gai's standard. Everyone blanched.

"An evil omen," said Wu Yong. "Choose another day for your expedition, brother."

"The wind snaps your standard, brother, just as you're about to set forth. It's not auspicious for military action," said Song Jiang. "Wait a bit longer and then deal with those knaves. There'll still be time."

"The movement of wind and clouds is nothing to be alarmed about," retorted Chao Gai. "Now is the time, in the warmth of spring. If we wait until they build up their strength and then attack, it will be too late. Don't try to stop me. I'm going, come what may!"

Song Jiang couldn't dissuade him. With his troops, Chao Gai ferried across the river. Sunk in gloom, Song returned to the fortress. He sent Dai Zong down to watch developments and report.

Chao Gai with his five thousand men and twenty chieftains neared the village of Zengtou. Confronting them was stockaded camp. The following morning Chao went with the chieftains for a closer look. Clearly, the village was strongly fortified.

Suddenly, from a grove of willows seven or eight hundred men emerged. At their head was a bold fellow—Kui, fourth son of the Zeng family.

"You bandits from Liangshan Marsh are all rebels," he shouted. "I've been meaning to turn you over to the authorities and claim the reward, and now Heaven sends you right into my arms! Get off your horses and be bound. What are you waiting for!"

Chao Gai was very angry. As he turned his head he saw one of the chieftains riding forth to do battle with Kui. It was Lin Chong, the first to form the chivalrous band on Mount Liangshan.

The two horses met, and the warriors fought more than twenty rounds, with neither vanquishing the other. Kui realized he was no match for Lin Chong. He wheeled his mount and lance in hand, rode for the willow grove. Lin Chong reined in his steed and did not pursue. Chao Gai led his forces back to camp. There, they discussed strategy for attacking the village.

"Let's go tomorrow and provoke a battle," Lin Chong proposed.

"We'll see what their strength actually is, then we can talk some more."

The next morning they marched with five thousand men to the broad plain outside the entrance to Zengtou, took up positions, beat their drums and shouted. Cannon thundered from the village and a large body of men rode forth, led by seven bold fellows in a single line. In the middle was the instructor Shi Wengong. To his left was his assistant Su Ding; to his right the eldest son, Tu. Continuing to the left were Mi and Kui; further right were Sheng and Suo. All were clad in armor from head to foot. An arrow fitted to his bow, Shi sat the thousand-Zi Jade Lion horse. He held also a crescent-bladed halberd.

After three rolls of the drums, several cage carts were pushed out from the Zeng family position and placed to the fore. Tu pointed at his adversaries.

"Rebellious bandits," he shouted, "do you see these carts? If we simply kill you, we won't be real men. We're going to nab every one of you, lock you in the carts and deliver you to the Eastern Capital, just to show you how tough we Five Tigers really are! Surrender now, while you still have the chance, then we'll see!"

Chao Gai, enraged, levelled his lance and galloped towards Tu. To protect him, the other chieftains also charged, and the two sides were soon locked in combat. The Zeng family forces retreated step by step into the village. Lin Chong and Huyan Zhuo slew mightily to east and west, providing close cover for Chao Gai. But Lin could see that the prospects were poor. He hastily pulled back and reassembled his men. Both sides were strewn with casualties. Chao Gai returned to camp very depressed.

"Don't take it to heart, brother," the chieftains urged. "Worry will only injure your health. Brother Song Jiang also has setbacks at times in battle, but he wins in the end. The fighting was confused today. Both sides suffered casualties. But we haven't lost. No need to feel bad!"

Chao Gai said: "I'm not in a good mood, that's all." He remained in camp for three days. Though each day his troops went to challenge the foe, not a man came forth from Zengtou.

On the fourth day, two monks called on Chao Gai. They were escorted by several of the brigand soldiers. Chao received them outside his tent. The two dropped to their knees and kowtowed.

"We are custodians of the Fahua Monastery east of Zengtou," they said. "Those Five Tiger sons constantly harass our monastery, demanding gold and silver and money. There's nothing they won't do. We know their layout in detail, and we've come to show you how to get inside and take their fortifications. If you can eliminate them it will be a blessing."

Chao Gai was very pleased. He invited the monks to be seated, and had them served wine.

"Don't believe them, brother," Lin Chong advised. "How do you know it isn't a trick?"

"We are men who have renounced the material world. We wouldn't dare to deceive," protested the monks. "We've long known of the righteous behavior of the men of Liangshan Marsh. You never harm the common people wherever you go. We've come to join you. Why should we want to fool you chieftains? Besides, the Zeng family forces could hardly defeat your great army. Why be suspicious?"

"You needn't doubt them, brother," said Chao Gai. "We'll miss a big opportunity. I'll go myself, tonight, to see."

"Please don't, brother," Lin Chong urged. "Let me raid the village with half our men. You wait outside with reinforcements."

"If I don't go personally, would our forces be willing to attack? You remain with half our troops as reinforcements."

"Who will you take with you?"

"Ten chieftains and twenty-five hundred men."

That evening a meal was prepared and eaten. The bells were removed from the horses' bridles, the men wore stick gags, for a swift night march. Silently, they followed the two monks to the Fahua Monastery. It was very ancient. Chao Gai dismounted and went inside. There was no one around.

"Why are there no monks in a monastery of this size?" he queried.

"Those animals of the Zeng family caused so much trouble that most of them were compelled to return to secular life. Only the abbot and a few retainers remain. They're living in the courtyard where the tower is. Stay here temporarily. A little later, we'll lead you into the stockade of those rogues."

"Where is it?"

"There are four stockades. The Zeng brothers are in the northern one. If you take that, the others won't matter. The remaining three will quit."

"When shall we go?"

"It's now the second watch. We'll go at the third, and take them by surprise."

From Zengtou, they heard the measured beat of the watchman's drum. Later, they heard the drum sounding the half-watch. After that, they listened no more.

"The soldiers are all asleep," said the two monks. "We can go now."

They led the way. Chao Gai and the chieftains mounted and, with their men, left the monastery and followed. Before they had gone five *li,* the two monks had disappeared into the shadows.

The van was afraid to continue. The paths on all sides were tortuous and difficult. No homes or people could be seen. The forward troops became alarmed and informed Chao Gai.

Huyan Zhuo ordered a retreat. They had marched less than a hundred paces when on every side gongs crashed and drums pounded. Resounding yells shook the ground. Torches everywhere sprang to light.

Chao Gai and the chieftains hurriedly led their men in a withdrawal. They had just traversed two turns in the road when they ran into a troop of enemy cavalry, who showered them with arrows. One struck Chao Gai in the face, and he fell from his horse.

Huyan Zhuo and Yan Shun galloped off at top speed. Liu Tang and Bai Sheng behind them, put Chao back on his steed and fought their way out of the village. At the village entrance Lin Chong rushed up with reinforcements. Only then were they able to stem the foe. A wild melee continued until dawn, when both sides retired to their bases.

Lin Chong made a count of the troops. The three Ruan brothers, Song Wan and Du Qian had escaped by crossing the stream. Of the twenty-five hundred men who had gone in with Chao Gai only twelve or thirteen hundred were left. They had followed Ou Peng back to camp.

The chieftains came to see Chao Gai. An arrow was stuck in his cheek. They pulled it out. Blood flowed, and he fainted. On the arrow was the name of the instructor Shi Wengong. Lin Chong directed that a salve made for metal weapon wounds be applied. Chao Gai had been hit by a poisoned arrow. The venom was working, and he was unable to speak.

Lin Chong ordered that he be placed on a cart, and that the three Ruan brothers, plus Du Qian and Song Wan, escort him back to the mountain fortress. The fifteen chieftains remaining in the camp conferred.

"Who would have thought when brother Chao Gai the Heavenly King came down the mountain that such a thing would happen," they said. "The wind snapped the pole of his standard, and this was the fulfillment of that bad omen. We'll simply have to return to the stronghold. Zengtou Village can't be taken in a hurry."

"We'd better wait for orders from brother Song Jiang before pulling our troops out," Huyan Zhuo said.

The chieftains were morose, the men had no heart for battle. All wanted to go back to the fortress. That night at the fifth watch, as the earliest faint light began to appear, the fifteen chieftains were still sunk in gloom. For indeed, a snake cannot travel without a head, a bird without wings cannot fly. The chieftains sighed. They had no assurance that either an advance or a retreat would succeed.

Suddenly, a picket guarding the road rushed in and reported: "Five enemy columns heading this way. Their torches are without number!"

Lin Chong immediately mounted. Torchlight had turned the hills on three sides as bright as day. Shouting foe were rapidly advancing. The chieftains did not resist. At Lin's orders, they broke camp and withdrew. The Zeng family forces pursued them fiercely. The two sides fought a running battle for sixty *li* before the brigands could break free. They counted their men. They had lost nearly seven hundred. It was a heavy defeat.

They hurriedly resumed the march in the direction of Liangshan Marsh. Halfway there, they were met by Dai Zong, who transmitted a command: They were to bring their troops back to the stronghold. There, new plans would be formulated.

The chieftains complied. On their arrival, they went to see Chao Gai. He was no longer able to eat or drink, and his whole body was swollen. Song Jiang wept by his bedside. He personally applied poultices and fed Chao medicines. The chieftains all kept vigil outside the tent. By the third watch of the third day a great weight seemed to be depressing Chao's body. He turned his head to Song Jiang.

"Preserve your health, brother," he said. "Let whoever captures the bowman who slew me become the ruler of Liangshan Marsh." Chao Gai closed his eyes and died.

To Song Jiang it was as if he had lost one of his parents. He cried until he was faint. The chieftains helped him out of the tent. They urged him to look after the stronghold's affairs.

"Don't grieve so, brother," Wu Yong and Gongsun Sheng advised. "Life and death are man's destiny. Why take it so hard? There are important matters awaiting your attention."

Song Jiang ceased his weeping. He directed that the body be leaved in fragrant water, dressed in burial garments and hat, and displayed in Fraternity Hall. The chieftains performed sacrificial ceremonies. A coffin and inner casket were built and, after an auspicious day was selected, placed in the main hall. A spirit curtain was hung and a memorial tablet put before it, in the center. The inscription read: *Memorial Tablet of the Venerable Chao the Heavenly King and Leader of Liangshan Marsh.*

All the chieftains, from Song Jiang on down, dressed in deep mourning. The junior officers and the rank and file wore mourning head kerchiefs of white. The fatal arrow, broken in a vow of vengeance, lay before the altar. A long white banner was raised. Monks were invited to the citadel from a nearby monastery to offer prayers for the departed. Every day Song Jiang led the outlaws in mourning. He had no heart to attend to the affairs of the fortress.

Lin Chong, with Gongsun Sheng and Wu Yong, discussed the matter with the other chieftains. They decided to make Song Jiang their leader and take their orders from him. The following morning, bearing flowers, lanterns and candles,

Lin Chong and the others invited Song Jiang, the Defender of Chivalry, to be seated in the Hall of Fraternity.

"Hear us, brother," said Wu Yong and Lin Chong. "A country cannot be governed without a sovereign, a household cannot be ruled without a master. Chao Gai, leader of our mountain stronghold, has gone to Heaven. There is no one to make decisions. Your name, brother, is world renowned. We wish to choose an auspicious day and invite you to become our leader. We will obey your commands."

"Remember the dying wish of Chao the Heavenly King: 'Let whoever captures the bowman who slew me become the ruler of Liangshan Marsh,'" said Song Jiang. "You all know about it, you mustn't forget. I haven't avenged him, or wiped out this debt. How can I accept?"

"That is what Chao said," Wu Yong admitted. "But we still haven't caught the culprit, and the stronghold cannot be without a leader. If you don't take over, brother, who else would dare? Who will command our forces? His wish was as you say. Why don't you accept temporarily? We'll work something out later."

"Putting it that way is reasonable. I'll accept the post for the time being. When Chao Gai is avenged, when someone captures Shi Wengong, no matter who, he must become our ruler."

Li Kui the Black Whirlwind shouted: "Not only are you right for leadership of Liangshan Marsh, brother—you'd make a fine emperor of the Song Dynasty!"

"You're talking wildly again, you wretched oaf. Stop your raving or I'll cut your tongue out!"

"Why should you do that? I'm inviting you to become emperor, not the head of some little group worshipping a local god!"

Wu Yong intervened. "The scamp has no sense of proportion. Don't trouble yourself with the likes of him. Please deal with important affairs."

Song Jiang burned incense and sat in the chair of the supreme leader. On his left was Wu Yong, on his right was Gongsun Sheng. The row to the left was headed by Lin Chong, Huyan Zhuo headed the row to the right. All paid their respects and took their seats. Song Jiang addressed them:

"I have accepted this post temporarily. I am completely reliant on your support, brothers. We must be of one heart and mind, united in our efforts, as close as bone and marrow, acting together to carry out Heaven's will. Today our fortress has many men. It's no longer like it was before. I'm asking you brothers to command six sets of fortifications. Fraternity Hall shall be known from now on as Loyalty Hall. We shall have four sets of land fortifications, front and back, left and right. On the rear of the mountain will be two small forts. On the front of the mountain will be three fortified passes. We'll also have a fort on the water at the foot of the mountain, plus small fort on each of the banks. We shall ask you brothers to take charge.

"In Loyalty Hall I shall temporarily occupy the first position. Second shall be Military Advisor Wu Yong; third, Taoist Reverend Gongsun Sheng; fourth, Hua Rong; fifth, Qin Ming; sixth, Lu Fang; and seventh, Guo Sheng. The left set of fortifications shall be commanded by Lin Chong, Liu Tang, Shi Jin, Yang Xiong, Shi Xiu, Du Qian and Song Wan, in that order. The right by Huyan Zhuo, Zhu Tong, Dai Zong, Mu Hong, Li Kui, Ou Peng and Mu Chun. The front set of fortifications shall be under Li Ying, Xu Ning, Sagacious Lu, Wu Song, Yang Zhi, Ma Lin and Shi En. Guarding the rear will be Chai Jin, Sun Li, Huang Xin, Han Tao, Peng Qi, Deng Fei and Xue Yong. The water defenses will be under Li Jun, Ruan the Second, Ruan the Fifth, Ruan the Seventh, Zhang Heng, Zhang Shun, Tong Wei and Tong Meng. These forty-three chieftains shall be the leaders of the six inner defenses of the stronghold.

"The first pass at the front of the mountain shall be held by Lei Heng and Fan Rui, the second by Xie Zhen and Xie Bao, the third by Xiang Chong and Li Gun.

"The small fort on the Shore of Golden Sands shall be commanded by Yan Shun, Zheng Tianshou, Kong Ming and Kong Liang. Duck's Bill Shore's small fort shall be under Li Zhong, Zhou Tong, Zou Yuan and Zou Run.

"As to the two small forts on the rear of the mountain, the one on the left shall be led by Stumpy Wang, Ten Feet of Steel and Cao Zheng; the one on the right by Zhu Wu, Chen Da and Yang Chun.

"In Loyalty Hall in the row of rooms on the left Xiao Rang shall be in charge of documents; Pei Xuan, rewards and punishments; Jin Dajian, seals and letters; and Jiang Jing, money and grain accounts. In the row of rooms on the right, Ling Zhen shall be in charge of cannon; Meng Kang, shipbuilding; Hou Jian, clothing and armor manufacturing; and Tao Zongwang, walls and ramparts.

"In the rooms of the two wings behind the Hall, we'll have the following supervisors: Li Yun, housing; Tang Long, iron smithery; Zhu Fu, wines and vinegars; Song Qing, feasts and banquets; Du Xing and Bai Sheng, miscellaneous.

"The four taverns which serve as lookout places for us shall continue to be run by Zhu Gui, Yue Ho, Shi Qian, LiLi, Sun Xin, Mistress Gu, Zhang Qing and Sun the Witch. Yang Lin, Shi Yong and Duan Jingzhu shall buy horses from the north.

"These are our dispositions. Let everyone respect them and none disobey."

From the day Song Jiang assumed the leadership of the stronghold in Liangshan Marsh, every chieftain, large and small, was happy and content. All gladly acceded to his directions.

One day Song Jiang conferred with them. He wanted to avenge Chao Gai and lead troops against the village of Zengtou. But Wu Yong was opposed.

"The mourning customs of the people must be respected, brother," he advised. "You must wait a hundred days before going into battle. It won't be too late."

Song Jiang heeded his words and remained in the stronghold. Every day he had prayers offered for Chao Gai's safe passage into Heaven.

One day he invited a monk whose Buddhist name was the Beatified and who was a member of the Longhua Monastery in Darning the Northern Capital. The Beatified, on his way to Jining, had been passing through Liangshan Marsh, and had been asked to the fortress to conduct services for the departed. During a vegetarian meal, Song Jiang, in the course of conversation, inquired whether the Northern Capital had any places or people of note.

"Surely you've heard of the Jade Unicorn of Hebei?" the monk retorted.

Song Jiang and Wu Yong suddenly remembered. "We're not yet old. We shouldn't be so forgetful at our age," Song exclaimed. "There's a rich man in the Northern Capital called Lu Junyi. His nickname is the Jade Unicorn. He's one of the Three Remarkable Men of Hebei Province. He lives in the capital city and is highly skilled in the martial arts. With cudgel and staff he has no equal. If we could get him to join our stronghold, we'd need have no fear of any government troops or police sent to catch us."

Wu Yong laughed. "Why so despondent, brother? You want him up here? There's nothing hard about that!"

"He's the head of one of the leading families of Darning. How can we induce him to become an outlaw?"

"I've been thinking of this for some time, though for the moment I'd forgotten. I have a plan that will bring him up the mountain."

"You're not known as the Wizard without cause. Will you tell us, please, Military Advisor, what your plan is?"

Calmly, with two fingers pressed together, Wu Yong related his plan. And as a result, Lu Junyi cast aside embroidered banners and beaded drapes and entered instead the dragon's pool and tiger's den. Truly, to bring one man into the Marsh, warfare was inflicted on the entire population.

How did Wu Yong trick Lu Junyi into coming up the mountain? Read our next chapter if you would know.

CHAPTER 61

WU YONG CLEVERLY TRICKS THE JADE UNICORN

ZHANG SHUN AT NIGHT ROILS GOLDEN SANDS CROSSING

"With the aid of this facile three-inch tongue of mine, I shall go fearlessly to the Northern Capital and persuade Lu Junyi to come to our mountain," Wu Yong avowed. "It will be as easy as taking something out of a bag. You just put your hand in and you've got it. All I need is a rough courageous companion to go with me."

Before he had finished speaking, Li Kui the Black Whirlwind shouted: "Take me, brother Military Advisor."

"Desist, brother," Song Jiang cried. "If someone was needed for arson or murder, pillaging homes or raiding towns, you would be just right. This is a careful delicate operation. You're much too violent."

"You all scorn me because I'm ugly. That's why you won't let me go."

"It's not that. Darning is full of police. If anyone should recognize you, you'd be finished."

"That doesn't matter. No one is better suited for what the Military Advisor wants."

Wu Yong intervened. "I'll take you if you'll promise me three things. If you don't, you'll just have to stay here in the stronghold."

"I'll promise you not three, but thirty!"

"First, you're like wildfire when you're drunk. From today on, you've got to quit drinking. You can begin again when we get back. Second, you'll go as a Taoist acolyte serving me. When I tell you to do something, you do it. Third,—and this is the most difficult— starting tomorrow you're not to say another word, you're to become a mute. If you promise these three things, I'll take you along."

"I can promise not to drink, and to act like an acolyte. But if I can't talk, I'll stifle!"

"If you open your mouth you'll get us into a muddle."

"Of course, it's easy. I'll keep a copper coin in my mouth. That'll do it."

The chieftains laughed. Who could persuade Li Kui to remain behind?

That day a farewell feast was given in Loyalty Hall. In the evening, all retired. Early the next morning Wu Yong gathered a bundle of luggage and directed Li Kui, disguised as an acolyte, to tote it down the mountain on a carrying-pole. Song Jiang and the other chieftains saw them as far as the Shore of Golden Sands. They urged Wu Yong to be careful, and to keep Li Kui out of scrapes. Wu Yong and Li Kui took their leave. The others returned to the stronghold.

The two travelled four or five days, stopping at inns in the evening and rising at daybreak, when they cooked breakfast and continued their journey. Li Kui was a constant irritation to Wu Yong. After several days, they arrived at an inn on the outskirts of the city. They spent the night there, and when Li Kui went down to the kitchen to cook their evening meal he hit the waiter so hard the fellow coughed blood.

The waiter went to their room and complained to Wu Yong. "That mute acolyte of yours is too rough, I was just a little slow in lighting the stove and he gave such a punch I spit blood!"

Wu Yong apologized and handed the man a dozen strings of cash for his pains. He berated Li Kui. Of that we'll say no more. They rose the next morning at dawn, cooked breakfast and ate. Wu Yong summoned Li Kui to the room.

"You pleaded to be taken along, and all you do is aggravate me. We're going into the city today. It's no place for fooling around. I don't want you to cost me my life!"

"I wouldn't dare!"

"Now remember this signal. If I shake my head, you're not to move."

Li Kui promised. The two left the inn and set out for the city in disguise. Wu Yong wore a black crinkled silk head kerchief that came down to his eyebrows, a black Taoist cassock trimmed in white, and a multicolored girdle. His feet were shod in square-toed cloth shoes, and he carried a pole with a bronze bell which shone like gold. Li Kui's bristly brown hair was wound up into two coils on either side of his head. His black tiger body was clad in a short brown gown. A multicolored short-fringed sash bound his bear-like waist. He wore a pair of open-work boots for climbing mountains. On a pole with a curved end a strip of paper dangled, reading: "Fortunes told. One ounce of silver." At that time robbers marauded throughout the land, and every prefecture and county had to be defended by troops. Since the Northern Capital was the leading city in Hebei, it was garrisoned by an army under the personal command of Governor Liang. It was a neatly laid out metropolis.

Wu Yong and Li Kui swaggered up to the gate. The forty or fifty soldiers on guard were gathered around an officer seated in a chair. Wu Yong approached and bowed.

"Where are you from, scholar?" one of the soldiers asked.

"My name is Zhang Yong. This is Li, my acolyte. I'm a wandering caster of horoscopes. I've come to this great city to tell fortunes." Wu Yong produced his false license and showed it to the soldier. "That acolyte has wicked eyes," some of the other soldiers said. "Shifty, like a thief."

Li Kui, who overheard, was ready to burst into action. Wu Yong hastily shook his head, and Li Kui lowered his gaze.

"It's a long story," Wu Yong said apologetically. "He's a deaf mute, but he's terribly strong. He's the son of one our family's bondmaids. I had to take him along. He has no manners at all. Please forgive him."

Wu Yong strolled on through the gate, with Li Kui plodding at his heels. They walked towards the center of the city. Wu Yong rang his bell and chanted:

Gan Luo won fame early, Zi Ya late,

Peng Zu and Yan Hui, each a different life span,
Fan Dan was poor, Shi Chong rich,
Fortune varies for every man.

"Fortune, destiny, fate. I predict life, I foretell death, I know who shall rise high and who shall fall low," cried Wu Yong. "I'll tell your future for one ounce of silver." Once more he vigorously rang his bell.

Fifty or sixty laughing children trailed behind. Singing and giggling, they passed the gate of Magnate Lu's storehouse. Soon Wu Yong returned and marched by again, followed by the hooting youngsters.

Lu was seated in the office, watching his stewards check merchandise in and out. Hearing the noise, he asked the man in charge for the day: "What's all that racket outside?"

"It's really very funny," the man replied. "Some Taoist fortune teller from out of town is walking the streets offering his services. But he wants an ounce of silver. Who would give that much! With him is an acolyte, a sloppy looking fellow who walks like nothing human. Kids are following them and laughing."

"He wouldn't venture to make such large claims if he wasn't a man of learning. Invite him in."

The steward went out. "Sir priest," he called. "The magnate asks you in."

"Who is he?"

"The magnate Lu Junyi."

Wu Yong told Li Kui to come along, raised the door curtain, and entered the office. He instructed Li Kui to sit down on a goose-necked chair and wait. Then he approached Lu and bowed.

Lu bowed in return. "Where are you from, sir priest? What is your name?"

"My name is Zhang Yong. I call myself the Mouth That Talks of Heaven. I'm from Shandong, originally. I can cast horoscopes for emperors, I can predict births and deaths, high position or poverty. For an ounce of silver I can tell your fortune."

Lu invited Wu Yong to a small alcove in the rear of the hall. They seated themselves as host and guest. After tea was served, Lu ordered the steward to bring an ounce of silver.

"Please, sir priest, tell me my humble fate."

"When were you born?"

"A gentleman asks only about misfortune, not fortune. So you needn't talk of prosperity. Just tell me what else is in store," said Lu. "I'm thirty-two." He stated the year, month, day and hour of his birth.

Wu Yong took out an iron abacus, calculated a moment, then slammed it down. "Fantastic!" he exclaimed.

Startled, Lu demanded: "What lies ahead for me?"

"I'll tell you frankly, if you won't take it amiss."

"Point out the road to the lost traveller, sir priest. Speak freely."

"Within the next hundred days, bloody tragedy will strike. Your family wealth will be lost, and you will die at the sword."

Lu Junyi laughed. "You're wrong, sir priest. I was born in the Northern Capital and grew up in a wealthy family. No male ancestor ever broke the law, no female widow ever remarried. I conduct my affairs with decorum, I do nothing unreasonable, I take no tainted money. How can I have incurred a bloody fate?"

Wu Yong's face hardened. He returned the silver piece, rose, and walked towards the door. "People always prefer to hear what pleases them," he sighed. "Forget it. I'm willing to point out a smooth road, but you take my good words as evil. I'll leave you now."

"Don't be angry, sir priest. I was only joking. I'd like to hear your instructions."

"If I speak directly, don't hold it against me."

"I'm listening carefully. Hold nothing back."

"Your fortune has always been good, magnate. But your horoscope conflicts with this year's fate god, and the result is evil. Within a hundred days, your head shall be separated from your body. This has been destined. There is no escape."

"Isn't there any way to avoid it?"

Wu Yong again calculated on the abacus. He said: "Only if you go to a place one thousand *li* southeast of here. Although you may suffer some shocks and alarms, you will not be injured."

"If you can arrange that, I'll gladly reward you!"

"I'll tell you a four line prediction verse. You must write it on the wall. When it comes true, you'll appreciate my mystic powers."

Lu called for a brush pen and ink slab. Wu Yong sang these four lines and Lu wrote them on the white calcimined wall:

A boat sails through the reeds,
At dusk a hero wanders by,
Righteous to the very end,
Out of trouble you must fly.

Wu Yong collected his abacus, bowed and turned to go. Lu Junyi urged him to stay, at least until the afternoon.

"Thank you for kindness," said Wu Yong, "but I must get on with my fortune telling. I'll come and pay my respects another day."

Lu saw him to the gate. Li Kui took up the pole with the curved end and went out. Wu Yong bid Lu farewell. Followed by Li Kui, he departed from the city and returned to the inn. There he paid their bill and collected his luggage. Li Kui carried the fortune telling sign.

"The main job has been done," Wu Yong exulted, after they had left the inn. "Now we must hurry back to the stronghold and prepare our welcome for Lu Junyi. Sooner or later, he'll come."

To return to Lu Junyi, every evening at dusk he stood in front of his hall and gazed unhappily at the sky, sometimes muttering unintelligibly to himself. One day he impatiently summoned his stewards. Before long, they all arrived.

The chief steward was named Li Gu. Originally from the Eastern Capital, he had come to join a friend living in Darning. But the man was nowhere to be found and, after a time, Li Gu fell, frozen, outside the magnate's gate. Lu Junyi saved his life and took him into the household. Because Li Gu was diligent, could write and calculate, Lu put him in charge of household affairs. Within five years he rose to the post of chief steward. He managed all matters of both household and outside business, and had forty or fifty clerks working under him.

These now followed Li Gu into the hall and respectfully greeted the magnate. Lu looked them over and asked: "Where is that man of mine?"

The words were scarcely out of his mouth, when a person came before him. Over six feet tall, he was twenty-four or five years of age, was adorned with a thin mustache and goatee, and had a slim waist and broad shoulders. The kerchief on his head was twisted into the shape of a papaya, with his hair coming up through a hole in the middle. His white gown had a round silk collar of filagreed silver thread. Around his waist was a girdle woven of fine spotted red thread. His feet were shod in brown oiled leather boots. A pair of gold rings shaped like animals dangled from the back of his head. His neckerchief was of fragrant silk. A fan inscribed by a famous calligrapher was tucked slantwise at his waist. Over one ear hung an all-season flower.

The young man was a native of the Northern Capital. After losing his parents as a child, he had been adopted by the Lu family. Because he had pure white skin, Lu engaged a skilled tattooist to decorate his body. The result was kingfisher blue added to white jade. No one could match the young man in beauty of physique. Not only was he gorgeously tattooed, but he could blow and strum musical instruments, sing and dance, and play word games. There was nothing he didn't know, nothing he couldn't do.

He could speak various dialects, knew the special jargon of many different trades. As for the fighting arts, no one could touch him. Hunting in the outskirts of the city, he could bring down any game with his bow. He used only three short arrows, and never missed. Wherever his arrow struck, there his quarry fell. Returning to the city in the evening, he seldom brought back less than a hundred birds. In archery contests, he cleaned up all the prizes.

His mind, too, was quick and agile. You had only to mention a problem and he gave you the answer. His name was Yan Qing. People of the Northern Capital were fond of quips, and they called him the Prodigy. He was Lu Junyi's most trusted adviser.

The men Lu summoned greeted him respectfully and stood in two lines. Li Gu headed the line on the left, Yan Qing headed the line on the right. Lu the Magnate addressed them.

"Last night a fortune teller predicted that unless I took refuge a thousand *li* southeast of here, I would suffer a bloody disaster within a hundred days. I remember now that southeast of here in Tai'an Prefecture, there's a temple on Mount Taishan called the Golden Temple of the Match-Heaven God. This god governs births and deaths and man's disasters. I shall go there and burn incense to expiate my sins and avoid the calamity. At the same time I can do a bit of business and admire the scenery. Li Gu, I want you to get me ten large carts and load them with our Shandong local products. Pack your luggage, because you're going with me. Yan Qing, you stay and look after the household and our storehouses. Li Gu will turn over his duties to you. I'm leaving in three days."

"Master, you're making a mistake," said Li Gu. "Everybody knows fortune tellers are slick talkers. You shouldn't listen to that fellow's claptrap. Remain at home. What's there to be afraid of?"

"My fate has been determined. Don't try to stop me. Once disaster strikes, it's too late to be sorry."

"Please listen to my humble opinion, master," said Yan Qing. "The road to Tai'an runs pass Liangshan Marsh, which is infested with bandits under Song Jiang. Though they rob and pillage, government soldiers and police can't get near them. Wait until times are more settled, if you want to burn incense. Don't believe that fortune teller's wild story. He's probably a plant from Mount Liangshan, sent to stir you up so that they can trick you into joining them. It's too bad I wasn't home last night. With two or three phrases I could have exposed the fellow and made him a laughing stock."

"You're both talking rot. Who would dare to deceive me! Those oafs in Liangshan Marsh—what do they matter? I can scatter them like grass, in fact I'll go and nab them. My prowess with weapons will show them what a real man is like!"

Before he had finished speaking, a woman emerged from behind a screen. It was his wife Jia.

"Husband," she said, "I've been listening to what you've been saying. 'Better to stay at home than even one *li* roam,' as the old saw goes. Ignore that fortune teller. Why put your vast family affairs aside and expose yourself to shocks and alarms in a den of tigers and lair of dragons just to do some business? Stay at home, be calm and content, relax quietly, and naturally nothing will go wrong."

"You don't know anything about it, woman! My mind is made up. I don't want to hear any more from any of you!"

Yan Qing said: "Basking in the reflection of your good fortune, master, I have been able to learn a little skill with weapons. I don't mean to boast, but if you take me with you and any bandits happen along, I should be able to knock off forty or fifty. Leave Chief Steward Li to look after things at home and let me accompany you."

"Li Gu knows trade practices I don't understand. He'll save me a lot of trouble. That's why I'm taking him and leaving you here. I have others to keep the accounts. All you have to do is take charge of the manor."

"My feet have been bothering me quite a lot lately," said Li Gu. "It's hard for me to walk any distance."

Lu was very angry. "Soldiers are trained for months for the sake of a few days of battle. I want you to go with me on this trip, and you've got all kinds of excuses. The next man who defies me is going to get a taste of my fists!"

Li Gu, frightened, looked towards the mistress. But she only walked sadly into an inner room. Yan Qing was even less inclined to speak.

Silently swallowing his humiliation, Li Gu went to pack the luggage. He got ten drivers, ten large carts, and forty or fifty animals to haul them. He loaded on the luggage, and had the merchandise securely tied in place.

Lu Junyi put his own affairs in order. The third day, he burned paper prayers, dispersed money to the male and female members of his family, and gave instructions to each. That evening he directed Li Gu to finish up quickly and prepare to leave the city first with two servants. Li Gu went off. The magnate's wife, seeing the carts, wept.

At the fifth watch the following morning, Lu rose, washed, and put on a complete set of new clothes. He gathered his weapons and went to the rear hall, where he burned incense in farewell to his ancestors. He instructed his wife: "Take good care of things at home. At the latest I'll be back in three months; at the earliest, only forty or fifty days."

"Be careful on the road, husband. Write to us when you can, so that we'll know how you're getting on."

Yan Qing came forward and bowed, in tears. Lu had orders for him as well.

"Be diligent in all things. Don't go running off to roister in houses of pleasure."

"Since you'll be away, master, I certainly won't slacken."

Staff in hand, Lu left the city. He was met by Li Gu.

"You and the two servants go on ahead," Lu directed. "When you find a clean inn have them prepare food, so that it's ready for the drivers and porters when they get there, and we won't be delayed."

Li Gu also carried a staff. He set off with the two servants. Lu and other servants followed with the carts. They passed splendid mountains and elegant waterways, travelling broad roads and level plains.

"I couldn't have enjoyed such scenery if I remained at home," Lu thought pleasurably.

After travelling forty *li* or more he was met by Li Gu, and they had a pastry lunch. Li Gu went on again. Another forty or fifty *li* and they reached an inn, where Li Gu had arranged quarters for the night for all.

Lu went to his room, leaned his staff, hung up his felt hat, removed his knife, and changed his shoes and stockings. It goes without saying that he rested and dined. The company rose early the next morning and cooked breakfast. When everyone had eaten, the animals were hitched to the carts and the march resumed.

They proceeded in this manner for several days, stopping at dark and continuing at dawn. Again, they put up at an inn for the night. The following morning they were preparing to go on when one of the waiters addressed Lu Junyi.

"I must tell you, sir, that less than twenty *li* from here the road passes an entry to Liangshan Marsh. The lord of the mountain is Song Jiang. Although he doesn't harm travellers, rather than suffer frights and alarms it's best to go by quietly."

"So that's how it is," Lu exclaimed. He told a servant to fetch his trunk. Lu unlocked it and took out a bundle from which he extracted four white silk banners. He ordered the waiter to bring four bamboo poles and attach the banners, one to each. On them, Lu wrote this series of lines:

From the Northern Capital Lu the Bold
Transports merchandise a long, long way,
Determined is he to catch the robbers,
Fully his manliness to display.

Li Gu and the others groaned. "Are you a relative of Song the mountain lord, sir?" asked the waiter.

"I'm a magnate from the Northern Capital. What relation would I be to those crooks! I've come specially to nab that lout Song Jiang."

"Speak softly, sir," begged the waiter. "Don't get me involved. This is no joke. Even with ten thousand men, you'll never get near Song Jiang!"

"Bullshit. You oafs are probably all in cahoots with him!"

The waiter was beside himself with despair The drivers and porters were dumbfounded. Li Gu and the other servants knelt at the magnate's feet.

"Master, have pity on us. Save our lives, go back. Rather that than prayers for our departed souls!"

"What do you know!" Lu barked. "Would those little finches dare contend with an eagle? I've always wanted to show my prowess with arms, but I've never met a foe worthy. Today, I have my chance, here and now. Why wait! In those bags on my cart I've got some good hemp rope. The bandits I don't kill I'll knock down with my halberd. You tie them up and put them on the carts. If necessary abandon the merchandise. We'll use the carts for transporting prisoners. I'll deliver their chief to the capital and claim the reward. That will satisfy my wish of a lifetime. If a single one of you refuses to go along with me now, I'll slaughter you right here!"

The four banners were affixed to the four leading carts. The remaining six carts followed. Li Gu and the rest, weeping and sniveling, had no choice but to obey the magnate. Lu took out a halberd head and tied it to his staff tightly with three strong knots. He hastened the carts forward in the direction of Liangshan Marsh. Li Gu trembled with every step he took on the winding mountain road, but Lu pushed on relentlessly.

They marched from early morning till almost noon. In the distance they saw a big forest, with trees larger than a two-man embrace. When they reached the edge of the forest a shrill whistle pierced the air, terrifying Li Gu and the two servants. They didn't know where to hide.

Lu Junyi ordered that the carts be pulled to one side, under guard. The drivers and porters, bemoaning their fate, crawled beneath the carts. "When I knock the robbers down, you tie them up," Lu shouted. Before the words were out of his mouth, four or five hundred outlaws emerged from the edge of the forest. Behind them the crashing of gongs could be heard. Another four or five hundred brigands cut off Lu's retreat. Cannon boomed in the woods, and out leaped a bold warrior.

"Do you recognize the mute acolyte, Magnate Lu?" he called, brandishing a pair of axes.

Lu suddenly understood. "I've often thought of capturing you robbers," he cried, "and I'm here today to do it. Bring that knave Song Jiang down the mountain to surrender. Any tricks and I'll kill you all. I won't spare a one!"

Li Kui laughed. "Magnate, you've fallen for a clever ruse by our Military Advisor. Come and take your place in a chieftain's chair."

Enraged, Lu twisted his halberd and charged. Li Kui met him with axes swinging. Before they had fought three rounds Li Kui jumped from the combat circle, turned, and headed for the forest. Lu pursued, halberd level. Li Kui ran into the wood, zigzagging left and right. In a towering fury, Lu plunged in after him. Li Kui flew into a grove of pines. By the time Lu got there, his adversary was gone.

He was turning away when a group of men appeared from the side of the grove and a voice called: "Don't go, Magnate. Do you know me?"

Lu looked and saw a big fat monk, dressed in a black cassock and carrying an iron Buddhist staff by its lower end.

"Who are you, monk?" the magnate shouted.

The man laughed. "I'm Sagacious Lu the Tattooed Monk. I'm here on orders from brother Song Jiang to welcome you and lead you up the mountain."

"Bald donkey," Lu exploded, "how dare you be so rude!" Twisting his halberd, he rushed the monk.

Sagacious met him with whirling staff. Before they had fought three rounds, the monk parried Lu's halberd, turned arid ran. Lu gave chase. At that moment Wu Song the Pilgrim stepped forth from among the brigands. He charged, brandishing two swords. Lu abandoned his pursuit of Sagacious and battled with Wu Song. They had fought less than three rounds when the Pilgrim hastened away.

Lu Junyi laughed. "I won't chase you. You louts aren't worth it!"

But then someone on the mountain slope called out: "You don't understand, Magnate. Haven't you heard that man fears falling into the water, just as iron fears falling into the fire? Our Military Advisor has made his plan. How can you escape?"

"Who are you, rogue?" Lu yelled.

The man laughed. "Liu Tang the Red-Haired Demon."

"Petty crook, don't try to get away," the magnate fumed. He dashed at Liu, halberd in hand.

They had just battled three rounds when a voice off at an angle shouted: "Gallant Mu Hong the Unrestrained is here!" And Liu Tatig and Mu Hong, each with a halberd, attacked Lu Junyi.

Before they had gone three rounds, Lu heard footsteps behind him. "At you!" he exclaimed. Liu Tang and Mu Hong fell back a few paces, and Lu whirled to face the adversary in his rear. It was Li Ying the Heaven-Soaring Eagle. From three sides Lu's foes assailed him. But he was completely unruffled, in fact the more he fought the stronger he became.

As they were belaboring each other, gongs crashed on the mountain top. The three chieftains feinted with their weapons and swiftly withdrew. Reeking of sweat from his exertions, Lu did not pursue. He returned to the edge of the forest to seek his carts and drivers. But the ten carts, their drivers and all the animals had vanished. Lu groaned.

He clambered to a high point and looked around. Far in the distance at the foot of a slope he saw a group of brigands driving the carts and animals before them. Li Gu and the others, tied in a line, followed. To the beat of drums and gongs, they were being led to a grove of pines.

Lu's heart burst into flames, rage engulfed him like smoke. Halberd in hand, he chased after the procession. When he was not far from the slope two bold fellows shouted at him: "Where do you think you're going?" One was Zhu Tong the Beautiful Beard, the other Lei Heng the Winged Tiger.

"Small-time robbers," Lu yelled back. "Return my carts and drivers and animals!"

Zhu Tong twiddled his beard and laughed. "How can you be so dense, Magnate? Our Military Advisor often says: 'A star can only fly down, it can never fly back.' The way things stand, you might just as well come with us to the fortress and take your place in a chieftain's chair."

Infuriated, Lu charged the two with levelled halberd. Zhu Tong and Lei Heng met him with their own weapons. Before they had fought three rounds the former constables turned and fled.

"I'll never get my carts back unless I knock one of those bandits over," thought Lu. He pursued them recklessly around the bend of the slope. But the two had vanished. Instead, he heard the sound of clappers and flutes wafting down from the mountain top. He looked up. Fluttering in the breeze was an apricot yellow pennant on which was embroidered the words: *Righteous Deeds on Heaven's*

Behalf. And there beyond, beneath a gold-spangled red silk umbrella, was Song Jiang, with Wu Yong to his left and Gongsun Sheng to his right. They were accompanied by a column of sixty or seventy men. All politely hailed Lu Junyi.

"Magnate, we trust you've been well!"

Lu grew very angry, and he cursed them by name. Wu Yong tried to soothe him.

"Calm yourself, brother. Song Jiang has long known of your virtue, and holds you in the greatest respect. He sent me to call at your gates and lure you up the mountain so that we might perform righteous deeds for Heaven together. Please don't take it amiss."

"Presumptuous bandits," yelled Lu. "How dare you trick me!"

From behind Song Jiang emerged Hua Rong with bow and arrow. "Magnate," he called, "don't force a showdown between us. Let me demonstrate my archery."

Before he had finished speaking, the arrow whizzed straight into the big red tassel atop Lu's broad-brimmed felt hat. Astonished, the magnate turned and fled. On the heights, drums shook the ground. From the east side of the mountain, led by Qin Ming the Thunderbolt and Panther Head Lin Chong, came a body of yelling mounted men, banners waving. A similar troop, also shouting and waving banners, charged out from the west side of the mountain, led by Two Rods Huyan Zhuo and Metal Lancer Xu Ning. Lu was so frightened he didn't know which way to go.

It was growing dark. Lu's feet hurt, and he was hungry. Frantically seeking an escape route, he hurried along a small mountain path. At dusk, mist veiled the distant waters, fog locked the deep mountains. The moon and stars were dim, the vegetation a pale blur. Lu was reaching the ends of the earth, if not the limits of the sky.

He looked around. There was nothing but reeds here, and misty water. Lu raised his face to the sky and sighed. "I wouldn't listen to good advice, and now I'm in a terrible mess!"

A small boat slid out from among the reeds, sculled by a fisherman. "You're very brave, sir traveller," the fisherman called. "This is the entry to Liangshan Marsh. What are you doing here in the middle of the night?"

"I've lost my way and can't find a place to spend the night. Save me!"

"This region is very broad, but there is a market town. It's over thirty *li* if you go by land, and the road is tortuous and difficult to follow. By water, though, it's only four or five *li*. Give me ten strings of cash and I'll take you there in my boat."

"Get me to an inn in the market town and I'll give you plenty of silver."

The fisherman rowed up to the shore and helped Lu on board, then shoved off with his iron-tipped bamboo pole. When they had gone four or five *li*, they heard the sound of an oar in the reeds ahead. A small craft flew out. On it were two men. The one in the prow, buff naked, gripped a long punting pole. The one in the stern was wielding a sweep oar. Pole held athwart, the man forward sang this song:

> Though poems and books I cannot read,
> And in Liangshan Marsh I dwell,
> I shoot fierce tigers with snarebows and arrows,
> Fresh baited hooks bring me fish as well.

Lu Junyi, startled, didn't dare utter a sound. From reeds on the right, two more men rowed out on another small boat. The man in the stern plied a creaking sweep oar. The man in the bow held horizontally a long punting pole. He sang this song:

My favorite pastime is killing men, A rogue I've been since the day I was born, Thousands in gold means nothing to me, I'm determined to nab the Jade Unicorn.

Lu the Magnate groaned. Now, from the middle reeds a third boat came skimming towards him. The man in the prow was holding an iron-tipped wooden pole upside down, and he was singing this song:

> A boat sails through the reeds,
> At dusk a hero wanders by,
> Righteous to the end,
> Out of trouble you must fly.

The men on all three craft hailed Lu respectfully. The one in the center was Ruan the Second. Ruan the Fifth was on the boat to the left, Ruan the Seventh was on the boat to the right. The three craft approached. Lu was very alarmed. He knew he couldn't swim.

"Land me on the nearest shore," he urged the fisherman.

The man laughed. "By the blue sky above and the green waters below, I was born on the Xunyang River, came to Liangshan Marsh, and have never concealed my name. Meet Li Jun the Turbulent River Dragon! If you don't surrender, Magnate, you'll be throwing your life away!"

Lu was astonished. "It's either you or me!" he shouted, and he lunged at Li's heart with his halberd. Li saw the blade coming. Hands on the sweep oar, he flipped over in a back somersault and landed kaplonk in the water. The boat spun around in a circle and the halberd fell overboard.

Suddenly, at the stern, a man shot up from under the water with a shout. It was White Streak in the Waves Zhang Shun. Treading water, he grasped the rudder and gave a quick twist. The boat turned turtle, and the hero landed in the drink. Could he live through this?

Truly, a plan had been laid to catch a phoenix and cage a dragon, a pit had been dug for a heaven-startling, earth-shaking man.

After falling in the water did Lu Junyi survive? Read our next chapter if you would know.

CHAPTER 62

SNIPING WITH ARROWS YAN QING SAVES HIS MASTER

LEAPING FROM A BUILDING SHI XIU SNATCHES A VICTIM FROM THE EXECUTION GROUNDS

Zhang Shun wrapped and arm around Lu's waist and swam with him towards shore. They soon reached the bank. Fifty or sixty men were waiting with lighted torches. These gathered round, removed Lu's dagger and stripped him of his wet clothes. They were about to bind his arms when Dai Zong the Marvellous Traveller transmitted an order.

"Lu the Magnate is not to be harmed," he shouted.

An attendant gave Lu a silken embroidered tunic and gown to wear. Eight brigands brought a sedan-chair, assisted Lu into it, and set forth. Seen in the distance were twenty or thirty red silk lanterns, illuminating a mounted troop which was approaching to the accompaniment of drams and music. At the head was Song Jiang, Wu Yong and Gongsun Sheng. They were followed by many chieftains.

All dismounted. Lu Junyi hastily got down from his sedan-chair. Song Jiang knelt. The other chieftains, in rows, did the same. Lu also dropped to his knees.

"Since I have been captured, I request an early death."

Song Jiang laughed. "Please sit in your sedan-chair, Magnate."

The chieftains resumed their saddles. To the sound of music, the procession climbed through the three fortified passes and went directly to Loyalty Hall. There, the hosts dismounted and led Lu into the hall. It was brightly lit by lanterns and candles.

"Your fame, Magnate, has long thundered in my ears," said Song Jiang. "Being able to meet you today is one of the greatest good fortunes of my life. My brothers behaved rudely a little while ago. We beg your forgiveness."

Wu Yong stepped forward and said: "The other day, on orders from brother Song Jiang, I called at your gates disguised as a fortune teller. My aim was to lure you up the mountain so that you might join us in our mutual endeavors to act on Heaven's behalf."

Song Jiang invited Lu Junyi to be seated in the highest chieftain's chair. Lu's reply was courteous.

"I've no talent, knowledge or ability, and I've offended your prestige. Ten thousand deaths would be a light retribution. Why do you make sport of me?"

Song Jiang smiled. "Who would dare? Because of our genuine respect for your great virtue, Magnate, we have hungered and thirsted for your arrival. We pray you do not scorn our humble mountain fortress. Be our leader. We will unquestioningly obey your every command."

"Then let me die immediately, for I cannot accede to your wish."

"Let's talk about it again another day," Wu Yong suggested.

Wine was brought for the magnate. Lu had no way out, and he drank several cups. Lesser brigands conducted him to the rear hall to rest.

The next day sheep and horses were slaughtered and Song Jiang invited the magnate to a large feast. After much polite refusal, Lu consented to sit in the middle. When several rounds had been drunk, Song Jiang rose, goblet in hand.

"Last night we offended you, and for this we beg your pardon. Although our stronghold is small, and not a worthy place to water your horse, we hope you will consider our sincere fidelity. I gladly relinquish my position to you, Magnate. Please do not refuse."

"You're making a mistake, sir chieftain. There are no crimes against my name, and my family has a bit of property. A man of the great Song Dynasty I was born, a ghost of the great Song Dynasty I will die. I prefer death to accepting your proposal!"

Wu Yong and the other chieftains also joined in Song Jiang's pleas. But Lu was determined not to become an outlaw.

"If you're not willing, Magnate," Wu Yong finally said, "we can't force you. You would be with us in body but not in spirit. Since we have the rare privilege of having you here, even if you won't join us, at least stay a while. Then we'll escort you home."

"Why not let me go right now? My family has had no news of me. I'm afraid they'll worry."

"No problem about that. We'll have Li Gu return first with the carts. You can go a few days later."

Lu turned to his chief steward. "Are your carts and merchandise all there?"

"Not a thing is missing."

Song Jiang ordered that two large silver ingots be presented to Li Gu, and two small bits of silver be given to the servants, and ten ounces of silver be distributed among the carters. The recipients expressed their thanks.

"You know my difficulties," Lu said to the chief steward. "When you get home, tell my wife not to worry. Say I'll be returning in four or five days."

Li Gu, who wanted only to get away, readily assented. "I certainly will," he promised. He bid farewell and left Loyalty Hall. Wu Yong rose.

"Set your mind at ease, Magnate," he said. "Keep your seat while I see Li Gu off. I'll be back soon."

Wu Yong mounted and went on ahead to the Shore of Golden Sands and there waited for the chief steward. Soon Li Gu, the two servants, the draught animals and their drivers, came down the mountain. Wu Yong, who had five hundred brigands with him, hemmed the procession in on two sides. Seated in the shade of a willow tree, he summoned Li Gu before him.

"Your master has already talked it over with us and agreed. Today he's taken the second chieftain's chair. Even before he came up the mountain, he wrote a four line rebellious verse on the wall of a room in his house. Note the first word of each line. In the first it's 'Lu', in the second it's 'Jun', in the third it's 'Yi', in the fourth it's 'rebels'—'Lu Junyi rebels.' Now you know what he's doing in our fortress! At first we were going to kill you all, but then we thought it would give our stronghold a bad name. So we're letting you go. Travel day and night and hurry home. But don't nourish any hopes that your master will return."

Li Gu fervently kowtowed. Wu Yong ordered that boats take the men and animals across the river. They shortly were speeding along the road to the Northern Capital.

We'll leave Li Gu for the moment and talk of Wu Yong after he went back to the banquet in Loyalty Hall. He besieged Lu Junyi with clever and persuasive arguments. The feast didn't end till the second watch. Another feast was laid the following day.

"I appreciate the good intentions of you chieftains in keeping me here," said Lu, "but for me every day is like a year. I must leave today."

Song Jiang replied: "I'm a man of no talent, and have been very fortunate to meet you, Magnate. I'd like to use my own money to give you a small dinner where we can have a heart to heart chat. Please don't refuse."

Another day passed. The following day Song Jiang laid a feast, the next day it was Wu Yong, and the day after it was Gongsun Sheng. To tell it briefly, there were over thirty chieftains, and each day each of them in turn gave Lu a banquet. Time slipped away, the sun and moon shuttling across the sky. More than a month went by. Again Lu proposed to leave.

"We'd like to keep you," said Song Jiang, "but if you really must go, we'll have a few modest drinks in farewell in Loyalty Hall."

The next day, Song Jiang again paid for the feast out of his own pocket. The other chieftains protested to Lu Junyi.

"Though our brother respects you one hundred per cent, we respect you one hundred and twenty," they said. "But you go only to his banquet! Just because you have regard for the substantial brick, that doesn't mean you should scorn the thin tiles!"

And Li Kui shouted: "I risked my life in the Northern Capital to invite you here, and you won't allow me to feast you. I'm going to hang on to your tail until you agree!"

Wu Yong laughed. "Who ever heard of that kind of an invitation? How crude! Magnate, forgive him. But, in view of their sincerity, you really ought to stay a little longer."

Almost unnoticed, another four or five days expired. Lu was determined to go. Then Zhu Wu the Miraculous Strategist approached him with a group of chieftains in Loyalty Hall. "Although we are of lesser rank," said Zhu, "we have expended some efforts for our brother Song Jiang. There isn't any poison in our wine! If you take offense and refuse to dine with us, I won't make any trouble. But I'm afraid my brothers will react badly. Then, being sorry will be too late!"

Wu Yong rose to his feet. "You men behave! I'll speak to the magnate for you. I'm sure he can stay on a bit longer. Why not? 'Advice offered, wine goblet in hand, is never ill-intentioned,' as the old saying goes."

Lu could not withstand the importunities of so many. He agreed to remain another short while. This stretched into an additional nearly forty days. It had been the fifth lunar month when Lu left the Northern Capital, and by now he had spent more than two months in the mountain fortress. Golden wheat rustled in the breeze and the dew was cool. Autumn Festival time was rapidly approaching.

Lu longed to go home, and he spoke to Song Jiang about it. Obviously, his wish was intense.

"That's easy enough," said Song. "Tomorrow, I'll see you to the Shore of Golden Sands."

Lu Junyi was delighted. The next day, his clothing and weapons were restored, and a column of chieftains escorted him down the mountain. Song Jiang presented him with gold and silver on a platter.

"I don't mean to boast," said Lu, "but my family has money and goods in plenty. I'll take only enough to get me to the Northern Capital. I don't want the rest."

Song Jiang and the other chieftains escorted Lu to the Shore of Golden Sands. There, they bade him farewell and returned to the stronghold. Of that we'll say no more.

We'll speak rather of Lu Junyi, who strode along at a rapid clip. In ten days he reached the suburbs of the Northern Capital. Since it was already dusk he didn't enter the city but put up for the night at an inn. Early the next morning he left the village hostel and hastened towards the city.

Before he had gone a *li* he met a fellow in tattered head kerchief and ragged clothes. The man, on seeing Lu, dropped to his knees and kowtowed. It was Yan Qing the Prodigy.

"What are you doing in this condition?" cried the magnate.

"This isn't the place to talk."

The two rounded the corner of an earthen wall and Lu started to question Yan Qing.

"Not long after you left, master," the young man related, "Li Gu returned and said to the mistress, 'The master has thrown in with Song Jiang in Liangshan Marsh. He's accepted the chair of the second chieftain.' Li Gu went to the authorities and accused you. They began living together and, claiming that I was disobedient, threw me out. They confiscated all my clothes and drove me from the city. And they warned all my friends and relations that they would go to court and prosecute anyone who gave me shelter, even if they had to spend half the family fortune doing it! As a result, no one dared have anything to do with me. Having no place to stay in the city, I've been wandering around in the outskirts, begging. I've had to live in a rear lane. Take my advice, master, and return to Mount Liangshan.

Don't even consider anything else. If you go into the city, you'll surely be trapped."

"My wife isn't that kind of a woman," Lu shouted. "You're just farting, you oaf!"

"You don't have eyes in the back of your head, master, how could you have seen? You spent most of your time developing your physique, you never had much interest in sex. The mistress has been having an affair with Li Gu for a long time. Now they can shut the door and be together as husband and wife. If you go home, master, they're bound to do you dirty."

Lu was furious. "My family has lived in the Northern Capital for five generations. Everyone knows us! How many heads has Li Gu got to spare that he would dare pull such a thing? You've probably been up to some wickedness yourself, and you're telling me this to put me off! I'm going home and get to the bottom of this, and then I'll settle with you!"

Yan Qing wept bitterly and kowtowed, clinging to his master's garments. Lu kicked him aside and strode on towards Darning.

He entered the city and went directly home. His stewards gaped in amazement. Li Gu hurried forward to welcome him. He escorted Lu into the hall, dropped before him and kowtowed.

"Is Yan Qing here?" Lu inquired.

"Don't ask, master. It's a long story and you've had a tiring journey. Why don't you rest first, then I'll tell you."

Lu's wife emerged, weeping, from behind a screen. "Don't cry," urged Lu. "Just tell me what's happened to young Yan."

"Don't ask now, husband. It's a long story and you've had a tiring journey. Why don't you rest first, then I'll tell you."

The magnate was growing suspicious, and he demanded an answer.

"Why not change your clothes, worship in the family chapel, and have some breakfast," Li Gu suggested. "Then it will be time enough for us to speak." He had food laid out for the magnate.

As Lu was raising his chopsticks, he heard shouts at the front and rear gates.

Two or three hundred policemen came charging in. They promptly bound the astonished Lu and drove him with blows of their batons to the residency of the governor of the Northern Capital.

Governor Liang was at that moment holding court. In lines to his left and right were seventy or eighty policemen like wolves and tigers, and these brought Lu before him. Lu's wife and Li Gu both knelt to one side.

"You were one of the Northern Capital's good citizens, you knave," shouted the governor. "Why did you join the bandits in Liangshan Marsh and accept the second chieftain's chair? You came to link forces within and without so that they can attack the city! Now that you've been captured, what do you have to say?"

"In a moment of stupidity I let Wu Yong from Mount Liangshan, posing as a fortune teller, into my house. With lying words, he beguiled me to Mount Liangshan, where I was detained for more than two months. Fortunately, I was able to get away and come home. I have no evil intent. I pray Your Excellency will see into my heart."

"Do you expect anyone to believe that! If you're not in league with them, why did you stay there so long? The wife you abandoned and Li Gu have both exposed you. Would they make false accusations?"

"Since it's come to this, master, you'd better confess," Li Gu advised. "That poem you wrote on the wall at home has a hidden rebellious meaning. It's overwhelming proof. There's no need to say any more."

"We don't want to injure you," said Lu's wife, "but we're afraid you'll involve me. You know the old saying: 'When a man rebels, his family and all his relations must pay with their lives.'"

Kneeling before the governor, Lu cried that he was being wronged. "Don't say that, master," Li Gu urged. "If the charge is true, you can't escape it. If it's false, you'll easily clear yourself in the end. But first confess, and you won't have to suffer a beating."

Lu's wife agreed. "It's hard to get a false charge into court, husband, and it's equally hard to deny the facts. If you've committed a crime, you'll be the death of me! Will your sensitive skin be able to withstand the feelingless rods? Confess, and your sentence will be lighter!"

Li Gu had spread bribes high and low, and now Zhang the court clerk spoke up. "That stubborn villain! If he's not beaten he'll never confess!"

"Right," said Governor Liang. "Beat him," he shouted.

Policemen flung Lu Junyi face downward and pounded him till his skin split, his flesh protruded and blood flowed in rivulets. Three or four times he fainted. Finally, he could bear it no longer.

"I was destined for a violent death," he sighed. "I'll make a false confession."

As soon as the clerk obtained the confession, he had a hundred-catty rack for the condemned placed around Lu's neck and directed that he be taken to prison, to the distress of all spectators inside and outside the court. That same day Lu was pushed through the prison gates, led to a pavilion and forced to kneel. Seated on a bed was the superintendent of the city's two prisons, who was also the official executioner. He was Cai Fu, a native of the Northern Capital, known as Iron Arm for his strength with the executioner's blade.

Standing beside him was his brother Cai Qing, one of the guards. The people of Hebei Province like to make quips, and they gave Cai Qing the nickname Single Blossom because of his fondness for hanging a flower over one ear. Holding a courier's staff, he stood at his brother's side.

"Lock this condemned prisoner up," Cai Fu said. "I'm going home for a while. I'll be back later."

Cai Qing led Lu away.

Cai Fu rose and left the prison. He was passing through the gates when a man rounded a wall ahead. He was carrying a container of cooked rice and looked worried. It was Yan Qing the Prodigy.

"What are you up to, young brother?" Cai Fu asked.

Yan Qing dropped to his knees and wiped the tears rolling down his cheeks. "Brother Superintendent, have pity on my master Lu the Magnate," he pleaded. "He's been wrongfully convicted and has no money to pay for food. I begged this half container of rice outside the city so that he'll have something to stem his hunger, permit me to give it to him, brother Superintendent, and you'll be doing a good deed!" Yan Qing, his voice choking, prostrated himself.

"I know about this case," said Cai Fu. "You can bring him the rice."

Yan Qing thanked him and entered the prison. As Cai Fu was crossing the prefectural bridge, a waiter hailed him respectfully.

"There's a customer upstairs in our tea-house, Superintendent. He's waiting to speak to you."

Cai Fu went upstairs with the waiter and found Li Gu the chief steward. The two exchanged courtesies.

"What can I do for you, Chief Steward?"

"I've never concealed from you my good side or my evil. You know all about me, Superintendent. Tonight, I want you to finish him off. I've no other way to show my respect, but here are fifty ounces of gold in scallion shape. I'll take care of the other court officials and functionaries myself."

Cai Fu laughed. "Haven't you read what's carved on the tablet in front of the court? *It's easy to oppress the people but hard to deceive Heaven.* You're so crooked you cheat yourself. Do you think I don't know? You've taken over his property and stolen his wife, and you offer me a paltry fifty ounces of gold to kill him! If the Inspector General came down here and checked on me, I hate to think of the charge I'd have to face!"

"If it's not enough, Superintendent, I can add another fifty."

"Li Gu, you're the kind who would feed his cat its own tail! Are you trying to tell me that Lu Junyi, well-known magnate of the Northern Capital, is worth only one hundred gold ounces? Get this straight— I'll need five hundred ounces of gold, if you expect me to do him in!"

"I have them here. You can have the whole amount, as long as you do the job tonight."

Cai Fu took the gold and concealed it on his person. He stood up. "You can call for the body tomorrow morning." Li Gu thanked him, and happily departed.

Cai Fu returned home. No sooner had he arrived than a man raised the door curtain and entered.

"How do you do, Superintendent," the visitor said. A handsome man, he wore a round-collared gown the deep green of a raven's wing, a girdle with a buckle of mutton-fat jade. His turban was like the crown of a crested goose, his shoes were encrusted with pearls. He kowtowed before Cai Fu.

The superintendent hastily returned the salutation. "What is your name sir," he asked, "and what do you want to see me about?"

"It would be better if we talked inside."

Cai Fu invited his visitor into a conference alcove, where they seated themselves as host and guest. The caller opened the conversation.

"Don't be alarmed, Superintendent. I'm from the Heng hai Shire of Cangzhou Prefecture. My name is Chai Jin. I'm a direct descendent of the Zhou emperors, and I'm known as the Small Whirlwind. Because I'm chivalrous and generous, I've become acquainted with members of the gallant fraternity everywhere. Unfortunately, I committed a crime and had to take refuge in Liangshan Marsh. I'm here today on orders of brother Song Jiang to inquire about Lu the Magnate. Who would have thought that due to the connivance of corrupt officials, an adulterous wife and her wicked lover, he would be cast into a cell for the condemned! His life is hanging by a thread, and his fate is in your hands. I'm calling at your home to tell you this, with no fear of the consequences to myself. If, with Buddha-like compassion, you keep Lu in this world, we shall not forget your great virtue. But if you permit an error even half the size of a grain of rice to occur, our soldiers will surround your city, our generals will arrive at your moats, and we'll smash our way in and slaughter the entire population, good and bad, old and young! We have long known that you are a bold fellow who is chivalrous and faithful. For want of a proper gift, we can present you only with a thousand ounces of gold. Now, if you want to arrest me, go ahead. Bind me with ropes. I swear I won't so much as frown."

In a cold sweat, Cai Fu was afraid to speak. Chai Jin rose. "When a gallant man does something, he doesn't dilly-dally. Let's have your answer."

"Please go back, sir. I can handle this."

"We have your promise. Your kindness will be rewarded." Chai Jin stepped out the door and summoned his companion. He took from him the gold and placed it in Cai Fu's hands. Then he bid the superintendent a courteous farewell and departed. The companion was none other than Dai Zong the Marvellous Traveller—another man not easily put off!

But Cai Fu wasn't sure how to go about it. He thought for some time, then returned to the prison and conferred with his brother.

"Ordinarily, you're good at making decisions," said Cai Qing. "A small matter like this—what's so hard about it! As the old saying goes: 'Prove a killing with a show of blood, a rescue must be thorough or it's not any good.' Since we've got a thousand ounces of gold, we'll spread some of it around, high and low. Governor Liang and Clerk Zhang both have itchy palms. Once they've taken the bribes, they'll naturally spare Lu's life, and simply exile him to some distant place or other. Whether he's rescued or not is up to the bold fellows of Liangshan Marsh. We can only do our part."

"That suits me fine. Transfer Magnate Lu to a better place of confinement, and see to it that he gets good food and drink every day. Let him know what we're doing."

The two brothers came to an agreement. They secretly dispensed gold high and low, judiciously placing their bribes.

The next day, learning that nothing had happened, Li Gu went to Cai Fu's home and urged him to take action. Cai Qing said: "We were about to do it, but Governor Liang wouldn't permit us. He has ordered that Lu's life be spared. You work on the higher-ups. If they give us the word, there won't be any problem."

Li Gu sent an intermediary with money to see Governor Liang. But the governor only said: "This is a matter for the superintendent in charge of the prisons. Am I supposed to kill him myself? In a day or two I'll tell him to see to it."

Thus the governor and the superintendent each pushed the decision off onto the other. Clerk Zhang, who had received money from Li Gu, kept postponing a final disposition of the case. But Cai Fu came to him with another bribe and urged him to get it settled. Zhang drafted a judgment and brought it to Governor Liang.

"How shall we dispose of this?" asked the governor.

"It seems to me that although there's a complaint against Lu, there isn't any real evidence. He did stay in Liangshan Marsh for a long time, true, but he was inveigled into it, and we can't get at the real culprit. Give him forty blows and exile him three thousand *li*. How does that sound to Your Excellency?"

"Very intelligent. It suits me perfectly."

The governor directed Cai Fu to bring Lu Junyi before him. In open court he had the rack removed, read aloud the confession, and imposed a beating of forty blows. A leafed iron rack of twenty catties was then locked around Lu's neck and the governor sentenced the prisoner to Shamen Island. He instructed Dong Chao and Xue Ba to escort him there under guard.

These two originally had been policemen in Kaifeng Prefecture, and been ordered privately to kill Lin Chong while taking him to Cangzhou. Because they failed to do so, Marshal Gao Qiu had found an excuse for banishing them to the Northern Capital. Governor Liang, discovering that they were a competent pair, had added them to his staff. Now he directed them to escort Lu into exile.

Dong and Xue received the official sentence document and took Lu the Magnate from court to the dispatch office, and there had him detained. The guards then went home to pack their luggage and prepare for the journey.

When Li Gu heard about this, he groaned. He sent a man to invite the two guards for a chat. Li Gu received Dong Chao and Xue Ba at a tavern, conducted them to seats in a private room, and there served them with food and wine. After each had drunk three cups, Li Gu spoke.

"I won't try to deceive you—Lu the Magnate is my enemy. He is being banished to Shamen Island, which is a long way from here, but he hasn't a penny, and you two will have to foot all your own travel expenses. Even if you move very quickly, the round trip will take you at least three or four months. I haven't any proper gift, only these two silver ingots to burden your hands. When you reach a convenient place, a number of *li* away, or at most two stages from here, kill him. Bring back the tattoo on his face as proof and I'll give you each fifty ounces of gold in addition. All you have to do is write up some false report. I'll attend to the people in the governor's office."

Dong and Xue looked at each other. There was a long silence. The large silver ingots were a strong temptation.

"I'm only afraid we couldn't bring it off," Dong said.

"Brother," Xue remonstrated, "Master Li is a fine gentleman. We ought to do this for him. If ever we have any problems, he'll surely look after us."

"I never forget a favor," said Li Gu. "I'll gradually repay you."

The two guards accepted the silver, said goodbye, returned to their quarters, and gathered their luggage. The same night, they set out.

"I'm still in pain from the beating I had today," said Lu. "Couldn't we start tomorrow?"

"Shut your friggin mouth," said Xue. "It's rotten luck for gents like us to be stuck with a pauper like you! To Shamen Island and back is over six thousand *li*. Travel expenses are going to be enormous, but you haven't a penny. How are we going to manage!"

"Have pity. I've been wrongfully convicted."

"You rich usually won't even give a fellow a hair off their hide," said Dong. "Well, Heaven isn't blind, and now you're getting what you deserve! Don't complain. We'll help you walk."

Lu could only swallow his anger and move along. They left through the East Gate, and the guards hung their luggage and umbrellas on Lu Junyi's rack. As a prisoner, there was nothing he could do about it.

By dusk, they had covered fourteen or fifteen *li*. There was a town ahead, and they looked for a place to spend the night. The waiter led them to a room in the rear and they set down their bundles.

"We are, after all, gentlemen of the police," Xue Ba said to Lu. "Are we to dance attendance on a prisoner? If you want to eat, cook up some rice!"

Lu had no choice but to go to the kitchen, with the rack around his neck, and ask the waiter for fuel stalks. He twisted these into a bundle and made a fire in the stove. The waiter put rice on to boil and washed bowls and chopsticks for him. Lu had been born rich, and he didn't know how to do these things. The fuel was wet. It didn't burn well, and kept going out. Lu blew hard to keep it alight, and got his eyes full of ashes.

Dong grumbled and scolded. When the rice was cooked, the two guards helped themselves. Lu dared not take anything. The two finished eating, and allowed Lu to have the remainder of their soup and their cold rice. Xue cursed him continuously.

The meal over, Xue ordered Lu to heat water so that they could wash their feet. Only when the water was boiling hot did Lu venture to sit down in the room. The guards finished bathing their feet, then brought a basin of sizzling water for Lu. The moment he removed his straw sandals, Xue plunged his feet into the water. The pain was agonizing.

"A gentleman waits on you, and you have the nerve to grimace," snarled Xue.

The guards chained Lu behind the door, where he groaned all night. They themselves slept on the brick *kang* bed. At the fourth watch they got up and ordered the waiter to make breakfast. They ate, gathered their bundles and prepared to set forth. Lu's feet were blistered from the scalding. He could scarcely stand.

What's more, it was a rainy autumn day, and the road was slippery. Lu skidded and stumbled with every step. Xue drove him on with blows of his staff, while Dong pretended to urge leniency. Xue complained and grumbled all along the way. They travelled more than ten *li* and came to a large forest.

"I really can't move," said Lu. "Have pity and let me rest."

The guards led him into the forest as the east was turning light. No one else was abroad.

"My partner and I got up very early this morning," Xue Ba said to Lu. "We're quite tired and would like to take a nap. But we're afraid you'll run away."

"Even if I sprouted wings I couldn't escape."

"We're not going to let you trick us. I'll tie you up." With the rope he had hanging at his waist Xue bound Lu around the middle to a pine tree, then pulled his feet back and fastened them as well.

"Go to the edge of the forest and keep watch, brother," Xue said to Dong. "Cough as a signal if anyone comes."

"Brother, do the job quickly!"

"Don't worry. Just keep watch."

Xue raised his official staff. "You mustn't blame us two," he said to Lu. "Your steward Li Gu told us to kill you during the journey. You'd die anyway after you got to Shamen Island. It's better to dispatch you here. Don't complain about us in the Nether Regions. A year from now will be the first anniversary of your death!"

His tears falling like rain, Lu lowered his head and waited to die. Xue raised his staff with both hands and started a blow at Lu's temple. Dong, on the edge of the forest, heard a thud, and he hurried back to look. The magnate was still tied to the tree, but Xue was lying face up at Lu's feet, the staff dropped to one side.

"Strange," Dong muttered. "Did he swing so hard that he tripped and fell?"

Dong tried to help him up, but couldn't budge him. Then he saw that blood was flowing from Xue's mouth, and three or four inches of a slender arrow protruded from his chest. Before Dong could yell, a man sitting in a tree to the northeast cried: "Here it is!" A bowstring twanged and an arrow lodged itself in Dong's throat. His feet flew up and he landed heavily.

The man leaped down from his perch, whipped out a dagger, cut the ropes binding Lu, and smashed open the rack around his neck. Then he threw his arms around the magnate and wept aloud. Lu opened his eyes and recognize Yan Qing.

"Is this my ghost meeting you now?" Lu cried.

"I waited outside the chancellery and followed you and the guards," said Yan Qing. "The rogues wanted to kill you in this forest! But with two arrows from my crossbow I finished them both. Did you see it?"

"You've saved my life," said Lu. "But killing those two guards makes my crime more severe. Where can I go?"

"It was Song Jiang who started all this trouble. Where else except Mount Liangshan?"

"My wounds still hurt from the beating and my feet are torn. I can't walk."

"You mustn't delay. I'll carry you on my back."

Yan Qing kicked the two bodies aside, picked up his crossbow, tucked his dagger in its sheath, collected the official staves, lifted Lu onto his back, and headed east. By the time he had walked ten *li* or so, he was exhausted. They saw a small village inn, entered, and asked for a room. They bought some meat and wine to appease their hunger. For the time being, they remained at the inn.

Passers-by found the bodies of the two guards in the forest. The chief of the nearby hamlet informed the local village head, who in turn notified Darning Prefecture. An officer sent to investigate identified the victims as Dong Chao and Xue Ba, police guards in the governor's chancellery.

Governor Liang, on receiving the report, instructed the Inspector of Police of Darning to apprehend the criminals within a fixed time. Police, examining the scene of the crime, said: "These crossbow arrows are clearly Yan Qing's. We'd better move fast." Nearly two hundred policemen went separately to every home and inn in every town and village far and near and put up "Wanted" posters describing the two culprits in detail.

Lu Junyi, unable to walk, stayed at the inn recovering from his wounds. When the waiter heard about the murder, he could talk of nothing else. He noted the resemblance of his guests to the sketches in the "Wanted" posters, and hurried to the hamlet chief.

"There are two strange men staying at our inn," he said. "I wonder whether they could be the ones?"

The hamlet chief relayed this information to the authorities.

In search of something tasty, Yan Qing went with his crossbow to the nearby fields and shot some game. On his return, he found the whole village in an uproar. He hid in a grove of trees and watched. Two hundred policemen, armed with spears and swords, surrounded Lu Junyi, who was bound on a cart which was being pushed away. Yan Qing wanted to rush out and save him, but he had no military equipment, and could only groan.

"If I don't go to Mount Liangshan and get Song Jiang to come to the rescue," thought Yan Qing, "I'll be throwing my master's life away!"

He left immediately. He was still travelling by the middle of the night. He was hungry, but he hadn't any money. Yan Qing came to a small hill. It was covered with underbrush and had a few trees. He went into a grove and slept till daylight. He awoke very depressed. A magpie was chattering in a tree.

"If I can shoot that down," he thought, "I can beg some boiling water from a villager and cook it. That will ease my hunger pangs."

Emerging from the grove, he looked up. The bird cawed at him raucously. Yan Qing softly removed his crossbow from its sheath and offered a silent prayer: "I've only this one arrow. If my master is going to be saved, let it bring the magpie down. If my master is fated to die, let the magpie fly away unscathed."

He fitted the arrow to the string and shouted: "Bow, don't fail me!" The trigger mechanism twanged and the arrow hit the bird in the tail. It flew down the hill, the arrow trailing from its rump. Yan Qing gave chase, but he lost sight of his quarry.

While he was searching, he saw two men coming his way. The one in the lead wore a turban shaped like a pig's snout. Gold-traced silver rings dangled at the back of his head. A gown of fragrant black silk was bound at the waist by a gold-figured sash. He was shod in hempen sandals over soft stockings that reached his knees, and he carried a staff as high his eyebrows. The man behind had a broad-brimmed white felt hat on his head, a tea-colored gown with embroidered sleeves, a pink purse at his middle, and heavy leather shoes. On his back was a bundle of clothing. He carried a short cudgel. A knife hung at his waist.

They passed so close by, they almost brushed shoulders with Yan Qing. He turned and looked after them and thought: "I have no travelling money. If I knock those two down and take the purse it will be easier for me to get to Liangshan Marsh."

He hung his bow behind him and followed. The two, heads down, were concentrating on walking. Yan Qing caught up with the rear man in the felt hat. He punched him square in the back and knocked him down. But before he could hit the man in front, the fellow raised his staff and cracked Yan Qing on the left shin, tumbling him to the ground. The rear man meanwhile got up, planted a foot on Yan Qing, pulled out a dagger and poised to stab.

"Bold fellow," Yan Qing cried, "it doesn't matter if I die, but who will deliver my message?"

The man hesitated and lowered his arm, then pulled Yan Qing up. "What message have you, knave?"

"Why do you ask?"

The other man grasped Yan Qing's hand and pulled it forward, exposing the tattooing on his wrist. "Aren't you Yan Qing, the one they call the Prodigy, in the household of Lu the Magnate?" he asked.

Yan Qing thought: "One way or another, I'm going to die. I might as well tell the truth and let him arrest me, so that I can go to the next world with my master!" Aloud, he said: "Yes, I am!"

The two men laughed. "It's a good thing we didn't kill you. So you're young brother Yan! Do you know who we are? I am Yang Xiong the Pallid. And this is Shi Xui the Rash."

"We've been ordered by brother Song Jiang to proceed to the Northern Capital and inquire about Lu the Magnate," said Yang Xiong. "Our Military Advisor and Dai Zong have also come down from the mountain and are waiting for news."

Yan Qing told them everything that had transpired, and Yang said: "In that case I'll take you to brother Song Jiang in the fortress and we can decide what to do. You, Shi Xiu, go on to the Northern Capital, see what you can find out, and report back."

"Right," said Shi Xiu. He gave Yan Qing a muffin and dried meat to eat, and left him his bundle to carry.

The Prodigy went with Yang Xiong. They travelled through the night to the mountain fortress, where Yan Qing met Song Jiang and told the story in full. Shocked, Song Jiang summoned his chieftains for a conference.

We'll talk now of Shi Xiu. With only the clothes he wore on his back, he arrived at the outskirts of the Northern Capital. It was already turning dark and he was unable to enter the city, so he rested that night outside. He went in the next morning after breakfast.

He observed that people were sighing, and seemed quite downcast. Puzzled, he proceeded to the center of town. The door of every home was closed. He asked an old man what was wrong.

"Traveller, you wouldn't know," the old man replied. "Here in the Northern Capital we have a Lu the Magnate. He's one of our richest men. He was snatched away by the robbers of Liangshan Marsh and managed to escape. But when he came home he was convicted on a wrongful charge and sentenced to Shamen Island. Somehow, on the way, the two guards escorting him were killed. Last night, Lu was captured again, and today, at the third quarter after noon, he's going to be executed here in the middle of the city! You'll be able to see it."

To Shi Xiu the news was like a douse of icy water. He walked on. At the main intersection was a two-storied tavern. He entered, went up the stairs, and sat down in a small room overlooking the street.

"Are you having other guests, or are you drinking alone, sir?" the waiter asked.

Shi Xiu glared. "A big bowl of wine and a large platter of meat. Just bring them and let's not have any friggin questions!"

Startled, the waiter poured two measures of wine and sliced a large platter of beef. Shi Xiu ate and drank steadily. Before long, he heard a growing hubbub in the street below. He looked out the window. The door of every home and shop was shut tight.

The waiter came up the stairs and said: "You must be drunk, sir! There's going to be a public execution down there. Pay your bill and go someplace else, quickly!"

"That stuff doesn't scare me. Get out of here before I give you a taste of my fists!"

Not daring to reply, the waiter went back downstairs.

On the street gongs crashed and drums thundered. Shi Xiu watched from his window. Crowds jammed all sides of the execution place. A dozen pairs of guards, bearing swords or staves, pulled and pushed Lu forward and compelled him to kneel outside the tavern building. Iron Arm Cai Fu carried the official sword of execution. Single Blossom Cai Qing held Lu's rack.

"Magnate Lu," said Cai Fu, "you can see for yourself. It isn't that we two didn't want to save you. Circumstances are forcing us to do this! We've already arranged a seat for you in that Temple of the Five Saints ahead. Your soul can go there and claim it."

From the crowd a voice shouted: "It's three quarters after noon!"

Cai Qing removed Lu's rack and grasped his head. Cai Fu raised the executioner's sword. The clerk read in a loud voice the crimes listed on the condemned man's placard. The crowd of spectators gasped in anticipation.

And with that sound, Shi Xiu, dagger in hand at the upstairs window of the tavern, let out a yell:

"The bold fellows of Liangshan Marsh are all here!"

Cai Fu and Cai Qing pushed Lu aside, grabbed the ropes which had bound him, and ran. Shi Xiu leaped down from the window and wielded his steel knife, killing men like hacking melons and slicing vegetables. He downed a dozen or more before they could get away. He grabbed Lu with one hand and pushed south. Shi Xiu didn't know the Northern Capital streets, and Lu was too stunned to do more than stumble along.

Governor Liang was astounded when he heard the news. He immediately summoned his highest commanders and directed them to have their soldiers seal off all four city gates. He sent his entire police force after the fugitives.

Pursued by fast horses and powerful troops, could Shi Xiu and Lu the Magnate scale the high city walls and towering ramparts? Where could they go? They had no claws for burrowing into the ground, and no wings to fly them up to the blue sky.

Did Lu the Magnate and Shi Xiu escape? Read our next chapter if you would know.

CHAPTER 63

SONG JIANG ATTACKS THE NORTHERN CAPITAL WITH TROOPS

GUAN SHENG DISCUSSES HOW TO TAKE MOUNT LIANGSHAN

There was no way for Shi Xiu and Lu the Magnate to get out of the city. Police surrounded them and snared them with long hooked poles and looped ropes. In spite of their courage, the two couldn't resist overwhelming numbers. They were caught and brought before the governor, their captors crying that here was the rogue who had raided the execution grounds.

Shi Xiu was hustled into court. He stood, glaring. "You're a crook who ruins the country and injures the people, a slave of a slave," he shouted at Liang. "Soon my brother Song Jiang and his army will attack your city and trample it flat and hack you into three pieces! I've been sent on ahead to notify you louts!"

The onlookers were stupefied at Shi Xiu's revilement of the governor in open court. But Liang listened. For several minutes he was sunk in thought. Finally he ordered that a big rack be fastened on each of the prisoners and that they be cast into the jail for the condemned. He put Cai Fu in charge, warning him against any slip-ups.

Cai Fu wanted to be on good terms with the gallants of Mount Liangshan. And so he detained his charges in a cell together, and every day served them good food and wine. As a result, they did not suffer, in fact they lived quite well.

Liang then summoned Wang, the newly appointed prefect, and asked him for a list of the casualties in the fracas. Seventy or eighty had been killed, and innumerable others had sustained head injuries, lacerations and fractured limbs. Liang dispensed government funds for medical treatment for the wounded and cremation for the dead.

The next day news began coming in of dozens of proclamations which had been posted inside and outside the city by the Mount Liangshan forces. Citizens, not daring to conceal them, reported the proclamations to the authorities. Governor Liang read one, and his soul flew up to Ninth Heaven in fright. It ran as follows:

Song Jiang, a Liangshan Marsh fighter for righteousness, hereby notifies the authorities of Daming and all its inhabitants: Lu Junyi of the Northern Capital is a man of honor. We recently invited him to our mountain stronghold to carry out together with us the Will of Heaven and dispatched Shi Xiu to inform you of this. To our surprise you seized them both. If they are not harmed, and you turn over to us the adulterous wife and her lover, we will not intervene. If however you injure these men who are our wings, our limbs, we shall descend from our fortress in full force and take vengeance, incinerating and destroying everything, good or bad. Heaven and Earth will support us, and the spirits will assist. We shall wipe out the treacherous and exterminate the stubborn. Easily we shall enter the city, but not lightly will our wrath be appeased. Virtuous husbands and wives, filial sons and grandsons, righteous citizens and clean officials need have no fear. They may go peacefully about their affairs. Let all be thus advised.

Liang again summoned Prefect Wang. "How shall we deal with this?" he queried.

Wang was a weak and timid person. "The imperial court sent soldiers to arrest that gang on Mount Liangshan several times, but they failed," he said. "What can a small city like ours do? If those wild villains attack before imperial forces come to the rescue, we'll be finished. I have a suggestion. Spare the lives of the two prisoners, but write a plea to the imperial court and notify his excellency Premier Cai. At the same time send our local troops out to prepare to repel any raiders. This will preserve the city and protect its inhabitants. If we execute those two, the brigands may attack immediately before reinforcements can arrive. The imperial court will blame us and the citizens will be thrown into a panic. It will be a nasty situation."

"Your proposal is quite sound," said Governor Liang. He summoned superintendent Cai Fu and gave him his instructions.

"Those two are no ordinary culprits," he said. "If you're too hard on them, they may die. If you're too soft, they may escape. I want you and your brother to watch them day and night. Be flexible, but keep them under constant guard. Don't relax for a moment."

Cai Fu was delighted with this order, since it fitted in precisely with what he had in mind. On leaving the governor he went to reassure the two prisoners. Of that we'll say no more.

Governor Liang then called his generals, Wen Da the Mighty Sword and Li Cheng the King of the Skies, to his residency for a conference. He told them of the proclamations from Liangshan Marsh and what Prefect Wang had proposed. Li Cheng was contemptuous.

"So those petty bandits may dare to emerge from their lair," he said. "It's nothing for you to be concerned about, Excellency. I'm not talented, and I've eaten much of the public larder without performing any meritorious deeds. Now I would like to do my utmost. Let me lead my soldiers forth and encamp outside the city. If the bandits don't come, we can discuss what to do next. Though strong, their days are numbered. I'm not boasting, but if they do venture out and attack, I guarantee not one of them will return alive!"

Liang was very pleased. He rewarded the commanders with gold and silks. The two thanked him, took their leave, and returned to their respective posts.

The following morning Li Cheng summoned his officers to his tent to confer. From among them Suo Chao, a handsome, impressive man came forward. He was known as the Urgent Vanguard, and his weapons were a pair of golden battle-axes.

"The bandit Song Jiang is coming soon to attack our Northern Capital," Li Cheng said. "Muster your soldiers, march them thirty-five *li* from the city and make camp. I will follow with more troops."

The next morning Suo Chao did as ordered. He halted at a place called Flying-Tiger Valley, and built a fortified encampment at the foot of the hills. Li Cheng, the day after, left the city with leaders of his middle and flanking units, marched twenty-five *li* to Locust Tree Slope, and there set up a stockaded camp. Both camps bristled with spears and knives. Branched stakes, like sharp deer antlers, were firmly embedded on the perimeters. On three sides deep pits were dug. The soldiers rubbed their hands in anticipation, eager to distinguish themselves and win glory for the emperor.

We'll divide our story into two parts. Those proclamation notices were written by Wu Yong after hearing the news from Yan Qing and Yang Xiong. On learning from Dai Zong that Lu the Magnate and Shi Xiu had been captured, he had them put up when no one was around on bridges and roadways. Dai returned to the mountain fortress and told the chieftains in detail what had transpired.

Song Jiang was shocked. He at once had the drums sounded to summon the chieftains to Loyalty Hall. They took their seats in order of rank. Song addressed himself to Wu Yong.

"You meant well at the time, inviting Lu the Magnate up the mountain to join our band. But because of this, today he's in trouble, and brother Shi Xiu as well. What can we do to rescue them?"

"Don't worry, brother. I'm not talented, but I have a plan. We can use this opportunity to relieve the Northern Capital of its money and grain for our own use! Tomorrow is an auspicious day. Divide our chieftains into two. Leave half here to guard the fort. Give me the other half to attack the city."

Song Jiang directed Ironclad Virtue Pei Xuan to muster the necessary forces to march the following day.

"These two big axes of mine haven't had any action for a long time," said Li Kui the Black Whirlwind. "I'm glad to hear we're going to fight and pillage again. Let me have five hundred men and I'll take the Northern Capital, hack Governor Liang into mincemeat, dismember the corpses of Li Gu and that adulterous female, and rescue Lu the Magnate and Shi Xiu! The 'mute acolyte' will get his revenge. I'll do a thorough job of it."

"Although you're brave, brother," Song Jiang replied, "the Northern Capital isn't like other prefectures. What's more, Governor Liang is the son-in-law of Premier Cai, and his generals Li Cheng and Wen Da are of matchless courage. They're not to be underestimated."

"You knew I'm quick to speak, yet you let me go disguised as a mute," Li Kui yelled. "But now, though you know I like to kill, you won't let me be the vanguard. Do you want to aggravate me into my grave!"

"Since you insist," said Wu Yong, "you can go as a vanguard. Take five hundred bold fellows and set up an advance position. You can start tomorrow."

That evening Song Jiang and Wu Yong decided on the number of men to be used in the campaign. Pei Xuan wrote a notice which he dispatched to various installations on the mountain, outlining the order of march according to contingents and directing prompt execution.

It was then the end of autumn and the beginning of winter, a comfortable time for wearing armor, and the horses were sleek and fat. For a long time the men had not seen battle, and they longed for action. The hatred they felt was intense, and they were determined to wreak vengeance. Happy with their mission, they gathered their weapons, and saddled and bridled their steeds. They rubbed their hands, ready to start down the mountain at the appointed hour.

The first contingent, the vanguard, consisted of five hundred men under Li Kui the Black Whirlwind. The second, under Two-Headed Snake Xie Zhen, Twin-Tailed Scorpion Xie Bao, Kong Ming the Comet and Kong Liang the Flaming Star, consisted of a thousand men. The third also contained a thousand men and was led by the girl Ten Feet of Steel, and her lieutenants Sun the Witch and Mistress Gu the Tigress. The fourth was headed by Li Ying the Heaven-Soaring Eagle, assisted by Nine Dragons Shi Jin and Sun Xin the Junior General, and also contained a thousand men.

Song Jiang was the commander-in-chief of the central army, with Wu Yong as his military advisor. His four aides were Lu Fang the Little Duke, Guo Sheng the Second Ren Gui, Sun Li the Sickly General and Huang Xin the Suppressor of the Three Mountains. Qin Ming the Thunderbolt led the forward army, seconded by Han Tao the Ever-Victorious General and Peng Qi the Eyes of Heaven General. Panther Head Lin Chong commanded the rear army, and his lieutenants were Ma Lin the Elfin Flutist and Deng Fei the Fiery-Eyed Lion. The left army was commanded by Two Rods Huyan Zhuo, assisted by Golden Wings Brushing the Clouds Ou Peng and Yan Shun the Elegant Tiger. Hua Rong led the right army, aided by Chen Da the Gorge-Leaping Tiger and Yang Chun the White-Spotted Snake.

Also on the expedition were the cannon expert Heaven-Shaking Thunder Ling Zhen, who was in charge of grain for the men and fodder for the horses, and Dai Zong the Marvellous Traveller who was responsible for collecting military intelligence.

Each contingent, under its respective leader set out at daybreak in the prescribed order. Only the Deputy Military Advisor Gongsun Sheng was left behind with a body of men to guard the fortress and its three passes, assisted by Liu Tang, Zhu Tong and Mu Hong. The waterside fort was held by Li Jun and others. Of that we'll say no more.

We'll speak now of Suo Chao, seated in his camp in Flying-Tiger Valley. A horseman sped up like a meteor and announced that Song Jiang was approaching with an army of countless thousands. They were only twenty or thirty *li* away. Suo Chao immediately sent word to Li Cheng on Locust Tree Slope. The general hurriedly relayed the information to the city. At the same time he mounted his charger and rode directly to the forward camp. Suo Chao greeted him and told him the news in detail.

At dawn the next day the defenders breakfasted. When it was light they broke camp, moved forward to the Yu Family Hamlet, and deployed fifteen thousand infantry and cavalry in battle positions. Li Cheng and Suo Chao, in full armor, reined their horses beneath a pennant-decorated arch. Far to the east more than five hundred men could be seen flying towards them in a cloud of dust. Riding in the fore was Black Whirlwind Li Kui, a battle-ax in each hand. Glaring, he ground his teeth and shouted: "Your lord Black Whirlwind from Mount Liangshan is here!"

Li Cheng turned to Suo Chao with a laugh. "Every day we hear about the bold fellows from Liangshan Marsh. Why, they're just a pack of dirty bandits, not worth mentioning! Vanguard Commander, why don't you nab the louts?"

Suo Chao smiled. "There's no need for me to act. We have plenty of field officers eager for glory."

Before the words were out of his mouth, a senior officer named Wang Ding, twirling a lance, galloped forward with a hundred horsemen. Li Kui and his men couldn't withstand the united cavalry charge, and they fled in all directions. Suo Chao and his forces chased them past Yu Family Hamlet.

Behind the hill, gongs and drums suddenly resounded, and two cavalry troops rode forth. On the left was Xie Zhen and Kong Liang, on the right was Kong Ming and Xie Bao, and each troop contained five hundred fierce riders.

Startled by the appearance of these reinforcements, Suo Chao stopped his pursuit and hastily returned.

"Why didn't you capture the bandits?" Li Cheng demanded.

"We chased them beyond the hill and were about to take them when the rogues were reinforced. Their support had been waiting in ambush. We couldn't follow through."

"They're only bushwhackers. What's there be afraid of!"

Li Cheng led his entire forward army in a charge past Yu Family Hamlet. Ahead he saw banners wave, and heard yells and the thunder of drums and the crash of gongs. Another cavalry troop appeared. At the head of this one was a girl warrior, very smartly accoutred. On the red banner in front of the unit she was leading, the words *Female General Ten Feet of Steel* were inscribed in letters of gold. Mistress Gu was on her left, Sun the Witch on her right, and together they led a force of over a thousand. Their men were of every size and description and hailed from many different parts of the country.

When Li Cheng saw them he said to Suo Chao: "Soldiers like that are absolutely useless. Go at them directly, while I surround them with my troops."

Grasping his golden axes, Suo Chao struck his horse and galloped forward. Ten Feet of Steel turned her mount and raced for a hollow in the hills. Li Cheng, who had spread out his force, tore after her.

Suddenly, he heard earth-shaking yells. Charging towards him was Li Ying the Heaven-Soaring Eagle, flanked by Shi Jin and Sun Xin. Hastily, he and his soldiers retreated into Yu Family Hamlet. But then they were assaulted from the left by a contingent led by Xie Zhen and Kong Liang, and from the right by the unit under Xie Bao and Kong Ming. Meanwhile, the three women commanders had wheeled their troop around and were catching up from the rear.

So hot was the pursuit that Li Cheng and his men were scattered.

They pressed desperately on to return to camp. Ahead, they found Li Kui the Black Whirlwind blocking their path. Li Cheng and Suo Chao managed to dash through. By the time they reached the camp, they had suffered huge losses.

Song Jiang and his army did not chase them any further. They reassembled for a short rest, then made camp.

Li Cheng and Suo Chao hurried to the city and reported to Governor Liang. That same night Wen Da was rushed to the battle area with local reinforcements. Li Cheng received him in the camp on Locust Tree Slope and raised the question of a withdrawal strategy. Wen Da laughed.

"Those bandits are only a slight itch. They're nothing to worry about!"

That night they agreed on a plan and instructed the troops. At the fourth watch everyone had breakfast, at the fifth they donned their armor, at daylight they marched. Thrice the battle drums rolled as they broke camp and advanced towards Yu Family Hamlet.

Soon they saw Song Jiang's army, sweeping towards them like the wind. Wen Da the Mighty Sword spread his troops out in battle formation, and ordered his archers to shoot and stop the front ranks of the advancing foe. Song Jiang selected one of his senior officers to go forth. He bore a red banner with the words writ large in silver: *Qin Ming the Thunderbolt.*

Qin Ming reined his horse and shouted: "You corrupt officials of the Northern Capital, listen! We've been intending to attack your city for a long time. Only a fear of hurting its good people has prevented us. Turn over Lu Junyi and Shi Xiu, surrender the adulterous pair, and we'll withdraw and swear we won't encroach. If you are stubborn, you'll bring fire down on your own heads that will melt jade and stones! Those are your only prospects. If you've anything to say, speak now, without delay!"

"Who will seize that varlet for me?" Wen Da furiously cried.

Before he had finished speaking, Suo Chao advanced to the front and shouted: "You were an officer appointed by the imperial court. How has the government ever wronged you? Instead of behaving like a proper person you've become a wretched bandit! I'm going to pulverise you when I catch you today!"

To Qin Ming the words were like coal in a stove, oil on a fire. He clapped his horse and charged, whirling his wolf-toothed cudgel.

Suo Chao spurred his mount to meet him. Two spirited horses collided, two sets of weapons clashed, the armies on both sides yelled. The contestants fought more than twenty rounds, with neither the victor.

Han Tao moved up on horseback from the ranks of Song Jiang's vanguard unit. He fitted an arrow to his bow, aimed, and let fly. The arrow struck Suo Chao in the left arm. He dropped his axes, turned and cantered back to his position.

Song Jiang pointed with his whip and all three armies surged forward. Corpses soon covered the plain, blood flowed in rivers. It was a crushing defeat. The Song Jiang forces chased the running foe past Yu Family Hamlet, then captured Locust Tree Slope. Wen Da fled all the way to Flying-Tiger Valley. When he counted his soldiers, he found he had lost a third.

On Locust Tree Slope Song Jiang made camp. Wu Yong said: "Beaten troops are always frightened. We ought to go after them before they recover their nerve. It's too good a chance to miss."

"You're quite right, Military Advisor," replied Song Jiang. He circulated the order that his crack victorious forces should that evening divide into four columns and march through the night to attack the city.

As to Wen Da, he had just caught his breath after returning to Flying-Tiger Valley, when a junior officer entered and announced a row of fires on a nearby hilltop. Wen Da mounted his horse and went out with a troop of soldiers to look. There, on a hill to the east, countless torches were turning the hills and the surrounding fields red.

To the west, too, fires gleamed. Wen Da led his men hastily in that direction. Suddenly, from behind he heard thunderous shouts. Racing in pursuit from the east was Hua Rong, followed by Yang Chun and Chen Da. Panic-stricken, Wen Da led his soldiers quickly back to Flying-Tiger Valley.

But then, from the glowing torches in the west Two Rods Huyan Zhuo, with Ou Peng and Yan Shun as his second in command, came charging downward. Pincers from east and west were closing in. And from the rear, there were more yells, and Qin Ming the Thunderbolt, aided by Han Tao and Peng Qi, raced up to join the fray. Shouting men and neighing horses milled in the firelight without number.

Wen Da's army was thrown into confusion. They broke camp and left. Again they heard yells, this time before them. There were bursts of flame Heaven-Shaking Thunder Ling Zhen and his assistants had slipped around to the side of Flying-Tiger Valley via small paths and were bombarding with their cannon.

Wen Da and troops plunged through and raced for the city. Ahead of them drums pounded. A troop of cavalry was blocking their way. In the firelight Panther Head Lin Chong moved forward, aided by Ma Lin and Deng Fei. On all sides drums thundered in unison and fierce flames erupted. The government soldiers, in turmoil, fled for their lives.

Swinging his sword, Wen Da was hacking his way through when he ran into Li Cheng. The two joined forces and fought a withdrawal action. By dawn they had battled to the outskirts of the city.

When Governor Liang heard the news, his soul was shaken from his body. He hastily mustered troops and sent them out to bring in the defeated soldiers. Then he locked the city gates and tightened his defenses.

The following morning Song Jiang's forces arrived. They pushed straight up to the East Gate and there made camp. They prepared to attack.

In the city's military headquarters Governor Liang called a conference. It was difficult to see any solution.

"The brigands are at our gates," said Li Cheng. "The situation is desperate. If we delay any longer, we'll be lost. You must immediately write a personal family letter, Excellency, to the premier, and send it by trusted emissary tonight. The premier will then be able to petition the emperor in the morning court to dispatch crack troops to our rescue. That would be best. Second, you should also officially notify all neighboring prefectures and counties to send relief troops quickly. Third, instruct the Darning Prefecture to conscript civilians to go up on the walls of the Northern Capital and help defend the city. Let them keep in readiness throwing logs, ballista stones, blinding lime and molten metal. Have them cock the crossbows, and be vigilant day and night. In this manner we can guarantee against mishaps."

"I can write the letter easily enough, but who will carry it?" Said the governor. That same day he designated one of his leading commanders, Wang Ding. Wang donned full armor, selected a couple of cavalrymen, and took the letter. The city gate was opened, the drawbridge lowered, the messengers went off to the Eastern Capital at flying speed. Neigh boring prefectures and counties were officially notified to rush relief troops. Prefect Wang was directed to muster civilians for the defense of the city walls. Of that we'll say no more.

Song Jiang divided his forces and established camps on the north, east and west of the city, leaving only the approaches to the south gate open. Every day he attacked, at the same time urging the mountain stronghold to send grain and fodder for a long siege. He was determined to break into Darning and rescue Magnate Lu and Shi Xiu. Every day Li Cheng and Wen Da came out with soldiers and gave battle, but they were unable to win. Suo Chao was recuperating from his arrow wound, which had not yet healed.

Wang Ding and the other two riders arrived at the residency of the premier with the private letter and dismounted. The keeper of the gate went in and reported. The premier directed that Wang Ding be allowed to enter. Wang went directly to the rear hall, kowtowed and presented the message. Premier Cai Jing opened the letter and read it. Shocked, he closely questioned Wang Ding. The emissary related the story of Lu Junyi in detail, adding, "Song Jiang has surrounded the city with a huge force of bandits. We can't cope with them." He told also of the murderous battles at Yu Family Hamlet, Locust Tree Slope and Flying-Tiger Valley.

"You've had a tiring ride," said Cai. "Go to the government hostel and rest. I must hold a conference of officials."

"The Northern Capital is in a terrible dilemma, Your Excellency. It faces disaster. If it should fall, what will happen to the rest of Hebei Province? We hope Your Excellency will send troops quickly and destroy the rebels!"

"No need to say any more. You may go."

Wang Ding withdrew. The premier at once directed his officer of the day to summon the Chancellor of Military Affairs to an urgent conference on a military matter of the utmost importance. Shortly thereafter, Tong Guan, the Chancellor, accompanied by three marshals, arrived at the hall of state and presented themselves to the premier. Cai Jing told them in detail of the emergency in the Northern Capital.

"We need a plan, and a first-rate general, to drive off the marauding bandits and preserve the city," he said.

The assembled officers looked at one another with frightened expressions. From behind the infantry marshal a man stepped forward. A commander of the palace guards, his name was Xuan Zan. His face was as black as the bottom of pot, his nostrils were aimed at the sky, he had curly hair and a reddish beard. A massive fellow, he wielded a steel blade. His skill with weapons was out of the ordinary. Formerly married to the daughter of a prince, he had been known as the Ugly Son-in-Law. The prince, impressed by his winning several archery matches in a row, had given him his daughter in marriage. But Xuan Zan's ugliness had so revolted the girl that she died.

As a result he was held in low esteem and never rose above his rank of guards' commander. Tong Guan, a wily sycophant and courtier, considered himself infinitely superior, and treated him with contempt.

But at this moment Xuan Zan felt he had to speak, and he addressed the premier.

"I became friends with a man when I was in the rural areas. He is a direct descendant of Guan Yu, famed general at the end of the Han Dynasty, when the country split into three. His name is Guan Sheng, and he bears a striking resemblance to his noble ancestor. His weapon is a crescent-shaped halberd, and so people call him Guan Sheng the Big Halberd. He's now a, lowly patrol officer in Pudong, but he's studied books of military lore since childhood, is thoroughly versed in weaponry, and is a man. Of matchless valor. If he is presented with money and raised to senior officer rank, he can expunge the water-girt fortress and destroy the wild rebels. This man is essential to the preservation of our country and peace in our land. He awaits only your command."

Cai Jing was delighted. He appointed Xuan Zan his emissary to ride like a comet through the night to Pudong with an invitation to Guan Sheng to come to the capital and confer. The assembled officials withdrew.

Xuan Zan immediately set out, accompanied by four or five other horsemen. In less than a day they arrived at the headquarters of the Pudong patrol and dismounted. Guan Sheng was there, discussing the rise and fall of prominent figures in ancient and current times with his friend Hao Siwen. When he was informed that an emissary had come from the Eastern Capital, he went out with Hao to welcome him. Guan exchanged courtesies with his caller and invited him into the hall and asked him to be seated.

"We haven't seen each other in a long time," said Guan. "What brings you all this distance today?"

"The Mount Liangshan bandits are attacking the Northern Capital. I've told the premier that you had a strategy for keeping the country tranquil, and a skill capable of destroying all enemy officers and troops. By imperial decree, and on orders of the premier, I bring you these gifts of money and satins and a fine saddle, and request you to set forth. You mustn't refuse, brother. Get your things together and we'll start for the capital."

Guan Sheng was extremely pleased. "This is Hao Siwen," he said. "He and I are sworn brothers. His mother dreamed she was entered by the spirit of a wild dog shortly before she became pregnant with Hao. And so, today, he is known as Wild Dog Hao. He's skilled in all eighteen of the military arts. Since I've been summoned by the premier, why shouldn't I take him with me, so that we can serve the country together?" Xuan Zan gladly consented. He urged them to commence the journey quickly.

Guan Sheng gave parting instructions to his family, collected his weapons, horse, helmet, armor and luggage, and set out that same night with Hao and a dozen big fellows from West of the Pass, all accompanying Xuan Zan. On reaching the Eastern Capital, they rode directly to the premier's residency and dismounted. The keeper of the gate announced them and they were invited in. Xuan Zan led Guan Sheng and Hao Siwen to the hall of state. They kowtowed to the premier, then stood respectfully at the foot of the dais.

Premier Cai Jing looked Guan Sheng over. He saw a tall, powerfully built man with a fine beard divided into three strands, eyebrows that extended to his sideburns, eyes turned up at the corners, a face as ruddy as jujubes, and crimson lips. Cai was very pleased.

"How old are you, officer?" he asked.

"Thirty-two, sir."

"Bandits from Liangshan Marsh have surrounded the Northern Capital. Tell me, please, do you have any good plan for breaking the siege?"

"I heard a long time ago that those bandits have taken over the Marsh and prey on the people and raid the towns. Now they've dared to leave their lair and seek their own destruction. It would be a waste of energy merely to relieve the Northern Capital. If you will give me an army of crack troops, I'll first take Mount Liangshan, then capture the bandits. Thus, neither of their forces will be able to help the other."

Cai Jing was delighted. "Besieging the kingdom of Wei to relieve the kingdom of Zhao—the strategy used in ancient days! Exactly what I was thinking." He directed the Council of Military Affairs to muster fifteen thousand crack soldiers from the provinces of Shandong and Hebei, and let Hao Siwen lead the vanguard and Xuan Zan the rear contingent, with Guan Sheng in over-all command. Duan Chang the infantry marshal was given charge of grain and fodder supplies. The premier highly rewarded the three new commanders and set a date at which they were to proceed directly and in force against Liangshan Marsh.

But the dragon's home is the sea; it cannot ride the mist and clouds. The tiger on the unfamiliar plain cannot fully use its teeth and claws. Truly, while gazing longingly at the autumn moon one can easily lose the glowing jewel in its casket.

What finally befell the forces of Song Jiang? Read our next chapter if you would know.

CHAPTER 64

HUYAN ZHUO DECEIVES GUAN SHENG ON A MOONLIT NIGHT

SONG JIANG CAPTURES SUO CHAO ON A SNOWY DAY

Guan Sheng took his leave of the premier and assumed command of the fifteen thousand men. He divided them into three contingents and, with them, left the Eastern Capital, heading for Liangshan Marsh.

Meanwhile, Song Jiang and his commanders attacked the Northern Capital every day. Li Cheng and Wen Da dared not come out and confront them. Suo Chao's arrow wound had not yet healed. There was no one to fight.

Song Jiang was unable to crack the city. He grew morose. They had been away from the mountain stronghold for some time, but victory remained elusive. Sitting gloomily in his tent one night, he lit a candle and started to read over the Heavenly Books given him by the Mystic Queen. It struck him as odd that no army had been sent to relieve the long besieged city. And why hadn't Dai Zong, whom he had dispatched to the mountain fortress, returned? Song Jiang's mind was troubled. He could neither eat nor rest.

A junior officer came in and said: "The Military Advisor is here." Wu Yong entered the central tent.

"We've been surrounding the Northern Capital for quite a while. Why hasn't any army been sent to its rescue?" he queried. "And no one comes out to do battle. We know that three horsemen had left the city. Governor Liang must have dispatched emissaries to the Eastern Capital to report the emergency. Surely Premier Cai, his father-in-law, would send an army under an able general to his rescue. Could they be using the 'besieging Wei to relieve Zhao strategy'? Instead of relieving this place, they could be attacking our Mount Liangshan stronghold. That must be it. You've good cause for worry. We should call in our forces, but not withdraw all."

Just then Dai Zong the Marvellous Traveller arrived. He reported to Song Jiang. "The premier has engaged the services of Guan Sheng the Big Halberd, direct descendant of the immortalized Guan Yu. He's leading an army in a raid on Mount Liangshan. The chieftains in our fortress don't know what to do. They hope you, brother, and the military advisor will return with our forces quickly and come to their aid."

"Even so," cautioned Wu Yong, "we mustn't be too hasty. Tonight, we'll have the infantry withdraw first. But we'll leave two cavalry units in ambush on both sides of Flying-Tiger Valley. When they learn in the city that we're pulling out, they'll certainly chase us. This is the plan we must follow. Otherwise, our army will fall into disorder."

"You've spoken well, Military Advisor," said Song Jiang.

He ordered Hua Rong to place five hundred troops in hiding on the left side of the valley, and Lin Chong to conceal another five hundred on the right. Huyan Zhuo he directed to take twenty-five horsemen and Ling Zhen to set up some artillery about a dozen *li* from the city. When the pursuing soldiers came out they were to fire their cannon. This would be the signal for the troops lying in ambush to close in for the kill.

At the same time, Song Jiang's forward contingent would pull back, with dragging banners and muffled drums, like drifting clouds after rain, like retreating troops who refused to fight.

The infantry rose in the middle of the night and began marching away, in order of their units. Not until early the next morning did the bugles sound for a general withdrawal.

All this was observed from atop the city walls—the dragging banners, the shouldered halberds and axes, the obvious intent to return to the mountains, the noisy bustle, the dismantling of the camps. The news was reported to Governor Liang.

"The Liangshan Marsh army has called in its troops. They're all leaving."

Governor Liang summoned Li Cheng and Wen Da.

"Evidently the premier has sent an army to capture their Mount Liangshan," said Wen Da, "and the knaves are afraid of losing their lair, so they're rushing to get back. This is our chance to slaughter them and nab Song Jiang."

Before the words were out of his mouth, a mounted messenger arrived with a directive from the Eastern Capital to join in exterminating the bandits. Pursue them, it said, if they retreat. Governor Liang promptly ordered Li Cheng and Wen Da to lead two contingents and harry Song Jiang's forces from the east and the west.

At the head of the withdrawing units, Song Jiang observed the soldiers pouring out of the city to give chase. He and his men moved quickly, as if their lives depended on it. Li Cheng and Wen Da pursued, straight to the side of Flying-Tiger Valley. Then cannon boomed behind them.

Li Cheng and Wen Da, startled by the blast, reined in their horses and looked. To their rear they saw a bristling array of banners and heard the wild thunder of battle drums. It was completely unexpected. Then five hundred men under Hua Rong, and an equal number under Lin Chong, surged towards them from left and right in a murderous charge.

It was too late to take defensive action. The government commanders knew they had been tricked, and led a full speed retreat. They ran right into a troop of cavalry, under Huyan Zhuo, which slaughtered them savagely. Li Cheng and Wen Da, their helmets gone, their armor in shreds, fled back to the city and bolted the gates.

Song Jiang's troops resumed their orderly withdrawal. As they neared Liangshan Marsh, they found Xuan Zan the Ugly Son-in-Law blocking their road. Song Jiang directed his army to halt and make camp. At the same time he sent a messenger secretly across the river and up the mountain with an order for relief units both by land and by water.

Inside the stronghold, Zhang Heng the Boat Flame, chieftain of the water forces, said to his brother Zhang Shun, White Streak in the Waves: "We haven't performed any meritorious deeds since coming here. Now Guan Sheng the Big Halberd of Pudong is attacking our fortress in three columns. Why don't we two raid his camp, capture him, and cover ourselves with glory? Then we'll be able to hold our heads up before our brothers."

"Our only job is to command these water forces," said Zhang Shun. "If we don't relieve a brother unit in danger, people will laugh at us."

"Don't be so finicky, otherwise we'll never distinguish ourselves. If you don't want to, that's up to you. Tonight, I'm going."

All Zhang Shun's pleas were to no avail. That night Zhang Heng put four or five men each on more than fifty boats. They were garbed for a stealthy raid, and carried bamboo spears and short daggers. Moonlight shone faintly on the cold dew. It was very still, around the second watch, when the small craft reached the shore.

Guan Sheng was in the central tent, reading by the light of a lamp. A junior officer on sentry duty came in quietly and reported: "Forty or fifty small boats have entered the reeds. The men on them are armed with spears. They're hiding there on both sides. We don't know what they're up to."

Guan Sheng smiled coldly. He turned to the commanding officer and whispered a few words.

Zhang Heng, leading between two and three hundred men, advanced on tiptoe from the reeds to the edge of camp. They pushed aside the pronged barriers, and continued directly to the center of headquarters. They saw in a tent Guan Sheng stroking his beard as he read beside a lamp.

Happily, Zhang Heng charged into the tent, spear in hand. At once gongs crashed and soldiers yelled, raising a terrible din. It sounded as if heaven and earth were falling, mountains and rivers collapsing. From four sides the soldiers in ambush spewed forth. Not one of the three hundred or so raiders got away. They were bound and pushed before the general's tent.

Guan Sheng looked them over and laughed. "Lawless rebels, petty scoundrels! Dare you come here and insult me?" He had Zhang Heng confined in a prisoner's cart. As to the others, he put them in jail, intending to deliver the lot to the capital after he had captured Song Jiang.

At this time the three Ruan brothers, in the fort by the waterside, were considering sending to Song Jiang for instructions. Zhang Shun came in.

"Although I begged him not to," he said, "my brother raided Guan Sheng's camp. He was caught and put in a prisoner's cart."

Ruan the Seventh uttered an exclamation. "We're all in this to the death, together through thick and thin. He's your flesh and blood brother. How could you let him be captured? If you don't rescue him, we Ruan brothers will!"

"I don't dare make a move without orders," said Zhang Shun.

"While you're waiting they'll chop him into mincemeat," cried Seventh.

"That's right," Second and Fifth agreed.

Zhang Shun couldn't convince them otherwise. He was forced to agree.

That night, at the fourth watch, all the chieftains of the water forces, large and small, were put in command of a hundred or more craft. Rapidly, they set sail for Guan Sheng's camp. To the sentry on the shore they looked like a swarm of ants. As they neared the bank, he hurriedly reported to the Big Halberd.

"Stupid thieving slaves," laughed Guan Sheng. He again whispered instructions to his commanders.

With the three Ruan brothers in the lead and Zhang Shun bringing up the rear, the yelling raiders charged into the camp. But not an enemy was in sight. Startled, the Ruan brothers turned to leave. Gongs crashed before the tents. From left and right government infantry and cavalry, in eight columns, closed in like giant scoops and dustpans.

Quickly alert to the danger, Zhang Shun dived into the water. The three Ruan brothers rushed along the path for the shore. Their pursuers caught up, and hooked poles snaked out and nooses flew, catching the Devil Incarnate Ruan the Seventh and dragging him away. Second, Fifth and Zhang Shun were rescued by Turbulent River Dragon Li Jun, Tong Wei and Tong Meng at the risk of their own lives.

The naval forces informed Mount Liangshan what had happened. Liu Tang told Zhang Shun to go by water directly to Song Jiang's camp and report. Song Jing conferred with Wu Yong. How were they to drive back Guan Sheng?

"The coming battle will be decisive. On it victory or defeat will depend," said Wu Yong.

Before the words were out of his mouth, they heard battle drums thundering. Xuan Zan the Ugly Son-in-Law was leading his three contingents in a frontal assault. Song Jiang and his forces advanced to meet them. Xuan Zan appeared beneath an arch of pennants and reined in his horse.

"Who will go forth and seize that rogue?" cried Song Jiang.

Hua Rong promptly clapped his steed and attacked, holding his lance. Xuan Zan met him with whirling blade. Back and forth they fought, up and down the field, for ten full rounds. Hua Rong executed a feint, turned his mount and rode away. Xuan Zan pursued and began to catch up. Hua Rong set his steel lance in the rings of his saddle and took out his bow and arrow. Twisting around, he extended his powerful arms and released the feathered shaft. Xuan Zan heard the twang of the bow and, as the arrow sped towards him, raised his weapon. It pinged off the blade.

Hua Rong notched a second arrow to his string. His foe was closer now. He aimed at his chest and let fly. Xuan Zan ducked low over his stirrups, and the missile whizzed past. But the Ugly Son-in-Law was thoroughly impressed with his marksmanship. Abandoning the chase, he pulled his steed around and galloped back towards his position. Hua Rong wheeled his horse and pursued. As he narrowed the gap between them, Hua Rong winged a third arrow at Xuan Zan's back. It clanged against protective armor and bounced off.

Xuan Zan raced to his position and sent a messenger to Guan Sheng to report what had happened. The Big Halberd immediately called for his battle charger. He grasped his sword, mounted, and rode to the front, emerging beneath the arch of pennants.

Song Jiang commented quietly to Wu Yong on Guan Sheng's noble appearance. Turning to his chieftains, he said: "A heroic general, worthy of his fame!"

Lin Chong was angered by this remark. He said: "We brothers have fought sixty or seventy engagements since coming to Liangshan Marsh, and always with honor. Such a comparison reflects on our prestige!" He rode out at Guan Sheng, lance extended.

The Big Halberd shouted: "Swamp bandits, how dare you rebel against the imperial court! I challenge Song Jiang alone to a battle to the death!"

Song Jiang, from beneath his side's arch of pennants called Lin Chong to stop, and himself rode forth. He bowed to Guan Sheng.

"I am Song Jiang, a petty functionary from the town of Yuncheng," he said. "I respectfully present myself so that the general may criticise my shortcomings."

"A small official like you—how dare you rebel against the throne?"

"His Majesty has been deluded. He's given power to corrupt ministers and officials who harm the people. My brothers and I seek only to perform righteous deeds for Heaven and emperor. We have no evil intent."

"The emperor's soldiers are here before you, and you still resist! Your smooth talk can fool no one. Dismount and surrender, or I'll pound you to mincemeat!"

Qin Ming the Thunderbolt was infuriated. Brandishing his wolf-toothed cudgel, he sprang into the saddle and rushed forward. The Big Halberd galloped out to meet him. Lin Chong, afraid he would lose a chance to distinguish himself in combat, also flew to attack Guan Sheng. The three battled savagely in a cloud of dust like revolving figures on a carrousel lantern.

Song Jiang was concerned lest they injure Guan Sheng. He ordered the buglers to blow recall. Lin Chong and Qin Ming returned to the position.

"We were about to grab the lout," they said. "Why did you call us back and halt the battle?"

"Brothers," said Song Jiang, "we fight in righteous self-defense. We never use our strength against the weak. If it took two of you to capture him, he wouldn't acknowledge it as a fair defeat, and people would laugh at us. I consider him a courageous general, an able, loyal statesman, a descendant of an immortalized ancestor. If he would consent to go up the mountain, I'd gladly relinquish my place to him."

The two chieftains were very dissatisfied. That day, both sides withdrew their forces.

Guan Sheng, returning to his camp, dismounted and removed his armor. "I couldn't hold out against those two commanders. It was plain I was about to lose," he mused. "But Song Jiang called them back. I wonder why?" He directed that Zhang Heng and Ruan the Seventh be brought to him in their prisoner carts, and he questioned them:

"Song Jiang was only a petty functionary in Yuncheng. Why do you fellows support him?"

"Our brother is famed throughout Shandong and Hebei," Ruan the Seventh retorted. "He's called the Timely Rain and the Defender of Chivalry. A crude oaf like you wouldn't know that!"

Guan Sheng, with lowered head, did not reply. He ordered that the carts be taken away.

He brooded in his tent that night, unable to sleep or rest. He walked out and gazed at the moonlit sky. Frost covered the ground. Guan Sheng sighed. A scout approached him and reported.

"A bearded commander, riding alone and carrying only a whip, wishes to see you."

"Did you ask him who he is?"

"He bears no armor or weapons. He won't give his name. He says only that he wants to speak to the commander-in-chief."

"Very well. Bring him to me."

The man was escorted to Guan Sheng's tent. He looked vaguely familiar in the lamplight. Guan Sheng asked him who he was.

"Please dismiss your attendants."

Guan Sheng laughed. "If a general of a great army isn't of one heart and mind with his troops, how can he command them? In headquarters or out, high rank or low, we all know how to keep secrets. You can speak freely."

"My name is Huyan Zhuo. I was formerly the commander of the imperial linked-up cavalry which attacked Liangshan Marsh. But I was deceived by a bandit trick and lost the initiative. I was unable to return and report to the emperor. When I heard that you had come, General, I was overjoyed. On the battlefield this morning Song Jiang saw that Lin Chong and Qin Ming were about to capture you, and he called them back before they could do you an injury. He's long had the desire to surrender, but his bandits don't agree. He and I have conferred secretly on a way to compel them. If you are willing, General, tomorrow night take a light bow and short arrows, ride a swift horse along a small path into the bandits' camp, and seize Lin Chong and other brigand chieftains. Then you can turn them over to the authorities in the capital. Not only will you be performing a great deed, but Song Jiang and I will have our crimes forgiven."

Very pleased, Guan Sheng invited Huyan Zhuo to drink. Huyan told him that Song Jiang's main concern was loyalty to the emperor, and that it was unfortunate he had become involved with brigands. Guan Sheng stroked his beard and poured wine. The two spoke freely and without suspicion.

The next day, Song Jiang again mustered his forces to do battle.

Guan Sheng said to Huyan Zhuo: "Tonight, we'll put our plan into operation. But first we must defeat some of their top commanders."

Huyan donned some borrowed armor, mounted, and rode with the Big Halberd to the field of battle. The moment he set eyes on him, Song Jiang cried: "I never gave you an iota less than your due. Why did you steal away in the night?"

"Knavish bandits," Huyan replied. "You'll never amount to anything!"

Song Jiang ordered Huang Xin the Suppressor of the Three Mountains to fight him. Grasping his death-dealing sword, Huang vaulted into the saddle and rode against Huyan. The chargers met and the contestants battled. They had fought less than ten rounds when Huyan raised one of his rods and knocked Huang to the ground. Song Jiang's men rushed onto the field and carried Huang back. Delighted, Guan Sheng commanded all three contingents to attack and annihilate the foe.

"Don't do that," Huyan urged. "That knave Wu Yong is sure to have some scheme. If we pursue, we'll fall into their trap."

Guan Sheng immediately recalled his troops, and they returned to camp. In the central tent, he treated Huyan to wine and asked about Huang Xin the Suppressor of the Three Mountains.

"He originally was an important official in the imperial court and a district commander in Qingzhou Prefecture. He and Qin Ming and Hua Rong became brigands at the same time. Killing that bandit today has taken the edge off their prestige. When we slip into their camp tonight we're sure to succeed."

Guan Sheng was very pleased. He ordered that Xuan Zan and Hao Siwen head two columns as reinforcements. He himself would command a unit of five hundred cavalry armed with light bows and short arrows. Huyan Zhuo would lead the way. They would set out at the second watch, and by the third reach the middle of Song Jiang's camp.

At the boom of a signal cannon they would attack simultaneously from within and without.

The moonlight was as bright as day. At dusk they had put on their armor and removed the bells from their horses' bridles. The soldiers were equipped for stealthy action. When they mounted, each man gripped a short stick in his teeth to ensure silence. Huyan led the way and the others followed.

For half a watch they travelled a mountain path. Forty or fifty soldiers who had been lying in concealment rose up by the side of the road. "Is that you, General Huyan?" a low voice asked.

"No talking," Huyan snapped. "Follow behind my horse."

He rode on ahead, with Guan Sheng in his rear. They proceeded through a mountain gap. Huyan pointed with his lance. A red lamp glowed in the distance.

Guan Sheng reined in his steed. "What place is that?"

"Song Jiang's central army." Huyan urged on his horse.

As they neared the red lamp a cannon boomed. Guan Sheng and his cavalry charged. But when they reached the lamp, there wasn't a soul in sight, and Huyan had disappeared. Guan Sheng, startled, realized he had been tricked. Hastily, he pulled his mount around. On the surrounding hills, drums pounded and gongs crashed. Scrambling for any escape path, the soldiers fled for their lives. Guan Sheng galloped away, followed only by a few other riders.

They hurried through the mountain gap. On the edge of the grove behind them again a cannon boomed. Hooked poles shot out from every side and dragged Guan Sheng from his saddle. His weapon and horse were taken, he was stripped of his armor, and pushed and jostled into the main camp. Lin Chong and Hua Rong and a troop of horsemen cut off Hao Siwen. Attacked by the two chieftains, Hao fought them twenty or thirty rounds. He felt his strength ebbing and turned to flee. From obliquely behind him the girl warrior Ten Feet of Steel hotly pursued. She snared him with a crimson noose and dragged him from his steed. Brigand infantry rushed forward, grabbed him, and hauled him to the main camp.

In the meanwhile, Qin Ming and Sun Li, out after Xuan Zan with a troop of cavalry, ran into him on the road.

Xuan Zan rode forward. "Wretched bandits," he fumed. "Who resists me dies, who avoids me lives!"

Qin Ming was furious. He spurred his mount forward, brandishing his wolf-toothed cudgel, riding full tilt towards Xuan Zan. The chargers met and the contestants battled several rounds. Then Sun Li began closing in from the side. Xuan Zan grew flurried, he lost his old skill. He was knocked from his saddle by Qin Ming's cudgel. The three brigand contingents cheered. They rushed over and seized him.

While all this was going on, Li Ying the Heaven Soaring Eagle was raiding Guan Sheng's camp with a large force and rescuing Zhang Heng, Ruan the Seventh and the other captured naval brigands. They also seized a quantity of grain, fodder and horses, and induced many of the defeated foe to surrender.

At dawn Song Jiang and his forces returned to the mountain. The east was gradually turning light when he and his chieftains seated themselves according to rank in Loyalty Hall. Guan Sheng, Xuan Zan and Hao Siwen were brought in. Song Jiang hastily came down, ordered the guards back and personally untied them. He seated Guan Sheng in the central chair of the highest leader and kowtowed.

"This lowly criminal has accidentally offended against Your Excellency's authority," he said humbly. "I beg forgiveness."

Huyan Zhuo also came forward. "I was acting under orders and could not refuse. I pray you, General, excuse my presumptuous behavior."

Guan Sheng was nonplussed by the chivalrous attitude of the chieftains. He turned to Xuan Zan and Hao Siwen. "We're here as captives. What shall we do?"

The two replied: "Whatever you decide, General."

"We've no face to return to the capital," said Guan Sheng. "We ask only an early death."

"Why talk like that?" said Song Jiang. "If you don't scorn us as too insignificant, why not join us in performing righteous deeds on Heaven's behalf? Of course, if you'd rather not, we won't keep you. We'll send you back to the capital today."

"People call you Song Jiang the Loyal and Righteous, and you're certainly worthy of your name,, A man must requite the friend who understands him. Since we can no longer return home or to our posts, we'll gladly serve as ordinary soldiers under your command."

Song Jiang was delighted. He had a big feast of celebration laid that day, and sent men out to assure the scattered government troops of good treatment if they surrendered. Six or seven thousand responded. The remainder were allowed to go. Of the soldiers who capitulated, those who had families were given some silver and permitted to return home. Xue Yong, dispatched with a letter to Pudong, was instructed to fetch Guan Sheng's family to the stronghold. Of that we'll say no more.

During the feast, Song Jiang suddenly remembered Lu Junyi the Magnate and Shi Xiu, still incarcerated in the Northern Capital, and tears came to his eyes.

"Don't feel badly," said Wu Yong. "I have a plan. Muster our troops and attack Darning tonight. We're sure to succeed."

Guan Sheng rose and said: "As thanks for your not having killed me, I would like to march in the forward echelon."

Song Jiang was very pleased. The next morning he instructed that Xuan Zan and Hao Siwen's original troops be restored to them and that they serve as the forward unit's vanguard. Not one of the captured commanders was unwilling to join in the attack on the Northern Capital. Li Jun and Zhang Shun were directed to follow up with armored naval forces. All set forth in the order prescribed.

In the city Governor Liang was drinking with Suo Chao to celebrate his recovery from his wound. The sky was dull, and the wind howled. A cavalry scout entered and reported.

"Guan Sheng, Xuan Zan and Hao Siwen and their men have been captured by Song Jiang, and have joined his band. The Liangshan Marsh army will reach here today."

Governor Liang goggled, his mouth agape. Goblets toppled, chopsticks fell.

"Those bandits gave me an arrow wound," said Suo Chao. "Now I can get my revenge!"

Liang rewarded him with warm wine and directed him to lead city soldiers against the foe. He ordered Li Cheng and Wen Da to follow with reinforcements.

It was mid-winter and the weather was cold. For days the sky had been overcast with red clouds. A strong wind howled and moaned. Suo Chao marched to Flying-Tiger Valley and made camp.

The next day Song Jiang, with Lu Fang and Guo Sheng, mounted a bluff to watch Guan Sheng fight. Three times the big drums sounded, and Guan Sheng rode onto the field. At the opposite end Suo Chao appeared on horseback. He didn't recognize Guan Sheng.

An aide said: "That's Guan Sheng the Big Halberd who's just gone over to the rebels."

Suo Chao silently gripped his lance and rode at his opponent. Guan Sheng clapped his horse and galloped to meet him, brandishing his sword. The two had fought less than ten rounds when Li Cheng intervened. He had been watching from the government's central contingent and saw that Suo Chao's play with axes could never defeat Guan Sheng. Flourishing his blade, he joined in the assault.

Xuan Zan and Hao Siwen moved in with their weapons to help the Big Halberd. Now five horsemen were involved. Song Jiang on the bluff pointed with his whip. His entire army rolled into action. Li Cheng's soldiers suffered a crushing defeat. Severely mauled, they retreated into the city that night and barred the gates. Song Jiang's troops chased them to the foot of the walls, then made camp nearby.

The next day Suo Chao again surged out with a contingent of government soldiers. Wu Yong instructed his field officers to go through the motions of putting up a fight, but to retreat if the enemy advanced. Suo Chao, fooled by this display, returned to the city triumphant.

In the evening the clouds massed and the wind was fierce. When Wu Yong came out of his tent, it was snowing heavily. He dispatched infantry to a narrow stretch between a stream and a hillside and had them dig a pit, cover it over and conceal it with earth. That night the snow continued to fall. The next morning everything was covered with a white mantle two feet thick.

To the watchers on the city wall Song Jiang's forces looked frightened. They seemed to keep shifting from one position to another. Suo Chao, seeing this, mustered three hundred cavalry and sallied forth.

The outlaws scattered and withdrew. Song Jiang directed naval chieftains Li Jun and Zhang Shun to go lightly armed towards the foe. Restraining their mounts, lances athwart, when they neared Suo Chao they cast their weapons aside and fled in the direction of the pit, with Suo Chao in hot pursuit. An impatient man, he threw caution to the winds.

Here the path ran close to the stream. Li Jun abandoned his steed and leaped into the water. He swam forward. "Brother Song Jiang, run!" he yelled.

Suo Chao galloped recklessly across the narrow stretch. On the hillside behind a cannon boomed, and startled horse and rider tumbled into the trap. Brigands who had been hiding immediately swarmed around. Even if Suo Chao had three heads and six arms he couldn't have warded off the seven injuries and eight wounds inflicted upon him.

Truly, deep silvery snow concealed a snare, beneath ivory jade flakes a pit trap lay.

What was in store for Suo Chao the Urgent Vanguard? Read our next chapter if you would know.

CHAPTER 65

TOWER-SHIFTING HEAVENLY KING APPEARS IN A DREAM AS A SPIRIT

ON THE WATER WHITE STREAK IN THE WAVES GETS HIS REVENGE

Suo Chao was seized. The remainder of his cavalry fled back to the city and reported that he had been captured. Governor Liang was panic stricken. He ordered his commanders to defend the city, but not go forth to give battle. He considered executing Lu Junyi and Shi Xiu, but was afraid of angering Song Jiang. The capital could not rush support troops to him in an emergency and he might only get into deeper trouble. He therefore kept the two in prison and sent a dispatch to the capital that he was awaiting instructions from the premier.

Song Jiang returned to camp and seated himself in his central army tent. The outlaws who had caught Suo Chao brought him before Song Jiang's standard. Very pleased, Song Jiang ordered his men back, and personally untied the prisoner. He invited him into the tent and served him wine.

"Take a look at my brother chieftains here. More than half were once imperial military officers," he said comfortingly. "Because the emperor has been deluded and permits corrupt officials to hold power and harm the people, they have all volunteered to help me act on Heaven's behalf. If you don't scorn us, General, join our cause of righteous loyalty."

Yang Zhi came forward and paid his respects. He told Suo Chao what had happened since they parted. Clasping hands, they wept. The situation being what it was, Suo Chao had no choice but to submit. Song Jiang was pleased. That night, they drank in the tent in celebration.

The next morning they discussed how to take the city. But assaults several days in a row produced no results. Song Jiang was depressed. As he sat alone in his tent that night, a strange wind suddenly rose, reducing the lamp flame to the size of a pea. A figure appeared in the shadows. Song Jiang raised his head and looked. Chao Gai the Heavenly King was standing hesitantly in the entrance way.

"Brother," he said to Song Jiang, "you still haven't gone back. What are you waiting for?"

Song Jiang was astounded. He quickly got up and asked: "Where have you come from, brother? I still haven't avenged your wrongful death, and I'm uneasy about it day and night. Nor have I performed the sacrificial rites. And so your spirit appears, to berate me."

"It isn't that," Chao Gai replied. "Step back a bit, brother. Your life aroma stifles me. I don't dare draw any closer. I have come especially to tell you this: You're due for a hundred days of blood aura calamity. Only an earthly fiend star south of the Yangzi can cure you. The best thing you can do is call in your troops, quickly."

Song Jiang sought clarification. He pressed forward and said: "You come as a spirit from the Nether World, brother. Tell me the whole truth."

But Chao Gai gave him a push, and he suddenly wakened, as if from a dream. He shouted for a junior officer to invite the Military Advisor. Wu Yong soon arrived. Song Jiang told him the strange thing that had transpired, and asked him to interpret the dream.

"So Chao the Heavenly King appeared as a spirit. That's something you can't ignore," said Wu Yong. "The weather is cold and the ground is frozen. Our forces can't stay here much longer. It would be better to return to the stronghold for the winter. When spring comes and the snow melts we can attack the city again. It will be time enough, then."

"What you say is correct. But Lu the Magnate and brother Shi Xiu are still languishing in jail. Every day must seem like a year, while they wait for us to rescue them. If we go back now, I'm afraid those scoundrels will kill them. It's a bad situation whether we stay or leave."

No decision was reached.

The next day Song Jiang was dispirited and weary, he ached all over, his head felt as if it was split by an ax, his body burned with fever. He lay down and couldn't get up. The chieftains all came in to see him.

"My back is hot and painful," he said.

They looked and found a red swelling as big as a griddle.

"It's either an ulcer or a carbuncle," Wu Yong proclaimed. "I read a medical book once that said green bean powder protects the heart and prevents poisons from entering. We'd better buy some and feed it to brother. If only we could get a doctor! But we'll never find one here, with a war going on."

White Streak in the Waves Zhang Shun thought of something. "When I lived on the Xunyang River my mother developed a backache, but no medicine seemed to help," he said. "Finally, we called in An Daoquan, a doctor of Jiankang District, and he cured her immediately. I later sent him some silver. Now, brother is so ill. That doctor is the only one who can treat him. Though the road is far and one can't travel very quickly, I'll hurry day and night and bring him here as fast as I can."

"In brother's dream Chao Gai told him he would have a hundred days of disaster, and that only an earthly fiend star south of the Yangzi could cure him. Could that man be the one?" Wu Yong wondered.

"If you know such a person, bring him to me, swiftly," Song Jiang begged. "Never mind the difficulties. This is the time to show your fraternal devotion. Travel day and night and fetch him. Save my life!"

Wu Yong gave Zhang Shun a hundred ounces of gold in leekstrip form to present to the doctor, plus thirty ounces of silver for travel expenses, and said: "Leave today. Come what may, bring him. Let nothing delay you. We're pulling up camp and returning to the fortress. Bring the doctor there. Be as quick as you can."

Zhang Shun said goodbye, shouldered his pack and set forth.

Wu Yong notified the chieftains to call in the troops and return to the stronghold. Song Jiang was transported on a cart. They left that same night. Having been caught in one ambush, the defenders in the Northern Capital guessed this was another trick, and didn't venture out.

Governor Liang, on hearing news of the departure, was at a loss.

Li Cheng and Wen Da said: "That knave Wu Yong is full of crafty schemes. We'd better remain here on the defensive, and not go after them."

As to Zhang Shun, he travelled day and night in his hurry to save Song Jiang. It was then the end of winter, and when it didn't rain it snowed. The road was hard going. But Zhang Shun pushed on, regardless.

When he reached the shore of the Yangzi, not a ferry boat was in sight. Zhang Shun groaned, but continued skirting the banks. Finally, he saw cookfire smoke rising from a cove of withered reeds.

"Boatman," he called, "bring your ferry and take me across."

The reeds rustled and a figure emerged. He was wearing a conical straw hat and a coir raincape. "Where do you wish to go?" he asked.

"I've urgent business in Jiankang. I'll pay you extra if you ferry me over."

"That's no problem. But it's late. When you get to the other side you won't find any place to sleep. You'd better rest on my boat. At the fourth watch, when the wind has died and the moon is bright, I'll take you across. You'll have to pay me a little more."

"What you say makes sense."

With the boatman, Zhang Shun entered the reeds. A small boat was moored to the bank. Beneath its canopy a thin youth huddled beside a fire. The boatman helped Zhang Shun aboard. Zhang went into the cabin, removed his wet clothes, and asked the youth to dry them over the fire. He opened his bundle, took out a quilt, wrapped himself in it, and lay down.

"Can you get any wine around here?" he called to the boatman. "It would be fine if you could buy some."

"There's no place that sells wine, but if you want rice I can give you a bowl."

Zhang Shun finished the rice, lay down and slept. For one thing he was weary from days of continuous travel, for another he was very careless. By the first watch he was sound asleep.

The thin youth who was warming his hands over the charcoal embers pointed pursed lips towards Zhang Shun. "Big brother," he said to the boatman, "have you had a look?"

The boatman circled around to the bundle on which Zhang's head was resting. He squeezed and felt hard metallic objects. He gestured with his hand. "Untie the boat. We'll do him in when we get to the middle of the river."

Parting the reeds, the youth leaped to the bank, loosed the mooring rope, jumped back aboard, and shoved off with a bamboo pole. Then he plied a creaking sweep oar and propelled the small craft to the river's center.

Softly the boatman bound Zhang Shun with ropes in the cabin, and brought out a cleaver from beneath the deck. Just then Zhang awoke and found his hands tied. He couldn't move. The boatman pressed him down and raised the big knife.

"Spare me, bold fellow, and I'll give you all my money!"

"I want your gold and silver, and I want your life as well!"

"Let me die in one piece and my ghost won't come back to haunt you!"

The boatman put down the cleaver and tossed Zhang Shun into the river. He opened the bundle and found a large amount of gold and silver. Frowning thoughtfully, he called the thin youth.

"Come here," he said. "I want to speak to you."

The youth entered the cabin. The boatman seized him with one hand and hacked him cruelly with the cleaver, bringing him to a sorry end. Then he pushed the body into the water, wiped up the blood-stains and rowed on.

Zhang Shun could stay under water for days. When he was thrown in, he sank down and gnawed open the ropes, then swam to the south bank. He saw a lamp gleaming in grove of trees. He climbed the bank and, dripping wet, entered the grove. Ahead was a rustic tavern. The proprietor had got up in the middle of the night and was pressing wine. The light of his lamp shone through a crack in the wall.

Pushing open the door, Zhang Shun saw an old man. He promptly kowtowed.

"Were you robbed on the river?" the old fellow asked. "And did you save your life by jumping into the water?"

"I wouldn't fool you, grandpa. I was on my way from Shandong to Jiankang on business and it was late. I found a ferry, but the two bad men on it robbed me of my clothes and money and threw me in. I'm a good swimmer, so I managed to escape. Grandpa, please help me."

The old man conducted him to the rear of the house, gave him a quilted coat, dried his wet clothes over the fire, and heated some wine for him to drink.

"What's your name?" he asked. "What's a Shandong man doing in these parts?"

"My family name is Zhang. Dr. An of Jiankang District is a close friend of mine. I've come to see him."

"In Shandong you must have passed Liangshan Marsh?"

"I went right by there."

"Song Jiang, the leader on that mountain, doesn't rob travellers or harm the people. He does only meritorious deeds on Heaven's behalf."

"He's loyal and righteous. He never attacks good persons, only corrupt officials."

"I've heard his band is truly righteous. They succor the poor and old, not like the knavish bandits we have here! Our people would be happy if he came. Then we wouldn't have to take any more abuse from crooked overlords."

"Don't be alarmed, grandpa, but I'm Zhang Shun the White Streak in the Waves. Brother Song Jiang has developed a carbuncle on his back, and I was sent with a hundred ounces of gold to invite Dr. An. But I was careless and fell asleep on the boat and those two scoundrels tied my hands and threw me in the river. I gnawed the ropes open and here I am."

"So you're a bold fellow from Mount Liangshan! I'll call my son. He'll want to meet you."

A young man shortly emerged from the rear. On seeing Zhang Shun, he bowed and said: "I've long known of your fame, brother, but never had the chance to meet you. My family name is Wang, and I'm the sixth in our line. Because my movements are swift, I'm called Lightning Wang Dingliu. I've always liked swimming and jousting with staves, but could never find a teacher who would accept me. I've been spending my days selling wine here on the banks of the river. I know those two who robbed you. One is Zhang Wang the River Blockade Demon. The thin young fellow, who is from Huating County, is called Oily Mudfish Sun the Fifth. Those villains are always robbing people on the river. Don't worry, brother. Stay here a few days. When the rascals come to drink, I'll avenge you."

"I appreciate your good intentions. But I'm very anxious about brother Song Jiang. I only wish I could fly back to the fortress in a single day! I must enter the city as soon as it's daylight and request Dr. An to go with me."

Wang Dingliu gave his own clothes to Zhang Shun, and feted him with chicken and wine. Of that, no more need be said.

The next morning the sky cleared and the snow vanished. Zhang Shun was given a dozen ounces of silver and escorted into Jiankang District. He went directly to the foot of Elm Tree Bridge and found Dr. An selling medicines in the doorway of his shop. Zhang Shun entered and kowtowed.

"It's been years, brother," the doctor said. "What wind blows you here?"

Zhang Shun followed him inside and related his adventures, from the trouble in Jiangzhou until he went with Song Jiang up the mountain. He said that the outlaw leader had developed a carbuncle on his back, and that he, Zhang, had been dispatched to fetch Dr. An. He apologized for not bringing a fee, but explained that he had been robbed and nearly lost his life on the river.

"I should go immediately, since it's Song Jiang the renowned fighter for righteousness," said the physician. "But my wife died and I've no one at home. I can't just walk off and leave everything."

Zhang Shun pleaded with him. "If you won't go, I can't return to the mountain."

"We'll discuss it again, later."

Only after much urging did Dr. An finally consent.

An spent a great deal of time with a local prostitute called Clever Pet Li. The doctor doted on her. That evening he took Zhang Shun to eat and drink at her place. Clever Pet hailed the young man respectfully as "brother."

After four or five cups, An was half drunk. He said to the girl: "I'll spend the night here. Tomorrow morning I'm off with this brother for Shandong. I'll be away from twenty days to a month. I'll come and see you when I get back."

"I don't want you to go! If you won't listen to me, stay away from my door!"

"My medicine kit is packed and I'm ready to go. I leave tomorrow. Cheer up. I won't be gone long."

In a childish tantrum the girl threw herself on An's chest. "If you don't listen to me, and go. I'll curse you till the flesh flies from your bones!"

White Streak in the Waves was infuriated by these goings-on. He wanted to swallow Clever Pet down in one gulp.

It was growing dark. An was very drunk by now. He staggered into the girl's room and collapsed on her bed.

"Go home," Clever Pet said to Zhang Shun. "There's no place for you to sleep here!"

"I'll wait till brother sobers up. We'll leave together."

Since she couldn't get rid of him, the girl put him in a small room near the front door.

Zhang Shun was burning with impatience. How could he sleep? Around the first watch he heard a knock on the door and peered out through a crack in the wall. He saw a man slip in and speak to the old bawd who tended Clever Pet.

"You haven't been around in a long time," she said. "Where have you been? Tonight, the doctor's sleeping drunk in her room. What can we do?"

"I've brought her ten ounces of gold. She can have them made into hairpins. You must do something, old mother, to get us together."

"Wait in my room. I'll call her."

Zhang Shun recognized the man in the light of the lamp. It was Zhang Wang the River Blockade Demon. He had come to spend on Clever Pet some of the wealth he had recently acquired on the river.

Zhang Shun could scarcely contain his rage. He continued to watch. He saw the old bawd carry food and wine into her room, then fetch Clever Pet. He wanted to dash in after her, but he was afraid he'd mess things up and the robber would get away.

By the third watch the two servants in the kitchen were also drunk. The old bawd, who had been reeling around, sat in an intoxicated stupor beneath the lamp. Zhang Shun softly opened the door of his room and tiptoed to the entry to the kitchen. He saw a gleaming cleaver lying on the oven and the old bawd sprawled in a drunken slumber on a bench with her head to one side.

He crept into the kitchen and picked up the cleaver. First he killed the old bawd. He wanted to destroy the two servants next. But the cleaver had not been sharp to begin with, and hacking the old woman had turned its edge. Then he caught sight of an ax for chopping kindling. He grabbed it. Before the servants could cry out, he finished them both with one blow each.

Clever Pet, hearing the noise, hurriedly opened the door of her room. She found herself confronted by Zhang Shun. He swung the ax and split her chest asunder.

Zhang Wang saw, by the light of the lamp, the girl fall dead. He pushed open the rear window, leaped over the wall, and escaped.

White Streak in the Waves was frantic, but there was nothing he could do about it. Recalling what Wu Song had done under similar circumstances, he tore a strip from the edge of his tunic, dipped it in the blood, and wrote on the wall: "The killer is An Daoquan." He wrote it in dozens of places.

Around the fifth watch, as dawn was breaking, he heard An wake from his drunken slumber and call Clever Pet.

"Don't shout, brother," said Zhang Shun. "There's something I want to show you."

An got up. When he saw the four bodies he was paralyzed with fright. He trembled uncontrollably.

"Brother," said Zhang Shun, "do you see what's written on the wall?"

"You're ruining me!"

"Only two roads are open to you. Either you raise a rumpus, and I leave, and you pay for the crimes with your life. Or, if you want nothing to come of this, you go home, get your medicine kit, and rush with me to Mount Liangshan and save my brother. Take your choice."

"You're too reckless!"

When it was daylight, Zhang Shun wrapped some money for travel expenses and escorted An home. The doctor knocked till someone opened the door. He collected his medicine kit and left the city with Zhang Shun. They went directly to Lightning Wang's tavern.

"Yesterday, Zhang Wang passed this way," the proprietor said. "Unfortunately, I didn't see you anywhere."

"I met him too, but I didn't take any action. I'm on an important mission. Who has time for petty vengeance!"

Before the words were out of Zhang Shun's mouth, Lightning Wang exclaimed: "Here he comes again!"

"Don't alarm him. See where he goes."

They watched while Zhang Wang went down to his craft by the shore. Wang Dingliu hailed him.

"Hey, brother Zhang, bring your boat over. Two relatives of mine want to cross."

"If they want to board my boat, they'll have to hurry."

Lightning told Zhang Shun.

"Brother An," Zhang Shun said to the doctor, "you and I must exchange clothes. That way, we can get on board."

"How?"

"I have an idea. Don't ask."

The two put on each other's garments. Zhang Shun tied a kerchief around his head, and over this a large conical straw hair which shadowed his face. Lightning carried the medicine kit on his back. They walked down towards the boat.

Zhang Wang brought the craft to the bank and the three men went aboard. Zhang Shun crept to the poop deck and lifted up the boards. The cleaver was still there. He took it and returned to the cabin.

Zhang Wang plied the creaking sweep oar and the vessel glided to the middle of the river. Zhang Shun removed his hat and upper garments.

"Boatman, come quick," he called. "This cabin has blood stains."

"Don't joke," said Zhang Wang.

Not realizing it was a trick, he stuck his head in. Zhang Shun wrapped his arms around the boatman's neck.

"Robber," he shouted. "Do you recognize the passenger you ferried that snowy night?"

Zhang Wang stared, speechless.

"You duped me out of a hundred ounces of yellow gold and tried to kill me! Where's that thin young man?"

"I didn't feel like sharing the money with him and I was afraid he'd argue. So I killed him and threw his body in the river."

"You robber! I was born on the banks of the Xunyang and raised at the foot of Little Melon Hill. I sold fish for a living. Everybody knew me! Because I raised a row in Jiangzhou I had to go to Liangshan Marsh and join Song Jiang. We marauded all over. Everybody feared me! You tricked me onto your boat, tied my hands, and threw me in the river. If I wasn't a good swimmer, I'd be dead! We meet today as enemies. I can't forgive you!"

He pulled the boatman into the cabin, trussed his hands behind his back and tied them to his ankles. Then he heaved him into the Yangzi, exclaiming: "I didn't cut you up, either!"

Lightning Wang sighed as the river robber sank beneath the waves. Zhang Shun found his gold pieces and wrapped them up.

The three men rowed for shore. Zhang Shun said to Wang Dingliu: "I'll never forget your chivalry, brother. If you don't scorn me, perhaps you and your father will dispose of the tavern and come to Mount Liangshan where we can seek righteousness together. What do you say?"

"Nothing would please me better!"

At that, they parted. Zhang Shun and Dr. An changed back into their own clothes and disembarked on the north shore. Lightning Wang bid them farewell and rowed the boat home. He packed his belongings and prepared to catch up.

The other two, carrying the medicine kit, started on their journey. An was a man of letters who had always been a doctor. He wasn't used to walking. After about thirty *li,* he was worn out. Zhang Shun invited him to an inn and bought wine. While they were drinking, a man entered and approached them.

"Why have you been so long, brother?" he exclaimed.

Zhang Shun looked up. It was Dai Zong the Marvellous Traveller, disguised as a merchant. Hurriedly, Zhang introduced him to An, then inquired about Song Jiang.

"He's only semi-conscious and can't eat or drink. He seems to be dying. The crisis will be soon."

Zhang Shun wept, but An queried: "How is his complexion?"

"Haggard. He groans constantly. The pain never stops. I don't think he can last much longer."

"If he still feels pain, I can cure him. I'm only afraid I won't reach him in time."

"That's easy," said Dai Zong. He affixed two charms to An's legs and shouldered the medicine kit. "You come at your own pace," he said to Zhang Shun. "I'll go on ahead with the doctor."

Dai and An left the inn. Using the marvellous travel method, they sped off.

Zhang Shun remained at the inn for another two or three days. Sure enough, Lightning Wang, carrying their luggage, arrived with his father.

Delighted, Zhang Shun said: "I've been waiting for you."

"Dr. An?" asked Wang.

"Dai Zong the Marvellous Traveller came here to meet me. He's gone off with the doctor."

Lightning Wang, his father, and Zhang Shun left together for Liangshan Marsh.

Dai and An, using the marvellous travel method, reached Mount Liangshan the same night. Chieftains, big and small, welcomed them and led them to Song Jiang's bedside. He was scarcely breathing.

But Dr. An, after taking his pulse, said: "You needn't worry, chieftains. His pulse is all right. Although his body is depressed, there's nothing very serious. I don't like to boast, but in ten days he'll recover."

The chieftains all kowtowed. An burned some artemisia over the carbuncle to draw out the poison, then applied a draw poultice externally and gave growth-stimulating medicines internally.

In five days the patient regained his rosy complexion, his flesh became tender, his appetite improved. Before ten days were up, although the wound wasn't completely closed, he was eating and drinking as usual.

Zhang Shun arrived with Lightning Wang and his father. After greeting Song Jiang and the chieftains, he told how he had been robbed and got his revenge, both times on the river.

"You nearly delayed brother Song Jiang's recovery," said the outlaw leaders with a sigh.

As soon as he was better, Song Jiang conferred with Wu Yong on how to attack the Northern Capital and rescue Lu Junyi the Magnate and Shi Xiu, as was their duty in chivalry. Dr. An had reservations.

"Your wound still isn't fully closed," he said. "You mustn't be too active. It interferes with the healing process."

Wu Yong added his own urgings. "Don't concern yourself about this, brother. It will only upset you. Just rest and regain your strength. I have no talents, but now that spring is here I definitely will crack open the Northern Capital, rescue Lu the Magnate and Shi Xiu, and capture the adulterers. We guarantee to avenge you."

"With you aiding me so solicitously, Military Advisor, though I die, I'll be able to close my eyes."

Wu Yong issued his orders in Loyalty Hall. And as a result the Northern Capital was turned into a fiery inferno, a forest of spears, and before the governor's residency lay a mountain of corpses, a sea of blood. Truly, his casual remarks caused demons to tremble in fear and gallant commanders to be overwhelmed with admiration.

What was the plan Military Advisor Wu Yong had evolved? Read our next chapter if you would know.

CHAPTER 66

SHI QIAN BURNS THE JADE CLOUD MANSION

WU YONG BY A RUSE TAKES DARNING CITY

"Fortunately, you're all right now, brother," Wu Yong said to Song Jiang. "Having Dr. An here treating your illness is a great blessing for our stronghold. While you were confined to bed, I frequently sent scouts into the Northern Capital to nose around. They say Governor Liang has got the jitters. He's afraid we're going to attack. I also had men put up proclamations in all the market places in and around the city assuring the ordinary people that they would not be harmed. We say that each wrong has its avenger and every debt has its creditor, and promise that when our army enters Darning we'll seek out only certain specific enemies. The result is that Governor Liang is more worried than ever. Premier Cai in the Eastern Capital has heard that Guan Sheng has come over to us, but he doesn't dare mention this in the presence of the emperor. Cai favors giving us amnesty and official posts. He feels that will solve everything. He keeps writing to Governor Liang, urging him to spare the lives of Lu the Magnate and Shi Xiu as a sign of conciliation."

On hearing this, Song Jiang wanted to go down the mountain immediately and attack the Northern Capital. Wu Yong had another idea.

"It's now the lunar New Year and the Lantern Festival Day is rapidly approaching," he said. "It's the custom in the Northern Capital to put on a big display of lanterns. I'd like to take this opportunity to slip some men into the city, first, then attack. Coordinating inside and out, we can break through the defenses."

Song Jiang agreed. "Please work out the details," he said to the brigand commanders.

"The most important thing is to set a blaze inside the city as a signal. Which of you brothers will venture to go in and do it?" Wu Yong queried.

A man walked up to the foot of the platform. "I will!" Everyone looked. It was Shi Qian, known as Flea on a Drum.

"I lived in the Northern Capital as a child," he said. "There's one big tavern called Jade Cloud Mansion. Upstairs and down it has well over a hundred rooms. It's bound to be very lively the night of the Lantern Festival Day. I'll sneak into the city before that, and on the fifteenth of the first lunar month I'll climb to the top of the building and light a signal fire. Then the Military Advisor can dispatch forces to raid the prison. That's the best way."

"Just what I was thinking," said Wu Yong. "Start down the mountain tomorrow at daybreak. At the first watch on Festival night, if you can set a fire on top of the Mansion you'll win a lot of credit."

Shi Qian promised to carry out his mission, and departed.

The next day Wu Yong ordered Xie Zhen and Xie Bao to disguise themselves as hunters and go into the city with presents of game for the officials. When they saw the signal fire on the night of the fifteenth they were to stand in front of the government office and stop any officer or soldier who tried to report it. The two consented and left.

Wu Yong then told Du Qian and Song Wan to assume the garb of rice merchants and push two barrows into the city and find quarters. The moment they saw the signal blaze on the fifteenth they were to seize the city's East Gate. They promised and departed.

He instructed Kong Ming and Kong Liang to disguise themselves as beggars. They were to sleep under the eaves of some building in the busiest section of the city. When they saw the fire on the Mansion, they were to hurry and lend a hand. The two consented and left.

Wu Yong directed Li Ying and Shi Jin to dress as travellers, and to put up at an inn outside the East Gate. On seeing the signal blaze they were to kill the soldiers guarding the gate, take it over, and keep it for a convenient exit. The two promised and departed.

He told Sagacious Lu and Wu Song to move into a temple outside the city in the guise of itinerant monks. At the signal they were to go to the South Gate and block the government troops attempting to charge out. They agreed and left.

Wu Yong ordered Zou Yuan and Zou Run to pretend to be lantern sellers and put up at an inn in the center of the city. When they saw the fire on the roof top they were to go to the front of the prison and support the raiders. The two promised and departed.

He told Liu Tang and Yang Xiong to disguise themselves as policemen and take rooms in front of prefectural headquarters. When they saw the signal fire they were to prevent anyone from going in to report it, and thus cut the connection between the municipal administration's head and its tail. The two consented and departed.

He directed the Taoist Gongsun Sheng to assume the garb of a wandering priest, with Ling Zhen disguised as his acolyte, move into a secluded part of the city with hundreds of fireworks, and set them off when they saw the signal blaze. They agreed and left.

Zhang Shun was to enter the city with Yan Qing through the water gate via the moat and seize the adulterers in the home of Lu the Magnate.

Stumpy Tiger Wang, Sun Xin, Zhang Qing, Ten Feet of Steel Hu, Mistress Gu and Sun the Witch were to be three country couples coming to see the lantern display. They were to set fire to Lu's house.

Chai Jin and Yue Ho, dressed as army officers, would go to the home of Cai the prison superintendent and demand that he guarantee the safety of the two prisoners.

When all these dispositions had been made, the chieftains set out upon their various missions. It was then the beginning of the first lunar month.

We'll speak not of the bold fellows who departed, one by one, down the mountain, but tell instead of Governor Liang, as he summoned Li Cheng, Wen Da, Prefect Wang, and other high officials for a conference.

"Every year we put on a big display of lanterns to celebrate the first full moon, and make merry with the populace just as they do in the Eastern Capital," said the Governor. "But the Liangshan Marsh bandits have raided us twice, recently. I'm afraid a lantern festival might attract trouble. I'm considering calling it off. How do you gentlemen feel about that?"

"I think the robbers have stealthily withdrawn," said Wen Da. "Those proclamations of theirs prove that they're at their wits' end. There's nothing else they can do. You needn't let them concern you, Excellency. If we don't have our lantern display this year and those varlets find out about it they're sure to sneer at us. I propose that you issue an edict calling for even more fancy lanterns and celebrations than last year, and construct two hills of lanterns in the center of the city, Follow the example of the Eastern Capital and celebrate the Lantern Festival for five full days, from the thirteenth to the seventeenth, inclusive, with revels all through the night. Have the prefect check to make sure that everyone takes part. You too must join, Excellency, and celebrate with the people. I'll lead a cavalry unit to Flying-Tiger Valley, and there guard against the bandits pulling any tricks. District Commander Li can patrol with his Iron Cavalry around the outskirts of the city, to ensure that the populace is not disturbed."

Governor Liang was pleased with this suggestion. After he and his officials had discussed and agreed upon it, he had public proclamations issued accordingly.

Darning, known as the Northern Capital, was the largest city in Hebei and a thriving metropolis. Merchants and traders flocked there in droves. When they heard there was to be a lantern festival, all came to take part.

On the streets and in the lanes, local officials daily inspected the preparations. Wealthy families vied with one another in their displays, travelling anywhere from one hundred to three hundred *li* to buy handsome and flowery lanterns. Many vendors brought lanterns to the city annually. Families built special sheds in front of their doors, where they hung up their best lanterns and set off fireworks. Inside the courtyards other sheds were erected. Here, amid beautiful screens and revolving lights, pictures by famous artists graced the walls, and rare antiques and intricate toys were placed on view.

Every household in every street and lane had lanterns ready. Beside the prefectural bridge near the governor's residency an artificial hill had been built. Two paper dragons, one red and the other yellow, coiled around it. Each scale of their bodies was a small lantern, and water spewed from their mouths. Countless lanterns also illuminated both approaches to the bridge.

An artificial hill was erected in front of the Bronze Buddha Monastery. Around this coiled a blue dragon, lit by hundreds of lanterns.

Before the Jade Cloud Mansion was another artificial hill. On it was a white dragon, with innumerable lanterns on all sides. The Mansion was actually a tavern, the finest in the province. Three eaved stories high, with carved beams and decorated pillars, it was an extremely handsome structure of more than a hundred rooms. From morning till night the Mansion resounded with music and song.

All the temples and monasteries were festooned with lanterns to celebrate a prosperous new year. Needless to say, the displays in the houses of joy and amusement were more lavish still.

Scouts reported the news to Mount Liangshan. Wu Yong was delighted. He informed Song Jiang. Song wanted to lead personally an attack on the Northern Capital. But Dr. An disapproved.

"Your wound isn't entirely closed," he said. "You mustn't move about too much. If anger seeps in, the cure will be difficult."

"Let me go in your place," Wu Yong proposed. He and Ironclad Virtue Pei Xuan then mustered eight contingents.

The first was led by Two Rods Huyan Zhuo, assisted by Han Tao and Peng Qi, with Huang Xin, Suppressor of the Three Mountains, commanding the reserve. This was entirely a cavalry outfit. Actually, Huyan's forward unit was not going to fight. It was a ruse to draw Guan Sheng into battle.

The second contingent had Panther Head Lin Chong leading the forward unit, aided by Ma Lin and Deng Fei, with Hua Rong commanding the reserve. This too was entirely cavalry.

The third contingent, also fully mounted, had Guan Sheng the Big Halberd leading the forward unit, seconded by Xuan Zan and Hao Siwen. Sun Li the Sickly General brought up the rear.

The fourth contingent, again fully cavalry, had Qin Ming the Thunderbolt in command of the forward unit, assisted by Ou Peng and Yan Shun. Yang Zhi the Blue-Faced Beast led the reserve.

Mu Hong the Unrestrained, an infantry commander, was at the head of the fifth contingent. His lieutenants were Du Xing and Zheng Tianshou.

Another infantry commander, Li Kui the Black Whirlwind, headed the sixth contingent, assisted by LiLi and Cao Zheng.

Infantry commander Lei Heng the Winged Tiger, aided by Shi En and Mu Chun, led the seventh contingent.

The eight contingent was led by infantry commander Fan Rui the Demon King Who Roils the World, seconded by Xiang Chong and Li Gun.

The eight companies were ordered to march that same day and to brook no delays. They were to reach the city walls by the second watch of the fifteenth of the first lunar month, infantry and cavalry advancing together.

When the command was given, the eight contingents set forth down the mountain. The other chieftains remained with Song Jiang to guard the fortress.

Now Flea on a Drum Shi Qian was a man who flew along eaves and walked atop walls. He didn't enter the Northern Capital on the regular road but clambered over the city wall at night. Unable to find accommodations at an inn for a single traveller, he wandered the streets all day and at night rested beneath the pedestal of a god in a temple. On the thirteenth he went to the center of town and watched the citizens erecting their sheds and hanging their lanterns.

He saw Xie Zhen and Xie Bao, carrying game, also strolling and looking. He observed too Du Qian and Song Wan coming out of a house of pleasure. Shi Qian went to an upper floor of the Jade Cloud Mansion and walked around. Down in the street again, he met Kong Ming, dirty, his hair dishevelled and wearing a tattered sheepskin coat, begging with a staff in his left hand, a bowl in his right. Kong Ming nudged him to go to the back and talk.

"You don't look a bit like a beggar, brother," said Shi Qian, "a big robust fellow like you, with a fair skin and rosy complexion! This city is full of policemen. If any of them sees through your disguise, our whole project may be delayed! You'd better stay out of sight."

While he was speaking, another beggar approached from the edge of a wall. Shi Qian looked at him closely. It was Kong Liang.

"You're another one with a snowy white skin," said Shi Qian. "Nobody would believe you were starving. They'll surely spot you as a fraud." Suddenly, two men grabbed them from behind and barked: "A fine thing you three are up to!"

They turned and saw Yang Xiong and Liu Tang. Shi Qian breathed a sigh of relief. "You nearly scared the life out of me!"

"Come with me," said Yang Xiong. He led them to a secluded spot and said reproachfully: "Don't you have any sense? How could you talk there? It's lucky it's only we two who saw you. If it was one of those sharp-eyed fast-moving policemen, brother Song Jiang's big plan might have to be postponed. We've seen the other brothers. There's no need for you to roam the streets any more."

"Zou Yuan and Zou Run are out selling lanterns," said Kong Ming. "Sagacious Lu and Wu Song have put up in a temple outside the city. That's enough talk. Let each man do his job when the time comes."

In front of a temple they met a Taoist priest coming out. "What are you five doing here?" he cried. It was Dragon in the Clouds Gongsun Sheng. Behind him was Ling Zhen, disguised as an acolyte. The seven exchanged significant glances, nodded in agreement, and went their separate ways.

With the festival day almost upon them, Governor Liang directed Wen Da the Mighty Sword to lead his mounted, troops out of the city and set up a position in Flying-Dragon Valley to guard against the bandits. On the fourteenth he ordered Li Cheng the Heavenly King to take five hundred Iron Cavalry, in full armor, and patrol the outskirts.

The next day, the fifteenth, the Lantern Festival Day, was clear and bright. At dusk, the moon rose, gilding the avenues and streets with silver. Crowds watched the rockets and admired the beautiful shining lanterns.

That night Superintendent Cai Fu instructed his brother to keep an eye on the prison. "I'm going home for a while. I'll be back soon."

As he was entering the door of his house, two men moved in after him. The first was dressed as an army officer. The other appeared to be a servant. But when

Cai Fu looked at them in the light of a lamp, he saw that the first was Chai Jin the Small Whirlwind and the second Iron Throat Yue Ho. Cai Fu knew Chai Jin, and he invited them in and started to lay out wine cups.

"No wine, thanks," said the Small Whirlwind. "We've come with an urgent request. We know you've been taking excellent care of Lu the Magnate and Shi Xiu, and for that we can't thank you enough. While all the festivities are going on we'd like to slip into the prison and see them. May we trouble you to lead the way? Please don't refuse."

Cai Fu was an experienced officer. He could guess pretty well what Chai Jin intended. If he refused and the outlaws succeeded in breaking into the city, not only he but his whole family would be exterminated.

He had no choice but to risk the dangerous consequences. He gave them some old clothes to wear and disguised them as policemen. Then he changed his head kerchief and led them directly to the prison.

Around the first watch Stumpy Tiger, Ten Feet of Steel, Sun Xin, Mistress Gu, Zhang Qing and Sun the Witch, masquerading as three couples from the country, mingled with the crowds entering the city through the East Gate. Gongsun Sheng and Ling Zhen, carrying large hampers on shoulder-poles, went into the Temple of the City God and sat down on the veranda. The temple was next door to the prefectural government office.

Zou Yuan and Zou Run strolled towards the center of town bearing lanterns for sale. Du Qian and Song Wan, each trundling a wheel barrow, proceeded directly to the front of the governor's residency and merged with the revellers there. The residency was on the avenue leading to the East Gate.

Liu Tang and Yang Xiong, each holding a policeman's staff and with a weapon concealed on his person, sat down on either side of the prefectural bridge. Yan Qing and Zhang Shun swam into the Northern Capital beneath the water gate and concealed themselves in a secluded spot. Of all this we'll say no more.

Soon, the second watch was sounded in the drum tower. Shi Qian appeared with a basket on his arm. In it were sulphur and nitrate and things to ignite them, covered over by velvet ornaments for ladies' hair. He entered Jade Cloud Mansion and walked up the stairs. In every room pipes were tootling, drums and clackers beating, and games being played, as merry-makers noisily celebrated the Festival of the Lanterns. Pretending to be selling his hair ornaments, Shi Qian went from room to room. He met Xie Bao and Xie Zhen in the hallway carrying steel pitchforks from which rabbit game were suspended.

"It's time," said Shi Qian. "Why isn't there any activity outside?"

"We've just been out front and saw a mounted scout go by," said Xie Zhen. "Our troops have probably arrived. You just do your job."

Before the words had left his mouth a clamor arose in front of the building. Someone exclaimed: "The men of Liangshan Marsh are at the West Gate!"

"Hurry," Xie Zhen said to Shi Qian. "We're going to take our posts outside the government office."

He and Xie Bao hurried to their destination and found it crowded with defeated soldiers who had fled back to the city. They said: "Wen Da the Mighty Sword lost his position in a surprise raid. The bandits are headed this way!"

Li Cheng, who was patrolling atop the city wall when he heard the news, galloped to garrison headquarters. He mustered more troops, and ordered that the gates be closed and the city defended.

Prefect Wang had led over a hundred policemen, with chains and fetters, to suppress any disturbances. He returned to garrison headquarters hastily on learning of the impending attack. Governor Liang, who had been seated at his ease outside his residency, had not been alarmed when the first news reached him. But when, less than half a watch later, mounted scouts came flying back like comets, he was shaken to the depths of his soul. He hurriedly called for his horse.

At that moment Shi Qian ignited the sulphur and nitrate on the roof of Jade Cloud Mansion. An enormous flame shot into the sky, paling the moon. Governor Liang hastily mounted and started to ride to the scene. But two big fellows pushed over their wheel barrows, blocking the road, then proceeded to pour oil on them from lamps which had been hanging on the barrows and set them on fire.

Liang headed for the East Gate. Two other big fellows shouted: "Li Ying and Shi Jin are here!" and strode murderously forward, twirling halberds. The guards at the gate fled, but not before a dozen of them had been wounded. Du Qian and Song Wan then joined in, and the four, together, captured the East Gate.

Governor Liang saw he was no match for them. With his retinue he flew to the South Gate. There, he heard voices crying: "A big fat monk with a Buddhist staff and a beast-face pilgrim with a pair of sharp knives are yelling and slaughtering their way in!"

Liang turned his steed and went back to his residency. He saw Xie Zhen and Xie Bao felling men left and right with their steel pitchforks. He thought to go to prefectural headquarters, but dared not draw any closer. Prefect Wang tried to come out to him. Liu Tang and Yang Xiong brought their policemen's staves down on Wang's head with such force that his brains spattered and his eyes bulged, and he fell dead in front of the prefecture. His officers and clerks fled for their lives.

The governor hurriedly rode to the West Gate. The concerted boom of explosives in the City God Temple shook the earth. At the same time Zou Yuan and Zou Run with torches on long bamboo poles began setting fires to the eaves of houses, while Stumpy Tiger and Ten Feet of Steel, in front of the southern brothel section, came fighting forward, aided by Sun Xin and Mistress Gu who had pulled out concealed weapons. Zhang Qing and Sun the Witch barged into the Bronze Buddha Monastery, clambered up the artificial hill and set it ablaze.

All over the city, the people were scurrying in terror. Screams and wails shivered in every household. In a dozen places flames brightened the sky. Confusion reigned.

As Governor Liang was rushing to the West Gate he met Li Cheng and his cavalry, and they all raced to the top of the city wall above the South Gate. Li reined in his steed, mounted the Drum Tower and peered out. Approaching was a huge array of men and horses and a banner inscribed with the words: *General Huyan Zhuo.* The general was a spirited and courageous figure in the firelight. To his left was Han Tao, to his right Peng Qi, while Huang Xin brought up the rear. Spread out like wings of a goose, the ruthlessly advancing contingent was nearly at the gate.

Unable to leave the city, the governor and Li Cheng concealed themselves beneath the archway of the North Gate and watched the brightly leaping flames. They could see a mounted force of unknown number flying towards them. It was led by Panther Head Lin Chong, who held a lance athwart as he urged on his horse. To his left was Ma Lin, to his right Deng Fei. Hua Rong brought up the rear.

Liang went again to the East Gate. Amid an advancing army of torches he could see Mu Hong the Unrestrained, with Du Xing on his left and Zheng Tianshou on his right. These three gallant infantry commanders, halberds in hand, were rapidly closing in on the city with over a thousand men.

Throwing all caution to the winds, the governor dashed through the South Gate. In the light of torches on the side of the drawbridge he could see Li Kui the Black Whirlwind, with LiLi on his left and Cao Zheng on his right. Buff naked, Li Kui swarmed up from the moat, brandishing his axes. LiLi and Cao came with him.

Li Cheng carved a bloody path out of the city to cover the governor's escape. Murderous cries arose on their left. From amid an army of countless torches, Guan Sheng the Big Halberd rode forth. Clapping his spirited roan and waving his blue steel blade, he galloped directly towards Liang.

Li Cheng, grasping his two knives, advanced to meet the foe. But he had no heart for the fight, and soon pulled his horse around and withdrew. From the left a combined force under Xuan Zan and Hao Siwen, with Sun Li bringing up the rear, charged fiercely. In the ensuing battle, Hua Rong advanced swiftly from behind, fitted an arrow to his bow and brought a lieutenant beside Li Cheng tumbling from his saddle. The startled Li turned and fled.

Before he had gone more that half a bowshot, drums pounded and gongs crashed on his right. In the firelight he saw Qin Ming the Thunderbolt, waving his cudgel on a spirited mount, murderously advancing with Yan Shun and Ou Peng, followed by Yang Zhi. Li Cheng fought as he retreated, still protecting the governor. They managed to break through.

Meanwhile, in the city Du Qian and Song Wan slaughtered the governor's family, old and young, good and bad. Liu Tang and Yang Xiong wiped out the family of Prefect Wang. Kong Ming and Kong Liang had climbed the rear wall of the city prison and were about to go in. Zou Yuan and Zou Run planted themselves at the front of the prison to prevent anyone from entering.

Inside, Chai Jin and Yue Ho recognized the signal fire. "Did you brothers see that?" they called to Cai Fu and Cai Qing. "What are you waiting for?"

Cai Qing was on guard at the door, but Zou Yuan and Zou Run smashed it open and shouted: "The whole band of bold fellows from Liangshan Marsh is here! Bring out Lu the Magnate and Shi Xiu!"

Cai Qing hastily reported to his brother, but by then Kong Ming and Kong Liang had already jumped down from the top of the building. Chai Jin, regardless of whether the Cai brothers were willing or not, pulled out an implement, opened the fetters and released the two prisoners.

"Come with me, quick, to Lu's house and protect his family," Chai Jin said to Cai the Superintendent.

All rapidly emerged through the prison gate, where they were joined by Zou Yuan and Zou Run, and hurried to the home of Lu Junyi. The Magnate led the five Mount Liangshan men in a search for his wife and his steward Li Gu.

When Li Gu heard that an army of bold fellows from Liangshan Marsh had entered the city and saw the fires rising on all sides, his eyes twitched and he consulted with Lu's wife. They packed some valuables and hurried through the door. But then they heard front gates being knocked down and an unknown number of men rushing in. They turned in fright and stole out through the rear gate. They tiptoed along the wall and headed for the river, hoping to find a place of concealment.

On the bank Zhang Shun shouted: "Where does that woman think she's going!"

Panic-stricken, Li Gu jumped into a boat to hide. As he was about to plunge into the cabin, a hand suddenly reached out and grabbed him, and a voice shouted: "Li Gu, do you remember me?"

The steward recognized the voice of Yan Qing. "Young Prodigy," he cried, "we've never been enemies! Don't pull me ashore!"

Zhang Shun, on the bank, already had the woman clapped under one arm. He dragged her down to the boat. Yan Qing held on to Li Gu, and all went towards the East Gate.

Lu the Magnate, when he found his wife and steward gone, ordered his servants to pack his gold and silver and precious things, load them on carts and take them to the mountain fortress for distribution.

Chai Jin went with Cai Fu to his house where the superintendent collected his family and belongings. They prepared to leave for the mountain stronghold.

"You must save the ordinary people of the city, Excellency," said Cai Fu. "Don't let them come to any harm."

Chai Jin relayed his request to Wu Yong. But though the Military Advisor immediately issued appropriate orders, by then half the population had been killed or wounded.

The sky was already light. Wu Yong and Chai Jin, in the city, had the trumpets blow the call to assemble. The chieftains and Lu the Magnate and Shi Xiu all gathered at the governor's residency. The released prisoners praised Cai Fu and Cai Qing for their kindness and said they owned them their lives. Yan Qing and Zhang Shun brought forward Li Gu and Lu's wife. The Magnate told Yan Qing to keep them under guard until their disposition could be decided upon. Of that we'll say no more.

We'll talk rather of Governor Liang, fleeing the city under the protection of Li Cheng. They ran into Wen Da, returning with the remnants of his defeated army, and joined forces and travelled south together. Suddenly, the forward units set up a clamor. Fan Rui the Demon King Who Roils the World, with Xiang Chong on his left and Li Gun on his right—three infantry commanders—were advancing on them with flourishing knives and spears. And behind the fugitives appeared Lei Heng the Winged Tiger, plus Shi En and Mu Chun, each leading a thousand foot soldiers and cutting off their retreat.

Truly, the keeper sends the prisoner back to jail, the doctor orders the patient to return to bed.

Were Governor Liang and his men able to escape? Read our next chapter if you would know.

CHAPTER 67

SONG JIANG REWARDS HIS THREE ARMIES

GUAN SHENG DEFEATS THE WATER AND FIRE GENERALS

Fighting desperately, Governor Liang's forces broke through the strong encirclement and fled west. Fan Rui, plus Xiang Chong and Li Gun, tried to catch them in vain. Finally, with Lei Heng, Shi En and Mu Chun, they returned to the Northern Capital to await further orders.

Military Advisor Wu Yong, in the city, directed that proclamations be posted reassuring the citizenry and that the fires be extinguished. All the members of the families of Governor Liang, Li Cheng, Wen Da and Prefect Wang were either killed or ran away. No one bothered to inquire. The prefectural treasury was broken open, and its gold, silver, precious objects, silks and satins were loaded on carts. The conquerors also opened the granary. They distributed relief grain to the entire populace and loaded the remainder on carts also, for removal to the Mount Liangshan fortress.

Wu Yong ordered his commanders and men to prepare to march. Li Gu and the wife of Lu the Magnate were placed on prisoner carts and the cages nailed fast. The outlaw forces were divided into three contingents, then all set out for Liangshan Marsh. Dai Zong went on ahead to inform Song Jiang.

Song Jiang summoned the generals in the stronghold and they descended the mountain to greet the returning chieftains and escort them to Loyalty Hall. On meeting Lu the Magnate, Song Jiang kowtowed. Lu Junyi returned the courtesy.

"It was our desire to invite you here, Magnate, to join us in striving for righteousness," said Song. "We never thought we would encounter such difficulties and that you would nearly lose your life. Our hearts were torn with anxiety! But Heaven protected you, and we meet again. We are infinitely relieved."

Lu bowed. "Thanks to brother's prestigious power and the virtue of his chieftains, with united hearts and strength you have saved my humble self. I could never adequately express my gratitude, though I scattered my innards on the ground."

He presented Cai Qing and Cai Fu to Song Jiang and said: "If it weren't for these two I would not be here!"

Song wanted Lu to take over as leader. The Magnate was astonished. "How could a man like me command the mountain fortress?" he said. "Let me be your groom, brother, an ordinary soldier, to return your kindness in saving my life. That would be my greatest pleasure."

Song Jiang continued to press him, but Lu wouldn't hear of it. Li Kui protested.

"If you hand over the leadership to someone else, brother, I'm going to start killing!"

And Wu Song added his complaint. "You're always trying to give your command away. It chills us brothers to the heart!"

"What do you varlets understand," Song Jiang shouted. "Stop your chatter!"

"You mustn't insist, brother," Lu said hurriedly. "You're making me very uneasy."

Li Kui had a suggestion. "Everything is quiet, now," he said. "You be emperor, brother. Let Lu the Magnate be your prime minister. Make us all big officials. We'll fight our way into the Eastern Capital and seize the friggin throne! That would be a lot better than friggin around here!"

Song Jiang was furious. He swore at Li Kui.

"Let Lu the Magnate rest in the east wing as our guest," Wu Yong offered soothingly. "Later on, when he has performed some meritorious deeds, we can talk again about relinquishing the leadership."

Only then did Song Jiang cool down. He told Yan Qing to share quarters with Lu, and provided accommodations for Cai Fu and Cai Qing and-their households. Guan Sheng's family had already been brought to the fortress by Xue Yong.

Song Jiang ordered that a big feast be laid. He generously rewarded his cavalry, infantry and naval forces. He directed his commanders, high and low, to provide wine for their various units. Inside Loyalty Hall the chieftains, politely deferring to one another, drank and made merry.

Lu the Magnate rose to his feet. "The adulterous pair have been caught and are awaiting disposition."

Song Jiang smiled. "I'd forgotten. Bring them here!"

Men opened the cages of the prison carts and dragged the captives into the Hall. Li Gu was bound to the main pillar on the left, Lu's wife to the main pillar on the right.

"There's no need to interrogate these rascals," said Song. "Lu the Magnate, do with them what you will."

A dagger in his hand, Lu walked over to the culprits and cursed them furiously. He carved out their hearts, cut off their limbs and cast their bodies to the ground. Then he returned to the banquet and thanked the assemblage. The chieftains congratulated him and complimented him profusedly.

Meanwhile, Governor Liang, hearing that the outlaw forces had withdrawn, returned to the city with Li Cheng and Wen Da and their defeated army. The three found that nine-tenths of their families had been killed, and they loudly lamented. Armies arrived from neighboring towns to chase the men of Mount Liangshan, but by then they were far away. Governor Liang told the armies to return.

His wife had concealed herself in a flower garden in the rear and had escaped with her life. She advised Liang to petition the emperor to dispatch an army and wipe out the bandits and obtain vengeance, and at the same time to write a letter to her father the premier letting him know. Liang did so, reporting that over five thousand civilians had been killed and innumerable people wounded, with losses to the military exceeding thirty thousand.

The governor's emissary reached the premier's chancellery in a few days. He dismounted and was announced. The premier ordered that he be allowed to enter. The emissary went directly to the ceremonial hall, kowtowed, and presented the secret missive addressed to the throne. He related how the brigands had broken into the Northern Capital, and said they were a large and powerful foe.

Originally, Premier Cai Jing favored an amnesty. The credit Governor Liang would receive for effectuating it would also reflect favorably on himself. But the mission had failed miserably—a fact which could not be concealed. Now Cai wanted an all-out war.

"You may withdraw," he snapped.

At the Fifth watch the following morning the Imperial Bell sounded, and civil and military officials gathered in the Waiting Court. Premier Cai stood at their head. Approaching the Jade Dais, he offered Governor Liang's petition to the Virtuous Sovereign. The emperor read it and was shocked.

Zhao Ding, a counsellor, stepped forward and said: "We've sent soldiers after those bandits a number of times, but always suffered heavy losses. That's because the terrain is in their favor. In my humble opinion, it would be better to grant them amnesty, recall them to the throne, give their leaders high rank and put them to the defense of our borders. That would solve it."

Cai Jing was very angry. "You're an imperial counsellor," he shouted, "yet you want to destroy our imperial discipline! Lowly madman, you deserve to die!"

"I order you to leave this court at once," said the emperor. He divested Zhao Ding of his office and returned him to the status of ordinary citizen.

No one dared to offer any other proposals.

"Those bandits are outrageous," the emperor said to Cai Jing. "Who can we send to capture them?"

"They're only a gang of robbers in the wilds. We've no need for a large army. I'd like to recommend two officers—Shan Tinggui and Wei Dingguo, both commandants of Lingzhou Prefecture. If Your Majesty will issue an order and dispatch an emissary to fetch them and their men at all speed, they will be able to sweep away the filth."

Very pleased, the emperor issued commissions and directed the Council of Military Affairs to have them executed. Rising, the monarch left the chamber, followed by the multitude of officials. Many of them smiled sceptically to themselves.

The next day Cai Jing chose a chancellery official to deliver the imperial commissions to Lingzhou.

In the mountain stronghold, Song Jiang distributed among his infantry, cavalry and naval forces the valuables obtained from the treasury of the Northern Capital. Cows and horses were slaughtered, and feasts were held several days in succession to welcome Lu the Magnate. Although they had no fine delicacies, there were mountains of meat and seas of wine. The chieftains imbibed until they were half drunk-

"For the sake of Lu the Magnate," said Wu Yong, "we damaged the Northern Capital, slew many of its people, robbed the treasury, and chased Governor Liang and his generals out of the city. Surely, he'll report to the emperor. He won't let the matter drop, particularly since his father-in-law is the premier. They're bound to dispatch an army against us."

"There's reason for your concern, Military Advisor," said Song Jiang. "Let's send a man to the Northern Capital tonight to ferret out the news. Then we'll know how to prepare."

Wu Yong laughed. "I've already done that. He should be back soon."

While they were still discussing the problem at the banquet, the spy returned. "Governor Liang has petitioned the throne for a punitive army," he reported. "Counsellor Zhao Ding proposed an amnesty, but Cai Jing cursed him and had him kicked out of office. The emperor has commissioned Shan Tinggui and Wei Dingguo, commandants of Lingzhou Prefecture, to proceed against us with their soldiers."

"How shall we confront the foe?" asked Song Jiang.

"Let them come," said Wu Yong. "We'll take them all in one swoop."

Guan Sheng rose and addressed the two. "I'm deeply grateful for the hospitality you brothers have extended to me ever since I arrived at this mountain," he said. "But I haven't done anything in return. I met Shan and Wei many times when I was still in Pudong, and I know all about them. Shan is very clever at using water to inundate enemy troops, and so everyone calls him the Water General. Wei is skilled with fire in his attacks. He employs flame-throwers on the battlefield, and so he's known as the Fire General.

"I have no talent, but if you'll let me have five thousand men, I'll stop those two on the road before they can get started. If they're willing to surrender, I'll bring them here. If they're not, I'll capture them and deliver them as my gift. There's no need for you brothers to use a large heavily armed force and tax your energies and spirits. I wonder whether you would consider my idea?"

Song Jiang was delighted. He instructed Xuan Zan and Hao Siwen to go along, and consented to give Guan Sheng the five thousand men he requested. The following morning Song Jiang and his chieftains feasted and saw the three commanders off at the Shore of Golden Sands, where they departed with their troops.

The chieftains returned to Loyalty Hall and Wu Yong said to Song Jiang: "Guan Sheng has gone, but we don't guarantee his devotion. We'd better have some good commanders follow and keep an eye on him. They can act as support forces."

"He seems a highly chivalrous person to me. He's shown no sign of wavering. You shouldn't doubt him."

"I'm afraid his heart might not be the same as yours, brother. I say let Lin Chong and Yang Zhi, with Sun Li and Huang Xin as their lieutenants, go down with another five thousand men."

"I want to go, too," said Li Kui.

"There's no need for you this time," said Song Jiang. "We already have enough good commanders."

"I'll get sick if this idleness keeps on! If you don't let me go along, I'll go on my own!"

"You listen to orders or I'll have your head!"

Sulkily, Li Kui left the Hall.

Lin Chong and Yang Zhi led troops down the mountain to support Guan Sheng. The next day an officer came and reported: "Black Whirlwind Li Kui left last night at the second watch with his two axes. No one knows where he's bound."

Song Jiang groaned. "All because I said a few harsh words! He's probably gone to join another band!"

"You're wrong, brother," said Wu Yong. "Li Kui may be rough and crude, but his sense of chivalry is very strong. He'd never join anyone else. He'll be back in a day or two. Don't worry."

But Song Jiang was very upset. He first sent Dai Zong after Li Kui, and later Shi Qian, Li Yun, Yue Ho and Wang Ding with four more separate search parties.

When Li Kui went down the mountain with his two axes during the night, he followed a small path in the direction of Lingzhou. "So many men and horses to fight two friggin generals!" he muttered. "I'll charge into the town and kill them with one chop of the ax each! That'll shake up brother Song Jiang, and raise my prestige again with the others!"

After walking half a day, he grew hungry. He groped in his waist purse and found that he had left the mountain in such a hurry he'd forgotten to take any money.

"It's a long time since I've robbed anyone," he thought, "but now I'll have to find some oaf to vent my anger on."

By the side of the road he saw a rustic tavern. He went in, sat down, consumed three measures of wine and two catties of meat, then rose and started to leave. The waiter stopped him and asked for money.

"I'll give it to you soon," said Li Kui. "Wait till I do a little business up ahead." He turned to go.

A huge ferocious-looking fellow came in. "You've got your nerve, you swarthy villain," he shouted. "Who runs a tavern so that you can eat for free!"

Li Kui glared. "This lord eats for free wherever he goes."

"When I tell you who I am, you'll be pissing and farting in terror. This lord is Han Bolong of Liangshan Marsh. The money to open this tavern was given to me by brother Song Jiang personally."

Li Kui grinned inwardly. "Our stronghold never even heard of this friggin lout," he thought.

As a matter of fact Han, who originally was a robber, had wanted to join the band on Mount Liangshan. He had sought out Zhu Gui the Dry-Land Crocodile and requested that he lead him to Song Jiang. But because Song first developed a growth on his back and then became very involved in warfare, he had been too busy to see anyone. Zhu Gui had told Han to carry on with his tavern business.

Now, Li Kui took one of the axes from his belt and offered it to Han Bolong. "Keep this as a pledge," he said.

Han didn't know it was a trick. As he reached for the ax, Li Kui whipped out its mate and cracked open Han's forehead with a splitting crunch. What a pity that Han Bolong, who'd been a bold ruffian half his life, should die at the hands of Li Kui!

The two or three waiters fled into the village, sorry that they had been born with only two legs. Li Kui took whatever money he could find, set fire to the thatched building, and continued on towards Lingzhou.

He had travelled less than a day when a big fellow approached from the side of the highway and examined him from head to toe.

"What are you looking at this lord for, varlet?" Li Kui demanded.

"Whose lord are you?" the man retorted.

Li Kui rushed him. With one blow of his fist the fellow knocked Li Kui flat on his backside.

"He throws a nice punch," thought Black Whirlwind, sitting on the ground. He raised his face and asked: "What's your name?"

"This lord hasn't any name. But if you want to fight, come on! Do you dare get up?"

Enraged, Li Kui prepared to jump to his feet. But a kick in the ribs from the big man sent him sprawling. "I can't lick this fellow," cried Li Kui. He hauled himself erect and started to leave.

The man shouted for him to halt, and asked: "What's your name, swarthy fellow?"

"Since I've lost, I'd rather not say. But you're a gallant fellow, so I won't deceive you. I'm Li Kui the Black Whirlwind of Liangshan Marsh."

"Are you, really? Don't lie, now."

"If you don't believe me, look at these two axes."

"What are you doing out alone, if you're a Mount Liangshan man?"

"Big Brother squelched me, so I'm going to Lingzhou to kill two fellows named Shan and Wei."

"I hear that a force from the stronghold is already heading that way. Can you tell me who's in it?"

"Guan Sheng the Big Halberd is in command. He's followed by reinforcements under Panther Head Lin Chong and Yang Zhi the Blue-Faced Beast."

Convinced, the man dropped to his knees and kowtowed.

"Truly," said Li Kui, "what is your name?"

"I was born in the district of Zhongshan. My family have been wrestlers for three generations. Our ways of striking with hands and feet have been passed down from father to son. We don't teach outsiders. But I've never had any good connections, and no one I've tried to throw in with would have me. I'm known all through Shandong and Hebei as Jiao Ting the Merciless.

"Recently, I heard that in Kouzhou Prefecture there's a place called Withered Trees Mountain, and on it is a robber who loves to kill. Though his name is Bao Xu, everyone calls him the God of Death. He goes forth from his mountain to rob and pillage. I'm on my way to join his band."

"A man with your skill ought to be joining Song Jiang, our Big Brother."

"I'd been hoping to go to your fortress for a long time, but I never had anybody to introduce me. Now that I've met you, brother, I'll be glad to join Big Brother Song Jiang."

"I've got to show him a thing or two, first. I've come all the way down the mountain and I haven't killed a single person. I can't return empty-handed. We'll go to Lingzhou, kill the two commandants Shan and Wei, then head back to our fortress together."

"Lingzhou is a fortified town. It's full of soldiers. With all our skill, just the two of us attacking wouldn't be any use. We'd only be throwing our lives away. We'd be better off going to Withered Trees Mountain and persuading Bao Xu to join the band with us on Mount Liangshan. That would be best."

While they were talking, Shi Qian approached behind them. He called to Li Kui: "Big Brother has been very worried about you. Please come back to the mountain. Four parties are out searching for you."

Li Kui introduced Jiao Ting.

"Big Brother is waiting for you," Shi Qian persisted.

"Enough," cried Li Kui. "Jiao Ting and I have it all settled. We're going to Withered Trees Mountain, first, and get Bao Xu to join us."

"You can't. Big Brother is waiting. We have to return to the stronghold now."

"If you won't come with me, tell Big Brother what I'm doing. I'll be back soon."

Shi Qian was afraid of Li Kui. He returned to the mountain fortress alone. Jiao Ting and Li Kui proceeded to Kouzhou Prefecture and headed towards Withered Trees Mountain.

As to Guan Sheng, with Xuan Zan and Hao Siwen and five thousand brigands, he neared Lingzhou. The prefect had already received the imperial mandate to transfer troops to the Eastern Capital, plus a directive from the premier. He summoned commandants Shan and Wei to a conference and transmitted the directive to them. The two officers mustered their soldiers, issued arms, had the horses saddled and bridled, drew grain and fodder, and fixed a date for departure.

Suddenly, a messenger arrived and announced: "Guan Sheng the Big Halberd of Pudong has arrived with troops and is invading our prefecture."

Shan and Wei were furious. At the head of their soldiers, they rode forth to confront the foe. As the two armies drew near they could see each others' drams and flags. From beneath an arch of pennants, Guan Sheng rode forward. On the far side, as drums thundered, the Water General, astride a black steed, appeared, gripping a black lance. His helmet, his armor, his robe, his boots—all were black. He was preceded by a man carrying a northern-style black banner which bore the inscription: *Water General Shan Tinggui.*

On the near side, bridle bells jingled as the Fire General Wei Tingguo rode out. His accoutrements were mainly red, and he was preceded by a soldier carrying an embroidered red banner in the southern style which bore the inscription: *Fire General Wei Tingguo.*

The two commandants entered the combat area together. Astride his horse, Guan Sheng greeted them courteously: "It's been a long time since we met, commandants."

Shan and Wei laughed. They pointed at Guan Sheng and reviled him: "Talentless, mad rebel! You're unworthy of the emperor's kindness. You've besmirched your ancestor's name! Now you recklessly lead troops here. It's completely inexcusable!"

"Commandants, you're mistaken," Guan Sheng replied. "Our sovereign has been deceived. Treacherous ministers have taken power. They employ only their intimates, they reprove only their enemies. But brother Song Liang is a man of virtue and benevolence who performs righteous deeds on Heaven's behalf. He has sent me here to invite you to join us. If you don't consider me too lowly, permit me to escort you to our mountain stronghold."

His words infuriated the commandants. Together, they charged, one like a dark cloud from the north, the other like a ball of flame from the south. As Guan Sheng waited to meet them, Xuan Zan flew out from his left and Hao Siwen burst forth from his right, and clashed with the two attackers, head on. Sword against sword flashed icily in ten thousand streaks, lance against lance filled the air with the chill of death.

Guan Sheng, watching from a distance, was full of admiration for the commandants. Suddenly, they broke off the engagement, turned their horses, and rode back into their own position. Hao Siwen and Xuan Zan closely pursued. Wei turned to the left, Shan to the right, followed respectively by Xuan and Hao.

As Xuan Zan gave chase, four or five hundred foot soldiers, with pennants and armor of red, stretched out in a single line and surrounded him. Hooked poles extended, nooses flew, and both horse and rider were snared.

Hao, pursuing Shan to the right, was also surrounded by five hundred infantry, only these had black pennants and armor. They surged up from behind and captured him.

While the two were being led off towards Lingzhou, Shan and Wei, with five hundred troops each, again came racing forth. Guan Sheng was unable to cope. He fell back with his men. Wei and Shan clapped their horses and pursued. Then, ahead of him, Guan Sheng suddenly saw two chieftains galloping in his direction. They were Lin Chong and Yang Zhi, and they swept around his flanks and plunged in among the Lingzhou soldiers, slaughtering and scattering them. Guan Sheng halted his remnant contingent, and united it with the Lin and Yang forces. He met the two, and was joined subsequently by Sun Li and Huang Xin. All made camp together.

The Water and Fire Generals, with Xuan Zan and Hao Siwen as captives, returned triumphantly to the town. Prefect Zhang received them, and had wine served in congratulation. He ordered that cage carts be built for the two prisoners, and directed an aide to set out that very night and deliver them to the Eastern Capital, with a guard of three hundred foot soldiers, and report the arrest to the imperial court.

The party followed a winding road towards the Eastern Capital. They came to a mountain covered with withered trees and dried reeds. To the crash of gongs, a gang of robbers suddenly appeared. The man in the lead brandished a pair of battle-axes, and he had a voice like thunder. It was Li Kui the Black Whirlwind of Liangshan Marsh. And behind him was Jiao Ting the Merciless. They and their outlaws blocked the road and, without a word, seized the prisoner carts.

As the aide turned to flee, Bao Xu the God of Death, with an iron face and bulging eyes, closed in from behind. He swung his sword and hacked the aide from his steed. The rest of the escort party abandoned the carts and ran for their lives.

Li Kui saw that the prisoners were Xuan Zan and Hao Siwen, and he asked how they came to be in such a predicament.

"But what are you doing here?" Xuan countered.

"Big Brother wouldn't let me join in the slaughter, so I came down the mountain on my own. First I killed Han Bolong, then I ran into Jiao Ting, and he brought me here. Bao Xu was like an old friend as soon as we met. He's been treating me like a brother. We'd just agreed to attack Lingzhou when a lookout on the mountain spotted soldiers convoying prisoner carts in this direction. I figured that government troops had captured some bandits, but I never dreamed it was you."

Bao Xu invited everyone into his stronghold and feasted them with mutton and wine. Hao Siwen said to him: "Since you're willing to join us in Liangshan Marsh, brother, why not combine forces in an attack on Lingzhou? That would be an excellent arrangement."

"Brother Li Kui and I were talking about going in together. Combining with you is even better. I also have two or three hundred good horses I can give."

Bao Xu led his six or seven hundred men, and the five bold fellows set out together for Lingzhou.

Soldiers in the escort who had fled back to the town hurried and reported to Prefect Zhang: "Robbers intercepted us on the road. They seized the prisoner carts and killed our officer."

Shan and Wei were enraged. "We'll capture those rogues," they vowed, "and bring them here for execution!"

Then they heard that Guan Sheng was outside the town with troops and challenging them to battle, Shan rushed to be the first to respond. The city gate was opened and the drawbridge lowered and he rode forth at the head of a thousand cavalry. From an arch of pennants five hundred horsemen in black armor sped to the battlefield, with the Water General in the lead. He was an imposing figure as he loudly reviled Guan Sheng.

"Traitorous failure, you're going to die!"

Waving his halberd, Guan Sheng clapped his horse. They fought only twenty rounds when Guan Sheng pulled his steed's head around and quickly departed. Shan chased him for more than ten *li*. Guan Sheng flung some words over his shoulder.

"You'd better dismount and surrender! What are you waiting for?"

Shan thrust his levelled lance at Guan's back. But Guan Sheng, with his fabulous agility, parried the weapon with a sharp rap, shouting at the same time: "Down you go!" The diverted momentum brought Shan out of his saddle to the ground. Guan dismounted and helped him to his feet.

"I beg your pardon, General," he cried.

The frightened Shan kowtowed. He begged for his life and surrendered;

"I have spoken of you often to Big Brother Song Jiang." said Guan. "He's dispatched me specially to invite you two generals to join us in striving for righteousness."

"Talentless though I am, I will gladly do my humble utmost to work together on Heaven's behalf."

The two rode side by side and continued to talk. Lin Chong saw them and asked what had happened. Guan Sheng said nothing of victor or vanquished.

"We met in the mountains and got to chatting about old times, and I persuaded him to come with us," he merely remarked.

Lin Chong and the others were delighted. Shan returned to the front and shouted a command. Five hundred yelling soldiers in black armor swarmed over to the outlaws' side. The remainder fled back to town and hurriedly reported to the prefect.

Wei was greatly angered by the news. The next day he rode out with his troops to give battle. Shan, Guan Sheng and Lin Chong proceeded directly to the front. From the arch of banners opposite, the Fire General advanced on his battle charger. He cursed when he saw Shan following Guan Sheng.

"Ungrateful traitors, conscienceless wretches!"

With a laugh, Guan Sheng clapped his steed and rode forward to meet him. The two clashed, brandishing weapons. They had fought less than ten rounds when

Wei galloped back to his position. Guan Sheng started to follow. He was stopped by a shout from Shan.

"Don't go after him, Commander!"

The Big Halberd quickly reined in. Five hundred fire soldiers, dressed in red, came flying from Lingzhou, and all carried incendiary implements. To the front and rear of their ranks were fifty carts piled high with very inflammable dry reeds. Each man had on his back an iron flask containing sulphur, nitrate and other incendiaries. The fire soldiers set all these ablaze and dashed among their foe. Men and horses, seared by the flames, fell dead or wounded. Guan Sheng's forces scattered in every direction. They retreated forty *li* before they halted and made camp.

Wei called in his troops and turned towards the town. He found it billowing with flames and smoke. What had happened was that Black Whirlwind Li Kui, together with Jiao Ting and Bao Xu and the robbers of Withered Trees Mountain, had approached Lingzhou from the rear and broken through the North Gate. They tore into the town, setting fires and pillaging Lingzhou's granary and treasury.

When Wei learned of this, he dared not enter. He hastily withdrew his troops, harried from behind by Guan Sheng who had again caught up. Communications between front and rear were disrupted. In any event, Lingzhou was already lost. Wei retreated to Zhongling, a county seat, and settled in. Guan Sheng surrounded the town and ordered his commanders to attack. Wei kept the gates closed and refused to come out.

"He's a brave man," Shan said to Guan Sheng and Lin Chong. "He'd rather die than submit to pressure. Go easy and you'll succeed. You won't get anywhere being impatient. I'm willing to go into the town, whatever the risks, and try to persuade him to surrender."

Guan Sheng was very pleased. He agreed to let Shan go in alone. An officer reported Shan's arrival. Wei came out to greet him and invited him into the hall.

"The imperial court has no lustre and the land is in turmoil," said Shan. "The emperor is confused, wicked ministers hold power. We're now serving Song Jiang, in Liangshan Marsh. Later, when the treacherous ministers have been deposed? there will be time enough to return to court and stamp out evil and restore correctness."

Wei considered this-in silence for several minutes. Finally, he said: "I'll surrender only if Guan Sheng asks me to, in person. Otherwise, I'd rather die than submit."

Shan mounted his horse and returned with the reply. Guan Sheng said: "I'm a person of no consequence. The general rates me too highly." He prepared to set out, accompanied only by Shan.

"You'd better think it over, brother," said Lin Chong. "A man's mind is hard to fathom."

"The brave fear nothing," said Guan Sheng. He rode directly to the county government office. Wei, receiving him with joy, kowtowed and surrendered.

They talked of old times together, and Wei entertained Guan Sheng at a feast. That same day, he went with him to the brigands' camp, accompanied by five hundred of his fire soldiers. There he was introduced to Lin Chong, Yang Zhi and the other chieftains. The outlaw forces were re-assembled and all set out for the mountain fortress.

Song Jiang had sent Dai Zong to meet them on the road. When the Marvellous Traveller saw Li Kui he said: "Because you sneaked off down the mountain, we brothers have had to do a lot of wasted running around. Shi Qian, Yue Ho, Li Yun and Wang Dingliu have already gone back. I'd better return too and tell Big Brother, so he won't worry about you any more."

Dai Zong went on ahead. Guan Sheng and the others proceeded to the Shore of Golden Sands, where the naval unit in several trips ferried them across.

A man came running towards them, panting and exhausted. They all recognized him. It was Duan Jingzhu the Golden Dog.

"Didn't you go Up north with Yang Lin and Shi Yong to buy horses?" asked Lin Chong. "Why have you come back in such a flurry?"

Duan's reply was brief, but as a result Song Jiang dispatched an army to attack a certain place. An old debt was expunged, vengeance was attained. Truly, he knew very well his words were a hook and line that once more would fish out trouble.

What then was it that Duan said to Lin Chong and the others? Read our next chapter if you would know.

CHAPTER 68

SONG JIANG ATTACKS ZENGTOU VILLAGE AT NIGHT

LU THE MAGNATE CAPTURES SHI WENGONG

"I went north with Yang Lin and Shi Yong to buy horses," Duan said, "and I picked over two hundred strong, well-sinewed, fine-coated steeds. But on the way back, while passing through Qingzhou Prefecture, we were set upon by a gang of robbers, headed by Yu Baosi, known as the Spirit of the Dangerous Road. There were more than two hundred of them. They stole all our animals and took them to Zengtou Village. I don't know where Shi Yong and Yang Lin have gone. I fled through the night and am hastening to the stronghold to report."

Lin Chong agreed that it was necessary to discuss the matter with Big Brother. They all forded the river and repaired to Loyalty Hall, where they met Song Jiang. Guan Sheng introduced Shan and Wei to the various chieftains. Li Kui told how, after going down the mountain, he killed Han Bolong, met Jiao Ting and Bao Xu and, with them, broke into Lingzhou. Song Jiang was very pleased with the addition of these four brave men.

But he grew very angry when Duan related the robbery of the horses. "They did this sort of thing to me before," he cried, "and now they've behaved discourteously again! I've been unhappy day and night because I haven't avenged the death at their hands of Chao Gai the Heavenly King. If I still don't avenge him now, I'll be the butt of ridicule and shame!"

"Spring is here," said Wu Yong, "the ideal season for battle. When we attacked them before, we failed to utilize the terrain. This time we must be clever."

"I hate them to the marrow of my bones. I'll get my revenge or, I swear, I'll never return!"

"Shi Qian can fly over eaves and skim atop walls. Send him in to scout around. When he comes back, we'll confer."

Flea on a Drum was dispatched to Zengtou. Two or three days later, Yang Lin and Shi Yong, who had escaped, arrived at the fortress. They said that Shi Wengong had been boasting in Zengtou that there was no room on this earth for both him and the outlaws of Liangshan Marsh. Song Jiang was in favor of mustering their troops immediately.

But Wu Yong said. "Wait till Shi Qian comes back and reports. It will be time enough, then."

Song Jiang, filled with rage, was thirsting for revenge. He couldn't contain himself. He sent Dai Zong to fly to the village and report back quickly with all the news he could find. In only a few days Dai Zong returned.

"Zengtou wants to avenge itself for Lingzhou," he said. "They're raising an army and setting up a big emplacement at the village entrance, with headquarters in the Fahua Monastery. Banners mark their outposts for hundreds of *li* around. I don't know how we can get in there."

The following day Shi Qian returned and reported: "I made very detailed inquiries. They've built five forts. More than two thousand men are guarding the entrance, under Shi Wengong. This is the main fort. The north fort is commanded by Zeng Tu, with Su Ding as his lieutenant. Zeng Mi, the second Zeng son, is in charge of the south fort. Zeng Suo, the third son, commands the west fort. The east fort is under Zeng Kui, the fourth son. The central position, in the village itself, is held by the fifth son Zeng Sheng and the father Zeng Nong. Yu Baosi the Spirit of the Dangerous Road is a huge fellow with an enormous girth. He's feeding those horses he stole inside the monastery grounds."

Wu Yong summoned the chieftains to a conference. "Since they've got five forts," he said, "we'll divide into five columns and attack each separately."

Lu the Magnate rose. "I have not yet shown my gratitude for being rescued and brought here. I would now like to go forward and give my all. Would that, I wonder, meet with your respected approval?"

Song Jiang was delighted. "If you're willing to go down the mountain, Magnate, you may lead the vanguard."

"The Magnate has arrived only recently," Wu Yong intervened. "He has no battle experience, the mountain paths are tortuous and ill-suited for riding. Rather than lead the vanguard, he would be better at the head of a contingent in ambush on the plain. When he hears the sound of our central unit's cannon, he can reinforce us."

Wu Yong was afraid that Lu would capture Shi Wengong and Song Jiang would feel constrained to fulfil the dying wish of Chao Gai that leadership be given to whoever caught his killer. Song Jiang, on the contrary, hoped that Lu would make the capture precisely so that he could turn over command of the stronghold to him out of respect to Chao Gai. But Wu Yong was adamant. He directed Lu to go with Yan Qing and five hundred infantry to paths upon the plain and await the signal.

Wu Yong divided the outlaw forces into five columns. Against the fort due south of Zengtou would go three thousand cavalry under Qin Ming the Thunderbolt and Hua Rong, seconded by Ma Lin and Deng Fei. The fort east of the village would be attacked by three thousand infantry under Sagacious Lu the Tattooed Monk and Wu Song the Pilgrim, with Kong Ming and Kong Liang as their lieutenants. Yang Zhi the Blue-Faced Beast and Nine Dragons Shi Jin, seconded by Yang Chun and Chen Da, would lead three thousand cavalry against the fort north of Zengtou. Sent against the fort to the west were three thousand infantry under Zhu Tong the Beautiful Beard and Lei Heng the Winged Tiger. Zou Yuan and Zou Run were their seconds in command. The central fort would be attacked by five thousand troops under commander-in-chief Song Jiang, Military Advisor Wu Yong, and Gongsun Sheng, accompanied by LU Fang, Guo Sheng, Xie Zhen, Xie Bao, Dai Zong and Shi Qian. Bringing up the rear would be a five thousand man unit of mixed infantry and cavalry under Li Kui the Black Whirlwind and Fan Rui the Demon King Who Roils the World, with Xiang Chong and Li Gun as their lieutenants. The remaining chieftains would stay to guard the mountain stronghold.

The five columns led by Song Jiang advanced rapidly. Scouts reported their approach to Zeng Senior, who summoned Shi Wengong and Su Ding for a military conference.

"All we have to do is dig a lot of concealed pits and we'll catch their toughest commanders and fiercest men," said Shi. "That's the best way to deal with those scruffy bandits!"

Zeng Senior ordered his vassals out with mattocks and shovels to dig pits all round the entrance to the village, and cover them over with mats and earth. Then he had soldiers lie in ambush near the pits and wait for the arrival of the enemy. He had a dozen of so pits also dug around the northern approach to the village.

While Song Jiang's army was on the march Wu Yong sent Shi Qian ahead to scout. A few days later, Flea on a Drum returned and reported: "Pits have been dug north and south of Zengtou, I don't know how many, to trap us."

Wu Yong laughed. "Nothing remarkable about that!" He led the troops on until they were quite near the village.

Around noon that day the advance unit saw a rider passing by. Bronze bells tinkled on his horse's neck, and pheasant plumes were tied to its tail. The rider wore a black hat and white robe, and he carried a short spear.

Men of the vanguard wanted to give chase, but Wu Yong stopped them. He ordered them to make camp where they were, dig a deep moat on all four sides, and lay out a perimeter of iron spikes. Each of the five columns was directed to do the same.

For the next three days no one came forward from the Zengtou forts to give battle. Wu Yong once again sent Shi Qian, this time disguised as a junior officer manning one of the ambushes, to find out why. Flea on a Drum made a mental note of the concealed pits, how far they were from the various forts, and how many of them there were in total. In a single day, he had all the information required, in detail, and he returned and reported.

The next day Wu Yong instructed the vanguard infantry to divide into two units, equipped with mattocks. He also directed that one hundred carts be loaded with reeds and dry brushwood and be concealed among the central column.

That night he ordered that the infantry columns first attack the forts to the east and west of Zengtou at mid-morning the following day. The cavalry under Yang Zhi and Shi Jin should spread out in a straight line before the northern fort. If the foe there beat drums and waved banners, they should put on a display of fight, but under no circumstances advance. Wu Yong's orders were transmitted.

Shi Wengong was hoping that Song Jiang's forces would attack the south fort and fall into the concealed pits. The road before it was narrow.

Where else could they go?

At mid-morning the next day the sound of cannon was heard up ahead. Pursuit troops gathered at the south gate. Then a messenger arrived from the east fort.

"A monk with an iron staff and a pilgrim brandishing a pair of long knives are attacking us front and rear," he reported.

"They must be Sagacious Lu and Wu Song of Liangshan Marsh," said Shi Wengong. He sent part of his soldiers to support Zeng Kui.

From the west fort another messenger arrived. "A big fellow with a long beard and a robber with a face like a tiger, with banners reading *Beautiful Beard Zhu Tong* and *Winged-Tiger Lei Heng,* are pressing us hard," he said.

Shi Wengong sent a portion of his men to aid Zeng Suo. Once more cannon boomed ahead. Shi had no more troops to spare. He could only wait for his adversaries to advance and tumble into the pits, at which time his soldiers hiding behind the hills would come out and help Shi nab them.

But Wu Yong swept forward around the hills in two flanking movements. The infantry guarding the fort was afraid to leave it. The soldiers flushed out of ambush were driven towards the fort by Wu Yong's pursuing troops, and large numbers of them fell into the pits.

Shi Wengong was about to sally forth when Wu Yong pointed with his whip. Gongs crashed and from the midst of the outlaw forces a hundred carts were pushed out and set ablaze. The conflagration of reeds, brushwood, sulphur and nitrate concealed the sky with smoke and flames. By the time Shi and his soldiers emerged their road was blocked by burning carts. They could only avoid them and hastily retreat. Gongsun waved his sword and conjured up a mighty wind which blew the flames into the south gate of the fort. Several buildings and part of the stockade burst into blaze and were destroyed.

A victory had been won. Trumpets summoned the outlaws to reassemble. They returned to their camps and rested. That night Shi repaired his gate and both sides secured their positions.

The next day Zeng Tu said to Shi Wengong: "If we don't kill their leaders it will be hard to wipe those bandits out." Telling his tutor to defend the fort, he donned his armor, mounted, and rode out at the head of his troops to challenge his adversaries to battle.

When Song Jiang heard who it was, he proceeded to the front, escorted by Lu Fang and Guo Sheng. He saw Zeng Tu under an arch of banners, and he burned with hatred. He pointed at him with his whip.

"Who will take that scamp for me and get me my long-awaited revenge?"

Lu Fang the Little Duke clapped his steed and rode against Zeng Tu, holding upright his crescent-bladed halberd. The antagonists met amid a clash of weapons. They fought over thirty rounds. From beneath the arch of pennants Guo Sheng could see that Lu Fang was weakening. He had fought well for the first thirty rounds, but his movements had become clumsy, and he was forced on the defensive.

Fearful that Lu Fang would be defeated, Guo Sheng suddenly mounted and, twirling his own crescent-bladed halberd, flew onto the battlefield and joined in the attack on Zeng Tu. The three horsemen locked in combat.

A panther's tail, with spots like gold coins, dangled from the head of each of the halberds. Both were lifted as the two outlaws closed in to seize their opponent. Zeng Tu had a quick eye. He raised his lance and entangled the tails, but the crimson tassel on his own weapon was also caught. He couldn't pull them apart. All three men were wrenching to free them.

Hua Rong, watching from the outlaws' position, was afraid his two companions would suffer. He rode forward, his left hand grasping his bow, his right hastily fitting a long slim arrow. He bent the bow and let fly at Zeng Tu. At that very moment Zeng Tu had extricated his lance, while the halberds were still entangled and, quicker than it takes to say, was thrusting at Lu Fang's neck. The arrow struck him in the left arm, knocking him from his saddle. Lu Fang and Guo Sheng's halberds swiftly took his life.

A dozen horsemen galloped back and reported to Shi Wengong, who reported in turn to the central fort. Zeng Senior wept aloud. The warrior beside him, his son Zeng Sheng, was enraged. A man of superb skill with arms, he wielded a pair of swords with such deadliness that no foe dared come near him. He ground his teeth in fury.

"Prepare my horse," he yelled. "I'm going to avenge brother!"

His father couldn't stop him. In full armor, he took his swords, mounted, and rode to the front fort.

"You mustn't underestimate the enemy," Shi Wengong warned him. "Song Jiang has many intelligent bold officers. In my humble opinion we should continue holding our five forts while secretly dispatching an emissary to Lingzhou to request that the throne be petitioned immediately for a relief army. One half of it should be sent to attack Mount Liangshan, the other to defend Zengtou. That will take the heart out of the bandits. Their only thought will be to rush back to their stronghold. Then, though I am a person of no talent, I shall be glad to join with you and your brothers in pursuing and exterminating the brigands. We're sure to attain great distinction."

Before he had finished speaking, assistant instructor Su Ding arrived from the north fort. He agreed with Shi's proposal. "That scoundrel Wu Yong is full of tricks," he said. "He mustn't be considered lightly. Defense is the best course. When the relief army arrives, we can discuss long-range plans again."

"They killed my brother," Zeng Sheng shouted. "He must be avenged! Why should we wait! Delay will only give the enemy time to gather strength and make them harder to defeat!"

Neither Shi nor Su could dissuade him. Zeng Sheng mounted and, with a few dozen horsemen, flew from the fort to challenge the foe.

Song Jiang was notified. He instructed the advance force to give battle. Qin Ming, on receiving the order, started to go out, brandishing his wolf-toothed cudgel, against Zeng Sheng. But suddenly Li Kui, axes in hand, rushed forward without a word to anyone and occupied the center of the arena.

One of the enemy recognized him. "That's Li Kui the Black Whirlwind," he said.

Zeng Sheng directed his archers to shoot. Ordinarily, Li Kui went naked into combat, and he relied on the shields of Xiang Chong and Li Gun for cover. But this time he rushed out alone, and an arrow struck him in the leg. He fell like a collapsing Mount Taishan. The horsemen behind Zeng Sheng galloped forward to seize him, while Qin Ming and Hua Rong raced from the opposite side, followed by Ma Lin, Deng Fei, Lu Fang and Guo Sheng. Since Song Jiang's men outnumbered him, Zeng Sheng was afraid to continue the engagement. He and his soldiers returned to the fort. Song Jiang called his forces back to camp.

The next day, Shi Wengong and Su Ding opposed any further combat.

But they had no affect on Zeng Sheng. "Brother must be avenged," he insisted. Shi had no choice but to don his armor and mount. His horse was the famous White Jade Lion That Glows in the Night which he had taken forcibly from Duan Jingzhu. Song Jiang rode out with his chieftains to meet him.

Shi raced fiercely towards them. Qin Ming, eager for first honors, flew forward. The animals met and weapons clashed. After twenty rounds Qin Ming faltered, and he rode back towards his original position. Shi, pursuing, thrust with his lance. He hit Qin Ming in the leg, and the Thunderbolt fell from his saddle. Lu Fang, Guo Sheng, Ma Lin and Deng Fei raced to his defense. Although they managed to rescue Qin Ming, the enemy inflicted casualties. They withdrew and made camp ten *li* from the fort.

Song Jiang ordered a cart for the Thunderbolt and had him escorted back to the mountain fortress to rest. Then he conferred with Wu Yong. They sent word to the stronghold for Guan Sheng the Big Halberd, Xu Ning the Metal Lancer, Shan Tinggui and Wei Dingguo to come and lend a hand.

Song Jiang burned incense and prayed, and cast divining sticks. Wu Yong looked at the omens and said: "Since this place is penetrable, enemy soldiers will surely slip into camp tonight."

"We'd better prepare, then."

"Don't let it trouble you, brother. Simply order the chieftains of three camps to combine them into two, one east, one west, and place Xie Zhen on the left and Xie Bao on the right of this one. Let the remainder conceal themselves in ambush on all sides."

This was done. That night, the sky was clear and the moon was bright. There was no wind or clouds.

Shi Wengong, in his fort, said to Zeng Sheng: "The bandits today lost two commanders. They must be frightened and depressed. This would be a good time to raid their camp."

Zeng Sheng immediately ordered Su Ding in the north fort, Zeng Mi in the south, and Zeng Suo in the west, to come at once with their soldiers and join in the attack. Around the second watch, they stealthily posted pickets, removed the bells from their horses and the clanking armor from the men, and crept into Song Jiang's central camp. No one was in sight. The camp was empty.

Realizing they'd been tricked, they turned to beat a hasty retreat. But from the left came Two-Headed Snake Xie Zhen and from the right came Twin Tailed Scorpion Xie Bao, with Hua Rong appearing in the rear, and all closed in together. In the darkness, Zeng Suo was skewered by Xie Zhen's steel trident, and tumbled dead to the ground.

Torches were applied to Shi's fort to the rear and wild shouts rose as outlaw troops smashed into the stockade from the east and the west. A savage melee raged through half the night. Shi Wengong clawed out an escape route and fled.

Zeng Senior's agitation doubled on learning of the death of his son Suo. The next day he asked Shi to write a letter of surrender. The instructor, who was also very frightened, did so, and dispatched it by emissary to Song Jiang's camp. Song Jiang opened it and read:

Zeng Nong, lord of Zengtou Village, bows his head and respectfully greets Song Jiang, commander-in-chief. My sons in a moment of rashness wrongly offended your prestige. When Chao Gai the Heavenly King came with troops and reasonably demanded our submission, one of my underlings dared to snipe at him with bow and arrow. We also criminally stole your horses. There aren't words enough to express my apologies. All of this was against my wishes.

Now that dog of a son is dead, and I sent this emissary to request peace. If you will end the fighting and retire your troops, I will return all of your horses and highly reward your forces with gold and cloth. It is my sincere desire to avoid casualties on both sides. I pray you give this matter your consideration.

By the time he finished reading, Song Jiang was in a rage. "He killed my brother Chao Gai," he fumed. "'Why should I quit! I'll raze that village to the ground!"

The emissary, lying prostrate, trembled uncontrollably. Wu Yong hastily intervened.

"You're wrong, brother," he said. "We contended with them because they abused us. But now they are asking for peace. Can we abandon principle because of a moment of anger?"

A reply was written and ten ounces of silver given to the emissary who returned to the village. Zeng Senior and Shi Wengong opened the missive and read:

Song Jiang, commander-in-chief of Mount Liangshan, sets his hand in reply to Zeng Nong, lord of Zengtou: Since ancient times a country without credibility must perish, a man without virtue must die, wealth gained without rectitude must be confiscated, generals without courage must suffer defeat. Originally there was no enmity between Liangshan Marsh and Zengtou Village. Each stayed within its own boundaries. But your evil deeds aroused our hostility. If you seek peace you must return the horses you stole on two occasions, turn over the thief Yu Baosi; and reward our soldiers with money and cloth. Let your generosity demonstrate your sincerity. If you change your mind, we shall have to take other measures.

Zeng Nong and Shi were both shocked and depressed. The next day Zeng Nong dispatched an emissary with another message: "If you want Yu Baosi, please send a man as hostage."

Song Jiang and Wu Yong dispatched Shi Qian, Li Kui, Fan Rui, Xiang Chong and Li Gun as an earnest of a desire for negotiations. Just before they left, they were told what to do in the event of an emergency, and urged to act promptly. The five departed.

Guan Sheng, Xu Ning, Shan Tinggui and Wei Tingguo arrived from the mountain stronghold. After a reunion with the other chieftains they were stationed in the central column.

Meanwhile, Shi Qian and the four bold fellows met with Zeng Senior. "Big Brother has ordered us here to discuss peace," said Flea on a Drum.

"If Wu Yong sends five men he must be up to some trick," said Shi Wengong.

Li Kui angrily grabbed Shi and commenced to beat him. Zeng Senior hurriedly intervened.

Shi Qian said: "Li Kui may be crude, but he has Big Brother's fullest trust. He was specially chosen. You have no need for suspicion."

Zeng Senior was very anxious for peace. Ignoring Shi, he served the five wine and invited them to rest in the camp in the Fahua Monastery, and posted a guard of five hundred soldiers front and rear. He then appointed his son Zeng Sheng his negotiator and sent him to Song Jiang's camp with Yu Baosi.

After presenting themselves at the central column, they delivered the horses they had stolen, plus a quantity of gold and bolts of cloth.

"These are the latest horses you rustled," said Song Jiang. "Where is White Jade Lion That Glows in the Night that you snatched from Duan Jiangzhu the previous time?"

"My instructor Shi Wengong has been riding it," said Zeng Sheng. "That's why we didn't bring it."

"You hurry up and write a letter, and say I want that horse back, quickly!"

Zeng Sheng penned a missive and sent a man with it to the fort. When Shi was informed, he said: "Any other horse he can have, but not this one!"

Several times the messenger shuttled back and forth. Song Jiang absolutely insisted. Finally, Shi dispatched a reply.

"If he really must have my horse, let him withdraw his army first, and I'll give it to him."

Song Jiang went into a huddle with Wu Yong. While they were conferring a man suddenly arrived and reported: "Armies from Qingzhou and Lingzhou are on their way!"

"When those rascals in Zengtou hear about this, they're sure to pull a switch!" Song Jiang averred.

He secretly ordered Guan Sheng, Shan and Wei to engage the Qingzhou army, and Hua Rong, Ma Lin and Deng Fei to engage the forces from Lingzhou. He also summoned Yu Baosi privately, reassured him and treated him with great kindness.

"If you're willing to perform meritoriously, I'll make you a chieftain in our mountain stronghold," said Song Jiang. "Vengeance against you for stealing our horses will be forgotten. I'll break an arrow in pledge. If you won't co-operate, Zengtou will soon be destroyed. It's up to you." Yu decided to give in and accept orders. Wu Yong told him of his plan.

"Pretend to have escaped and run back to your fort. Say to Shi Wengong: 'I was in Song Jiang's camp with Zeng Sheng, negotiating peace. From what I heard, I now have the true picture. Song Jiang's only purpose is to get back his Fine horse. He's not interested in peace. Once you return the animal, he's going to turn on us. He's heard that relief armies are on the way from Qingzhou and Lingzhou, and he's in a terrible flap. You must take advantage of this situation and act. It's too good to miss.' If Shi heeds your advice, we'll be ready for him."

Yu went to Shi's fort and spoke as directed. Shi led him to Zeng Senior and said that Song Jiang had no intention of making peace, and that this was a good time to attack his camp.

"But Sheng is there," the father protested. "If we change, they're sure to kill him."

"We'll smash into the camp and rescue him, come what may. Tonight we'll order all of our forts to muster their full complement of men and go with us against Song Jiang's camp. Once we cut off the snake's head its body—the rest of the bandits—will be immobilized. When we return there will be time enough to kill Li Kui and the other four."

"An excellent plan, instructor."

Su Ding in the north fort, Zeng Kui in the east fort and Zeng Mi in the south fort were notified to join in the raid. Yu managed to slip into the fort in the Fahua Monastery and see Li Kui and the others. He surreptitiously told Shi Qian what was going on.

Meanwhile, Song Jiang said to Wu Yong: "I wonder how our plan is working out?"

"If Yu doesn't come back, that means they've fallen for it," said the military advisor. "Tonight, they'll probably raid our camp. We'll pull out, first, and lie in ambush on both sides. At the same time we'll send Sagacious Lu and Wu Song with foot soldiers against their east fort, and infantry under Zhu Tong and Lei Heng against their west fort, while Yang Zhi and Shi Jin attack the north fort with cavalry. This method is called 'The Foreign Hunting Dog Waits for the Quarry in Its Den'. It never fails."

That night Shi Wengong set out with Su Ding, Zeng Mi, Zeng Kui and their soldiers. The moon was hazy, the stars were dim. Shi and Su were in the lead, Mi and Kui covered the rear. Bells had been removed from the horses and clanking armor from the men. All advanced quietly towards Song Jiang's camp.

They found the gates open and not a soul inside. It was completely still. The raiders knew they had been duped, and quickly departed. As they hurried back towards their fort they heard gongs clashing and cannon booming in Zengtou. Shi Qian, who had climbed into the bell tower of Fahua Monastery, had clangorously tolled the big bell. This was the signal for outlaw artillery to open fire on the East and West Gates of the village. With a roar, countless brigands poured through the blasted portals, slaughtering as they came. In the monastery, Li Kui, Fan Rui, Xiang Chong and Li Gun vigorously fought their way out.

Shi was anxious to return to the fort, but he couldn't find the road. The fort itself was a scene of mad confusion. Zeng Senior, on being informed that the men of Liangshan Marsh were charging murderously in from two directions, hung himself in despair.

Zeng Mi, hastening to the west fort, died from a thrust of Zhu Tong's halberd. Zeng Kui, fleeing to the east fort, was trampled to jelly in the chaos by horses' hoofs.

Pursued by Sagacious Lu and Wu Song, Su Ding rushed pell-mell through the North Gate, outside of which were innumerable concealed pits. He ran into Yang Zhi and Shi Jin, who killed him with arrows. The men and horses fleeing in his wake tumbled one on top the other into the pits, countless numbers dying in their fall.

Shi Wengong's White Jade Lion steed was fleet. He galloped through the West Gate into the wilderness. A black mist curtained the sky. Shi couldn't tell north from south. He rode on for twenty *li,* not knowing where he was.

A gong crashed in a wood and four or five hundred troops surged out. The commander at their head held a long staff, which he swung at the legs of Shi's mount. The magnificent stallion, before the blow could land, leaped over its attacker's head and galloped on.

Shi continued to race through the night. Dark clouds massed, chill vapors floated, a black mist spread, a fierce wind blew. In the emptiness, wherever he turned he was dogged by Chao Gai's spirit. Shi resumed his original road, and he ran into Yan Qing the Prodigy and Lu Junyi the Magnate.

"Where do you think you're going, wretched thief!" shouted Lu. With one thrust of the halberd into Shi's leg, he brought him from his saddle. Lu tied him up and marched him to Zengtou. Yan Qing led the famous steed to the main camp.

Song Jiang was both delighted and angry. While glad that Lu Junyi had distinguished himself, he was enraged to see Shi Wengong, who had slain Chao Gai the Heavenly King.

First he had Zeng Sheng decapitated and every member of the Zeng family slaughtered, old and young, without exception. Then he stripped the village of all gold, silver, valuables and grain and loaded them onto carts for delivery to the mountain stronghold, where they would be distributed as rewards among the chieftains and troops.

Meanwhile, Guan Sheng drove off the army from Qingzhou, and Hua Rong scattered the soldiers from Lingzhou, and they and their forces returned to the village. Not a chieftain, big or small, had been lost, and Song Jiang had regained the White Jade Lion That Glows in the Night, to say nothing of large quantities of booty.

Shi Wengong was locked in a cage cart, the outlaw troops were assembled, and all headed back for Mount Liangshan. None of the towns, villages or hamlets en route were molested.

On arriving at Loyalty Hall, they gathered before Chao Gai's spirit tablet. Xiao Rang the Master Hand, at Song Jiang's direction, wrote the memorial address. The chieftains wore mourning and wept. Shi Wengong's heart was cut out and offered as a sacrifice to the departed. The ceremony was completed.

Song Jiang then discussed with the chieftains the question of Chao Gai's successor.

"You, brother, should be the supreme leader, with Lu Junyi the Magnate as second in command," said Wu Yong. "The remaining brothers should retain their original ranks."

"Don't you remember Chao Gai's dying wish? 'Let whoever captures Shi Wengong become the ruler of Liangshan Marsh.' Today, Lu Junyi caught the knave and brought him up the mountain as a sacrifice to brother Chao Cai. Vengeance has been attained. It is only proper that he command. There's no need for a lot of talk."

"I'm lacking in both virtue and talent," Lu protested. "I wouldn't dare to assume such a position. Even if I were given the lowest rank, it would be too much."

"I don't mean to be overly modest," said Song Jiang, "but in three respects I am your inferior. First, I'm short and swarthy, ugly and incompetent, while you are handsome, stalwart, and of noble men. Second, I was only a petty functionary who committed a crime and had to flee. Because these brothers didn't scorn me, I was allowed to rule temporarily. But you are the son of a powerful family, and renowned for gallantry. Although you were in a bit of danger for a while, Heaven has defended you, and you're now out of trouble. Third, I can neither maintain stability in civil affairs nor win the support of troops in military matters. I haven't the strength to strangle a chicken, or draw a bow as much as an inch, whereas you can deal with a thousand enemies at once. You understand the present and are learned in the past. There's no one who doesn't concede your superiority. Because of your talent and virtue it is entirely fitting that you be the ruler of our mountain stronghold. Later, when you return to the service of the emperor and through merit build your career, you surely will become a high official, and we brothers will bask in your reflected glory. My mind is made up. You mustn't refuse any longer."

Lu Junyi respectfully and humbly kowtowed. "Brother, say no more," he begged. "Even if I die for it, I cannot accede to your order!"

"Remain as leader, let Lu be second in command," Wu Yong urged, "and everyone will be satisfied. You'll chill our men's hearts if you keep on relinquishing like this!" He had already noted the expressions on the faces of the others before making this statement.

Li Kui the Black Whirlwind raised his voice loudly: "I risked my life at Jiangzhou to come here with you. We've given you your way in everything. I'm not afraid of Heaven itself, so I ask you: Why do you keep trying to give up the friggin command? I'll start killing again! We can dissolve the gang!"

Wu Song also took Wu Yong's hint. "There are many high military officers under you, brother," he said, "who once took their orders from the emperor. They'll listen to you, but not to anyone else."

Liu Tang said; "There were seven of us when we first came up the mountain. It was our intention then to make you our leader. We couldn't serve another now."

"If you give up command, brother," Sagacious Lu shouted, "I say we should pack it in and each go his separate way!"

"Enough," Song Jiang cried. "I have a method. Whatever is Heaven's will, we'll act accordingly."

"What is your proposal," said Wu Yong. "Please tell us."

"It involves two matters," said Song Jiang.

And because of these, two heroes were added to Mount Liangshan, and the district town of Dongping was stricken by calamity. The stars of Heavenly Spirits joined in loyal righteousness, and in Liangshan Marsh the stars of Earthly Fiends gathered.

What were the two matters of which Song Jiang spoke? Read our next chapter if you would know.

CHAPTER 69

NINE DRAGONS SHI JIN IS TRAPPED IN DONGPING PREFECTURE

SONG JIANG CHIVALROUSLY RELEASES GENERAL TWO SPEARS

"We're short of money and grain," Song Jiang said to the assembled chieftains, "but to the east of here are two prefectural towns where they have both. One is Dongping, the other is Dongchang. While we've never disturbed their people, when we asked them to lend us some grain, they flatly refused. I'm going to have the names of these towns written on separate slips of paper. Lu Junyi and I will each draw one. Whoever first conquers his town will become the ruler of Liangshan Marsh. Agreed?"

"Good," said Wu Yong. "We'll abide by Heaven's will."

"Don't talk like that," said Lu. "Big Brother must remain as leader. Otherwise I won't accept the mission."

But Lu was over-ruled. Ironclad Virtue Pei Xuan wrote out the slips. Prayers were offered and incense burned. Then the drawing was made. Song Jiang picked Dongping, Lu got Dongchang. All of the chieftains were satisfied.

That day a feast was laid. While they were drinking wine, Song Jiang announced the disposition of the forces to be used in the attacks. His own command would consist of twenty-five chieftains including himself. They would lead an army of ten thousand infantry and cavalry. The three Ruan brothers—Second, Fifth and Seventh, would support them with a naval flotilla.

Under Lu Junyi would be another twenty-four chieftains. They too would command an army of combined infantry and cavalry numbering ten thousand, and would be supported by a naval flotilla under Li Jun, Tong Wei and Tong Meng.

The other chieftains, and those convalescing from wounds, would remain to guard the fortress. The dispositions having been made, the two armies set forth against the prefectural towns.

It was the first day of the third lunar month. The days were warm, the wind mild, the grass green, the turf soft—perfect conditions for battle.

We'll speak First of Song Jiang, as he marched on Dongping, Forty *li* from the town, he and his forces came to a village called Anshan, and there made camp.

"Cheng Wanli the governor of Dongping and his district military commander are both natives of Shangdang County, east of the river. The commander's name is Dong Ping. Because he's skilled with a pair of spears, he's known to everyone as General Two Spears. He has the courage often thousand," said Song Jiang. "Although we're going to attack his town, we should treat him courteously. I want to dispatch two men with a written declaration of war. I shall urge him to surrender and avoid a battle. If he refuses, no one will be able to blame us for the carnage. Who dares to deliver my message?"

A man stepped forward. He was Yu Baosi. "I know Dong Ping by sight," he said. "I'll be glad to deliver the declaration."

Another man emerged from the ranks of the chieftains. His name was Wang Dingliu. "I haven't proven my mettle to the stronghold yet," he said, "and so I'd like to go with him on this mission."

Song Jiang was very pleased. He wrote his letter and gave it to the two volunteers. It stated only a request for grain.

When Governor Cheng of Dongping heard that an army under Song Jiang was camped in Anshan, he summoned his district commander, General Two Spears to discuss the military situation. Just as they had sat down, the gate-keeper entered and said: "Messengers from Song Jiang are here with a declaration of war."

Cheng directed that they be allowed in. Yu and Wang entered and presented the letter. Cheng read it. He turned to the general.

"They're demanding money and grain. What shall we do?"

The general was furious. He shouted for the emissaries to be taken out and decapitated. Cheng intervened.

"No! Since ancient times messengers between hostile states have never been killed. It would be highly improper. Let them each be beaten twenty strokes and sent back. We'll see what Song Jiang does next."

But the general was still fuming. He had the two bound and beaten till their skin split and their flesh burst asunder, and then had them driven from the town.

They returned to the camp, weeping. "That lout of a general has no sense of fitness," they complained. "He holds our fortress in contempt."

Anger filled Song Jiang's breast. He longed to level the town immediately. He instructed Yu and Wang to return to the stronghold and rest. Nine Dragons Shi Jin rose and said:

"I used to live in Dongping and was sweet on a girl in a pleasure house there. Her name is Li Shuilan. We were having a really warm affair. If I take some gold and silver and slip into town, I can stay in her house. I'll set a time, Big Brother, and you can attack. As soon as General Two Spears goes out to fight, I'll climb up into the Drum Tower and start a fire. Operating from within and without, we'll win a big victory."

"Excellent," cried Song Jiang.

Shi Jin put some gold and silver in a bundle, concealed a weapon on his person, and bid a respectful farewell.

"I won't move my troops, brother, until you pick an appropriate moment," Song Jiang informed him.

Nine Dragons entered the town and went directly to the home of Li Shuilan in the western pleasure house district. The pander of the establishment was startled to see him. He led Shi Jin inside and called the girl. Shuilan escorted Shi Jin upstairs and they sat down.

"I haven't seen so much as your shadow in ages. How come?" she queried. "I hear you're a big chieftain in Liangshan Marsh now. There's a notice out for your arrest. The last couple of days the streets have been buzzing with talk that Song Jiang is going to raid the town for grain. What are you doing here, anyway?"

"The truth is I am a chieftain on Mount Liangshan, but I haven't distinguished myself yet. Big Brother plans to attack the town for grain, all right. I told him about your place and he sent me here to spy. I've brought you some gold and silver. You're not to breathe a word. After this is over, I'll take you and your family up the mountain, and we'll be happy."

Shuilan glibly promised to do everything he asked. She accepted the money and served him food and drink. But later she discussed it with the bawd who was the pander's wife.

"When he was a regular caller, he was a good person," the girl said. "His coming here didn't matter. But now he's gone bad. If there's trouble, it won't be any joke for us."

"It's dangerous to provoke those bold fellows of Song Jiang in Liangshan Marsh," the pander cautioned. "They can take any town they like. When they break in here, they'll wreck everything. They'll go hard on us if we don't keep our word."

"Old idiot," his wife the bawd swore. "You're just ignorant! If there's a wasp in your bosom, pluck it out, as the old saying goes. Informants are never prosecuted—that's the universal rule. Go to the district court, quick, and inform on Shi Jin. Let them take him. Then, whatever happens, we won't be involved."

"He's brought us a lot of money," the pander said hesitantly. "What's the point of it if we don't do anything for him?"

"Animal," his wife exclaimed. "Your words are just farts! We bawds have harmed thousands! What's one more? If you don't inform on him I'll go down there myself and cry for justice—against you, as well!"

"Control yourself," urged the pander. "Tell Shuilan to hang on to him. We don't want to stir the grass and alarm the snake. He mustn't get away. I'll report to the police first, and let them nab him. Then I'll inform the court."

Shuilan went back upstairs. Shi Jin was struck by her alternating flushes and pallor.

"Is anything wrong? Why do you look so frightened?"

"I missed my step on the stairs and nearly fell. My heart's all aflutter."

Suddenly they heard footsteps running up the stairs and shouts outside the window. Dozens of policemen burst into the room. They hustled Shi Jin like a bound lion down the stairs, and rushed him to the district court of Dongping.

"You impudent scoundrel," shouted the governor. "How dare you come here to spy? If Li Shuilan's protector hadn't informed, you might have caused severe damage to our citizenry? Tell us the whole story, quickly! What did Song Jiang send you to find out?"

Shi Jin didn't speak.

"Rogues like that never talk unless you clout them," growled the general.

"Police and jailors, beat the villain," shouted Governor Cheng.

Shi Jin's captors spewed cold water on him, then struck him a hundred blows with big rods on each leg. He endured it, and didn't say a word.

"Put a heavy rack on the lout and put him in the cell for the condemned," said General Two Spears. "When we catch Song Jiang we'll deliver them both to the Eastern Capital for punishment!"

To return to Song Jiang. After Shi Jin left, he wrote a letter to Wu Yong saying that Shi Jin had gone to the home of Li Shuilan the doxy to spy. The military advisor was shocked. He hastily conferred with Lu Junyi and hurried to Song Jiang that same night.

"Who told Shi Jin to go?" he demanded.

"It was his own idea. He said that the girl had been his mistress, that they were very close."

"You've made a mistake, brother. If I were here, I never would have agreed. Courtesans become intimate quickly, but they like new things and tire of the old. They've harmed countless talented men. They're as unstable as water. Even if she felt some genuine affection for him, she'd have a hard time going against her procuress. Shi Jin is sure to have come to grief."

Song Jiang asked what they could do about it. Wu Yong summoned Mistress Gu and gave her instructions.

"We must trouble you to go into Dongping. Disguise yourself as a poor beggar woman and slip into town. If anything's stirring, report back at once. If Shi Jin is in prison, approach one of the jailors and say you want to bring him some food, for the sake of past kindness. After you get inside, tell Shi Jin secretly. 'We're breaking into town the last day of the month around dusk. During the excitement, find a way to get yourself free.' The night of the last day of the month, you, Mistress Gu, start a fire as a signal. That's when we'll launch our raid."

Wu Yong turned to Song Jiang. "First, you must attack the county town of Wenshang, brother. The people are bound to flee to Dongping. Mistress Gu can mingle with the refugees and go in with them. No one will recognize her."

The military advisor mounted his horse and returned to Dongchang.

Song Jiang mustered five hundred men and sent them against Wenshang, under Xie Zhen and Xie Bao. Sure enough, the residents, supporting the old and carrying the young, scurried to Dongping to escape the battle. The town was thrown into confusion.

Mistress Gu, her hair dishevelled, her clothes in tatters, mingled with the crowds and entered the town. She begged along the streets until she came to the prefectural government compound. Her queries revealed that Shi Jin was indeed in prison.

The next day, carrying a jug of rice, she walked back and forth in front of the prison, waiting. Finally, an elderly policeman came out. She dropped to her knees and kowtowed, her tears falling like rain.

"What are you crying about, woman?"

"My former master Shi Jin is in there. It's been ten years since he left us. I heard only that he was travelling around as a merchant. I can't imagine what he's doing in jail. Nobody's sending him anything to eat, so I want to bring him this mouthful of food I've begged. Have pity, brother. Take me in. You'll be performing a greater blessing than building a seven-story pagoda."

"He's a bandit from Liangshan Marsh, and he's committed a capital offense. No one would dare to take you in there."

"He must accept what he deserves, even if it's death by slow slicing. But have pity on an old woman who only wants to deliver a mouthful of food for the sake of kindness in the past." Again Mistress Gu wept.

The old policeman thought to himself: "If it were a man, I couldn't do it. But what harm is there in a woman?" He led Mistress Gu into the prison where she found Shi Jin wearing a heavy rack on his neck, and iron chains around his waist.

Nine Dragons was amazed to see her, but he remained silent. Mistress Gu pretended to weep and sob as she fed him from the jug. Jailors hastened towards them.

"That's a condemned evil-doer," they shouted. "Not even the wind gets in here. Who let you bring him food? Get out, quick, and save yourself a beating!"

There were too many people around. She couldn't say much, but only had time to whisper: "We're breaking into the town the last night of the month. Fight to free yourself."

Before Shi Jin could ask her what time of the night, the jailors drove her with blows out of the prison door. He remembered only "last night of the month."

It happened that the third lunar month had thirty days that year, instead the usual twenty-nine. But when Shi Jin asked one of the jailors, "What's the date?" the man remembered wrongly and said: "The last day of the month. I must buy some spirit paper to burn for the wandering souls."

Shi Jin could scarcely wait. Near evening, he got one of the keepers, who was half drunk, to take him to the latrine.

"Who's that behind you?" Shi Jin suddenly exclaimed.

As the man turned, Shi Jin wrenched open the rack and struck him on the forehead with a corner of it, knocking him to the ground. With a brick Shi Jin smashed the wooden fetters on his feet. Falcon eyes glaring, he charged into the central pavilion, where several policemen were sodden with drink. He killed a few, the others fled.

Nine Dragons opened the prison gate, in anticipation of rescue from the outside. He released all the inmates, about fifty or sixty men. They came cheering out of their cells.

When the situation was reported to Governor Cheng, his face turned an earthen hue. Hastily, he sent for his district commander.

"There must be an enemy spy in town," General Two Spears averred. "Dispatch guards at once to surround the scoundrel! I'll seize this opportunity to lead troops out and capture Song Jiang. Defend the town well, Excellency. Send a dozen men to hold the prison gate. Let no one escape!"

The general mounted, mustered his troops and set forth. Cheng formed a force of keepers and guards, armed with spears and staves, and dispatched them to prison gate, where they stood, shouting. While Shi Jin didn't dare to come out, neither did they have the courage to go in. Mistress Gu could only bemoan the miscarriage of the plan.

General Two Spears, sallying out with his infantry and cavalry at the fourth watch, raced murderously towards Song Jiang's camp. A scout reported their approach.

"Mistress Gu must have run into trouble," Song Jiang said. "Now the foe is attacking. We'll give them a hot welcome!" He ordered his army to get ready.

By dawn the contending hosts were deployed in battle positions. General Two Spears Dong Ping rode forward.

Clever and ingenious, he was a man of considerable accomplishments. There were few skills he hadn't mastered, including the playing of string instrument* and bamboo flutes. Throughout Shandong and Hebei he was famed as the dashing General Two Spears.

He cut a fine figure, and Song Jiang was filled with admiration. Attached to the General's arrow quiver was a pennant reading: *Heroic General Two Spears, noble lord often thousand families.* Song Jiang ordered Han Tao to joust with him.

Han Tao's weapon was a long lance. Grasping it firmly, he cantered towards Dong Ping. The General wielded his two spears with dazzling artistry. Han Tao was unable to cope.

Song Jiang next ordered Xu Ning the Metal Lancer into battle with his hooked weapon to replace Han Tao. Xu Ning at once galloped forward and locked Dong Ping in fierce combat. They fought desperately in a cloud of dust for over fifty rounds, with neither emerging the victor.

It was lasting too long. Song Jiang was afraid Xu Ning would lose. He had the trumpeter sound retreat, and Xu Ning turned his steed and rode back. General Two Spears closely pursued him right into the midst of the outlaws' position. Song Jiang waved his whip, and from all sides his troops closed in.

He rode to the top of a bluff and watched Dong Ping, surrounded by the outlaws. When the General headed east, Song pointed east with his pennant and the troops moved east and cut him off. When he tried to go west, Song pointed west with his pennant, and the troops shifted west and blocked him again.

Dashing first one way, then another, General Two Spears fought until late afternoon, when he finally broke through. Song Jiang did not give chase.

It was clear by then to Dong Ping that he could not wrest victory. He withdrew his forces into the town that same evening. Song Jiang moved his army up during the night and surrounded the walls. Inside the town Mistress Gu dared not light a signal fire and Shi Jin was unable to come out. Both were stalemated.

Now, Governor Cheng had a daughter of exceptional beauty, and Dong Ping, who was unmarried, had frequently sent intermediaries to plead his suit. But Cheng would not consent. As a result, there was some hostility between the two men, though they spoke to each other pleasantly enough. The morning after Dong returned to the town with his soldiers, he again sent a spokesman to press for the girl's hand.

"I'm a civil and he's a military official. Such a marriage would be ideal," said Cheng. "But I'd be a laughing stock if I consented now, with bandits at our gates and the situation so dangerous. Let's wait until we've driven them off and the safety of town preserved. It won't be too late then to talk about marriage."

The spokesman reported Cheng's reply. "Well put," said Dong, but in his heart he was very annoyed. He wasn't at all sure Cheng would agree later on.

Song Jiang, after arriving during the night, was intensifying his attack. The governor requested Dong Ping to go out and fight. Angrily, General Two Spears donned his armor and mounted. With three armies he marched from the town.

Beneath an arch of pennants on the field of battle, Song Jiang shouted: "How dare you, a lone general, oppose me? I've a hundred thousand men under me and thousands of able commanders, all united in carrying out Heaven's will to succor the needy and rescue the endangered! Better surrender now and avoid being killed!"

"Little clerk with the criminal tattoo on his cheek, death-deserving rogue," Dong fumed, "you're raving mad!"

Spears in hand, he galloped towards Song Jiang. From the left of his target Lin Chong and, from the right Hua Rong, rode out to meet him, each of them armed. They fought several rounds, then the two chieftains withdrew, while the outlaw army beat a confused retreat, as if already vanquished. Dong clapped his horse and courageously pursued.

Song Jiang pulled back to the border of Shouchun County, with General Two Spears closely following. When they were about a dozen *li* from the county seat, they came to a village. The post road running through its center was lined by thatched huts. Dong, racing after them on his horse, didn't know it was a trap. Out of healthy respect for Dong's power as a warrior, the night before Song had placed Stumpy Tiger Wang, Ten Feet of Steel, Zhang Qing, Sun the Witch and over a hundred men in ambush in the huts. They had laid ropes across the road and covered them with earth. At the sound of a gong, they were to raise and pull them taut, trip the steed, and catch the general.

When Dong reached the stretch of road, he heard Kong Ming and Kong Liang shout behind him: "Don't harm our ruler!" A gong crashed in front of the huts, the doors flew open, and ropes sprang up athward the road. As Dong's horse turned, more ropes rose behind it. Down went the animal and its rider. From the left Stumpy Tiger and Ten Feet of Steel leaped out, from the right Zhang Qing and Sun the Witch. Together they seized Dong and stripped him of his helmet, armor and spears, and removed his horse. The two women generals bound his hands behind him and, each bearing swords, led him under guard to meet Song Jiang.

Song Jiang, who had gone past the thatched huts, reined in beneath a leafy poplar and watched the two women chieftains approaching with their prisoner.

"I instructed you to invite General Dong Ping here," he shouted. "Who told you to tie him!"

The two murmured apologies and withdrew, as Song Jiang hastily dismounted and removed Dong's bonds. He took off his own armor and robe and gave them to the general to wear, prostrated himself and kowtowed. Dong hurriedly returned the courtesy.

"If you don't scorn us as too lowly, General," said Song Jiang, "please be the ruler of our mountain stronghold."

"I am your prisoner. Even death would be too light a punishment. If you are willing to spare me, I will consider myself infinitely fortunate!"

"Recently, we've run short of grain, and so we requested Dongping Prefecture to lend us some. We had nothing else in mind."

"That lout Cheng was once just a tutor in the house of Lord Tong Guan. Now he uses his high position to oppress the populace. If you'll allow me, brother, I'll fool them into opening the gates. You can charge in and take their money and grain as my thanks for your kindness."

Song Jiang was delighted. He ordered that Dong's possessions be returned. General Two Spears put on his armor and mounted. He rode back to Dongping Town, followed by the outlaw army, its banners and pennants rolled.

"You, on the walls," shouted Dong. "Open the gates!"

The soldiers above the gates brought torches and, in their light, recognized the district commander. They opened the big gates and lowered the drawbridge. Dong rode over and smashed the iron lock. Song Jiang and his army surged into the town.

They went directly to the prefectural government compound. An order was quickly transmitted that none of the ordinary people were to be killed, or their homes burned. Dong burst into Cheng's residency, slaughtered the governor and his entire household and took the daughter. At Song Jiang's direction, the prison was opened and Shi Jin rescued.

Song Jiang then looted the treasury of its gold and silver and valuables, and had grain from the government granary loaded onto carts, with instructions that it be delivered to the Shore of Golden Sands for the three Ruan brothers to take up the mountain.

Shi Jin led a party to the home of Li Shuilan in the western pleasure section. He hacked her, and her pander and bawd, to pieces.

Song Jiang distributed Cheng's private possessions among the populace and put up proclamations which read: "We have executed the tyrannical governor. Good citizens go about your business in peace." He then withdrew his army.

Bai Sheng the Daylight Rat hurried towards the chieftains when they reached the town of Anshan. He told of a battle in the district of Dongchang. Song Jiang frowned, and his eyes grew large with anger.

"Brothers," he cried, "we won't return to the mountain. Come with me!"

Truly, the heroes of the Marsh in powerful assault marched again on Dongchang, a town of lavish and elegant riches.

Were Song Jiang and his army able to effect a rescue? Read our next chapter if you would know.

CHAPTER 70

FEATHERLESS ARROW ASSAULTS HEROES WITH STONES

SONG JIANG ABANDONS GRAIN TO CATCH A WARRIOR

Bai Sheng said: "Lu Junyi has had two failures in a row in besieging Dongchang. The town is defended by a fierce general named Zhang Qin. He hails from Zhangte Prefecture and began his career in the cavalry. He flings stones with remarkable accuracy, hitting the mark every time. People call him the Featherless Arrow. Under him are two commanders. One is Gong Wang the Flowery-Necked Tiger, so named because he had a tiger tattooed all over his body, with its head decorating his neck. He throws a spear while riding. The other is Ding Desun the Arrow-Struck Tiger. His face is scarred from his cheeks to his throat. He throws a trident while riding.

"Lu waited outside the town for ten days, but no one came forth to fight. A few days ago, Zhang Qin emerged and Hao Siwen fought him for many rounds. Zhang then withdrew and Hao gave chase. A stone hit Hao on the temple and knocked him from his saddle. Yan Qing managed to strike Zhang's horse with an arrow, and so we were able to save Hao's life. That was our first failure.

"The next day, Fan Rui the Demon King Who Roils the World rode forth with Xiang Chong and Li Gun, who brandished their shields. Unexpectedly, in an underhand pitch, Ding flung his trident and struck Xiang Chong. That was our second failure.

"Both men are nursing their wounds on one of our boats. Our general Lu Junyi has sent me here to request you to come to his aid."

Song Jiang sighed. "How unlucky he is. I even dispatched Wu Yong and Gongsun Sheng to help him. I was sure he'd succeed in battle and thus gain face in our stronghold. Who'd have thought he'd meet his match'. But that being the case, I and my brothers will have to go to his rescue."

He ordered the three armies to march. The chieftains mounted and went with Song Jiang to the outskirts of Dongchang. Lu met them and related what had transpired. Then all made camp.

While they were conferring, a junior officer entered and reported: "Zhang Qin the Featherless Arrow is challenging us to personal combat."

Song Jiang and his chieftains rose and proceeded to a wide plain and deployed their troops. Three times the drums thundered, and Zhang Qin the Featherless Arrow rode forward. Back and forth, from one end of the line to the other, he cantered, his animal's hoofs churning dust. Gong Wang the Flowery-Necked Tiger emerged abruptly from the left side of the enemy's arch of pennants. From the shadows on the right came the Arrow-Struck Tiger Ding Desun. The three rode onto the field of battle. Zhang Qin pointed at Song Jiang.

"Robber varlet of the swamp, I challenge a fight to the death!" Song Jiang asked his chieftains: "Who will contend with Zhang Qin?" Angrily aroused, one of the heroes beside him leaped into the saddle and galloped forward, brandishing a sickle-bladed lance. It was Xu Ning the Metal Lancer.

"Just the man!" thought Song Jiang approvingly. The two horses met, the two weapons vied. After less than five rounds Zhang Qin retreated. Xu Ning pursued. Featherless Arrow raised the lance in his left hand as if to thrust, while with his right he quietly extracted a stone from an embroidered pouch. Xu Ning was quite close. Zhang Qin suddenly twisted around and let fly with the stone. He hit poor Xu Ning squarely between the eyes, knocking him from his horse.

Gong Wang and Ding moved up to grab him. But Song Jiang's forces were many, and Lu Fang and Guo Sheng both rushed out with their crescent-bladed halberds and snatched the victim back to safety.

The shocked Song Jiang turned pale. "Who will take on that scoundrel?" he asked.

Before the words were out of his mouth, from behind him a horse flew forward. It was Yan Shun who next contended. He fought many rounds, but there was no holding Zhang Qin, and Yan turned and withdrew. Zhang Qin, racing in pursuit, pulled out a stone and threw. It clanged against the back plate of Yan's armor. Bending low over his saddle, Zhang Qin cantered away.

"That wretch is nothing to be afraid of!" a voice among the outlaws shouted. And a chieftain clapped his steed and flew on to the field, holding a long lance. Han Tao the Ever-Victorious General engaged Zhang Qin without another word!

A mighty cheer went up as the horses met. Han Tao wanted to display his skill before Song Jiang. Concentration all his energies, he battled with Zhang Qin. But after less than ten rounds, Featherless Arrow withdrew. Han, wary of his stones, did not give chase. When Zhang looked back and saw he was not being followed, he wheeled his mount. Han Tao advanced with levelled lance. Zhang Qin stealthily extracted another stone. His hand rose and the missile struck Han Tao on the bridge of the nose. Blood streaming from the offended organ, Han fled back to his position.

Peng Qi was furious. Without waiting for Song Jiang's orders, waving a three-pointed, two-edged blade, he galloped towards Zhang Qin.

But before the two horses could meet, Featherless Arrow once more threw a stone concealed in his hand. Peng Qi was clunked on the forehead. He dropped his three-pointed, two-edged sword, and returned to the position in great haste.

One defeat after another. Panic gripped Song Jiang's heart. He was about to call a retreat. Then a mighty voice shouted from behind Lu Junyi the Magnate: "If our prestige is broken, how will we be able to fight in days to come? Let's see if those stones can hit me!"

It was Xuan Zan the Ugly Son-in-Law. He kicked up his horse and flew towards Zhang Qin, waving his blade.

"Singly come, singly go. Doubly come, flee in pairs," cried Featherless Arrow. "Haven't you seen my trick with stones?"

"You've hit others," retorted Xuan Zan, "but you'll never hit me!"

Even before he had finished speaking, Zhang Qin flung the stone in his hand. He struck Xuan Zan on the side of the mouth and tumbled him from his saddle. Gong Wang and Ding Desun advanced to seize him, but the outlaw forces, who outnumbered them, got there first and brought him back.

Song Jiang was consumed with rage. Sword in hand, he rent his gown and swore: "I'll either take Zhang Qin personally or I won't return to my army!"

Huyan Zhuo heard him make the vow. "What use are we brothers if you have to go forth yourself," he exclaimed. Astride his Ebony Steed Which Treads in Snow, he rode onto the field and reviled Zhang Qin.

"Over-rated scamp! What have you got except a bit of strength and courage? Do you recognize the great warrior Huyan Zhuo?"

"Traitor and vanquished general! See what you can do with this!" Featherless Arrow sent a stone sizzling through the air.

Huyan hastily raised his rods to ward it off and it struck him a paralyzing blow on the wrist. Since he could no longer swing the steel rods he returned to his base.

"All of the cavalry chieftains have been wounded," said Song Jiang. "Who of the infantry dares to capture Zhang Qin?"

Liu Tang, twirling his halberd, strode onto the field of battle. Zhang Qin laughed.

"Puny commander! I've beaten your cavalry. What good are footsloggers!"

Enraged, Liu Tang charged. Featherless Arrow turned his steed and cantered towards his position. Liu Tang raced after and caught up. With a swift hack, he struck the animal. It lashed out with its rear hoofs and switched its tail across Liu Tang's eyes, blinding him temporarily. A stone from Zhang Qin felled him to the ground. As he struggled to rise, government soldiers pounced on him and dragged him away.

"Who will rescue Liu Tang?" Song Jiang yelled.

Yang Zhi the Blue-Faced Beast, brandishing his halberd, rode out against Zhang Qin. Featherless Arrow feinted with his lance. Yang Zhi swung, Zhang Qin ducked down to his stirrups, and the blade struck empty air.

"Take that!" cried Zhang Qin, with a quick underhand toss.

The stone clanged against Yang Zhi's helmet, chilling him to the marrow. Bending low over his saddle, he hurriedly withdrew.

"If we lose our manhood today, how can we return to Liangshan Marsh?" thought Song Jiang. Aloud, he said: "Who will work off this rage for me?"

Zhu Tong looked at Lei Heng. "They've taken Liu Tang. So what!" he said. "If one man can't deal with Zhang Qin, we'll attack him together!"

Both men carrying halberds, they advanced murderously, Zhu Tong on the left, Lei Heng on the right. Zhang Qin laughed.

"One's not enough, so you've added another. Even if there were ten of you, it wouldn't matter!" Not a flicker of fear crossed his face. In each hand he concealed a stone.

Lei Heng reached him first. Zhang Qin's arm rose in god-like stance, and the stone flew so quickly it was impossible to dodge. Before Lei Heng knew what was happening the missile struck his cheek and knocked him flat on his back. As Zhu Tong rushed to the rescue, a stone hit him in the neck.

Guan Sheng, from the position, saw that both were wounded. Gathering all his might, he galloped out on his swift roan, brandishing his dragon sword. Zhang Qin, who had just driven off the other two, returned to the field. Again he threw. Guan Sheng hastily raised his weapon to ward off the stone, and it nicked the edge, striking sparks. His taste for battle vanished. Guan Sheng pulled his roan around and went back to base.

When General Two Spears Dong Ping saw this, he said to himself: "I surrendered to Song Jiang only recently. If I don't display some of my military skill, people won't think much of me when we go up the mountain." He galloped onto the field, his set of spears in hand.

Zhang Qin rebuked him harshly. "Yours and mine are neighboring prefectures, as close as lips and teeth. Together we exterminated robbers, which was only fitting and proper. Why have you turned against the imperial court? You ought to be ashamed!"

Furious, Dong Ping charged. The horses met, the weapons rose. It was lance against spears, with four arms wildly darting. Sixty or seventy rounds they fought, then Zhang Qin rode away.

"Others may fear your stones," said Dong Ping, "but they can't touch me!"

Featherless Arrow set his lance in its socket, pulled a stone from his embroidered pouch, and threw. But Dong Ping's eyes were sharp and his hands fast. He flicked the missile aside. Zhang Qin extracted a second stone and threw again. Again, Dong Ping evaded it. Two stones had missed their mark. Zhang Qin was growing panicky. Dong Ping's steed pounded in hot pursuit of his own, almost nose to tail.

As Zhang Qin neared the left side of his army's arch of pennants, General Two Spears thrust at his hack. Twisting, Featherless Arrow ducked low over his stirrups, and the blade went harmlessly by.

The two steeds were now racing parallel. Zhang Qin set aside his lance. With both hands he grasped Dong Ping, his arms and spears, and tugged. But he couldn't budge him. The two men grappled on horseback.

Suo Chao, watching from Song Jiang's position, hurried to the rescue, brandishing his big ax. Gong Wang and Ding Desun galloped out from the opposite position and intercepted him. They fought savagely. Zhang Qin and Dong Ping were locked in inseparable combat, while the mounts of the other three milled furiously about.

Lin Chong, Hua Rong, Lu Fang and Guo Sheng advanced together, two with lances, two with crescent-bladed halberds, to assist Dong Ping and Suo Chao. Zhang Qin saw that the situation was worsening. He abandoned Dong Ping and rode quickly back to his own position. But Dong Ping would not give up. He rode after Featherless Arrow right into the midst of the enemy, forgetting all about the stones. Zhang Qin stealthily pulled one from his pouch and waited for Dong Ping's horse to draw nearer. Then, "Take that!" he cried.

General Two Spears hastily dodged, and the stone whizzed past his ear. He returned to his base. Suo Chao left Gong Wang and Ding Desun and hurried after him Zhang Qin didn't use his lance but softly extracted a stone and flung it at Suo Chao. It struck him in the face before he could avoid it. Streaming blood, he returned to base with his ax.

Meanwhile, Lin Chong and Hua Rong had Gong Wang pinned down on one side, and Lu Fang and Guo Sheng had engaged Ding Desun on the other. Flurried, Gong Wang cast his javelin, but it hit neither of his opponents. He was weaponless now, and Lin Chong and Hua Rong captured him easily and took him back to their position.

Ding Desun twirled his trident and contended desperately with Lu Fang and Guo Sheng. He was unaware that Yan Qing was watching him from the arch of pennants.

"They've defeated fifteen of our chieftains in a row," thought the Prodigy. "We'll lose face if we don't nab at least one lieutenant."

He cast aside his staff, took up his bow, fitted an arrow, and let fly. It whistled into the hoof of Ding's mount, which stumbled to the ground. Lu and Guo immediately seized the fallen rider.

Zhang Qin wanted to go to his rescue, but the foe were too many. He returned to Dongchang with Liu Tang under guard. The prefect, from the town wall, had seen Featherless Arrow vanquish fifteen Mount Liangshan chieftains in succession. Although Featherless Arrow had lost Gong and Ding, he had captured Liu Tang. The prefect proceeded to his office and celebrated his victory with wine. Then he had Liu Tang put in jail with a rack around his neck, and sat down to confer with Zhang Qin.

As to Song Jiang, he returned with his army to camp. Gong and Ding he sent to the stronghold in Liangshan Marsh under escort. Afterwards, he consulted with Lu Junyi and Wu Yong.

"In the Five Dynasties period, Wang Yanzhang of the Great Liang beat thirty-six Tang commanders before the sun so much as moved their shadows," he said. "Today, Zhang Qin vanquished fifteen of our chieftains. Truly, a splendid general, no less a man than Wang Yanzhang!"

The others had no reply, and Song Jiang continued.

"It seems to me he relies completely on Gong and Ding to cover his flanks. Now that we've captured them, we ought to be able to think of some good way to catch him as well."

"You can rest assured, brother," said Wu Yong. "I've been observing his movements, and I have it all worked out. Send the wounded chieftains back to the fortress, and direct Sagacious Lu, Wu Song, Sun Li, Huang Xin and LiLi to bring as many of our naval forces as they can muster. We want carts and boats so that we can advance both by land and water, coordinate navy and cavalry, and trick Zhang Qin. In this way we Will succeed." And Wu Yong explained how the forces were to be deployed.

In the town, Zhang Qin was saying to the prefect: "Although we won, the robbers' strength is still intact. Send scouts to investigate, then we'll decide what to do."

When the scouts returned, they reported: "Northwest of their camp there's vast amount of grain. We don't know where it came from, but it's loaded on over a hundred carts and five hundred boats, large and small, on the river. Both convoys are moving forward, under several supervisors along the way."

"Can those scoundrels be up to something?" the prefect pondered. "We must be careful that they don't trick us. I'll send out more scouts to make sure it's really grain they're carrying."

The next day a junior officer returned and said: "Those carts are laden with rice. Some of it spilled out. And although the cargoes on the boats are covered, we could see the ends of grain sacks."

"I'm leaving tonight," said Zhang Qin. "First, I'll stop the carts along the bank, then I'll seize the boats upon the river. If you'll lend a hand, Prefect, we'll capture them before the first beat of the watch drum!"

"An excellent plan. Just make sure you time it right." The prefect directed that the soldiers, after eating and drinking their fill, put on armor and take plenty of empty sacks.

Holding his long lance, Zhang Qin quietly left the town at the head of a thousand men. Though the moon was faint, the sky was studded with stars. Before the expedition had gone ten *li* they saw a convoy of carts and a banner reading: *Righteous Loyalty Grain of the Marsh Fortress.* Walking in the lead was Sagacious Lu. He carried his Buddhist staff. His cloak was girt up around the waist.

"I'll bounce a stone off the skull of that bald-pate!" muttered Zhang Qin.

By then Lu had seen him, but he pretended to be unaware, and continued striding forward. But he forgot to take precautions against Zhang Qin's stones.

"Speed!" shouted Featherless Arrow, astride his steed.

The flying stone struck Lu's head, drawing blood and knocking him flat. Zhang Qin's cheering soldiers charged. Wu Song whipped out his two knives, rushed forward find rescued Sagacious, then fled, abandoning the carts.

Featherless Arrow seized them. They were indeed laden with grain. Too pleased to bother pursuing Sagacious Lu, he brought the carts into the town. The delighted prefect took them over. "Now for the grain boats," said Zhang Qin.

"Be sure you time it right," the prefect admonished.

Featherless Arrow mounted and rode to the South Gate. Grain boats without number could be seen on the river. He shouted for the gate to be opened. Yelling, his army charged down to the river's edge. Suddenly, heavy clouds gathered and a dark mist spread and covered the sky. Zhang Qin's soldiers, infantry and cavalry, couldn't see a thing. Gongsun Sheng had worked a magic spell.

Zhang Qin grew flurried, and his eyes dimmed. He wanted to go back, but there was no way open to either advance or retreat. Wild shouts rose on every side. He had no idea where the attackers came from. Lin Chong, leading his Iron Cavalry, drove Zhang Qin, horse and rider, into the water. Waiting for him in a line in the river were eight naval chieftains: Li Jun, Zhang Heng, Zhang Shun, the three Ruan brothers and the two Tongs. Zhang Qin could not struggle loose. The three Ruan brothers grabbed and bound him, and took him into camp. The naval chieftains hurried to report his capture to Song Jiang.

At Wu Yong's urging, the outlaws attacked the town the same night. It was impossible for the prefect to withstand them by himself. On four sides outside the town cannon boomed. The gates swung wide. The terrified prefect had nowhere to run.

Song Jiang's forces surged into the town. First, they freed Liu Tang. Then they broke open the granaries, sent part of the grain and money to the mountain stronghold, and distributed the rest among the people. They spared the life of the prefect, since he ordinarily had been a decent official.

Song Jiang and chieftains gathered in the prefectural office. The naval commanders brought forward Zhang Qin. He had wounded many of their brothers, and the chieftains, grinding their teeth in rage, wanted to kill him. But Song Jiang ordered that he be untied, and came down the steps to greet him.

"We offended your mighty prestige by mistake," he apologized. "Please don't hold it against us." He invited Featherless Arrow into the hall.

Before the words were out of his mouth, Sagacious Lu, his head bound with a kerchief, rushed up with raised staff to smite Zhang Qin. Song Jiang blocked him and shouted at him to stand aside.

Moved by Song Jiang's chivalry, Featherless Arrow kowtowed and declared his surrender. Song Jiang poured wine upon the ground and broke an arrow.

"If you brothers insist on vengeance, Heaven will not protect you, and you'll die beneath the sword!" he prophesied.

The chieftains had no reply. They smilingly relaxed and acceded. Everyone was pleased. The troops were mustered in preparation for the return to the mountain. Zhang Qin had a suggestion.

"In Dongchang district there is a veterinary named Huangfu Duan," he said. "He's a good judge of horses, and knows the causes of their chills and fevers. With potions and needles, he cures them all. His skill is truly remarkable. He's from Youzhou Prefecture, originally. He has blue eyes and blond hair and foreign features, and is known as the Purple Beard. We could use him on Mount Liangshan. We could tell him to bring his family and come with us, if that meets with your approval."

Song Jiang agreed with pleasure. "If Huangfu Duan is willing to join us, we'll be glad to have him."

Happy that Song Jiang manifested such a clear fondness for him, Zhang Qin summoned the veterinary. Song Jiang and the chieftains were favorably impressed. Huangfu Duan was certainly out of the ordinary. His blue eyes had two pupils each, and his curly beard extended down below his waist. Huangfu was received with such chivalry that he willingly agreed to join the band. Song Jiang was more than content.

Having restored internal harmony, he ordered the chieftains to muster the carts, laden with grain and gold and silver, and set out for the mountain fortress. The two armies, front and rear, also marched.

The return journey was uneventful, and they soon reached Loyalty Hall. Song Jiang summoned Gong Wang and Ding Desun and spoke to them kindly. The two kowtowed and declared their allegiance. Huangfu Duan became the stronghold's official veterinary. General Two Spears Dong Ping and Featherless Arrow Zhang Qin were enrolled as chieftains.

Extremely pleased, Song Jiang called for a feast of celebration. Each took his place in Loyalty Hall according to rank. There were exactly one hundred and eight of them.

"Brothers," said Song Jiang, "from the time we began to gather on this mountain, we have never had any real losses anywhere. This is due to Heaven's beneficence, not to the ability of any man. I am leader today only thanks to the courage of you brothers. Joined here in righteous assembly, I have a few words I would like to say. I hope you brothers will listen."

"Please speak, Big Brother," said Wu Yong. "We'd like to hear you."

Song Jiang expounded his ideas before the chieftains. And as a result the thirty-six stars of Heavenly Spirits confirmed their destined number and the seventy-two stars of Earthly Fiends tallied with the divine design.

What, then, did Song Jiang propose? Read our next chapter if you would know.

CHAPTER 71

IN LOYALTY HALL A STONE TABLET BEARS A HEAVENLY SCRIPT

THE HEROES OF LIANGSHAN MARSH TAKE SEATS IN ORDER OF RANK

"After my trouble in Jiangzhou I came up the mountain," said Song Jiang, "and later, thanks entirely to the support of you heroic brothers, I was made leader. Gathered here today we have a total of one hundred and eight chieftains. I am very happy. Since brother Chao Gai's death, on each of the occasions we led troops down the mountain we always returned intact. This is because Heaven defended us. It was not due to the talent of any man. Whenever one of us was captured by the enemy, whether imprisoned or wounded, he always came back safely. All of this was the work of Heaven. None of us can claim any credit. And here we are today, one hundred and eight of us gathered in righteous meeting. Truly an event rarely witnessed from ancient times to the present!

"These are days when armed soldiers roam, slaughtering at will and committing unpardonable crimes. I'm thinking of holding a great mass to thank the spirits of Heaven and Earth for their protective benevolence. We should pray first that they continue to preserve our health and security. Second, that the emperor will pardon our terrible crimes and allow us to serve our country loyally to the death. Third, that Chao Gai's ghost may soon become a spirit in Heaven so that in later reincarnations we may meet again.

"We should pray also that those who died by violence—the burned, the drowned, the murdered innocents—be allowed to cross over into Heaven.

"This is what I'd like to do. I wonder what you brothers think of the idea?"

"Excellent," said the chieftains. "A fine thing that can bring only good."

"Let Taoist mentor Gongsun Sheng conduct the mass," suggested Wu Yong. "Send men down to invite Taoist priests of high attainment to attend and bring the necessary paraphernalia. Have someone buy scented candles and paper horses, plus fruit and flowers, vegetables and other meatless dishes, and all things required for the sacrifices."

It was decided to hold the mass for seven days, starting the fifteenth of the fourth lunar month. The stronghold spent money freely and made full preparations. As the time drew near, four banners were hung in front of Loyalty Hall. Inside, three high altars were built, and idols of the Seven Precious and Three Clean Saints were set. On either side stood the Spirits of the Twenty-Eight Constellations and the Twelve Watches—for these were the true officiators over all important masses. Outside the hall were placed idols of the guardian generals Cui, Lu, Deng and Dou. Then the paraphernalia was laid out and the Taoist priests invited to begin. Including Gongsun Sheng, they numbered forty-nine.

It was a clear, bright day, pleasant and mild, with the moon white in the summer sky and the breeze gentle. Song Jiang and Lu Junyi lit the incense first, followed by Wu Yong and the other chieftains. Gongsun Sheng, officiating over the sacrifices, handed out the required texts and orders. He and the forty-eight Taoist priests would conduct mass thrice daily for seven days. Then they would disperse.

Song Jiang begged Heaven for a sign. He asked Gongsun Sheng to burn special prayers written on paper three times daily, so that their smoke would waft them to the Emperor of Heaven. And so, the third watch of the seventh day found Gongsun Sheng on the first tier of the altar, the other priests on the second, and Song Jiang and the chieftains on the third. The lesser commanders and officers stood below. All were earnestly entreating Heaven for a sign.

Suddenly, there was a sound like the ripping of fabric in the northwest corner of the sky. Everyone looked. They saw an object resembling an upended golden platter, narrow at both ends and broad in the middle. Known as Heaven's Gate, or Heaven's Eye, it was dazzlingly bright and resplendent as sunset clouds. A column of fire, shaped like a willow basket, twirled down from the center of the Eye towards the altar. It circled the altar once, then plunged into the earth near the southern end of the hall.

Heaven's Eye was closed by then, and the Taoist priests descended from their altar. Song Jiang ordered men to dig with shovels and mattocks where the fire had vanished. At a depth of three feet, they found a stone tablet. It was inscribed on both sides with mystic writing. Song Jiang ordered that the ashes of the paper prayers be scattered.

At dawn the next day, after the priests had their breakfast, he gave them gifts of gold and cloth. Only then did they examine the stone tablet. It was covered with weird squiggles, like tadpoles, which no one could decipher. But one of the priests, named Ho, was skilled in the occult.

"I have a set of books at home, handed down from my ancestors," he said, "which teaches how to read Heavenly writing. Since ancient times, it's always been this tadpole script, and I've learned how to decipher it. Let me have a look and I'll tell you what it says."

Pleased, Song Jiang handed over the tablet. The priest perused it for some time. Finally, he spoke.

"These are names of all of you gallant warriors. On one side it says: 'Act in Heaven's Behalf.' On the other: 'Complete Loyalty and Righteousness.' At the top are diagrams of the Great and Small Dippers. Below that are your names. If there's nothing unfavorable, I'll read them aloud, one by one."

"How fortunate that you can solve the mystery. We're extremely thankful. If you can enlighten us, we'll owe you our deepest gratitude. Please don't hesitate even if it contains criticism. Hold nothing back. We want to hear every word."

Song Jiang told Xiao Rang the Master Hand to take notes on yellow paper.

Ho the Taoist priest said: "The thirty-six lines on the front are names of stars of Heavenly Spirits. The seventy-two lines on the back are names of stars of Earthly Fiends." He gazed at them for several minutes, then told Xiao Rang to copy as he dictated.

On the front of the stone tablet were the names of the 36 stars of Heavenly Spirits. They are:

Song Jiang, Tiankui Star, *the Timely Rain*
Lu Junyi, Tiangang Star, *the Jade Unicorn*
Wu Yong, Tianji Star, *the Wizard*
Gongsun Sheng, Tianxian Star, *the Dragon in Clouds*
Guan Sheng, Tianyong Star, *the Big Halberd*
Lin Chong, Tianxiong Star, *the Panther Head*
Qin Ming, Tianmeng Star, *the Thunderbolt*
Huyan Zhuo, Tianwei Star, *the Two Rods*
Hua Rong, Tianying Star, *the Lesser Li Guang*
Chai Jin, Tiangui Star, *the Small Whirlwind*
Li Ying, Tianfu Star, *the Heaven-Soaring Eagle*
Zhu Tong, Tianman Star, *the Beautiful Beard*
Sagacious Lu, Tiangu Star, *the Tattooed Monk*
Wu Song, Tianshang Star, *the Pilgrim*
Dong Ping, Tianli Star, *General Two Spears*
Zhang Qin, Tianjie Star, *the Featherless Arrow*
Yang Zhi, Tian'an Star, *the Blue-Faced Beast*
Xu Ning, Tianyou Star, *the Metal Lancer*
Suo Chao, Tiankong Star, *the Urgent Vanguard*
Dai Zong, Tiansu Star, *the Marvelous Traveler*
Liu Tang, Tianyi Star, *the Red-Haired Demon*
Li Kui, Tiansha Star, *the Black Whirlwind*
Shi Jin, Tianwei Star, *the Nine Dragons*
Mu Hong, Tianjiu Star, *the Unrestrained*
Lei Heng, Tiantui Star, *the Winged Tiger*
Li Jun, Tianshou Star, *the Turbulent River Dragon*
Ruan the Second, Tianjian Star, *the Ferocious Giant*
Zhang Heng, Tianjing Star, *the Boat Flame*
Ruan the Fifth, Tianzui Star, *the Recklessly Rash*
Zhang Shun, Tiansun Star, *the White Streak in the Waves*
Ruan the Seventh, Tianbai Star, *the Devil Incarnate*
Yang Xiong, Tianlao Star, *the Pallid*
Shi Xiu, Tianhui Star, *the Rash*
Xie Zhen, Tianbao Star, *the Two-Headed Snake*
Xie Bao, Tianku Star, *the Twin-Tailed Scorpion*
Yan Qing, Tianqiao Star, *the Prodigy*

On the back of the stone tablet were written the names of 72 stars of Earthly Fiends:

Zhu Wu, Dikui Star, *the Miraculous Strategist*
Huang Xin, Disha Star, *the Suppressor of Three Mountains*
Sun Li, Diyong Star, *the Sickly General*
Xuan Zan, Dijie Star, *the Ugly Son-in-Law*
Hao Siwen, Dixiong Star, *the Wild Dog*
Han Tao, Diwei Star, *the Ever-Victorious General*
Peng Qi, Diying Star, *the Eyes of Heaven General*
Shan Tinggui, Diqi Star, *the Water General*
Wei Dingguo, Dimeng Star, *the Fire General*
Xiao Rang, Diwen Star, *the Master Hand*
Pei Xuan, Dizheng Star, *the Ironclad Virtue*
Ou Peng, Dikuo Star, *the Golden Wings Brushing the Clouds*
Deng Fei, Dihe Star, *the Fiery-Eyed Lion*
Yan Shun, Diqiang Star, *the Elegant Tiger*
Yang Lin, Di'an Star, *the Elegant Panther*
Ling Zhen, Dizhou Star, *the Heaven-Shaking Thunder*
Jiang Jing, Dihui Star, *the Magic Calculator*
Lu Fang, Dizuo Star, *the Little Duke*
Guo Sheng, Diyou Star, *the Second Rengui*
An Daoquan, Diling Star, *the Skilled Doctor*
Huangpu Duan, Dishou Star, *the Purple Beard*
Wang Ying, Diwei Star, *the Stumpy Tiger*
Hu Sanniang, Dihui Star, *Ten Feet of Steel*
Bao Xu, Dibao Star, *the God of Death*
Fan Rui, Diran Star, *the Demon King Who Roils the World*
Kong Ming, Dichang Star, *the Comet*
Kong Liang, Dikuang Star, *the Flaming Star*
Xiang Chong, Difei Star, *the Eight-Armed Nezha*
Li Gun, Dizou Star, *the Flying Divinity*
Jin Dajian, Diqiao Star, *the Jade-Armed Craftsman*
Ma Lin, Diming Star, *the Elfin Flutist*
Tong Wei, Dijin Star, *the Dragon from the Cave*
Tong Meng, Ditui Star, *the River Churning Clam*
Meng Kang, Diman Star, *the Jade Flagpole*
Hou Jian, Disui Star, *the Long-Armed Ape*
Chen Da, Dizhou Star, *the Gorge-Leaping Tiger*
Yang Chun, Diyin Star, *the White-Spotted Snake*
Zheng Tianshou, Diyi Star, *the Fair-Faced Gentleman*
Tao Zongwang, Dili Star, *the Nine Tailed Tortoise*
Song Qing, Dijun Star, *the Iron Fan*
Yue He, Dile Star, *the Iron Throat*
Gong Wang, Dijie Star, *the Flowery-Necked Tiger*
Ding Desun, Disu Star, *the Arrow-Struck Tiger*

Mu Chun, Dizhen Star, *the Slightly Restrained*
Cao Zheng, Diji Star, *the Demon Carver*
Song Wan, Dimo Star, *the Guardian of the Clouds*
Du Qian, Diyao Star, *the Skyscraper*
Xue Yong, Diyou Star, *the Sick Tiger*
Shi En, Difu Star, *the Golden-Eyed Tiger Cub*
Li Zhong, Dipi Star, *the Tiger-Fighting General*
Zhou Tong, Dikong Star, *the Little King*
Tang Long, Digu Star, *the Gold-Coin Spotted Leopard*
Du Xing, Diquan Star, *the Demon Face*
Zou Yuan, Diduan Star, *the Dragon from the Forest*
Zou Run, Dijiao Star, *the One-Horned Dragon*
Zhu Gui, Diqiu Star, *the Dry-Land Crocodile*
Zhu Fu, Dizang Star, *the Smiling Tiger*
Cai Fu, Diping Star, *the Iron Arm*
Cai Qing, Disun Star, *the Single Blossom*
LiLi, Dinu Star, *the Hell's Summoner*
Li Yun, Dicha Star, *the Black-Eyed Tiger*
Jiao Ting, Di'e Star, *the Merciless*
Shi Yong, Dichou Star, *the Stone General*
Sun Xin, Dishu Star, *the Junior General*
Mistress Gu, Diyin Star, *the Tigress*
Zhang Qing, Dixing Star, *the Vegetable Gardener*
Sun Erniang, Dizhuang Star, *the Witch*
Wang Dingliu, Dilie Star, *the Lightning*
Yu Baosi, Dijian Star, *the Spirit of the Dangerous Road*
Bai Sheng, Dihao Star, *the Daylight Rat*
Shi Qian, Dizei Star, *the Flea on the Drum*
Duan Jingzhu, Digou Star, *the Golden Dog*

When he had finished, the chieftains stared at the list in amazement. "Who would have thought," Song Jiang mused, "that a petty functionary like me would be the highest of all the stars. And you, brothers, originally were with me up in the sky together. Today, Heaven has indicated that it is right for us to be united in chivalry. We've reached our full number, and our ranks have been decided by Heaven, with a general division into higher and lower. We've been listed in order, under the star categories of Heavenly Spirits and Earthly Fiends. Each of you chieftains must keep to his particular rank. Let there be no squabbling. Heaven's edict must be obeyed."

"Who would dare go against Heaven's will!" said the chieftains.

Song Jiang rewarded priest He with fifty ounces of gold. He also gave some payment to the other priests. They collected their paraphernalia for the mass and departed down the mountain.

Song Jiang then conferred with Wu Yong and Zhu Wu. They decided to hang a tablet reading "Loyalty Hall" on the building of that name, put another sign on Unity Pavilion, and build stockades around all three passes in front of the stronghold. Behind the hall they would level a "V" shaped terrace up the slope, and construct a large pavilion at the apex, with building wings extending down on the east and the west. In the pavilion they would place the spirit tablet of Chao Gai. Song Jiang, Wu Yong, Lu Fang and Guo Sheng would occupy the east wing. Lu Junyi, Gongsun Sheng, Kong Ming and Kong Liang would occupy the west.

New pennants and banners were made. On the very top of the mountain an apricot-yellow banner was stretched reading: "Act in Heaven's Behalf." In front of Loyalty Hall were two banners. One said: "Defender of Justice from Shandong," the other: "Jade Unicorn from Hebei," meaning Song Jiang and Lu Junyi, respectively. In addition there were banners of dragons, tigers, bears and panthers rampant; pennants of blue dragons with white tigers, vermilion birds on black backgrounds; golden axes with white tassels, blue banners and black umbrellas, and large fringed banners of black. These were for the use of the armies.

There were also banners of the Four Stars in the Big Dipper, Central Heaven and the Four Directions, the Three Essentials and the Nine Elements, the Twenty-Eight Constellations, the Sixty-Four Diagrams, the Nine Heavens and the Eight Diagrams—in all a hundred and twenty-four Heaven-governing banners, all made by Hou Jian. Metal tallies and seals were forged by Jin Dajian.

When everything was ready, an auspicious day was chosen, and oxen and horses were slaughtered in sacrifice to the Spirits of Heaven and Earth. The signs "Loyalty Hall" and "Unity Pavilion" were hung, and the apricot-yellow banner "Act in Heaven's Behalf was also put in place. To the pillars on either side of the entrance to the hall two Vermilion vertical tablets were attached. Reading downward, and continuing from the right tablet to the left, they said: "Be ardently righteous and loyal always, never covet wealth or harm the people."

That day Song Jiang ordered a huge feast. He took up his tallies and seals of office and addressed the gathering. "Brothers," he said, "let each of you carry out your duties of leadership, and hearken without fail to orders. To do otherwise would harm our chivalry. Whoever willfully disobeys shall be punished according to military law. None will be let off lightly."

He then read the chain of command, which was as follows:

General Commanders:

Song Jiang the Defender of Chivalry and Lu Junyi the Jade Unicorn

Chiefs of Staff:

Wu Yong the Wizard Wu Yong and Gongsun Sheng the Dragon in Clouds

Officers for Money and Grain Control:
Chai Jin the Small Whirlwind and Li Ying the Heaven-Soaring Eagle

Officers in Charge of Main Cavalry:
Guan Sheng the Bid Halberd; Lin Chong the Panther Head; Qin Ming the Thunderbolt; Huyan Zhuo the Two Rods and Dong Ping the General Two Spears

Officers in Charge of Light Cavalry and Vanguard:

Hua Rong the Lesser Li Guang; Xu Ning the Metal Lancer; Yang Zhi the Blue-Faced Beast; Suo Chao the Urgent Vanguard; Zhang Qin the Featherless Arrow; Zhu Tong the Beautiful Beard; Shi Jin the Nine Dragons and Mu Hong the Unrestrained

Officers in Charge of Distant Scouting and Picket Cavalry:

Huang Xin the Suppressor of Three Mountains; Sun Li the Sickly General; Xuan Zan the Ugly Son in Law; Hao Siwen the Wild Dog; Han Tao the Ever-Victorious General; Peng Qi the Eyes of Heaven General; Shan Tinggui the Water General; Wei Dingguo the Fire General; Ou Peng the Golden Wings Brushing the Clouds; Deng Fei the Fiery-Eyed Lion; Yan Shun the Elegant Tiger; Ma Lin the Elfin Flutist; Chen Da the Gorge-Leaping Tiger; Yang Chun the White-Spotted Snake; Yang Lin the Elegant Panther and Zhou Tong the Little King

Senior Infantry Officers:

Sagacious Lu the Tattooed Monk; Wu Song the Pilgrim, Liu Tang the Red-Haired Demon; Lei Heng the Winged Tiger; Li Kui the Black Whirlwind; Yan Qing the Prodigy; Yang Xiong the Pallid; Shi Xiu the Rash; Xie Zhen the Two-Headed Snake and Xie Bao the Two-Tailed Scorpion

Junior Infantry Officers:

Fan Rui the Demon King Who Roils the World; Bao Xu the God of Death; Xiang Chong the Eight-Armed Nezha; Li Gun the Flying Divinity; Xue Yong the Sick Tiger; Shi En the Golden-Eyed Tiger Cub; Mu Chun the Slightly Restrained; Li Zhong the Tiger-Fighting General; Zheng Tianshou the Fair-Eyed Gentleman; Song Wan the Guardian of the Clouds; Du Qian the Skyscraper; Zou Yuan the Dragon from the Forest; Zou Run the One-Horned Dragon; Gong Wang the Flowery-Necked Tiger; Ding Desun the Arrow-Struck Tiger; Jiao Ting the Merciless and Shi Yong the Stone General

Officers in Charge of Four Water Defense Forts:

Li Jun the Turbulent River Dragon; Zhang Heng the Boat Flame; Zhang Shun the White Streak in the Waves; Ruan the Second the Ferocious Giant; Ran the Fifth the Reckless Rash; Ruan the Seventh the Devil Incarnate; Tong Wei the Dragon from the Cave and Tong Meng the River Churning Clam

Officers in Charge of Four Information-Gathering and New Arrival-Welcoming Inns:

Dongshan Inn: Sun Xin the Junior General and Mistress Gu the Tigress
Xishan Inn: Zhang Qing the Vegetable Gardener and Sun Erniang the Witch
Nanshan Inn: Zhu Gui the Dry-Land Crocodile and Du Xing the Demon Face
Beishan Inn: LiLi the Hell's Summoner and Wang Dingliu the Lightning

Chief Scout:

Dai Zong the Marvelous Traveler

Officers in Charge of Delivery of Secret Messages for Infantry:

Yue He the Iron Throat; Shi Qian the Flea on the Drum; Duan Jingzhu the Golden God and Bai Sheng the Daylight Rat Cavalry

Officers Guarding Central Army Headquarters:

Lu Fang the Little Duke and Guo Zheng the Second Rengui

Infantry Officers Guarding Central Army Headquarters:

Kong Ming the Comet and Kong Liang the Flaming Star

Officers in Charge of Punishments and Executions:

Cai Fu the Iron Arm and Cai Qing the Single Blossom

Cavalry Liaisons Among the Three Armies:

Wang Ying the Stumpy Tiger and Hu Sanniang the Ten Feet of Iron

Deputy Chief of Staff:

Zhu Wu the Miraculous Strategist

The following are officers who were assigned administrative jobs:
Dispatches and Orders: Xiao Rang the Master Hand
Military and Civil Awards and Punishments: Pei Xuan the Ironclad Virtue
Money and Grain Accounting: Jiang Jing the Magic Calculator
Boat Building: Meng Kang the Jade Flagpole
Tally and Seal Making: Jin Dajian the Jade-Armed Craftsman
Manufacture of Banners and Robes: Hou Jian the Long-Armed Ape
Veterinary and Horse Attending: Huangpu Duan the Purple Beard Huangpu
Doctor of Medicine and Surgery: An Daoshun the Skilled Doctor
Weapons and Armor Making: Tang Long the Gold-Coin Spotted Leopard
Manufacture of Cannon: Ling Zhen the Heaven-Shaken Thunder
House Construction and Maintenance: Li Yun the Black-Eyed Tiger
Butchery: Cao Zheng the Demon Carver
Banquet Supervision: Song Qing the Iron Fan Wine and Vinegar Brewing: Zhu Fu the Smiling Tiger Erection of Walls and Fortifications: Tao Zongwang the Nine-Tailed Tortoise
Chief Standard Bearer: Yu Baosi the Spirit of the Dangerous Road

And one each to the following sixteen supervisory positions: dispatches and orders, military and civil awards and punishments, money and grain accounting, boat building, tally and seal making, manufacture of banners and robes, veterinary, doctor of medicine and surgery, weapons and armor making, manufacture of cannon, house construction, butcher, banquet supervisor, brewer, erector of walls and fortifications, and chief standard bearer.

The decree was dated "a lucky day of the fourth lunar month, in the second year of the Xuan He Period, at the great meeting on Mount Liangshan, when assignment of duties was proclaimed."

Each chieftain then received his appropriate tallies and seals and the feasting ended. Everyone was very drunk. The chieftains left to take up their posts. Those who had not yet been appointed retired to quarters before and behind the "V" terrace to await orders.

Song Jiang selected another auspicious day, burned incense, and ordered drums beaten to summon the chieftains. When all had assembled in the hall, he addressed them.

"This is no ordinary occasion. I have something to say. Since we have come together as the stars of Heavenly Spirits and Earthly Fiends, we must vow before Heaven to unite to the death without reservation, rescue one another from danger and aid one another in misfortune, while striving jointly to defend the country and preserve peace for the people."

The chieftains heartily concurred. They too lit incense and knelt together in the hall, Song Jiang continued.

"I was only a petty functionary, and have neither learning nor ability. But thanks to the protection of Heaven and Earth and the illumination of the sun and the moon, we brothers have gathered here on Mount Liangshan in the Marsh and formed a heroic host. There are now one hundred and eight of us, which conforms to the number ordained by Heaven and is pleasing to the hearts of men. From this day on, if any of us acts in a deliberately unvirtuous manner, or offends our code of chivalry, we pray that Heaven and Earth scourge him, that the spirits and men destroy him, that he never again be reincarnated in human form and remain forever sunk in the depths. We vow to serve our country in righteous loyalty, act in Heaven's behalf, defend our borders and secure our people. Heaven examine us, and by Your Luminance reply."

In chorus the chieftains swore their eternal unity. That day, they reaffirmed their fraternity in a blood oath. They imbibed heavily of wine before the convention finally disbanded.

This, reader, was the grand confluence of chivalry in Liangshan Marsh. The origin of these men and their assignments was preordained. We shall not repeat ourselves.

The gallant fellows often went down the mountain, alone or at the head of a body of men, or simply a few of the chieftains together, and patrolled the roads. Ordinary travellers and merchants were not molested. But if they encountered a high official, they lightened his coffers of their gold and silver. Not a member of his family was left alive. Loot was delivered to the mountain stronghold and put in the treasury for collective use. Trifling items of booty were divided among the men.

Ranging within a radius of three hundred *li,* the outlaws openly plundered the wealth of prominent families which oppressed the people. Who dared to oppose! They raided the accumulations of such persons and newly rich upstarts, near and far, and carried them up the mountain. They staged well over a thousand such raids. No one could resist them, and they Cared nothing about possible public lamentations by their victims. In any event, no one spoke out and they were never exposed.

Song Jiang remained on the mountain after the oath of unity. The scorching heat of summer was replaced by the cool of early autumn. The Ninth Day of the Ninth Lunar Month Festival was fast approaching. Song Jiang directed Song Qing to lay a feast at which the brothers could enjoy the flowering chrysanthemums. All those who were away from the fortress were summoned back.

There was a mountain of meat and a sea of wine that day. Quantities were first dispensed among the outlying forces of the cavalry, infantry and navy, and among the junior commanders, so that they might form their own gatherings and dine together.

Chrysanthemums were banked in Loyalty Hall, where the chieftains sat according to rank, wine cups in hand. In the front of the hall, on either side, gongs crashed and drums pounded. The chieftains revelled, to the clink of cups and chopsticks, with much noise and laughter. Ma Lin played the flute and sang, Yan Qing strummed the *zheng* lute.

Before they knew it, it was dusk. Song Jiang, very drunk, called for paper and a brush-pen, determined to write a poem. When he had finished, he sang it to musical accompaniment. It went like this:

Welcoming the Double Ninth
 With newly distilled good wine,
We gaze at the blue waters, red bills,
 Yellow reeds and dark bamboo.
The grey in my hair is ever increasing,
 But a yellow chrysanthemum is tucked over one ear.
Let us savor out friendship,
 More precious than gold or jade.
We've controlled the savage foe and can defend our borders,
 Our orders are wise, our discipline tight.
We want only to repel the barbarian invaders,
 Defend the people and our country.
Constantly we burn with loyal ardor, though wicked officials
 Are blind to our exploits.
May the emperor soon hand down an amnesty,
 Then will our hearts be fully at ease.

"Day in and day out you talk about amnesty," Wu Song shouted. "You're cooling our enthusiasm!"

And the Black Whirlwind glared and exclaimed: "Amnesty, amnesty, who needs a friggin amnesty!" He kicked over the table, smashing everything on it.

"How dare that swarthy oaf behave so rudely," Song Jiang cried. "Guards, take him out and cut his head off!"

The chieftains dropped to their knees. "He's drunk. Forgive him, brother," they pleaded.

"Rise, brothers. Put him in jail, then."

The chieftains were relieved. A few jailors approached Li Kui.

"Are you afraid I'll resist?" the Black Whirlwind demanded. "I wouldn't complain if Big Brother had me sliced to ribbons! He could have me killed and I wouldn't care! Though Heaven itself can't scare me I'll listen to him."

He walked off with the guards to the jail. The incident shook Song Jiang into sobriety. He was very depressed. Wu Yong spoke to him soothingly.

"Everyone is enjoying this feast you ordered. Li Kui's a crude fellow and goes a little wild when he's drunk. Why take it to heart? Join our brothers in their revelry."

Song Jiang said: "When I got drunk in Jiangzhou and wrote that rebellious poem, he fought for me. Today I wrote another and nearly had him killed. Luckily, you brothers spoke up. My emotional ties with Li Kui are the strongest. We're as close as flesh and bone. I can't help having tears in my eyes."

He turned to Wu Song. "Brother, you're an intelligent man. I advocate amnesty so that we can return to a respectable life and become government officials serving our country. Why should that cool your enthusiasm?"

"All the ministers today, whether civil or military, are crooks," said Sagacious Lu, "and they've got the emperor fooled. Those rogues are as black as my cassock. Who can wash the imperial court clean? An amnesty won't solve anything. Let's have a ceremonial parting, and tomorrow each can go his separate way and be done with it."

"Listen to me, brothers," said Song Jiang. "The emperor is sacred and pure. Because he's surrounded by corrupt ministers he's temporarily confused. But the day will come when the clouds will part and the sun will emerge again. He'll know that we act on Heaven's behalf and never harm the people, and he'll pardon our crimes. We'll serve the country with one heart and strive to distinguish ourselves. What could be finer? That's why I hope we'll be amnestied soon. I want nothing else."

The chieftains thanked Song Jiang profusely. They drank heartily and with good cheer. The banquet broke up and they returned to their respective posts.

Early the next morning chieftains went to see Li Kui. He was still asleep. They awakened him.

"You were drunk yesterday," they said, "and you swore at Big Brother. Today, you're going to be executed."

"I wouldn't dare swear at him even in my dreams," said the Black Whirlwind. "But if he wants to kill me, let him."

They led him into the hall and asked Song Jiang what punishment he should be given. Song Jiang berated Li Kui sternly.

"I have many men under my command. We'd have no law and order whatever if they all behaved as rudely as you! For the sake of these brothers, I'll suspend sentence on your execution. But it will go hard with you if you misbehave again!"

Li Kui, murmuring submissively, withdrew. The chieftains also departed.

The days were uneventful as the winter solstice drew near. Snow fell, mantling the world with silver. The sky cleared and a man came up from below and reported: "Seven or eight *li* from here we captured a group from Laizhou transporting lanterns for the Eastern Capital. What shall we do with them?"

"Don't bind them," said Song Jiang. "Bring them up here." Not long after, the travellers were led into the hall. Two were government bailiffs, eight or nine were lantern artisans. Their wares were on five carts. The leader of them spoke.

"I'm a bailiff in Laizhou. These fellows are lantern artisans. Every year the capital orders three sets of lanterns from our prefecture. This year they've asked for two more in addition. The lanterns are the Jade Shed Intricate Nine-Hued type."

Song Jiang treated the travellers to wine and food, then asked them to display the lanterns. The artisans hung the Jade Shed lanterns, a total of eighty-one, on four sides. Suspended in Loyalty Hall, they extended from the rafters to the floor.

"I'd keep all your lanterns," said Song Jiang, "if I weren't afraid it might get you into difficulty. Just leave me one Nine-Hued lantern set, and you can deliver the rest to the officials. And here are twenty ounces of silver for your trouble."

The travellers thanked him and departed. Song Jiang had the lanterns lit and placed in Chao Gai's memorial hall. The next day he spoke to the chieftains.

"I was born in Shandong and I've never been to the capital. I hear that the emperor is having a big lantern show, with public merry-making and a celebration of the first full moon of the new year. Manufacture of the lanterns began in the winter solstice and has finished only now. I'd like to go into the city secretly with a few brothers and take a look at the lanterns."

"That's not feasible," said Wu Yong. "The Eastern Capital has more police than anywhere. If anything went wrong, what could we do?"

"I'll stay out of sight in an inn during the day. I'll only go into the city at night. What could happen?"

The chieftains tried to dissuade him in vain. Song Jiang insisted.

And because Song Jiang went to see the lanterns, a theater was reduced to rubble and a street of brothels became a battlefield. Truly, bold tigers approached the Imperial Palace, fierce stars encroached on Reclining Ox Fort in the night.

How did Song Jiang cause a disturbance in the Eastern Capital? Read our next chapter if you would know.

CHAPTER 72

CHAI JIN WEARS A COCKADE AND ENTERS THE FORBIDDEN COURTYARD

LI KUI ON FESTIVAL NIGHT DISTURBS THE EASTERN CAPITAL

In Loyalty Hall that day Song Jiang announced the disposition of those who would go to see the lanterns: "I will travel with Chai Jin, Shi Jin with Mu Hong, Sagacious Lu with Wu Song, and Zhu Tong with Liu Tang. The rest of you will remain and guard the fortress."

"They say the lanterns of the Eastern Capital are a pretty sight," said Li Kui. "I want to go too."

"Impossible," said Song Jiang.

Li Kui insisted stubbornly. There was no refusing him. Finally, Song Jiang relented.

"All right. But only on condition that you don't make any trouble. Dress as a servant."

He told Yan Qing to accompany them also, with the specific task of keeping a watchful eye on Li Kui.

You will remember, reader, that Song Jiang's face bore the tattoo of the criminal. How could he appear in the capital city? After the skilled doctor An Daoquan had arrived at the stronghold he had removed the mark with a powerful caustic. Later, he treated the wound with good medicines. When a red scar formed he removed this gradually with daily applications of poultices containing powdered gold and ground jade. That is what medical books refer to when they talk of "obliterating blemishes with fine jade."

Song Jiang instructed Shi Jin and Mu Hong to go first, disguised as travellers. Sagacious Lu and Wu Song would go next, as wandering monks. Lastly would be Zhu Tong and Liu Tang, in the garb of merchants. All wore swords and carried halberds and, needless to say, had concealed weapons on their persons. Song Jiang himself and Chai Jin pretended to be vacationing officials. Dai Zong went as a lieutenant. In the event of any emergency, he could rush back to the stronghold with a report.

Li Kui and Yan Qing, the "servants," transported the luggage of the "officials" down the mountain on carrying-poles. The chieftains saw the travellers off to the Shore of Golden Sands. Wu Yong cautioned Li Kui. "Whenever you set out on your own you get into a jam. This time you're going to the Eastern Capital with Big Brother to see the lanterns. It's not your usual jaunt. You're not to drink on the road. Behave with caution and curb your temper. If you provoke any clashes, we brothers may have to terminate our relationship."

"Don't worry, Military Advisor," said the Black Whirlwind, "I won't stir up anything."

They parted, and the travellers set out. They touched Jizhou, passed Tengzhou, went through Danzhou, reached Caozhou, and at last arrived at an inn outside the Wanshou Gate of the Eastern Capital, where they took quarters. It was the eleventh day of the first lunar month. Song Jiang conferred with Chai Jin.

"I don't dare enter the capital tomorrow in daylight," he said. "I'll wait until the evening of the fourteenth, when the celebration is noisiest, and go in then."

"I'll scout out a route for you with Yan Qing tomorrow."

"Excellent."

The following day Chai Jin dressed handsomely, bound his head in a fresh kerchief, and put on clean shoes and stockings. Yan Qing also garbed himself fashionably. The two left the inn. The suburban households were festive and gay as they prepared to enjoy the lantern festival and celebrate the peaceful atmosphere. Chai and Yan reached the gate without incident and entered the city.

They strolled along Imperial Road, taking in the sights, and came to the area adjoining the palace's East Glory Gate. Here were many taverns and tea-houses, patronized by people richly garbed in silks and satins, each in a distinctive color. Chai Jin led Yan Qing to a small tavern. They went upstairs and sat down in a room overlooking the street.

They could see attendants going in and out of the palace grounds. Each wore a cockade in the shape of a flower with jade-green leaves tacked to the side of his head kerchief. Chai whispered some instructions in Yan's ear. Yan nodded, went swiftly down the stairs and left the tavern. Fortunately, the attendant he approached was rather simple-minded. Yan hailed him respectfully.

"I don't know your face," the man said. "We've never met."

"My master is an old friend of yours. He's sent me to invite you to join him. Aren't you Inspector Zhang?"

"My name is Wang."

"Oh, Inspector Wang, of course. That's the name. I was in such a hurry, I forgot."

Wang went with Yan into the tavern and up the stairs. Yan raised the door curtain and announced: "Inspector Wang is here." He gave Chai a hidden signal with his hand.

The two men exchanged courtesies. Wang looked at Chai Jin. He didn't know him. "My eyesight is poor," he said. "I'm afraid I don't remember Your Excellence. Would you be good enough to tell me your name?"

Chai Jin smiled. "We were friends as children. You'll think of it without me saying." He summoned the waiter and ordered wine.

Tasty dishes were served, and Yan Qing saw to it that the attendant's cup remained filled. When the man was half drunk, Chai questioned him.

"What is the meaning of that cockade?"

"Today, the emperor is celebrating the first full moon. There are twenty-four companies of us palace attendants, nearly fifty-eight hundred men in all. We've each been issued a new robe, a cockade in the shape of green leaves and a golden flower, and a small metal badge pinned above it reading: 'Celebrate with the People.' We're on call at all times. Only those with this palace cockade and robe are allowed in."

"I didn't know that," said Chai Jin. They downed several more cups, and Chai said to Yan Qing: "Get us a pot of warm wine."

Before long, Yan brought the wine. Chai Jin rose and addressed Attendant Wang, cup in hand.

"Drink this round I respectfully offer and you'll know my name."

"I just can't think of it. Please tell me."

Wang raised his cup and drained it. Almost instantly he began to drool from the corners of his mouth. His feet flailed, and he fell back off his bench. Chai quickly stripped Wang of his head kerchief, clothing and footwear, and put them on, including the cockade and the colored silk robe.

"If the waiter should ask," he said to Yan Qing, "tell him the attendant is drunk, and that the other gentleman will be back soon."

"No need to instruct me. I'll handle it."

Chai Jin left the tavern and went to the East Glory Gate of the palace. Because of the cockade and the color of his robe, no one stopped him from entering. It was a splendid, lavish place of glorious hues, a paradise on earth. Chai passed a number of compounds whose gates were closed and fastened with golden locks. Then, off to a side, he saw a sign in letters of gold, "Hall of Deep Thought." This was the imperial library.

Its vermilion doors of ornately carved wood were open. Chai Jin entered. Directly opposite was an imperial chair, flanked by tables on which lay brush-pens with ivory handles, decorated paper, imperial ink-slabs, and the famous grinding stones from Duanxi. Innumerable sets of books lined the walls, each with ivory fastenings. Behind the chair was a screen decorated with a scenic panorama in lovely colors. Chai Jin walked around to the back of the screen. It was blank, except for a listing of the four major outlaws, as follows: "Song Jiang of Shandong, Wang Qing west of the River Huai, Tian Hu of Hebei, Fang La south of the Yangzi."

"We are the ones who are ravaging the country," Chai Jin reflected. "It has been written here so that no one will forget." He drew a concealed knife and cut out the words "Song Jiang of Shandong" and hastily quit the building. Others were already entering.

Chai Jin left the inner grounds, departed through the East Glory Gate, and returned to the tavern. Attendant Wang was still in a drugged slumber. Chai took off Wang's clothes and put on his own. He directed Yan Qing to pay the bill and give the waiter a large tip.

As he and Yan were leaving he said to the waiter: "Attendant Wang and I are close friends. He's drunk, so I signed in for him at the palace. He still hasn't come to, but I have to go outside the city and must leave before the gates close. You can keep the change. Wang's clothing and identification are all here."

"I'll take care of everything, sir," the waiter assured him.

Chai and Yan left the tavern and exited from the city through the Wanshou Gate.

Towards evening the attendant awakened, Since his identifying robe and cockade were still with him, he didn't suspect what had happened. The waiter told him what Chai Jin had said. Still befuddled with drink, Wang returned home.

The next day a colleague informed him: "The words 'Song Jiang of Shandong' have been removed from the Hall of Deep Thought. Today security at every gate is as tight as the bands on a bucket. Anyone going in or out is closely checked."

Wang at last understood. But he didn't dare breathe a word.

On reaching the inn, Chai told in detail what he had seen in the palace, and handed over the "Song Jiang of Shandong" which he had cut from the imperial writing. Song Jiang examined it with many sighs. On the evening of the fourteenth he and several of his men went into the city to view the lanterns.

During the Song Dynasty the Eastern Capital was the leading metropolis. It grew prosperous and rich under the Taoist Sovereign.

At dusk that day a bright moon rose in the east in a cloudless sky. Song Jiang and Chai Jin were disguised as vacationing officials. Dai Zong wore the garb of a lieutenant. Yan Qing tagged along as servant. Only Li Kui remained at the inn.

The four men mingled with the noisy crowds swarming in through the Fengqiu Gate and wandered about the streets and marts. It was a warm evening with gentle breezes, ideal for strolling. On the main thoroughfare sheds had been erected in front of every door and hung with lanterns, which vied for beauty and turned the night into day. The buildings too were decked with lanterns, and the streets thronged with carriages and people.

The four men turned away from Imperial Road to a street lined on both sides with signboards denoting establishments of "misty moonlight." The four were struck by one house midway down. Its doorway was covered by a blue cloth drape, behind which was a curtain of spotted bamboo. Green silk gauze screened the windows on either side. Between them and the doorway hung two vertical plaques reading: "A Fairy Maid of Song and Dance, A Flower of Surpassing Grace."

Song Jiang and his companions went into a tea-house opposite and sat down. "Which courtesan's place is that?" they asked the waiter.

"The leading lady of her profession in the Eastern Capital, Li Shishi. And in the house next door to us is Zhao Yuannu."

"Isn't Li the one who's having a hot affair with the emperor?" Song Jiang asked.

"Not so loud," said the waiter. "There are eyes and ears all around."

Song Jiang leaned close to Yan Qing and whispered: "I want to meet Li Shishi and arrange something with her privately. Invent some story to get us in. We'll wait for you here." He remained with Chai Jin and Dai Zong, drinking tea.

Yan Qing walked up to the door of the courtesan's residence, pushed aside the drape, raised the bamboo curtain, and entered. He saw fine smoke rising from a bronze incense burner on a rhinoceros-hide table beneath a hanging duck and drake lamp. On two of the walls were scenic paintings by four famous artists. Below stood four armchairs, also covered by rhinoceros hide.

There didn't seem to be anyone around. Yan Qing crossed a small court-yard into another parlor. Here were three small beds of ornately carved camphor wood, cushioned with purple mattresses bearing a fallen-petals-in-a-flowing-stream design. A fine lamp hung on a jade stand, here and there were rare antiques.

Yan Qing coughed softly. A serving maid rounded a folding screen, saw Yan Qing and curtsied.

"What is your name, big brother? Where are you from?"

"Can I trouble you, sister, to ask mama to come out? I have something to say."

The girl left and, a few moments later, returned with the bawd. Yan urged her to be seated. He kowtowed four times. "What is your name, young brother?"

"You've forgotten me, mother. I'm Zhang Xian, son of Zhang the Second. I've been away from the city since childhood. I only returned today."

Zhang was a very common name. The bawd thought for several moments. She couldn't see the young man clearly in the lamplight. Suddenly, she imagined she remembered.

"Not little Zhang Xian near the Taiping Bridge? Where have you been? I haven't seen you in ages."

"Of course not. I've been away. Today, I'm looking after a guest from Shandong. He's got more property than words can say. He's probably the richest man in his province. He's here on business. One, he wants to enjoy the lantern fes-tival; two, he's visiting relatives here in the capital; three, he's buying and selling merchandise; and four, he's longing to meet your lady. He asks only to sip tea at the same table, and he'll be satisfied. I wouldn't dare ask otherwise. I'm not kid-ding —that man has thousands in gold and silver, and he'd like to present some of it to this house."

The greedy bawd was very fond of money. Yan Qing's story went to her heart. She hastily called out Li Shishi and introduced her to Yan. He could see in the lamplight that the girl truly had a form that could sink fish and down geese, a face that eclipsed the moon and put the flowers to shame. Yan dropped to his knees and kowtowed. The bawd relayed his story to Shishi.

"Where is the gentleman now?" asked the girl.

"In that tea-house across the way," said Yan.

"Invite him to have some tea here."

"He wouldn't dare enter without your permission."

"Hurry over and ask him," said the bawd.

Yan Qing went to the tea-house and related the news in Song Jiang's ear. Dai Zong paid the bill and the three men followed Yan to the courtesan's house,

On entering, they were escorted to the main parlor, where Li Shishi stood with hands folded demurely.

She greeted Song Jiang politely and said: "Zhang Xian has just been talking about your munificence. Your visit brings luster to our humble dwelling."

"I'm an ignorant man from an obscure mountain hamlet," replied Song. "To be able to gaze upon your beauty is my greatest good fortune." The courtesan asked him to be seated. "Who is this other gentleman?" she queried, indicating Chai Jin.

"My nephew Sheriff Ye," said Song. He also instructed Dai Zong to greet the girl.

Song Jiang and Chai Jin were ushered to guest seats on the left Side of the table, and Li Shishi took her place on the right, as hostess, while the bawd brought in the tea things. The girl poured for each of the four men personally. The tea leaves were finer than birds' tongues, the brew was as fragrant as dragon's saliva. When they had finished and the tea service was removed, they chatted pleasantly.

The bawd entered and said: "His Majesty is waiting in the rear."

"I'm afraid I can't keep you any longer, today," the courtesan said to her guests. "But he's due to visit the Upper Purity Temple soon and won't be able to come here for some time. Once he goes, you gentlemen will be welcome to call again and join me in a few cups of wine."

Song Jiang bid her a respectful farewell and departed with his three companions.

When they had left her door Chai Jin said: "The emperor has two mistresses, Li Shishi and Zhao Yuannu. We've met one, what about the other?"

They went to the building next to the tea-house and raised the door curtain. Yan Qing spoke to Zhao Yuannu's bawd.

"These two gentlemen are wealthy merchants from Shandong. If they could meet your lady, they would present her with a hundred ounces of silver."

"My girl hasn't any luck. She's sick in bed and can't receive company."

"We'll try again another time," said Song Jiang.

The bawd saw them to the door and bid them farewell. Leaving the street, they headed towards Tianhan Bridge to view the massed lanterns display. As they neared the Fanlou Restaurant building they heard the shrilling of pipes and the beat of drums. Lanterns dazzled the eye, people swarmed in and out like ants.

Song Jiang and Chai Jin went upstairs, found a room and sat down. They ordered drinks and side dishes. Sipping their wine, they admired the lanterns gleaming outside in the night. They had downed only a few cups when they heard someone making up lyrics and singing them in the adjoining room:

Though our courage surges to the stare,
Our heroic task is unfulfilled.
With dragon sword grasped firm in hand,
We won't quit till every scoundrel's killed!

Song Jiang knew that voice. He hastily entered. There was Nine Dragons Shi Jin and Mu Hong the Unrestrained, quite drunk and talking wildly.

"You brothers frightened the wits out of me," Song Jiang said sharply. "Pay your bill and get out. If it was some policeman instead of me who heard you, you'd have been in a fine mess. I never expected you two to be so careless. Leave the city without delay. After the formal lantern display tomorrow night, I'm leaving too. That's the best way. We don't want to stir up any trouble."

Shi Jin and Mu Hong had nothing to say. They paid their bill, went down the stairs, and departed from the Eastern Capital.

Song Jiang and his three companions had a few more cups. They were a bit tipsy. Dai Zong paid the bill. Flipping their long sleeves, they left the restaurant. They returned to the inn outside Wanshou Gate and pounded on the door. Li Kui peered at them with sleepy eyes.

"What's the good of letting me come to the Eastern Capital?" he grumbled to Song Jiang. "You only make me stay here and watch the room. While I'm penned up in this friggin place, you fellows are out having a good time."

"It's because you have a bad disposition and are so ugly. I'm afraid if I take you into the city you'll only create a disturbance."

"Don't take me, then! Why make a lot of excuses? When did my looks ever scare anybody's family to death?"

"All right, tomorrow night, the fifteenth, and no more. We'll see the lanterns and leave immediately."

Li Kui laughed happily.

The next day, Lantern Festival Day itself, was bright and clear. Towards evening, huge crowds of celebrants gathered. It was a time of national peace and prosperity, when peasants toiled contentedly in their fields. Song Jiang and Chai Jin, in the guise of vacationing officials, followed by Dai Zong, Li Kui and Yan Qing, went into the city through the Wanshou Gate.

Although there was no curfew that night, each of the gates was guarded by soldiers in full armor, equipped with weapons at the ready. Their bows were strung, their swords were unsheathed, and every post was manned. Five thousand cavalry under the personal command of Marshal Gao Qiu patrolled atop the city walls.

Song Jiang and his four companions jostled through the crowds into the Eastern Capital. He whispered some instructions in Yan Qing's ear, and added: "I'll be waiting in the tea-house."

Yan Qing went to the home of Li Shishi and knocked on the door. The prime-ranking courtesan and her bawd received him.

"Ask your master, the magnate, to please forgive us," they said. "We never know when His Majesty is liable to drop in privately. We must be diligent."

"My master apologizes for disturbing you. Shandong is only a remote province by the sea. It doesn't have anything of value. What it does produce wouldn't be worth presenting to you. All he can do is send you one hundred ounces of gold as a token of his esteem. Perhaps the lady can have ornaments made out of them for her hair. If he comes across something attractive later on, he'll send it with his respects."

"Where is the magnate now?" asked the bawd.

"He's waiting for me at the end of the lane. We're going to see the lanterns."

There was nothing the bawd loved more in the world than wealth. When Yan Qing took out two gold nuggets, gleaming like live coals and put them on the table, she was overjoyed.

"This is Lantern Festival Day," she said, "and my girl and I are celebrating it at home with a few cups of wine. If the magnate wouldn't think our fare too meager, perhaps he'd visit our humble abode for a chat. Do you think he might come?"

"I'm sure he will. I'll pass on your invitation."

Yan Qing went to the tea-house and informed Song Jiang. They all repaired to the home of Li Shishi. Song Jiang told Dai Zong and Li Kui to wait at the front door.

The three entered the large parlor where Li Shishi received them. "We've only just met," she said to Song Jiang. "You shouldn't give such an expensive gift. It really isn't right."

"We have nothing of value in my rustic mountains. I can only offer this trifle as an expression of thanks."

The courtesan invited them into a small adjoining room, and asked them to be seated. Maids served rare fruits, fine food, vintage wine, and tasty delicacies. The crockery was of the best, the table was laid beautifully. Shishi approached them and bowed, wine cup in hand.

"I must have been lucky in my previous incarnation or I wouldn't be able to meet you two gentlemen today. With this simple wine, I pledge to you, my elders." Song Jiang said: "Although I have a bit of property in my mountain area, I have never seen anything so lavish as you have here. Your fame is known throughout the land, lovely and charming lady. An interview with you is more difficult to obtain than reaching Heaven. Yet here I am, actually chatting and drinking with you personally!"

"How extremely kind of you, magnate. You praise me too highly. I am unworthy!"

Both drank, and Shishi directed her personal maid to pour wine in tiny gold cups. Then the courtesan relaxed and gossiped about members of her profession. To all her remarks it was Chai Jin who replied. Yan Qing, who was standing off to one side, offered quips that made everyone laugh.

After several rounds Song Jiang became more loquacious. He rolled up his sleeves and gesticulated as he talked in the free manner of the brigands of Mount Liangshan.

"My brother is always like this after he's had some wine," Chai Jin smiled. "Pray don't laugh at him, lady."

"Drinking is for pleasure," said Shishi. "Why stand on ceremony?"

"One of those two servants at the front door," a young maid said, "the one with the yellow beard who's so weird-looking he scares you, is muttering curses."

"Tell them both to come in," said Song Jiang.

Dai Zong soon entered the side room with Li Kui. When the Black Whirlwind saw Song Jiang and Chai Jin sitting and drinking with Shishi, he glared.

"Who is this fellow?" Shishi asked. "He looks like one of those imps standing before the judge in the temple statuary."

Everyone laughed except Li Kui. He didn't know what she was talking about.

"He's the son of one of our family servants," said Song Jiang.

"It doesn't matter," said the courtesan with a laugh. "I have no refinement."

"The lout is a skilled warrior," Song explained. "He can tote two or three hundred catties and fight forty or fifty men."

Shishi called for large silver flagons and gave Li Kui and Dai Zong three rounds each. Yan Qing was afraid Li Kui would say something coarse, and he directed the two to return to their posts at the front of the house.

"When a real man drinks," said Song Jiang, "he doesn't use small cups." He picked up a large silver flagon and downed several rounds.

In a low voice Shishi murmured a song by the poet Su Dongpo to the melody of *Xijiangyue*. His senses heightened by wine, Song Jiang called for brush-pen and paper. He ground the ink thick and black, dipped his pen, and spread the paper.

"Though I have no learning," he said to the courtesan, "I'd like to scrawl a few words to express the sadness in my heart. I beg of you to hear me, foremost flower."

Taking up his pen, Song Jiang, then and there composed a *yuefu* poem. It ran as follows:

North and south,
Where under Heaven is there a place for this wild traveller?
My misty mountain stronghold
Is but a base for future status in the imperial capital.
Jade sleeves and swirling incense,
Red brocades and snow-white cuffs...
One smile from you is worth
A thousand ounces of gold.
Fairy maid, your beauty
Is more than I can bear!
Six times six in wild goose formation,
Plus eight times nine,
Waiting only for news

From the Golden Cock.
Our chivalry Heaven-embracing.
Earth-shaking our loyalty,
Yet recognized by none
Within the Four Seas.
Morose and sad at separation,
I drink,
And in a single night
My hair turns white.

When he had finished, he handed the poem to Li Shishi. She read it a few times, but didn't understand. He was about to explain when the courtesan's personal maid entered.

"His Majesty has arrived at the rear door through the tunnel," she announced.

"I won't be able to see you off," Shishi said hastily to her guests. "Please forgive me." She hurried to receive the emperor.

The young maid quickly gathered the cups and utensils, carried away the small table, and swept the floor. Song Jiang and the others concealed themselves in a dark corner of the side room. From it they could see Shishi in the parlor kneeling before the sovereign.

"Your Majesty must be weary from affairs of state."

The emperor's head was covered by a silk gauze kerchief in the Tang style. He wore an imperial dragon robe.

"I've just returned from the Upper Purity Temple," he said. "I directed my son the prince to dispense wine to the populace at Xuande House and my younger brother to attend the fair at the Thousand Paces Esplanade. I had arranged to meet Marshal Yang, but he never showed up, though I waited a long time. So I came here. Approach, beloved, let us talk together."

"If we miss this chance, we may never get another," Song Jiang whispered to his cohorts in the darkness. "Why don't we three go forward and beseech an amnesty? What would be wrong with that?"

"Impossible!" said Chai Jin. "Even if he agreed, he could always reverse himself later."

Meanwhile, Li Kui's wrath was growing. Song Jiang and Chai Jin had sat drinking with the beauty, but he and Dai Zong had been sent to watch the door! Li Kui's hackles rose. His fury reached a boiling point.

Just then, Marshal Yang raised the hanging screen and pushed open the double doors. He was about to Step in when his eyes Ml on Li Kui, Standing inside the entry.

"Who are you, knave? How dare you come here?" he barked.

Without a word, Li Kui picked up an armchair and flung it at Yang's head. The startled marshal tumbled backwards, knocking over another two chairs. Dai

Zong rushed to intervene, but he was too late. Li Kui ripped pictures off the wall and set fire to them with a candle. Smashing left and right, he spread the blaze. Incense table, chairs, benches—he pulverized them all.

Song Jiang and his companions hurried out when they heard the tumult. They found the Black Whirlwind, stripped to the waist, going on a rampage. By the time they got outside the door, Li Kui was tearing down the street with a cudgel he had grabbed somewhere. Song Jiang decided to leave the city immediately with Chai Jin and Dai Zong, lest the gates be closed before they could escape. He directed Yan Qing to remain behind and look after Li Kui.

The moment the fire broke out in Li Shishi's home, the emperor was off like a streak of smoke. Neighbors who hurried to fight the blaze also rescued Marshal Yang. Of that no more need be said.

The sounds of the yelling and shouting reached Marshal Gao, who was patrolling above the North Gate. He hastened down with his soldiers to give chase. Li Kui, battling madly, ran into Mu Hong and Shi Jin. They were joined by Yan Qing, and the four fought their way to the inner side of the city wall.

Soldiers rushed to close the gate. But from the outside up charged Sagacious Lu with his iron staff, Wu Song with his double swords, and Zhu Tong and Liu Tang, swinging halberds. They hacked a path into the city and saved their four mates.

They got through the gate just about the time Gao and his mounted force were reaching it. Song Jiang, Chai Jin and Dai Zong had vanished. The eight chieftains grew alarmed.

Now it so happened that Wu Yong, the outlaws' military advisor, suspecting Song Jiang would have difficulty, had decided to raid the Eastern Capital. He fixed a time and dispatched a thousand armored cavalry under the five Tiger Chieftains. In the outskirts they met Song Jiang, Chai Jin and Dai Zong, and provided them with horses they had brought for that purpose. Then the other eight arrived and were also given mounts. But there was no sign of Li Kui.

Marshal Gao and men were preparing to charge forth. Five of Song Jiang's commanders—Guan Sheng, Lin Chong, Qin Ming, Huyan Zhuo and Dong Ping, galloped up to the edge of the moat.

"All the gallants of Mount Liangshan are here," they shouted. "Surrender the city and save yourselves from death!"

Gao dared not come out. He hurriedly pulled up the drawbridge and retreated with his soldiers to defensive positions atop the city wall.

"You're Li Kui's best friend," Song Jiang said to Yan Qing. "Wait for the swarthy oaf and bring him back. I want to return to the stronghold with our men tonight before the foe can intercept us."

Song Jiang and the outlaws departed. Yan Qing, watching beneath the eaves of a house, saw Li Kui emerging from the inn with his luggage on his back. An ax in either hand, he leaped forth from the inn gate with a yell and headed, alone, to attack the Eastern Capital.

Truly, he left the inn roaring like thunder, flourishing axes to split the city gate.

How did Li Kui the Black Whirlwind assault the Eastern Capital? Read our next chapter if you would know.

CHAPTER 73

BLACK WHIRLWIND PRETENDS TO CATCH A SPIRIT

THE MOUNT LIANGSHAN HERO PRESENTS TWO HEADS

Yan Qing flung his arms around Li Kui's waist. With one twist, he threw him to the ground, head down and feet to the sky. Yan Qing then dragged him up, let go, and strode off along a path. Li Kui followed.

Why did Li Kui go with him? Because Yan Qing was the first among wrestlers. For that reason Song Jiang had dispatched him to control Li Kui. If the Black Whirlwind didn't listen, Yan Qing needed only one swift motion to floor him. Li Kui had had more than one taste of his hands and feet. He was afraid of Yan Qing and had to obey.

They dared not travel the highway. If pursuing government troops caught up, they'd have a hard time resisting. They made a wide detour in the direction of Chenliu County. Li Kui put on his clothes again and concealed his axes beneath them. Since he had no head kerchief, he parted his scorched-brown hair and did it up in two buns in the manner of a Taoist priest. They walked until daylight. Yan Qing had some money, and bought meat and wine in a village tavern. After eating, they continued on.

In the Eastern Capital that morning, confusion reigned. Marshal Gao led troops forth, but they were unable to apprehend the fugitives and had to return. Li Shishi claimed she knew nothing about anything. Marshal Yang also came back and rested. A check revealed that four or five hundred people in the city had been injured. Innumerable others, who had fallen or been knocked down, suffered bruises and contusions. Gao met with Tong Guan, head of the Council of Military Affairs, and they both conferred with the premier about petitioning the emperor. Troops were sent to pursue and catch the outlaws.

As to Li Kui and Yan Qing they reached a village called Four Willows. It was already late in the day, and they approached a large manor and knocked on the gates. They were ushered to a thatch-roofed hall, where Squire Di, who owned the manor, received them. He saw the buns of hair on Li Kui's head, but observed that he was not wearing a Taoist gown and was very ugly. Not knowing what to make of him, the squire addressed himself to Yan Qing.

"Where does this reverend come from?"

Yan Qing laughed. "He's a strange person. None of you have ever heard of him. We'd like something to eat, and to spend the night. We'll leave in the morning."

Li Kui didn't speak. The squire kowtowed before him.

"Help me, Reverend," he pleaded.

"What do you want me to do? Tell me frankly."

"There are over a hundred people in this household, including my wife and my twenty-year-old daughter. For the last six months the girl has been possessed by a spirit. She never leaves her room, and doesn't even come out to eat. If anyone tries to go near her, he's showered with bricks and stones. Many of us have been hurt. We've had the magistrate down several times, but he's never been able to catch the spirit."

"Squire, I'm a disciple of Abbot Lou of Qizhou. I know how to ride the clouds and capture demons. If you don't mind spending a bit, I'll nab him for you tonight. I'll need a pig and a sheep, first, for sacrifice purposes."

"We've got all the pigs and sheep you want, to say nothing of wine."

"Pick a couple of fat ones, and slaughter and roast them, and bring them here. I need also a few bottles of good wine, to make my arrangements. Tonight, at the third watch, I'll capture your spirit."

"If you want any written prayers or paper paraphernalia, Reverend, I have some."

"I've got my own magic. I don't need any of that friggin stuff. I'll just go to her room and snatch him."

Yan Qing could barely restrain his laughter. The squire had nothing but praise for Li Kui.

By midnight the roasted animals were laid out in the hall. Black Whirlwind called for a large bowl, and lined up a dozen bottles of heated wine. He lit two candles and ignited good incense in a burner. Then he dragged over a bench and sat down in the middle. But instead of reciting prayers, he pulled out one of his axes, hacked open the pig and sheep, and proceeded to tear off large chunks and eat them.

"Join me, young Prodigy," he said magnanimously.

Yan Qing only smiled coldly, and Li Kui continued gorging until he was full of meat and had consumed five or six bowls of fin wine, to the astonishment of the squire.

"Share this bounty with me," Li Kui said to the squire's vassals. In the twinkling of an eye he handed out the remaining meat. "Bring a bucket of warm water. I want to wash my hands and feet," he directed.

His orders were soon obeyed. After completing his ablutions, he demanded tea from the squire and said to Yan Qing: "Have you eaten yet?"

"I've had plenty," Yan Qing replied.

"We've finished the wine and meat, and tomorrow we must be on our way," Li Kui said to the squire. "We lords are going to sleep now."

"But this is terrible," cried the squire. "When are you going to catch the spirit?"

"You really want me to do that? Then lead me to your daughter's room."

"But that's where the demon is. Bricks and stones come flying out. Who dares to go!"

Li Kui grasped his two axes and directed men to stand with torches at a distance and light his path. He strode up to the house. It was faintly illuminated inside by a lamp. He peered in. A young fellow was holding a girl in his arms and they were talking.

With one kick the Black Whirlwind burst open the door and charged in swinging his axes. The lamp seemed to leap into a thousand slivers of light, shattered by Li Kui's blow. They young man tried to flee. Li Kui yelled, and hacked him down. The girl plunged under the bed and hid. Li Kui cut the man's head off, carried it over to the bed, and rapped on the frame with his ax.

"Come out, quick, woman. Otherwise I'll chop you and this bed to pieces."

"Spare me, I'll come out!"

No sooner had the girl poked her head out than Li Kui grabbed her by the hair and pulled her over beside the corpse. "Who is this fellow I've killed?" he demanded.

"Young Wang, my lover."

"Where did the bricks come from, and the food you ate?"

"I used to give him my gold and silver hairpins, and he would slip over the manor wall late at night and buy things."

"You filthy slut, what use are you!" Li Kui dragged her to the bed and cut her head off. He tied the two heads together by their hair, then placed the bodies side by side.

"I had a full meal. I need some exercise to help digest it." He stripped to the waist and flailed the two bodies with his axes as if he was drumming. Li Kui grinned. "That pair won't come back to life."

He stuck his axes into his girdle, picked up the heads, and returned to the hall. "I've caught two demons," he shouted, flinging down the heads.

The whole manor, astonished, gathered round to stare. They recognized the squire's daughter, but they didn't know who the other head belonged to. Finally, one of the vassals spoke.

"He looks something like Young Wang the bird-catcher from East Village."

"You've got sharp eyes," said Li Kui.

"How did you find out, Reverend?" asked the squire.

"Your daughter was hiding under the bed. I hauled her out and questioned her. She confessed he was her lover, Young Wang. Their food, he used to bring in. After I got all the information, I took action."

The squire wept. "Reverend, you should have spared my daughter."

"Stupid old ox! Your daughter takes a lover and you want me to spare her! Instead of thanking me, you weep and blame me. I'll settle with you tomorrow."

Yan Qing found a room, and he and Li Kui retired.

The squire led a group of people with lanterns and candles into his daughter's room. They saw the dismembered parts of the headless bodies scattered all over the floor. The squire and his wife wept distractedly. They ordered that the bodies be taken to the rear and burned.

Li Kui slept until daybreak. He jumped out of bed and sought the squire.

"Yesterday, I caught the spirit for you. Why don't you show your thanks?"

Squire Di had no choice but to wine and dine him. After Li Kui and Yan Qing finished eating, they left. The squire went back to managing his manor.

On departing from Four Willows Village Li Kui and Yan Qing set out again along the road. This time of the year the grass was withered and the fields denuded, branches had fallen and the hills were empty.

The journey was uneventful. They continued in a wide detour towards the northern end of Liangshan Marsh. They were still seventy or eighty *li* from the stronghold, not far from the town of Jingmen. The mountain was not yet in sight, and it was growing late. They went up to a large manor, knocked on the gate, and asked for shelter.

"Why don't we find an inn and put up there?" said Yan Qing.

"We're much better off with a leading family like this," Li Kui retorted.

Before the words were out of his mouth, the vassal returned and said: "My master the squire is very distraught. You two had better rest someplace else."

Li Kui barged right in and headed for the thatch-roofed hall. Yan Qing was unable to restrain him.

"Passing travellers ask to spend the night," Black Whirlwind bellowed. "What's so friggin important that it's got your squire all upset! I want to speak to him."

The squire, peering out, saw how fierce Li Kui looked. He sent a man to invite him to a wing of the hall. There, a side room was provided for the two visitors. Later, a meal was served, after which they went to bed.

Not having had any wine, Li Kui couldn't sleep. As he tossed and turned on the earthen *kang,* he heard the squire and his wife, in the adjoining room, weeping and sobbing. Thoroughly irritated, Li Kui didn't close his eyes a minute.

When at last it was light, he jumped out of bed and strode to the front of the hall. "Who was crying all night and preventing this lord from sleeping?" he demanded.

The squire heard him, He came out and explained: "We have an eighteen-year-old daughter and someone has taken her. That's why we're upset."

"Stupid old ox. All boys and girls must marry when they reach a certain age. What's there to be upset about?"

"We don't agree to the match. He snatched her away by force."

"More funny business! Who is the man?"

"When I tell you you'll fart and pee in your pants with terror. He's the supreme commander of Liangshan Marsh, Song Jiang. One hundred and eight bold fellows are the chieftains there, and they have a considerable army."

"What I want to know is how many of them came here?"

"Two days ago, their leader arrived with a young fellow, both riding horses."

Li Kui called Yan Qing over. "Listen to this old man. It seems our Big Brother says one thing and does another. He's not a good person."

"Big Brother wouldn't commit wrong. I'm sure there's nothing in this."

"Didn't he go to the house of that Li Shishi in the Eastern Capital? Why wouldn't he pull something dirty here?" Li Kui turned to the squire. "You've got food in your manor. We want to eat. I'm Li Kui the Black Whirlwind of Liangshan Marsh. This is Yan Qing the Prodigy. If Song Jiang has taken your daughter, we'll bring her back."

The squire kowtowed his thanks.

The two returned to the mountain fortress. The trip was without incident. They went directly to Loyalty Hall, where Song Jiang received them.

"Where have you been, brothers," he queried. "You must have lost your way many times to be coming back only now."

Li Kui glared. Without a word he took his axes and cut down the apricot-yellow banner inscribed with "Act in Heaven's Behalf and ripped it to shreds. Everyone stared in amazement.

"What are you doing, you swarthy rogue?" Song Jiang shouted. Axes in hand, Li Kui charged across the hall towards Song Jiang. Guan Sheng, Lin Chong, Qin Ming, Huyan Zhuo and Dong Ping hurriedly blocked him, wrenched away his axes, and hustled him to the lower end of the chamber.

"That oaf is acting up again," Song Jiang cried angrily. He turned to Black Whirlwind. "Tell me, what have I done wrong?"

Li Kui was speechless with rage. Yan Qing stepped forward and related what had transpired from the time they left the Eastern Capital to their arrival at the manor near Jingmen.

"Squire Liu told us that two days ago Song Jiang and a young companion rode up to the manor," Yan Qing continued. "When he heard that they were men who acted in Heaven's behalf, he ordered his eighteen-year-old daughter to serve them wine. They ate and drank far into the night, then ran off with the daughter. Brother Li Kui, hearing this story, believed it to be true. I kept telling him: 'Big Brother isn't that kind of a person. Somebody must be impersonating him, and misbehaving in his name.' But Brother Li said: 'I saw him in the Eastern Capital hanging around that hussy Li Shishi like he couldn't bear to part. Of course he's the man.' That's why he's so furious."

"You've got it all wrong about Li Shishi. I didn't realize," Song exclaimed to Li Kui. "Why didn't you say something?"

"I considered you a chivalrous man. Who'd have thought you were such an animal! Imagine doing a thing like that!"

"Listen to me: I came back in the company of three thousand cavalry. If two horsemen dropped out, everyone would have noticed. And if I captured a woman, she'd be here in the stronghold. You can search my house, goon!"

"That's friggin nonsense, brother, and you know it. Every man in the fortress is under your command, and most of them would cover for you. She could be hidden anywhere. I used to respect you for not being a skirt-chaser. Actually, you're crazy about wine and women. Your killing of Yan Poxi was just a little show. The real thing was when you lusted after Li Shishi in the Eastern Capital. Don't try to deny it. Return his daughter to old Squire Liu, and we can still come to terms. If you don't, sooner or later I'll kill you."

"Take it easy. Squire Liu isn't dead yet, and all his vassals are still there. I'll go and confront him. If he identifies me as the man, I'll stick out my neck for your ax. If he says I'm not the culprit, what should your penalty be, disrespectful varlet?"

"If I can't pin this on you, you can have my head."

"Good. All you brothers are witnesses." Song Jiang directed Ironclad Virtue Pei Xuan to write out two orders of execution as pledges for the bet, and each man signed one. Song Jiang handed his pledge to Li Kui. Black Whirlwind gave his to Song Jiang.

"That young fellow the squire spoke of must be Chai Jin," said Li Kui. "It can't be anyone else."

"I'll go too, then," said Chai Jin.

"That you will, never fear. If the squire identifies you, you'll get a taste of my axes, too, lord or no lord!"

"That's all right with me," said Chai Jin. "You go first and we'll follow, so there won't be any funny business."

"Right," said Li Kui. He called to Yan Qing. "We'll go on ahead. If they don't come, it's because they know they're guilty. We'll come back and have this out!"

Yan Qing and Li Kui proceeded to the manor. "Any news, bold fellows?" the squire asked.

"Our Song Jiang is coming here today for you to identify him," said the Black Whirlwind. "I want you and your wife and your vassals to take a good look. If it's him, speak up, don't be afraid. I'll be responsible."

A vassal announced: "A dozen horsemen are at the gates."

"That's them," said Li Kui.

While the others waited outside, Song Jiang and Chai Jin entered. They went directly to the thatch-roofed hall and sat down. Li Kui stood to one side with his axes, ready to strike as soon as the old man recognized the culprit. But Squire Liu walked over to Song Jiang and kowtowed.

"Is this the man who kidnapped your daughter?" the Black Whirlwind queried.

Squire Liu opened wide his weak old eyes and examined Song Jiang carefully. "No."

"What do you say to that?" Song Jiang asked Li Kui. "You two gave him a look and scared him. He doesn't dare speak."

"Call his vassals, then, and ask them.'

Li Kui summoned the vassals. In one voice they all said: "He's not the man."

"Squire Liu," said Song Jiang, "I am Song Jiang of Liangshan Marsh. This brother is Chai Jin. Your daughter was probably kidnapped by an impostor. If you find out where she's gone, let our stronghold know. We'll take care of it for you."

To Li Kui he said: "This is no place for us to talk. When you get back to the fortress I'll have something to say." He and Chaj Jin and their escort left first for the stronghold on the mountain.

"A fine mess, brother," said Yan Qing.

"It's my fault for being too impatient. Since I've forfeited my head, I might as well cut it off and have you present it to Big Brother."

"You've no reason to kill yourself. I have a way out. It's called 'Bearing the Thomstick and Requesting Punishment'."

"What do you mean by 'Bearing the Thomstick'?"

"You remove your clothes, have your hands tied, carry a thomstick on your bare back, and prostrate yourself before Loyalty Hall. You call out: 'Let Big Brother beat me as he will.' Of course, he won't have the heart. That's 'Bearing the Thomstick and Requesting Punishment'."

"Not bad, but it's kind of embarrassing. I'd rather cut my head off and get it over with."

"All of us in the stronghold are your brothers. Who would laugh at you?"

Reluctantly, Li Kui returned with Yan Qing to the fortress.

Song Jiang and Chai Jin reached Loyalty Hall first. They were just talking about Li Kui with the other chieftains when they saw him approaching. He was buff naked, and on his back he bore a thomstick. He knelt mutely outside the hall, with lowered head.

"Why are you bearing a thomstick, you swarthy scoundrel?" Song Jiang smiled. "Do you think that way I'll have to let you off?"

"I was wrong. Take this big stick and beat me, brother."

"I bet against your head. Why bring me a thomstick?"

"If you won't forgive, brother, cut my head off. It will be what I deserve."

The chieftains all apologized on Li Kui's behalf. "I'll forgive him on one condition: that he capture the two impersonators and find Squire Liu's daughter and bring her home."

Li Kui jumped to his feet. "I'm off. It'll be as easy as catching turtles in a jug. I only have to put out my hand."

"There are two of them, and they're mounted. You're all alone. How are you going to get near them? Take Yan Qing along."

"I'll be pleased to go, brother, if those are your orders," said Yan Qing.

He went to his quarters and got his bow and a staff as tall as his eyebrows. With Li Kui he went once again to the manor of Squire Liu.

Yan Qing questioned him carefully. "They came when the sun was in the west," said the squire, "and left at the third watch. I don't know where they went. I didn't dare follow. The leader was short, thin, and dark-complected. The other was a big strong fellow, with a short beard and large eyes."

The two chieftains queried further, then said: "Don't worry, squire. We're going to return your daughter to you, come what may. Our Big Brother Song Jiang has ordered us to find her, and we must obey."

They asked for boiled meat and steamed muffins and put these in ration bags which they slung across their shoulders. Leaving the manor, they first searched due north. It was a desolate area, devoid of human habitation. In two days they found not a trace of their quarry.

Next they tried the east. A two-day search proved fruitless, though they ranged as far as Gaotang in Lingzhou Prefecture. Li Kui grew more irritable, and his face was flushed as they turned around and headed west. But in the next two days they again discovered nothing.

That night the two took shelter in an ancient temple at the foot of a hill, and bedded down on the big altar table. Li Kui, too annoyed to sleep, sat up. He heard someone walking by, outside. He jumped down from the table, opened the temple door, and looked. A man with a halberd was staring up the hill behind the temple. Li Kui followed.

Yan Qing, who heard him moving about, took his bow and staff and caught up with Black Whirlwind. "Don't chase him, brother," he said. "I have another way."

It was night, and the moon was hazy. Yan Qing handed his staff to Li Kui. The man was now some distance away, head down, walking rapidly. Yan Qing soon narrowed the gap between them until he was fairly close behind. Fitting an arrow to his bow, he pulled the string tight and let fly, crying. "Bow, don't fail me!" The arrow struck the man in the right leg and brought him down.

Li Kui raced forward, seized the fellow by the collar and hauled him back to the temple. "Where have you hidden Squire Liu's daughter?" he yelled.

"I don't know anything about it, sir," the man replied. "I haven't taken anyone's daughter. I'm only a petty highwayman, doing a very modest business. I wouldn't dare go in for anything big, like snatching a man's daughter."

Black Whirlwind tied the fellow securely and raised his axes menacingly. "If you don't tell the truth I'll cut you into twenty pieces!"

"Let me up and we'll talk this over," the man exclaimed.

"I'll remove the arrow from-you," said Yan Qing. He allowed the man to rise. "Frankly, now, who was it who stole Squire Liu's daughter? Though you're only a highwayman, you must have heard something."

"I'm only guessing, I don't actually know. But about fifteen *li* northwest of here is a place called Ox Head Mountain, and on it is an old Taoist temple. Recently, two tough characters, one named Wang Jiang and the other Dong Hai, both minor bandits in the greenwood, killed all the priests and acolytes in the temple, and moved in with their gang. There are only six or seven of them. They specialize in robbery and plunder. Wherever they go, the leader calls himself Song Jiang. My guess is that the two chiefs have taken the girl."

"There's reason in what you say," Yan Qing averred. "Don't be afraid of us. I'm Yan Qing the Prodigy of Liangshan Marsh, and this is Black Whirlwind Li Kui. I'll treat your arrow wound, and you lead us to where those two are staying."

"All right," said the man.

Yan Qing returned his halberd and bound his wound. Then, in the light of the hazy moon, supported by Yan Qing and Li Kui, the man conducted them along the road for fifteen *li*. They came in sight of the mountain. It wasn't very high, and did indeed resemble a reclining ox with its head on the ground.

As the three began climbing, the sky was not yet light. At the top they found an area enclosed by an earthen wall. Within was a moderately sized building of about twenty rooms.

"I'll go in and have a look," said Black Whirlwind.

"Better wait till daylight," Yan Qing advised.

But Li Kui had no patience. He jumped over the wall. Someone shouted. The door of the house opened, and a man with a halberd rushed out and charged Li Kui. Afraid that their rescue operation would be ruined, Yan Qing, holding his staff, also leaped the wall. The wounded highwayman streaked away like a wisp of smoke.

Yan Qing crept up to the bruiser who was fighting with Li Kui and cracked him on the cheekbone with his staff, knocking him into Li Kui's arms. With one whack of his ax on the fellow's back, the Black Whirlwind felled him to the ground. Not another person emerged from the building.

"There must be a rear exit," said Yan Qing. "I'll guard the back door and you watch the front. Don't go blundering in."

Yan Qing hid in the darkness beside the rear gate of the wall. He saw a man open the back door of the house and approach the rear gate with a key in his hand. Yan Qing advanced to meet him. The man spotted Yan Qing and skirted around the house towards the front.

"Stop him," Yan Qing yelled.

Li Kui dashed up and planted his ax in the man's chest. He cut the heads off the two bodies and tied them together. His blood lust aroused, he charged into the building, bowling men over like clay idols. Several of them cowered beside the stove. With one blow of his ax each, the Black Whirlwind dispatched them all.

In a room in the center of the building, sure enough, they found the girl, sobbing on a bed. She had misty hair and a flowery complexion. An alluring beauty.

"Aren't you Squire Liu's daughter?" said Yan Qing. "I am," the girl replied. "About ten days ago two robbers brought me here, and took turns ravishing me every night. I wept constantly and wanted to kill myself, but they watched me very closely. Now you two generals have saved me. You're like my father and mother reborn."

"Where are their two horses?"

"In the east wing."

Yan Qing saddled the animals and led them out. He collected the gold and silver hidden in the house—about five thousand ounces—and told the girl to mount. He wrapped up the money and tied it, along with the two heads, on the other beast.

Li Kui twisted grass into a torch, lit it on a lamp below a window of the building, and set the thatched roof afire from four sides. Then they pushed open the wall gate, escorted the girl down the mountain, and delivered her to the manor.

Her parents were overjoyed. All their cares vanished. They couldn't kowtow and thank the two chieftains enough.

"Don't thank us," said Yan Qing. "Go up to the fortress and thank our Big Brother Song Jiang."

The two refused the wine and food offered. They mounted the horses and hastened back to the stronghold. By the time they traversed the three fortified passes the rising sun was just crimsoning the rim of the mountains. They led the animals, laden with gold and silver and the two heads, directly to Loyalty Hall. Yan Qing reported to Song Jiang what had transpired.

Very pleased, Song Jiang ordered that the heads be buried, the gold and silver placed in the treasury, and the horses cared for with the rest of the cavalry steeds.

A feast was given the next day to congratulate Yan Qing and Li Kui. Squire Liu brought gold and silver to Loyalty Hall and tried to present it to Song Jiang in thanks. But Song Jiang would have none of it. After the wining and dining, he told the squire to take the money back with him to the manor.

Of that we'll say no more. A period of peace settled upon the mountain fortress.

Time passed quickly. Soon the willows were gosling yellow, gradually the river waves were a turquoise green. The cheeks of the peaches glowed pink, the faces of the apricots showed a faint smile. On the mountain, front and rear, flowers began to sprout, branches started to bud. Life returned to the duckweed on the ponds and the reeds along the shores. It was a time of grain rains and clearing skies, of the mellow, comfortable weather of the third lunar month.

As Song Jiang was quietly seated one day, he saw a group of men being led up from below the pass under armed escort. An outlaw arrived first and reported: "We've captured some fellows who are built like oxen. They have seven or eight handcarts and a number of staves."

The captives—big, hulking men—knelt at the lower end of the hall. "We're from Fengxiang District," they said, "and we're on a pilgrimage to Tai'an Prefecture to burn incense. The twenty-eighth of this month is the anniversary of the birth of the Emperor of Heaven. We're also going to take part in the staves contest. It lasts for three days, and there'll be hundreds of competitors. This year the famous wrestler Ren Yuan of Taiyuan will be there. He's ten feet tall and calls himself the Sky-Supporting Pillar. 'No one can match me,' he boasts. 'I'm the best wrestler in the world.' We hear he's been undefeated in the temple fair contests for the past two years, and has won some valuable prizes. He's put up an announcement, offering to take on all comers. We thought we might see him in action, and also pick up a few pointers on fighting with staves. Pray, great chieftain, favor us with your benevolence."

Song Jiang summoned a junior officer. "Take these men down the mountain at once. They're not to be harmed. From now on you're not to frighten persons on their way to burn incense in temples or returning. Let them pass freely."

The travellers kowtowed and thanked Song Jiang for sparing their lives, and departed.

Yan Qing then approached and said a few brief words. And as a result, all of Tai'an Prefecture was alarmed, and the county of Xiangfu was thrown into turmoil. Truly, two tigers battled in the Temple of the East Sacred Mountain, a pair of dragons fought in Jianing Hall.

What is it that Yan Qing said? Read our next chapter if you would know.

CHAPTER 74

YAN QING CLEVERLY DEFEATS SKY-SUPPORTING PILLAR

LI KUI PLAYS THE MAGISTRATE IN SHOUZHANG COUNTY

Although the last of the thirty-six Stars of Heavenly Spirits, Yan Qing was more quick-witted, well-informed, and adaptable than the other thirty-five. He addressed Song Jiang.

"Since childhood I have followed Lu Junyi the Magnate and learned from him the art of wrestling. In all the gallant fraternity, I have never met my match. Now there is a good opportunity. It will soon be the twenty-eighth of the third lunar month. I would like to go, alone, to the competition platform and try my skill against the Sky-Supporting Pillar. If I lose, I don't care if I die in the process. If I win, I'll earn a bit of glory for Big Brother. It's sure to stir up plenty of excitement. Maybe you could send some men to support me."

"I hear the fellow is ten feet tall," said Song Jiang, "as solid as steel, and enormously strong. You're short and thin. I know your technique is good, but how will you ever get near him?"

"His height and huskiness don't bother me. I'm only afraid he won't fall for my tricks. 'In wrestling use strength if you've got, use wiles if you've not,' as the old saying goes. I'm not boasting, but I'm very quick to seize an advantage. I won't necessarily lose to that big lout."

Lu Junyi the Magnate said: "This young Prodigy has indeed been good at wrestling since an early age. Let him go if he wants to. After the contest I'll see to it that he gets back."

"When do you want to leave?" Song Jiang asked Yan Qing.

"Today's the twenty-fourth. I'll bid you farewell tomorrow, brother. The journey will take a day or so. I'll reach the temple fair grounds on the twenty-sixth and spend the twenty-seventh inquiring around. Then, on the twenty-eighth, I'll fight him."

The following day, Song Jiang gave Yan Qing a farewell banquet. He was dressed like a rustic, but he wore embroidered clothes under his simple padded robe. Disguised as a Shandong pedlar, he had a drum-rattle tucked in his sash and carried his merchandise on a long shoulder-pole. The chieftains laughed at his appearance.

"Since you're made up as a pedlar," said Song Jiang, "give us a Shandong pedlar's song."

Yan Qing complied, twirling his drum-rattle in one hand, and beating out rhythm with wooden clappers in the other, giving a very creditable imitation. Everyone laughed. They drank till all were pleasantly mellow. Then Yan Qing took leave of the chieftains and went down the mountain. Crossing at the Shore of Golden Sands, he struck out along the road to Tai'an Prefecture.

Towards evening, as he was looking for an inn to spend the night, he heard a voice shouting behind him: "Brother Prodigy, wait for me!"

Yan Qing rested his carrying-pole and looked. Li Kui the Black Whirlwind was hastening after him.

"What do you want?" Yan Qing demanded.

"You stayed with me twice when I went to Jingmen Town. I saw you leave alone and I was worried about you. So I didn't ask Big Brother's permission, but just sneaked off to keep you company."

"I don't need you. Go on back."

"You're a fine one! I come to help you, and you act like that. I'm friggin well going with you!"

Yan Qing couldn't be ungracious in the face of Li Kui's chivalrous concern. "I don't mind your coming along," he said, "but they'll be celebrating the Emperor of Heaven's birthday and the town will be jammed with people from all over. Many of them might recognize you. I'll let you come on three conditions."

"All right."

"On the road we walk one before and one behind, and when we put up at an inn you're not to leave the door. That's one. Two, when we stop at an inn near the fair grounds you're to play sick. Cover your head with your quilt and pretend to snore. Don't make any other sound. Three, the day of the contest when you stand among the watching crowd, you're not to raise any rumpus. Brother, can you agree to that?"

"Easy! I'll do anything you say."

That night, they slept at an inn. They rose the next day before dawn, paid the bill, travelled a distance, and cooked breakfast.

"You go on ahead half a *li,* brother," said Yan Qing, "and I'll follow."

There were many people on the road going to the temple to burn incense, or returning. Several talked about the redoubtable Ren Yuan. "For two years he hasn't been beaten at the East Sacred Mountain Temple fair," they said. "This is going to be the third year."

Yan Qing listened. He would remember that. In late afternoon, as he neared the temple, he saw other travellers stopping by the roadside and reading something. He rested his load, pushed through the gathering to the front and looked. Stretched across two upright red poles like an ornate street arch was a pink signboard. On it was written: "Sky-Supporting Pillar Ren Yuan of Taiyuan, Wrestler." In smaller script on either side were the words: "Puncher of the fierce tiger on the South Mountain, kicker of the writhing dragon in the North Sea."

Yan Qing raised his carrying-pole and smashed the board to splinters. Without a word he again shouldered his pole and proceeded towards the temple. Several of the watchers, eager to stir up excitement, flew to Ren Yuan and reported that a man had shattered his signboard in challenge.

Yan Qing caught up with Li Kui and they looked for an inn. The temple fair was very lively. A hundred and twenty trades were all displaying their wares, fourteen to fifteen hundred inns were welcoming guests from many different parts, and a goodly number were full at this festival time. Yan Qing and Li Kui finally found a place at the far edge of the fair grounds. The prodigy rested his load, while Black Whirlwind rolled himself up in a quilt on the bed.

"A pedlar from Shandong come to do some business at the fair, are you, brother?" said the inn attendant. "I wonder if you have enough money for the room?"

"You shouldn't underestimate people," said Yan Qing, in the manner of a country bumpkin. "How much can a little room cost? Even if it were a large room, whatever others give, I can pay the same."

"Don't be offended, brother. This is our busiest season. It's better to have a clear understanding, first."

"This is a business trip. It doesn't matter about me. I can sleep anywhere. But I met this relative from my home village on the road, and he's come down with asthma. I've brought him to your inn so that he can rest. Here are five strings of cash, on account. Go to the kitchen and make us something to eat. I'll give you a tip when we leave."

The attendant took the money and went out to prepare the food. Of that no more need be said.

Not long after there was a hubbub at the inn door, and twenty or thirty big fellows entered. "What room is the man in who smashed the signboard as a challenge?" they asked the attendant.

"We don't have any such person."

"Everyone says he's here."

"We've only two rooms for rent. One is empty. The other is occupied by a Shandong pedlar and his sick relation."

"It's the pedlar who smashed the sign."

"Don't make me laugh! He's a slim young fellow. What use would a challenge from him be!"

"Take us to his room and let's have a look at him."

"It's that room down in the corner."

The men walked over, but the door was locked. They peered in through the window. All they could see was the feet of two men, sleeping. They didn't know what to think.

One of them said: "Since he had the courage to smash the sign and challenge the champion, he's surely no ordinary person. He's afraid someone will try to harm him before the match, so he pretends to be sick."

"That's probably it," the others agreed. "But there's no use guessing. We'll see when the time comes."

By dusk at least twenty or thirty such groups had called at the inn to inquire. The attendant's lips were dry and cracked with denials. That evening, when he brought the two guests their food, Li Kui poked his head out of the bedding.

"Aiya!" the attendant yelped. "The challenger!"

"He isn't the challenger. He's sick," said Yan Qing. "I'm the one who's challenging."

"Don't kid me. Ren Yuan could swallow you in a single gulp."

"You needn't smile. I have a trick that will hand you all a good laugh. When I come back from the match, I'll give you a present."

When the two had finished eating, the attendant collected the bowls and dishes and took them to wash in the kitchen. He didn't believe a word of what the Prodigy had told him.

The next morning, while they were having breakfast, Yan Qing said to Li Kui: "Brother, lock the door and sleep."

He mingled with crowds going into the Temple of the East Sacred Mountain. Located on the slopes of Mount Taishan, it was one of the most lavish and magnificent temples in the world. He wandered around a while, and offered four kowtows when he emerged from a thatched pavilion.

"Where can I find Teacher Ren, the wrestler?" he asked one of the worshippers.

"He instructs two or three hundred pupils in that big inn at the foot of the Welcome Benevolence Bridge."

Yan Qing, arriving at the bridge, found twenty or thirty wrestlers sitting on the railing. Ahead were gold-trimmed pennants and banners, embroidered canopies, and man-high backrests. He entered the inn yard. Ren Yuan was sitting in a pavilion in the center. He was indeed as huge and imposing as a temple guardian idol. Seated sideways on a bed with exposed had chest, he was every inch a tiger killer and mover of mountains as he watched his pupils perform.

One of them softly told him that this was the man who had shattered the signboard. Ren Yuan jumped up and fanned out his elbows.

"Anyone who wants to die this year can come and risk his life at my hands," he announced.

Yan Qing lowered his head and hurriedly departed. He could hear the gales of laughter behind him. He returned to Li Kui, and they drank and dined together.

"All this sleep is suffocating me," Black Whirlwind grumbled.

"Only one more night," Yan Qing consoled him. "Tomorrow's the showdown."

They chatted about various things of no interest to us.

Around the third watch the thud of drums sounded. Worshippers in the temple had commenced burning incense in celebration of the Emperor of Heaven's birthday. At the fourth watch, Yan Qing and Li Kui rose and ordered the attendant to fetch hot water so that they could wash their faces. They combed their hair smooth, removed their padded gowns, wrapped their legs in knee-length bindings, and put on silk trousers, hemp sandals, and a clean shirt each, binding this round the waist with a sash.

"We're leaving our luggage here," they said to the attendant. "Look after it for us."

"Nothing will be missing. Come back soon a winner!"

Staying at the inn were twenty or thirty pilgrims who had come to burn incense. "Think it over, young fellow," they urged Yan Qing. "Why throw your life away?"

"When everyone is cheering my victory, you can collect some gifts for me," the Prodigy replied.

The pilgrims departed for the temple.

"I might as well bring my two axes," said Li Kui.

"You can't do that," said Yan Qing. "If anyone recognizes you it will defeat our main purpose."

They mingled with the crowds and found an inconspicuous place for themselves on one of the temple porches. The grounds were jammed with worshippers. Huge as it was, the Temple of the East Sacred Mountain was soon filled to overflowing. Even the ridges of the roofs were lined with spectators.

Facing Jianing Hall a shed had been erected, and in it were gold and silver trophies and prizes of silks and satins. At the door of the hall five beautiful horses were hitched, all with fine saddles and bridles.

The prefect directed that no more worshippers be allowed to enter the temple, and settled down to watch the wrestling match in honor of Buddha. An old referee, holding a bundle of bamboo rods, mounted the platform outside the hall and worshipped the god. Then he called this year's wrestlers to come forth and contend.

Before the words were out of his mouth a tide of humanity surged forward. Preceded by a dozen staff-bearing guards and four embroidered pennants, Ren Yuan approached seated on a litter. In the van and to the rear were twenty or thirty stalwarts with tattooed arms. Surrounded by a jostling crowd, the procession reached the platform. The referee invited Ren Yuan to step down, and greeted him with a few warm words of welcome.

"I have won the championship at the temple for the last two years and earned a few unmerited prizes," said Ren Yuan. "This year I must fight stripped to the waist."

While he was speaking a man came with a bucket of water. Ren Yuan's disciples were standing around the platform in a dense circle. Their master opened his sash, removed his head kerchief, draped his padded Sichuan silk tunic over his shoulders, and loudly and respectfully hailed the Emperor of Heaven. He drank two mouthfuls of the holy water and discarded the tunic. Admiring cheers went up from thousands of throats.

How was Ren Yuan attired? A topknot done up in red thread crowned his head. He wore a jade green silk tunic fastened at the waist over a shirt with triple rows of jade buttons and trimmed with gold ruffles. His knee-length pants were plated with bronze and had a bronze crotch protector. Iron plates and rings encircled the calves of his legs. His wrists were firmly taped. Kicking shoes shod his feet. This, then, was the Sky-Supporting Pillar, who could lift the seas on earth and conquer the demons below.

"You've been the unrivalled champion here at the temple for the last two years, Teacher," said the referee. "This is the third year. Is there anything you would be willing to say to the assembled worshippers?"

"From four hundred prefectures and regions, from over seven thousand counties, good people come to burn incense in honor of the Buddha. All bring gifts which I have so unworthily won as prizes during the last two years. This year, after making my devotions, I am returning to my country home, and shall not be coming to this mountain again. From where the sun rises in the east to where it sets in the west, beneath the sky where sails the sun and moon, from the land of the barbarians in the south to the remote regions of Yan in the north, is there a man who dares to contend with me for prizes?"

Before Ren Yuan's voice had died away, Yan Qing raised himself up on the shoulders of the men on either side of him and shouted: "Yes, there is!" He flew to the platform across the backs of the throng. The crowd shouted.

"What is your name, young fellow?" the referee asked. "Where is your home? Where have you come from, now?"

"I'm Zhang the pedlar, from Shandong, and I've come especially to challenge him."

"Your end is near, young fellow, don't you realize that? Have you a sponsor?"

"I'm my own sponsor. No one has to be compensated for my life if I die!"

"Strip down and let's have a look at you."

Yan Qing whipped off his head kerchief. His gleaming hair was tied up in a topknot. He took off his straw sandals and squatted by the side of the platform and, unwound his leggings. Jumping up, he removed his shirt and struck a pose.

The turbulent spectators shouted their approval. They were astounded. Ren Yuan, at the sight of Yan Qing's finely muscled body, felt a thrill of fear.

On the Moon Terrace outside the hall sat the prefect, keeping order. Surrounding him, at his beck and call, were seventy or eighty pairs of black-clad police. Yan Qing came down from the platform and approached the terrace. The prefect was favorably impressed by his jade-smooth physique.

"Where are you from, young man?" he asked. "What brings you here?"

"My name is Zhang. I'm a first son, and I hail from Laizhou Prefecture in Shandong. I heard that Ren Yuan has challenged all wrestlers, and I made the trip specially to contend."

"The horse with full equipage over there is my prize. Suppose I give them to Ren Yuan. The trophies in the shed I propose to let you and him share, half and half. I'll also raise you up and let you serve at my side."

"Prefect, I don't care about the prizes. All I want is to dump him and give everyone a laugh, and hear the plaudits of the crowd."

"He's as huge as a temple guardian idol. I doubt if you'll be able to get near him."

"I'll willingly die in the attempt." Yan Qing again mounted the combat platform and faced Ren Yuan.

The referee asked Yan Qing to sign a waiver, then pulled out a list of rules, which he read. "You understand?" he said to the Prodigy. "No dirty tricks."

Yan Qing laughed coldly. "He's loaded with protective gear. I'm wearing only these thin silk pants. How could I do anything?"

The prefect summoned the referee. "That's a splendid young man. It's a pity," he said softly. "Tell him you'll call it a draw, with no need to contend."

Returning to the platform, the referee said to Yan Qing: "I'll let you go back to your village alive, young fellow. I'll declare this contest a draw."

"You're taking too much for granted! How do you know whether I'd win or lose?"

The area was jammed with spectators. Thousands of worshippers lined either side in dense rows like the scales on a fish. People were sitting on every inch of space atop the esplanades and on the roofs, all avidly awaiting the match.

Ren Yuan seethed with hatred. He longed to throw Yan Qing into the clouds so that he would be smashed in the fall.

"Since you're both determined to go ahead," said the referee, "we shall proceed with this wrestling match in honor of the Emperor of Heaven. Be careful and pay attention to the rules."

By this time the early morning mist had dissipated and the sun was beginning to rise. Holding his bundle of bamboo rods, the referee gave final instructions.

"Commence!" he shouted.

It's important to be clear in describing this wrestling-match, with its various moves. Telling it is slow, but things happened as quickly as a meteorite flashing across the sky.

At first Yan Qing only crouched on the right, while Ren Yuan stood on the left like a door god. Yan Qing didn't stir, and the space between them remained empty. Ren Yuan edged around to the right, but Yan Qing only watched the ground on three sides of his rival.

"If that's all he's going to do," mused the champion, "I won't have to move a hand. With one kick, I'll boot him off the platform."

Ren Yuan drew nearer. He feinted with his left foot. "None of that!" cried Yan Qing. Before Ren could close in, he slipped low past the big man's left side. Angrily, Ren whirled, but Yan weaved and dodged back past the right ribs of his opponent.

Turning his huge body again and again, Ren grew confused, and his feet stumbled. The Prodigy darted forward, grasped Ren's shoulder with his right hand, his crotch with his left, shoved his shoulder under Ren's chest, and lifted. Five times he spun with his hapless foe, who was dangling, feet in the air, to the edge of the platform.

"Down you go," he yelled, and tossed Ren, head first, to the ground.

This gambit is called the Pirouetting Pigeon. The crowd cheered wildly. Ren Yuan's disciples, seeing their master thrown, knocked over the shed and seized the trophies. Loud quarrels and fist fights broke out among the crowd. Twenty or thirty of Ren's wrestling pupils clambered onto the platform. The prefect hadn't a chance in the world of keeping order.

No one expected that this scene would incense a mighty figure. Li Kui the Black Whirlwind, his strange eyes widening in a glare, watched angrily from the side, bristling like a tiger. He had no weapon, so he pulled up a pine sapling as easily as plucking a scallion and snapped it in two. With one segment in each hand, Li Kui commenced flailing. Some of the spectators recognized him, and called out his name. This brought policemen, who were outside, pouring into the temple.

"Don't let the Black Whirlwind of Liangshan Marsh get away!" they shouted.

When the prefect heard this, he scooted out of the rear of the hall so fast the three souls in his head and the seven spirits beneath his feet vanished With him. Some people crowded around the platform, but most of the worshippers hurried from the temple.

Ren Yuan was lying in a daze at the foot of the platform, barely breathing, when Li Kui reached him. Black Whirlwind pried up a stone slab and pounded Ren Yuan to a pulp. He and Yan Qing battled to the temple gate, where they were met by a hail of arrows. Climbing to the roof of a temple building, they hurled tiles at their assailants.

A clamor arose at the gate, and a body of men fought their way forward. Their leader wore a wide-brimmed hat of white felt and a white silk gown, and carried a dagger at his waist. In his hands was a halberd. It was Lu Junyi, the Jade Unicorn of the Northern Capital. Behind him were Shi Jin, Mu Hong, Sagacious Lu, Wu Song, Xie Zhen and Xie Bao, with a thousand men. Forcing open the gate, they surged in to the rescue.

Yan Qing and Li Kui leaped down from the roof and joined them, and all left together. Li Kui returned to the inn for his axes, and went on a killing rampage. By the time prefectural government troops arrived at the scene, the outlaws were far gone. The soldiers knew that the men of Liangshan Marsh were difficult adversaries, and were afraid to give chase.

Lu Junyi ordered that Li Kui be collected and the return journey commenced. But during a half day's march, they saw no sign of him on the road. Lu laughed.

"That trouble-maker. Someone will have to find him and bring him back to the mountain."

"I'll do it," Mu Hong volunteered.

"Fine," said Lu.

Meanwhile, Li Kui, axes in hand, proceeded to the county town of Shouzhang. The court had just adjourned for the noon recess when he walked up to the gate of government headquarters.

"The lord Black Whirlwind of Liangshan Marsh is here!" he shouted.

The staff of the county office was paralyzed with fright. Theirs was the closest town to the outlaw stronghold, and mothers had only to say "Black Whirlwind Li Kui" to scare crying children into silence. And now, here he was, in person. A terrifying situation!

Li Kui went in and sat down on the magistrate's official chair. "A few of you had better come out and talk," he called. "Otherwise, I'll set fire to the place."

People in the corridor held a hasty conference. They decided they'd have to comply. "He might really do it," they said. Two of their number were selected and sent into the hall.

They kowtowed four times and, still on their knees, spoke. "Since you've come, chieftain, you must have some instructions."

"I don't want to disturb your county. I was passing by and thought I'd stop a while and fool around. Call your magistrate. I want to see him."

"When he heard you'd come, he left through the back door. We don't know where he's gone."

Li Kui didn't believe them. He wandered through the rear chambers, looking for the magistrate, and came upon the clothing wardrobe. He twisted open the lock, took out the official hat, affixed the corner attachments, and put it on. Next, he slipped into the green robe of office, tied the belt, exchanged his hemp sandals for elegant boots, took up the elmwood tablet, and walked back into the hall.

"All you officers," he called, "come in here and see this!" They had no choice but to obey. "How does this outfit look on me?"

"Very appropriate."

"Now, I want you to summon court for me. If you don't, I'll level this town to the ground."

The officers were afraid of him. They called a number of functionaries, who beat three rolls on the big drums with bone and ivory sticks, then all advanced and hailed Li Kui respectfully.

Black Whirlwind laughed heartily. "Now, let two litigants argue their case."

"No litigant would dare to appear before the chieftain."

"Then a couple of you can act the parts. I won't hurt you. It's just for fun."

The functionaries conferred, and picked two jail keepers to play the roles. Local people crowded the gate of the county office to watch. The two litigants knelt at the front of the hall.

"Pity me, magistrate," said the plaintiff. "That man struck me."

"He cursed me, first," retorted the defendant. "That's why I hit him."

"Who is the one who was hit?" Li Kui queried.

"I, sir," said the plaintiff.

"And who is the one who hit him?"

"He swore at me," said the defendant, "so I clouted him."

"The man who did the hitting is a good fellow," said Li Kui. "Let him go. The other is a spiritless lout. Why did he allow himself to be struck? Put a rack around his neck and parade him before the populace in the street outside the office."

Li Kui rose, fastened the green official gown, tucked the elmwood tablet in his belt, grasped his big axes, and went out to supervise the affixing of the rack around the neck of the plaintiff. Only after the man was put on exhibition at the county office gate, did Black Whirlwind stride on. He was still wearing the magistrate's splendid clothes and boots. The people who had been watching at the gate couldn't restrain their mirth.

He wandered around the town for a while, and then he heard pupils chanting their lessons. He raised the door curtain of the schoolroom and went in. The terrified teacher leaped out of the window and fled. Pupils wept, screamed, ran, or hid. Chuckling, Li Kui departed. Just outside the door he ran into Mu Hong.

"Everyone has been worried stiff about you, and here you are playing the fool! Come back to the mountain at once!"

Mu Hong dragged Li Kui off without any ceremony. Black Whirlwind was compelled to leave Shouzhang County and return to Liangshan Marsh. Crossing the Shore of Golden Sands, the two arrived at the fortress. Everyone laughed at the sight of Li Kui's attire. Song Jiang was holding a celebration for Yan Qing in Loyalty Hall when Black Whirlwind, enveloped in a green magistrate's robe, discarded his axes, swaggered in, and kowtowed before him, elmwood tablet in hand. As he began his prostrations, he trod on the gown, ripping it, and fell sprawling. The assembled chieftains roared with laughter.

"You've got a nerve, sneaking down the mountain without my permission," cried Song Jiang. "For that, you deserve to die! Every place you go, you make trouble. I'm saying this in front of all our brothers—I won't forgive you the next time!"

Li Kui sang out a respectful acknowledgment, and withdrew.

The succeeding period on Mount Liangshan was uneventful. The men practiced daily with their weapons, the infantry and cavalry maneuvered, the naval forces polished their skills. In each of the forts they busily manufactured more war machines, clothing, armor, blades, bows and arrows, banners and pennants. Of that we'll say no more.

Meanwhile, Tai'an Prefecture had sent a report to the imperial court in the Eastern Capital. The Council for Reports to the Throne had been receiving reports from the various prefectures and counties, and they all were complaints about the depredations of Song Jiang and his forces. The minister decided to present them together.

The day the imperial audiences were to be held, at the sound of the Jingyang Bell all the high officials gathered in the Hall of the Water Clock to await the arrival of the emperor at the morning court. It was a month since the Taoist Sovereign had last conducted such a session.

At three raps of the rod in the imperial ante-chamber, the civil and military officials formed in two bodies at the foot of the golden stairs. The holy ruler appeared. All kowtowed, and the chief of ceremonies called: "If anyone has a petition, let him come forward. If there are none, this court will adjourn."

The Minister of the Council for Reports to the Throne advanced and said: "Our council has received a great many reports from the various prefectures and counties complaining about Song Jiang and his robber chieftains. These brigands openly attack towns and cities, pillage treasuries and granaries, kill soldiers and civilians. They are insatiable, but wherever they go no one seems able to defeat them. If they are not destroyed soon, they will cause tremendous damage. We pray that Your Majesty take appropriate measures."

"Last year at the first Lunar Festival, they raided this capital," said the emperor. "This year they're causing disturbances everywhere, not just in prefectures and shires near their lair. I ordered the Council of Military Affairs to send troops against them, but have not yet received any reports."

Cui Qing, the Inspector General, stepped forward and said: "We hear that in Liangshan Marsh they have a banner which reads 'Act in Heaven's Behalf.' It tends to delude the common people. Because the people sympathize with them, it is not feasible to send troops among them. Moreover, Tartar Liao armies are attacking our borders, and our outposts are not able to cope with them all. It would be very inconvenient for us to divert soldiers at this time to a punitive expedition against the bandits. In my humble opinion, those deperadoes in the mountains, lawbreakers all, have gone into hiding and are committing wicked acts because they have no other way out. If a royal amnesty could be issued, and a high minister, bearing a dispensation of imperial wine and food, could go to Liangshan Marsh and speak kind words and offer the amnesty on condition that they fight against the Liao, both the public and private interests would be served. We pray that Your Majesty take appropriate measures."

"There is reason in what you say," replied the emperor. "It has my approval."

He designated Marshal Chen Zongshan as emissary, and directed him to proceed to Mount Liangshan with the symbolic imperial wine and an amnesty for all. Court was adjourned, and Marshal Chen took the royal decree and returned home to prepare for the journey.

And because Marshal Chen went with the amnesty, thousands of weapon blades and armored cavalry covered the mountain, and vast armadas of fighting ships crowded the waterways. Their thunderous clashes flushed out the demons and angered the King of Hell. Truly, fragrant imperial wine turned to stomach-burning gall, a royal pardon led to a declaration of war.

How did Marshal Chen deliver the amnesty to Song Jiang? Read our next chapter if you would know.

Chapter 75

The Devil Incarnate Upsets the Boat and Steals the Imperial Wine

The Black Whirlwind Rips Up the Pardon and Curses Emperor Hui Zong

As Marshal Chen was preparing for his journey, several people came and said: "Your mission will serve the government and remove a burden from the populace. Both the army and the people will benefit. The men of Liangshan Marsh place loyalty to the throne above all. They await only the emperor's amnesty. Speak sweet words, Marshal, and reassure them. Your clean name will be renowned for ten thousand generations."

Just then the majordomo of the premier's chancellery arrived. "The premier would like to speak to you, Marshal," he said.

Chen mounted his sedan-chair and went directly to the chancellery on New Song Gate Avenue. The majordomo led him to the study in the inner sanctum, where the premier received him. Chen sat down politely to one side. They had some tea, then Premier Cai spoke.

"I hear the emperor is sending you to Mount Liangshan with an amnesty. That's why I've asked you for a talk. You mustn't relax our imperial discipline when you get there, or violate our national laws. Remember what the *Analects of Confucius* say: 'When on a mission, wherever you go, abuse not the sovereign's command, and be a worthy emissary.'"

"This I know. Please give me your instructions, Premier."

"I've directed my majordomo to accompany you. He's well acquainted with the law. If you run into any snags, he'll be able to remind you."

"I'm deeply grateful for your consideration," said Chen. He took his leave of the premier, left the chancellery with the majordomo, got into his sedan-chair, and returned home.

He had just settled down to rest, when his gate-keeper entered and announced: "Marshal Gao is dismounting at the gate." Chen hastened out to welcome him, and invited him to be seated in the hall. After an exchange of pleasantries, Gao came to the point.

"If I had been present when the imperial court was considering an amnesty for Song Jiang, I would have opposed it. Those brigands have insulted the court time and again, and their crimes reach the sky! Pardoning them and letting them come into the capital is sure to provoke disaster. I wanted to submit my own petition, but the royal decree had already been announced. Well, we'll see what happens. If those bandits still have no conscience and stall on the amnesty, return to the capital quickly, Marshal. I'll petition the emperor to muster a large army, which I'll lead personally, and wipe them out, root and branch! That's my fondest wish. I have a captain under my command who's a clever and competent speaker. Give him one question, and he'll answer you ten. He can go with you and lend you a hand."

"I'm grateful for Your Excellency's concern."

Marshal Gao rose, and Chen escorted him to the gate of the residency. There, Gao climbed on his horse and departed.

The next day Premier Cai's Majordomo Zhang and Marshal Gao's Captain Li arrived at Chen's headquarters. Marshal Chen's horses were already saddled and bridled and his soldiers mustered. Ten generals placed ten bottles of imperial wine into hampers decorated with dragons and phoenixes, and these were carried by bearers on shoulder-poles and preceded by imperial yellow banners.

Marshal Chen mounted. Accompanied by a trusted entourage of five or six, plus Zhang and Li, also on horseback, and with the emperor's decree carried in the lead, he led the procession through the New Song Gate. The officials who were seeing them off returned to the city.

The party wound its way to Jizhou. Prefect Zhang Shuye met them and invited them into the prefecture, where a feast had been laid. He inquired about the amnesty, and Marshal Chen told him the story.

"In my humble opinion, it's the best solution," said the prefect. "There's just one thing: you must speak to them pleasantly and reassure them with kind words. Nothing else matters so long as you accomplish the main objective. Your good name will be famed to all posterity. Several of those outlaws are very hotheaded. If you say one word that triggers them off, the whole deal may be spoiled."

"Nothing can go wrong with us two along," said Majordomo Zhang and Captain Li. "You talk only of caution and affability, Prefect. What about our imperial discipline? Those worthless fellows must be constantly chastened. If you let them get too cocky they'll set a bad example to others."

"Who are these two?" the prefect queried.

"This is Premier Cai's majordomo, and this is a captain under Marshal Gao."

"It would be better if they didn't go."

"They're trusted confidants. If I don't take them, the premier and the marshal will get suspicious."

"I'm only trying to help. I'm afraid your journey will be futile."

"With us two along," the majordomo interjected, "though there be ten thousand fathoms of water, not a drop will escape!"

The prefect was afraid to say any more. After feasting his guests, he escorted them to the hostel for officials, to rest.

The next day the prefecture sent a man to inform Mount Liangshan of the mission. Song Jiang had been conferring daily with his chieftains in Loyalty Hall on the military situation. Spies had already reported to him that an amnesty was being offered and, although he had not yet seen any proof of this, he was overjoyed.

Now, the messenger arrived from Jizhou and said: "Marshal Chen, an emissary from the royal court, has reached our prefecture. He brings ten bottles of imperial wine and a vermilion decree of amnesty. Prepare to welcome him."

Song Jiang was delighted. He rewarded the messenger with wine and clothing material and ten ounces of silver, and sent him back.

"We're going to be pardoned and become government officials," he said to the chieftain. "Our hardships have not been in vain. At last we will attain our just rewards."

"To my mind the amnesty won't go through," said Wu Yong. "Even if it does, they consider us with contempt. Better wait till the scoundrels come at us with a big army and we give them a good drubbing. We'll slaughter their men and down their horses till we terrify them even in their dreams. That's the time to accept an amnesty. Then we can do it with dignity.'

"You shouldn't talk like that," said Song Jiang. "It goes against our principle of 'loyalty.'"

"High court officials coming here," mused Lin Chong. "They're up to something, and it's not necessarily good."

"There's sure to be some threat in the decree, to frighten us," said Guan Sheng.

"These fellows must be Marshal Gao's men." said Xu Ning.

"Stop being so sceptical, all of you," Song Jiang ordered. "Get ready to welcome them."

He instructed Song Qing and Cao Zheng to prepare a feast, and Chai Jin to supervise all arrangements, "in proper style." He directed that a dwelling be provided for Marshal Chen, with silk and satin furnishings, and colored decorations hung throughout. He sent Pei Xuan, Xiao Rang, Lu Fang and Guo Sheng down the mountain and twenty *li* along the road to welcome the arrivals. The chieftains of the naval forces were to moor large boats by the shore to ferry them across.

"Don't make a move without my orders," Wu Yong warned the chieftains.

Xiao Rang and his three companions, with another five or six carrying wine and tidbits, all completely unarmed, advanced twenty *li* as a welcoming party.

During that stage of Marshal Chen's journey, Majordomo Zhang and Captain Li did not ride, but walked ahead of the horses. Two or three hundred government troops followed. These included a dozen military officers from Jizhou, riding in ranks to the fore. Next came the imperial wine bearers, and then the mounted purveyor of the Vermilion decree, which was in a casket strapped to his back. Fifty or sixty jail-keepers from the prefecture tagged along, hoping to pick up a little graft from the outlaws.

The procession was greeted by the welcoming party, who prostrated themselves, then knelt by the roadside.

"Your Song Jiang thinks pretty highly of himself," said Majordomo Zhang. "The emperor has sent an amnesty. Why isn't he here to receive it? This is an insult! You're all criminals who deserve to die. An imperial amnesty would be wasted on you. Marshal, let's go back."

The four brigands again prostrated themselves. "Our stronghold has not seen the amnesty yet," they explained. "We don't know if it is true or not. Song Jiang and all the chieftains are waiting to welcome you on the Shore of Golden Sands. Pray don't be angry, Marshal. The main thing is to carry this matter through for the sake of our country. Please forgive us."

"Even if we don't carry it through, I see no danger of you robbers flying up to Heaven," sneered Captain Li.

"What kind of talks is that," Lu Fang and Guo Sheng muttered. "They're only trifling with us!"

Xiao Rang and Pei Xuan continued to plead with the emissaries. The wine and tidbits they offered were refused. But the government expedition went with them to the river, where three warships were waiting. On one the horses were loaded; on the second, Pei Xuan and his party; on the third, the marshal and his entourage. The amnesty and the imperial wine were placed in the bow of this last craft. It was commanded by the Devil Incarnate Ruan the Seventh.

Seated on the prow of his vessel, Ruan gave directions to his twenty-some-odd naval oarsmen, each armed with a dagger at his waist. When Marshal Chen first came on board he was very lofty and aloof as he took a seat in the center. Ruan called to his sailors to row, and the men on both sides sang as they bent to their oars.

"Donkeys!" swore Captain Li. "His Excellency is present. Absolutely no sense of discretion!"

The sailors ignored him, and went on singing. Li threatened them with a rattan cane, but they stared at him fearlessly.

"If we feel like singing, what's it to you!" several of them said. "Wretched rebellious bandits, how dare you talk back to me!" Li fumed. He flailed wildly with his cane. Sailors on both sides promptly leaped into the water.

"You beat my oarsmen and force them overboard," Ruan the Seventh called from the bow. "How is this boat going to move?"

Two swift craft were seen to approach from upstream. Ruan had previously partially flooded the hold of his boat. Now, as the two vessels closed in behind him, he pulled out the plug and yelled: "We're leaking!"

Water poured into the hold. As Ruan cried for help, it was already over a foot deep. The two craft pulled alongside, and Marshal Chen was hastily assisted over to one of them. All efforts were concentrated on getting away. No one had time to think about the imperial wine or the emperor's amnesty. The two light boats rowed on swiftly ahead.

Ruan ordered his men to bail out the hold and mop it dry. "Bring me a bottle of that imperial wine," he called. "I want to see what it tastes like."

A sailor fetched a bottle, opened the sealed cap, and handed it to Ruan. Its fragrance tickled his nose.

"It may be poisoned," he said, "but I'll take the risk and try it!" He put the bottle to his lips and kept swallowing till he drained it dry.

"A pleasant bouquet," he said. "But one bottle is hardly enough. Bring me another!" He drank that one, too. Now that his throat was moistened, he finished off two more. Suddenly, he realized that he had created a problem.

"What am I going to do?" he said.

"There's a cask of liquor in the bow," one of the men suggested.

"Fetch me a bailing scoop and I'll give you fellows a share," said Ruan.

What he did was to distribute the remaining six bottles of imperial wine among the sailors, and when they had consumed them, filled the ten empty bottles with cheap rustic liquor from the cask. Resealing the caps, he put the bottles back in the royal hampers decorated with dragons and phoenixes. Then the men plied their oars mightily and sent their craft skimming along.

They reached the Shore of Golden Sands just as the others were disembarking. Song Jiang was waiting to welcome the royal emissary with incense and flowers and colored lanterns. Gongs crashed, drums pounded, and the fortress band made joyful music. The imperial wine was placed on a table which was carried by four men. The emperor's amnesty was similarly transported on another table. As Marshal Chen stepped ashore, Song Jiang kowtowed before him.

"I'm a former petty functionary whose face is marked with the criminal's tattoo, and my wicked deeds obscure the sky. Though Your Excellency has demeaned himself to come here, I cannot entertain you properly. I humbly crave your pardon."

"The marshal is a high official of the imperial court," said Captain Li. "He brings you men an amnesty. This is no small affair. How could you dispatch a leaky boat commanded by an ignorant rustic? You nearly endangered His Excellency's life!"

"We have plenty of good boats. We'd never dare send a leaky craft for His Excellency."

"Are you trying to deny it?" demanded Majordomo Zhang. "The hem of the marshal's robe is soaking wet!"

Song Jiang's five Tiger Cavalry chieftains pressed close behind to left and right, his eight Cavalry Picket commanders ranged themselves fore and aft. The insolence of Zhang and Li enraged them, and they would gladly have slain them were it not for the restraining presence of Song Jiang.

Only after Song Jiang's repeated entreaties did Marshal Chen get into the sedan-chair provided. Horses were brought for Majordomo Zhang and Captain Li. The two continued to behave with disgusting arrogance. Song Jiang persuaded them to mount and the procession, with much shrilling of pipes and beating of drums, proceeded upward through the three passes. Song Jiang and over a hundred chieftains followed.

All dismounted on reaching Loyalty Hall, and the marshal was invited in. The imperial wine and the amnesty were placed in the center at the upper end of the building. The marshal, the majordomo and the captain stood on the left side. Xiao Rang and Pei Xuan stood on the right. Song Jiang called the roll of chieftains. One hundred and seven men—only Li Kui was missing.

It was the fourth lunar month, and they were wearing light battle robes of lined silk as they knelt in the hall to hear the reading of the amnesty. Marshal Chen took the document from its casket and handed it to Xiao Rang. Pei Xuan officiated. At his call, the chieftains kowtowed. Xiao Rang unrolled the decree and read it out in a loud voice:

Edict: The country is governed by both civil and military means. The earliest emperors used both ceremony and punitive wars to preserve our territory. Matters may go smoothly or with difficulty. People may be clever or stupid. As I carry on the rule of my ancestors over this great empire, on which the sun and the moon always shine brilliantly, stretching so vast under the heavens, there is none who does not give me homage.

Recently, Song Jiang and his gang have been roistering over the wooded hills and pillaging the shires. Originally, I was going to suppress them with soldiers, but I feared this would cause harm to the people. I have therefore sent Marshal Chen forward with my amnesty. On receipt of it the bandits must turn over all their money, grain, weapons, horses and boats to my officials, destroy their lair, and be led into the capital. I will then pardon their crimes. If they lack conscience and oppose this decree I shall dispatch troops and wipe them out, young and old. Let this amnesty be proclaimed so that all may know.

In the early summer, fourth month of the third year of the reign of Xuan Ho.

Amnesty hereby proclaimed.

Xiao Rang finished reading. Anger darkened the countenance of Song Jiang and his men. Suddenly, Li Kui the Black Whirlwind leaped down from an overhead beam. He snatched the amnesty from Xiao Rang's hands and tore it to shreds. Then he grabbed Marshal Chen and commenced pummeling him with his fist.

Song Jiang and Lu Junyi threw their arms around Li Kui, and finally managed to separate him from the marshal.

"Who is this varlet," shouted Captain Li. "How dare he behave like this!"

Black Whirlwind was just looking for someone to hit, and he turned his attentions to Li. Punching him, he demanded: "Whose words are those, written in that amnesty?"

"It's an imperial decree from the emperor," said Majordomo Zhang.

"Your emperor doesn't understand anything about us bold fellows here! Pardoning us—what crust! Your emperor's name is Song. So's my Big Brother's. Your Song is an emperor. Why shouldn't my Song be an emperor too! Don't you come stirring up this Black Whirlwind, or I'll kill every one of you amnesty-writing officials!"

The others pulled him away from the emissaries and hustled him out of the hall.

"Don't take it to heart, Marshal," Song Jiang urged. "Not the slightest rudeness will be allowed. Bring the imperial wine and let everyone savor the emperor's kindness."

A golden goblet inlaid with jade was produced. Pei Xuan first poured wine from an imperial bottle into a silver testing bowl. It was cheap rustic liquor. The contents of the other nine bottles were similarly examined. All were of the same crude brew.

Shocked, most of the chieftains stalked out of the hall. Sagacious Lu brandished his iron staff and swore.

"Mother-rapers! This is going too far! Trying to give us watered liquor for imperial wine!"

Red-Haired Demon Liu Tang rushed forward with his halberd. Advancing together came Pilgrim Wu Song with his swords, plus Mu Hong the Unrestrained and Nine Dragons Shi Jin. The six commanders of the naval forces walked out, cursing.

Plainly, the situation was tense. Song Jiang blocked off his men with his body and ordered a sedan-chair and horses for the marshal and his escorts. They were to be escorted down the mountain immediately, and no one was to harm them. Most of the chieftains were in a towering rage. Song Jiang and Lu Junyi were compelled to mount their own steeds and see the marshal through the three passes personally. Kowtowing, Song Jiang begged forgiveness.

"It's not that we don't wish to surrender," he said. "The fact is that the framers of the amnesty don't realize how complicated our situation is here. If only the decree contained a few comforting words, we would gladly die ten thousand deaths to serve our country! Please explain that, Marshal, when you report to the throne."

The emissaries were hastily ferried across. Farting and pissing in terror, they fled back to Jizhou.

Song Jiang returned to Loyalty Hall and summoned the chieftains to a feast. "Although the court decree wasn't very intelligent, you shouldn't have behaved so impetuously," he said.

"Don't delude yourself, brother," said Wu Yong. "There will be an amnesty some day. But why reproach the brothers for getting angry? The court's attitude was too contemptuous. Forget about all that for now. Order full equipment for the cavalry, weapons for the infantry, and a refurbishment of our naval vessels. Sooner or later the government is going to send a big punitive army against us. We've got to slaughter their soldiers and down their horses in one or two battles, so that they're bereft of their armor and fear us in their dreams. That will be the time to talk about amnesty again."

"Absolutely right," said the chieftains. The feasting ended, and they retired to their respective quarters.

Meanwhile, Marshal Chen reached Jizhou. He told Zhang Shuye what had transpired in the mountain stronghold.

"Perhaps you said something you shouldn't?" suggested the prefect.

"I didn't dare open my mouth!"

"In that case, it was just a waste of effort. In fact, it made matters worse. Hurry back and report to the throne, Marshal. You mustn't delay."

Marshal Chen, Majordomo Zhang, Captain Li and the entourage returned to the Eastern Capital that night. Chen related to the prime minister in detail how the bandits of Liangshan Marsh had ripped up the decree. Cai was furious.

"How dare those petty robbers be so rude! We'll teach them to insult the great Song Dynasty!"

Chen wept. "If I hadn't been protected by your emanations, Premier, my shattered bones would be lying in the bandit fortress right now! Fortunately, I escaped with my life and was able to see your beneficent countenance again!"

The premier summoned the Chancellor of Military Affairs Tong Guan, and Marshal Gao and Marshal Yang to a military conference. They soon reported to the White Tiger Inner Sanctum. When they were seated, Cai sent for the majordomo and the captain, who told how the imperial decree was torn to shreds in the Mount Liangshan stronghold.

"Why should such scoundrels be amnestied!" cried Marshal Yang. "Which official recommended such a thing?"

"If I had been present, I surely would have opposed it," said Gao. "I never would have agreed!"

"Thieving rats and marauding dogs, contemptible rabble," fumed Tong. "I have no talent, but just let me lead an expedition personally, set a time limit, and I'll wipe them off the earth!"

"We'll petition the throne tomorrow," said the others. The meeting disbanded.

At the morning court the next day, high officials waited on the imperial stairs. Three times the rods rapped in the imperial hall, and officials divided into civil and military sections. Three times they called: "Long live the emperor," and made their obeisances. Premier Cai stepped forward and reported the outcome of the amnesty mission. The emperor was very angry.

"Who was it who proposed that I issue an amnesty?" he demanded.

"The Inspector General Cui Qing," someone replied.

The emperor ordered Cui to report to the Ministry of Justice and ask for punishment. He turned to the premier. "Those bandits have wreaking havoc for a long time. Who can we send to annihilate them?"

"We cannot succeed without a large force. In my humble estimation, the Chancellor of Military Affairs should lead the expedition personally. He can attain victory within an allotted time."

The emperor summoned Tong Guan and asked: "Are you willing to lead troops and seize the brigands of Liangshan Marsh?"

Kneeling, Tong replied: "As the ancients put it: 'The filial son must do his utmost, the loyal minister must stake his life.' I am ready to give my all to eradicate this canker in our hearts."

Marshal Gao Qiu and Marshal Yang Jian pledged their support. The emperor then issued a decree directing that gold seals and military tallies be issued to Tong Guan, that he be raised to the rank of Grand General, and that troops be drawn from various sources and placed under his command for use against the bandits of Mount Liangshan. A date was fixed for him to set forth.

And because Tong Guan marched with his army, thousands of cavalry filled the mountains and valleys, and innumerable fighting ships rode the green waters. Truly, only three thousand horsemen, bold as tigers, rolled up countless soldiers, courageous as leopards.

What lay in store for Tong Guan's big army? Read our next chapter if you would know.

CHAPTER 76

WU YONG LAYS OUT FOUR-DIPPER POSITIONS AND FIVE-PENNANT ARCHES

SONG JIANG SETS TROOPS IN NINE SEGMENTS WITHIN AN OCTAGON

Tong Guan proceeded to the Council of Military Affairs to muster troops and issue tallies. He ordered each of the eight military districts under the jurisdiction of the Eastern Capital to dispatch ten thousand men, headed by the district commander. The capital guards were to provide twenty thousand soldiers to protect the main body. Tong turned the running of the Council of Military Affairs over to his deputy. From the imperial garrison he selected two good generals to lead the forces on his left and right flanks.

Within ten days preparations were completed. Marshal Gao designated an official who would be responsible for quartermaster supply. Tong Guan, who maintained overall command, directed the officers of his three armies to get ready. He had weapons issued from the armory, and selected an auspicious day for departure. Marshals Gao and Yang gave him a farewell banquet. The imperial court directed the Council of Administration to dispense money among the soldiers.

Tong Guan ordered his commanders to set forth with the troops the following day. He bid farewell to the emperor, vaulted into the saddle, and left the city. Five *li* beyond the gate he found Marshals Gao and Yang waiting for him with a large body of officials. Tong dismounted, and Gao handed him a ceremonial cup of wine.

"Military Affairs Chancellor," said Marshal Gao, "you will undoubtedly distinguish yourself for the throne and return victorious. But you mustn't underestimate the bandits who conceal themselves in the marsh. First, store up a good supply of grain and fodder and build strong stockades, then you can lure them down from the mountain. Send suitable persons to scout out what they are up to before advancing. Capture every one of them alive. Don't let the imperial court down. I hope you will consider what I say."

"The words from your vast learning will remain engraved on my heart. I will not forget."

The two men drank. Marshal Yang came forward with ceremonial flagon and addressed Tong.

"The chancellor has read books on military lore and is deeply versed in strategy. Ordinarily, he would catch the bandits as easily as turning over his hand. Unfortunately, they operate in a marsh, and have the terrain in their favor. I trust, Chancellor, that you have a good plan."

"I will strike when the opportunity presents. I have my own methods," said Tong.

The two officials drank to him, and said: "Here, outside the capital's gate, we pledge you this: We shall look forward eagerly to news of your victory." They bid one another farewell and got on their horses.

Gao, Yang, and the other dignitaries returned to the city. The numerous minor officials who were also seeing Tong Guan off gradually dwindled away.

The three armies marched, every man bristling with martial spirit. They kept well-formed ranks. Discipline was strict. Leading the expedition was a vanguard of four divisions, commanded by a general. The rear unit was also comprised of four divisions, under another general. Covering the left and right of the eight divisions were flanking units headed by more generals. In addition to the main body commanded by Tong Guan directly, the twenty thousand infantry and cavalry guarding the flanks were all crack members of the imperial garrison. Holding his baton, Chancellor Tong supervised the march. The weapons advanced like a turbulent river, men and horses seemed to sail with the wind.

After fifty *li,* they made camp. The next day they resumed the march along the winding road. In less than two days they reached the boundaries of Jizhou Prefecture. Zhang Shuye, the prefect, emerged from the city to greet them. The armies camped outside the walls.

Tong Guan, with a troop of light cavalry, rode in and dismounted before prefectural headquarters. Zhang invited him into the main hall. The prefect kowtowed and was raised to his feet. He stood courteously before the Chancellor of Military Affairs.

"Those swamp bandits kill good citizens and rob travelling merchants. They're committed many a wicked crime," said Tong Guan. "Time and again we've tried to catch them, but we've never done so, and they've been allowed to spread. I come at the head of a hundred commanders and a hundred thousand troops. I shall eradicate the mountain stronghold, capture the brigands, and restore peace to the populace."

"The bandits operate in the marsh, Chancellor," said Zhang. "Although they're only mountain outlaws, there are some intelligent and courageous men among them. Don't let yourself be governed by anger. Devise careful plans, and you will succeed."

"It's timid, weak officials like you, leery of weapons and scared of death, who harm the nation and allow such brigandage to exist!" Tong shouted in a rage. "I'm here, now! You've nothing to fear!"

Zhang dared say no more. He lavishly wined and dined his guest, and Tong Guan left the city. The following day, at the head of his huge force, Chancellor Tong neared Liangshan Marsh.

Song Jiang had been informed by his spies of the coming attack some days before. With Wu Yong he worked out an airtight strategy, and they awaited the arrival of the big army. They instructed the outlaw chieftains to obey orders and allow no slip-ups.

Tong Guan had designated Duan Pengju, district commander of Suizhou Prefecture, as leader of the vanguard, with Chen Zhu, district commander of Zhengzhou, as his deputy. District Commander Wu Bingyi of Chenzhou was named leader of the combined rear; his deputy was Li Ming, district commander of Xuzhou. Han Tianlin, district commander of Tangzhou, and Wang Yi, district commander of Dengzhou, were put in charge of the left patrol; district commander Ma Wanli of Ruzhou and Zhou Xin, district commander of Songzhou, led the right patrol. Generals Feng Mei and Bi Sheng commanded the flanks of the central army. Tong Guan, the commander-in-chief, in full armor, exercised personal control over all operations.

Three times the battle drums thundered, and the army resumed its march. Before it had gone ten *li,* an enemy patrol was seen approaching in a rising cloud of dust. Thirty or so outlaw riders, the bells on their horses jingling, drew near. Black kerchiefs bound their heads, and they wore green battle robes. Their steeds were decked in red tassels and dozens of copper bells. Plumes protruding from the animals' hindquarters. The men carried long thin lances banded with silver, and light bows and arrows.

The standard of the leader bore the inscription: *Patrol Commander Zhang Qin the Featherless Arrow.* To his left was Gong Wang, to his right Ding Desun. About a hundred paces from Tong Guan's advance unit, the patrol reined in and turned back. The two commanders of the vanguard were unable to act, since they had no orders. They reported to the central command. Tong Guan rode forward personally. Before he had finished his inspection, Zhang Qin again advanced. Tong Guan was about to send men after him when one of his aides issued a warning.

"He has stones in an embroidered bag behind his saddle. When he throws, he never misses. Better let him alone."

Featherless Arrow rode out three times. Tong Guan made no move. Zhang Qin and his patrol went away.

Again the government army marched. Before it had gone five *li* gongs sounded behind the hills and around the bend came five hundred outlaw infantry. They were led by Black Whirlwind Li Kui, Fan Rui the Demon King Who Roils the World, Xiang Chong the Eight-Armed Nezha, and Li Gun the Flying Divinity. At the foot of the slope the brigands spread out in a straight line, round shields neatly in place.

Tong Guan at the head of his army waved his fly-whisk baton, and his soldiers surged rapidly forward. Li Kui and Fan Rui divided their infantry unit into two, both of which withdrew around the bend, all carrying their shields reversed. The government troops pursued them through a gap in the hills.

Reaching the other side they found a broad level plain, and there they began setting up their battle positions. In the distance Li Kui and Fan Rui scaled a height and disappeared into a forest.

Tong Guan's men erected a tall wooden command platform. Two military experts climbed to the top. In response to Tong's orders they directed soldiers to left and right, high and low, moving them into four positions shaped like hollow scoops.

No sooner was this done than cannon boomed on the rear of the mountain, and out flew a body of brigand cavalry. The government vanguard, already in position, waited to meet the foe. Ordering an aide to hold his horse, Tong Guan climbed to the top of the command platform. He saw a column of horsemen surging from the east side of the mountain. The foremost troop carried red flags, the second had striped ones, the third bore blue flags, the fourth also carried flags that were striped.

Another cavalry unit was sweeping around the west side of the mountain. The first troop carried striped flags; the second, white; the third, also striped; and the fourth, black. Behind each of the flag bearers streamed massed pennants of yellow.

Hurriedly the government generals repaired to the center of the army and established defensive formations. They could see the raiders clearly now, advancing from the south. Bearing flags of flaming red the lead riders were dressed in red gowns and armor; their roan-colored horses were festooned with red tassels. The red standard in the lead was embroidered above in gold thread with the six-starred Southern Dipper, and below in cinnabar with the emblem of a bird. On it was written: *Vanguard General Qin Ming the Thunderbolt,* and Qin suddenly emerged from the sea of red banners. On his left was deputy commander Shan Tinggui the Water General, on his right deputy commander Wei Dingguo the Fire General. Twirling their weapons astride their roan steeds they halted at the edge of the battlefield.

To their east were riders bearing blue flags. They wore blue gowns and armor, and blue tassels decorated their blue-grey horses. The blue standard in the lead was embroidered above in gold thread with the four-starred Eastern Dipper, and below in blue thread with a dragon. On it was written *The Big Halberd Guan Sheng, General of the Left Army,* and from the sea of blue banners Guan suddenly emerged. Beside him were his deputy commanders. On his left was Ugly Son-in-Law Xuan Zan, on his right Hao Siwen the Wild Dog. The three, weapons in hand, astride their blue-grey mounts, halted at the edge of the battlefield.

To the west appeared a troop of horsemen bearing white banners and wearing white gowns and armor, and riding white horses with white tassels, The white standard in the lead was embroidered above in gold thread with the five-starred Western Dipper, and below with a white tiger. On it was written *Panther Head Lin Chong, General of the Right Army,* and from the massed white banners Lin surged forth, flanked by his deputy commanders. On his left was Huang Xin Suppressor of the Three Mountains, on his right Sun Li the Sickly General. Twirling their weapons astride their white steeds they reined in at the battlefield.

Behind came cavalry with black banners. The gowns and armor of the men were black, as were the horses and their tassels. On the black standard in the lead the seven-starred North Dipper was embroidered above in gold thread, with the symbol for the Seven Northern Constellations below. It bore the words: *Two Rods Huyan Zhuo, General of the Combined Rear,* and Huyan suddenly emerged from amid the sea of black banners. With him were his deputy commanders. Ever-Victorious General Han Tao was on his left, the Eyes of Heaven General Peng Qi was on his right. Weapons in hand they halted their black steeds at the edge of the field of battle.

From the shadows of an arch of pennants to the southeast a troop rode forth carrying blue banners and wearing red armor. Embroidered on the standard in the lead in gold thread was the wind symbol above and a flying dragon below. Written on it were the words: *General Two Spears Dong Ping,* and Dong emerged with his deputy commanders from amid the banners. On his left was Ou Peng Golden Wings Brushing the Clouds, on his right Fiery-Eyed Lion Deng Fei. They reined in at the battlefield, weapons in hand.

A troop with red banners and white armor emerged from the shadows of an arch of pennants to the southwest. Embroidered on the lead standard in gold thread was the earth-symbol, and below that a winged bear. It bore the words: *Urgent Vanguard Suo Chao, General of the Cavalry,* and Suo rode forth from the banners, accompanied by his deputy commanders. On his left was Elegant Tiger Yan Shun, on his right Ma Lin the Elfin Flutist. Weapons in hand, the three halted their chargers at the battlefield.

Through an arch of pennants to the northeast came a body of horsemen with black banners and blue armor. On the lead standard embroidered in gold thread was the symbol for mountain, and below that a flying panther. On it was inscribed: *Cavalry General Nine Dragons Shi Jin,* and Shi emerged from the sea of banners with his deputy commanders. On his left was Gorge-Leaping Tiger Chen Da, on his right White-Spotted Snake Yang Chun. Weapons in hand, they halted at the battlefield astride their chargers.

From the northwest, through an arch of pennants came a cavalry unit with white banners and black armor. The symbol for Heaven was embroidered in gold thread on the upper half of the lead standard; below it was a flying tiger. *Cavalry General Yang Zhi the Blue-Faced Beast* read the standard, and Yang emerged from amid the banners, accompanied by his deputies. Yang Lin the Elegant Panther was on his left. On his right was Zhou Tong the Little King. The three reined in their chargers at the edge of the field of battle, holding their weapons.

The outlaw forces were thus laid out in a huge iron octagon, cavalry grouped with cavalry, infantry with infantry, all bristling with weapons, banners in neat rows—a formidable array! In the center were flags of apricot yellow, interspersed with sixty-four long banners, each bearing the octagon diagram.

At the four points of the compass the octagon was broken by four arches. Cavalry massed at the southern end, and in the shadows of the arch of pennants were two commanders, in ordinary dress astride yellow-brown horses. The first was Beautiful Beard Zhu Tong, the second was Lei Heng the Winged Tiger. All the riders in the troop carried yellow banners, wore yellow robes and yellow bronze armor, and sat yellow-brown steeds decked with yellow tassels.

The interior position was also open at four corners. Shi En the Golden-Eyed Tiger Cub commanded the eastern opening, the western entry was under

Zheng Tianshou the Fair-Faced Gentleman, Song Wan the Guardian of the Clouds held the southern, and Xue Yong the Sick Tiger the northern.

In the center of the yellow pennants was an apricot-yellow banner reading: *Act in Heaven's Behalf.* From the pole to which this was attached ran four woolen cords, and these were grasped by four tall stalwarts to hold the pole firm. Also guarding the banner was a man on horseback, Yu Baosi the Spirit of the Dangerous Road.

Behind these was an artillery platform under the command of cannoneer Ling Zhen the Heaven-Shaking Thunder. He was assisted by well over twenty men who surrounded the platform. To their rear was a section of outlaws armed with hooked poles and nooses for snaring the enemy.

Next was another massing of banners and pennants, seven each on four sides, a total of twenty-eight, embroidered with twenty-eight different constellations. In the center of these was a wool-napped, gosling-yellow flag bordered with pearls, with golden bells hanging from its lower edge and topped with plumes, indicating the headquarters of the highest commander.

Guarding this flag was Jiao Ting the Merciless, assisted by Kong Ming the Comet and Kong Liang the Flaming Star, both mounted and both in ordinary dress. In ranks to their front and rear were twenty-four brigands in iron armor and armed with wolf-toothed cudgels.

Next were embroidered generals' flags, with twelve men on each side carrying square-bladed decorated halberds. The embroidered flag on the left read: *Lu Fang the Little Duke.* The embroidered flag on the right was inscribed: *Guo Sheng the Second Rengui.* Both commanders were mounted.

Between the rows of halberdiers were infantry armed with steel pitchforks. They were led by the brothers Xie Zhen the Two-Headed Snake and Xie Bao the Twin-Tailed Scorpion, both of whom were in ordinary dress, and guarded the central army. Next, on finely saddled steeds, were two civil officers in charge of rewards and punishments. One was Xiao Rang the Master Hand, who looked after documents on Mount Liangshan. The other was Ironclad Virtue Pei Xuan, who was the chief secretary of the stronghold.

These were followed by twenty-four security guards dressed in purple and armed with wide-bladed sabres. They were led by two executioners wearing silks and satins, who stood between the rows. The first was Iron Arm Cai Fu. The second was his brother Cai Qing, known as the Single Blossom. They stood to the fore, with sword carriers to their left and right.

Behind, in two rows, were twenty-four brigands with gold and silver lances. Each row was under a mounted commander. The twelve in the left row bore gold lances, and their commander, also bearing a lance of gold, was Xu Ning the Metal Lancer. The twelve in the right row all bore silver lances, including their mounted commander Hua Rong the Lesser Li Guang. Both leaders had a gallant yet dangerous air. Their Lancers all wore black gauze turbans with ornaments of jade leaves and gold flowers tucked under in front of the ear. The twelve gold lancers in the left row wore green, the twelve silver lancers in the right row wore purple.

Still further back were pairs in silk clothes and colorful hats, groups in pink gowns and embroidered tunics. On either side were tents of jade green, vermilion panoplies and black umbrellas, yellow axes and white whisks, floating greens and flashing purples, then two lines of twenty-four ax-halberdiers, and twenty-four in pairs bearing rods. Between these, in a single line, were three umbrellas embroidered in gold thread and three fine horses in brocaded trappings. *

Two heroic figures stood before the middle steed. The man on the left, of noble visage, was that incomparable chieftain Dai Zong the Marvellous Traveller. He held a gosling-yellow flag inscribed with the word *Order*, and was responsible for the swift transmission of all military information and troop movement directives.

The man on the right was strikingly unusual in appearance. He was that dashing chieftain so skilled at secret activities, Yan Qing the Prodigy. Slung across his back was a powerful bow and sharp-tipped arrows. He held an eyebrow-high staff and was responsible for the security of the central army.

On the far right side of the army, seated on a handsomely equipped mount beneath a blue silk canopy embroidered in gold thread was that famed Taoist of high virtue Gongsun Sheng the Dragon in the Clouds. A true reverend, he could summon the wind and call the rain, order about demons and work magic. Attached to his back were two excellent swords, and the reins in his hands were of silk.

On the far left, astride a richly caparisoned steed beneath a blue silk canopy embroidered in gold thread, was that agile-minded, ever-victorious righteous general Wu Yong the Wizard, a remarkable strategist and tactician. He held a feathered fan. A set of bronze chains hung from his waist.

In the exact center, seated on the White Jade Lion That Glows in the Night, under a bright red canopy embroidered with gold thread, was the loyal and virtuous commander-in-chief Song Jiang, originally a citizen of Yuncheng, a county seat in Jizhou Prefecture in the province of Shandong. Known as the Timely Rain and Defender of Justice, he was in full armor and carried a sword of the finest Kunwu steel. Astride his gold-saddled white horse, he observed the battlefield and directed the central army.

Behind him, on battle chargers, were thirty-five lieutenant-generals in symmetrical ranks, armed with halberds, swords, bows and arrows. Next were twenty-four trumpeters and a complete military band. Beyond the battlefield, commandoes crouched in ambush on either side.

Leading the flanking forces on the left of the central army Mu Hong the Unrestrained, seconded by his younger brother Mu Chun the Slightly Restrained, had fifteen hundred men under his command. An equal number were led by Liu Tang the Red-Haired Demon on the right, aided by Tao Zongwang the Nine-Tailed Tortoise.

In the rear position was a female contingent, all on horseback, consisting of Ten Feet of Steel in the middle, Mistress Gu the Tigress on the left, and Sun the Witch on the right. Also covering the rear were their husbands Wang Ying the Stumpy Tiger, with Sun Xin the Junior General to his left, and Zhang Qing the Vegetable Gardener to his right.

Infantry and cavalry together, the outlaw forces totalled two thousand. But their manner of deployment was not to be underestimated. From his command platform Chancellor Tong Guan looked over their nine segments within an octagon, the brigands' bold cavalry, their heroic infantry, and his soul flew from him in fright, and his heart dropped.

"I couldn't understand why government troops were defeated each time they sought to capture these bandits," he cried. "Who knew they were so formidable!"

He watched for a long time, and heard the steady beat of the gongs and war drums of Song Jiang's army. Tong Guan came down from the platform, mounted his horse and rode to the front.

"Who dares to go fiercely forth and challenge combat?" he asked his generals.

A bold vanguard commander vaulted into the saddle and bowed to Tong Guan. "I will be glad to," he said. "Please give the order."

The speaker was Chen Zhu, district commander of Zhengzhou Prefecture. He wore a white robe and silver armor. His horse was bluish-white and decked with brown tassels. Chen, who wielded a long-handled sword, was deputy leader of the vanguard.

Tong Guan directed that three rolls be beaten on the golden drums, and that the red flag of the vanguard be broken out on the command platform. Chen Zhu galloped forward from the arch of pennants. Both armies set up a cry. Chen reined in, holding his blade horizontal.

"Wicked bandits, rebellious traitors," he shouted, "the emperor's soldiers are here! Surrender, or your bones and flesh will be ground to mud! Regrets will be too late!"

From the southern end of the outlaws' position, vanguard commander Qin Ming the Thunderbolt raced his steed to the field of combat. Without a word, he rode directly at Chen Zhu, brandishing his cudgel. The horses met, weapons waved, the cudgel struck, the blade slashed. Four arms contended, eight hoofs churned the turf.

Back and forth they fought, for more than twenty rounds. Qin Ming feinted, and let Chen Zhu move in. Chen's sword sliced the empty air. Thunderbolt raised his cudgel and brought it down with full force, smashing his opponent's helmet and cranium with a single blow. Chen Zhu fell dead beneath his steed. Shan Tinggui and Wei Dingguo, Qin Ming's deputy commanders, rode out quickly, seized the mount of the fallen foe, and escorted Qin Ming back to the outlaw lines.

Beneath the southeastern arch of pennants, General Two Spears Dong Ping watched Qin Ming win the first contest. "This has taken the wind out of the sails of the government army," he thought. "What would be a better time than now to dash over and capture Tong Guan!"

With a thunderous roar, a spear in either hand, he smote his steed and charged across the field. Tong Guan turned his horse and rode in amid his central army. At that same moment Suo Chao the Urgent Vanguard, beneath the southwest arch of pennants, uttered a shout.

"Let's nab Tong Guan! What are we waiting for!" He galloped across the field, waving his big ax.

Since both ends were already in motion, Qin Ming ordered his entire troop of red-bannered cavalry to charge and take Tong Guan.

Truly, all of the chancellor's misdeeds came home to roost. They pursued him like black eagles chasing a purple swallow, like savage tigers after an innocent lamb.

What was the fate of Chancellor Tong Guan? Read our next chapter if you would know.

CHAPTER 77

THE MEN OF MOUNT LIANGSHAN LAY AMBUSH ON ALL SIDES

SONG JIANG TWICE VANQUISHES CHANCELLOR TONG GUAN

Three units of Song Jiang's vanguard raced across the field. They ploughed into Tong Guan's army with swords and axes and inflicted a crushing defeat. Badly mauled, the government forces scattered, abandoning arms and equipment, yelling in fright. More than ten thousand soldiers were cut down. The rest fled thirty *li* before they halted and made camp.

Wu Yong had the trumpeters blow assembly. His order was transmitted: "Stop the pursuit and slaughter. We only want to give them a sample!" The outlaws returned to their stronghold, where they reported their exploits and claimed rewards.

Tong Guan was very disturbed over the losses his army had sustained, and he summoned his generals for a conference. Feng Mei and Bi Sheng reassured him.

"Don't worry, Chancellor," they said. "The bandits, when they learned we were coming, were able to lay out their battle positions ahead of time. Our forces were unfamiliar with the situation here, and the brigands were able to trick us. With the mountain as their base, they can move troops around and create diversions. We've had a temporary set-back because of the terrain. We'll reorganize and rest for three days to let our men regain their morale and give our horses a breather. Then we'll stretch our entire army into a long line, all on foot, and advance. We'll be like a mountain snake: If the head is attacked, the tail will come to the rescue; if the tail is attacked, the head will come to the rescue; if the middle is attacked, both head and tail will support it. Each section will be part of a continuous whole. This next battle we're sure to win."

"An excellent plan," said Tong Guan. "Just what I was thinking, myself."

He issued appropriate orders. The soldiers were re-grouped and given further training.

At the fifth watch on the third day the government troops rose and ate a hearty breakfast. The horses were equipped with leather armor, the men wore iron plate. Swords and axes, bows arid arrows, all were readied. Truly, weapons flowed in a rapid stream, infantry and cavalry sped like the wind.

Generals Feng Mei and Bi Sheng led the government army, militant and imposing, in a rapid march on Liangshan Marsh. The eight columns divided into a left and right. Three hundred armored cavalry rode as advance scouts. After a while they returned and reported to Tong Guan: "We haven't seen a single enemy soldier on the field where we fought the other day."

Suspicious, the chancellor summoned his generals and demanded: "Shall we withdraw?"

"Don't even consider it," Feng Mei urged. "Just keep pushing on. In our long snake deployment what have we to fear?"

Forward wound the government expedition until it came to the edge of the marsh. Not an adversary was in sight. They saw only a body of water and misty reeds. On the summit of the mountain stronghold in the distance an apricot-yellow flag unfurled, but there was no other movement.

A small boat glided out of the reeds along the opposite shore. Its lone occupant, in a conical hat and coir cape, sat sideways with his back to the government troops, fishing.

"Where are the robbers?" the soldiers hailed him.

He did not respond. Tong Guan ordered his archers to shoot. Two mounted men rode down to the edge of the river, fitted arrows to their bows, and let fly. The first arrow pinged off the conical hat and dropped into the water. The second clanged against the coir cape and also landed in the river.

The marksmen were two of Tong Guan's best archers. Startled, they wheeled their steeds around and trotted back. They bowed from the saddle and reported: "Both arrows scored a hit, but they didn't penetrate! We don't know what he's wearing!"

Tong Guan dispatched three hundred crack archers of the mounted vanguard. They spread out along the river bank and shot their feathered shafts, together. The fisherman remained unperturbed. Though most of the arrows fell short, several reached the boat. But those which struck the conical hat or coir cape bounced off harmlessly.

Since the target couldn't be killed by arrows, Tong Guan sent soldiers who could swim to capture him. Forty or fifty divested themselves of their armor and clothing and plunged into the river.

From the noise to the stern of his boat, the fisherman knew they were coming. Calmly he set down his tackle and picked up the oar which was lying beside him. As each swimmer drew near, he cracked him with the oar—on the temple, the crown, or the forehead—driving him beneath the waves. The others hastily returned to the bank and sought their clothes and armor.

Tong Guan was furious. He ordered five hundred more soldiers to the river and demanded that they capture the fisherman; whoever retreated would be cut in two! The soldiers stripped on the shore and jumped in, shouting. The fisherman turned the craft around and pointed at Tong Guan on the bank.

"Thieving minister, disrupter of the nation, animal who ravages the people! So you've come here to die! Don't you know you're as good as dead!"

Enraged, Tong Guan bellowed for his cavalry archers to shoot. The fisherman laughed.

"They'll never get here in time!" He flicked off his coir cape and conical hat and dove deep.

The five hundred soldiers by then had reached the boat. Suddenly, there were wild yells among them, as they began to sink. For the fisherman was White Streak in the Waves Zhang Shun. Under his hat and cape had been a bronze helmet and bronze armor. Encased like a turtle in its shell, he had been impervious to arrows. Now with his dagger he was killing soldiers, one after another, and the river was red with blood. Those who could, fled for their lives, while Tong Guan goggled from the shore in stupefaction.

"That yellow flag on top of the mountain seems to be moving," an officer beside him said, pointing.

The chancellor peered. Neither he nor his generals could fathom the significance. Feng Mei had a suggestion.

"How about dividing three hundred armored cavalry into two troops and sending them around both sides of the mountain to have a look at the rear?"

But as the horsemen neared the mountain, a cannon thundered from the reeds, spreading a pall of smoke. The cavalry quickly returned. "They're lying in ambush there!" they reported.

Tong Guan was stunned. Feng Mei and Bi Sheng ordered their men to stay out. Several hundred thousand soldiers waited, weapons in hand. Mounted messengers galloped to every section of the army, shouting: "Whoever runs will be executed!"

While the chancellor and his generals watched from their saddles, drums pounded on the rear of the mountain. Fierce shouts shook the heavens, and a large detachment came racing forward, all carrying yellow banners, with two valorous leaders at their head.

Riding golden brown horses were the heroic Zhu Tong the Beautiful Beard and his deputy commander Lei Heng the Winged Tiger. With them were five thousand men, mounted and on foot, eager to destroy the government soldiers. At Tong Guan's order Feng Mei and Bi Sheng rode forward to meet the foe. They drew rein at the field of combat, weapons at the ready, and swore.

"Surrender, you lawless bandits! What are you waiting for!"

Lei Heng laughed and shouted back: "Death is staring you in the face, dolts, and you don't even know it! How dare you venture to do battle with us!"

Bi Sheng was very angry. He clapped his steed and charged Lei Heng with levelled lance. The Winged Tiger spurred his mount. The horses met, the weapons clashed. Over twenty rounds the contenders fought with neither besting the other.

Feng Mei, seeing that Bi Sheng couldn't win, smote his mount and rode to join the fray, waving his sword. Zhu Tong uttered a cry and galloped, brandishing his blade, to intercept Feng Mei. Four horses, two sets of battlers, fought splendidly on the field of combat. Tong Guan kept exclaiming in admiration.

Just as the contest was reaching its climax Zhu Tong and Lei Heng executed a feint, turned their mounts, and rode towards their original position. Feng Mei and Bi Sheng, reluctant to let them go, gave chase. The outlaw force, shouting, withdrew in the direction of the rear of the mountain. Tong Guan led his army in hot pursuit past the foot of the mountain.

On the summit, trumpets blared. The government troops looked up. From before and behind, cannon balls whistled overhead. Tong Guan realized that enemy forces were hiding in ambush. He ordered a halt.

An apricot-yellow banner unfurled on the mountain top, embroidered with the words: *Act in Heaven's Behalf.* Skirting the side of the slope Tong Guan saw amid a phalanx of colored pennants and banners on the heights the figure of Song Jiang, world-renowned hero from Yuncheng County in Shandong and Defender of Justice. Behind him were his generals Wu Yong, Gongsun Sheng, Hua Rong and Xu Ning, plus his Gold and Silver Lancers.

Angrily Tong Guan ordered a contingent to go up and seize Song Jiang. Two columns prepared to ascend the slope. The sound of beating drums and hearty laughter floated down. Tong Guan's rage grew, and he ground his teeth.

"That robber dares to toy with me," he grated. "I'll capture him myself!"

"Chancellor, you must have a plan," Feng Mei said. "Don't go into danger personally. Call back our army and we'll investigate further. After that we can advance."

"Nonsense! We've already come this far. Why should we withdraw! We've been ordered to engage the bandits as quickly as possible. Now, we've seen them. We can't retreat!"

Before the words were out of his mouth, shouts were heard from the rear army, and a scout reported: "Due west, from behind the mountain, a strong force has emerged and split our rear army in two!"

Tong Guan, startled, hurried to the rescue with Feng Mei and Bi Sheng. At that moment behind the mountain on the east side drums sounded and out rushed another contingent. Half carried red banners, half carried blue. Five thousand infantry and cavalry, they were headed by two generals.

Qin Ming the Thunderbolt commanded the red banners, Guan Sheng the Big Halberd led the blues.

The two galloped up on their horses and shouted: "Tong Guan surrender your head!"

Enraged, the chancellor sent Feng Mei against Guan Sheng and Bi Sheng against Qin Ming. Angry shouts in his rear army intensified, but Tong Guan had the trumpets call assembly. He ordered his rear to fall back, and not be impatient for combat.

Zhu Tong and Lei Heng, leading a force of yellow banners, again attacked, this time in a pincers movement. The government troops were thrown into confusion. Feng Mei and Bi Sheng protected Tong Guan, and he fled for his life. An outlaw force, five thousand strong, cut in at an angle and intercepted them. Half of this unit bore white banners, the other half black. Commanding the blacks was Two Rods Huyan Zhuo, commanding the whites was Panther Head Lin Chong.

The two shouted from their horses: "Treacherous Tong Guan, where do you think you're going? Stand and be killed!" They charged in directly among the government soldiers.

Duan Pengju, district commander of Suizhou, took on Huyan Zhuo. Ma Wanli, district commander of Ruzhou, contended with Lin Chong. Ma commenced to weaken after only several rounds. As he turned to flee, Lin Chong uttered a roar.

Hopelessly flurried, Ma was pierced by Lin's thrust. He fell dead beneath his horse.

Duan Pengju lost his appetite for battle at the sight of his companion's body. He parried Huyan's rods, wheeled his mount around, and galloped away.

Huyan gave chase, and the two armies clashed in a general melee. Tong Guan scrambled to get back to his own forces. Wild shouts rose in the forward ranks. From behind the mountain a contingent of brigand infantry came running, and ploughed into the very center of the government army. It was led by a monk and a pilgrim, who yelled: "Don't let Tong Guan escape!"

The monk never read the scriptures but specialized in slaughter. He was Sagacious Lu, otherwise known as the Tattooed Monk. The pilgrim had killed the tiger on Jingyang Ridge. He was Wu Song, the boldest hero in the marsh-girt stronghold. Lu with his Buddhist staff, and Wu with his pair of swords, slashed into the government position.

The outlaw infantry charge shattered the imperial army into segments. Both advance and retreat were impossible. Tong Guan could only, with Feng Mei and Bi Sheng, break through the encirclement and hack a bloody path to the rear of the mountain. Just as they were catching their breath, they again heard the thunder of cannon and the pounding of drums. Another contingent of outlaw infantry, headed by two commanders, stopped them once more.

Xie Zhen and Xie Bao, each with a five-tined pitchfork, led their infantry in a headlong attack. Tong Guan and his men could not be checked. They broke through the barrier. But assailed from five sides by outlay forces on horse and on foot the government army was fragmented. Tong Guan fled, protected by Feng Mei and Bi Sheng.

The Xie brothers, with their pitchforks, rushed towards the mounted generals. Tong Guan clapped his horse and galloped off at an angle. Feng Mei and Bi Sheng, hurrying to cover his rear, met the district commanders of Tangzhou and Dengzhou—Han Tianlin and Wang Yi, and the four, together, fought their way out.

They hadn't gone very far, and were just catching their breaths, when they saw before them a cloud of dust and heard fierce yells. Out of a leafy green glade flew a mounted troop, headed by two commanders, and obstructed their road. General Two Spears Dong Ping and Urgent Vanguard Suo Chao charged directly at Tong Guan without a word.

Wang Yi, with levelled lance, tried to intercept them, but Suo Chao raised his ax and cut him from his steed. Han Tianlin, attempting a rescue, was pierced through by Dong Ping's spears. Feng Mei and Bi Sheng again galloped off with Tong Guan, striving desperately to save him. Drums beat on all sides. They had no idea from which direction the enemy was coming.

Tong Guan hauled his mount to the top of a bluff and looked. Four contingents of Liangshan Marsh cavalry, two auxiliaries and two units of infantry had surrounded the government troops and were sweeping through them like giant baskets and scoops, scattering them like clouds before the wind. The soldiers were running, panic-stricken, east and west.

A troop appeared at the foot of the slope. Tong Guan recognized the banners of district commanders Wu Bingyi of Chenzhou and Li Ming of Xuzhou. Their soldiers, beaten and bedraggled, carrying broken weapons, had come around Mount Linlang, seeking a place to hide. When Tong Guan hailed them, they turned their horses and started up the slope eagerly. But from the side of the mountain there were shouts, and a troop of cavalry charged forth. They bore two identifying banners and were led by Yang Zhi and Shi Jin. These two commanders, waving their blades, barred the way of the government officers.

Li Ming with levelled lance advanced on Yang Zhi. Wu rode against Shi Jin with crescent-bladed halberd. The two pairs fought up and down the slope and round and round, each man exerting his utmost skill. Tong Guan, reined in on the bluff, didn't know which to watch.

The four battled for over thirty rounds. Wu thrust at his opponent's heart. Shi Jin twisted, and the halberd slipped by his ribs, horse and rider following the impetus of the lunge. Shi Jin swung his blade, and a bloody head, still encased in its golden helmet, dropped to the ground. Wu's body collapsed beside it.

Li Ming decided he'd better go. But a terrible roar from Yang Zhi scared the soul out of him and set him to trembling so violently that his lance slipped from his nerveless fingers. Yang Zhi chopped with his sword. Li Ming dodged and the blade struck his horse's loins. As its rear quarters sank Li leaped from the saddle. He cast aside his lance and ran. But Yang Zhi with a swift slash cut him down. Poor Li Ming, half his life an army officer, and now it was all gone like a dream.

The two district commanders lay dead on the slope. Yang Zhi and Shi Jin pursued the demoralized government troops, cutting heads like melons.

Tong Guan, with Feng Mei and Bi Sheng on the bluff, dared not go down. At a loss he asked his two generals: "How can we break out of here?"

"Calm yourself, Chancellor," said Feng Mei. "I see an encampment of ours due south. As long as their flag still flies, we can be saved. Commander Bi will remain to protect you, and I will carve open a path and bring them to your rescue."

"The day is growing late," said the chancellor. "Watch for a suitable moment and dash over and return soon."

Grasping his long-handled sword, Feng Mei rode quickly down the slope, and galloped full tilt along the road south. He found the unit under district commander Zhou Xin of Songzhou. They were in a tight formation and were resisting staunchly. Feng Mei was led into the position.

"Where is the chancellor?" Zhou Xin asked.

"On that slope, ahead. He's waiting for your unit to rescue him. There's no time to waste! Get started immediately!"

Zhou Xin ordered his infantry and cavalry to coordinate closely. No one was to fall behind. Body and mind, all were to combine their efforts. With the two commanders leading the shouting troops, the detachment hastened towards the slope.

Before they had gone the length of an arrow-shot a unit cut in from the side. Feng Mei rode forward to engage them, waving his sword. But then he recognized Duan Pengju, district commander of Suizhou. The three joined forces and continued to the foot of the slope. Bi Sheng came down to meet them, and escorted them to the bluff.

They conferred with Tong Guan, who queried: "Shall we fight out of here tonight, or wait until morning?"

"We four will defend you to the death, Chancellor," Feng Mei assured him. "If we break through the encirclement tonight we'll be able to escape the bandits."

As darkness began to fall they heard yells without end on every side and the disorderly beating of drums. Around the second watch the moon was bright. With Feng Mei in the lead and all grouped around Tong Guan in a protective phalanx they made a concerted rush down the slope.

At once, voices shouted: "Don't let Tong Guan get away!"

The officers fought in a due southerly direction. By the fourth watch, after a confused battle, they finally broke through. Tong Guan, on horseback, pressed his fingers to his forehead and reverently thanked the gods of Heaven and Earth.

"How fortunate that we could escape this calamity!" He and his party pushed out of the area and hastened towards Jizhou. Just as they were congratulating themselves they saw on the slope of a mountain ahead a procession of countless torches. Behind them shouts rose once more.

In the light of the flaming brands they could see two bold fellows armed with halberds, walking in advance of a heroic general on a white horse. The rider, who carried a steel-tipped lance, was none other than Lu Junyi the Jade Unicorn, also known as Lu the Magnate. The halberdiers preceding him were Yang Xiong the Pallid and Shi Xiu the Rash. Their force of over three thousand, brimming with militant spirit, now intercepted the government unit.

Lu shouted: "Tong Guan dismount and be bound! What are you waiting for?"

"Enemy soldiers are before and behind us," the chancellor said to his cohorts. "What are we going to do?"

"I'll defend you with my life, Chancellor," said Feng Mei. "We officers will protect you and wrest a way to Jizhou! I'll fight that robber personally!"

Striking his mount, he cantered towards Lu, brandishing his sword. The horses met and the men battled. After only a few rounds Lu parried the big sword with his lance, closed in quickly, and grasped Feng around the waist, simultaneously lifting him from the saddle and kicking his steed away. Yang Xiong and Shi Xiu rushed to Lu's support, while outlaw troops dragged off the prisoner.

Bi Sheng, Zhou Xin and Duan Pengju, desperately defending Tong Guan, hurled their soldiers against the brigades preventing their passage, fighting as they advanced. Lu the Magnate gave chase. Tong Guan's beaten army scurried like a bereaved family's dog, darted like fish which escaped the net.

By dawn they had shaken off their pursuers. Jizhou was in sight when, from around the bend of a mountain ahead, a body of infantry shot out. They wore iron breastplates and pink silk turbans, and were led by four commanders.

Who were they? Li Kui with his two axes, Bao Xu holding a sword, and Xiang Chong and Li Gun each wielding spiked shields. They rolled down the slope like a ball of fire, slaughtering government soldiers left and right.

Tong Guan and his officers fled, fighting as they ran. Li Kui carved into the imperial cavalry and cut the legs of Duan Pengju's steed from under it. Raising his axes, with one blow he cracked Duan's skull, with another he sliced his throat. Duan was finished.

When the remnant government troops finally neared Jizhou they were in a sorry state, their helmets over one ear, their neck guards halfway up their cheeks. Men and horses were exhausted. They stopped at a stream to drink and water the animals. A cannon suddenly boomed, and arrows flew at them like a swarm of hornets. Hastily, the soldiers scrambled back up the bank. A troop of cavalry trotted out of a grove, headed by three heroes.

They were Featherless Arrow Zhang Qin, plus Gong Wang and Ding Desun, commanding well over three hundred horsemen. Little bronze bells tinkled on the bridles of the steeds, and they were bedecked with plumes and red tassels. The riders carried light bows and arrows, embroidered pennants and decorated spears. Led by their three commanders, they charged.

They were not a large force, and Zhou Xin rode forward to meet them, while Bi Sheng covered Tong Guan's hasty departure. Zhang Qin grasped Zhou's extended lance with his left hand. His right hand pulled back in a throwing position.

"Take that!" he cried, and a stone struck Zhou on the bridge of his nose, knocking him from his saddle.

Gong Wang and Ding Desun galloped up, and pierced Zhou's throat with their pitchforks. Like grass blighted by frost, like blossoms pelted in the rain, he expired beneath his horse's legs.

The fleeing Tong Guan and Bi Sheng dared not enter Jizhou, but led their remnant force instead through the night in the direction of the Eastern Capital. En route they picked up other escaping soldiers, and together made camp.

Song Jiang, a benevolent and virtuous man, who sought only to shun wickedness and become law-abiding again, had no desire to pursue and slaughter. Afraid his officers would be reluctant to abandon the chase, he immediately dispatched Dai Zong with an order to all his chieftains to gather their commands and return to the mountain stronghold and claim Everywhere trumpets sounded assembly. Commanders in the saddle rhythmically beat their weapons against their metal stirrups, and the infantry sang songs of victory as the outlaw troops, unit by unit, entered Liangshan Marsh and marched into the Water-Girt Fortress.

Seated with Wu Yong and Gongsun Sheng in Loyalty Hall, Song directed Pei Xuan to distribute the individual awards. Feng Mei, who had been captured by Lu the Magnate and delivered, bound, to the stronghold, knelt outside the hall. Song Jiang personally untied him, led him into the hall and invited him to be seated. He apologized for having inconvenienced him, and poured him wine to calm his fears. All of the chieftains had gathered, and that day there was general feasting and the dispensing of rewards to the troops.

After two days, Feng Mei was furnished with a saddled horse and preparations were made to escort him down the mountain. He was overjoyed. Song Jiang again apologized.

"Please forgive us for venturing to display our prowess on the battlefield, General," he said. "Our only desire is to obey the emperor and serve our country. Because we've been outlawed we've been compelled to behave in this manner. When you arrive at the imperial court, please explain for us. If we can some day bask again in the light of royal favor, we will never forget your great kindness, living or dead."

Feng Mei kowtowed and thanked Song Jiang for having spared him. Song Jiang supplied an escort which saw him out of the brigands' territory. Feng Mei went back to the capital. Of that we'll say no more.

Again in Loyalty Hall, Song Jiang conferred with Wu Yong and the other chieftains. All of the ambushes deployed during the battle had been planned by Wu Yong. So devastating had been the slaughter that Tong Guan was chilled with fear. Even his dreams were terror-ridden. He had lost two-thirds of his army.

"Once Tong Guan reaches the capital and reports to the emperor he's sure to raise another expedition," Wu Yong predicted. "We must send a man to learn what's going on. Then we can make suitable preparations."

"I agree completely," said Song Jiang. "But which of our brothers should it be?

"Let me go," said someone among those seated in the hall.

The others all looked, and they said: "He would be ideal. He's capable of big things."

And because this person went, hundreds of war craft were constructed outside the walls of Jizhou, and on Mount Liangshan a huge store of grain was added. Truly, battle chargers perished at the foot of the blue cliffs, boats cutting the waves sank in the weedy green waters.

Who was the man who went from Mount Liangshan to investigate? Read our next chapter if you would know.

CHAPTER 78

TEN COMMANDANTS CONFER ON TAKING LIANGSHAN MARSH

SONG JIANG DEFEATS MARSHAL GAO THE FIRST TIME

The volunteer was Dai Zong the Marvellous Traveller. Song Jiang said: "We depend entirely on you to find out all about their military preparations. But you'd better have someone to help."

"I'll be glad to go along," said Li Kui.

Song Jiang laughed. "You, Black Whirlwind who never stirs up trouble!"

"I won't make any trouble this time."

Song Jiang shouted at him to get out, then asked: "Which of you brothers will go?"

"How about me?" queried Liu Tang the Red-Haired Demon.

"Good," said Song Jiang. He was very pleased.

That day the two men packed some belongings and went down the mountain.

Meanwhile, Tong Guan and Bi Sheng neared the Eastern Capital with forty thousand men, all that was left of their beaten army. They ordered their commanders to lead the various units back to their camps. Tong Guan and Bi Sheng entered the capital with only the imperial guards. The chancellor removed his armor and went to call on Marshal Gao.

The two exchanged courtesies, and Tong was invited to be seated in a quiet alcove of the rear hall. He related in detail the defeats he suffered in two major encounters, the killing of his eight top commanders, his heavy losses in troops and horses, the capture of Feng Mei, and his own general dismay.

"Don't let it upset you, Chancellor," said Gao. "All you have to do is give the emperor a false report. Who would dare petition against you! I'll go with you to the prime minister. We'll work something out."

Tong and Gao mounted their horses and rode to the premier's mansion. An aide announced: "Chancellor Tong has returned." Prime Minister Cai Jing guessed that he had been defeated, and when told that Gao Qiu was calling with him, directed that they be ushered into his study. Tong kowtowed before the premier, his tears falling like rain.

"Don't take it so hard," said Cai. "I've heard you've had heavy losses."

"In that bandit marsh it's impossible to advance without boats," said Gao. "The chancellor had only cavalry and foot soldiers. That's why he lost the initiative and fell for the bandits' ruse."

Tong told about his defeat, and the premier said: "You lost an enormous number of troops, expended vast amounts of money and grain, and had eight column commanders annihilated. How dare I report this to the emperor?"

Tong Guan again kowtowed. "Cover up for me, Premier, I beg you! Save my life!"

"Tomorrow, at the royal audience, I will say only: 'The weather was extremely hot, our soldiers were not accustomed to it. So they discontinued the action and withdrew.' If he grows angry and says: 'This canker in our hearts must be eliminated, otherwise, the results will be calamitous.' how should I reply?" queried the premier.

"I don't mean to boast," said Gao. "But if you allow me to lead an expedition, I'll pacify those bandits in one engagement!"

"Since you're willing to go yourself, Marshal, naturally that's fine. I'll propose you tomorrow for commander-in-chief."

"There's just one thing. Besides an imperial decree mustering an army, I need boats. They should either be allocated from military and civilian craft, or I should be authorized to buy lumber at the official price and build my own ships of battle. Only by advancing simultaneously on land and on water, on boats and on horseback, will we be able to win the day."

"That won't be any problem," said Cai.

The keeper of the gate came in and said: "Feng Mei has returned."

Tong Guan was delighted. The premier directed that he enter. He asked the general what had happened.

Feng Mei kowtowed. "Song Jiang released as many as possible of those he captured and took the rest up the mountain. Not only didn't he kill us, but he gave us travel expenses and allowed us to return home. It is for that reason that I am able to see you noble countenance again."

"It's a bandit trick and an insult to our government," said Gao. "We shouldn't muster local troops, but go as far afield as Shandong and Hebei to select able men who'll go with me."

"Since we're all agreed," said Cai, "we'll meet again tomorrow and petition the emperor."

Tong and Gao returned to their respective headquarters.

They met again in the Waiting Chamber the following day at three strokes after the fifth watch. When the drums sounded, officials assembled in the imperial courtyard according to rank. All kowtowed, then arose and stood below the Jade Staircase in two groups—one civil, the other military.

The chief of ceremonies, holding his staff of office, called: "If anyone has a petition, let him come forward. If there are none, this court will adjourn."

Prime Minister Cai stepped forth and addressed the emperor. "We dispatched Tong Guan, Chancellor of Military Affairs, with a large army in a punitive expedition against the bandits of Liangshan Marsh. But the weather turned very hot and our forces had not yet adapted to it. Moreover, the bandit territory is all water and bogs. It's impossible to move without boats. Our infantry and cavalry were unable to advance. And so the expedition was called off and our forces returned to their camps, where they are waiting now for your imperial orders."

"How can they go again, since the weather is so hot?" cried the emperor.

"Tong Guan Will report to the Military Procurate for punishment. We propose appointing a new commander and sending out another expedition. We request your royal decree."

"Those brigands are indeed a canker in our heart. They must be exterminated. But who will undertake this task for me?"

Gao Qiu stepped forward. "Though I have no talents, I would gladly strain like a beast of burden to wipe out the bandits. I beg for your imperial command."

"Since you are willing to share my difficulties, I order you to muster an army."

"Liangshan Marsh is over eight hundred *li* in circumference. Without fighting ships it is impossible to advance. I request permission, therefore, to cut timber in the neighborhood of the marsh and have carpenters build boats. Either that, or grant me funds with which to buy civilian boats and convert them to military use."

"I authorize you to do whatever is necessary and possible. Only avoid causing harm to the people."

"I would never dare! Please don't set too strict a time limit, and I will endeavor to succeed."

The emperor called for silken robes and golden armor, and presented them to Marshal Gao Qiu. He also selected an auspicious day for the expedition to commence.

When the imperial audiences ended, Tong Guan and Gao Qiu saw the prime minister back to his mansion. Cai directed the Council of Administration to transmit the royal decree for the mustering of a new expeditionary army.

"There are ten commandants who distinguished themselves in expeditions against neighboring states like the Guifang, the Tangut, the Golden Tartars, or the Great Liao," said Gao. "They're excellent military men. I'd like you to appoint them my generals."

Premier Cai agreed. He issued a directive ordering the ten commandants to report at Jizhou with ten thousand crack troops each. All of the leaders had formerly been robbers in the greenwood. Later, they were amnestied, and rose rapidly to become high officials. Skilful and courageous, they won something of a reputation for themselves. Now, they received directives ordering them to Jizhou within a prescribed time, each heading a column of ten thousand, on pain of military discipline if they were late.

In the Jiankang district of Jinling was a naval unit. Its commanding officer was a man named Dragon Dream Liu, because his mother, when she conceived him, had dreamed that a black dragon had entered her womb. He grew up to be an excellent swimmer. Liu won distinction in a campaign against bandits on the Xiajiang River in Sichuan and was raised to the rank of admiral. He had fifteen thousand sailors under his command, and five hundred rowed vessels. His responsibility was the area south of the river.

Gao wanted this naval unit and its boats, and he ordered their immediate transfer. He also sent a trusted confidant, an infantry colonel named Niu Pangxi, to search up and down the river and along all its tributaries for more boats. Niu was to bring any craft he found to Jizhou where they were to be turned over for Gao's use.

There were many generals in Gao's headquarters. Two of the most able of these were brothers—Dang Shiying and Dang Shixiong, both field commanders and both extremely brave. From the imperial guards, Gao drew another fifteen thousand crack troops, bringing his total force up to a hundred and thirty thousand. He had grain delivered to the various columns, so that it could be issued to the troops during their march. Daily, he had armor and clothing put in order, and pennants and banners manufactured. But he still was not ready.

Meanwhile, Dai Zong and Liu Tang spent a few days in the Eastern Capital collecting information. Then they hastened back through the night to the mountain fortress and rendered a detailed report. When Song Jiang heard that Marshal Gao was personally going to lead an expedition against him, and that he had gathered a hundred and thirty thousand troops from all over, and that ten commandants would be serving as generals, he was shocked and frightened. He went into conference with Wu Yong.

"Have no fear, brother," said the military advisor. "Didn't Zhuge Liang defeat Cao Cao's army of a hundred thousand in ancient times with only three thousand men? I've heard of those ten commandants. They've served the imperial court well. Of course they appeared very heroic when there was no one around who could match them. But today, against our band of fine brothers—veritable wolves and tigers every one— they're out of date. You've nothing to worry about. Before the ten columns arrive, I'll give them a scare!"

"How will you do that?"

"They're to meet in Jizhou. I'll send two quick killers to wait in the outskirts. When the troops draw near, they'll slaughter a few."

"Who do you have in mind?"

"Featherless Arrow Zhang Qin and General Two Spears Dong Ping."

Song Jiang gave the two named chieftains a thousand men each. He ordered them to patrol the outskirts of Jizhou, and intercept and kill approaching government troops. He also directed his naval commanders to prepare to seize enemy boats. Assignments were given, as well, to other chieftains. No need to say what these were; you'll learn later on.

Although more than twenty days had passed Gao was still in the capital. The emperor sent a message urging him to march. Gao ordered his Imperial Guards force to leave the city first, and he directed some thirty-odd singers and dancers, girls and boys from the entertainment quarter, to go along for their amusement.

On the date of the Guards' departure, Gao pledged before the flag, took his leave of the emperor, and got ready to set forth. A month had gone by, and it was now typical early autumn weather. Government officials, large and small, were waiting at the pavilion ten *li* beyond the city gate to see them off. Marshal Gao, in full armor, rode a battle charger with a golden saddle. Preceding him were five auxiliary mounts with equipage encrusted with jade. To his left and right were the brothers Dang Shiying and Dang Shixiong. Behind came generals of the Imperial Guards, masters of arms, generals of defense, generals of militia, and other high-ranking officers. The army which followed marched in neat ranks.

At the pavilion Gao dismounted and bid the assembled officials farewell. The ceremonial wine-drinking send-off completed, he again climbed into the saddle and proceeded towards Jizhou. He allowed his soldiers to pillage freely en route, much to the detriment of the local population.

One after another the ten columns neared Jizhou. Commandant Wang Wente, at the head of his column, was more than forty *li* from his destination after a forced march. He was still driving hard when they reached a place called Phoenix Tail Slope. At the foot of the slope was a large grove. Wang's advance unit was just skirting this when they heard the crash of a gong.

From between the rear of the grove and the base of the hill a troop of cavalry trotted out and blocked the road. Its leader wore a helmet and armor and carried a bow and arrows. Attached to the sheath and quiver of these weapons were two small yellow pennants. One was inscribed: *Heroic General Two Spears.* The other read: *Gallant Duke of Ten Thousand Households.* In each hand he grasped a steel-tipped spear. It was none other than Dong Ping, the boldest assault leader in Liangshan Marsh, known as Dong the Brash.

He reined in his steed athwart the road and shouted: "Where are you from? Come down from your mounts and be tied. What are you waiting for?"

Wang checked his horse and laughed. "Even jars and jugs have two ears. You must have heard of us ten commandants. We've won scores of commendations, we're famous. I'm Wang Wente, the foremost among us."

Dong Ping laughed. "You're a rustic lout who couldn't kill anyone but his mother's lover!"

Commandant Wang was furious. "Rebellious bandit! How dare you insult me!"

He clapped his horse, levelled his lance and charged. Dong Ping, both spears horizontal, met him head on. They fought for thirty rounds, with neither emerging the victor.

Wang realized he couldn't defeat Dong Ping. "Rest a while," he shouted. He rode back to his position. Wang instructed his column not to remain and give battle but to break through.

With the commandant in the lead, the column smashed open the road block and, yelling, fought their way free. Dong Ping and his men followed in close pursuit. As the column passed the grove, another cavalry troop appeared suddenly before them. In the lead was Featherless Arrow Zhang Qin.

"Halt!" he shouted.

He flung a stone at Wang Wente's head. Wang tried to dodge, but it struck him on the helmet. Bending low over his saddle, Wang fled. The two chieftains gave chase. They had nearly caught up, when another unit cut in ahead at an angle. Wang recognized the column led by Commandant Yang Wen, hurrying to his rescue. Dong Ping and Zhang Qin dared not come any closer. They withdrew.

The two columns entered Jizhou, where they were received by the prefect Zhang Shuye. A few days later word came that Marshal Gao and his army were approaching. The ten commandants went out to meet him, and escorted him into the city. The prefectural office was converted temporarily into an army headquarters, and all rested.

Marshal Gao ordered the ten columns to camp in the outskirts of Jizhou. When Dragon Dream Liu arrived with his naval forces they would all set forth together. The columns did as directed, felling timber on the nearby hills and confiscating doors and windows of the villagers to build shelters and make beds for themselves. They caused severe losses to the local people.

Gao remained in his headquarters in the city, grabbing more recruits for his expedition. Anyone who had no silver for bribes was put in the foremost assault ranks. But if a man was able to spread a bit of money around he stayed in the central army and received frequent commendations for "valor." There was a great deal of this kind of corruption.

Dragon Dream Liu and his flotilla arrived after only a day or two, and Liu reported to Gao. The marshal summoned the ten commandants to join them in a strategy conference. Wang Huan had a proposal.

"Let the infantry and cavalry go ahead and lure out the bandits, then send in the naval forces to destroy their lair. They won't be able to fight on two fronts, and we'll capture them all."

Gao agreed. He ordered Wang Huan and Xu Jing to lead the vanguard, Wang Wente and Mei Zhan to bring up the rear, Zhang Kai and Yang Wen to command the left flank, Han Cunbao and Li Congji to command the right, Xiang Yuanzhen and Jing Zhong to be ready as reinforcements for front and rear. Dang Shixiong with three thousand crack troops joined the flotilla to aid Dragon Dream Liu and observe the battle.

Each unit now had its orders. After three days of preparation, they invited Gao to review them. The marshal came out of the city and personally inspected the columns, one by one. He then directed them, plus the naval forces, to set out for Liangshan Marsh.

Dong Ping and Zhang Qin returned to the fortress and gave a detailed report. Song Jiang and his chieftains led the outlaw army down the mountain. Before they had gone very far, they came within sight of the foe. The adversary forces halted within arrow shot of each another and set up their battle positions. Commandant Wang Huan rode forward from the government vanguard, carrying a long lance.

"Unrighteous bandits, desperate rustics," he shouted, "do you recognize General Wang Huan?"

The embroidered banners on the opposite side parted and Song Jiang rode forth. "Commandant Wang," he called respectfully, "you're of a venerable age. You shouldn't be going into combat for the state. Your opponent might make a slip and put an end to your blameless life. Go back. Send a younger man to fight."

Wang was furious. "The mark of the criminal is on your face, petty functionary! Dare you oppose Heaven's soldiers!"

"Don't insist, Commandant. These bold fellows of mine who 'act on Heaven's behalf' wouldn't necessarily lose to you."

Wang Huan's reply was to level his lance and charge. From behind Song Jiang a warrior rode out, his own lance horizontal, the bells on his steed's bridle jingling. It was Panther Head Lin Chong, and he galloped to engage his adversary.

The horses met, the soldiers yelled. Marshal Gao reined in his steed and watched from the front lines. The men on both sides shouted and cheered. Cavalrymen rose in their stirrups and infantrymen pushed back their helmets to get a better view. The contestants displayed their utmost skill.

Nearly eighty rounds they fought, with neither emerging the victor. Trumpets sounded and the combatants separated and returned to their positions. Commandant Jing Zhong went to the forward army and bowed from the saddle to Marshal Gao.

"I would like to have a go at the bandits. I request your permission."

Gao ordered Jing to proceed. Bridle bells behind Song Jiang again jingled and Huyan Zhuo rode out to meet the challenger. Jing, wielding a long-handled blade, was astride a melon-yellow steed. The contenders met and fought twenty rounds.

Huyan executed a feint, parried the big blade, and brought his steel rods with full force down on Jing's head, spattering his brain matter. Eyes bulging, Jing fell to the ground, dead.

Gao had lost one of his commandants. He urgently dispatched another — Xiang Yuanzhen. Xiang flew to the front with levelled lance. "Bandits," he cried, "who dares do battle with me?" General Two Spears Dong Ping surged to the front and engaged the enemy. Before they had fought ten rounds Xiang whirled his mount around and rode off, trailing his lance. Dong Ping clapped his horse and chased after him. Instead of entering his position, Xiang, apparently flurried, skirted its edge and continued to flee, with Dong Ping in hot pursuit.

Xiang socketed his lance, grasped his bow with his left hand, fitted an arrow with his right, and stretched the string to its full. Suddenly, he twisted around and shot. At the twang of the bow, Dong Ping threw up a warding hand, but the arrow struck him in the right arm. He dropped his lance and galloped back. Xiang, now the pursuer, readied another arrow. Huyan Zhuo and Lin Chong hastened out and escorted Dong to the safety of the position.

Marshal Gao ordered a mass attack just as Song Jiang was directing that Dong Ping be returned to fortress. The rear guard was unable to hold, and the outlaws scattered. Gao chased them as far as the water's edge. There he dispatched scouts to make contact with the government naval forces.

These, meanwhile, under Dragon Dream Liu and Dang Shixiong, were winding deep into the marsh. Mist and reeds obscured the creeks and rivulets. The masts of the government flotilla were strung out over a distance of ten *li*.

A cannon sounded from the mountain slope, and from every side small boats converged. The soldiers on the government craft, who were rather frightened to begin with, completely panicked when they saw the small craft swarming out from the depths of the reeds and cutting the government vessels off from each other. Most of them abandoned ship and fled. The bold fellows of Mount Liangshan were quick to take advantage of the confusion. Beating drums and gongs, they propelled their small boats forward.

Dragon Dream Liu and Dang Shixiong hastily turned their vessel around. But the shallow channel they had navigated earlier had been jammed with logs and brushwood by the outlaws, snagging oars and blocking passage.

More soldiers leaped into the water. Dragon Dream Liu divested himself of his armor, crawled up the bank, and struck out along a path. Dang Shixiong, unwilling to leave the vessel, ordered the sailors to row into a tributary.

Before they had gone two *li,* they saw ahead three small boats, command-ed by the three Ruan brothers, each of whom grasped a spear. As the boats neared the government craft, the remaining government soldiers jumped into the water. Dang stood alone on the prow with a long lance, facing Ruan the Second. As the boats of Ruan the Fifth and Ruan the Seventh pressed closer, Ruan the Second dived into the water. Dang realized his danger. He, too, jumped, abandoning his lance.

Suddenly, Zhang Heng the boat hand shot up from beneath. He grabbed Dang by the hair and around the waist, and tossed him dripping into the reeds. A dozen or so brigands who had been hiding there tied Dang securely and took him off to the fortress.

Gao saw that his entire flotilla was in disarray and that his men were flee-ing towards the mountains. His boats, all bearing the flag of Dragon Dream Liu, had been rounded up and captured. Gao's water approach had failed. He ordered his troops back to Jizhou. New measures would have to be considered.

It was late in the day when they started their march. All around cannon sud-denly thundered and Song Jiang's forces attacked from several sides. Marshal Gao could only groan in dismay.

Truly, happiness has not yet arrived when trouble returns, illness has just receded when misery descends again. A marshal became a man who had lost his way, ten columns of militant soldiers turned into a defeated rabble. And as a result, army-men could not return to their camps, naval forces fled to a dream world.

How did Marshal Gao and his ten-column army escape? Read our next chapter if you would know.

CHAPTER 79

LIU TANG BURNS THE SHIPS OF WAR

SONG JIANG DEFEATS MARSHAL GAO THE SECOND TIME

Although the artillery were only signal cannon firing blanks, and no outlaws were lying in ambush, Marshal Gao was frightened. He had no belly for further battle. He scurried back to Jizhou with his troops that same night. His infantry casualties were not high, but he had lost more than half his naval effectives, and not a single war ship returned.

Dragon Dream Liu managed to get back, after considerable difficulty. Sailors who were able to swim, had escaped. Those who could not, had all drowned.

His military prestige damaged, his energies depleted, Gao could only encamp in the city and wait for Niu Pangxi to arrive with fresh boats. He sent a dispatch to Niu urging speed: Niu was to seize any craft he could lay his hands on, bring it to Jizhou, and fit it out for the next expedition.

At the fortress Song Jiang returned first with Dong Ping. Doctor An Daoquan removed the arrow and dressed the wound with Golden Spear Ointment, and directed Dong to rest. Wu Yong and the other chieftains arrived next. Zhang Heng, head of the naval forces, brought Dang Shixiong to Loyalty Hall and claimed his reward. Song Jiang ordered that the prisoner be taken to the rear of the fortress and held under house arrest. The captured boats were to be distributed among the various chieftains commanding the water defenses.

In Jizhou Marshal Gao summoned his generals into council to discuss strategy against Mount Liangshan. Commandant Xu Jing spoke.

"I started wandering as a child," he said. "When I grew up and was giving exhibitions of arms and peddling medicines I made friends with a man. He's a skilled strategist and tactician, and has the talent of Sun Wu and Wu Qi—those ancient theoreticians of war—and the wisdom of Zhuge Liang. His name is Wen Huanzhang. He teaches school in the village of Anren on the outskirts of the Eastern Capital. If we could get him to be our chief of staff he could defeat Wu Yong's crafty schemes."

Gao at once sent a top-ranking general, with gifts of silks and a saddle horse, to invite the village teacher to come to Jizhou as quickly as possible and advise on military affairs. Only three or four days after the general departed, a report came from outside the city: "Song Jiang has arrived with his army. He challenges us to fight."

Marshal Gao was furious. He mustered the troops in the city and sallied forth. He also directed the commandants of the various forts to go out and give battle.

When Song Jiang saw Gao and his army approaching, he hastily drew back fifteen *li* to a broad, level plain. Gao closed in pursuit. Song Jiang's forces set up positions at the edge of a mountain slope. From a troop bearing red banners a fierce-looking commander burst forward. On his banner were the words: *Two Rods Huyan Zhuo.* He reined in his steed and halted at the edge of the battlefield, his lance held athwart.

"That's the fellow who commanded the emperor's chain-linked cavalry and sold out to the enemy," snarled Gao. He sent Commandant Han Cunbao, who wielded a crescent-bladed halberd, forth to meet him.

Without a word, the two clashed, one hacking with his halberd, the other thrusting with his lance, neither slackening for a moment. For more than fifty rounds they fought. Then Huyan executed a feint, broke away, struck his horse, and rode down the slope. Han, on racing steed, quickly followed.

Eight hoofs churned the turf like iron bowls. The chase continued for six or seven *li,* until the contestants were far from all the others. Han began closing the distance between them. Suddenly, Huyan turned his mount around, put up his lance and, brandishing his two rods, galloped to meet his pursuer. They battled for a dozen rounds. Again Huyan parried the crescent-bladed halberd and rode away.

"He can't get near me with his lance," thought Han Cunbao, "and can't beat me with his rods. I can take that thief alive! What am I waiting for!"

Han rapidly gave chase. But as he rounded a bend between two mountains, the path forked. Which direction had Huyan taken? He urged his steed up the slope and looked. He saw Huyan Zhuo riding off along a stream.

"Where do you think you're going, wretched robber," bawled Han. "Dismount and be bound, and I'll spare your life!"

Huyan halted and cursed Han fulsomely. Han rode in a wide circuit so that he came up behind Two Rods and cut off his retreat. On one side was the mountain, on the other side the stream. Their field of combat was the narrow space between, and it was there they met. The horses had little room to maneuver.

"Surrender now," called Huyan. "Why wait?"

"You're beaten already, and you want me to surrender!"

"I've lured you here because I want to capture you alive! That's your only hope for survival!"

"It's I who am going to capture you alive!"

The rage of the two men again flared. Han rained stabs against Huyan's chest and abdomen with his long halberd. Parrying left and right, Huyan countered with a whirlwind of thrusts from his lance.

For thirty more rounds they fought. As Han thrust at Huyan's ribs, Huyan lunged for Han's heart. Both dodged, and the weapons each went harmlessly by. But Huyan clapped the shaft of Han's halberd under his arm, and Han seized Huyan's lance with his hand. Both pulled and tugged with all their might from their saddles. The rear legs of Han's steed were in the stream. Huyan and his horse were dragged into the water.

The men struggled and wrenched, the horses kicked up spray till both combatants were drenched. Huyan abandoned his lance and, with Han's halberd still clamped under one arm, reached for his rods. At that moment, Han dropped

Huyan's lance and grabbed his arms. Locked in combat, the two tumbled into the water. Their horses spurted up the bank and galloped towards the mountains.

Weaponless, the men wrestled in the stream. Their helmets fell off, their armor hung in pieces. In the deep water they traded kicks and punches, moving gradually back to the shallow edge of the stream.

While the battle was raging, a troop of cavalry arrived at the bank, headed by Featherless Arrow Zhang Qin. They seized Han Cunbao and sent men to recover the horses. Hearing the neighs of the cavalry steeds, the animals returned themselves. The armor and weapons were retrieved from the stream and given to Huyan Zhuo. He mounted, dripping wet. Han was also put on a horse, his hands tied behind his back, and all rode quickly for the gap.

Ahead, they saw coming towards them another body of cavalry, searching for Han Cunbao. Both troops halted. In the fore of the government forces were two commandants—Mei Zhan and Zhang Kai. When these observed the bound and dripping Han mounted on a steed, Mei Zhan grew very angry. Brandishing a three-pronged two-edged blade, he charged at Zhang Qin.

Before they had fought three rounds, Zhang Qin broke and galloped away. Mei Zhan followed. Zhang Qin unlimbered his ape-like arms, twisted his wolf-like waist, and let fly with a stone. It struck Mei Zhan on the temple, drawing fresh blood. The commandant dropped his sword and covered his face with his hands. Zhang Qin wheeled his mount around. Zhang Kai fitted an arrow to his bow, pulled it to the full, and sped the feathered shaft. Zhang Qin yanked up his horse's head, so that it took the arrow in the eye. As the beast fell to the ground its rider leaped clear and prepared to fight on foot.

But Zhang Qin's only real military skill lay in throwing stones. With the lance he was slow. Zhang Kai, after rescuing Mei Zhan, came after Zhang Qin. The lance of the man on horseback darted like a thing bewitched. Zhang Qin defended himself as best he could, and when he could withstand no more, dashed for cover amid his own troop. Zhang Kai pursued, slaughtering horsemen left and right until he reached the site of Han Cunbao.

He was about to ride back with Han when he heard a clamor of wild yells. Two more cavalry troops were tearing through the mountain gap. One was led by Qin Ming the Thunderbolt, the other was headed by Big Halberd Guan Sheng, both chieftains riding fast and fierce. Zhang Kai, protecting Mei Zhan, departed hastily, abandoning their men. The cavalry cut in and again captured Han. Zhang Qin grabbed a riderless horse and mounted, but Huyan was exhausted and could only follow in the wake of the attackers. The impetus of the assault carried the men of Mount Liangshan to the fore of the government soldiers, and they harried them all the way back to Jizhou. There they ended the chase. They returned to the fortress with Han Cunbao that same night.

When Song Jiang, seated in Loyalty Hall with the other chieftains, saw the prisoner, he ordered his men to stand back and untied him personally. He invited Han to be seated at the head of the hall and treated him solicitously. Han was grateful beyond words. Song Jiang then asked Dang Shixiong to join them, and afforded Dang the same courteous treatment.

"You two generals may feel completely at ease," he said. "We have no evil intentions. We've come here only because corrupt officials have forced us to do so. If the emperor grants us amnesty we'll be happy to serve the government."

"But didn't Marshal Chen bring you an amnesty?" said Han. "Why didn't you take that opportunity to return to the path of righteousness?"

"Although it was an imperial amnesty, its terms were not clear. What's more, the emissaries had substituted a cheap rural brew for the imperial wine. My brothers were unconvinced. And that Majordomo Zhang and Captain Li dared to threaten and insult us!"

"Because no good person was in charge, a matter of importance to the state was delayed," Han said regretfully.

Song Jiang feasted his guests. The next day he presented them with saddled horses and saw them off to the mouth of the valley. The two spoke highly of him all the way to Jinzhou. By the time they neared the city it was late. They did not enter until the following morning.

They went to Marshal Gao and told him how Song Jiang had released them. Gao grew very angry.

"It's a bandit trick to soften our army's resolve! How can you two have the effrontery to see me? Guards, take them out and kill them!"

Wang Huan and the other officials dropped to their knees and pleaded: "It's not their fault. The scheme is Song Jiang's and Wu Yong's. If you execute Han and Dang, the bandits will laugh at us."

Gao finally let himself be persuaded. He rescinded his order, but he stripped both men of their ranks and directed them to report to the Military Procurate in the Eastern Capital for punishment. The two left under escort for the capital city.

Han Cunbao was the nephew of Han Zhongyan, a former premier. Many officials in the court had obtained their positions through him. One of these was Zheng Juzhong, originally a royal tutor, and now a censor in the court. Han Cunbao had great respect for him and told him about his problem. Zheng got into his sedan-chair and took Han to consult with Minister Yu Shen.

"We'll have to appeal to the prime minister," said Yu, "then we can petition the emperor."

He and Han went together to Premier Cai Jing and reported: "Song Jiang has no evil intentions. He's waiting only for an amnesty from the emperor."

"He destroyed the previous decree. Men so lacking in courtesy cannot be amnestied, they can only be wiped out or arrested."

"That was because the emissaries did not state the emperor's noble purpose and express his concern. They spoke harshly instead of kindly. For that reason the mission failed."

Only then did the premier consent to help.

The following morning when the Taoist Emperor opened court, Cai Jing again proposed offering an amnesty to Song Jiang and his men if they surrendered.

"Marshal Gao has asked Wen Huanzhang of Anren Village to be chief of staff, and Wen has already reported to the court for duty," said the emperor. "We shall send him as our emissary. If the brigands consent to submit, we will forgive their previous crimes. If not, we shall set a time limit within which we shall expect Marshal Gao to either exterminate them or bring them back to the capital as prisoners."

Cai Jing drafted the appropriate decree and, at the same time, invited Wen to dine with him in his mansion. Wen was a famous scholar, well known to most of the high ministers in the imperial court. Each of them drank to him in greeting. After the banquet Wen returned to his quarters and packed for his journey. He bid farewell to the emperor and set out the same day.

Meanwhile, in Jizhou Gao fretted impatiently. The gatekeeper entered and announced: "Niu Bangxi is here." Gao directed that he come in. Niu bowed respectfully and Gao asked: "What about the boats?"

"We confiscated along the way over fifteen hundred, large and small. They're all waiting below the lock."

Very pleased, the marshal rewarded Niu. He ordered that the craft be congregated in a wide bay and grouped in threes. Each group was to be decked with planks and chained together at the stern, so as to carry the maximum number of infantry. The cavalry would escort them along the banks.

By the time the dispersement of troops was settled and the soldiers had become adapt at boarding the craft half a month had gone by. Mount Liangshan already knew all about it.

Wu Yong instructed Liu Tang to strengthen defenses along the water courses. He told the naval chieftains to prepare small boats, nail iron plate to their prows, and fill their holds with brushwood sprinkled with sulphur and saltpetre. These would wait in the inlets.

He also ordered artillery expert Ling Zhen to place signal cannon on all the surrounding heights. Pennants were to be tied to tree-tops in the thickets along the river and gongs and drums and fireworks were to be readied there to create the impression that well-manned military encampments were at hand. Gongsun Sheng was asked to perform magic and raise the wind. The main forces would fight as three armies on the land.

Wu Yong's plan for the men of Mount Liangshan was completed.

In Jizhou, Marshal Gao hastened the departure of his contingents. His naval craft he placed under the leadership of Niu Bangxi, who again collaborated with Dragon Dream Liu and Dang Shiying as the three top commanders. Gao donned his armor, the drums thundered thrice and the boats in the bay set sail, while on land the cavalry swung into a trot. The craft sped forward like arrows, the horses seemed to fly, as the government troops pushed into Liangshan Marsh.

Gongs and drums beating, the naval vessels glided on, winding ever deeper into the marsh in an endless succession of masts. But not a single outlaw boat did they meet. As they neared the Shore of Golden Sands, they saw two fishing craft in a cove of lotus flowers. There were only two men on each, and they were clapping their hands and laughing uproariously.

Dragon Dream Liu, on the leading government vessel, ordered his archers to shoot. The fishermen dived into the river and swam underwater. Liu urged his flotilla on, and they gradually drew closer to the Shore of Golden Sands. A line of shady willows fringed the bank. Two brown oxen were tied to one of the trees, and three or four herd boys lay dozing on the grassy sward. In the distance a lad seated on the back of another ox was softly playing a flute.

Liu directed his assault squad to land first. The sleeping boys jumped up and, laughing merrily, disappeared into the willow grove. Six or seven hundred soldiers of the advance unit started clambering up the bank. A cannon boomed within the willows. On either side, war drums beat. A contingent in red armor, led by Qin Ming the Thunderbolt, burst into view on the left. On the right suddenly appeared a contingent in black armor, headed by Two Rods Huyan Zhuo. The two units, each comprised of five hundred men, swarmed towards the bank. By the time Dragon Dream Liu yelled for his troops to return to the boats he had already lost more than half.

Niu, hearing the agonized yells of the advance force, ordered his rear boats to pull back. But a string of cannon shots sounded on a hilltop and the reeds commenced to rustle. Gongsun Sheng, his long hair streaming down, his sword in hand, stood upon an astrological diagram on the summit, raising the wind. It moaned through the trees, gathering momentum, and pelted the soldiers with sand and stones and whipped up giant waves. Dark clouds enshrouded the earth, completely blocking out the sun. It was a wild, raging gale.

Dragon Dream Liu also hastily directed his vessels to retreat. From the criss-crossing inlets in the reeds and water lilies a number of small craft sped out and dispersed themselves amid the government flotilla. A drum sounded; and on each little boat torches were lit. This was in accordance with the plan Wu Yong had given to Liu Tang, whereby the naval chieftains would load the craft with dry reeds and brushwood sprinkled with oil, sulphur and saltpetre. In an instant, great flames were leaping skyward, and the small boats closed in on the larger vessels. Soon, from one end to the other, the entire government flotilla was ablaze.

Liu removed his helmet and armor and jumped into the water. Not daring to go near the shore, he headed for where the river was wide and deep, hoping thus to escape. A small craft, piloted by only one man, shot out of the reeds to intercept him. Liu flipped over and swam underwater. Someone seized him around the waist and hauled him to the boat, where he was dragged aboard. The man on the boat was Tong Wei the Dragon from the Cave. The one who had grabbed him was Li Jun the Turbulent River Dragon.

Meanwhile, Niu Bangxi, seeing all the government vessels in flames, also stripped off his armor and prepared to leap into the river. Suddenly, a man appeared on the prow holding a grappling hook. With this he snagged Niu and pulled him into the water backwards. The man was Zhang Heng the Boat Flame.

Corpses littered the waterways of Liangshan Marsh, their blood encrimsoning the waves. There were bashed and battered skulls without number. Dang Shiying, who was fleeing in a small craft, was killed by swarms of arrows from the reeds on both sides. Many of the soldiers could swim, and these escaped with their lives. Those who could not, died of drowning. Prisoners were escorted under guard to the fortress. Li Jun and Zhang Heng wee about to do the same with their captives Dragon Dream Liu and Niu Bangxi, but they were afraid Song Jiang would only let them go again. After talking it over, they killed the two by the roadside, cut off their heads and brought these to the mountain instead.

Meanwhile, Marshal Gao, leading his army as reinforcements to the water's edge, heard the continuous boom of cannon and the steady beat of drums. He guessed that the fighting was on the river, and he hastened forward, surveying both the banks and the nearby hills. He saw soldiers emerging from the water and crawling up the banks and running. Gao recognized one of the officers and asked him what had happened. The mail told how all the boats had been burned. He said he didn't know where the others were.

Gao's heart chilled with alarm. The yelling continued, and black smoke filled the sky. The marshal hastily led his troops back along the road they had come. Drums suddenly thundered on the hills ahead. A troop of horsemen burst forth and blocked their path. In the lead was Suo Chao the Urgent Vanguard, wielding a mountain-splitting battle-ax as he cantered towards them. At Gao's direction, Wang Huan, the commandant who was riding beside him, trotted out with levelled lance.

Before the two had fought five rounds, Suo Chao wheeled his mount and withdrew. Marshal Gao and his contingent pursued. But when they rounded the foot of a hill, Suo Chao had vanished. At that moment, they were attacked from behind by a troop led by Panther Head Lin Chong.

They suffered some casualties. They travelled another six or seven *li,* and a troop under Yang Zhi the Blue-Faced Beast caught up and inflicted further losses. After another eight or nine *li* Zhu Tong the Beautiful Beard harassed their rear, imposing still more casualties.

These were tactics devised by Wu Yong—not preventing retreat, but persistently raiding from behind. The battered government troops had no heart for battle. They wanted only to flee, and were incapable of protecting their rear.

Panic-stricken, Gao flew back to Jizhou. By the time he reached the city it was nearly midnight. Just then he saw flames rising from the fort in the outskirts and heard shouts of alarm. Shi Xiu and Yang Xiong plus five hundred foot soldiers lying in ambush had, with only a few torches, set the city ablaze, then slipped away.

Gao's soul leaped from his body in fright, and he hurriedly sent men to inquire. Only when they returned and reported: "They're gone," did he relax. A count of his troops showed he had lost more than half.

As Gao sat deep in gloom, a scout from a far outpost entered and reported: "An imperial emissary is arriving." Gao rode forth with his army and commandants to greet him. Wen Huanzhang, the emissary, told him of the proposed amnesty. When all the officers had been presented, they returned to headquarters in the city to confer. Gao ordered that a copy of the document be made.

The marshal had already suffered two heavy defeats and lost all his boats. If he delivered the amnesty now, he'd be ashamed to face people on his return to the capital. For several days he vacillated, unable to come to any decision.

It so happened that in Jizhou there was an old functionary named Wang Jin, a cruel, crafty fellow who was popularly known as "Cut Your Heart Out" Wang. He had been given to headquarters by Zhang Shuye, the prefect of Jizhou. Having read a copy of the amnesty, and learning that Gao was in a dilemma, Wang presented himself before the marshal.

"Your Excellency needn't worry about the amnesty," he said. "I have a way to cope with that. The Hanlin scholar who has drafted the document is surely on good terms with Your Excellency, since he has left the rear door open."

Gao was mystified. "What do you mean?"

"The most important part of the document is the line in the middle that reads: 'Obliterate Song Jiang, Lu Junyi and the other chieftains' crimes; we grant them amnesty.' This sentence is not clear. Have the copyist break it up into two sentences: 'Obliterate Song Jiang,' and 'Lu Junyi and the other chieftains' crimes, we grant them amnesty.' Then lure Song Jiang into the city, seize him as their leader, and execute him. Disband and scatter his followers. Since ancient times it has been said: 'A snake without a head cannot crawl, a bird without wings cannot fly.' Without Song Jiang, what good are the others! How does this strike Your Excellency?"

Gao was delighted. He immediately appointed Wang his chief advisor and told Chief of Staff Wen Huanzhang of the plan.

"An imperial emissary can act only in a righteous manner," Wen protested. "We cannot indulge in such deception! If any of Song Jiang's followers should learn of this and expose us, it would be extremely awkward!"

"Nonsense," cried Gao. "'The essence of military tactics is deception.' From the earliest days this has been the rule. There's no need to be so proper."

"This is a decree from the emperor, and so will be believed by everyone throughout the land. The words of the emperor are precious as jade. They cannot be tampered with. If we were to do what you say, and later it should be found out, we'd have no credibility in the future."

"We'll deal with the present, and worry about the future some other time," said the marshal.

He dispatched a messenger to Mount Liangshan directing Song Jiang and his entire complement to come to the walls of Jizhou to hear an imperial decree granting them amnesty.

After having again defeated Marshal Gao in battle Song Jiang instructed his junior officers to collect the remains of the burned boats and use them for firewood. Those that had been unscathed were to be turned over to the water defense positions. Captured enemy generals should be allowed to go back, at intervals, to Jizhou.

Song Jiang and his chieftains were conferring in Loyalty Hall when an officer entered and reported: "A messenger has come from Jizhou Prefecture. He says: 'The imperial court his sent an emissary with a decree granting amnesty and conferring official posts. I have been dispatched to announce this good news.'"

On hearing these joyous tidings from on high, Song Jiang smiled all over his face. He summoned the messenger into the hall.

"The royal court has granted an amnesty," the man said. "I have been sent by Marshal Gao to invite all of you chieftains to the walls of Jizhou for a ceremonial reading of the decree. We have no other intention. Please discard any doubts."

Song Jiang said he would discuss the matter with his generals. He rewarded the messenger with silver and satins and directed him to return to Jizhou. Then he ordered his chieftains to prepare to go and hear the reading of the imperial document.

"Don't be so hasty, brother," urged Lu Junyi. "Marshal Gao is probably up to something. You can't just rush into this!"

"If you men are always so suspicious, how will we ever return to the path of righteousness?" Song Jiang countered. "For better or worse, let's go."

Wu Yong smiled. "We've beaten that rogue Gao so badly his gall is chilled and his heart is shattered. No matter how elaborate a scheme he may have, it won't work. Besides, we're all gallant warriors. There's no need to worry. Just go along with brother Song Jiang down the mountain. I'll send Black Whirlwind Li Kui on ahead first with Fan Rui, Bao Xu, Xiang Chong and Li Gun and a thousand infantry to he in ambush on the east road to Jizhou. I'll also send sister Ten Feet of Steel with Mistress Gu, Sun the Witch, Stumpy Tiger Wang, Sun Xin and Zhang Qing and a thousand cavalry to he in ambush on the west road to Jizhou. If they hear a series of cannon shots they will charge to our rescue at the North Gate."

After Wu Yong's arrangements were carried out, the chieftains descended the slope. Only the naval commanders remained to guard the fortress.

And so, Marshal Gao, refusing to heed the advice of Chief of Staff Wen, lured the heroes from their stronghold. Who would have thought that this would convert the outskirts of Jizhou and the fringes of Liangshan Marsh to battlefields. The resulting melee was like wolves among a pack of dogs, tigers amid a flock of sheep. Truly, that single imperial decree stirred up the passions of the entire band of warriors.

How did the gallants wreak havoc in Jizhou? Read our next chapter if you would know.

CHAPTER 80

ZHANG SHUN DRILLS HOLES THROUGH THE PADDLE-WHEEL BOATS

SONG JIANG DEFEATS MARSHAL GAO THE THIRD TIME

Marshal Gao, seated in his headquarters in Jizhou, summoned Wang Huan and his other commandants into conference. He ordered them to strike camp and move with their contingents into the city. All were to remain on the alert and fully armed. No flags were to be displayed on the city walls, except above the North Gate, where an imperial yellow banner would be unfurled bearing the words: *The Emperor's Edict.* Gao, the emissary and the high officials then mounted the wall and awaited the arrival of Song Jiang.

From the mountain fortress Zhang Qin the Featherless Arrow set forth with an advance cavalry unit of five hundred, made a circuit of the city, and headed north. Then the Marvellous Traveller Dai Zong arrived and scouted on foot. This was reported to Marshal Gao, and he went personally to the ramparts of the outer wall, accompanied by a retinue of over a hundred. Flags were set up. An incense table was placed in the foreground.

Song Jiang's army could be seen approaching far to the north. First came trumpeters and drummers and many flagbearers, then the chieftains —in scoop and circle and "V" formations. On horseback, the foremost of these—Song Jiang, Lu Junyi the Magnate, Wu Yong and Gongsun Sheng, bowed from their saddles and hailed Marshal Gao.

On Gao's instructions an officer shouted from the wall-top: "The imperial court has deigned to pardon your crimes and has sent a special decree. Why do you come in armor?"

Song Jiang sent Dai Zong to the foot of the wall with the reply: "We have not yet heard the gracious statement and don't know what it contains. We therefore dare not come unprotected. If Marshal Gao will summon all the residents of the city and let them hear the decree with us together, we will then remove our armor."

Gao issued the appropriate order and, before long, all the citizens of Jizhou were assembled. Only then did Song Jiang and his chieftains advance. To a flourish of drums and trumpets, they dismounted. At a second flourish, they approached the city wall on foot. Behind, junior officers, leading the chieftains' horses, halted an arrow-shot away and assembled in neat ranks. At a third flourish, the chieftains stood with hands respectfully clasped and prepared to hear the decree. From atop the wall, the emissary read:

Edict: Each man's character is unique, a state has only one essential morality. People who behave well are proper citizens, those who do evil are rebels. For the latter, no good fate lies in store. We can only pity them. We bear that for a long time a band has congregated on Mount Liangshan, unresponsive to kindly exhortations to restore goodness to their hearts. We dispatch our emissary with this decree: Obliterate Song Jiang... Lu Junyi and the other chieftains' crimes, we grant them amnesty. Let the leaders report to the capital to give thanks, let their followers return home. Reject not the imperial decision. Let the emperor's benevolence expunge wickedness and restore righteousness to your hearts. Oppose not Heaven's will to replace the old with the new. Let this decree be proclaimed for all to know.

The Xuan He Period
Year—month—day—

When the words "Obliterate Song Jiang" were read out, Wu Yong said to Hua Rong: "Did you hear that?"

The moment the reading was completed, Hua Rong shouted: "Since you won't amnesty our Big Brother, why should we surrender!" He notched an arrow to his bow, pulled it to the full, and yelled at the emissary: "Take a look at Hua Rong's magic arrow!"

The feathered shaft struck the emissary between the eyes. Government officers tried urgently to save him, while the gallant outlaws below cried: "Down with them!" and loosed a volley of arrows at the men atop the city wall. Marshal Gao hurriedly took cover.

All four gates of the city opened, spewing out Jizhou troops. Drums pounded in the midst of Song Jiang's coterie. The outlaws mounted then-horses and withdrew. The municipal forces pursued them five or six *li,* then started back. Behind them cannon thundered and Li Kui came charging from the east with brigand infantry, while from the west Ten Feet of Steel led her cavalry in an attack. Both arms of the pincers closed in together.

Fearing an ambush, the government troops quickly withdrew into the city. Song Jiang and his unit then turned around and charged, so that the local Jizhou contingents were being attacked from three sides. Thrown into great confusion, they were slaughtered by the score as they fled towards the city. Song Jiang and his men did not pursue for long, but returned to Liangshan Marsh.

Gao wrote a report to the emperor stating that Song Jiang's bandits had killed the emissary and refused to submit to the royal decree. He sent in addition a personal letter to Prime Minister Cai, Chancellor Tong and Marshal Yang urging them to confer, and requesting the prime minister to petition the throne for immediate reinforcements for use against the brigands, and the right to requisition fodder along the way.

On receipt of Gao's letter, the premier obtained an audience with the emperor and told him what had transpired. The sovereign's face clouded.

"Those bandits have insulted the throne! They've rebelled against us repeatedly!" He ordered each of his armies to provide reinforcements, and to take their orders from Marshal Gao.

Marshal Yang, who already knew of the consecutive defeats, selected two generals from the Imperial Divisions. He also directed that five hundred crack infantry from each of the four camps at Dragon Fierce, Winged Tiger, Sun Lift, and Loyal Righteousness be mustered, totalling two thousand men, to go with the generals in aid of Gao against the brigands.

Who were these two generals? The first was Qiu Yue, Chief Arms Instructor of the Imperial Guards and Commander of the Left Echelon Protecting the Royal Person. The second was the Deputy Chief Arms Instructor of the Imperial Guards and Commander of the Right Echelon Protecting the Royal Person, Cavalry General Zhou Ang. Both men had been decorated many times for valor, were famed for their skill with arms, and enjoyed high prestige in the capital. Moreover, they were completely trusted by Marshal Gao.

Marshal Yang ordered them to depart immediately, and they went to take their leave of the prime minister. "Be prudent and win distinction soon, and we surely will raise you to more important posts," Cai said. The two generals thanked him.

From the four camps they chose, one by one, tall, stalwart men who were narrow of waist and broad of shoulder, superb specimens from the provinces of Shandong and Hebei who could climb mountains and swim rivers. Then they took their leave of Marshal Yang and various high officials, and announced they were departing the next day. The marshal presented them each with five excellent horses for their personal use in battle. He promised them a big send-off. The generals thanked him and went to their respective commands to prepare.

The following morning the troops, geared up for the march, assembled in front of Imperial Divisions headquarters. Qiu Yue and Zhou Ang divided them into four contingents. The thousand soldiers from Dragon Fierce and Winged Tiger, plus more than two thousand cavalry, were under Qiu Yue. Zhou Ang commanded the thousand from Sun Lift and Loyal Righteousness, in addition to another two thousand some-odd cavalry. Still another thousand foot soldiers were split into two follow-up support units.

By the time the sun was brightening the troops were formed in ranks. Marshal Yang examined them personally from the tower above the city gate. The junior officers looked imposing, the soldiers bold, as they stood behind their embroidered banners. And when, from amid the troops of cavalry, General Qiu Yue suddenly rode proudly forth to lead the column on the left, the capital's citizenry broke into cheers.

The men of Sun Lift and Loyal Righteousness stood also in smart formation, each contingent behind its embroidered banner. General Zhou Ang cantered forward from the midst of his assembled horsemen, stern and fierce, to lead his right column to the edge of the city.

There, he and Qiu Yue dismounted, bowed to Marshal Yang and bid farewell to the officials. Leaving the Eastern Capital, they set out with their troops for Jizhou.

In the city of Jizhou, Marshal Gao and Chief of Staff Wen conferred. They decided that, while waiting for the reinforcements to arrive, they would dispatch men to the surrounding hills to fell timber. They would obtain boat builders from nearby counties, set up a shipyard outside Jizhou, and construct vessels of war. They would also enlist bold fellows to serve as sailors.

It happened that a man named Ye Chun, a boat builder from Sizhou Prefecture, was living in one of the inns. On his way to Shandong he had passed Liangshan Marsh and had been waylaid and robbed by some of the petty bandits. Unable to afford the journey home, he now hung around the city. When he heard that Gao was felling timber for war craft to invade the marsh, he sketched a couple of vessels and went to call on him.

After courtesies had been exchanged, Ye said: "Why did the last naval expedition fail? Because your boats were simply confiscated from here and there, and used wind and oar power, neither of which are reliable. What's more, they were small, low-lying and narrow, so that it was difficult for their crews to use weapons.

"According to my plan, if you want to defeat the bandits you must build a few hundred big warships. The largest of these should be the type known as the Big Paddle-Wheeler. It has twelve paddle-wheels on each side and holds several hundred men. Twelve men turn each of the wheels. A bamboo screen along the gunwales wards off arrows. On deck will be towers for archers, and to these winches and pulleys will be attached.

"One rap on a bamboo segment in the ramparts of the bridge will be the signal to advance. All twenty-four paddle-wheels will immediately begin to rotate, and the boat will fly forward. The outlaws have no craft that can stop it. And when all our archers fire together, they'll never be able to block our arrows.

"The second type of vessel you need is known as the Small Paddle-Wheeler. It has a total of twelve wheels and holds a hundred or more men. A long spike protrudes from both its prow and its stern. It also has archer towers on each side and is also protected by a bamboo screen. This craft can be used in the narrower waterways of the marsh to prevent those rogues from laying ambushes. If you accept my plan, the bandits of Mount Liangshan will soon be subdued."

As Gao listened and examined the sketches, he was very pleased. He called for wine and food and clothing and rewarded Ye Chun. Gao put him in charge of the boat building project.

Gao pushed the men day and night, setting time limits within which to deliver the timber to Jizhou. Each county had to supply materials needed for the vessels' construction. Any man who was two days late in fulfilling his duties received forty strokes. If he was three days late, he got double. If he exceeded five days, he was executed according to military law. The pressure never let up. Many ordinary citizens were killed, and the people bemoaned their lot. A jingle going around ran like this:

A frog in a well can't see the whole sky,
Gao has taken advice from a jerk.
Paddle-wheelers won't win him victory,

A waste of money and exhausting work.

Sailors to be added to the fleet kept arriving in Jizhou, and Gao assigned them to the commandants of his various camps for training. Then one day the city gate-keeper announced: "Qiu Yue and Zhou Ang, the generals sent by the imperial court, are here." Gao directed his commandants to go outside the wall to greet them. When the two were ushered into his presence, Gao received them with food and wine. He entertained them and instructed an officer to reward their troops. The generals requested Gao's order to sally forth and do battle.

"Wait a few days, gentlemen, till the paddle-wheelers are ready," said Gao. "Then we can proceed on land and water together. With our combined naval and cavalry operation, we'll suppress the bandits in a single battle!"

"It will be child's play," boasted the generals. "Rest assured, Marshal? we surely will return to the capital victorious!"

"If you match your words with deeds, I shall petition the emperor to have you both promoted to important posts."

The feasting ended, the generals mounted their horses in front of Gao's headquarters and returned to their commands. They settled their troops in encampments and awaited orders.

When Song Jiang and his chieftains hurried back to Mount Liangshan after their rebellious outcry and murderous battle at the walls of Jizhou, Song Jiang was anxious. "Twice they've come with amnesties, and both times we injured the emissary," he said to Wu Yong. "That makes our crimes more serious than ever. What are we going to do? The court will surely dispatch an army to punish us."

He sent a scout down to find out what was happening and report back as soon as possible. In a few days the man returned with the details. Song Jiang and Wu Yong conferred in Loyalty Hall. They knew now that Gao had raised a navy, and that he had put Ye Chun in charge of building a fleet of hundreds of paddle-wheelers, large and small. Also that the Eastern Capital had dispatched reinforcements under Qiu Yue and Zhou Ang, both courageous generals.

"How can we stop ships that size when they come flying across the water?" said Song Jiang.

Wu Yong laughed. "What is there to be afraid of? All we need is a few naval chieftains. We have powerful warrior leaders to fight them on land. Anyhow, it will take them several weeks to build those big vessels. We've forty or fifty days yet. Send a couple of brothers down to get into their shipyard and stir them up a bit. Meanwhile, we'll gradually be thinking of a way to cope."

"Excellent. I'll tell Flea on a Drum Shi Qian and Golden Dog Duan Jingzhu to go."

"Better ask Zhang Qing and Sun Xin to disguise themselves as timber haulers and mix with the others and get into the yard also. And tell their wives Mistress Gu and Sun the Witch to dress up like the women food servers and go in with them. Flea on a Drum and Golden Dog can be their support."

Each of the pairs was summoned to the hall and instructed what to do. All were inordinately pleased and went separately down the mountains to carry out their missions.

Marshal Gao continued driving the boat builders day and night and conscripting people into his labor force. The entire area east of Jizhou was one vast shipyard. The several thousand artisans building the hundreds of large craft complained bitterly about conditions. But the rough soldiers threatened them with their swords, and forced them to work without rest.

Flea on a Drum and Golden Dog reached the shipyard first. "Since the other four will be setting fire to this place, you and I won't be making much of a show here," Flea said to Dog. "Let's just lay low till that happens. Then I'll wait outside the city gate. Troops are sure to be sent out. I can slip in when they open the gate, climb up to the wall tower, and set it to the torch. You, meanwhile, can be kindling a nice blaze in the fodder depot west of the city. They won't know where to rush first. We'll give them a good scare."

The two concealed incendiary powders on their persons, and separated to find safe resting places.

Zhang Qing and Sun Xin, on nearing Jizhou, saw four or five hundred men hauling lumber to the shipyard. They joined them and also laid their shoulders to the ropes. At the entrance to the yard over two hundred soldiers, each with a dagger at his waist, belabored the straining porters with sticks to greater speed.

Inside there was much confused activity. They whole area was enclosed by a large palisade and contained two or three hundred thatch-roofed work-sheds. Thousands of artisans were busily engaged. In one section men were sawing planks, in another carpenters were nailing them to the hulls, in a third others were caulking the cracks. Laborers without number were bustling about. Zhang and Sun drifted into dark corners of the kitchen-shed and kept out of sight.

Their wives, Sun the Witch and Mistress Gu, wearing soiled clothes and each carrying a jug of cooked rice, entered with other women noisily delivering food. Gradually, day waned and a bright moon rose. But most of the artisans went on working at their never-ending tasks.

Around the second watch Sun and Zhang set fire to the left side of the yard, while their wives started a blaze on the right. The thatched roofs burst quickly into flames. Yelling in alarm, the artisans and laborers knocked down the palisade and fled into the night.

Marshal Gao, who was sleeping, was aroused by a man hastening in and reporting: "The shipyard is on fire!" Gao got up quickly and ordered his army to the rescue. Qiu Yue and Zhou Ang, leading a contingent of municipal troops, hurried from the city to quench the blaze. Shortly thereafter flames began to dance on the wall tower. Gao mounted his horse and led troops personally up the wall. As they were fighting the fire another report came in: "The fodder depot to the west is in flames! The blaze has turned the sky as bright as day!"

Qiu and Zhou, by then rushing with their forces to the fodder depot, heard suddenly the thunder of drums and a chorus of murderous yells. Featherless Arrow Zhang Qin and five hundred cavalry, who had been hiding there in ambush, now dashed out, with Zhang heading directly for the two generals.

"Mount Liangshan's whole complement of heroes are here!" Featherless Arrow shouted.

Qiu Yue, angered, clapped his horse and waved his sword, and galloped towards Zhang Qin, who met his charge with levelled lance. Less than three rounds they fought, and Featherless Arrow turned and left. Eager to win glory, Qiu pursued. "Halt, bandit!" he cried.

Zhang socketed his lance and quietly drew a stone from his embroidered pouch. Twisting around, he waited till Qiu drew near, then let fly with a shout: "Here!"

The stone struck Qiu in the face, knocking him from his horse. Zhou Ang and several standard bearers tore pell-mell to the rescue. While Zhou engaged Featherless Arrow, the others got Qiu back into his saddle. Zhou and Zhang fought only a few rounds, when Zhang departed. Zhou did not pursue, and Zhang again returned. He saw approaching the four contingents under Wang Huan, Xu Jing, Yang Wen and Li Congji. Zhang waved his hand as a signal and led off his five hundred cavalry.

Fearing an ambush, the government troops did not give chase. They reassembled and went back to fighting the fires. The sky was already light by the time they extinguished the three blazes. Gao dispatched an officer to learn the state of Qiu's wound. The stone had hit him in the mouth, dislodging four of his teeth and lacerating his nose and lips. The marshal directed a doctor to treat him.

Qiu's injury intensified Gao's antipathy for the men of Liangshan Marsh. He hated them to the marrow of his bones. He sent an order to Ye Chun to hasten the construction of the boats, and instructed his commandants to set up camps around the perimeter of the yard and stay constantly on the alert.

Zhang Qing, Sun Xin and their wives were delighted. Flea on a Drum and Golden Dog returned. All six were met by cohorts who had come down to escort them back to the mountain fortress. On arriving in Loyalty Hall they told how they had set the fires. Song Jiang was very pleased. He gave a feast in their honor and handsomely rewarded them. Thereafter, he sent spies down frequently.

By the time the boats were built it was winter. But that year was warm. Marshal Gao was glad. He felt Heaven was helping him. He urged his naval officers to familiarize themselves with the use of the vessels, which were being launched one after another. Sailors, conscripted from all the surrounding areas, now numbered over ten thousand. One half was put to learning to propel the craft, the other half practised archery. In less than twenty days the necessary preparations were completed. Ye Chun invited Gao to inspect the fleet.

On the appointed day Gao arrived with his generals and commandants. More than three hundred paddle-wheelers lay in their moorings. A dozen or so were selected and decked with pennants, to the crash of gongs and the beat of drums. At a knock on the bamboo segment, the wheels on both sides of the vessels began to churn, and they skimmed forward at truly flying speed. Gao's heart warmed with joy.

"The bandits will never be able to stop boats as fast as these," he exulted. "We're sure to win!"

He rewarded Ye Chun with money and silks. He also paid the artisans travelling expenses and let them go home.

The next day Marshal Gao directed that fruits and animals and paper replicas of gold and silver ingots be prepared for a sacrifice to the Water Spirit. The generals formed ranks and invited Gao to light the incense. Qiu Yue, whose wounds had healed, was consumed by hatred. He longed only for a chance to capture Zhang Qin alive and wreak his vengeance. With Zhou Ang and the commandants he mounted and rode behind Gao to where the boats were moored. There, all dismounted and Gao conducted the sacrifice. After the incense was lit and the ceremonies completed, the paper money was burned and the generals offered their congratulations.

Gao directed that the singers and dancers who had been brought from the capital come on board and entertain, while the sailors practised propelling the large craft flying across the waters. The sound of music and revelry continued until well after dark. That night all slept on board.

The next day, and the day after there was more feasting and drinking. Still, the vessels did not sail. Suddenly a scout arrived and reported: "The Mount Liangshan bandits have written a poem and posted it in front of the City God Temple in Jizhou. Here is a copy." The poem ran as follows:

We'll capture Yang Jian and old Gao Qiu,
And mop up the prefectures on the Central Plain.
Even if your paddle-wheelers number ten thousand,
You won't leave Liangshan Marsh alive again!

Gao was furious. He wanted to set forth at once. "If I don't kill all those bandit rebels, I won't come back!" he raged.

"Cool your wrath, Marshal," Chief to Staff Wen urged. "I think they're actually afraid. That's why they bluster. It doesn't matter. Wait a few days. Decide exactly how you're going to use your troops on land and on water, then start. There's still time. Though it's already winter, the weather is warm. It's a blessing from Heaven, a sign of your prestige."

This kind of talk pleased Gao, and he went into the city to discuss troop movements. Zhou Ang and Wang Huan would lead a large army to follow along on land and give support to the navy. Xiang Yuanzhen and Zhang Kai would go with a force of ten thousand and block the large road in front of Mount Liangshan. The marsh had always been a place of mist and reeds and wild inlets. The road had been built, on Song Jiang's orders, only recently. Gao wanted to get his men in there first, and cut the connection with the mountain fortress. His Chief of Staff Wen, his other generals, his Chief Advisor Wang Jin, the boat builder Ye Chun, his standard bearers, his senior and junior officers, would all travel with Gao in the armada.

Wen objected. "You should supervise the cavalry advance on land, Marshal. Don't go with the fleet. It's too dangerous."

"There's nothing to worry about, retorted Gao. "The last two times not only didn't we capture any of the bandit leaders, but we took heavy casualties and lost many of our boats. This time we've got excellent craft. If I don't assume personal command how are we going to nab those rebels! We're going to fight them to the death! You need say no more."

The chief of staff dared not pursue the subject. He followed the marshal on board. Gao designated thirty large paddle-wheelers, with Qiu Yue, Xu Jing and Mei Zhan in command, as the van. Fifty small paddle-wheelers under Yang Wen, Chief Advisor Wang Jin and Ye Chun the boat builder, would go first to clear the way. A big red pennant on the lead craft bore the inscription in words of gold: *We roil the seas, stir the rivers and churn up white waves to pacify the country and suppress the torrent-causing demons.*

On a vessel in the central section of the fleet were Gao, Wen, and the boy singers and girl dancers. Green standards, generals' flags, pennants of yellow and white, and canopies of red and black broke out on all the boats, and arms were displayed in the central section. Vessels under Wang Wente and Li Congji brought up the rear.

It was the middle of the eleventh lunar month. The cavalry was given the order to march. Qiu Yue, Xu Jing and Mei Zhan, on the lead craft in the van of the armada, set sail. Like flying clouds and rolling mist, the government forces advanced on Liangshan Marsh.

The three generals in the van urged on their vessels, dispatching the small paddle-wheelers to both sides of the river to block the inlets, while the large paddle-wheelers proceeded full speed ahead. Eyes bulging, necks straining, the officers stared before them, as the craft wound swiftly deeper into the marsh.

Song Jiang and Wu Yong, who had been informed in detail about the enemy movements, had made careful preparations, and awaited the arrival of the government boats.

Gao's fleet could see in the distance a few small vessels approaching, each carrying fourteen or fifteen men dressed in armor. A captain sat in the middle of each craft, and on each was a white banner reading: *The Three Ruan Heroes of Liangshan Marsh.* Ruan the Second was on the boat in the center, Ruan the Fifth to his left, and Ruan the Seventh to his right. What appeared in the distance to be shining armor was actually only gold and silver paper.

The three vanguard generals shouted for the lead craft to open fire, and cannon balls, musket shots and rockets spewed forth. The three brothers and their crews waited fearlessly till the paddle-wheeler drew close enough to bring them within range, then, with a shout, dived into the river and swam away under water. Qiu Yue and his cohorts captured only three empty boats.

Before the fleet had proceeded another three *li,* three more skiffs were seen swiftly approaching. On the first were a dozen or so men, their bodies daubed with pigments of black, yellow and red. Their long hair hung unbound, and they whistled as they came. On the other two craft were six or seven men, and these were streaked red and yellow. Meng Kang the Jade Flagpole commanded the central vessel. Tong Wei the Dragon from the Cave commanded the boat to the left, Tong Meng the River Churning Clam captained the craft to the right.

Qiu Yue ordered his lead vessel to fire. With a shout, the painted figures dived into the river. Again the government forces took possession of only three abandoned vessels.

After proceeding another three or more *li* the van of the armada saw three medium-sized boats, propelled by eight men on each plying four oars. A dozen brigands, grouped around a captain who was seated in the prow of one of the vessels unfurled a red banner reading: *Naval Chieftain Li Jun the Turbulent River Dragon.*

On the craft to the left sat a captain holding an iron spear. Here, a green banner read: *Naval Chieftain Zhang Heng the Boat Flame.*

A bold figure stood on the craft to the right. Stripped to the waist and barefoot, he had several iron chisels tucked into his belt. In his hand was a bronze hammer. A black banner inscribed in silver read: *Chieftain Zhang Shun the White Streak in the Waves.*

"Thanks for delivering your boats to the marsh!" Zhang called.

The three vanguard generals shouted for their archers to shoot. Simultaneously with the twanging of the bowstrings, the men on the three craft somersaulted into the river.

It was early winter. None of the soldier and sailor conscripts on the government vessels cared to enter the icy water. While they hesitated, a volley of shots sounded from the signal cannon on the heights. Hundreds of little craft sped out from reeds on all sides like swarms of locusts. On each of these were four or five men and an unspecified cargo. The big paddle-wheelers tried unsuccessfully to ram them.

Obstructions, shoved in beneath the water, suddenly stopped the paddle-wheels from turning. Arrows shot from the archery towers were warded off by the men on the little craft with board shields.

They closed in on the big ships, caught their tillers with grappling hooks, hacked at the sailors at the wheels. Fifty or sixty brigands were already clambering up the lead ship. The frantic officers wanted to withdraw, but their retreat was cut off.

As the van vessels fought a confused battle, wild yells rose in the rear of the armada. Marshal Gao and Chief of Staff Wen, hearing the panic from their position in the center of the fleet, hurriedly sought to go ashore. A clamor of trumpets and drums shook the reeds. The soldiers on Gao's ship yelled: "We're leaking!" and jumped into the river.

Before and behind, all the paddle-wheelers were shipping water. Gao could see them sinking, while the little craft engulfed them like ants.

The government vessels were brand-new. How could they leak? Zhang Shun and a team of expert sailors had swum underwater with hammers and chisels and knocked holes in the bottoms, so that they were leaking like sieves.

Gao mounted the tiller deck in the stern and yelled for help to the boat behind. A figure spurted out of the river and leaped on the tiller deck. "I'll save you, Marshal," the man exclaimed. Gao stared. He had never seen him before.

The man strode forward. With one hand he grabbed Gao's head kerchief, with the other he grasped his belt. "Down you go," cried the swimmer. He tossed the Marshal into the river with a splash. How the mighty had fallen!

Two little craft came flying over, and Gao was hauled on board one. His captor was White Streak in the Waves Zhang Shun. In the water Zhang could take a man as easily as catching a turtle in a jar. He had only to extend his hand.

When the fleet was thrown into confusion, Qiu Yue, on the lead vessel, was anxious to escape. Suddenly, a naval officer emerged from among the outlaw sailors who had boarded the ship. Before Qiu could defend himself, the man bounded up to him and hacked him down with one sweep of his blade. The swordsman was Yang Lin the Elegant Panther. Xu Jing and Mei Zhan saw Qiu Yue die, and rushed to fight Yang Lin.

Four more lesser chieftains advanced on the generals: Zheng Tianshou the Fair- Faced Gentleman, Xue Yong the Sick Tiger, Li Zhong the Tiger-Fighting General, and Cao Zheng the Demon Carver. All came charging up from the rear.

It was too much. Xu Jing jumped overboard. To his surprise, someone was waiting for him beneath the waves, and he was taken.

Mei Zhan was stabbed in the thigh by Xue Yong, and fell into the hold. Eight chieftains were leading the outlaw naval forces. Three of these were still on their first boat. Li Yun the Black-Eyed Tiger, Tang Long the Golden-Coin Spotted Leopard, and Du Xing the Demon Face. Even if those government commandants had three heads and six arms apiece, they could never have got away. Song Jiang was in control of the Liangshan Marsh naval contingents. Lu Junyi the Magnate commanded the outlaw warriors on land.

At the time of the complete victory on the waterways, Lu was leading his army in an advance along the main road in front of Mount Liangshan. They ran into the government forces under Zhou Ang and Wang Huan.

Zhou Ang rode to the fore and shouted: "Rebellious bandit, do you recognize me?"

"You worthless officer," Lu yelled back. "Your death is before your eyes and you still don't know it!" He levelled his lance and galloped towards his foe.

Zhou Ang gave his mount full rein and raced to meet him, brandishing his battle-ax. They clashed on the road before the mountain.

Less than twenty rounds they fought, with neither the victor, when cries arose from the rear of the government troops. Outlaw forces, which had been lying in ambush in the forests on both sides of the road, had come charging out and were assailing the soldiers from all directions. Led by Guan Sheng and Qin Ming in the southeast, and by Lin Chong and Huyan Zhuo in the northeast, the brigand heroes closed in rapidly.

Commandants Xiang Yuanzhen and Zhang Kai couldn't stop them. They fought their way free and ran for their lives. Zhou Ang and Wang Huan dared not remain and give battle. Trailing their weapons, they turned their steeds and followed after the fleeing generals to the safety of Jizhou City. There, they quartered their troops and awaited further news.

After winning the naval engagement and capturing Gao Qiu, Song Jiang directed Dai Zong to transmit his urgent order: none of the prisoners were to be harmed. Chief of Staff Wen and the other officials still on the big paddle-wheelers, plus the singing boys and dancing girls and the rest of their company, were removed from the vessels. Then, trumpet calls signalled the outlaw forces to retire to the fortress with their captives.

Song Jiang, Wu Yong and Gongsun Sheng were in Loyalty Hall when Zhang Shun brought in the dripping Gao Qiu. Song Jiang hurried forward to meet him. He had fresh clothes of silks and satins brought for Gao to change into. Then he escorted the marshal to the interior of the hall and begged him to be seated in the central place of honor.

Dropping to his knees and murmuring that he deserved to die for his crimes, Song Jiang kowtowed. Gao hastily returned the courtesy. Song Jiang directed Wu Yong and Gongsun to help the marshal to his feet, and once again beseeched him to be seated. He instructed Yan Qing to transmit the order: "Whosoever, after today, kills any person shall be severely punished according to our military law."

One by one, the outlaw chieftains brought in their prisoners. Tong Wei and Tong Meng with Xu Jing; Li Jun and Zhang Heng with Wang Wente; Yang Xiong and Shi Xiu with Yang Wen; the three Ruan brothers with Li Congji; Zheng Tianshou, Xue Yong, Li Zhong and Cao Zheng with Mei Zhan; Yang Lin with the head of Qiu Yue; Li Yun, Tang Long and Du Xing with the heads of Ye Chun and Wang Jin; Xie Zhen and Xie Bao with Chief of Staff Wen, plus the singing boys and dancing girls and the entire theatrical company. Only four had escaped: Zhou Ang, Wang Huan, Xiang Yuanzhen and Zhang Kai.

Song Jiang directed that fresh clothes be provided to all, and that they be permitted to clean up a bit. He then invited everyone into the hall, and asked them be seated according to rank. He directed that the captured soldiers be allowed to return to Jizhou. For the singing boys and dancing girls and their company he provided a good boat, and told them to go back on their own.

Song Jiang ordered that cows and horses be slaughtered and that a feast be laid. To the strains of joyous music he rewarded his troops and, summoning his chieftains, presented them to Marshal Gao. He repeatedly toasted his guest, while Wu Yong and Gongsun kept their cups filled and Lu Junyi the Magnate and the others stood in attendance.

"I'm only a petty functionary with the tattoo of a criminal upon my face. I would never dare oppose our holy emperor," Song Jiang exclaimed. "I was forced to come here because of my many heavy offenses. Although I was twice approached with the emperor's benevolent forgiveness, the missions were perverted and corrupt. It's a long complicated story. Rescue me, Marshal, from the depths of the pit and let me see the sun again! Your kindness will be engraved upon my bones! I will pay for it with my very life!"

Gao looked around at the assembled gallants. Bold and heroic, intelligent and imposing, each and every one was handsomely dressed. Although they were no longer on the battle field, he was still half afraid of them, and he said: "Rest assured, Song Jiang. When I return to the court I will petition the emperor for a full amnesty. You will be pardoned and rewarded with an important post. Your warriors, high and low, will also enjoy the emperor's favor and become respectable officials."

Overjoyed, Song Jiang bowed and thanked the marshal. In the banquet that followed, although elegant dishes were lacking, there were mountains of meat and seas of wine. All of the chieftains, by turns, respectfully toasted their eminent guest of honor.

Gao's tongue was loosened by drunkenness, and he boasted: "I've been a wrestler since childhood. I'm the world's best."

Lu Junyi, also drunk, was irritated by Gao's bragging. He pointed at Yan Qing and said: "This young brother also knows how to wrestle. He won the East Sacred Mountain competitions three times."

Gao lumbered to his feet, took off his robe, and demanded that Yan wrestle with him. Because Song Jiang had been treating Gao respectfully as a marshal of the imperial court, the chieftains had tolerated his vainglorious talk. Now they saw his challenge to Yan Qing as a good chance to shut his mouth. They stood up.

"Good, good," they said. "Let's have the match." They swarmed noisily out of the hall.

Song Jiang was also in his cups. His mind was fuzzy. When the two contenders removed their outer garments and walked to the broad open porch, he ordered that a soft rug be put down.

The two struck poses, then Gao lunged. But Yan Qing's hands were swifter. He grabbed Gao and, with one twist, threw him so hard on his back that Gao lay stunned for several minutes, unable to rise. This grip is known as the life-saver. Song Jiang and Lu Junyi hurriedly raised Gao to his feet and helped him put on his clothes.

"You're a little drunk, Marshal," they said, smiling. "How can you wrestle in this condition? Please don't be offended."

Badly shaken, Gao returned to the banquet. He drank until far into the night, when he was assisted to quarters in the rear of the hall.

The next day, Song Jiang gave another banquet to soothe Gao after his shock of the previous night. The marshal announced he wished to leave.

"I have no intention of detaining Your Excellency," Song Jiang assured him. "May Heaven strike me dead if I'm deceiving you!"

"If, mighty warrior, you permit me to return to the capital, I and my whole family will be your guarantors before the throne. An amnesty will surely be granted and you will be given an important position. If I go back on my word, may I have no cover under Heaven and no hiding place on Earth and may I die pierced by spears and arrows!"

Song Jiang kowtowed in thanks.

"You may keep my generals here as hostage if you don't believe me.

"There's no need. How could I doubt a high noble like you? I'll have mounts prepared for them and send them back to their camps."

"We're grateful for your considerate treatment. And now I must go."

Song Jiang and his chieftains begged Gao to remain a bit longer. The next day they again feasted and talked until late, but on the third day the marshal insisted that he must leave. Song Jiang gave him a final farewell banquet.

"Send one of your more intelligent men along," Gao suggested. "He can accompany me when I petition the emperor and relate your circumstances here on Mount Liangshan. Then an imperial decree can be issued quickly."

Song Jiang wanted nothing more than an amnesty. After conferring with Wu Yong, he selected Xiao Rang the Master Hand for the mission.

"Better send Yue Ho the Iron Throat, too," Wu Yong recommended. "Let them both go."

"Although you trust me, warrior," said Marshal Gao, "I would like to leave Chief of Staff Wen here as a token of my word."

Song Jiang was very pleased. On the fourth day, he and Wu Yong and about twenty horsemen accompanied Gao and his commandants down the mountain and saw them off all the way to the Shore of Golden Sands, a distance of over twenty *li.* They bid the marshal farewell and returned to the fortress. From then on they watched for an emissary and listened for good tidings.

News of Gao's return preceded him, and Zhou Ang, Wang Huan, Xiang Yuanzhen, Zhang Kai, and Prefect Zhang Shuye came out of the city to greet him. After entering Jizhou, the marshal remained for several days. He instructed the local commandants to lead their troops back to camp to rest and await orders. Then, with General Zhou Ang, plus senior and junior officers, he set out for the Eastern Capital with his army, accompanied by Xiao Rang and Yue Ho. Prefect Zhang Shuye returned to Jizhou, where he maintained strict security precautions.

And because Gao took with him two representatives from Liangshan Marsh, gallant men met their sovereign in the ornate palace, bravos were entertained by high officials and lofty nobles. Their courage was sung at lavish banquets, they were conspicuous heroes amid the fiercest of generals.

On returning to the capital how did Gao stand as guarantor for Song Jiang and his cohorts when he petitioned for their amnesty? Read our next chapter if you would know.

CHAPTER 81

AT NIGHT YAN QING MEETS THE EMPEROR BY A TRICK

DAI ZONG RESCUES XIAO RANG

On Mount Liangshan the chieftains conferred. "I wonder what Gao Qiu will do," mused Song Jiang.

Wu Yong laughed. "He's a beady-eyed, slippery character, the kind who'll turn on you in a flash. He lost so many troops and wasted so much of the government's money and grain, when he gets back to the capital he's sure to claim that he's ill. He'll make some vague report to the emperor and order his army to rest. Xiao Rang and Yue Ho he'll keep under house arrest. So far as an amnesty is concerned, you're just hoping in vain."

"That's terrible! We won't get the amnesty, and we're harming two of our men besides."

"Pick two more clever fellows and send them to the capital with money and jewellery. Have them inquire what's going on and find a connection who can convey our wishes to the emperor. Then Gao Qiu won't be able to squirm out of it. That would be the best plan."

Yan Qing came forward. "Before we raised such a rumpus in the Eastern Capital last time, we managed to get acquainted with Li Shishi. I imagine she guessed pretty well what we're after. Since she's the emperor's mistress, of course he didn't suspect her of having anything to do with us. She probably simply said that we had found out where he went for his private pleasures and deliberately tried to frighten him. The incident was closed. Let me go to her again with money and jewellery. Pillow talk is the quickest way to get word to the emperor. It will be easy. One way or another, I'll persuade her."

"All right," said Song Jiang. "But you may run into danger."

"Let me go along and help," Dai Zong proposed.

"When we attacked Huazhou, you did a favor to Marshal Su," Zhu Wu the Miraculous Strategist reminded Song Jiang. "He's a good-hearted person. If he intervenes with the emperor for us, it will help a lot."

Song Jiang summoned Chief of Staff Wen and invited him to be seated. "Do you know Marshal Su Yuanjing?" Song Jiang queried.

"We were students together," Wen replied. "The emperor never goes a step without him. Su is extremely virtuous and generous, a kindly, amiable person."

"Frankly, we doubt whether Gao Qiu will really request the emperor for an amnesty when he returns to the capital. I met Marshal Su once when he was burning incense in Huazhou. I'd like to beg him to petition for us."

"If that's what you want, General, I'll write a letter which you can have delivered."

Pleased, Song Jiang called for paper and pen. At the same time, he lit fine incense, brought out the Heavenly Books of the Mystic Maid, prayed to Heaven, and cast bamboo prediction slips which revealed an extremely favorable omen. Then he drank with Dai Zong and Yan Qing to their successful journey.

Two large hampers were packed with gold and jewellery and silks, and the letter was concealed on the person of the emissaries, who bore also forged identity documents from the Kaifeng prefectural government. Both were disguised as bailiffs.

They took their leave, crossed at the Shore of the Golden Sands and headed for the Eastern Capital. Dai Zong carried an umbrella and wore a pack upon his back. Yan Qing, his bailiff's staff on his shoulder, toted the hampers, one at either end. His black gown was tucked up in front, a pouch hung at his waist. Puttees bound his legs to the knees, his feet were shod in hempen sandals. Except for pauses to eat or drink, the two halted only to sleep at night, pushing on again at dawn.

After many a day, they arrived at the Eastern Capital. Instead of going in directly, they circled round to the Wanshou Gate. A guard halted them. Yan Qing set down the hampers.

"What are you stopping us for?" he demanded in a countrified accent.

"Orders from headquarters. Men from Mount Liangshan may try to slip in with the crowds. At every gate all travellers must be questioned."

"You certainly know your duty," Yan Qing snickered, "questioning your own people! We have some business to do in Kaifeng Prefecture. I don't know how many thousands of times we've gone through this gate! You question us and turn a blind eye to the Mount Liangshan men strolling by right under your nose!"

He pulled out the forged documents and shoved them in the guard's face. "Can you recognize Kaifeng identity papers?"

The officer in charge of the gate shouted at the guard: "They've got Kaifeng papers. What are you questioning them for? Let them in!"

Yan Qing snatched back the documents, shoved them inside his gown, picked up the hampers and walked on. Dai Zong, with a cold laugh, followed.

They proceeded to the neighborhood in front of the Kaifeng government compound, sought out an inn, and retired.

The next day Yan Qing changed into a cloth gown, tied at the waist by a sash, and wore a hat at a rakish angle in the manner of a young idler. He took from the hamper a packet of gold and jewellery.

"I'm going to see Li Shishi, brother," he told Dai Zong. "If anything goes wrong hurry back to the stronghold."

Yan Qing proceeded to the courtesan's home. The carved railings were still there, and the green windows and vermilion doors had been repainted, prettier than before. He pushed aside the door curtain of spotted bamboo and entered.

The fragrance of incense greeted him. Pictures and calligraphy by famous artists had again been hung in the parlor; beneath the eaves were twenty or thirty trays of curiously shaped stones and miniature pines. Brocaded cushions were piled on couches of carved sandlewood.

Yan Qing coughed softly. A maid emerged, then informed the courtesan's "mama" that they had a caller. The bawd was startled to see him.

"What are you doing here again?"

"Please ask the lady to come out. I have something to say."

"The last time you called you got us into trouble and wrecked the house. If you've anything to say, say it."

"My words are for the lady's ears only."

Li Shishi, who had been listening outside the window, now entered. She was a lovely sight, her cheeks as rosy as dew-drenched apples, her waist as supple as a willow swaying in the breeze, a veritable Heavenly Maid, more beautiful than a Moon Fairy. Her skirt swirled as she glided lightly into the room.

Yan Qing stood up, placed the packet on the table, kowtowed four times before "Mama" Li, then twice before Leading Courtesan Li.

"You're too courteous," Shishi protested. "You shouldn't honor one so young."

Yan Qing rose and said: "Last time we gave you a fright. We've been uneasy ever since."

"Don't deceive me," exclaimed the girl. "You said you were Zhang Xian and that the other two were merchants from Shandong, and you created a terrible riot! Luckily, I was able to cajole the emperor. If it were anyone else but me, she and her whole establishment would have been ruined!"

"There were a couple of lines in that poem your magnate wrote which I wondered about:

Six time six in wild goose formation,
Plus eight times nine,
Waiting only for news
From the Golden Cock

I was about to question him, when the emperor arrived unexpectedly. Then the rumpus started, and I had no chance. Now that you're here, you can explain. Don't try to fool me. Tell me the truth. I won't be satisfied till you clear things up!"

"I'll tell it to you straight, but please don't be alarmed, Queen of Courtesans. That short swarthy fellow who sat at the head of the table was none other than Song Jiang the Defender of Justice. In the second seat, the fair-complexioned man with the mustache and goatee was the Small Whirlwind Chai Jin, descendant of Emperor Chai Shizong. The man dressed as a bailiff who stood opposite was Dai Zong the Miraculous Traveller. The one at the door who fought with Marshal Yang was Li Kui the Black Whirlwind. I myself am from Darning Prefecture, the Northern Capital. Everyone call me Yan Qing the Prodigy."

"Big Brother Song Jiang came to the capital to see you, and sent me first, disguised as Zhang Xian, to arrange it. He wasn't seeking to buy your smiles and charms, but wanted rather to reveal to you our story because he knows you're close to the emperor. We hope you'll tell His Majesty of our desire to act on Heaven's behalf, defend our country and preserve peace for the people. An early amnesty will prevent a further loss of lives. If our monarch will grant such a decree, you, my lady, will be the chief benefactor of the thousands of men on Mount Liangshan. Due to the interference of corrupt ministers, the true situation has been kept from the emperor. And so, we seek this path. We have no intention to frighten you, my lady. Big Brother has no proper gift to offer, only these small trinkets. He begs that you don't laugh at them, and accept."

Yan Qing opened the packet and spread upon the table gold and jewellery and precious plates. The bawd, who loved riches, was enchanted. She urged Shishi to accept, and led Yan Qing to a small private room and begged him to be seated. She served him fine delicacies and waited on him solicitously. Since no one knew when the emperor was likely to drop in, none of the young lords and rich young gentlemen ever dared to venture to the courtesans' house for tea. Li Shishi waited on Yan Qing personally.

"I'm a condemned criminal," he protested. "How dare I sit at the same table with the leading courtesan in the land?"

"Don't talk like that," exclaimed the girl. "You're a famous warrior. It's only because no good person has been able to speak up on behalf of you men that you've had to bury yourselves in the marsh."

"The first amnesty, which Marshal Chen brought, had no reassuring words, and he substituted cheap drink for the imperial wine. The second amnesty was phrased in such a way that it could be interpreted as excluding Song Jiang and Lu Junyi. For that reason, we didn't surrender. Next, Minister Tong came with an army, and we demolished them in two engagements. Finally, Marshal Gao mobilized thousands of people and built a great fleet and attacked. In three battles we wiped out more than half his forces. The marshal himself was captured and taken to our stronghold. Brother Song Jiang not only didn't kill him, but treated him royally and sent him back to the capital. All the prisoners were also let go. When he was on Mount Liangshan the marshal swore a great oath that he would petition the emperor for our amnesty. We dispatched two of our men with him—Xiao Rang the Master Hand and Yue Ho the Iron Throat. But it looks like the marshal has them confined in his residency and won't let them out. He'll never admit to the emperor that his losses were so heavy."

The girl agreed. "He wasted money and grain and the lives of his officers and men. He wouldn't dare tell the emperor the truth. I heard all about it. Let's have a few cups together and discuss this thing."

"I'm a very poor drinker."

"You've had a long, hard journey. Here you can relax. We'll drink some wine and then decide what to do."

Yan Qing couldn't get out of it. He had to match the courtesan cup for cup.

Li Shishi had made her start in life as a prostitute. She was a temperamental girl, and when she saw that Yan Qing was a fine figure of a man and an eloquent speaker she took an immediate liking to him. As they drank, she began dropping hints, which grew increasingly provocative. Yan Qing was a clever fellow, and he understood perfectly. But he was a dedicated warrior, determined to put through Song Jiang's grand plan. How could he respond?

"I've heard you're an excellent musician, brother," said the courtesan. "I'd love to hear you play."

"I have studied music a bit," Yan Qing admitted. "But I wouldn't have the nerve to perform in your presence, my lady."

"I'll play first, then, and you listen."

Shishi directed a maid to bring her flute. She took the instrument from its brocaded bag and blew softly. Truly a lovely sound, soaring into the clouds and seeping into the rocks.

Yan Qing was lavish in his praise. When Shishi had finished she handed him the flute.

"Now play something for me."

Yan Qing wanted to win her esteem. He accepted the instrument and performed with all his skill. The girl was enchanted.

"I didn't realize you were such a talented flutist!"

She took up a lute and played a little tune. The notes lingered in the air like a chorus of jade chimes, like a duet of orioles.

Yan Qing bowed his thanks and said: "I'll sing a song for your amusement, my lady." He had a beautiful voice, and he enunciated the lyrics clearly. At the conclusion of his song, he bowed again.

The girl raised her cup and drank to him. She thanked him in her most seductive tones. With lowered head, he murmured an acknowledgment. After a few more drinks, the courtesan addressed him with a smile.

"I hear that your body is artistically tattooed. Would you let me have a look?"

Yan Qing laughed. "It's true I have a few decorations. But how dare I disrobe in my lady's presence?"

"With a gallant gentleman like you, who worries about such things?"

At her insistent pleas, Yan Qing finally removed his robe. Shishi was delighted. She ran her jade fingers over the designs. The young man hastily put his robe on again.

Again she drank with him. Her suggestiveness was quite open now. Yan Qing was afraid she'd make a move he'd find hard to repel. Suddenly, he had an idea.

"How old is my lady this year?" he asked.

"I'll be twenty-seven."

"I'm two years younger, twenty-five. Since you're kind enough to give me your affection, I'd like to acknowledge you as my foster big sister."

Yan Qing dropped to his knees. Like pushing a golden mountain, like a toppling jade pillar, he kowtowed eight times.

This stymied the girl's wicked inclinations and enabled the grand plan to go forward. Anyone else so beguiled with drink and sexual allure would have brushed the grand plan aside. But Yan Qing had a will of iron. He was a real man!

Then Yan Qing asked "Mama" Li to come in, and he kowtowed to her too, and acknowledged her as his foster mother.

"Stay here with us," said Shishi. "There's no need to live at an inn."

"That's very kind of you. I'll go get my things."

"Don't keep me waiting, now!"

"The inn's not far. I'll be right back."

Yan Qing took his leave, went to the inn, and related to Dai Zong what had happened.

"Excellent," said the Miraculous Traveller. "I'm only afraid she'll arouse you and you won't be able to control yourself."

"A man who can be diverted by drink or sex when he's out on a mission is no better than a beast! May I die beneath ten thousand sword cuts if I let that happen to me!"

Dai Zong laughed. "We're both men of honor. No need to swear."

"But there is. You surely doubt me."

"Just go quickly. At a propitious time push the thing through and hurry back. Don't make me wait too long. We have to deliver that letter to Marshal Su."

Yan Qing packed some odd bits of gold and jewellery and silks and returned to Shishi's house. He gave half to "Mama" Li and distributed the rest among the servants and attendants. They all were very pleased. Quarters were prepared for him in a room adjacent to the parlor, and he moved in. Everyone fondly addressed him as "Young Uncle."

By fortunate coincidence that evening a man came and said: "The emperor is coming tonight." On hearing this, Yan Qing went to Li Shishi.

"Do me a favor, sister," he pleaded. "Arrange for me to meet the emperor so that I may request his imperial pardon in writing for my crimes. You'll be conferring a blessing."

"I can do that. Move him with your eloquence. I've no doubt he'll grant it."

Gradually, darkness fell. The moon was hazy, the air was filled with the fragrance of flowers and the musky scent of orchids. Accompanied by a young eunuch, the sovereign arrived through the secret tunnel at the rear door of the courtesan's house. He was dressed in the white garb of a scholar. Seating himself in the anteroom, he directed that the front and rear gates be locked and the lamps and candles brightly lit. Li Shishi, formally dressed and coifed, presented herself before his majesty. She curtsied, and they exchanged courtesies.

"Put on something more comfortable and entertain me," said the emperor.

Shishi did so, and led the monarch into her chamber. A table had already been laid with delicacies. The courtesan lifted her cup and urged him to drink.

"Come, beloved," he said happily, "sit beside me." He was obviously in a good mood.

"A cousin of mine, who has been wandering around, just arrived today," said Shishi. "He longs to see Your Majesty, but dares not present himself. He's asked me to make the request."

"Since he's your cousin, why not?"

The courtesan summoned Yan Qing. He dropped to his knees and kowtowed. The emperor was pleased by his handsome appearance. Shishi directed Yan Qing to entertain the sovereign with some flute music while he was drinking his wine. After a while she played the lute, then she told Yan Qing to sing. The young man again kowtowed before the monarch.

"I only know some naughty tunes, which I wouldn't dare sing!"

"Exactly what I need to cheer me," said the emperor. "I'm here privately in this house of pleasure. Go right ahead."

Yan Qing took up a pair of ivory clapper sticks, bowed again to the sovereign, and said to Shishi: "If I go off key, sister, please correct me." He cleared his throat and, keeping time with the clappers, sang:

> No news from him
> Since he left our village,
> Constant longing
> Tears at my heart.
> The swallows are gone,
> The flowers fade,
> In just one spring
> My waist grows thin.
> Faithless lover,
> When will he return?
> It would have been better
> If we never had met!
> In dreams we're together,
> But then I awake,
> Outside my window
> Orioles sing in the dawn.

Yan Qing was in excellent voice, and the emperor, delighted, bade him sing again. The young man kowtowed.

"I have another tune that's rather special."

"Good. Let's hear it." With feeling, Yan Qing sang:

> Hear my plea, hear my plea,
> Who knows how I've wandered,
> Who knows!
> In Heaven and on Earth
> The innocent oft are wronged,

In the Fiery Pit, 'tis said,
Are hearts that are loyal and true,
Loyal and true!
Surely the day will come
When great benevolence
Will be by men repaid!

"What's the meaning of this song?" asked the startled monarch.

Weeping bitterly, Yan Qing prostrated himself on the ground. The emperor was puzzled.

"If you'll tell me what's troubling you, perhaps I can find a solution."

"I've committed towering crimes! I dare not address my sovereign!"

"I forgive you. You may speak freely."

"All my life I've been a wanderer. While travelling with merchants in Shandong and passing by Liangshan Marsh, we were captured and taken to the bandit Stronghold. There I stayed for three full years. Only recently did I escape and return to the capital. Although I've seen Cousin Shishi, I dare not walk the streets for fear that someone will recognize me and report me to the police. How would I be able to explain?"

"He's been miserable," Li Shishi added. "You must help him, Your Majesty!"

"That's easy," the emperor laughed. "No one would dare molest the young cousin of Leading Courtesan Li."

Yan Qing gave the girl a significant glance. Shishi pouted and said to the monarch: "All I want is your written pardon. Then my cousin won't have to worry."

"How can I write it? I don't have my royal seal here."

"A pardon in your own hand is better than any document with a seal. Save my cousin! You'll be doing me a great favor!"

Unable to resist her blandishments, the sovereign called for pen and paper. "Mama" Li brought the writing materials from the study and Yan Qing ground the ink stick on the writing slab. The girl handed the emperor the ivory brush-pen with purple bristles. In a flourishing script he commenced to write on the imperial yellow paper, then paused.

"I'm afraid I've forgotten your name."

"I'm called Yan Qing."

"Ah." The emperor wrote: *Xuan Ho the Taoist Sovereign does hereby pardon Yan Qing of all crimes.* Let no official arrest or question him. At the bottom, he signed his name.

Yan Qing respectfully received the document and kowtowed. Shishi raised her cup and drank her thanks.

"Since you've been in Liangshan Marsh, you must know the situation there," said the monarch.

"Song Jiang and his band have *Act in Heaven's Behalf* written on their banner and their hall is called *Loyalty Hall.* They never attack a government seat or harm the people. They kill only corrupt and slanderous officials. They long for an early amnesty so that they can devote themselves to serving our country."

"But I sent them amnesties twice. Why did they reject them and refuse to surrender?"

"The first one contained no words of comfort, and the emissary substituted cheap local brew for the imperial wine. The second was read in a manner that excluded Song Jiang. The brigands suspected a trick, and that changed everything. Minister Tong led an army against them, but after two engagements only a few escaped with their lives. Marshal Gao organized a huge civilian force to build ships of war, and attacked, but he didn't gain so much as a broken arrow. In three engagements the bandits slaughtered his men and cut his army in two and captured the marshal. He vowed he would get them an amnesty, and they let him go, sending two of their men with him and keeping Chief of Staff Wen as hostage."

The emperor sighed. "I knew nothing of any of this. Tong Guan said his troops couldn't stand the summer heat; that's why they returned. Gao said he had come back to the capital temporarily because he was ill."

"Although you are a wise sovereign," said Shishi, "you live deep inside the palace. How can you know when dishonest ministers conceal the truth?"

Again the monarch sighed. It was growing late. Yan Qing took his pardon, kowtowed and withdrew. The emperor and Shishi went to bed, where they revelled in intimate union.

The monarch left with the waiting young eunuch before dawn. Yan Qing got up and, on the excuse that he had some matters to attend to early in the morning, went back to the inn. He told Dai Zong everything that had been said, word for word.

"It's developing very well," said the Miraculous Traveller. "Now, let's deliver the letter to Marshal Su."

"After we've eaten."

The two had breakfast, filled a hamper with gold and jewellery and silks, took the letter, and headed for Marshal Su's residency. They asked one of the neighbors whether he was home.

"The marshal hasn't returned from the palace yet," they were told.

"Why not?" said Yan Qing. "There are no audiences in session at this hour."

"He's our sovereign's closest companion. The emperor never goes a step without him. He may come home early, he may come home late. It's hard to say."

"There's the marshal now," someone exclaimed.

Very pleased, Yan Qing said to Dai Zong: "Brother, wait for me outside the residency. I'm going to speak to him."

Approaching was a sedan-chair carried by porters in brocaded garments and ornate hats. Yan Qing knelt in its path.

"I have a letter to present to the marshal," he called.

Su looked at him. "Come with me," he directed. Yan Qing followed the sedan-chair into the residency compound. It halted before a large hall. The marshal got down, entered an adjoining study and seated himself. He ordered Yan Qing to come in.

"On whose business are you?"

"I've come from Shandong with a letter from Chief of Staff Wen."

"Which Chief of Staff Wen?"

Yan Qing presented the letter. The marshal looked at the envelope.

"I couldn't imagine who it was! Why, it's Wen Huanzhang, my childhood schoolmate!" he opened the letter and read:

With hands washed clean, kowtowing a hundred times, I write this missive to the Respected Marshal. It's thirty years since I played in your home as a child. Recently, Marshal Gao appointed me Chief of Staff of his army. Unfortunately, he wouldn't heed my advice, and was defeated three times in succession. I'm ashamed to mention it. We both were captured and bound. But Song Jiang, in his benevolence, would not permit us to be harmed.

With Xiao Rang and Yue Ho—two men from Mount Liangshan, the marshals has now returned to the capital, promising to seek an amnesty. I have been left as hostage. I pray that you urge the emperor to pardon the crimes of Song Jiang and his cohorts, and let them make recompense through meritorious deeds. This will benefit not only our country, but the entire world! Your credit will resound through the ages!

Rescue me and allow me to live! I anxiously await your reply and trust you will understand.

In deepest gratitude, respectfully, Wen Huanzhang
The __ day of the first month, spring,
of the fourth year of the Xuan He Period

Marshal Su was astounded. "Who are you?" he demanded.

"Yan Qing the Prodigy from Liangshan Marsh." The young brigand went out for the hamper and brought it into the study. "I waited on you several times when you were burning incense in Huazhou, Marshal. How could you have forgotten? Brother Song Jiang sends you these paltry gifts as a small token of his esteem. He prays every day that you will save us. His sole desire is that the marshal will obtain our amnesty. If you can persuade the emperor to grant one, you will be the great benefactor of the thousands of men on Mount Liangshan. The time for my mission is limited. I must go back now."

Yan Qing kowtowed and left the residency. Marshal Su directed that the gifts be put away. He already had an idea.

Dai Zong and the Prodigy returned to the inn and Yan Qing said: "The first two parts of our mission succeeded pretty well. But Xiao Rang and Yue Ho are still detained in Gao's residency. How are we going to get them out?"

"We'll dress as bailiffs again and wait in front of Gao's place. When some officer comes out, we'll bribe him to let us see them. Once we've made contact, we'll decide what to do."

The two disguised themselves, took some money, and proceeded towards Taiping Bridge. At the gate of the residency they kept watch. Soon, a young captain came swaggering forth. Yan Qing approached him and bowed.

"Who are you?" the captain demanded brusquely.

"Shall we go to the tea-house where we can talk?"

Dai Zong was waiting in a private room, and the three sat down together and had tea. Yan Qing spoke.

"I'll come to the point. Marshal Gao brought two men back with him from Mount Liangshan. One is called Yue Ho. He's relative of this brother here, and I'd like to see him. So we're asking your assistance."

"I don't want to hear it! I don't know anything about what goes on in there!"

Dai Zong took from his sleeve a large silver ingot and placed it on the table. "There's no need for him to leave the residency," he said. "Just let us speak to him and you can have this ingot."

Stirred by the sight of the silver, the captain admitted: "Those two are there, all right. But the marshal has ordered that they must remain in the rear garden. If I let him out to talk to you, you must keep your word and give me the ingot."

"Naturally," said Dai Zong.

The officer hurriedly went back to the residency, while Yan Qing and Dai Zong waited in the tea-house. In less than half a watch, he returned, all in a flurry.

"First give me the silver. I've got Yue Ho in one of the side buildings."

Dai Zong whispered something in Yao Qing's ear and handed the captain the ingot. Yan Qing went with the officer to the side building and saw Yue Ho.

"Talk quickly, you two, then go," said the captain.

"I'm here with Dai Zong," Yan Qing said to Yue Ho softly. "We're planning to rescue you and Xiao Rang."

"They've got us in the rear garden. The wall is high and they've hidden the ladders. How are you going to do it?"

"Is there a tree anywhere near the wall?"

"There are large willows all along one side."

"Tonight, listen for a cough. We'll be outside and throw over the ends of two ropes. Tie them to the willows, and we'll pull our ends tight. Then you and Xiao Rang climb over. At the fourth watch. Don't be late."

"What are you so gabby about?" the captain called. "Go back inside and be quick about it!"

Yue Ho returned to the garden and quietly informed Xiao Rang. Yan Qing swiftly reported to Dai Zong. All waited for night to fall.

On the street Yan Qing and Dai Zong bought two thick lengths of rope and concealed them under their robes. They wandered to the rear of the residency to get the lay of the land. They found a stream and two empty boats moored not far from the bank. They hid in these craft until they heard the watchman's drum sound four times.

The two went ashore, circled round to the rear wall, and coughed. From within they heard an answering cough. Both sides were ready. Yao Qing threw over the rope ends. Giving them time to be secured, he and Dai Zong pulled their ends tight.

Yue Ho was the first to climb out, and he was followed by Xiao Rang. When both had slid down, they tossed the ropes into the garden. The four hid themselves in the boats until daybreak. Then they proceeded to the inn and knocked on the door. They packed their luggage, cooked and ate breakfast, paid the bill and left. As soon as the city gate was opened, they swarmed through and headed for Mount Liangshan to report their news. And if those four hadn't returned to the stronghold, would Marshal Su have petitioned the throne and obtained a full amnesty for Song Jiang and his men? Truly, when a high official reads a royal edict, heroes kneel before the imperial presence. How did Marshal Su appeal to the emperor? Read our next chapter if you would know.

CHAPTER 82

THE MOUNT LIANGSHAN FORTRESS DISTRIBUTES ITS WEALTH

SONG JIANG AND ALL OF HIS MEN ARE AMNESTIED

When Yan Qing didn't return that night, Li Shishi became suspicious. Marshal Gao's trusted subordinate, delivering breakfast to Xiao Rang and Yue Ho the next day, found the room empty. He hurriedly informed the chief steward. The steward searched the garden, and discovered the two ropes tied to the willow. The captives had escaped. He had no choice but to report to the marshal. Gao Qiu's gloom deepened at this startling news. He secluded himself in his residency, claiming he was ill.

The following day the Taoist Sovereign held court at the fifth watch and received the homage of his officials. He seated himself on the throne in the Hall of Culture and Virtue.

"Are the civil and military officials all assembled?' he asked.

"They await outside the hall, each in his respective group, civil on the left, military on the right," replied the chief of ceremonies.

The emperor ordered that the curtain be rolled up and that Tong Guan, Chancellor of Military Affairs, come forward.

"That punitive expedition of a hundred thousand troops you led personally against Liangshan Marsh, was it victorious or defeated?" queried the sovereign.

Tong Guan knelt and replied: "It wasn't that I didn't do my utmost! But it was the height of summer, and the soldiers weren't used to the surroundings and the climate. Many fell ill. Two or three out of ten died. With our forces dwindling, all I could do was bring them home for further training. Unfortunately on the way back more than half died of heat prostration. Your Majesty directed the bandits to surrender but, filled with false pride, they haughtily refused. Then Gao Qiu went after them with a naval armada, but he sickened and had to return."

"Inept, treacherous minister! Your failure to tell the truth has caused our nation great damage. How is it that in only two engagements the bandits utterly demolished the imperial forces! And that rascal Gao Qiu, after wasting who knows how much of the province's money and grain, not only lost many ships and a considerable number of troops, but was personally captured and taken to the bandits' mountain stronghold! Instead of killing him, Song Jiang and his lieutenants treated him courteously and let him go. Our royal orders were disgraced and made a laughing stock!

"I have heard that Song Jiang and his men neither attack local governments nor harm the people. They seek only an amnesty so that they can serve the country. Officials like you, who are jealous of the talents of others and deliberately conceal the facts, are the lowest of vermin! A fine Chancellor of Military Affairs! You should be ashamed! I ought to have you executed to appease the indignation of the people, but I'll spare you for the time being!"

The emperor shouted at Tong Guan to fall back. Silently, the chancellor withdrew to a side. The sovereign addressed his Hanlin Academy scholars.

"Prepare my personal imperial decree, and send it with a high official, ordering Song Jiang and his men to return from Mount Liangshan."

Marshal Su Yuanjing came forward and knelt before the throne. "Although I have no talent, I would be glad to go."

The sovereign was very pleased. "I'll write the document myself," he exclaimed. He ordered that a table be brought and the paper be spread.

After penning the decree, he called for the imperial seal and impressed it on the document. He directed the Keeper of the Royal Stores to draw thirty-six gold slabs and seventy-two slabs of silver, thirty-six bolts of red satin and seventy-two bolts of green satin, plus one hundred and eight bottles of yellow-sealed imperial wine, and entrust them to the marshal. He also gave Su twenty-four bolts of cloth for coats and linings and a banner proclaiming the imperial amnesty in letters of gold, and ordered him to set forth on the morrow.

The marshal took his leave of the emperor and left the Hall of Culture and Virtue. Court concluded, the officials withdrew, and Chancellor of Military Affairs Tong Guan slunk back to his residence in disgrace. He dared not attend any more royal audiences, and feigned illness. When Marshal Gao heard what had happened, he was terrified. He too was afraid to appear before the sovereign.

Marshal Su had the imperial wine and other gifts packed and shouldered by porters. Mounting his horse, he left the city. Officials saw him and his entourage out of the Nanxun Gate. The party proceeded towards Jizhou, flying the imperial banner with its inscription of gold.

Meanwhile, Yan Qing, Dai Zong, Xiao Rang and Yue Ho returned through the night to the stronghold and reported to Song Jiang and the other chieftains. Yan Qing showed them the pardon the emperor had personally written by hand.

"Good news is sure to come," said Wu Yong.

Song Jiang burned fine incense, brought out the Heavenly books given him by the Mystic Maid of Ninth Heaven, and raised his head and prayed. When he cast the divining sticks they revealed an extremely lucky omen.

"We're sure to succeed," cried Song Jiang. He requested Dai Zong and Yan Qing to go once more to the city, check on developments and report back immediately, so that adequate preparations could be made. A few days later, the two returned. "The emperor has entrusted Marshal Su with his royal decree," they said. "The marshal is also bringing imperial wine, gold and silver slabs, satin of red and green, and cloth for coats and linings. He's on his way to proclaim the amnesty and will be here soon."

Song Jiang was overjoyed. From Loyalty Hall he busily issued a series of orders: Men were to set up twenty-four shelters along the road from Liangshan Marsh to Jizhou, all decorated with bunting and filled with musical instruments. There, musicians—hired from neighboring shires —would play to welcome the procession. A lesser chieftain was to be in charge of each of the shelters. Others were sent out to buy fruit and sea delicacies and wine and tidbits to serve as snacks.

Marshal Su and his entourage, winding their way towards Mount Liangshan with the amnesty, reached Jizhou. Prefect Zhang Shuye came out to welcome them, and settled them in the hostel for officials. Politely, he raised his cup of greeting.

"Twice before the royal court sent amnesties. It was a serious loss to the country that they were not effectuated because their delivery was entrusted to the wrong persons. This mission of yours, Marshal, will surely be of great benefit."

"His Majesty has recently learned that the band on Mount Liangshan are interested primarily in righteousness. They neither raid the prefectures nor harm good people. They stress acting in Heaven's behalf. And so His Majesty has dispatched me with his hand-written decree, plus gifts of thirty-six slabs of gold, seventy-two slabs of silver, thirty-six bolts of red satin, seventy-two bolts of green satin, a hundred and eight bottles of yellow-sealed imperial wine, and twenty-four bolts of cloth for coats and linings, to deliver an amnesty. Do you think the gifts too trifling?"

"It's not a question of gifts with these people. They want to serve the nation faithfully so as to earn fame for their posterity. If only you'd been able to come earlier, Marshal, our country wouldn't have had to suffer such heavy losses in officers and soldiers, money and grain. Once these warriors return to the fold they certainly will perform meritorious deeds for the emperor."

"Can I trouble you to go to the fortress, Prefect, and tell them to prepare to receive my mission? I will wait here."

"Of course."

The governor mounted his horse and left the city with a dozen men. At the foot of the mountain he was met by lesser chieftains, who at once reported the news to the stronghold Song Jiang hastened down and escorted Prefect Zhang to Loyalty Hall.

"Congratulations," Zhang exclaimed. "The emperor has dispatched Marshal Su with his personally hand-written amnesty, together with valuable gifts. The marshal is already at Jizhou. Prepare, warrior, to welcome the imperial decree."

Pressing his fingers to his brow in a gesture of delight, Song Jiang said: "He is bringing us new life!" He begged Zhang to dine with him.

"I'd love to," said the prefect, "but the marshal would be annoyed if I were slow in getting back."

"At least have a drink, and accept these paltry things—I can hardly call them gifts." Song Jiang presented gold and silver on a platter.

"I wouldn't dare."

"A mere trifle, why refuse? Not nearly enough to express our thanks, but do take them as a small token of appreciation. Once the mission is completed, we shall offer something more substantial."

"I'm deeply grateful for your good intentions. But please keep them here, for now. I can always call for them later."

Prefect Zhang was absolutely incorruptible. He made strict demands upon himself.

Song Jiang directed his generals Wu Yong and Zhu Wu, plus Xiao Rang and Yue Ho, to escort Prefect Zhang to Jizhou, and there see Marshal Su. On the day after the morrow all chieftains, big and small, would wait to greet the emissary thirty *li* from the fortress.

Wu Yong and the others travelled through the night to return the prefect to Jizhou, and called on the marshal the next morning at the hostel for officials. They kowtowed and remained kneeling before him. Su directed them to rise and be seated. Deferentially, the four replied they wouldn't dare. The marshal asked their names.

"I am called Wu Yong," said the brigand military advisor, "and these are Zhu Wu, Xiao Rang and Yue Ho. We have been sent by brother Song Jiang to welcome Your Excellency."

"Why, Master Wu, how nice to see you again! It's been years since last we parted in Huazhou. Who would have thought that we'd meet again today'. I am fully aware of the fidelity and righteousness in your hearts. Corrupt ministers have used their authority to conceal the true facts from the emperor. But now he knows, and has dispatched me with his personal amnesty, imperial wine and various gifts. You need have no hesitation about accepting them."

The four kowtowed their thanks and said: "It is entirely due to the marshal's kindness that we crude rustics living in a mountain wilderness have the good fortune to meet Your Excellency and receive His Majesty's benevolence! It shall be engraved always on our hearts and bones! We don't know how we can ever repay!"

Prefect Zhang entertained them that night at a banquet.

Early the next morning in Jizhou three carts were laden with burning incense. A group of porters bore the imperial wine in a phoenix and dragon decorated case. Another group carried gold and silver slabs, and silks and satins of red and green. A miniature pavilion housed the emperor's decree. Marshal Su rode beside it as the procession headed east. Prefect Zhang, also on horseback, followed, with Wu Yong and the other three riding in his wake. Horsemen leading the way in the tightly packed assembly carried the gold-lettered imperial yellow banner, preceded by troops with fluttering pennants beating golden drums.

For nearly ten *li* they advanced along the winding road, and soon reached the first shelter. Marshal Su noted the gay bunting and the tootling musicians playing a welcoming tune. A few score li beyond they arrived at another decorated shelter. Ahead they saw, amid swirling incense, Song Jiang and Lu Junyi kneeling in the road, and behind them, also on their knees in neat ranks, all the other chieftains, big and small, waiting to welcome the imperial decree.

"Let everyone mount," the marshal directed.

They rode together to the water's edge, where many boats ferried them to the Shore of Golden Sands. Above and below the three passes music soared to the heavens. Soldiers, celebrants, in clouds of incense, flowed in long lines to Loyalty Hall.

There the riders dismounted, and the incense and the imperial decree in the miniature pavilion were carried into the hall. In the center stood three ceremonial tables skirted with imperial yellow gauze of dragon and phoenix design. The decree was placed on the central table before the tablet representing the emperor, which was in the exact middle of the room. The gold and silver slabs were set on the left table, the red and green satin on the right, while the imperial wine and the cloth for the coats and linings were placed before the tables on the floor. From a golden burner rose the fragrance of fine incense.

Song Jiang and Lu Junyi escorted Marshal Su and Prefect Zhang to the seats of honor. Xiao Rang and Yue Ho stood on the left, Pei Xuan and Yan Qing stood on the right. Lu and the others knelt before the dignitaries. At Pei Xuan's command, all kowtowed. Xiao Rang then read the decree:

Imperial Edict: From the day I assumed the throne I have ruled with virtue and righteousness, changing the world by ceremonial rectitude, bringing peace through punishments and rewards. Never have I ceased seeking good ministers or loving the populace. Broadly have I dispensed charity, endeavoring to bestow happiness equally upon all. The people enjoy my benevolence, even infants know my concern.

Song Jiang, Lu Junyi and their men are loyal and righteous, and do not engage in violent persecution. For a long time they have wished to return and display their gratitude. Although they have committed crimes, it was not without reason. In view of their sincerity, I sympathize with them deeply. I have directed Marshal Su to deliver my amnesty to Song Jiang and the other offenders presently residing in Liangshan Marsh. I bestow also on Song Jiang and his higher chieftains thirty-six slabs of gold and thirty-six bolts of red satin; to his lesser chieftains I give seventy-two slabs of silver and seventy-two bolts of green satin. From the date of this decree let them cast doubt aside, return quickly and submit. Important tasks will be given them.

Let this document be proclaimed so that all may know.
The second month, __ day, spring,
in the fourth year of Xuan He

"Long live the emperor!," shouted Song Jiang and his cohorts. They fell to their knees and kowtowed. As Pei Xuan called the roll, Marshal Su dispensed the gifts. The imperial wine was opened and poured into a huge silver tureen. From this it was ladled out, warmed and placed in a silver wine pot. Marshal Su filled a golden goblet and addressed the chieftains.

"On orders from our sovereign I have brought this imperial wine as a gift. Fear it not, warriors. See, I drink before you."

He drained the cup, and the chieftains voiced their thanks. Su filled it again and presented it to Song Jiang. Song dropped to his knees and drank. Lu Junyi, Wu Yong and Gongsun Sheng were each in turn handed the goblet. Finally, Su toasted all one hundred and eight chieftains together.

Song Jiang directed that the wine be poured, and invited Marshal Su to be seated in the center of the hall. The chieftains paid their respects. Song Jiang then approached.

"I had the honor of meeting you at the temple on the West Sacred Mountain. I'm profoundly grateful for your kindness. Thanks to your efforts with those close to the emperor, my men and I are able to see the sun again. We shall never forget."

"I knew how loyal you all are, and that you act in Heaven's behalf, but I didn't realize you were being wronged. And so I dared not put in a word for you before. I'm sorry for the delay. It wasn't until I received the letter from Chief of Staff Wen and your generous gift that I began to learn what was going on. While chatting with emperor in Mantled in Incense Hall one day I managed to tell him. He checked and found what I told him was correct. The following day, while holding court in the Hall of Culture and Virtue in the presence of all his officials, he severely castigated Chancellor of Military Affairs Tong Guan, and blamed Marshal Gao for having repeatedly failed. He called for his writing equipment, personally penned an amnesty, and entrusted me to bring it and present you and your chieftains with gifts. I hope you will wind up your business here quickly and report to the capital. You must show yourselves worthy of the emperor's benevolence."

All were very pleased and respectfully expressed their thanks. Song Jiang invited Chief of Staff Wen to join them. The happy reunion between Su and Wen spread joy throughout the hall. Wen and Prefect Zhang were seated opposite Marshal Su, and everyone took his place at banquet tables according to rank. Many toasts were drunk, while outside the band vigorously played. Although the fare was not elaborate, there were mountains of meat and seas of wine. All drank heavily, and had to be supported to their quarters to rest.

The following day, they feasted again, talking of things old and new, and chatting about their aspirations. On the third day they dined once more, and took the marshal on a tour of the mountain. They returned to their quarters at dusk, many sodden with wine. After several such days, though Song Jiang and his chieftains were reluctant to let him go, the marshal said he must leave for the capital.

"You don't understand," he explained. "It's been some time since I delivered the amnesty. If you heroes return promptly, all will be well. If you don't, false and jealous ministers will very likely gossip."

"We were hoping you'd stay a few days more," said Song Jiang, "but since you feel you must go, of course we won't detain you. Let's have one more day of drinking, and we'll see you off early tomorrow morning."

The chieftains joined in a merry feast, and again voiced their thanks in the course of toasts. Marshal Su spoke flattering and reassuring words. They caroused until night.

The next morning horses and carts were readied. Song Jiang brought gold and jewels on a platter to the marshal's quarters, and respectfully presented them. Only after Song Jiang's repeated urging did Su accept and place them in his chest of clothing. His luggage packed, his horse saddled, the marshal prepared to set forth.

Those returning with him were given food and wine by Zhu Wu and Yue Ho, and lavishly rewarded with money and clothing material, to their great delight. Gold and valuables were also presented to Chief of Staff Wen and Prefect Zhang. They accepted only after Song Jiang insisted. He ordered that Wen depart with Marshal Su.

To the beat of golden drums and the trilling of fifes the chieftains accompanied the marshal down the mountain, proceeding a distance of thirty *li* after crossing the river at the Shore of Golden Sands. There all dismounted and raised their wine cups in a farewell toast.

"When you see the emperor, Marshal, please give him an excellent report," said Song Jiang.

"Rest assured, warrior. Wind up your affairs and come to the capital as soon as possible. When your army nears the city be sure to send someone on ahead to notify me. I'll inform the emperor and dispatch a welcoming party. We want to do this in proper style."

"Excellency, I beg your indulgence. Wang Lun built the mountain stronghold in this small marsh of ours, and he was succeeded by Chao Gai. I, in turn, have ruled here for many years. Damage to the neighboring populace has been considerable. For the next ten days I'd like to distribute our wealth among them. Once that's done we'll hasten to the capital without further delay. Would you please convey this to the emperor so that he'll allow us a bit more time."

Marshal Su assented. He bid them farewell and, with his entourage, headed for Jizhou.

Song Jiang and his men returned to the stronghold. In Loyalty Hall the assembly drum was beaten. As the chieftains seated themselves all the officers gathered. Song Jiang addressed them.

"Brothers, ever since Wang Lun established the fortress and Chao Gai strengthened it this place has flourished. Many years have passed since you brothers rescued me at Jiangzhou and chose me as leader. Today we've been amnestied and have seen the face of the sun again. Soon we shall go to the capital, serve our country, win prestige and privileges for our wives and children, and enjoy the blessings of peace. Those of you who have things which should go in the storerooms deliver them there for our common use. The remaining property shall be divided equally among us in a righteous manner with no contention.

"We hundred and eight are all stars. We live and die together. The emperor's amnesty frees us of any crimes. Soon we shall go to the capital and see His Majesty. We must be worthy of his benevolence. As to you other officers, some of you came with the intention of joining us, some simply followed others, some are army officers who lost their commands, others were captured. If you wish to go with us to the capital, you may enroll. If you don't, you may resign. I will pay you off and you can return to civilian life."

On Song Jiang's instructions Pei Xuan and Xiao Rang prepared two registers. After discussion among the members of the three armies four or five thousand men resigned. Song Jiang gave them money and gifts and sent them on their way. Those who wished to remain registered for duty.

The next day Song Jiang had Xiao Rang write proclamations and sent men out to post them in all the neighboring towns and hamlets. Everyone was invited to come to the mountain for a ten-day close-out. The proclamation read as follows:

Notice from Song Jiang and his warriors in Liangshan Marsh: Because in the past we occupied these hills and groves we caused considerable disturbance among the neighboring populace. Now His Imperial Majesty has amnestied our crimes and we are returning to his service. As a recompense to you neighbors we are holding a close-out for ten days. We shall dispense our property among you, free of charge. This is absolutely true. Have no doubts. Please honor us with your presence. It will be our pleasure.

___ day of the third month of the fourth year of Xuan He
Song Jiang and his warriors of Liangshan Marsh

From the storerooms gold and jewels, silks and satins were distributed among the chieftains and officers and men. Another portion was selected as a gift for the government. The remainder was piled in the fortress for dispensation during the ten-day close-out.

This ran from the third to the thirteenth of the third month. Meat and wine were liberally served to the people, who came in droves, carrying empty bags and trays. Song Jiang ordered that they be compensated at the rate of ten times the damage suffered. Happily the recipients thanked him and departed.

When the close-out ended, the chieftains began packing for the trip to the capital. Song Jiang thought the men's families should return to their old homes. But Wu Yong had another idea.

"Better keep them here, brother," he said. "It will be time enough for them to go home after we've seen the emperor and been assured of his kindness."

Song Jiang saw the point. "You're right." He ordered the chieftains to get on with their packing and, at the same time, reorganize their troops.

They very soon set out, and quickly reached Jizhou where they warmly thanked Prefect Zhang Shuye. He gave a banquet for all the warriors and rewarded the ranks of the three armies.

Song Jiang thanked the prefect and they left the city. Preceded by an advance contingent of six or seven hundred they marched towards the Eastern Capital. Dai Zong and Yan Qing were sent on ahead to notify Marshal Su. The marshal promptly informed the emperor: "Song Jiang and his army are on their way."

The sovereign was very pleased. He directed the marshal and the imperial controller to greet the arrivals with pennants and standards. The two at once left the city.

The brigand forces were marching in smart formation. In the fore were two red banners, one reading *Obey Heaven,* the other *Defend the Country.* The chieftains were in full armor. The only exceptions were Wu Yong—who wore a black silk head kerchief, Gongsun Sheng— who wore a heron feathered Taoist coat, Sagacious Lu—in a fiery red Buddhist robe, and Wu Song—in a pilgrim's black cassock. All the others were in battle dress with metal fittings.

They had been marching for many a day, and now, as they neared the capital, the vanguard saw coming towards them the imperial controller with pennants and standards. Song Jiang was informed. He and his chieftains went first to greet Marshal Su then halted the army outside the New Official Gate, set up shelters, and waited for the emperor's summons.

Marshal Su and the imperial controller entered the city and informed the emperor.

"I've heard a lot about Song Jiang and his chieftains," said the sovereign. "A hundred and eight of them, bold and courageous, all corresponding to star spirits. Remarkable men. Today they have submitted and returned to the capital to become respectable citizens. I shall proceed with my officials to Xuante Tower. Let Song Jiang and his chieftains march in full armor at the head of their army and enter the city, but with not more than four or fire hundred troops. I will review them as they march from east to west. I also want the people and the officials, civil and military, to know these gallant heroes who are now our loyal subjects. Then let them divest themselves of their armor and weapons, put on the satin robes which I have presented to them, and enter the palace through East Glory Gate. I shall receive them in the Hall of Culture and Virtue."

The imperial controller went to the brigands' camp and transmitted the message to Song Jiang.

The next day Song Jiang had Ironclad Virtue Pei Xuan select six or seven hundred stalwart men, and before these place golden drums and colorful flags, then a corps of spear and sword and ax bearers, with the two red banners *Obey Heaven and Defend the Country* in between. Every man carried a sword and bow and arrows, and wore full armor. In ranks they entered the city's East Gate.

Civil and military, the whole populace had turned out, supporting the old and holding the young. They lined the roads and stared at the brigands as if they were gods. The emperor and his officials watched from the tower. They saw the golden drums and fluttering pennants, the swords and axes in gleaming array, the white fetlocked cavalry, and the red banners *Obey Heaven* and *Defend the Country*. In addition there was a band of thirty or so mounted musicians, drumming and blowing. Finally came the massed ranks of the stalwarts. Xie Zhen and Xie Bao cleared the road for the procession, Zhu Wu brought up the rear.

The emperor was delighted at this magnificent display. He said admiringly to his officials: "They are indeed heroes!"

He instructed the chief of ceremonies to tell Song Jiang and the chieftains to change into ceremonial clothes and be prepared to be received at court. The order was transmitted. Outside the place gate the men removed their armor, donned the satin robes of red and green, attached the slabs of gold and silver, put on the special hats and pale green boots worn at imperial audiences. Gongsun Sheng had tailored his red satin into a Taoist coat, Sagacious Lu had made a Buddhist robe, and Wu Song a pilgrim's cassock. All had used the material presented by the emperor. With Song Jiang and Lu Junyi in the lead, seconded by Wu Yong and Gongsun Sheng, and followed by the other chieftains, they entered the East Glory Gate. The ceremonial fittings and paraphernalia had already been placed in order.

By then it was early morning, and the sovereign arrived at the Hall of Culture and Virtue. The master of rites led Song Jiang and the chieftains into the royal presence. They formed lines and, in keeping with the commands of the chief of ceremonies, kowtowed and shouted, "Long live the emperor!" Pleased, His Majesty invited them to draw near and be seated according to rank. On his order, a banquet was laid by the imperial caterers. The emperor's vintners brought the wine, the Delicacies Department brought the entrees, the royal chefs did the cooking, and the official Banquet Bureau served the food, while in the background music played. The emperor, in his royal chair, joined them personally at the table.

The feasting went on until dusk. Song Jiang and the chieftains thanked the sovereign, and left the palace with flowers in their hair. Outside the West Glory Gate they mounted their horses and rode back to camp. The next day they again entered the city and went with the imperial master of rites to the hall of Culture and Virtue to express their gratitude. His Majesty, very pleased, was thinking of giving them official rank so that they would qualify for appointment to government posts. Again Song Jiang and the chieftains thanked him and returned to camp.

But the Chancellor of Military Affairs said to the emperor: "They've only just submitted and have not yet won any merit. They shouldn't be given rank so easily. They ought to distinguish themselves in battle, first. What's more, there are thousands of them camped outside our gates. That's a bad situation. Among Song Jiang's forces are officers of the capital garrison who fell into his hands. They should return to it. Officers and men from other armies should also go back to their original units. The remainder should be divided into five columns, and assigned to duty in different parts of Shandong and Hebei. That would be best."

The next day, the sovereign sent the imperial controller to the camp with a directive: *Song Jiang's forces shall be disbanded and returned to their original units.*

The chieftains were angry. They said: "Though we've submitted to the throne, not only aren't we given rank, but you want to split us brothers up! We chieftains have vowed to live and die together! If you insist on dividing us, we have no choice but to go back to Liangshan Marsh!"

Song Jiang hastily stopped them. He begged the controller to explain the situation to the emperor. The controller reported word for word, not daring to leave anything out. Startled, His Majesty summoned his Chancellor of Military Affairs.

"Although those fellows have surrendered, they haven't actually changed. Sooner or later, they're going to make serious trouble," said the chancellor. "It seems to me you should issue an order which will lure them into the capital, exterminate the whole hundred and eight, and then disband their army. This will save the country from disaster."

The sovereign hesitated. From behind a screen, a high official emerged, dressed in a purple gown and holding an ivory tablet.

"On every border the beacon fires burn continuously," he shouted, "and within the country there is danger of internal calamity! It's all because treacherous ministers like you are wrecking His Majesty's domain!"

Truly, only this voice calling for strengthening the nation and pacifying its borders could save our Heaven-startling, Earth-shaking heroes.

Who was this official who so timely appeared? Read our next chapter.

CHAPTER 83

SONG JIANG IS ORDERED TO SMASH THE LIAO TARTARS

AT CHEN BRIDGE STATION WEEPING HE EXECUTES A SUBORDINATE

That year the king of the Liao Tartars dispatched his armies over the mountains. First they occupied nine border prefectures. Then, in four columns, they swept down and pillaged Shandong, Shanxi, Henan and Hebei. Every prefecture and county sent petitions to the throne pleading for rescue. All such documents had to pass through the hands of Tong Guan, Chancellor of Military Affairs. He talked it over with Prime Minister Cai Jing, Marshal Gao Qiu and Marshal Yang Jian, and they decided not to forward the petitions. They only notified a few neighboring prefectures and urged them to send reinforcements and relief. This was as futile as trying to fill a well with snow. People knew about it, but they kept the facts from the emperor.

Then, the four crooked ministers hatched a scheme. They arranged for Tong Guan to propose to the sovereign a means that would destroy Song Jiang and his men. They hadn't expected that another important minister would intervene. The man who hurried out from behind the screen was Marshal Su Yanjing, and he appealed directly to the emperor.

"Your Majesty! Song Jiang and his bold fellows have just surrendered. The hundred and eight of them are extremely close and devoted. They'd never agree to being separated. They'd rather die, first. And now, some people want to have them killed! These gallant men are extremely brave and intelligent. If, when you bring them into the city, they rise up in revolt, then what? How will you deal with them?

"The Liao Tartars have occupied nine border prefectures with a hundred thousand troops, and every county is petitioning for relief. We have sent some units, but it's been like splashing water on ants. The enemy is too powerful. Our forces can't cope with them. We've lost every engagement. All this news has been kept from you.

"In my humble opinion if we dispatched Song Jiang and his fine generals and all the troops under their command to the border, they could defeat the Liao bandits. Sending them into battle will truly be of great advantage to our country. As a mere minister I cannot order this, myself, but I beg Your Majesty to consider."

Pleasure suffused the emperor's countenance. He queried his officials. All agreed that Su's proposal was reasonable. The sovereign angrily berated Tong Guan and his fellow conspirators.

"By your slanders and lies you've harmed our country. Your jealousy of talent has blocked the path of the meritorious. Your distortions have seriously damaged affairs of state! But I will forgive you this time and not pursue the matter."

The emperor personally drew an edict naming Song Jiang as the Vanguard General against the Liao Tartars, and stating that his chieftains would be awarded official rank in keeping with how they distinguished themselves. He directed

Marshal Su to deliver the edict to Song Jiang at his camp. The sovereign dismissed court and his officials withdrew.

Marshal Su brought the imperial document to Song Jiang's camp and told him the emperor's intention. Song Jiang hastily lit incense, kowtowed in thanks for His Majesty's benevolence, and opened the edict. It read as follows:

Edict: When Emperor Shun assumed the throne, he raised Gao Tao to enforce his rule. When Tang became sovereign, he appointed Yi Yin to maintain peace. From the time I established my reign I have been tireless in selecting men of excellence. Recently, Song Jiang and his cohorts have joined us. They wish to obey Heaven and defend the country. They are all honorable and entirely faithful. Such great talent should not be used lightly.

Now, the Liao armies have invaded our borders. I have appointed Song Jiang as the Vanguard General to smash them, and Lu Junyi as "Vice-Vanguard General. His other officers will be awarded appropriate rank when their meritorious deeds are reported to the throne. Let them all set out at once, go directly to the enemy's lair, castigate the evildoers, save the people, and purge our border regions. Each prefecture through which they pass shall supply them with money and grain. They are authorized to punish any official who fails to comply.

This imperial edict is hereby proclaimed.

__ *day of the fifth month of the fourth year of Xuan He*

Song Jiang, Lu Junyi, and the other chieftains, who had listened, kneeling, while the document was being read, were very pleased. They kowtowed, and Song Jiang expressed their thanks to Marshal Su.

"We've been hoping for a chance like this to serve out country," he said, "to win credit and position and become loyal officials. You've been kinder to us than our own parents, intervening with the emperor on our behalf. Our only problem is that we still haven't disposed of Chao Gai's spirit tablet on Mount Liangshan, and our families haven't yet returned to our homes. And our walls and battlements must be destroyed and our ships of war brought here. Would you please request His Majesty to allow us to return to the mountain and attend to these matters? Then we can get our arms and equipment in order and devote ourselves entirely to serving the nation."

Marshal Su gladly assented and reported to the emperor, who instructed the treasure to draw one thousand ounces of gold and five thousand ounces of silver, plus five thousand bolts of satin, and issue them to the chieftains. He ordered the marshal to handle the distribution at the camp. The gifts were to be given to the dependents of those with families, to guarantee their support for the rest of their lives. Chieftains without families would receive the gifts directly, to use as they saw fit.

Imperial order in hand, Song Jiang expressed his thanks and directed the distribution. As he was leaving for the palace, the marshal offered Song Jiang a few words of advice.

"Go to the mountain, General, but come back quickly. Let me know of your return in advance. There must be no delay."

Song Jiang and his chieftains then conferred on who should go. They decided that these should be Song Jiang, his chief generals Wu Yong, Gongsun Sheng, Lin Chong, Liu Tang, Du Qian, Song Wan, Zhu Gui, Song Qing and the three Ruan brothers—together with cavalry, infantry and naval forces of over ten thousand. The rest of the army would remain encamped near the capital under Vice-Vanguard General Lu Junyi. The journey to the mountain stronghold was uneventful. Seated in Loyalty Hall, Song Jiang instructed the families to pack and get ready to start for home. He also ordered that pigs and sheep be slaughtered, incense and candles lit, and ingots and horses of paper burned as sacrifices to the spirit of Chao Gai. Then the former leader's spirit tablet was also reduced to ashes and a feast laid for all the chieftains.

In carts and on horseback the families departed for their original homes. Song Jiang directed his retainers to escort their families and old Squire Song and his household back to their native village in Yuncheng County and become respectable citizens again.

He told the three Ruan brothers to select the most useful of the ships of war, and to distribute the remaining smaller craft among the neighboring populace. These could also dismantle the buildings and take the materials. The fortifications in the three passes and structures like Loyalty Hall were to be destroyed.

When all this was done and everything put in order, the armed forces were assembled. They returned swiftly to the capital.

The march was without incident, and they soon reached the camp where Lu Junyi and the others were waiting. Yan Qing was sent on to the city to inform Marshal Su that they were ready to take leave of the sovereign and commence the expedition. The marshal duly notified the emperor.

The next day His Majesty received Song Jiang and his chieftains with smiling countenance in the Hall of Martial Heroes. Libation cups were drunk, and the sovereign, extremely pleased, spoke.

"Go forth and crush the Liao Tartars. Let us hear news of victory soon. We shall make much important use of you. As to your generals, they shall be awarded rank according to their merit. Let there be no delay!"

Song Jiang kowtowed and offered thanks. "I was only a petty functionary who committed a heinous crime and was exiled to Jiangzhou," he said. "There, for rebellious words written while drunk, I was condemned to execution in the public square. These brothers rescued me, and since I had no place else to hide, I took refuge with them in Liangshan Marsh. For all these crimes I deserve ten thousand deaths! Yet Your Majesty, in your vast benevolence, has seen fit to pardon me. Though I split my liver and gall with exertion, I shall never be able to repay Your

Majesty's kindness! I shall certainly expend my utmost strength and devotion to carry out your royal order, or die gladly in the attempt'."

Very pleased, the sovereign again awarded cups of imperial wine. At his direction, Song Jiang was presented with a gold-embossed set of bow and arrows, a fully accoutered fine steed, and a precious sword. Song Jiang kowtowed and voiced his gratitude.

Then he took leave of the emperor and returned to camp with the imperial gifts. He ordered his commanders to prepare to march.

Emperor Hui Zong the following morning directed Marshal Su to transmit his order to the Council of Administration to dispatch two officials to Chen Bridge Station and there give send-off rations to Song Jiang's departing troops. Each man was to receive a bottle of wine and a catty of meat, and not an ounce less. The chancellor worked through the night, preparing the rations, then sent two officials to distribute them.

Song Jiang, after conferring with Wu Yong, divided his army into two groups, with the five Tiger and eight Wildcat chieftains leading the infantry in the van and the ten Charger chieftains leading the cavalry bringing up the rear. He himself, together with Lu Junyi, Wu Yong and Gongsun Sheng, would command the central forces. The three Ruan brothers, Li Chun, Zhang Heng and Zhang Shun, under whom would be Tong Wei, Tong Meng, Meng Kang, Wang Dingliu and the various sailor chiefs, would command the naval vessels, and sail from the Caiho River into the Yellow, and there proceed north. Song Jiang announced that the army would follow the highway from Chen Bridge Station, and instructed his chieftains to forbid any harassment of the local populace.

The two officials designated by the Council of Administration arrived at Chen Bridge Station to distribute the emperor's largesse to Song Jiang's forces. Shamelessly dishonest, they stinted for their own private gain. These bribe-taking back-biting liars gave out wine bottles that were only half full, and the catty of meat each man received weighed only ten ounces instead of sixteen.

After distributing to the forward group, the officials came to a rear unit whose troops wore black helmets and black armor. They were shield-bearers under Xiang Chong and Li Gun. Among these was a junior commander who discovered the chicanery and angrily berated the two officials.

"It's grafters like you who sabotage the emperor's benevolence!"

"What do you mean?" they cried.

"His Majesty ordered a bottle of wine and a catty of meat for each man, and you've cut them both! We don't like to quarrel, but your characters are a disgrace! You'd steal the gilt off the face of an idol of Buddha!"

"You've got a nerve! Slicing to death would be too good for you! You're still a Liangshan Marsh rebel!"

Furious, the young officer threw the meat and wine in their faces.

"Arrest that rascally robber!" they howled.

The young man drew his sword from the edge of his shield. The official pointed at him indignantly.

"Dirty bandit! Would you dare use that blade!"

"When I was on Mount Liangshan I was better than the best of your fighters! I killed thousands of them! Why would I scruple about a couple of crooks!"

"We dare you to kill us," they bawled.

The young commander stepped forward and slashed the face of one of them. He collapsed to the ground. The watchers cried out in alarm and fell back. The junior officer hacked again several more time. Clearly, the man was dying. It was too late for the troops to intervene.

Xiang Chong and Li Gun flew to inform Song Jiang. Startled, he exclaimed to Wu Yong: "What are we going to do?"

"The Chancellor of Administration doesn't like us. This thing gives him precisely the chance he's been looking for," mused Wu Yong. "All we can do is direct the execution of our officer, report the matter to the Council of Ministration, halt our march and await a disposition. Have Dai Zong and Yan Qing rush to the city and quietly notify Marshal Su. Request him to inform the emperor of the provocation. That will forestall the chancellor from twisting the facts. I guarantee nothing will come of it."

The strategy agreed upon, Song Jiang galloped to Chen Bridge Station. The junior officer was standing beside the body of the slain official. Song Jiang directed that wine and meat be taken from the hostel for officials and dispensed among the troops. Then he summoned the young officer into the hostel and questioned him.

"He kept cursing us and saying we were rebellious bandits from Liangshan Marsh, and that we all ought to be exterminated! I lost my temper and killed him. I'm waiting for your sentence, General."

"He was an official of the imperial court. I was afraid of him myself. How could you slay him? We're all sure to be implicated. Our march against the Liao Tartars had only started, we haven't yet won a bit of distinction, and you pull a stunt like this. What are we going to do?"

The young commander prostrated himself and waited for death. Song Jiang wept.

"From the time I came to Mount Liangshan I never harmed any of our brothers, big or small. But now that I'm an official I have no choice. I must obey the law. I know your aggressive spirit is still strong, but you shouldn't have given free rein to it as you did in the old days."

"I'm ready to die."

Song Jiang ordered the young officer to drink heavily of wine and hang himself from a tree. When this was done he had him decapitated.

The body of the official was formally encoffined, and a letter sent to the Council of Administration. Actually, the chancellor already knew all about it, but of that we'll say no more.

Dai Zong and Yan Qing hurried directly to Marshal Su's residency on entering the city and told him in detail what had happened. That evening the marshal went to the palace and informed the emperor. The following day His Majesty held court in the Hall of Culture and Virtue. When the drum boomed in the dragon tower and the bell sounded in the phoenix belfry, the seneschal rapped three times with his rod and the civil and military officials formed ranks in two groups at the foot of the stairs.

From among them the Chancellor of Administration came forward and said: "A soldier in the army of Song Jiang, who only recently surrendered to the throne, has killed an official our chancellery dispatched to distribute wine and meat. We hope Your Majesty will look into the matter."

"I entrusted your chancellery with a mission. The responsibility is yours," replied the sovereign. "Your men were untrustworthy. That was the cause. They deliberately cut the meat and wine ration. The Mount Liangshan soldier refused to be cheated, and a clash was the result."

"Who would dare cut the imperial wine?" the chancellor protested.

The emperor grew angry. "I've already sent an investigator, and I know the whole story. You can't deceive me with your subtle words and evasions! You dispensed only half bottles of my gift of imperial wine, the meat you gave only ten ounces to the catty. That is what enraged the soldier and caused the bloodshed!" Then His Majesty asked: "Where is the culprit?"

"Song Jiang has decapitated him and says that his head will be displayed. He has reported the matter to the chancellery, halted his march and is waiting for a disposition."

"Let his breach of discipline be noted. We shall settle the matter according to his merits when he returns from defeating the Liaos."

Silently, the chancellor withdrew. His Majesty dispatched an emissary to urge Song Jiang to continue his expedition after displaying the head of the decapitated young officer at Chen Bridge Station.

Song Jiang expressed thanks for the emperor's benevolence, hung up the head as directed and buried the body. Heart-brokenly, he wept. Then he wiped his tears, mounted, and headed north with his army.

Every day they covered sixty *li* before making camp. They caused no trouble in any of the counties and prefectures through which they passed. The march was uneventful, and after a time they neared the borders of the Liao Tartars.

"The Liaos have been invading us in four columns," Song Jiang said to Wu Yong. "Should we divide up and go after them, or attack their cities and towns?"

"It's a vast territory and thinly populated. If we split up we won't be able to coordinate. Better take a few cities first, then we'll see. If we hit them hard they'll naturally call back their soldiers."

"An excellent plan," approved Song Jiang. He summoned Duan Jingzhu and said: "You know the northern roads well. I'm going to let you lead the advance. Which is the nearest prefecture?"

"Tanzhou is right ahead. It's a vital entry to Liao territory. A deep river called the Lushui winds around the prefectural city and connects with the River Weiho. You'll need warships to attack Tanzhou. Once our flotilla arrives we can assault from land and water together, and take the city."

Song Jiang dispatched Dai Zong to urge Li Jun and the other naval chieftains to hasten their armada and assemble in the Lushui.

Dongxian Bojin, the man who commanded the Tanzhou garrison, was a vice-minister of the Kingdom of Liao. Under him were four fierce generals—Aliqi, Yaor Weikang, Chu Mingyu and Cao Mingji. All were absolutely fearless. When Vice-Minister Dongxian learned that Song Jiang and his entire army had been dispatched by the Emperor of Song and was nearing his territory, he reported at once in writing to the king. He requested aid from the neighboring prefectures of Qizhou, Bazhou, Zhuozhou and Xiongzhou, and at the same time sent his soldiers to meet the enemy. Aliqi and Chu Mingyu took leave of the duke and led forth thirty thousand men.

Meanwhile, Guan Sheng the Big Halberd was advancing with the forward section of the vanguard towards Miyun County, which was part of the prefecture of Tanzhou. The county magistrate hurriedly reported this to the two Tartar generals.

"The Song emperor's army is marching this way with banners flying. They're all amnestied brigands from Liangshan Marsh under Song Jiang."

Aliqi laughed. "They're only bandits. Why worry?" He ordered his soldiers to make camp and prepare to give battle outside Miyun.

The next day, Song Jiang heard that Liao forces were approaching, and he instructed his troops to engage them. "We'll test their mettle," he said. "But we don't want any unnecessary losses."

The chieftains donned their armor and mounted. Song Jiang and Lu Junyi rode personally to the front lines to observe. Far off they could see the Tartar forces, who carried black flags and banners, advancing in dark swarms that covered the earth and obscured the sky. Arrows from the bows of both sides stopped the contending hosts a distance apart.

The black flags separated. On a magnificent prancing horse a Tartar general rode forth. He was fair complected, with red lips, golden hair and green eyes, and was tall and powerful. The banner behind him read:

Aliqi, General of the Great Liao Kingdom.

Song Jiang looked. "That general is not to be underestimated," he said to his chieftains.

Before the words were out of his mouth, Xu Ning the Metal Lancer rode forth, his sickle-bladed lance held athwart. Aliqi hooted at the sight of him.

"The Song Dynasty is doomed! Sending scruffy bandits as officers! What brass to invade our great nation! Only death awaits you!"

"You worthless officer, disgrace to your country, how dare you insult us!"

The armies of both sides shouted as Aliqi and Xu Ning clashed in combat. For more than thirty rounds they fought, and Xu Ning realized he could not win. He withdrew towards his own lines, pursued by the Tartar general. Hua Rong hastily notched an arrow to his bowstring. But Zhang Qin, leaning on the pommel of his saddle, had already drawn a stone from his brocaded pouch, and now he flung it at the approaching general. Like a streaking meteor, like an arrow from a bow, it struck Aliqi near the left eye and knocked him head over heels to the ground. Hua Rong, Lin Chong, Qin Ming and Suo Chao galloped forward and caught first the fine steed, then Aliqi himself.

Chu Mingyu, Aliqi's second in command, wanted to rush to his rescue, but Song Jiang's entire army charged in a murderous assault that swept the Tartars from Miyun County. It inflicted such heavy losses that the defenders fled back to Tanzhou. Song Jiang did not follow. Instead, he made camp in Miyun.

He went to see Aliqi. The stone had hit him at the end of the eyebrow, near the temple, destroying the eye. The Tartar general died in great pain.

Song Jiang ordered that he be cremated, and had Zhang Qin credited with the First Merit in the record book. Aliqi's chain armor, his decorated lance of white pear wood, his jade-embossed belt with its lion's head buckle, his dappled silver-grey steed, plus his boots, robe, bow and arrows, were all given to Zhang Qin. That day the expeditionary force celebrated the victory with a feast in Miyun. Of that no more need be said.

The next day Song Jiang broke camp and ordered his army to march directly on Tanzhou. When Vice-Minister Dongxian was informed that they were advancing, and learned that they had killed one of his generals, he closed the gates and directed his troops to remain inside the city. Then he heard that a naval armada had also reached the walls, and went with his generals to look from the ramparts. He saw Song Jiang's chieftains, waving banners and brandishing weapons, shouting challenges as they stood in bold array.

"No wonder our young Aliqi was defeated," said the vice-minister.

"Who says he was defeated?" Chu Mingyu protested. "He was vanquishing the barbarian chieftain, chasing after him when a savage dressed in green knocked him from his horse with a stone. It took four barbarians with lances to capture him. Our side was caught unawares. That's why we lost."

"What does the stone-throwing savage look like?"

Someone pointed Zhang Qin out. "See that fellow with the black pouch, wearing our young general's clothes and armor and riding his steed? That's the one."

Dongxian leaned over the ramparts for a closer look. But Zhang Qin had seen him first. Galloping forward, he winged a stone. It grazed Dongxian's ear, scraping off a bit of skin. His retinue shouted in alarm.

"The savage has a formidable skill," muttered the vice-minister, nursing his painful ear. He came down from the wall and wrote a report to the Liao Tartar king. He also notified all the prefectures along the border to be on their guard.

For four or five days Song Jiang's army attacked, to no avail. They retired to Miyun and made camp. While Song Jiang was conferring in headquarters, Dai Zong came and reported that the naval chieftains had arrived at the Lushui River on ships of war. Song Jiang sent Dai Zong to summon them to headquarters. Before long, Li Jun and the others appeared.

"This is not like battling in the marsh," Song Jiang reminded him. "Find out first where the water is deep and where it is shallow, then advance. The Lushui current is swift. If anything goes wrong, we won't he able to save you. Proceed carefully. Keep your men concealed. Pretend you're delivering grain to Tanzhou. I want you chieftains to carry hidden weapons and stay under cover. Have only four or five men plying the oars and two on shore pulling the two ropes on each vessel. Move slowly towards the city and moor the boats on either shore outside and wait for our land forces. When the Tanzhou authorities see you they're sure to open the river gate to get the grain quickly. At that moment all of you burst out and capture the gate. You'll earn great distinction."

Li Jun and the naval chieftains acknowledged the order and departed. A junior officer entered and reported.

"A huge army is tearing in this direction from the northwest. They're carrying black flags. There are over ten thousand of them, and they're moving towards Tanzhou."

"They must be reinforcements from the king of the Liaos," said Wu Yong. "Let's send out a few chieftains to block and scatter them. We don't want them to stiffen the courage of the troops in the city."

Song Jiang mobilized Zhang Qin, Dong Ping, Guan Sheng and Lin Chong, with a dozen or so small chieftains and five thousand troops, and dispatched them at flying speed to meet the foe.

When the king of the Liao Tartars heard that the gallant Song Jiang of Liangshan Marsh had cut through with his army directly to Tanzhou and had surrounded the city, he ordered two of his nephews to lead a relief expedition. One was called Yelu Guozhen, the other Yelu Guobao. Both were Liao generals, both were royal nephews, and both were immeasurably brave. At the head of ten thousand men, they were rushing to support Tanzhou. As they drew near, they were met by the Song forces. The two sides spread out in battle positions, and the two Tartar generals rode forward.

They were brothers. They were dressed the same, and they carried the same lances. From Song Jiang's ranks, General Two Spears Dong Ping cantered to the fore. He shouted to them in a powerful voice. "Where do you hail from, barbarian officers?" This infuriated Guozhen. "You marsh bandits invade out great kingdom, and you have the nerve to ask where we hail from!"

Dong Ping said no more, but galloped directly towards Yelu Guozhen with spears at the ready. The young Tartar was hot-tempered and unyielding. He lowered his metal lance and charged. The two horses met, the three points whirled. In the cloud of dust, in that murderous frenzy, the wielder of the two spears displayed exceptional skill, the manipulator of the metal lance showed miraculous ability. Fifty rounds they fought, with neither emerging the victor.

Guobao feared his older brother was tiring. He beat the headquarters' gong, signalling a call to withdraw. Guozhen was more than willing. The struggle was getting too hot for him. But Dong Ping locked him between the two spears and wouldn't let him go. Because Guozhen's mind was racing, his hands faltered. Dong Ping with his right arm swept aside the heavy green lance, with his left spear he stabbed into the base of his opponent's throat. Poor Guozhen's golden crown fell from his head, his feet turned skyward, and he tumbled from his saddle to the ground.

With levelled lance, Guobao galloped to the rescue. To Zhang Qin the Featherless Arrow this was too good an opportunity to miss. Socketing his pear-wood lance, he drew a stone from his embroidered pouch. He clapped his steed and raced into the field of combat.

Quicker than it takes to say, when the two flying horses were about a hundred feet apart, and while the young Tartar was heedless of all but the coming clash, Zhang Qin drew back his arm and threw. "Take that!" he cried. The stone struck Guobao full in the face, and sent him somersaulting from his saddle.

Guan Sheng, Lin Chong and their troops swarmed forward. The Liao soldiers, leaderless, scattered in panic. Those of the ten thousand who escaped being slaughtered fled wildly. The fully caparisoned mounts of the royal nephews were captured, as were their golden standards. Guozhen and Guobao were Stripped of their jewelled crowns and robes and armor, and their heads were cut off.

Over a thousand battle chargers had been taken. These were driven to Miyun and presented to Song Jiang. Delighted, he rewarded his troops, and credited Dong Ping and Zhang Qin with the Second Merits. He would send a written report of the victory to the emperor after the capture of Tanzhou.

That night Song Jiang and Wu Yong worked out their strategy. Lin Chong and Guan Sheng were to lead a detachment of cavalry and assault Tanzhou from the northwest, Huyan Zhuo and Dong Ping would move with their horsemen from the northeast, Lu Junyi would attack from the southwest.

"I and our central forces will advance from the southeast. At the sound of our cannon, all strike together," said Song Jiang.

He directed Ling Zhen the Heaven-Shaking Thunder, Black Whirlwind Li Kui, Fan Rui the Demon King Who Roils the World, and Bao Xu the God of Death, together with shield officers Xiang Chong and Li Gun and over a thousand shield-twirling soldiers, to proceed to the foot of the city walls, and from there fire the signal cannons when the time came.

At the second watch, land and naval forces would go into action together. The orders given, all units prepared for the assault.

Meanwhile, Dongxian the vice-minister waited in Tanzhou for his relief. Remnants of the defeated army of the royal nephews straggled into the city and told him what had occurred.

"Prince Yelu Guozhen was killed by a man wielding two spears. Yelu Guobao was knocked from his horse with a stone thrown by a fellow in a green turban and then seized and slain."

The vice-minister stamped his foot in exasperation. "That savage again! He's caused the death of two royal nephews! How am I ever going to face the king! When I catch that green turbaned lout I'll pound him to bits."

That evening a scout reported: "Six or seven hundred grain boats have moored along both banks of the Lushui, and an army is approaching in the distance."

"Those barbarians don't know our waterways and have sailed their grain boats here by mistake," said the vice-minister. "Their army is surely after the grain."

He summoned Chu Mingyu, Cao Mingji and Yaor Weikang and gave the three generals his instructions: "Song Jiang and his barbarians have sent another large force against us. There are also a number of their grain boats in our river. Yaor Weikang, go out against the raiders with a thousand troops. Chu Mingyu and Cao Mingji, open the water gate and bring those vessels in here, fast. Even if we get two out of three, that will be fine. You'll earn great distinction."

At dusk that evening, Song Jiang's left flank infantry force, under Black Whirlwind and Fan Rui, advanced towards Tanzhou and began reviling the Tartars. Yaor Weikang, who had been ordered to go out against them by the duke, opened the city gate and lowered the drawbridge. But Black Whirlwind, Fan Rui, Bao Xu, Xiang Chong and Li Gun, with their thousand infantry, all fierce sword and shield men, dashed up and occupied the other end of the bridge, bottling the Tartars inside.

Ling Zhen had set up his cannon, and was waiting only for the time to fire them. Arrows were whizzing down from atop the city walls, but the shield bearers gave him protection. Bao Xu and the thousand men were yelling in the background. They sounded more like ten thousand from the noise they made.

When his soldiers couldn't get out of Tanzhou, the vice-minister grew frantic. He hastily ordered Chu Mingyu and Cao Mingji to open the water gate and seize the boats. Song Jiang's navel chieftains were lying motionless in the holds. As soon as the water gate opened, they pried up the deck boards and converted the craft into vessels of war.

On learning this, Ling Zhen fired a Blazing Wind cannon. The boats moored along either shore sailed forward to engage the enemy craft. From the left came Li Jun, Zhang Heng and Zhang Shun, rapidly plying their oars. From the right, the three Ruan brothers in their warships bore murderously down on the enemy boats.

Chu Mingyu and Cao Mingji realized they had fallen into an ambush. Hurriedly, they tried to beat a retreat. But it was too late. The Song fighters were already boarding their craft. They could only run for shore.

Song Jiang's six chieftains charged the water gate. They killed or drove off the defenders. The two Tartar generals fled for their lives. A torch waved atop the water gate, and Ling Zhen fired a Wagon cannon. Its projectile screamed across the sky.

Continuously the bombardment mounted, scaring the duke out of his wits. Black Whirlwind, Fan Rui and Bao Xu, leading Xiang Chong, Li Gun and their shield bearers, went tearing into the city.

The vice-minister and his general Yaor Weikang saw that all the gates had been taken and the Song troops were pouring in from every side.

They mounted and fled Tanzhou through the North Gate. Before they had gone two *li* they were intercepted by Guan Sheng the Big Halberd and Panther Head Lin Chong. The Tartar vice-minister and general had no choice but to give battle.

With a net spreading over Heaven and Earth, how could they escape? What, finally, was the vice-minister's fate? Read our next chapter if you would know.

CHAPTER 84

SONG JIANG ATTACKS QIZHOU CITY

LU JUNYI BATTLES IN YUTIAN COUNTY

Vice-Minister Dongxian and Yaor Weikang had no stomach for a fight after a brief fierce encounter with Lin Chong and Guan Sheng. Desperately, they broke through at an angle and fled. Since it was Tanzhou they were after, the chieftains did not pursue but moved quickly instead into the city.

After the Song forces took Tanzhou and scattered the remaining Tartar troops, Song Jiang posted notices guaranteeing that the local population would not be harmed in the slightest. He directed that as many as possible of his war vessels should sail into the city, then rewarded his soldiers. As to the Tartar officials, those who had some prestige he kept on in their original positions. The remainder he pressured to leave the city and return to the desert. He sent a written report to the emperor on the conquest of Tanzhou, together with the valuables he had removed from the city's treasury. He wrote also to Marshal Su, requesting him to convey the news to the sovereign.

The emperor, on being informed, was delighted. He ordered that Zhao Anfu, a commissioner from the Council of Military Affairs, proceed at once to the front with twenty thousand imperial cavalry troops.

Song Jiang and his chieftains, learning of Zhao's impending arrival, travelled a long distance from the city to meet him. They then escorted him to quarters in the prefectural residence, being used temporarily as the army's high command. All the generals came to pay their respects. Zhao Anfu, a direct descendant of the imperial Zhao family, was a man of benevolence and virtue who conducted his affairs in a correct and upright manner. It was this person, recommended by Marshal Su, that the emperor had chosen to oversee the military operations.

Zhao was very pleased to find Song Jiang such an honorable man. He said: "His Majesty is well aware how dedicated you and your officers and troops are. He has deputed me to supervise. He also sends you gifts of gold and silver and bolts of satin laden on twenty-five carts. I am to report to the throne the names of those who especially distinguish themselves and petition that they be awarded official rank. I shall also report again those prefectures and shires you have already taken. All of you commanders must do your utmost and cover yourselves with glory. When you return victorious to the capital, His Majesty will surely make important use of you."

Song Jiang expressed thanks and said: "Can I trouble Your Excellency to take over control of Tanzhou? I propose to divide my forces and attack the other major prefectures of the Kingdom of Liao, so that the enemy won't be able to coordinate."

He distributed the gifts among his officers, then called back all his troops and directed that they wait for orders regarding the forthcoming attack on the Tartar cites.

"Qizhou isn't far ahead," said Yang Xiong. "Beyond that is a vast area rich in money and grain, rice and wheat. It's truly the Liao treasury. Conquer Qizhou and you can get the rest."

Song Jiang thereupon requested his military advisor Wu Yong to confer with him.

Meanwhile, Vice-Minister Dongxian and Yaor Weikang, heading east, ran into Chu Mingyu and Cao Mingji and the remnants of their defeated army. Like a dog whose master has just died, like a fish which has escaped the net, they were scurrying along. All joined forces and hastened to the prefectural city of Qizhou. There they were received by Prince Yelu Dezhong, younger brother of the king. They told him of the large and mighty army commanded by Song Jiang, and of the remarkable barbarian stone thrower who flung his missiles with devastating accuracy and never missed. It was he who had killed the two royal nephews and General Aliqi.

"In that case you must help me destroy him," said the prince.

Before the words were out of his mouth a roving scout entered and reported: "Song Jiang has divided his army into two columns and is attacking our prefecture. One column is advancing on Pinggu County, the other is moving against Yutian County."

"Lead your troops to Pinggu," the prince said to the vice-minister, "but don't engage the foe. I'll wipe out the barbarians at Yutian with my army, then slip around and come at the ones near Yutian from the rear. They won't be able to get away."

He also notified the prefectures of Bazhou and Youzhou to send reinforcements immediately. He set out with a large army, accompanied by his four sons. They flew towards the beleaguered Yutian.

Commanding a column of thirty thousand men each, Song Jiang and Lu Junyi were advancing on the target county seats. When he neared Pinggu Song Jiang found the approaches firmly held. He did not venture to push on, but encamped west of the town.

Lu Junyi, with his force of thirty thousand strong, was soon within sight of the Tartar foe at Yutian. He conferred with his general Zhu Wu.

"I don't know this border area," he said. "I'm not familiar with the terrain. How should we go about it?"

"In my humble opinion being strangers to these parts we should proceed cautiously. Spread our troops in a long curved-snake formation. If the enemy attacks our head, our tail can come to its aid. If our head is attacked, our tail can aid. If our middle is attacked, both head and tail can provide support. They won't be able to break any link in our circle. In that way we won't have to worry about being unfamiliar with the terrain."

"My own feeling, exactly," said Lu, very pleased. He ordered his troops to advance.

In the distance, they could see the Liao soldiers swarming towards them, like a dense dark fog, like rolling yellow sand dunes. Their black flags were rows of raven clouds, their fine steeds were charged with a lethal spirit. Their broad-brimmed hats of green felt were like lotus leaves stirred by the breeze in a thousand ponds, their iron helmets were ten thousand leagues of ocean seas gleaming dully neath the winter sun. Each buttoned his tunic on the left side, wore his hair down to his shoulders, and dressed in double chain mail over a thick tightly woven robe. Stalwart, dark complected men, they had green eyes and brown hair.

The Tartar cavalry were broad-shouldered, with waists of steel and legs of iron, and they rode excellent mounts. Their bows were tipped with rams' horns, their poplar arrows had been scoured with sand. Their broad tiger skin capes contrasted with their narrow saddles of incised leather. Raised in the border regions, they grew up skilled in weaponry. For generations they had been riding the most spirited horses. Their infantry marched to the blare of bronze trumpets and the throb of sheepskin drums, their cavalry played flutes and fifes as they cantered along.

Prince Dezhong arrived at Yutian and deployed his troops for battle. Zhu Wu climbed a "cloud ladder" to observe them. He came down and reported to Lu Junyi.

"The barbarians have spread out in a 'Five Tigers Backed by a Mountain' position. Nothing special," said Zhu. He went up the ladder for another look.

Left and right he waved his signal flag, deploying the Song expeditionary forces. Lu watched, mystified.

"What battle position is this?"

"It's called 'Leviathan into Roc'."

"How can a 'leviathan become a roc'?"

"In our North Sea we have a fish known as the white leviathan. It can turn itself into a roc and fly ninety thousand *li*. This battle position at first glance appears quite small. But as soon as the fighting starts it can expand enormously. That's why it's called 'Leviathan into Roc'."

Lu Junyi heartily approved. Then the enemy's battle drums pounded, their pennant gate opened and the prince, the king's younger brother, rode forth together with his four sons, two on each side, all dressed alike. Small mirrors fringed by black tassels dangled from the young men's shoulders, and each carried a good sword and sat a swift horse. They reined in at the edge of the battlefield in a straight line. Behind the prince in deep ranks were many officers.

"How dare you marsh bandits invade our borders!" the sons shouted.

"The two armies are face to face," said Lu to his chieftains. "Which of our heroes will be the first to do combat?"

Almost before the words were out of his mourn Guan Sheng the Big Halberd rode forward waving his big blade. The prince's son Zongyun, brandishing his sword, clapped his horse and galloped to meet him. Before they had fought five rounds, another son, Zonglin, joined in the fray.

At this, Huyan Zhuo, swinging his rods, quickly engaged him. The other two sons, Zongdian and Zonglei, raced forward, to be met by Xu Ning and Suo Chao. The four pairs clashed in a wild melee.

Featherless Arrow Zhang Qin, meanwhile, rode quietly to the edge of the field of combat. Soldiers of the Tartar force which had been defeated at Tanzhou recognized him, and hurriedly reported to the prince.

"That savage in the green robe is the stone-thrower. He's coming close on his horse, and must be up to his old tricks!"

Tianshanyong, the famous Tartar bowman, overheard this and said: "Don't worry, Your Excellency. I'll give him a taste of my skill!" Tianshanyong used a painted crossbow and feathered iron bolts one foot long and shot from the saddle. His nickname was Drop of Oil.

Now he cocked the trigger and advanced stealthily, partly concealed by two Tartar officers who rode before him. But Zhang Qin caught sight of him, drew a stone from his pouch and flung it with a yell. It whizzed past the bowman's helmet. Tianshanyong slipped behind his horse's back and fitted a bolt to his crossbow. As soon as Zhang Qin was near enough, Tianshanyong fired.

"Aiya!" cried Zhang Qin. Hastily, he attempted to dodge. But the bolt struck him in the neck and knocked him from his saddle. General Two Spears and Nine Dragons Shi Jin, followed by Xie Zhen and Xie Bao, in a desperate rush, rescued him. The arrow was extracted, but a bandage around Zhang Qin's neck couldn't stop the flow of blood. Lu directed Zou Yuan and Zou Run to take him in a cart to Tanzhou and have him treated by the physician An Daoquan. They departed on the cart. Of that we'll say no more.

Shouts again rose at the front, and a scout reported: "A cavalry detachment is racing this way from the northwest. They don't respond to hails. They're just knocking everyone aside and plunging directly into the battlefield."

With Zhang Qin hit in the neck by an arrow, Lu had not much eagerness for combat. The four chieftains pretended to be losing, and retreated to their own lines, pursued by the four Tartar princelings. Meanwhile, Liao attackers were smashing through from the northwest like an avalanche. Nothing could stop them. The Song forces, split into fragments, were unable to come to each other's aid.

Lu Junyi, alone with his one mount and single lance, fought past the enemy lines. It was dusk, and he ran into the four Tartar princelings who were just returning. Fearlessly he fought them all. Suddenly he executed a feint and Zonglin closed in, hacking with his sword. Lu froze him with a yell. Before Zonglin could recover his wits, Lu's lance stabbed him from his horse. The other three, startled and a bit frightened, rode quickly away. Lu dismounted, cut off his adversary's head and hung it on his steed's neck. Vaulting into the saddle, he proceeded south.

Encountering a unit of Liao troops, well over a thousand, he charged them so savagely they broke and ran. A few *li* further on, he saw another detachment. In the dark moonless night he couldn't at first tell who they were. But then he heard voices speaking in his own Song accents.

"Whose army is that?" he called.

Huyan Zhuo answered. Lu was delighted. He joined them.

"We were broken up by the Tartars, and couldn't help each other." said Huyan. "The four princelings fought here with Han Tao and Peng Qi for a time. I don't know what became of them after that."

"I killed one, and three ran away. Then I barged into over a thousand more, and scattered them. I never thought I'd meet you here."

They all headed south. After travelling only about a dozen *li* they saw their path blocked by another detachment.

"We'd better wait till daylight," said Huyan. "There's no use attacking in the dark."

From the opposite side a voice sang out: "Is that you, General Huyan Zhuo?"

Huyan recognized the voice of Guan Sheng the Big Halberd. "Commander-in-Chief Lu is here too," he shouted.

All the chieftains dismounted and sat down on the grass to confer. Lu and Huyan told what had happened to them, after which Guan Sheng spoke.

"We lost the initiative and couldn't come to each other's aid. I and Xuan Zan, Hao Siwen, Shan Tinggui and Wei Dingguo were riding around looking for a road, and ran into a thousand of our troops. When we got here it was dark. We don't know the terrain and were afraid of falling into an ambush. We decided to wait for daybreak before travelling on. I never expected to meet you, brother."

The two units joined forces.

At dawn they wound their way south and once again reached Yutian town. They saw a body of men ahead, patrolling outside, and recognized General Two Spears Dong Ping and Metal Lancer Xu Ning. They had camped there after having been scattered by the Tartars.

"Hou Jian and Bai Sheng have gone to report to Song Jiang," they said, "but we don't know where Xie Zhen, Xie Bao, Yang Lin and Shi Yong are."

Lu ordered a count of those who had already arrived in Yutian, and found they were more than five thousand men short. He was quite disturbed. At mid-morning he was informed that the four missing chieftains had returned with over two thousand troops. Lu summoned the chieftains.

"We four managed to fight through and go deep into vital enemy territory," said Xie Zhen. "But we lost the road and didn't know which way to turn. This morning we ran into the Tartars again and killed a whole slew of them. Only then were we able to get here."

Lu ordered that the head of the princeling Zonglin be hung up on display in Yutian town, and rewarded the troops. Around dusk just as the men were preparing to rest, a young officer patrolling the roads entered and reported: "Liao soldiers are surrounding the town. We don't know how many."

Startled, Lu took Yan Qing to the top of the town wall for a look. They saw gleaming torches for a depth of ten *li*. A junior officer pointed out the princeling Zongyun, riding a fiery steed and supervising troop movement.

Yan Qing said: "Yesterday they hit Zhang Qin with a sneak arrow. Today we'll return the compliment."

He fitted an arrow to his bow and shot. The missile struck Zongyun on the bridge of his nose and knocked him from his saddle. His soldiers hastily rescued him. The Tartar troops retreated five *li*. Lu conferred with his generals in the town.

"They've pulled back a bit," he said, "but they'll surely encircle us again in the morning. We'll be closed in tighter than an iron bucket. How are we going to get out?"

"Song Jiang would rescue us if he knew," said Zhu Wu. "Striking from within and without, we could break the siege."

Truly, they had gone from the den of tigers and dragons into a snare net covering earth and sky. Was it victory or defeat which lay in store for them?

They waited until daylight and saw that the Liao contingents had surrounded them on all sides without a crack. A cloud of dust arose in the southeast as tens of thousands of soldiers marched towards them. The chieftains stared.

"It must be Song Jiang with our army," said Zhu Wu. "When he attacks south, we here will strike with our entire force!"

The opposing Tartars maintained the siege from mid-morning till mid-afternoon, but then they could withstand the flank attack no longer. They began pulling back from the perimeter of the town.

"After them," cried Zhu Wu. "What are we waiting for!"

Lu directed that the four gates of the county town be opened and led his troops out in hot pursuit. They slaughtered the Tartars and scattered them like falling stars and scudding clouds. Song Jiang also chased the fleeing enemy a long distance. Only at daybreak did he sound the trumpets to regroup and enter the county town.

When all the Song troops had gathered, Lu announced an offensive against Qizhou. Twenty-three chieftains were left with Commissioner Zhao to defend Tanzhou. The remainder were divided between left and right columns. Forty-eight went with Song Jiang who commanded the left, thirty-seven with Lu Junyi who commanded the right.

Both armies would march on Qizhou simultaneously, Song Jiang's column from Pinggu, and Lu's column from Yutian. Zhao Anfu and the twenty-three chieftains held Tanzhou. Of that no more need be said.

Originally Prince Yelu Dezhong the Tartar king's younger brother was defending Qizhou with the aid of his four princeling sons, a dozen generals, and over a hundred thousand troops. His chief general was called Baomisheng. The second in command was Tianshanyong.

Song Jiang's troops had campaigned several arduous days in a row. Song saw that they were weary and ordered a temporary rest. For the assault on Qizhou he already had a plan. But first he dispatched a man to Tanzhou to inquire about Zhang Qin's arrow wound.

"The injury is superficial. Tell our highest leader not to worry," was Dr. An's reply. "Once the pus is drained he'll recover quickly. But our soldiers are suffering from many ailments because of the heat. I've asked Commissioner Zhao to send Xiao Rang and Song Qing to the Eastern Capital to buy heat-stroke medicine in the Imperial Hospital. Huangfu Duan, our veterinary, wants medicine for our horses. They will attend to that, too."

Very pleased, Song Jiang consulted with Lu regarding the attack on Qizhou. "I had this plan before I knew you were surrounded at Yutian," he said. "Gongsun Sheng is a native of Qizhou, Yang Xiong used to be a bailiff in the local government, and Shi Xiu and Shi Qian both lived there for a long time. The other day when we defeated the Tartars, I instructed Shi Xiu and Shi Qian to mix with the remnants of their army and retreat with them into the town. Once they get there they'll have a place to stay.

"Shi Qian said to me: 'In Qizhou there's a big temple called the Baoyan Monastery. Its vestibule houses scriptures and precious objects. In the center of the compound is a magnificent hall, and in front of this is a fine tower that pierces the clouds.' And Shi Xiu said: 'I've told him to hide on the roof of the vestibule. I'll bring him food every day. For calls or nature he'll just have to wait till dark. As soon as you and our troops assault the town he'll set fire to the top of the tower.' Shi Qian is a veteran roof-climber and wall-sealer. He won't have any trouble concealing himself. When the time comes he'll put the prefectural government offices to the torch. They've talked it over and have already gone. I'm mobilizing our attack forces."

The next day, Song Jiang and his soldiers quit Pinggu County and joined Lu and his men. Together, they marched on Qizhou.

Meanwhile, the prince was raging over the loss of two of his sons. He conferred with his chief generals Baomisheng, Tianshanyong and the Vice-Minister Dongxian.

"Last time the relief columns from Zhuozhou and Bazhou both advanced widely spread out," he said. "But now Song Jiang has concentrated his forces at Yulian. Sooner or later he'll attack Qizhou. What are we going to do?"

"I'd have nothing against those barbarians if they hadn't invaded," said Baomisheng. "But since they have, I must fight them as enemies. I'm going out and capture a few. Otherwise, they'll never leave!"

"One of them wears a green robe and is fantastically good at throwing stones," said the vice-minister. "Be careful of him."

"I hit him in the neck with an arrow," said Tianshanyong. "He's probably dead."

"Except for that fellow," said the vice-minister, "the others don't matter."

A junior officer entered and said: "Song Jiang's army is rushing towards Qizhou."

The prince hastily mustered his troops and flew out to engage the foe. Thirty *li* from the town the opposing contingents met, and both deployed in battle positions. Baomisheng, his long lance held athwart, rode forth.

"Who will break him, seize his banner, and win the first distinction?" queried Song Jiang.

Before the words had left his mouth, Panther Head Lin Chong was in the field, contending with the Tartar general. They fought over thirty rounds, with neither the victor. Lin Chong wanted to be the first to distinguish himself. He closed in with his eighteen-foot lance and its snake-shaped point. Uttering a thunderous roar, he brushed aside his opponent's weapon and thrust into Baomisheng's neck. The Tartar general fell from his horse.

Song Jiang was very pleased. Both armies yelled. Tianshanyong rode forward next. From Song Jiang's ranks Xu Ning emerged to meet him, bearing a sickle-bladed lance. The two had fought less than twenty rounds when a thrust from Xu Ning brought his opponent tumbling to the ground.

Two generals vanquished in a row! Song Jiang was delighted. He waved his army into action. The Liao Tartars, frightened by the death of two top commanders, fled towards Qizhou. Song Jiang's forces pursued them a dozen *li* or so, then pulled back.

That night they set up camp and Song Jiang rewarded the troops. The following day they struck camp and headed for Qizhou. On the third day the prince, having lost two senior generals, grew very nervous when informed that Song Jiang's army was approaching. He hastily gave instructions to Vice-Minister Dongxian.

"Go out there and meet the foe! Take some of the pressure off us!"

The vice-minister couldn't very well refuse. He set forth with Yaor Weikang, Chu Mingyu, Cao Mingji and a thousand soldiers and deployed outside the town walls.

Song Jiang's contingents drew near and assumed a goose-wing formation. Their pennant gate opened and Suo Chao cantered forward, holding a large battle-ax. Yaor Weikang sped out from the Tartar ranks, lance in hand.

They met and fought for more than twenty rounds. The Tartar began to lose courage, and with it his taste for combat. He longed to get away. From the top of the town wall the prince saw him turn his steed and start for the Tartar position. But Suo Chao caught up, raised his big ax, and brought it down on Yaor Weikang's skull, cleaving it in two.

The vice-minister ordered Chu Mingyu and Cao Mingji to rush into the fray. They were both eight-tenths scared, but since they couldn't get out of it they advanced with their lances.

Nine Dragons Shi Jin, brandishing his sword, emerged to take on the two of them. Shi Jin was a great warrior. One sweep of his blade hacked Chu Mingyu from his saddle. Cao Mingji tried to flee, but Shi Jin caught up and, with another swing of his sword, cut him to the ground. Then he galloped directly into the Tartar position.

Song Jiang pointed with his whip, and his men rushed the drawbridge. In an ever-deepening gloom the prince ordered that all the gates be shut and every general take a stand on top of the walls. He sent a hurried report to the king, and dispatched emissaries to Bazhou and Youzhou requesting immediate assistance.

"They've locked the town up tight," Song Jiang said to Wu Yong. "What should we do?"

"We've got Shi Xiu and Shi Qian in there. They'll stay as long as necessary. Prepare scaling ladders and cannon on four sides for the attack. Have Ling Zhen launch an artillery bombardment first. If we hit them hard they're sure to crack."

"Precisely what I was thinking." Song Jiang ordered an offensive that very night.

The assault was intense. The prince directed that the entire populace man the walls. Shi Xiu, who for several days had been hiding in the Baoyan Monastery, bad been growing impatient at the lack of action. Now Shi Qian came to him excitedly.

"Brother Song Jiang is hitting the town hot and heavy. There'll never be a better time for setting those fires!"

They made their plans. Shi Qian would first put the top of the tower to the torch, then the monastery hall. "You burn the government offices," said Shi Qian. "When our forces at the South Gate see all these important places ablaze they'll strike even harder. They'll crack this town wide open!"

Both set out with powder, flint and steel, pipe length and coal, concealed on their persons. By nightfall Song Jiang's troops were assailing the town relentlessly.

The nimble Shi Qian could skim along eaves and skip over walls as easily as on level ground. He soon had the top of the tower in flames. Since it was the highest point around, the blaze could be seen plainly inside the town and out for a distance of over thirty *li,* like a fiery gimlet. Then Shi Qian ignited the monastery hall.

These two fires threw the town into an uproar. Among the citizenry, old and young panicked, boys cried, girls wept, and all ran for their lives. At this moment Shi Xiu climbed to the top of the government office and set it ablaze. The authorities realized the enemy had concealed agents at work. What did the populace care about defending the town walls? Nobody could stop them. They dashed off to look after their homes. Soon the monastery was also in flames. On the way out, Shi Qian had put it to the torch.

Four or five fires in less than half a watch told the prince that Song Jiang had operatives in the town. Hurriedly, he mustered some troops, took his wife and two children, loaded a cart, opened the North Gate and left.

Qizhou was in great confusion. Song Jiang urged his men to drive harder. Murderous yells rose inside the town and out. The attackers captured the South Gate. Vice-Minister Dongxian knew he couldn't hang on alone. He departed in the wake of the prince through the North Gate.

Song Jiang and his army surged into Qizhou. First, he had the fires extinguished. At daybreak, he posted notices reassuring the populace. He billeted as many of his troops as possible inside the town and issued them rewards. The achievements of Shi Qian and Shi Xiu were recorded in the distinguished conduct book for officers. Song Jiang sent a written dispatch to Zhao Anfu.

"We have taken the large prefecture of Qizhou. We would be pleased to have Your Excellency move your quarters here."

To which the commissioner wrote a reply: "I shall remain in Tanzhou temporarily, while Vanguard General Song Jiang holds Qizhou. Due to the severe summer heat, this is not a good time to shift troops. We can discuss this again when the weather is somewhat cooler."

Song Jiang then instructed Lu Junyi to encamp with his forces in Yutian County. The remainder of the army would occupy Qizhou. When the weather cooled, new orders would be given.

Meanwhile, Prince Yelu Dezhong and Vice-Minister Dongxian, together with their wives and children, fled to Youzhou. From there they went to Yanjing to report to the king. The monarch of the Liao Tartars was seated in his Golden Hall. Before him his civil and military officials stood in ranks. Court was just concluding.

The privy councellor announced: "The prince has arrived from Qizhou and awaits an audience."

The king immediately had them summoned. On entering the hall the prince and the minister prostrated themselves before the throne and wept aloud.

"Don't distress yourself, dear brother," said the king. "Whatever it is, tell me all about it."

"The Song emperor has sent an expeditionary army under Song Jiang against us. They're very strong. We can't seem to stop them. They've killed two of my sons and four Tanzhou generals. Then they rolled on and took Qizhou. We've come to Your Majesty to request death!"

"Rise, sirs," said the king. "We must talk this over. Who, after all, is this barbarian, Song Jiang? Just a bandit!"

Marshal Chu Jian the vice-premier came forward and explained. "I've heard about this fellow. Originally he was a bandit in a stronghold in Liangshan Marsh. But he never hurt good, ordinary folk, and sought always to act on Heaven's behalf. He killed only corrupt officials who harmed the people. Tong Guan and Gao Qiu led armies against him, but he completely smashed them in only five battles. No one has been able to arrest the gallant men in his band. Three times the emperor sent him offers of amnesty. Finally, he surrendered. He's been appointed vanguard general of the expeditionary force, but has not been given any official rank. The rest of his chieftains have no status either. These are the men who have been dispatched to slaughter us. I hear there are a hundred and eight of them, and each corresponds to a star in Heaven. They are formidable foes. Don't underestimate them, Your Majesty!"

"In view of what you say, what should we do?" exclaimed the king.

His elegant gown sweeping the floor, Minister Ouyang stepped forward confidently. "Long live Your Majesty," he said. "A son should be filial, a minister should be loyal. Although I am without talent, I have a small plan for driving back the Song invaders."

The king was pleased. "If you have any good suggestions, let's hear them."

Ouyang was brief, and as a result Song Jiang won great distinction, his name was inscribed in history, his deeds in the royal records. His forces returned from the border singing paeans of victory, beating time on their stirrups with their whips. Truly, their skill in defending their country vied with Lu Wang's, their righteous merit exceeded that of Zhang Liang.

What, then, was the proposal of Ouyang of the Kingdom of Liao? Read our next chapter if you would know.

CHAPTER 85

SONG JIANG AT NIGHT CROSSES YIJIN PASS

WU YONG BY A RUSE CAPTURES WENAN TOWN

Ouyang explained, "Song Jiang and his band are bold gallants from Liangshan Marsh. But the emperor of Song today is manipulated by Cai Jing, Tong Guan, Gao Qiu and Yang Jian. These four crooked ministers are jealous of real talent and block righteous conduct. If you're not their intimate you can't advance, if you don't give them money they don't want you. They'll never permit the Song Jiang faction to exist for long. In my humble opinion, Your Majesty should grant him high rank, bestow on him gold and silks, fine furs and horses. I'll be glad to go as your emissary and urge him to serve our great Liao kingdom. If he and his chieftains join us, Your Majesty can take the Central Plain as easily as turning over your hand! I beg you to consider!"

"What you say is quite true," mused the king. "You shall be my emissary. Take with you a hundred and eight fine saddle horses and a hundred and eight bolts of the best silk. Tell Song Jiang that he shall be a Grand General, the Supreme Commander of our Liao soldiery. As a sign of our faith in him, he shall also have a bountiful gift of gold and silver. Write down the names of the chieftains. They too shall be given official rank."

From the attending ranks Wuyan, the commander-in-chief, stepped forward and addressed the throne. "Why amnesty Song Jiang and his gang of petty bandits?" he cried. "I have under my command twenty-eight star-blest generals and eleven Heaven-guided officers. With our powerful army and bold commanders, what have we to fear? If the barbarians refuse to withdraw, I'll lead our troops personally and slaughter the lot!"

"You're a splendid warrior, a winged tiger, true," said the king. "But if we add them to our forces, your wings will be doubled. Don't try to prevent it."

After this rebuff, no one else dared speak. Wuyan was the country's leading general, versed in all eighteen branches of military art, an excellent strategist and tactician. Around thirty-five, tall and stalwart, he had a fair complexion and rosy lips, brown hair and green eyes, and was possessed of matchless courage and strength. In battle he used a long iron lance flecked with steel, and when in the thick of combat the iron slabs at his waist clanked fearsomely. Truly a formidable fighter!

On receipt of the governmental decree, Ouyang assembled the many gifts, mounted his horse and proceeded towards Qizhou where Song Jiang was resting his troops. Informed that a Liao emissary was approaching, Song didn't know whether this boded good or evil. He brought out the Books of the Mystic Maid and cast divining sticks. They fell in a pattern auguring great good fortune.

He told Wu Yong about the omen and said: "It probably means the Liao emissary will offer us an amnesty. What should we do?"

"If that is so, we can match their plan with one of our own. Accept it. Let Lu Junyi hang on to Qizhou, then take Bazhou prefecture. Once we've got Bazhou, the Liao kingdom is sure to crack. Tanzhou we already have. First become a high general of the Liao kingdom. The rest will be simple. Do the difficult things first and the easy things later. Don't let them suspect."

When Minister Ouyang arrived at the town, Song Jiang ordered that the gate be opened and the Tartar official be allowed to enter. Ouyang dismounted in front of the prefectural office and went directly to the main hall. Ceremonial greetings were exchanged. Host and guest took their seats.

"What brings you here, sir?"

"There is small matter. Could I speak to Your Excellency alone?"

Song Jiang directed his chieftains to withdraw. He led his visitor to a secluded room in the rear. Ouyang bowed.

"Our Liao kingdom has long known of your fame, General. Because of the vast distance between us, unfortunately we never had the opportunity to view your noble countenance. We have heard, too, that when you were in your mountain stronghold you acted always in Heaven's behalf, and that you and your brother chieftains were of one heart. Today, in the Song court evil ministers block the path of righteousness. If you dispense bribes among them you can obtain high office and important duties. If you don't, even though you do great deeds for your country, you are kept in obscurity and never rise in rank. This wicked clique holds power. They slander the upright, are jealous of ability, make no distinction between what is worthy of reward and what deserves punishment, and have sown confusion throughout the land. Bandits run wild south of the Yangzi, on both sides of the Zhejiang River and in the provinces of Shandong and Hebei. The people are so despoiled by them they can barely sustain themselves.

"Out of a desire to serve your emperor loyally, you surrendered with a hundred thousand crack troops. But you were given only the position of a mere vanguard general, and have not been elevated to official rank. Nor has any rank been granted to your brother chieftains, despite their devoted efforts to serve their country. Although you have led your army into the desert, suffered privations and performed meritorious deeds, the imperial court has bestowed no rewards. This is all due to the schemes of the wicked monsters. Only by sending whatever plunder you may acquire to Cai Jing, Tong Guan, Gao Qiu and Yang Jian can you be sure of attaining official rank and winning royal favor. Should you fail to do this, no matter how faithfully you perform and how conspicuously you distinguish yourself, when you return to the capital you will be branded a traitor.

"I have been dispatched as the emissary of the king of Great Liao to inform you of His Majesty's desire to designate you his Grand General and Supreme Commander of the Liao soldiery, and to present you with gold and silver plus a hundred and eight bolts of silk and a hundred and eight fine mounts. I am also to write down the names of all one hundred and eight of you so that official titles may be bestowed. I have no wish to cajole you, General. I am here because our king, who has long known of your virtue, has deputed me to invite you and your chieftains to accept an amnesty and submit to his rule."

Song Jiang heard him out, then replied. "What you have said, sir, is very true. Because I was born of mean estate and was just a petty functionary in Yuncheng City I had to flee after committing a crime and take temporary refuge in Liangshan Marsh. Yet the Song emperor offered me an amnesty three times, and finally pardoned my crimes. Although my position is lowly and I have not yet performed any meritorious deeds, I would like to repay the emperor for his kindness in forgiving me. The Liao king wishes to grant me high rank and present me with valuable gifts. I dare not accept. Please take them back. Since it is now the heat of summer, I have ordered my army to rest and have borrowed two of your monarch's towns to quarter them in. Let's wait until the cool of autumn. Then we can discuss this again."

"If you don't scorn them as too trivial, General, at least accept the gifts. I will come for another talk later on."

"You must realize there are a lot of eyes and ears among the hundred and eight of us. If word of this leaks out, there will be trouble."

"But power is firmly in your hands. Who would dare disobey?"

"You don't understand. The majority of my chieftains are fearless straightforward warriors. Better let me prepare them. When we're all agreed, there'll be time enough to give you an answer."

After wining and dining Ouyang, Song Jiang saw him out of the town. The emissary mounted and left. Song Jiang told Wu Yong what had transpired.

"What shall I do?"

Wu Yong sighed, head down, but did not reply.

"Why do you sigh, Military Advisor?"

"I've been wondering. Since you place loyalty first, I'm afraid to say too much. It seems to me there's a great deal of truth in Minister Ouyang's statements. Our Song emperor, though noble and intelligent, has lost much of his power to Cai Jing, Tong Guan, Gao Qiu and Yang Jian. What's more, he trusts them. Even if we distinguish ourselves, there's no assurance we'll be elevated. After three amnesty offers you, our leader, have been given only the empty title of Vanguard General. In my humble opinion going over to the Tartars at least would be better than maintaining a fortress in Mount Liangshan. Of course it might violate your sense of loyalty."

"You're badly mistaken! Going over to the Tartars is out of the question! Even if the Song Dynasty wrongs me, I can't wrong the Song Dynasty. I may not receive any rewards, but I'll leave behind a clean name. Heaven will not forgive me if I turn traitor! We ought to be loyal and serve our country unto death."

"Since that's how you feel, brother, we can use this opportunity to take Bazhou. But we'll have to rest our soldier and horses temporarily because of the summer heat."

The two reached agreement, but they didn't tell the other chieftains. They remained in Qizhou waiting for the heat to pass.

While chatting with Gongsun Sheng the following day Song Jiang said: "I've often heard you speak of your teacher Luo the Sage as a lofty scholar of a prosperous era. That time we attacked Gaotang Prefecture, and I sent Dai Zong and Li Kui to request your aid in countering Gao Lian's magic, you mentioned that Luo the Sage's occult skill was extremely effective. Could I trouble you, brother, to take me to his temple so that I may burn incense and pray, and wash the earthly dust from my soul? Would that suit you?"

"I've been thinking about going home to see my old mother and paying my respects to my old teacher at the same time. But I saw you were busy settling down our troops, and didn't dare ask. I was going to request leave today. It never occurred to me that you would want to go, too. We can start tomorrow morning. I'll present you to my teacher and go visit my mother."

The next day Song Jiang turned over command of the army to his military advisor, and prepared famous incense, fresh fruit, gold and jewels and fine silks. Together with Hua Rong, Dai Zong, Lu Fang, Guo Sheng, Yan Shun and Ma Lin, he and Gongsun set out for Two Fairies Mountain in Jiugong County at the head of five thousand infantry.

Astride their horses, the chieftains rode deep into the mountains. Green pines mantled the slopes, and the air was cool and clear. The summer heat was left far behind. Truly, mountains of great beauty. Gongsun pointed.

"That is called 'Fish Snout Mountain.'"

Gongsun led Song Jiang to the Temple of Purple Shades where all dismounted and straightened their clothes. A junior officer carrying the incense and gifts, they proceeded to the Crane Pavilion. Taoist priests greeted Gongsun and Song Jiang respectfully.

"'Where is my teacher?" Gongsun asked.

"For the past few days the master has been meditating in the rear," replied the priest. "He hasn't been seeing anyone and seldom comes to the temple."

With Song Jiang, Gongsun followed a hilly winding path behind the temple towards the sage's retreat. Before they had gone a *li,* they saw a fence of brambles. Outside it were green pines and cypress, within were pretty shrubs and flowers. In the center were three connected snow caverns. It was here that Luo the Sage read scriptures.

An acolyte, seeing them arrive, opened the gate and came out. Gongsun entered a thatched shack in front of the Crane Pavilion and kowtowed before his teacher, Luo the Sage.

"Song Jiang, my old friend from Shandong, has received an amnesty. By imperial order, he leads an army against the Liao, and has already reached Qizhou. Today, he has come specially to pay you his respects."

Luo directed that he be invited in. As Song Jiang entered, Luo came down from the dais to greet him. Song Jiang begged Luo to be seated so that he might kowtow before him.

"You are a mighty minister of our state, General," protested the Taoist, "with gold at your waist and purple in your clothes. You're on a mission for His Majesty. I'm only a poor rustic priest. How do I dare?"

But Song Jiang insisted, and Luo finally sat down. Song Jiang first placed the fine incense in the burner and lit it, then he kowtowed eight times. He summoned Hua Rong and the other chieftains, and they did the same.

Luo asked them all to be seated and instructed his acolyte to serve tea and fruit. After making a few polite inquiries about their journey, the Sage addressed himself to Song Jiang.

"You correspond to a star of Heavenly Spirit, General, you're famed throughout the Central Plain, you're surrounded by other Star Spirits, and together you act in Heaven's behalf. Recently you have submitted to the rule of the Song court, for which virtuous deed you shall be remembered for countless generations.

"My pupil Gongsun Sheng I introduced into our order personally, and he shunted off earthly interests and devoted himself to truth. Subsequently, he had no choice but to join you, since he too was a spirit descended from a star. Today you have deigned to visit me, General. I am not worthy. Please overlook my faults."

"I was just a petty functionary in Yuncheng, and had to run away to the mountains because I committed a crime. Fortunately, heroic companions came like the wind from every direction. We're of one voice, one breath, as close as bone and flesh, limbs of the same body. Only after Heaven sent a sign did we know that we were united as stars of Heavenly Spirits and Earthly Fiends.

"Three times the Song emperor granted us amnesty and forgave our crimes, and my chieftains joined me in submitting to imperial rule. I have been put in command of an expeditionary force against the Liao. Since we were passing your holy place, I thought I might take advantage of this lucky chance to offer my respects. If you could tell me what lies ahead, sir Sage, I would consider myself infinitely fortunate."

"Stay a while, General. Have a vegetarian meal with me. It's getting late. Spend the night in our crude thatched shelter and go back in the morning. What do you say?"

"I'm longing to have you unravel the mystery, Teacher. Only then will I be able to go on with peace of mind." At Song Jiang's signal, his retainers proffered the gold and jewels and silks to Luo the Sage.

"I'm an old man living quietly in a rustic retreat," said the Taoist. "I have no use for riches. A cloth gown to cover my body is good enough. I have never worn silks. As a commander of whole armies you have to spend thousands every day, General. Take back your gifts. Use them for your soldiers. I have no need for such things. I'll just keep the platters of fruit."

Song Jiang again kowtowed and begged Luo to accept, but the old man was adamant. A vegetarian meal was served. When they had finished eating, they drank tea. Luo told Gongsun to go home and see his mother.

"Come back early in the morning and accompany the general back to the city," he admonished.

That evening Luo chatted with his visitor. Song Jiang told in detail what was troubling him, and pleaded for a prophecy.

"You have a loyal heart, General, and you act in conformity with Heaven's will. God will surely protect you. Some day you will be entitled a noble. Have no doubt, after your death sacrifices will be made to your spirit in a temple. But in life your future is rather dim. It's far from perfect."

"Do you mean, Teacher, that I won't come to a good end?"

"Oh, no. You'll die in your bed, and be buried in a proper grave. It's just that in your life there are many abrasions among the smooth, more sorrows than joys. When you're at the height of your success, you should pull back a bit. Don't strive too long for wealth and rank."

"Such things have never been my desire. I want only to be together always with my brothers. If I can have that, I'll be content though I live in poverty. My sole wish is peace and happiness for all."

Luo the Sage smiled. "When the final parting comes, who of us can hope to stay!"

Song Jiang bowed and begged him for a prophecy. The old Taoist directed his acolyte to bring paper and pen. Then he wrote this eight-phrase prophecy and handed it to Song Jiang:

Few are the loyal,
Rare are true friends.
Success in the Northland
Is but the moon's sickly glow.
At winter's start
The geese fly away.
When dynasties change
Old titles must go.

Song Jiang didn't understand. He bowed to the Sage and said: "Please explain, Teacher. What's the meaning of this riddle?"

"It's decree from Heaven and cannot be revealed. When the time comes, you will know. The night is dark and the hour is late. Please return to the temple, General. We'll meet again in the morning. Some years ago I received something while asleep. I want to enter that dream again so that I can return it. Forgive me, General."

Concealing the eight-phrase prophecy on his person, Song Jiang took his leave of the sage and went back to the temple. The Taoist priests conducted him to their meditation hall, and there he spent the night.

Early the next morning, he again went to call on Luo the Sage. Gongsun was already waiting in the thatched shack. Luo had a vegetarian breakfast served. When it was over, he addressed Song Jiang.

"I have a request. My pupil Gongsun's mundane pursuits are only temporary. His destiny is to follow the Way. But if he remains here now to look after me, he'll be neglecting his brothers. I'll let him go with you, General, and achieve great merit. But when you return to the capital and report your victory to the throne, I hope you will allow him to come back here. Thus he will be able first to carry on the Way and then end his mother's constant longing. I have no doubt that as a gallant warrior, General, you behave in a righteous manner. I wonder whether you would be willing to accept my suggestion?"

"Teacher's word is my command! Whether brother Gongsun remains with me is up to him. I wouldn't dare interfere."

Luo the Sage and Gongsun Sheng in a pious gesture placed their palms together before their faces. "We thank you, General," they said, "for your golden promise."

The chieftains bid farewell to Luo. He saw them to the outside of the retreat. "Look after yourself, General. May we hear soon of your being entitled!"

Song Jiang bowed and departed. The horses had been fed and groomed, and were waiting for him and his chieftains in front of the monastery. The Taoist priests saw them off to the outskirts of the temple grounds, and there bid them farewell. The Visitors led their steeds to a level halfway down the slope. Then all mounted and rode back to Qizhou.

The journey was uneventful. They dismounted in front of the municipal government office in the center of town. Li Kui the Black Whirlwind was there to greet them.

"You went to see Luo the Sage," he said. "Why didn't you take me along?"

"Luo claims you tried to kill him. He's got it in for you."

"He gave me a hard enough time!"

Everybody laughed.

Song Jiang entered the government compound, and they all went to a hall in the rear. He showed the eight-phrase prophecy to Wu Yong, but no one could decipher it.

"Brother," said Gongsun, "this is a mystic decree from Heaven. Its meaning is not intended to be clear. Put it away, it will serve you all your life. Don't try to guess. Remember what my teacher said—when the time comes, you will know."

Song Jiang acceded to Gongsun's advice. He placed the decree inside the Three Heavenly Books for safekeeping. The army remained in Qizhou for the next month or more. There were no military developments.

In the latter half of the seventh lunar month a dispatch arrived from Commissioner Zhao in Tanzhou. He said the imperial court had sent a directive urging an offensive. Song Jiang talked it over with Wu Yong. They went first to Yutian and met with Lu Junyi and the others. They held practice maneuvers, got the weapons in order, and settled deployment details. Then they returned to Qizhou, offered sacrifices to their flags, and chose an suspicious day for setting forth.

At this moment an attendant announced: "An emissary from the Kingdom of Liao."

Song Jiang went out to receive him. It was Minister Ouyang. He was invited to the rear, and courtesies were exchanged.

"What brings you here, Minister?"

"I prefer to speak to you alone."

Song Jiang dismissed his orderlies.

"The King of Great Liao has exceeding admiration for your virtue, General. If you come over, he will surely be moved to give you rank and titles. But that is of relatively small import. What matters is that you join us early so that His Majesty may not be kept in suspense."

"No one else is here, I can speak freely. The last time you called, my chieftains all guessed your purpose. Half of them are not willing to submit. If I go to Youzhou Prefecture with you to visit the king, Lu Junyi, my Vice Vanguard General, is certain to pursue me with troops. And if we battle there outside the town, the old fraternal feeling among my brothers will come to nought! I must first take refuge in some city—it doesn't matter which—with some of my trusted cohorts. Then, if Lu learns what I've done, and comes after me, I can stay out of his way. If he refuses to take my advice, I can still fight him. If he doesn't know, and returns to the Eastern Capital, I'm going to have trouble anyway. But by then I will have seen the king. I'll have time enough to go forth at the head of a Great Liao army and engage the foe."

Very pleased, Ouyang said: "We're not far from Bazhou. There are only two approaches to it. One is called Yijin Pass. It's flanked by high steep cliffs, and through it runs a post road. The other is called Wenan Pass, and it also has ugly heights on either side. Beyond this is the county town. There two passes are the gateways to Bazhou from the flanks. You can, if you wish, take shelter in Bazhou. The city is ruled by Kangli Dingan, the king's brother-in-law. You can stay with him, General, and see what develops here."

"In that case, I'll send people to my home immediately to fetch my father, so that he won't be caught. You may dispatch men to me secretly, Minister, to lead the way. I'll start preparing tonight."

Ouyang was very happy. He bid Song Jiang farewell, left the government compound, mounted his horse and departed.

Song Jiang summoned Lu Junyi, Wu Yong and Zhu Wu to Qizhou, and they evolved a ruse for taking Bazhou. Lu then returned, and Wu Yong and Zhu

Wu gave secret instructions to the other chieftains. With fourteen of these Song Jiang readied a force often thousand. Now, they had only to wait for Minister Ouyang to reappear.

Two days later Ouyang came again at a gallop. "The king of Great Liao is convinced of your good intentions," he announced to Song Jiang. "With you on our side what have we to fear of the Song army! His Majesty will also be supported by cavalry from Yuyang and infantry from Shanggu. Since you're worried about your father we're sending people to invite him to Bazhou. He and the king's brother-in-law can keep each other company."

"The chieftains who are willing to go with me are all prepared. When shall we start?"

"Tonight. Please issue your orders."

Song Jiang directed that to ensure silence every metal part of the horses' equipment be muffled and that the men march with wooden gags in their mouths. They would be leaving that very night. He entertained the emissary until dusk, then he ordered that the town's West Gate be opened.

Ouyang led the way with a few dozen horsemen. Song Jiang and a body of troops followed. When they had gone something over twenty *li* Song Jiang suddenly uttered a cry of dismay.

"*Aiya!* I arranged with Wu Yong, my military advisor, to go over to the Great Liao together. We left in such a hurry, I didn't wait for him. Let's slow down a bit, and send someone to get him."

Around midnight, the gate of Yijin Pass loomed before them. Minister Ouyang shouted a command.

"Open the gate!"

The officer in charge complied. The army marched through and continued on to Bazhou. Shortly before dawn Ouyang invited Song Jiang to enter the city. Kangli Dingan, the king's brother-in-law, was notified of their arrival. Brother of the queen, he was extremely influential. What's more, he was possessed of remarkable courage. Serving under him in the defense of Bazhou were two ministers. One was called Jinfu, the other Yeqing.

When he heard that Song Jiang had come to surrender, Dingan ordered that the army camp outside the city, and that only Vanguard General Song Jiang be allowed to enter. Ouyang led Song Jiang into the presence of the Royal Brother-in-Law. Impressed by his handsome appearance, Dingan came down from the dais to greet him. After courtesies were exchanged in the Rear Hall, Dingan invited him to be seated.

"The Royal Brother-in-Law is a tree of gold branches and jade leaves, while I am only a small officer who surrenders. How dare I accept such ceremony? How can I ever repay?"

"Your fame as conqueror of the Central Plain is known throughout the land. You have won the admiration of our Liao king. He will surely make important use of you."

"Basking in your reflected glory, Royal Brother-in-Law, I shall do my utmost to display my gratitude for His Majesty's vast beneficence." Very pleased, Dingan ordered that a feast of congratulations be laid for Song Jiang, and that cows and horses be slaughtered to feted his soldiers. A house was provided in which Song Jiang and Hua Rong and the others could stay. Only then were the troops allowed into the city. The chieftains paid their respects to the Royal Bother-in-Law and the Tartar generals, then joined Song Jiang in their special quarters.

Song Jiang sent for Ouyang and said: "Would you please notify the officials at the pass gates to let Wu Yong through when he arrives. He will live here with me. I forgot about him last night, we travelled so quickly. Wu Yong is indispensable to me in major military affairs. He's equally adept in civil matters, and he knows every aspect of strategy and tactics."

Ouyang sent word to both Yijin and Wenan: Should a scholarly looking gentleman named Wu Yong appear, let him in.

From atop the gate at Yijin Pass the official in charge saw a huge cloud of dust stretching from earth to sky. It heralded the approach of a large army. The official primed his cannons and prepared to engage the foe.

In front of the mountain a lone horseman appeared. He looked like a scholar. With him, on foot, were a monk and a pilgrim. They were followed by about a dozen villagers. All hurried towards the gate. The horseman drew rein before it and raised his voice in a shout.

"I am Song Jiang's military advisor Wu Yong. I'm trying to find him. The Song troops are hot on my heels! You must open the gate and save me!"

"That's the man, all right," thought the official. He ordered that the gate be opened to admit Wu Yong. The monk and the pilgrim promptly barged in with him. Soldiers at the entrance tried to stop them. The pilgrim was well inside by now.

"We are two men who have spurned the material world," cried the monk. "The Song troops are on our trail. Please save us!"

Soldiers attempted to push them out. The monk and pilgrim lost their tempers. "We're not monks at all," they yelled. "We're Sagacious Lu and Wu Song the Lords of Slaughter!"

The Tattooed Monk began swinging his iron staff, cracking every skull he encountered. The Pilgrim wielded his pair of swords, killing soldiers like slicing melons and cutting vegetables. The dozen "villagers" were actually all chieftains. They rushed the gate and took it over. Lu Junyi and his army then poured through the pass into Wenan County. The officials at the gate couldn't stem the tide. The entire county soon fell to the attackers.

Wu Yong galloped to the walls of Bazhou. The officials at the gate reported his arrival. Song Jiang and Minister Ouyang went to meet him and led him to the presence of the Royal Brother-in-Law.

"I was a bit late getting started," Wu Yong explained. "I hadn't expected Lu Junyi to hear about my leaving the town. He came tearing after me, and chased me as far as the pass. Now I've reached this city. I don't know what Lu did after I escaped him."

Just then a mounted comet scout entered and reported: "The Song army has captured Wenan County and is heading this way!"

The Royal Brother-in-Law mustered troops and prepared to go out and meet the foe. "You needn't do that," said Song Jiang. "Wait till Lu reaches our walls. I'll try to persuade him to come over. If he doesn't agree, there'll still be time to fight him."

Another mounted scout reported: "They're not far from the city now."

Dingan the Royal Brother-in-Law and Song Jiang mounted the walls for a look. They saw the Song troops deployed in neat ranks outside the city. Lu Junyi, in helmet and armor, grasping his lance astride a spirited steed, was positioning his forces. An imposing martial figure, he reined in beneath his gate of pennants.

"Let Song Jiang, the opposer of the imperial court, come out," he shouted.

Standing in the ramparts beneath the watch tower, Song Jiang called back: "Brother, the Song court makes no distinction between what should be punished and what should be rewarded. Slanderers and intriguers hold power. I have already gone over to the king of Great Liao. Come and help me. Let's both support the king. Don't forget the many days we were together in Liangshan Marsh."

"I had a happy family and a prosperous business in the Northern Capital when you inveigled me up the mountain! Three times the Song emperor offered us amnesties. He's been more than kind to you. How could you betray him? You swarthy sawed-off incompetent! Come out and fight! We'll see who's the better man!"

Angrily, Song Jiang commanded the guards to open the gate. He directed Lin Chong, Hua Rong, Zhu Tong and Mu Hong to go forth and capture Lu Junyi. Lu restrained his officers from assisting him, and fearlessly charged directly at all four. They battled for more than twenty rounds. Then the four turned their mounts and withdrew towards the city. Lu waved his lance and swept forward with a large contingent in pursuit. Lin Chong and Hua Rong took a stand at the drawbridge over the moat. Then, feigning defeat, they retreated into Bazhou, still battling. The large Song army massed outside set up a mighty cheer.

Inside the city, Song Jiang and his forces immediately turned on the Tartars and joined in the assault. The slaughter was widespread. Many surrendered. Dingan the Royal Brother-in-Law stared, open-mouthed. He was utterly helpless. Together with his ministers, he was caught and bound.

Song Jiang led in the troops which were still outside the city and had a reunion with his chieftains in the prefectural government center. He sent for Dingan the Royal Brother-in-Law and Ministers Ouyang, Jinfu and Yeqing, invited them to be seated, and received them courteously.

"You Liaos didn't understand," he said. "You figured us all wrong. My band of gallants were never bandits racketing around in the wooded hills. Every one is a star spirit. They wouldn't betray their emperor. All we wanted was to capture Bazhou, and we took this opportunity to do so. Now that we have succeeded, you, Royal Brother-in-Law, may return to your native land. Have no fear. We have no intention of killing you. Those under you may also go back, with their families. Bazhou now belongs to our empire. Don't contend for it again. Our soldiers will be everywhere. We won't permit any interference."

Song Jiang directed all Tartar officials in the city to leave, and return with Dingan to Youzhou. He also posted proclamations reassuring the local populace, and instructed Lu Junyi to go back with half the troops and hold Qizhou. He himself remained in control of Bazhou with the other half. He sent a messenger with the news to Commissioner Zhao. Overjoyed, Zhao relayed the information in a report to the emperor.

Dingan and his three ministers, plus many officials, travelled to the Tartar capital in Yanjing. They told the king of Song Jiang's false surrender. "And as a result, the barbarians have conquered Bazhou!"

The monarch was furious. He cursed Minister Ouyang. "It's all because of your slavish intrigues, shifting everything around! You've lost us the vital city of Bazhou! How are we going to hold Yanjing!" He shouted an order: "Take him out and execute him!"

Wuyan the commander-in-chief came forward. "Don't worry, Your Majesty. There's no need for our country's king to exert himself over that rogue Song Jiang. We have a plan. Forgive Minister Ouyang. If Song Jiang finds out you had him killed, he'll laugh at us."

The monarch pardoned Ouyang, then questioned Wuyan. How could he defeat the barbarians and recapture the cities?

"I shall go with twenty-eight star-blest generals and eleven Heaven-guided officers and deploy in battle formation. We'll flatten those barbarians in a single action!"

Before the words were out of Wuyan's mouth, Commanding General Ho stepped forward and added his guarantee. "Rest assured, Your Majesty. It seems to me the old saying is correct: You don't kill a chicken with an ox-slaughtering knife. Why use our regular army for a thing like this? I have a little plan that will send all the barbarians to a graveless death!"

"We shall be delighted to hear it, my dear Minister," said the king, very pleased.

Opening his mouth and wagging his tongue, Ho detailed his shrewd plan. And as a result, Lu Junyi was lured to a place where the horses had no fodder and the soldiers no grain. The entire Song army almost perished, a band of heroes nearly came to an end.

What was the plan General Ho expounded before the Tartar king? Read our next chapter if you would know.

CHAPTER 86

SONG JIANG BATTLES ON LONE DEER MOUNTAIN

LU THE MAGNATE IS TRAPPED IN STONY VALLEY

Ho Zhongbao, the commanding general, ranked second after Wuyan, the commander-in-chief of the Great Liao armed forces. Very tall, powerfully built, a shrewd strategist, he wielded a three-pointed two-edged sword. He was responsible for the defense of Youzhou Prefecture, and was in charge of every branch of military service.

"We have a place in Youzhou called Stony Valley," he told the king. "Hemmed in on all sides by high mountains, a single road goes in and ends there. I intend to use a dozen or so cavalrymen to lure the barbarians into that valley and then surround it with troops. The enemy won't be able to go forward, and won't be able to retreat. We'll starve them to death."

"How will you get them to come?" asked Wuyan.

"They've taken three of our big prefectures, and are feeling very proud of themselves," said Ho. "They're sure to want Youzhou, next. If I dispatch troops to provoke them, they'll certainly give chase. We'll lead them into the valley, and they'll be stuck!"

"Your plan is incomplete. Once you get them there, you must send a large force in to slaughter them. Now let's see how you go about it."

General Ho took his leave of the king, donned his armor, buckled on his sword and mounted his horse. He returned to Youzhou at the head of a column of infantry. There he mobilized his soldiers and divided them into three units. One was to defend Youzhou, the other two were ordered to attack Bazhou and Qizhou. These were placed under the commands of Ho Chai and Ho Yun, respectively, younger brothers of the commanding general. They were not to win. In fact they were to pretend defeat and draw the Song army across the line into Youzhou, where the next move of the plan would go into effect.

Meanwhile, in Bazhou, Song Jiang received the report: "The Liaos are assaulting Qizhou. We're in danger of losing it. We hope you'll send relief forces at once."

"Since they're attacking, we've no reason to be resting," said Song Jiang. "We'll use this opportunity to conquer Youzhou."

Leaving behind a small unit to defend the city, he and the rest of the army broke camp and headed for Qizhou. There, they would join forces with Lu Junyi the Magnate's contingent, and set a date for their offensive.

The Tartars under Ho Chai continued their advance on Bazhou. They ran into Song Jiang's troops after they had left the city and were halfway to Qizhou. They clashed only two or three times, and Ho Chai led his soldiers away in a retreat. But Song Jiang did not pursue. He was informed that Ho Yun had assailed Qizhou, and had also withdrawn when Huyan Zhuo came out to give battle.

Song Jiang conferred in his tent with Lu Junyi on how to take Youzhou. Wu Yong and Zhu Wu had some words of caution.

"The enemy wouldn't have split their soldier into two columns if they weren't trying to lure us in. We mustn't fall for their tricks."

"You're wrong," Lu protested. "We've beaten them time after time. Why should they want to pull us towards them? If we don't conquer Youzhou now, when we can, it may not be so easy later. Move immediately, I say. What are we wailing for!"

Song Jiang agreed. "The rogues are exhausted. What kind of plan could they have? This is our chance."

He ignored Wu Yong and Zhu Wu's advice and marched on Youzhou, dividing his forces into three columns, large and small. Soon, the advance unit sent back word: "Liao soldiers ahead, blocking the road." He rode forward to look.

He saw coming around the side of the mountain a swarm of black flags. Song Jiang ordered his advance unit to spread out. The Tartar army rolled towards them, covering the earth. Bearing their embroidered black flags, they separated into four columns and deployed in front of the mountain slope. As Song Jiang, Lu and the chieftains watched, from the hundreds of thousands of Tartars massed like black clouds, a high general emerged. Holding athwart his three-pointed, two-edged sword, he halted his steed at the opposite end of the field of combat. On his banner were inscribed the legend: *Vice Commander-in-Chief of the Great Liao Army Ho Zhongbao.*

"He must be an excellent warrior," said Song Jiang. "Who dares to vie against him?"

Before the words were out of his mount, Guan Sheng the Big Halberd, waving his crescent-shaped blade, galloped forward on his roan pinto. No talk was exchanged between the two. They met in instant battle.

Truly, they were two dragons contending for a treasure, a pair of tigers fighting over prey. To and fro they twisted like the turning body of a phoenix, up and down they flailed like the beating wings of a fabulous *luan.* Sword clanged against sword, flashing yards of icy fire. Steed pounded against steed, shaking half the sky with their murderous power.

More than thirty rounds the warriors battled. But Commanding General Ho, instead of intensifying his efforts, turned and rode towards his own lines. Guan Sheng galloped in pursuit. Ho led his troops back around the mountain. Song Jiang and his army chased them for forty or fifty *li.*

Suddenly, on all sides war drums began to thunder. Song Jiang hastily shouted for his army to withdraw. But a contingent of Tartars, pouring down the slope on the left, blocked his retreat. As he agitatedly divided his forces to meet the threat, another Tartar contingent charged from the right. Ahead, General Ho wheeled his soldiers around to attack from the front. Song Jiang's men were completely enclosed in a giant pincers. The Tartars had cut the Song dynasty army in two.

The rear half, fighting hard under Lu Junyi, could no longer see the forward elements. They desperately sought an opening through which to pull back. Another Liao unit assailed them from the side. The Tartar soldiers, yelling savagely, were now attacking all around, tightly hemming them in. Lu sent his chieftains in charges to left and right, front and rear, urgently trying to break through. They fought with magnificent valor.

Dark clouds suddenly massed, blotting out the sky and turning day into night. The men lost all sense of direction. Lu was panic-stricken. Leading his-troops, he struggled to smash free. The Tartars, hearing ahead the tinkling of bridle bells, galloped to meet the foe.

Lu and his men reached a gap in the mountains. He could hear the voices of the Tartars and the neighing of their horses inside the gap, and he urged his army forward. A wild gale arose, whipping up sand and gravel, blinding both sides. Lu battled in this maelstrom until nearly midnight. Only then did the wind fade and the clouds part, revealing a sky full of stars.

The Song soldiers took their bearings. All around were high trackless mountains and steep pathless cliffs. Only twelve chieftains and five thousand troops could be accounted for. Hemmed in by cliffs all around, they sought in vain for a way out.

"The men are weary after fighting all day," Lu thought. "We'll rest here tonight and continue searching tomorrow."

When the dark clouds gathered and the wind blew, Song Jiang's forces were also blinded by sand and gravel and unable to see one another. Gongsun Sheng, on horseback, recognized it at once as a magic spell. He waved his precious sword and muttered an incantation, then shouted: "Speed!" He pointed with his precious sword, and the clouds dispersed and the gale subsided. The Liao army pulled back without giving battle, and the broad evil miasma gradually vanished.

Having broken clear of the encirclement, Song Jiang and his troops withdrew to a high mountain. There they linked up with more of their forces and placed their grain carts in a wide circle to form a rough stockade. A count of the chieftains revealed that thirteen of them, including Lu Junyi the Magnate, were missing, as well as five thousand troops.

At daybreak, Song Jiang sent Huyan Zhuo, Lin Chong, Qin Ming and Guan Sheng with soldiers to look for them. But after searching all day, they could find no trace. He then took out the Three Heavenly Books of the Mystic Maid of Ninth Heaven and lit incense and cast divining sticks. "The general omen isn't bad," he said, "but they seem to have fallen into an evil area and can't get free."

Worried, he sent Xie Zhen and Xie Bao, disguised as hunters, to scour the mountains. He also ordered Shi Qian, Shi Yong, Duan Jingzhu and Cao Zheng to travel around and see if they could pick up any news. The Xie brothers, wearing tiger skin robes and carrying steel fork-spears, pushed deep into the mountains. By dusk they saw no sign of human habitation, only an endless jumble of heights.

They crossed another few mountains. By then it was night. In the misty moonlight, they saw a pin-point of lamplight on a far slope.

"Someone must live there," they thought. "We'll go and ask for something to eat."

They strode swiftly in the direction of the lamplight. After walking a *li* or more, they reached their destination. Beside a grove was a dilapidated shack of two or three rooms. They could see the lamp burning through a crack in the wall. Pushing open the door, they found an old woman of about sixty. They set down their fork-spears and bowed in greeting.

"I thought it was my sons coming home," said the woman. "I never expected guests. No need for courtesy. Where are you from, hunters? What brings you here?"

"We're from a family of hunters in Shandong," said Xie Zhen, "but we came to these parts to do bit of trading. Who knew we'd run into armies fighting and killing all over the place? We lost our capital and haven't been able to earn a living. So we've been hunting in these mountains for a little wild game to feed ourselves with. But we don't know the paths and we've lost our way. Could you put us up for the night, old mama?"

"Nobody can carry his home with him, as the old saying goes. My two boys are also hunters. I'm expecting them back today. Just sit yourselves down and I'll make you some supper."

The Xie brothers thanked her. "We're grateful to you, old mama."

She went inside, and they sat down outside the front door. Before long, two men appeared, carrying a roebuck. "Ma, where are you?" they called.

The woman came out and said: "So you're back, boys. Put that deer down and meet our guests."

Xie Zhen and Xie Bao hastily bowed. The other two returned the courtesy and asked: "Where are you from, sirs? What brings you here?" The Xies repeated what they had told the mother.

"We live here," said the young men. "We're called Liu the Second and Liu the Third. Our father was Liu the First, but unfortunately he died. Only our mother is left. Our family has been hunting for a living for twenty or thirty years. The paths here are tricky. We don't know them all ourselves. You say you're from Shandong? Why come here to seek a living? Don't try to fool us. You're not really hunters, are you?"

"Since it's come to this, there's no use pretending," said the Xies. "We'll tell you brothers the truth." Falling on their knees, they explained. "We are indeed hunters from Shandong. We're brothers named Xie Zhen and Xie Bao. But for a long time we've been following our brother Song Jiang in Liangshan Marsh. Recently, we were amnestied, and we've come with him to smash the Tartars of Great Liao. The other day General Ho scattered one of our units in a big battle, and we don't know what's become of them. We two have been sent out to inquire."

The Liu brothers laughed. "So you both are bold gallants. Rise, please. We'll show you the way. Rest a while. We'll cook you a haunch of venison and warm some local wine. You're our guests."

The meat was soon cooked and the Lius served the Xie brothers. Over the wine they said: "We've long heard how Song Jiang of Liangshan Marsh acts on Heaven's behalf and never harms good people. His fame has spread all the way to the kingdom of Liao."

"Our brother takes loyalty and righteousness as his main guide. He's vowed never to trouble honest folk. He kills only corrupt officials, and uses his strength to aid the weak."

"That's what we heard. So it's really true!"

All four were very pleased. They formed a deep mutual affection.

"That missing contingent of ours," said the Xie brothers. "It has more than a dozen chieftains and four or five thousand men. We can't imagine what's become of them. They must be trapped somewhere."

"You're not familiar with our terrain. This section is under the rule of Youzhou Prefecture. We have a place called Stony Valley. A dead-end road runs into it, and there are steep cliffs on both sides. If that entry is blocked, whoever has gone in can't come out. That's where your unit must be. No other place is broad enough to hold so many troops. Where Vanguard General Song Jiang is camped is called Lone Deer Mountain. Before it is a broad plain where you can fight freely, and from the summit you can see foes approaching from any direction.

"If you want to rescue your unit, you have to crack open Stony Valley at all costs. The enemy must have a large force bottling up the entry. That section is full of cypress trees, and the two tallest ones, looking like big umbrellas, mark the entrance to the valley. You can see them from a long way off. Rut be careful. Commanding General Ho can work magic spells. General Song Jiang must cope with them."

The Xie brothers thanked the Liu's and travelled through the night to return to their camp.

"What have you heard?" Song Jiang asked, the moment he saw them.

They told him what the Liu brothers had said. Startled, he summoned Wu Yong to a conference. While they were talking, a junior officer entered.

"Duan Jingzhu and Shi Yong are here with Bai Sheng."

"Bai Sheng was trapped together with General Lu. It's a wonder he was able to get away," exclaimed Song Jiang. He summoned the three to his tent.

Duan Jingzhu spoke first. "I was scouting with Shi Yong among some high mountains," he said, "when I saw a bundle of felt rolling down from a summit. We watched it roll to the foot of the slope. It looked like a big ball of felt clothing, all tied with cord. We walked over to the edge of the grove, where it stopped, and found Bai Sheng inside."

Bai Sheng explained. "General Lu and twelve of us chieftains were engaged in a fierce battle. Suddenly the sky darkened and the sun lost its lustre.

We couldn't tell one direction from another. We heard voices and the neighing of horses. Lu ordered us to charge. Before we knew it we were deep in a cul-de-sac surrounded by high cliffs and no way out, cut off from any grain or fodder. Our whole column is truly in a bad situation. General Lu directed me to roll down the mountain and try to get through to report. Luckily, I ran into Shi Yong and Duan Jingzhu. We hope you'll send reinforcements quickly, brother, and get us out of there. We're sure to die if you don't."

That very night Song Jiang mustered his troops and, with Xie Zhen and Xie Bao leading the way, headed for the two big cypresses, that is, the entrance to Stony Valley. His order was that the infantry and cavalry fight with all their might. Come what may, they had to smash open the valley.

All night they marched, and by daybreak they could see the two big umbrella-like trees in the distance. A troop under the Xie brothers hastened directly towards the entry. Commanding General Ho spread out his soldiers. The two brothers were eager to be the first to give battle, and Song Jiang wanted to launch a general offensive, but Panther Head Lin Chong galloped swiftly to the fore and engaged Ho Chai, After only two rounds, a thrust in the belly from Lin Chong brought him tumbling from his saddle.

Song Jiang's infantry, seeing that the cavalry had drawn first blood, now raced forward. Li Kui the Black Whirlwind, swinging his pair of battle-axes, carved a path through the Liao soldiers. Behind him came Fan Rui the Demon King Who Roils the World, Bao Xu the God of Death, plus Xiang Chong and Li Gun and their ferocious shield fighters, all wielding their weapons with lethal effect.

Black Whirlwind Li Kui made for Ho Yun. He rushed under his mount and broke its leg with one blow of the ax. Animal and rider fell to the ground. Li flew at them with his axes, hacking them both into mincemeat. The Liao soldiers swarmed forward, but they were stopped cold by Fan Rui, Bao Xu and their shield fighters.

Commanding General Ho had seen his two brothers die. He muttered a magic incantation. A wild gale rose and black clouds covered the mountain-tops, plunging the entire valley into darkness. Song Jiang summoned Gongsun Sheng. The Taoist, seated on his horse, murmured a few words, grasping his precious sword. Then, in a loud voice, he shouted: "Speed!"

Strong winds from all sides blew the clouds away to reveal a brightly shining red sun. In full force, Song Jiang's troops tore into the Liao army. His magic having failed and the enemy attacking with such vigor, General Ho could only wave his sword, clap his horse and gallop from the field. The two armies clashed in savage battle. Finally, the Tartars broke and fled helter-skelter.

The cavalry chased them, while the infantry opened up the entry to the valley. The Tartars had piled it high with big stones, blocking the road. After removing the stones, the foot soldiers pushed in quickly. Lu Junyi, when he saw them, cried out that he was ashamed.

Song Jiang ordered a halt to the pursuit of the Liao troops. "Call everyone back to Lone Deer Mountain," he said. "Our men and horses need rest."

Lu wept aloud. "If you hadn't come to my rescue, I surely would have died!"

Song, Lu, Wu Yong and Gongsurt rode back to camp side by side. There, the men removed their armor and rested. The next day, Wu Yong had a proposal.

"We ought to use this opportunity to take Youzhou. If we can do that, we'll have the Liao kingdom in the palm of our hand."

Song Jiang directed Lu Junyi and the twelve chieftains and their forces to proceed to Qizhou and rest there temporarily. Leading the other chieftains and troops personally, he left Lone Deer Mountain and set out for Youzhou.

By then Commanding General Ho had retreated into the city, very distressed by the loss of his two brothers. A cavalry scout reported: "Song Jiang's army is advancing for an attack." Ho grew even more upset.

Tartar soldiers mounted the city walls and looked. From the northeast a contingent bearing red banners, and from the northwest a contingent bearing green banners, were moving rapidly towards Youzhou. General Ho was shocked when the news was transmitted to him. He went up on the walls to see for himself. To his relief, he recognized the banners as Liao standards.

Inscribed with letters of silver, the red banners were those of Taizhen Xuqing, the Royal Son-in-Law, with an army of over five thousand. The green banners, written in gold and decorated with pheasant feathers, belonged to Security General Li. Keeper of the Palace and Vice Minister of Royal Security, Li Ji was a hereditary noble descended from the famous Han Dynasty official LiLing. His headquarters were in Xiongzhou, and he had more than ten thousand troops under his command. It was he who conducted the major raids on the Song borders. When he heard that the king of Liao was losing his cities, he hurried to the rescue.

General Ho sent this message to both columns: "Do not enter the city, but conceal yourselves north of the mountains. When I sally forth against Song Jiang's forces, close in on them from left and right." He then marched from Youzhou with his army.

As Song Jiang neared the city Wu Yong said: "If they bar the gates and don't come out that means they're not prepared. If they march to meet us that means they've laid an ambush, for sure. In that case, we should divide into three columns, one to continue the advance on the city, the other two to guard against flank attacks by the ambushers."

Truly, soldiers must meet all assaults, whether by land or water. Song Jiang instructed Guan Sheng, aided by Xuan Tan and Hao Siwen, to lead the left column, and Huyan Zhuo, with the assistance of Shan Tinggui and Wei Dingguo, to lead the right. Each would consist of more than ten thousand men, and would advance slowly along the paths behind the mountains. Song Jiang would command the main force and march directly on Youzhou.

Meanwhile, General Ho moved out with his troops to meet the attackers. The two armies confronted each other, and Lin Chong rode forth and engaged the general. After less than five rounds, Ho turned and rode away. Song Jiang's soldiers pursued. General Ho split his army into two columns. But instead of entering Youzhou, they skirted round it and continued on.

With a cry of "Halt!" Wu Yong ended the chase. Almost before the command had left his lips, Taizhen the Royal Son-in-Law charged down from the left, to be met by Guan Sheng's column. Huyan Zhuo engaged Security General Li's assault from the right. Three battles were raging at once. Corpses covered the plain, and blood flowed in rivers.

It was obvious to General Ho that the Tartars could not win. He wanted to return to Youzhou, but he encountered Hua Rong and Qin Ming, who engaged him in fierce combat. He tried to get to the West Gate, but he was blocked by General Two Spears Dong Ping, and another savage clash ensued. He turned towards the South Gate, but there Zhu Tong compelled him once again to fight a pitched battle. Not daring to continue in his attempts to reach the city, he struck out north along the main road. He was quite unprepared when Huang Xin the Suppressor of the Three Mountains charged, waving his big sword.

Panic-stricken, Ho became flurried. A blow from Huang struck his horse's head. The general abandoned the animal and ran. Two infantry chieftains, Yang Xiong and Shi Xiu, unexpectedly rushed him from the side and threw him flat on his face. At the same time Song Wan galloped up with levelled lance. Rather than disrupt their fraternal unity in contending to be the general's captor, they killed him on the spot.

The Tartar troops scattered and ran for their lives. The Royal Son-in-Law saw Ho's army banner fall and the soldiers flee. He knew the situation was bad. With his red-bannered column, he skirted round the rear of the mountains and hastily departed. Security General Li, engaged in the frontal battle, guessed that something had gone wrong when he could no longer see the red banners. He led his green bannered soldiers to the rear of the mountains and also withdrew.

All three enemy columns were in full retreat. Song Jiang drove directly on Youzhou. He took it without a struggle. Once inside the city, he billeted his troops and issued proclamations reassuring the local populace. He then dispatched an urgent message to Tanzhou, reporting the victory to Commissioner Zhao and requesting him to send troops to hold Qizhou. The naval chieftains and their craft were to come to Youzhou and await further orders. Lu Junyi the Magnate was to use part of his contingent to defend Bazhou.

Four major cities under Song control—Commissioner Zhao was delighted. He immediately sent a report to the emperor and made the necessary troop deployments to Qizhou and Bazhou. The situation was becoming critical for the Kingdom of Great Liao. Commissioner Zhao instructed the naval chieftains to get ready to sail. The big cities of the north were restored to Song rule—a remarkable feat.

The king of Great Liao in his palace summoned his top officials, civil and military. He conferred with Youxi Bojin the premier, vice-premier Chu Jian, and all the highest generals.

"Song Jiang has invaded our borders and taken four major cities. If he could conquer Youzhou, what's to prevent him from attacking our capital? Yanjing will be hard to defend! Commanding General Ho and his two brothers were all killed and Youzhou has been lost. Our country is beset by troubles. What do you ministers think we ought to do?"

Wuyan, the commander-in-chief, stepped forward. "Have no fears, Your Majesty. Several times I have requested to be sent with troops, but always I was prevented. As a result, the brigands are running amok and causing calamity. I beg a royal decree commissioning me to march with an expeditionary force against the foreign invaders and setting a time limit for their defeat. I shall seize Song Jiang and his chieftains and recapture our fallen cities."

The king acceded to his request. He issued to Wuyan the pearl-encrusted tiger standard, a gold seal and a royal decree, yellow and white panoplies, and banners of red and black. The monarch's orders were strict.

"Everyone—regardless of noble birth, royal kinship, or military affiliation—shall obey the commands of my beloved minister Wuyan. Muster an army quickly and set forth."

Wuyan, carrying the royal seal and official tallies, went to the training field, summoned his generals, and ordered them to gather all the Tartar forces and bring them to the capital. His eldest son, Yanshou, approached him in the reviewing pavilion with a suggestion.

"While you're raising this huge army, father, why not let me go first with a number of fierce generals, join forces with Taizhen the Royal Son-in-Law and Security General Li, and attack Youzhou. We'll slaughter eight tenths of the barbarians, and when you come you'll mop up the rest as easily as catching turtles in a jug! How does that strike you, father?"

"A good idea, my son. Take five thousand cavalry and twenty thousand crack infantry, and go. Since you're joining with the Royal Son-in-Law and the Security General, it should work out well. If you succeed, let me know by urgent dispatch."

Happily, Yanshou mustered his troops and left for Youzhou.

And because Wuyan's son dared the Song army to combat, the outskirts of Youzhou became the approaches to the Nine Li Mountains, and the banks of the Wanshui River became busy fording points.

Truly, Heaven and Earth tremble when cavalry legions race, demons quake when hordes of infantry charge.

How did Yanshou challenge battle? Read our next chapter if you would know.

CHAPTER 87

SONG JIANG WAGES A BIG BATTLE AT YOUZHOU

HUYAN ZHUO FORCIBLY CAPTURES A TARTAR GENERAL

Yanshou, leading twenty thousand men, after joining forces with Taizhen the Royal Son-in-Law and Security General Li, had thirty-five thousand soldiers under his command. He made sure their arms and equipment were all in order, and then set forth. A scout soon reported this to Song Jiang in Youzhou. Song conferred with Wu Yong, his military advisor.

"We've defeated the Liao forces several times in a row. They must be sending their crack troops and best generals against us. What should our tactics be?"

"Station our army outside the city and wait. Challenge them when they arrive. If we show them up as incompetent, they'll of course withdraw."

"Clever and clear, Military Advisor." Song Jiang ordered his contingents to leave the city.

Ten *li* from Youzhou is a flat plain called Fangshan. It is fringed by mountains and streams. Here, the army deployed into a Nine-Unit Octagon battle position.

Before long, the Tartars came into sight, in three columns. The one under young commander Yanshou, Wuyan's son, carried black banners. The Royal Son-in-Law's column bore red banners. Green were the banners of the Security General's column. All three spread out in battle positions when they saw Song Jiang's army.

Yanshou had learned military tactics under his father's personal tutelage. His knowledge was profound, his skill tricky. He viewed Song Jiang's battle formation, then directed his red and green banner contingents to deploy to left and right and build fortifications. He himself mounted a "sky ladder" amid his central column and observed Song Jiang's position. He came down with a superior smile on his face.

"Why are you smiling, General?" his lieutenants asked.

"That Nine-Unit Octagon of Song Jiang—who doesn't know that! It can't fool anybody. I'll just give him a scare."

He ordered three flourishes on the decorated battle drums, and had a command platform erected. Mounting the platform, with two flags he signalled deployment instructions to his left and right columns. Then he came down, got on his horse, directed his top officers to spread out the army, and rode to the front to confront Song Jiang.

He shouted: "You Nine-Unit Octagon can't deceive anyone! Do you recognize my formation?"

So the Tartar commander wanted to vie in deployment positions, did he? Song Jiang directed that "sky ladders" be erected, and he, Wu Yong and Zhu Wu climbed up to have a look at the Liao contingents. The three columns were linked, with left and right near enough to provide mutual support.

Zhu Wu recognized it immediately. "That's called the Great Monad and Three Powers—Heaven, Earth and Man," he told Song Jiang.

Leaving the other two on the command platform, Song Jiang came down and rode to the front. He pointed with his whip at Yanshou.

"You've set out a Great Monad and Three Powers position," he called. "There's nothing special about that."

"So you recognize it," said the young Tartar. "Watch us change, and see if you still know it." He turned and rode back to his command platform, mounted it and signalled a change with his flags.

Wu Yong and Zhu Wu, from their platform, saw that the foe had assumed a Four Elephants formation. They sent word to Song Jiang. Meanwhile, Yanshou had again emerged and sat his steed, weapon athwart.

"Do you recognize our position?" he demanded.

"You've converted into a Four Elephants formation."

The young Tartar shook his head in surprise and laughed coldly. Again he climbed his platform and signalled with his flags, while Wu Yong and Zhu Wu watched from their own platform. "That's the Revolving Octagon," said Zhu Wu. Again he notified Song Jiang.

Once more the young Tartar appeared at the front. "Can you recognize that?"

Song Jiang laughed. "It's only the Revolving Octagon! Nothing unusual!"

Thoughtfully, Yanshou said to himself: "I learned these deployments from teachers in secret, yet he identified them all. He must have some talented people on his staff."

Again he returned to his central column, got down from his horse, climbed the platform, and signalled with his flags. His army broke into eight eights, or sixty-four units, with no opening on any side. Zhu Wu, on the "sky ladder," recognized it.

"That's the Eight-Sector Diagram of Zhuge Liang," he told Wu Yong. "Head and tail are both concealed. No one knows where they are." They dispatched a man to request Song Jiang to come up and see for himself!

"Don't underestimate that Liao general," they advised him when he had joined them on the platform. "Those four are all traditional battle positions. They've been passed down without change. The first was the Great Monad and Three Powers. From that came the Four Elephants, which then produced the Revolving Octagon, which converted to the Eight-Sector Diagram. An incomparable progression, a matchless deployment!"

Song Jiang came down from the platform, mounted, and rode to the front. The Tartar general stabbed his halberd into the ground and reined in.

"Can you recognize our position?" he shouted.

"You are only a young commander with narrow vision, like a frog at the bottom of a well! All you know is these few deployments. Moves like your Eight-

Sector Diagram, with its concealed head, couldn't deceive even a child of the Song empire!"

"Since you know all of my battle positions, why not lay out a marvellous one of your own? See if you can fool me!"

"I only know the Nine-Unit Octagon. It may not be very profound, but dare you attack?"

The young Tartar laughed. "A small operation, nothing to it! Don't pull anything sneaky. Just watch us knock you over!"

He ordered the Royal Son-in-Law and the Security General to be ready with a thousand men each. "After I drive into their position," he told them, "you reinforce me." His battle drums began to pound.

Song Jiang also ordered three flourishes on his battle drums, and directed that the gate of pennants be opened and the young general be allowed to enter.

Yanshou assembled a task force of around twenty junior officers and a thousand armored cavalrymen. He calculated on his fingers that this was a "fire" day, and therefore decided not to attack from due south. He led his contingent around to the left to a point southwest of his objective, unfurled his white banners, and charged. Only half his unit was able to penetrate the Song lines. A shower of arrows halted the rear half and sent it back to its own position.

The young Tartar drove directly into Song Jiang's central column. Suddenly, a silvery metal barricade seemed to rise all around him. He blanched and thought: "Where did that wall come from?" He ordered his men to push out the way they came in.

But when they turned they saw behind them a misty silvery sea. Everywhere was gurgling water, but no path. Increasingly agitated, Yanshou led his troops due south, but a ball of fire, spewing long rays like sunset beams, rolled before them. Not a single enemy soldier was in sight. The young Tartar dared not advance in that direction.

They swerved to the east, only to be confronted by leafy trees and tangled undergrowth and, at either end, stakes of branches sharpened like deer antlers. They'd never get through there! But when they turned north a black mist covered the sky and somber clouds hid the sun. They couldn't see their hands in front of their faces. It was as dark as the chambers of Hell.

Yanshou was completely stymied. "Song Jiang must be working some magic," he said to himself. "It's hopeless. All we can do is smash our way out, or die trying!" He gave the command and his men charged, yelling.

"Where do you think you're going, infant general!" boomed the voice of a big commander who suddenly broke through from the side. A rod flew down towards Yanshou's forehead. Sharp-eyed and nimble, he parried the blow with his crescent-bladed halberd. But immediately a pair of rods struck, snapping his weapon in two. Before he could resist, the foe closed in swiftly, locked him effort-lessly in ape-like arms and, with a single twist of his wolf-like waist, lifted him from his saddle and captured him.

Blocked, his cavalry troop obeyed when they were shouted at to dismount. They could see nothing in the stygian darkness. They had no choice but to get down from their horses and surrender. The man who had taken Yanshou prisoner was none other than Tiger Chieftain Two Rods Huyan Zhuo. Gongsun Sheng, who had worked the magic, on learning that the young Tartar general had been caught, put an end to the spell. The sun once more shone on the battlefield from a clear blue sky.

Meanwhile, Taizhen the Royal Son-in-Law and Security General Li, each with a thousand soldiers, waited for news so that they could bring up their reinforcements. But since, to their surprise, they heard nothing, they didn't venture to move. Song Jiang now appeared at the front and called to them.

"Surrender, you two units. What are you waiting for? We've already captured Yanshou." At his order, his swordsmen pushed the young Tartar general forward.

Security General Li spurred his horse and galloped to rescue Yanshou with levelled lance. Qin Ming the Thunderbolt, brandishing his wolf-toothed cudgel, rode out to meet him. They clashed, weapons flailing, as the two armies set up a mighty yell.

Li lost his nerve, and his hands faltered. One blow from the wolf-toothed cudgel shattered his helmet and his skull together. He fell in a heap to the ground.

The sight was too much for the Royal Son-in-Law. He retreated rapidly with his unit. Song Jiang ordered his men to pursue. The great Liao forces fled in utter defeat. More than three thousand cavalry mounts were captured that day. Fallen banners and weapons filled the valley. Song Jiang led his troops on to Yanjing, determined to roll up the rest of the foe and win back all imperial territory under Liao domination.

Remnants of the defeated Tartar contingent reached Commander-in-Chief Wuyan and told him that his son Yanshou had been captured in battle and all his officers had surrendered. Security General Li had been killed by a blow of Qin Ming's club and his troops had fled, no one knew where. Taizhen the Royal Son-in-Law had also run for his life. There was no news of him, either.

Wuyan was shocked. "My son studied military art since childhood. He was very adept," he said. "How could that rogue Song Jiang have captured him?"

"And all he had was a Nine-Unit Octagon defense. Nothing remarkable," Wuyan's lieutenants added. "Yet when our young general formed four different deployments, that barbarian knew every one of them. He said to him: 'You recognized my Nine-Unit Octagon, but dare you attack?' And when we charged from the west with over a thousand cavalry, he deluged us with arrows so that only half our men got through, and somehow he captured our young general."

"That Nine-Unit Octagon is easy enough to hit," mused Wuyan. "He probably converted it into something else."

"We could see from our command platform—he didn't move his troops and his flags didn't change," the commanders assured him. "But a black cloud covered the battlefield."

"He must have used magic. If we don't muster our army, the scoundrel is sure to come here. I'll win victory or kill myself! Who dares to lead soldiers as my vanguard general?"

Two high-ranking officers promptly stepped forward and volunteered. One was Qiong Yaonayan, a national army general. The other was Kou Zhenyuan, a general of the Yanjing city contingent.

Wuyan was pleased. He said: "Proceed cautiously. Take a vanguard of ten thousand and open a road through the mountains. Where necessary, build bridges. Our main force will follow."

The two departed. Wuyan then appointed eleven senior generals and twenty-eight lieutenant-generals as commanders of the expeditionary force. It would consist of over two hundred thousand crack troops— all the country's available soldiers. He would petition the king himself to lead it.

Meanwhile, Qiong and Kou advanced through the mountains with their ten thousand men. A scout reported to Song Jiang in Youzhou the approach of this formidable foe. Startled, Song Jiang notified Lu the Magnate to bring as many men as possible. He also ordered the transfer of troops from Tanzhou and Qizhou, and invited Commissioner Zhao to come and observe the operations. He directed his naval chieftains to call their sailors ashore, and assemble in Bazhou before continuing their march.

Commissioner Zhao, under the protection of the naval chieftains, arrived last. All required forces were now congregated in Youzhou. After greetings had been exchanged, Commissioner Zhao complimented Song Jiang.

"You're so tireless, General, a pillar of our country! Your fame, your irradicable virtue, shall be known for countless generations. When I return to the capital, I shall recommend you highly to the emperor."

"A useless small official like me is not worth mentioning. Basking in the reflected glory of our great emperor and benefiting from Your Excellency's splendid prestige, I have made some small accomplishments. Anyone could have done the same. I have recently been informed that Tartar Commander-in-Chief Wuyan, by draining his nation's military manpower, has raised an army of over two hundred thousand, and is heading this way. Victory or defeat depends on the coming battle. I propose that you build a fort fifteen *li* from here, Commissioner, and observe how my brothers and I exercise our utmost fidelity and strength in this decisive engagement! Sustained by the emperor's overflowing virtue, we sure shall win victory to show our gratitude for His Majesty's benevolence!"

"Use your opportunities well, General. Sun Zi said: 'More calculation or less calculation determines victory or defeat.' Plan your strategy carefully. Consider every detail."

Song Jiang bid farewell to the commissioner and set off with Lu the Magnate at the head of a large army. They skirted Yongqing County, which is part of Youzhou Prefecture, set up camp and built fortifications. All the chieftains assembled in the headquarters tent for a conference.

"Wuyan is leading the entire Liao army against us," said Song Jiang. "This is no small matter. The battle will decide our life or death. You brothers must push forward and never retreat. The smallest merit will be reported to the court, and the emperor's rewards will be mutually shared. No one person will reap the benefits."

The chieftains rose and said: "We would never dare disobey your orders. We shall do our best in gratitude for your great kindness."

A junior officer entered. "A Liao emissary is here with a battle challenge."

Song Jiang directed that he be brought to the tent to present the document. Opening it, Song Jiang read that Generals Qiong and Kou, who were under Commander-in-Chief Wuyan of the Kingdom of Liao, as leaders of a vanguard force challenged the Song army to a decisive battle on the morrow. Song Jiang noted his acceptance on the bottom of the document. He ordered that the emissary be given food and wine and allowed to return to his own encampment. At daybreak the following day victory or defeat would be determined.

It was late autumn and early winter then. The men wore heavy armor, hide coverings protected the horses. The Song troops finished breakfast before dawn. When the sun topped the horizon, they broke camp and marched. Before they had gone five *li* they saw the Liao army in the distance. Amid the foe's embroidered black flags, two vanguard banners glistened. Battle drums thundered, the gate of pennants opened, and General Qiong rode forth. Lance athwart his prancing horse, he halted at the edge of the field of combat.

Song Jiang, beneath his own gate of pennants, was impressed by Qiong's heroic appearance. "Who will vie with this general?" he asked.

Nine Dragons Shi Jin, sword in hand, galloped forward on bounding steed. The two chargers met and their riders battled, sword against lance in a dazzling pattern of motion. Four arms thrust and flailed, eight hoofs churned the turf. Twenty or thirty rounds the men fought. Shi Jin felt his strength ebbing. He turned his horse and headed back towards his own position, with Qiong in hot pursuit.

Hua Rong, who had been directly behind Song Jiang, notched an arrow to his bowstring and rode to the front. When the Tartar was close enough, Hua Rong let fly. The arrow struck Qiong in the face and knocked him from his saddle. Shi Jin, hearing him fall, wheeled his mount around and raced back. With one sweep of the sword, he dispatched Qiong Yaonayan. Though an able warrior, the poor Tartar official nevertheless lost his life.

When Kou saw Qiong cut down, fury rose in his heart, rage flooded his gall. With levelled lance he urged his steed to the front.

"What bandit dared kill my brother with a sniper's arrow?" he cried.

Sun Li the Sickly General galloped out to engage Kou. Pounding battle drums shook the heavens, the air rang with ear-splitting yells. Sun Li's lance darted like a thing possessed. Kou was eight-tenths afraid. After only twenty or so rounds, he turned his horse and fled. Rather than disturb his army's front, he circled to the northeast.

Sun Li, eager to distinguish himself, didn't slacken his chase. Kou was well in the lead. The Sickly General set his lance in its socket, took his bow in his left hand, notched an arrow with his right, and drew the bow to its full. Aiming at Kou's back, he let fly.

The Tartar heard the twang and threw himself prone. As the arrow whizzed by, he snatched it. Sun Li silently applauded his foe. Kou laughed scornfully.

"The rogue thinks he's an archer!"

He clamped the arrow between his teeth and set his lance in the saddle rings. Quickly, he grasped a stiff bow in his left hand, fitted the arrow with his right, twisted around in the saddle and shot at Sun Li's chest.

The Sickly General had seen what the Tartar was up to, and had been riding a zig-zag course. He flung himself back as the arrow neared him, and it flew harmlessly past. His steed couldn't be checked. It careened onward at an all-out run.

Kou slung the bow over his shoulder. He looked back and saw Sun Li lying prone on his horse.

"That arrow must have got him," he thought.

But Sun Li was only pretending. His powerful legs gripped his animal's middle in a tight clasp which prevented him from falling off. Kou slowed his mount and turned to capture his pursuer. When the two horses were only a few meters apart, Sun Li suddenly sat up.

"If I don't take you now," he yelled, "you'll surely run away!"

Kou was stunned. But he shouted back: "You dodged my arrow, let's see you avoid my lance!"

He thrust at Sun Li with all his force. Sun Li swelled his chest and let the point clang against his armor and slide off to the side, then he moved in swiftly and grappled with his opponent. He raised the steel rod hanging from his wrist and brought it down in a crushing blow which tore away half of Kou's pate. The Tartar commander who for most of his life had been an official in Zhenyuan, died at Sun Li's hand, and his corpse lay at his horse's feet.

With upraised lance, Sun Li returned to the front. Song Jiang and his army charged the foe. Leaderless, the Tartars fled in all directions.

Song Jiang was still pursuing them when he heard ahead a volley of cannon fire. He ordered his naval chieftains to take a contingent and block the water approaches. Just as he was directing Hua Rong, Qin Ming, Lu Fang and Guo Sheng to ride to the top of the mountain and keep watch, he saw the Tartars rumbling towards them in swarms which covered the earth. Song Jiang was terrified. His three souls shook and his seven spirits trembled.

Truly, no matter how clever a man may be, it is difficult to escape danger. Whose was this great army now approaching? Read our next chapter if you would know.

CHAPTER 88

COMMANDER-IN-CHIEF YAN SETS UP A ZODIAC DEPLOYMENT

THE MYSTIC QUEEN INSTRUCTS SONG JIANG IN A DREAM

From a bluff Song Jiang viewed the powerful Liao army, then rode quickly back to his own position. He ordered a withdrawal to a mountain pass in Yongqing County. There, in his tent, he conferred with Lu the Magnate, Wu Yong and Gongsun Sheng.

"Although we defeated them in battle and killed two of their vanguard generals," he said, "the army I saw from the bluff is huge and strong. They're coming in endless lines. Only a tremendous force can deal with them. But we're comparatively few. What can we do?"

"Skilled generals among the ancients were able to defeat larger foes and do it beautifully," said Wu Yong. "In the old days, Xie Xuan of the state of Jin, with fifty thousand troops, beat back Fu Jian with twice that number. There have been many such cases. What are you worried about! Order out soldiers to go into battle with pennants tightly ranked, arrows notched to the bows, swords out of their scabbards. Set deer antler stakes in depth, alertly defend our camps. Construct good trenches and fortifications, have our weapons all laid out, our ladders and cannons in working order, and everything in proper readiness. We'll deploy simply in the Nine-Unit Octagon. This will be our defense. Though they come with a million soldiers, they won't dare to attack!"

"Well put, Military Advisor," said Song Jiang. He transmitted his instructions and directed his chieftains to await his orders.

Breakfast was before dawn the next day, and they broke camp when the sun cleared the horizon. They marched to the border of Changping County, spread out in battle formation, and set up new encampments. Foremost were the cavalry. Then came the infantry under Tiger General Qin Ming, with Huyan Zhuo to the rear, Guan Sheng on the left, Lin Chong on the right. Suo Chao was southeast, Xu Ning northeast, Dong Ping southwest, and Yang Zhi northwest. Song Jiang commanded the central contingent. The other chieftains maintained their original posts. The rear infantry established another position, under the command of Lu Junyi the Magnate, Sagacious Lu and Wu Song.

Amid their thousands of troops, the chieftains, talented militarists every one, rubbed their hands and prepared for the slaughter. The positions were laid out. They were ready for the Tartars.

Before long, they saw the Liao contingents moving forward in the distance. First came six units, serving both as an opening wedge and a defensive shield, three to the left and three to the right, five hundred men in each, the relative positions of the units shifting constantly.

Behind these the main force followed, their numbers covering the earth. The lead contingent was a sea of black flags and it stretched out in a row of seven cavalry troops, with a thousand riders in each, and each led by a senior commander. How were the commanders attired? Black helmets, armor and robes, astride ebony steeds and bearing ordinary arms. Each troop was designated by one of the Seven Northern Constellations.

The commanding general of all seven had on his standard the Mystic Militant Water Planet of the North. How was he dressed? A brown bandanna which covered his forehead bound his long silky black hair. Over a sleeveless black robe was silver armor chilling to behold. A lion's head belt clasped the darkly gleaming metal. He sat his spirited stallion firmly in a saddle of tooled leather. Hanging from his shoulder, the quiver bearing his arrows and hard bow of scoured poplar was decorated with animals rampant and flying fish. He held a three-pointed, two-edged, four-sided, eight-ringed sword. His name was Quli Chuqing and his personal troop consisted of three thousand horsemen with black shoulder-length hair, and their standard was the Five Vapors Constellation of the North. Supporting the black bannered contingent were infantry without number.

Green dragons writhed on the banners of the left contingent, which advanced in a row of seven cavalry troops, with a thousand riders in each, and each led by a senior commander. How were these commanders dressed? In four-seamed helmets, scaled armor in the shape of poplar leaves covering robes of kingfisher green. They rode horses with manes dyed green, and carried regular weapons. The Seven Eastern Constellations were the standards for the seven troops, and over them all was a commanding general whose standard was the Green Dragon Wood Planet of the East.

How was he attired? A lion's head helmet, armor from the hide of a fleet horse over a fine green robe, bound by a girdle of gold and green jade. He sat a saddle of tooled leather, a quiver of bow and arrows hung from his waist, and his hawk's beak boots were planted in stirrups of precious metal. In his hand was a crescent-bladed battle-ax with a filigreed gold handle, and his dragon horse was of the Clear Jade breed. His name was Zhi'er Folang and his personal troop contained three thousand cavalrymen bearing green banners. Their standard was the Nine Vapors Constellation of the East. Supporting the green bannered contingent were countless foot soldiers.

The right contingent, bearing white tiger banners, contained seven cavalry troops in a row, with a thousand riders in each, and each led by a senior commander. How were these commanders attired? In water-burnished helmets, and shining silver armor over plain silk robes. They rode snowy white horses and carried hand-gripped weapons, and their seven troops were designated by the Seven Western Constellations.

Over all seven was a commanding general whose standard was the Gold Planet of the Deep Pool of the West. How was he dressed? In a conical helmet with phoenix feathers, and double hooked armor of patterned silver plus a coldly gleaming jade belt over a fitted plain silk robe of flying snowflakes design. He rode a fleet steed of the Jade That Shines in the Night breed, and wielded a silver halberd of pure steel. His name was Wuli Kean, and his personal troop contained three thousand horsemen bearing white-tasseled silk pennants. Their standard was the Seven Vapors Constellation of the West. Before and behind the white bannered contingent were supporting infantry without number.

Pink banners marked the rear contingent—seven cavalry troops in a row, each with a thousand horsemen, each led by a senior commander. How were these commanders attired? In conical hats of ochre red and robes dyed the color of orangoutan blood, over which was chain and fish-scale armor of peach pink. They rode roan chargers called Red Rabbits and carried grip-handled weapons. The troops were named after the Seven Southern Constellations. Over all was a commanding general whose standard was the Ochre Peacock Fire Planet.

How was he dressed? In a stitched cap with shiny red tassels, and a purple-sheened pink robe covered by armor with a sunset design, and boots basted with red thread. A red leather belt encrusted with precious stones bound his waist, a quiver containing a hard bow and arrows hung from his shoulder. He carried an eight-foot-long dragon sword in his hand and rode a rough-red steed. He was General Dongxian Wenrong, and he led a personal troop of three thousand horsemen bearing red silk pennants. Their standard was the Three Vapors Constellation of the South. Supporting the pink-bannered contingent were foot soldiers without number in red-tasseled, red-stitched clothes.

In front of the Liao fixed position to the left were five thousand fierce horsemen, wearing caps stitched with gold thread and gold-plated armor over pink robes with crimson tassels. They bore fiery-red banners and rode roan steeds. The commander wore a stitched gold cap of hibiscus and sceptre pattern, and golden chain mail of linked animal faces over a fiery red embroidered robe, bound by a girdle encrusted with gold and precious stones. He carried a matched set of Sun and Moon swords and rode a Five Luminances red horse. He was Prince Yelu Dezhong, Royal Brother of the King of Liao. His standard was the Sun.

To the right in front of the Liao fixed position were five thousand women cavalry. They were dressed in patterned silver caps, silver hooked armor over plain robes of tasseled silk, and bore white pennants, rode white horses, and wielded silver-handled blade-lances. Their commander had in her hair, on opposite sides of her head, two pins of phoenix design trailing green silk. Around her forehead was a red silk band with precious stone sequins. The cloud pattern on her shoulders was tastefully set off by the brocade of her skirt. Over her silver armor she wore a tunic embroidered with dragons. Her small flowered boots rested firmly in her stirrups. In her diaphanous sleeve she carried a light jade-handled whip. She bore a Seven Star precious sword and rode a spirited silver-white horse. She was Dalibo, Royal Princess of the Kingdom of Liao. Her standard was the Moon.

Between the left and right cavalry units, amid a mass of yellow banners, were generals in golden armor, riding gold-hued horses. Their robes and armor formed a swath of yellow clouds, their embroidered yellow turbans were a mist covering half the sky. Four of these generals held the highest rank. Each commanded three thousand soldiers, and each defended one of the four corners of a square.

In the southeast corner was Royal Nephew Yelu Derong. He wore golden armor and an animal-face belt over a robe of black. Three pins held his golden cap in place. He carried a bow and arrows and a black-tasseled lance, and rode a pale dark steed. His standard was the Mouth of the Net Constellation.

Royal Nephew Yelu Dehua was in the southwest corner. He wore silver armor and a simple belt over a purple robe, and precious ornaments decorated his cap. He carried a stiff bow and arrows, wielded a precious sword and rode a black-maned, black-tailed roan. His standard was the Commemorative Constellation.

In the northeast corner was Royal Nephew Yelu Dechong. He was dressed in a green robe, silver armor, and wore a purple cap and precious belt. Hanging from his waist were a dragon bow and phoenix arrows. He grasped a crescent-bladed halberd and rode a Five Luminances yellow steed. His standard was the Purple Vapor Constellation.

The northwest corner was defended by Royal Nephew Yelu Dexin. He wore bronze armor over a white robe. A red band shot with black thread bound his forehead, and he was adorned with a gold-inlaid, gem-encrusted belt. A carved bow and arrows hung from his waist. In his hand he held a Seven Star precious sword, and he rode a jet-black steed with snowy white fetlocks. His standard was the Lunar Comet.

From among the yellow banners a general emerged whose standard was the Central Control Star. To his left were green flags, to his right were white banners. Before him were red panoplies, behind were black umbrellas. Encircling him were flags representing the twenty-four solar terms, and the sixty-four sections of the Octagon, plus the Southern Aurora, the Northern Dipper, the Flying Dragon, the Flying Tiger, the Flying Bear, and the Flying Panther—all blending in a confusing array which obscured the Jade Firmament.

How was this general attired? In a purple and gold cap encrusted with precious gems, in tortoise-back armor of gleaming gold over an embroidered silk gown from Sichuan, in a girdle of charming jade from Lantian. His bow, hanging on his left side, had a steel center and was etched in gold. His arrows, in a quiver on his left, had phoenix feathers and barbed heads. He was shod in hawk-beak-patterned, cloud-soled boots, and he rode an iron-backed, silver-footed horse. He sat a decorated saddle, the purple silk reins wrapped around the pommel, his feet firmly in the stirrups. At his waist hung his sword of command, in his hand he held his general's baton.

As he rode to the fore, he grasped the ochre-decorated shaft of his crescent-bladed halberd. Amid that gold and glittering array he was clearly the leader, for he was Wuyan, Commander-in-Chief of the Combined Forces of the Kingdom of Great Liao.

Behind the yellow banners was a royal phoenix and dragon carriage, surrounded by seven concentric rings of fully armed soldiers. In the center were thirty-six pairs of yellow-turbaned warriors who pushed the carriage. Preceding it, on the trace horses, were nine postillion riders in saddles of gold. Eight pairs of warriors in embroidered garments brought up the rear.

Seated on a throne in the middle of the carriage was the King of Great Liao, on his head a tall conical turban, his body encased in a nine-dragon robe of royal yellow, a Lantian jade girdle around his waist, red court boots upon his feet. Flanking him were his ministers. Youxi Bojin, the premier was on his left. Marshal Chu Jian, the vice-premier was on his right. Both wore ornate caps, fiery-skirted ochre gowns with purple fringes and gold slabs, and girdles of ivory and jade. On either side of the throne stood richly dressed boys and girls, holding jade and ivory implements. Royal Guards closely surrounded the carriage. For his standard the king had personally selected the North Star Which Reigns Imperially over All. The ministers to his left and right flew banners showing accompanying constellations.

The Liao army was now in position, spread out in an egg-shaped celestial deployment, anchored firmly like an overturned basin. Flags in four corners, weapons on eight sides, locked in shifting rings, the Tartars were able to advance or withdraw at will.

Song Jiang first pinned down the enemy's forward pickets with arrows from his archers. Then he and Wu Yong and Zhu Wu climbed a sky-ladder for a look. What he saw astonished him. Wu Yong didn't recognize the Tartar layout, but Zhu Wu said it was a Zodiac Deployment.

"It's called the Great Monad," he explained.

"How should it be assaulted?" Song Jiang asked.

"It keeps changing all the time. It's very difficult to come to grips with it," said Zhu Wu. "I don't know how to assault it."

"If we can't crack it open, how are we going to drive them back?"

"The trouble is we don't really understand their set-up," said Wu Yong. "How can we attack?"

While they were conferring, Wuyan the Tartar commander-in-chief was issuing his orders. "Today is a 'gold' day," he said. "We'll therefore have four officers—Gold Dragon Zhang Qi, Gold Ox Xue Xiong, Gold Dog Aliyi and Gold Ram Wang Jing—go with the Great White Gold Star General Wuli Kean and attack Song Jiang."

At the battle front, Song Jiang and his chieftains observed the seven Tartar troops to the left. Their pennant gates now opened, now closed, while drums thundered. Within their position, they seemed to be moving about a lot. The commander's banner travelled from east to north, to west, to south.

"The Celestial Platter is turning to the left," said Zhu Wu, "and today is a 'gold' day. That means they're going to attack."

Before the words were out of his mouth, five cannons boomed in unison, and soldiers surged out of the enemy position. In their center was the Gold Star General and his four satellites. With the force of an avalanche they led five troops in a murderous charge. Nothing could stop them. Taken by surprise, Song Jiang's forces hastily retreated, while trying to stem the foe's advance. But the Tartars caught them in a pincers, and they suffered heavy losses. They scrambled back to their fortified camp. The Liao army did not pursue.

A check revealed that Kong Liang had received a sword wound, Li Yun had been hit by an arrow, Zhu Fu had been injured by shrapnel, and Shi Yong had been stabbed by a lance. Among the troops there were wounds without number. The casualties were loaded onto carts and sent to a rear camp for medical treatment by Dr. An Daoquan. Song Jiang instructed his forward echelons to lay iron brambles and plant deer antler stakes and defend the camp's approaches.

"We took a beating today," Song Jiang said to Lu Junyi moodily. "What are we going to do? If we don't go out and challenge them, they're sure to launch an offensive."

"Use two columns to hit the units defending their flanks, while another two assault the seven troops due north," Lu proposed. "Then have our infantry pour in through the middle. We'll see what the knaves have got in there."

"All right."

The next day, in accordance with Lu's suggestion, they put their fortified camp in order, opened the gates wide, and moved forward with their assault contingent. As they neared the Liao position, the six units in charge of defense spotted them. Song Jiang ordered Guan Sheng to move up from the left, Huyan Zhuo from the right. He himself advanced in a frontal drive. Soon, they were in contact with the foe. Song Jiang then dispatched two more contingents to strike at the black-bannered seven troops in the center from the left and right. Sure enough, they broke them, and inflicted heavy casualties.

The black-bannered troops were in disarray. Song Jiang now ordered the five hundred shield warriors under Li Kui the Black Whirlwind to strike, to be followed by an infantry charge led by Sagacious Lu and Wu Song. It was a chaotic battle. Cannon thundered on all sides. Two columns from east and west, and the king's own yellow-bannered troops directly ahead, smashed into Song Jiang's forces. The pressure was too great. They turned and fled. The rear guard couldn't hold. It was badly mauled by the time it reached the fortified camp.

A check showed that more than half of Song Jiang's effectives had been destroyed. Du Qian and Song Wan were severely wounded. Li Kui was missing— as he hacked his way into the enemy position Black Whirlwind had been pinned down by hooked poles and captured. The news distressed Song Jiang. He ordered Du Qian and Song Wan to the rear camp for medical treatment. Injured horses were led off to be tended by Huangfu Duan.

"Today we lost both Li Kui and the battle," Song Jiang said to Wu Yong. "What can we do?"

"We captured Wuyan's son, the young general, a few days ago. We can make an exchange."

"If we do that now, how will we be able to save other chieftains we may lose in the future?"

"Why worry ahead of time, brother? Let's solve first things first."

A junior officer entered and announced: "A Liao emissary is here with something to say."

Song Jiang directed that he be brought in. As soon as he was presented, the emissary delivered his message.

"Our commander-in-chief has ordered me to inform you that today we captured one of your chieftains. Instead of killing him, our commander wined and dined him. He offers to exchange him for his son, the young general. If you are willing, we will return your chieftain."

"We'll bring the young general to the front tomorrow and make the exchange," Song Jiang promised.

The Tartar emissary mounted his horse and departed.

"We have no plan for breaking the enemy position," said Song Jiang. "It would be good if we could use the exchange to get a respite in the hostilities."

Wu Yong agreed. "Our army needs a rest. If we can work out some new strategy in the meanwhile, we can always hit them later."

That evening, men were sent to fetch the young general to headquarters, and an emissary was dispatched to Commander-in-Chief Wuyan.

The Tartar general was seated in his tent when a junior officer announced: "A messenger is here from Song Jiang." Wuyan ordered that he be allowed in. The emissary, on entering, spoke his piece.

"Our Vanguard General Song Jiang conveys his respects to Your Excellency. He is ready to exchange the young general for our chieftain. Since the weather is bitterly cold and the soldiers are weary, to prevent frostbite and suffering he proposes an armistice and a renewal of discussions in the spring. We request the Commander-in-Chief's approval."

"So you've captured that stupid, worthless son of mine," Wuyan shouted. "Even if he lives, he'd never have the effrontery to face me! We don't need any exchange. Take him out and kill him for me. If Song Jiang wants an end to hostilities, let him surrender, bound hand and foot, and save you all from death! Otherwise, I'll come with my mighty army and not a single blade of grass will be left standing! Now get out!"

The emissary flew back on his horse to the fortified camp and reported the conversation to Song Jiang.

Alarmed, and afraid that he would lose the chance to rescue Li Kui, Song Jiang left camp with the young Tartar general and hurried to the front.

"You can release our chieftain," he called. "I'm returning your young general. If you don't want an armistice, that's all right with us. We'll fight it out with you to the death!"

From the Liao position Li Kui was quietly placed on a horse and led to the fore. On this side, the same was done with the young general. Without another word from either adversary, the exchange was made. Li Kui returned to camp. The young general rode away. Neither side took hostile action that day. Song Jiang withdrew to camp with his soldiers and celebrated with Li Kui.

Later, he conferred with his chieftains in his tent. "The Liao force is powerful and we have no plan for cracking it," he said. "I'm anxious and worried. Each day seems like a year. What shall we do?"

Huyan Zhuo had a proposal. "Divide into ten columns. Leave two to hold our position, and hit them with the other eight, together, in a decisive battle."

"I rely entirely on your united hearts and strength, brothers," said Song Jiang. "That is the method we'll employ."

"We couldn't budge them in the last two engagements," said Wu Yong. "It would be better to wait till they attack us."

"That doesn't sound like a good idea to me. As long as the brothers are determined to combine against the foe, there's no reason why we should be defeated."

Orders were issued the same day. The following morning they broke camp, separated into ten columns, and marched out at a rapid pace. Two columns first established a back-up position. The remaining eight, disdaining any preliminary palaver with the foe, plunged into the Zodiac Deployment, shouting and yelling, banners waving.

At once cannon rumbled, forty-eight pennant gates opened, and Tartar soldiers charged in a wide snaking line. Song Jiang's men were taken by surprise. They retreated in disorder, trailing banners and lances, their trumpets and drums askew. They lost many troops before reaching their fortified camp.

Song Jiang ordered his chieftains to defend the mountain pass with pallisaded fortifications, dig a deep moat around the camp, and plant deer-antler stakes. The gates were to be kept closed. No one was to go out. The army would spend the winter in camp.

In response to repeated petitions to the throne by Commissioner Zhao Anfu, the emperor granted winter clothing to the expeditionary force. These were to be delivered by Wang Wenbin, formerly an arms instructor in the Imperial Guards and now the garrison commandant at Zhengzhou. Wang, an intelligent and courageous man, was highly qualified in both civil and military affairs. He left the capital with over ten thousand armored troops and a convoy of civilian drivers and nearly two hundred carts laden with five hundred thousand items of clothing, heading first for Chen Bridge Station. He was instructed to urge Song Jiang to resume hostilities and push for an early victory; delay would be a punishable offense. A yellow banner at the head of the convoy was emblazoned with the words *Imperial Gift Clothing*. Officials along the route supplied food and fodder.

The journey took many a day. At the Border Hall, Wang met Commissioner Zhao, to whom he handed a document from the Council of Administration. Zhao read it. He was very pleased.

"You've come just at the right time, General! Song Jiang has failed repeatedly in his assaults on the Zodiac Deployment laid out by Wuyan, the Liao commander-in-chief. Many of his chieftains were wounded. They are here right now, being treated by Dr. An. Song Jiang has built a fortified camp in Yongqing County and doesn't dare sally forth. He's very depressed."

"That's why the emperor has sent me. He wants him to resume the offensive in a combined operation with my men. Although Song Jiang has suffered several defeats, I can't go back to the Council of Military Affairs and simply report this to the emperor. I'm not very clever, but I've read a few books on military lore and know a bit about strategy. I'd like to go to the front and try a few tactics. Perhaps I could take some of the burden off Song Jiang in a decisive battle. Would that meet with Your Excellency's approval?"

Commissioner Zhao was delighted. He gave a feast for the commandant and rewarded the carters. He told Wang to deliver the clothing to the troops, but first dispatched an emissary to inform Song Jiang.

When the man arrived, Song Jiang was brooding in his tent. He was advised that Wang Wenbin, the garrison commandant at Zhengzhou, had arrived from the capital with fifty thousand items of winter clothing, and that Wang was authorized to join in a combined offensive. Song Jiang immediately sent a man to lead Wang to his tent, where he welcomed him with wine. After they had downed several cups, Wang asked what seemed to be the difficulty.

"When I was ordered to this border area by the court, thanks to the emperor's beneficent emanations I conquered four big cities," said Song Jiang. But then, in Youzhou Prefecture, Wuyan, commander-in-chief of the Great Liao Kingdom, laid out a Zodiac Deployment. Two hundred thousand troops, in neat array, like stars in the sky, with the king himself taking personal command! I've lost several engagements in a row. I can hold defensively, but I've no plan for attack. I dare not move. Fortunately, you've come, General. I hope you will teach me."

"There's nothing wonderful about that Zodiac Deployment! I have no talent, but I'd like to go to the front with you and take a look at it. Then we can decide."

Song Jiang gladly agreed. He directed Pei Xuan to turn the clothing over to the chieftains for distribution. When all were warmly dressed, they faced south and gratefully shouted long live the emperor. That day a feast was laid for General Wang and his soldiers were rewarded.

The next morning the reinforced army set out. Wang Wenbin mounted and proceeded to the front in full armor. Tartar soldiers opposite, watching their approach, reported it to headquarters. Trumpets and drams promptly sounded in unison, and loud shouts arose. Six cavalry units moved out from the Liao position. Song Jiang dispatched units which drove them back. Wang climbed the command tower for a look.

"It's just an ordinary deployment," he said, after coming down the ladder. "I don't see anything startling."

Actually, he didn't recognize the enemy deployment, and was only putting on a show of knowledge. He directed that the drums of the forward echelon pound out a challenge. The drums and trumpets of the adversaries responded in kind. Song Jiang reined in his steed.

"We don't want dogs and wretches," he shouted. "Have you got any real men who will fight?"

Even before he had finished speaking, the fourth gate of the black-bannered troop opened and an officer flew out. His hair, which hung loose, was bound at the forehead by a strip of yellow silk. He wore darkly gleaming armor of metal hoops over a sleeveless black robe. On a raven-black horse, a three-pointed sword in hand, he rode briskly to the front. Behind him came innumerable junior officers. At the head of their procession, a black banner bore the inscription in letters of silver: *General Quli Chuqing.*

"What better place than here for me to display my skill," Wang said to himself. With levelled lance he cantered into the field and, without any preliminaries, charged the Tartar general.

Wang lunged with his weapon, the Tartar parried with his blade. They had contended for about twenty rounds when the Tartar turned and fled. Wang raced after him. The Tartar had not really been vanquished. It was only a trick to lure Wang into pursuit. Brandishing his big sword, the Tartar waited till Wang was close, then turned swiftly and hacked. He cleaved Wang clean through from shoulder to chest, tumbling him dead at his horse's feet.

Hurriedly, Song Jiang called back his troops, while the Liao soldiers advanced. They fought a sharp engagement until the Song forces retreated to their camp in disorder. The death of Wang Wenbin had shocked both officers and men, and they stole glances at one another.

Song Jiang wrote a report to Commissioner Zhao: "Wang Wenbin went voluntarily into combat and was killed. Half the soldiers he brought with him have returned to the capital." Zhao was depressed by the news, go and extremely worried. He could only relay the information to the emperor and to the Council of Military Affairs.

Brooding in his camp, Song Jiang wracked his brain for a means to break the Liao army. He ate and slept badly, he was restless and disturbed. It was a bitterly cold winter night, and he sighed as he sat huddled over a single candle. Around the second watch, he wearily stretched out with his clothes on. Outside, the wind howled. The chill ate into his bones. He sat up.

Suddenly, he saw before him a green-clad girl acolyte, her palms pressed together in salutation.

"Where did you come from?" he queried.

"I'm here on orders from our queen. She extends her invitation. Can I trouble you to come a short distance with me, General?"

"Where is your queen?"

"Not far."

Song Jiang went with the acolyte out of the tent. A glow—an interplay of gold and jade—suffused the upper and lower sky. There was a fragrant breeze and a soft mist. The weather was like spring.

They walked only two or three *li* and Song Jiang saw ahead, in a large grove of pine and cypress and purple osmanthus, a stone-balustraded winding path overhung by lush bamboos and swaying willows. Crossing a stone bridge, they passed through a gate with a cinnabar-red lintel. Inside the courtyard were buildings with beautifully painted walls, decorated rafters and beams, red gold-studded doors, jade-tiled roofs and heavy eaves, curtains like delicate prawn tendrils and tortoise-backed window sills.

The acolyte led Song Jiang east along a corridor to a room on the left. She pushed open the vermilion door and asked him to be seated for a few minutes. On all sides of the room were quiet cloud windows and sunset-hued daises. It was filled with the scent of heavenly flowers and rare incense.

The girl went away, but returned very quickly. "Our queen invites the star lord to join her," she said.

The seat of Song Jiang's chair was scarcely warm. He rose immediately. Two fairy maids came in, wearing garlands of hibiscus and jade. Their garments were of red silk and gold thread, their faces were like the full moon, their hands like tender bamboo shoots. They glided towards Song Jiang and greeted him. He dared not look at them directly.

"You needn't be so modest, General," they said. "Our queen is just changing her clothes. She wants to discuss some affairs of state. Please come with us."

Assenting, Song Jiang followed them.

A bell sounded and chimes rang as a green-clad girl welcomed Song Jiang outside a large hall. The two fairy maids preceded him up the stairs on the east side. They approached a pearl curtain. Song Jiang could hear the tinkling of little jade chimes stirring in the breeze. The green-clad girl invited him in. He knelt before an incense table.

Then he raised his eyes and looked around. Amid fresh clouds and purple mist, directly opposite on a couch carved with nine dragons, there sat the Mystic Queen of Ninth Heaven. On her head was a crown of nine dragons and flying phoenixes. She wore a gossamer blouse of pale brown decorated with precious gems in dragon and phoenix design and a sun and moon skirt. Her feet were shod in pearl-studded cloud pattern slippers. She held a rod of flawless white jade. In attendance were twenty or thirty fairy maids.

"It's been several years since I gave you the Three Heavenly Books," said the Mystic Queen. "You have kept them well and observed them faithfully. Now the Song emperor has sent you against the Tartars. Are you succeeding?"

Song Jiang prostrated himself before her and replied: "I have respected the Books and kept their secret ever since Your Majesty presented them to me. On orders of the emperor I have been campaigning against the Tartars, but I have failed several times in attacks on the Zodiac Deployment laid out by Wuyan, the enemy's commander-in-chief. I've no idea how to crack it. We're in a precarious situation."

"Don't you know the magic formula?"

Song Jiang again kowtowed. "I do not. I'm just a crude ignorant fellow. Pray, instruct me, Your Majesty."

"The Zodiac Deployment is arranged like the solar system. Simply bludgeoning will never break it. You have to follow the Laws of Harmony and Antagonism. The black-bannered contingent, for example, centers around the Water Planet, and has the Five Vapors Constellation of the North as its standard. You should select seven of your chieftains and equip them with flags, armor, clothing and steeds the color of yellow earth, and have them drive against the contingent's seven cavalry troops. Then order one of your fiercest generals, also dressed in earth-yellow, to go in and capture the foe's Water Planet General. Don't we say that earth conquers water?

"Send white-robed soldiers under eight chieftains against the green-bannered troops on the left, since metal conquers wood. Send red-robed soldiers under eight chieftains against the white bannered troops on the right, since fire conquers metal. Send eight chieftains with black-bannered soldiers against the red-bannered rear contingent of the Liaos, since water conquers fire.

"Then send nine chieftains at the head of a green-bannered unit to cut into the foe's very center and take their yellow-bannered commander-in-chief. Wood conquers earth. Dispatch a unit carrying embroidered banners and dressed in flowery robes to crack the foe's sun contingent, and another unit bearing purple banners and dressed in silver armor to smash their moon contingent. On twenty-four carts, corresponding to the twenty-four solar terms, set cannon and shot, and bombard the center of the Tartar forces. Have Gongsun Sheng raise an astral storm and under its cover push directly up to the king of Great Liao.

"In this manner you will win total victory. But you must not operate during daylight. Wait until the darkness of night. Lead your troops yourself. Take personal command of your central army. Exhort your men. One concerted effort will do it.

"My words must be kept secret. Defend the country and bring peace to the populace and never slacken.

"There is a limit to dealings between celestials and mortals. At this point we part on earth forever. When you come to abide in the Heavenly Palaces we shall meet again. Return quickly now to your camp. Do not linger."

The Mystic Queen ordered the green-clad girl to serve tea. Song Jiang drank. She directed the girl to escort Star Lord Song Jiang back to camp. He kowtowed and expressed his deep gratitude, and left the hall. The girl led him down the stairs on the west side, then through the gate with the cinnabar-red lintel to the path. They crossed the stone bridge to the grove of pines. The green-clad girl pointed.

"The Liao soldiers are there. That is where you can break through."

Song Jiang looked. The girl gave him a sudden push, and he awakened. He had been dreaming in his tent. In the stillness he heard the watchman's drum strike the hour. It was already the fourth watch.

He summoned his military advisor to interpret his dream. When Wu Yong entered the tent, Song Jiang asked: "Have you a plan for breaking the Zodiac Deployment?"

"I'm afraid not."

"I saw the Mystic Queen in a dream and she gave me a secret method. I've decided upon it and would like your advice. We can call our chieftains and give them their assignments. For this battle we must use our best."

"I'd like to hear it."

Song Jiang described the method briefly. And as a result, the king of Great Liao surrendered, hands extended together, and Commander-in-Chief Wuyan lost his life. Truly, celestial strategy was employed and clever tactics adopted; in an astral battle, the Song armies broke through the magic pass.

What method did Song Jiang use, how did he crack the deployment? Read our next chapter if you would know.

Chapter 89

Song Jiang Cracks the Foe's Deployment

Marshal Su Bestows the Emperor's Pardon

Word for word, Song Jiang related to Wu Yong the method given to him by the Mystic Queen of Ninth Heaven in his dream. When they had agreed upon a course of action they informed Commissioner Zhao. They had twenty-four gun carriages built of planks and iron sheeting, with oil-soaked faggots stored below in each and a cannon mounted above. Artillery men worked through the night to finish the job.

Song Jiang then assembled his commanders and issued his battle orders:

The central division cavalry in earth-yellow robes would, headed by General Two Spears Dong Ping, strike at the heart of the Water Planet contingent, while units under seven other chieftains would hit the seven black-bannered cavalry troops to the left and right.

The center of the Wood Planet position would be assaulted from the west by cavalry in robes of white and gold under Panther Head Lin Chong, while the seven green-bannered Liao units to the left and right were being attacked by seven other chieftains.

Cavalry in robes of fiery red, led by Qin Ming the Thunderbolt, would go against the Metal Planet position from the south, simultaneously with raids by seven other chieftains on the seven white-bannered Tartar sections to the left and right.

From the north, cavalry in robes of water-black, commanded by Two Rods Huyan Zhuo, would raid the Fire Planet position. At the same time seven other chieftains would charge the red-bannered enemy units to the left and right.

Cavalry in robes of woody green under Guan Sheng the Halberd would strike from the south at the Earth Planet position held by the Tartar commander-in-chief. The yellow-bannered troops of the foe's central army to the left and right would be assailed by eight other chieftains.

A contingent carrying embroidered banners and dressed in flowery robes would, commanded by seven chieftains, go against the Sun division on the left, while another seven chieftains leading a unit in purple robes and silver armor would move against the Tartar's Moon division on the right.

A fierce, bold force headed by six chieftains would cut through directly to the foe's center and capture the king. Another five would provide cover for the cannon carriages moving up to the middle.

The naval chieftains and their forces would sail as close to the battlefield as possible and lend support.

Eight five-sided flags would be issued, and the Song forces would deploy in their usual Nine-Unit Octagon.

When Song Jiang had finished issuing his orders, the commanders returned to their respective contingents and made ready. The twenty-four gun carriages were laden with their equipment and pushed to the front. Truly, it was a strategy that would startle Heaven and Earth, and shake the very fiends and demons.

Meanwhile, Wuyan, commander-in-chief of the Liao army, mystified by Song Jiang's failure, day after day, to give battle, dispatched pickets who advanced as far as the perimeters of the expeditionaries' camp. Song Jiang continued with his preparations and set a date for the offensive.

Then, late in the day, determined, he marched with his men. As they drew near the Liao emplacements, they spread out in a straight line. Powerful bowmen to the fore kept the enemy at a distance while the Song forces waited for evening.

At dusk, wind massed thick clouds, bringing darkness before it was night. Song Jiang ordered his troops to gag themselves with reed sticks and wait for whistle signal. That night he sent forth four columns, retaining at the front only his earth-yellow horsemen. The columns dispersed the Liao pickets, then circled round towards the northern end of the enemy position.

A volley of cannon fire broke from the Song army about the first watch. Huyan Zhuo's contingent smashed in and took the Fire Planet. Guan Sheng then carved through the foe's central army and captured the Earth Planet. Lin Chong drove into the left army and seized the Wood Planet. Qin Ming grabbed the Metal Planet after cutting into the right army. Dong Ping, hitting the lead unit, took the Water Planet.

Gongsun Sheng waved his sword, casting an astral spell, and released five thunderbolts. The night wind blew with such force from the south that the tops of trees touched the ground. Stones rolled and sand flew, the God of Thunder streaked the sky with lightning. The twenty-four gun carriages, protected by five hundred shield warriors commanded by five chieftains, trundled into the Liao position. Ten Feet of Steel struck with her soldiers into the center of the Sun emplacement, while Sagacious Lu the Tattooed Monk drove with his men into the position of the Moon. Following the gun carriages, Lu Junyi the Magnate and his troops hit the Tartars' central army in a direct drive. Each unit pursued and slaughtered its own quarry.

Cannon roared in the night, thunder exploded overhead. In that murderous atmosphere rocks rolled and gravel flew. So great was the killing that the stars moved in the sky, the sun and moon grew dim. Fiends wept, demons cried, as soldiers clashed in wild confusion.

Wuyan the Tartar commander-in-chief was busily shifting his generals when he heard yells and tumult on all sides and the sounds of combat. By the time he mounted, the gun carriages had already reached his central army. Flames spurted into the sky as the boom of cannon shook the ground. Guan Sheng and his cavalry smashed through to the commander-in-chief's tent. Grasping his crescent-bladed halberd, Wuyan rode at Guan Sheng and gave battle. Zhang Qin the Featherless Arrow, flinging his stones, knocked down aides left and right. Many were injured, and fled for their lives, pursued by four chieftains who inflicted further devastation with their swords. His aides gone, Wuyan turned his steed and raced north. Guan Sheng galloped after.

Hua Rong, who saw the Tartar commander-in-chief run, also gave chase. Fitting an arrow to his bow, he let fly at Wuyan and hit him squarely in the back. The arrow clanged against the metal back plate, showering sparks. Before Hua Rong could shoot again, Guan Sheng caught up and swung his Green Dragon Halberd. The commander-in-chief was wearing three layers of armor—steel mail nearest his body, then a suit of sea animal hide, and all covered by a suit of golden chain mail. Guan Sheng's blow cut through the two outer layers. As he raised his blade to strike again, Wuyan closed in beneath its shadow and attacked with his crescent-bladed halberd.

They had fought four or five rounds when Hua Rong reached them. He sped an arrow at Wuyan's face. The commander-in-chief hurriedly dodged, but the missile nicked off the tip of his ear and scraped through his phoenix-plumed metal helmet. Wuyan fled.

Zhang Qin, in hot pursuit, flung a stone at Wuyan's head. It knocked him prone on his horse's back, but he continued riding away, trailing his halberd. Guan Sheng again caught up and again swing his Green Dragon Halberd. He sliced upwards through the commander-in-chief's waist, bones and all, right to his head. Wuyan tumbled to the ground. Hua Rong caught his fine horse and exchanged it for his own. Zhang Qin pierced the fallen Tartar with his lance. Thus expired a commander-in-chief, a gallant warrior, after only one hack of a halberd and one thrust of a lance! Poor Tartar hero. All passed as in a dream.

Sagacious Lu, leading Wu Song and five other chieftains, charged yelling into the Sun position. Yelu Dezhong, turning to flee, was tumbled from his steed when Wu Song broke the animal's neck with one blow of his blade. Wu Song seized the Liao general by the hair and cut off his head. Dezhong's two sons fled for their lives. The Sun position was smashed, its men scattered.

"We'll push on to the center, take the Liao king, and that will be the end of it," said Sagacious Lu.

In the Moon position, the Royal Princess, hearing the murderous shouts on all sides, hurriedly mustered her female warriors to ride to the rescue. But they were beset at their tents by Ten Feet of Steel, brandishing her pair of swords and leading Mistress Gu and five other chieftains. After many rounds, Ten Feet of Steel put aside her swords and closed with the princess, wrapping her arms around her waist. The two wrestled on horseback, tightly locked. Wang the Stumpy Tiger rode up and captured the princess. Mistress Gu and Sun the Witch killed and scattered the female soldiers, while the three men chieftains aided from the side. Poor highborn pampered princess, to thus fall captive, bound and tied!

Lu Junyi and his troops also cut into the Liao central army, killing Tartar officials and generals while Xie Zhen and Xie Bao cut down the "headquarters" flag. The king, closely guarded by his ministers and captains, withdrew towards the north. But his nephews Yelu Derong and Yelu Dexin were hacked from their mounts and killed. Nephew Yelu Dehua was captured. Nephew Yelu Dechong disappeared, no one knew where. The Liao army was completely surrounded, and the slaughter continued till the fourth watch. Not a single man of the more than two hundred thousand Tartar forces was left alive.

At daybreak the chieftains returned. Song Jiang sounded the trumpets recalling his men to camp. He directed that those who had taken captives turn them over and receive their rewards. Ten Feet of Steel came forward with the royal princess; Lu Junyi with nephew Yelu Dehua; Zhu Tong with Quli Chuqing the Water Planet; and other chieftains with five more generals. Heads of innumerable slain foes were also presented.

Song Jiang placed the eight prisoner generals in the charge of Commissioner Zhao of the Song central army. Captured horses were distributed among the chieftains.

The king of Great Liao, retreating in a panic to Yanjing, hurriedly ordered that the four gates of the city be closed, the moat defended, and that no one go out to confront the enemy. On learning that the king had withdrawn to Yanjing, Song Jiang directed his army to break camp. They marched to the Liao capital and surrounded it. Song Jiang invited Commissioner Zhao to observe the coming battle from the rear camp. He instructed his troops to ring Yanjing with scaling ladders, cannon and shot, to build fortifications and prepare for the attack.

Very nervous, the king summoned his ministers to a conference. They all said: "The situation is dangerous. The best thing would be to submit to the Song empire." The king agreed. He had a flag of surrender flown from the ramparts and dispatched an emissary to the Song camp with the message: "We will pay cattle and horses, pearls and gems, every year. We will never invade the Middle Kingdom again."

Song Jiang led the emissary to Commissioner Zhao in the rear camp, where he repeated the Tartar proposal.

"This is a matter of prime national importance," said Zhao. "Only the emperor can decide. I haven't the authority. You'll have to send a high minister to the Eastern Capital and request an audience. Only if the emperor formally approves the surrender in writing and pardons your crimes will we be able to end the war and withdraw our troops."

The emissary returned to Yanjing and reported to the Liao king. The sovereign summoned his civil and military officials to confer. Chu Jian, the vice-premier, spoke.

"Our army is weak, our generals few, our soldiers are virtually gone. How can we resist the foe?" he said. "But in my humble opinion at this critical juncture we can still win men's hearts with bribes of gold and silks. I would be willing to go to Song Jiang's camp personally with lavish gifts. We'll have him halt the fighting and call off the attack on the city. At the same time we must give expensive presents to top ministers in the Eastern Capital and buy them over. Then they will speak for us before the emperor and obtain a milder disposition. Cai Jing, Tong Guan, Gao Qiu and Yang Jian have great power, and they're all rogues. The boy emperor listens to their advice. Bribe them with gold and silks and buy their support. We'll surrender and be pardoned. The Song forces will be pulled back and the war ended."

The Liao king approved his vice-premier's proposal.

Chu Jian left the city the following day and proceeded to Song Jiang's camp. Song Jiang received him in his tent and asked what brought him. Chu Jian spoke of the surrender, and proffered a number of valuable gifts.

Song Jiang heard him out, then said: "If we hit your capital day after day, you can be sure we'll take it. And when we do, we won't spare even the roots of the grass* lest resistance grow again! I've seen your surrender flag, and I've called a halt to the fighting. Since ancient times in wars between two countries there has always been the right to capitulate. You are allowed to surrender. I, therefore, have checked my troops. I permit you to go to the imperial court to request sentencing and offer tribute. Do you think Song Jiang is the sort who can be bribed? Don't ever try that again!"

The Liao vice-premier was frightened. Song Jiang continued.

"Go to the imperial court and obtain a decree. I will keep my troops out of action temporarily. Go at once and come back quickly. Don't delay."

Chu Jian thanked Song Jiang, left the camp, mounted his horse, returned to Yanjing and reported to the king. All the important ministers conferred and reached an agreement. The following day the king and his ministers contributed fine curios, gold and silver, precious gems and glittering pearls, and these were loaded on carts for delivering by the vice-premier and fifteen other officials to the Eastern Capital. Over thirty saddle horses were readied for the journey and a petition to the emperor written.

On leaving Yanjing the delegation first called on Song Jiang. He led Chu Jian to the presence of Commissioner Zhao and told him of the mission. Zhao entertained the emissary courteously. After consulting with Song Jiang, he also wrote out a report to the emperor regarding their military progress. He deputed Chai Jin and Xiao Rang to turn it in to the Council of Military Affairs for transmission to the throne, and directed them to accompany Chu Jian to the capital.

For many days they were on the road. At last, they arrived. Ten cartloads of valuable gifts, the carts and their drivers were put up in the official hostel. Chai Jin and Xiao Rang handed in to the Council of Military Affairs the report on the military situation.

"Our army has Yanjing surrounded," they said. "We can take it at any time. The Liao king has hung a surrender flag on his ramparts and dispatched his vice-premier Chu Jian to petition for permission to capitulate, and to implore a pardon and an end to the war. We dare not decide on our own. We request an imperial decree."

"Stay with Chu Jian in the official hostel for the time being," said the council officer. "We here have to consider the long-range implications."

Cai Jing, Tong Guan, Gao Qiu and Yang Jian, as well as the heads of the other departments, large and small, were all avid for gain. Chu Jian the emissary from Great Liao and his entourage, needing their assistance, called first on Cai Jing the premier and the three top ministers, then on the heads of various other departments. To all of these officials they paid bribes and presented gifts.

The following day the emperor conducted his morning audience in the palace. All the assembled high officials, civil and military, kowtowed. Tong Guan, head of the Council of Military Affairs, addressed the throne.

"Our vanguard leader Song Jiang has destroyed and driven back the Liao soldiers, and has advanced as far as Yanjing, their capital, which he now has surrounded. It is likely to fall to us at any time. The king of Liao has hung out a flag of surrender and seeks to capitulate. He has sent here his emissary Chu Jian with an offer to become our tributary. They will submit to our terms, but beg for a pardon and peace, and plead that we withdraw our troops and end the war. They promise to pay tribute every year without fail. None of the ministries dares to decide on its own. We request an imperial disposition."

"If we talk peace and halt the hostilities, they will still exist as a nation," said the sovereign. "What do you ministers think we should do?"

Cai Jing the premier stepped forward.

"We have reached a consensus," he said. "Since ancient times the barbarians beyond our borders have never ceased harassing us. In our humble opinion, Liao should retain its identity as a nation and serve as a buffer state in the north, the lips to our teeth, so to speak. Their annual tribute will be to our advantage. We should permit them to surrender on our terms, end the hostilities, and summon our troops back to defend the capital. But we ministers cannot presume to intervene. We beg Your Majesty to decide."

The emperor approved the premier's proposal. "Bring the Liao emissary before me," he directed.

The order was transmitted summoning Chu Jian and his entourage. They knelt in a line at the far end of the hall and fervently kowtowed. A minister brought forward their petition and unrolled it on the imperial table. The Royal Petition Speaker read it in a loud voice:

Yelu Hui, Ruling Lord of the Kingdom of Great Liao, kowtows one hundred times and states to Your Majesty: Born in the desert and raised in a barbarian land, I was unfamiliar with the great laws of Your Majesty and never studied the major social duties of civilized man. Deficient in culture and military talents, I was surrounded by vicious sycophants, men greedy and corrupt, short-sighted as rats but crafty as roebucks. I was ignorant, they rapacious. We invaded your borders, provoking your army's reprisal. Mere ants cannot stir Mount Taishan, rivers cannot be halted in their flow to the sea. Although we still possess a few desolate cities, we have not enough provisions for even half a year.

Today, I dispatch my emissary Chu Jian to venture into your awesome presence and surrender out lands and request punishment. If Your Majesty will pity us and spare our poor lives and not destroy our ancestral inheritance, your name shall be engraved on our bones. With the utmost exertion we shall serve forever as a guard of your borders and a buffer for your imperial reign. You will give new life to our young and old, and all our descendants will be eternally grateful. Yearly, we will pay tribute. We vow never to fail.

Trembling, we wait with bated breath! In sincerity and fear, we bow our heads and kowtow! Respectfully submitted.

The __day of the Winter Month in the fourth year of Xuan He
Yelu Hui, Ruler of the Kingdom of Great Liao

The ministers heard the petition with pleasure, and the emperor directed that imperial wine be served to the emissary. Chu Jian and his entourage present-ed tributes of gold and silks to the royal court. The emperor ordered that the Treasury receive them, and that it accept thereafter annual tribute of money and cattle. He, in turn, gave gifts of silk and feasted the emissaries in the Hall of Imperial Caterers. He instructed them to go back to Liao.

"I will dispatch an official who will accept your surrender," he said.

Chu Jian and his party thanked the emperor, took their leave and returned to the official hostel. When the imperial audience ended they called at the various ministries to complete the necessary formalities and dispense more bribes.

Cai Jing reassured Chu Jian. "You go back," he said. "The four of us will see to everything."

Chu Jian thanked the premier and returned to the kingdom of Liao.

At the imperial audience the following day, Cai Jing entered at the head of the corps of officials. He petitioned the throne to pardon the Tartars. The emperor consented, and directed the scholars of the Hanlin Academy to draw up a docu-ment of pardon. He ordered Marshal Su to deliver and read it, and Commissioner Zhao to instruct Song Jiang to cease hostilities and return to the Eastern Capital. He was to release all prisoners, give back the captured cities, and restore to the Liao authorities whatever had been taken from their treasuries.

Royal court ended and the attending officials withdrew. The next day they called on Marshal Su and set a date for seeing him off. Su did not wish to delay the imperial decree. He had sedan-chairs and horses and attendants readied for the journey, took his leave of the emperor, bid the ministry officials farewell, and departed for Liao with Chai Jin and Xiao Rang.

It was the depths of winter. Masses of clouds hung heavy in the sky. The envoys passed Chen Bridge Station and headed for the frontier. Snow blanketed the plains, powdering the trees and garbing the vast open spaces in silver. Through snow and wind, Marshal Su and his party wound their way forward.

The snow still had not melted when they reached the border area. Chai Jin and Xiao Rang sent a mounted courier on ahead to inform first Commissioner Zhao, and then Song Jiang, of their arrival. Carrying ceremonial wine, Song Jiang and an escort party travelled fifty *li* and knelt by the roadside in greeting. Marshal Su and the officials in his party were very pleased by this welcome. They were invited into the camp, where Song Jiang had a feast laid. He and the marshal discussed affairs in the imperial court.

"Cai Jian, Tong Guan, Gao Qiu, Yang Jian and other high ministry officials have all been bribed by the Tartars," said Su. "Because of their urgings, the emperor has agreed to a surrender and an end to the fighting. Your troops are being called back to guard the capital."

Song Jiang sighed. "I have no criticism of the court. It's just that our accomplishments here seem to have been in vain."

"Don't distress yourself, General," said the marshal. "When I return to the capital, I shall speak highly of you to the emperor."

"And when he hears my testimony," added Commissioner Zhao, "he surely will show his appreciation for your deeds."

"There are a hundred and eight of us, doing our utmost for our country," said Song Jiang. "We have no personal ambitions, or any desire to impose on His Majesty's benevolence. As long as we can remain together in our labors, that will be our greatest happiness. If you can propose that for us, Commissioner, we shall be deeply grateful."

That day all dined and made merry. Only at evening did the feasting end. A messenger was dispatched to the king of the Liaos, notifying him to prepare to receive the decree.

The next day Song Jiang selected ten generals to escort Marshal Su and the decree into the kingdom of Liao. They were dressed in silk robes and golden armor and were fully armed. Guarding the marshal with a complement of three thousand infantry and cavalry, front and rear, they marched into the city.

The residents of Yanjing burned fragrant incense and hung festive lanterns before the doorway of every home. The king himself led his civil and military officials, all mounted and formally dressed, outside the South Gate to welcome the decree. Then they proceeded to the Royal Hall, where the ten Song generals arraigned themselves on either side, and Marshal Su took a stand to the left of the Dragon Pavilion. The king and his officials knelt before the hall. At a call from the Chief of Ceremonies, they kowtowed. The Liao chamberlain requested the decree. He then read it aloud:

The Emperor of Great Song proclaims: Since the days of our earliest kings and emperors there never was a sovereign who did not govern his subjects, nor subjects who did not sustain their sovereign. The Middle Kingdom has its ruler. Surely you barbarians have one too!

In violation of celestial laws, you Liaos have repeatedly invaded our borders. For this, you deserve to be instantly extinguished. But your petition has moved me to pity. I have not the heart to destroy you, and shall permit you to remain as a nation.

Effective from the day you receive this edict, all captured commanders shall be returned to Liao, your cities shall be restored once again to Liao rule.

But annual tribute must be delivered without fail. Respect our great country, venerate Heaven and Earth. This is the duty of you barbarians. Never forget!

We issue this decree so that all may know.

The __day of the Winter Month
of the fourth year of Xuan He

The king of the Tartars and his officials kowtowed and voiced their thanks. The imperial decree, on its dragon platform, was carried past, and the king and Marshal Su formally met. They exchanged courtesies, and the king invited the marshal to the rear of the hall, where a lavish feast of many delicacies was laid. While the Tartar officials poured wine and toasted their guests, beautiful girls played military airs on fifes and drums, or languorously turned in slow native dances.

When the banquet ended, Marshal Su and his party were provided quarters in the hostel for officials. Each member of the entourage received a gift.

The next day the king directed Chu Jian, his vice-premier, to go to the camp and invite Commissioner Zhao and Song Jiang into Yanjing to dine. On conferring with Military Advisor Wu Yong, Song Jiang decided it would be inappropriate for him to go. Commissioner Zhao, therefore, went without him to accompany Marshal Su. The king of the Tartars entertained the imperial emissaries at a grand banquet. Mulled grape wine was poured into silver goblets, delicious antelope meat was piled high on golden platters. Everywhere was tasty fruit and floral decorations of many hues.

And when it was nearly over, the king presented Marshal Su and Commissioner Zhao with curios on a golden platter. They feasted until far into the night.

To the accompaniment of martial music, the king and his officials the following day escorted Marshal Su and Commissioner Zhao out of the city and saw them off to camp. Again Vice-Premier Chu Jian was sent to call on Song Jiang. This time he brought gifts of cattle, sheep, horses, gold, silver and colorful silks. At a large meeting, he rewarded the troops and gave valuable presents to the commanders.

Song Jiang ordered that the Royal Princess and her company be released and permitted to go home. He also restored to Liao sovereignty the cities of Tanzhou, Qizhou, Bazhou and Youzhou. He saw off Marshal Su, who was returning to the capital. After reassembling his entire force, he dispatched his central army to serve as an escort for Commissioner Zhao. He then gave a banquet in the camp at which he rewarded his naval chieftains. He instructed them to sail back to the Eastern Capital and wait there for further orders.

He invited the premier of the Tartars and his deputy for a chat. The king directed premier Youxi Bojin and Vice-Premier Chu Jian to call on Song Jiang in his headquarters. Song Jiang received them in his tent, and host and guests took their respective places.

"Our soldiers have neared your capital's walls, our commanders are at your moat. Victory is at hand," he said. "Originally, we had no intention of letting you surrender. We were going to smash in and obliterate everything. It would have been quite reasonable for us to do so. But, granting your request, I permitted you to appeal to the imperial court. The emperor took pity on you and decided not to wipe you out. He is allowing you to surrender, unconditionally, and is giving you very generous terms.

"I am about to return to the Eastern Capital. Don't make the mistake of thinking we couldn't have defeated you. Don't provoke us again. Pay your annual tribute without fail. Behave yourselves. Commit no more crimes. If our army has to come again, we won't let you off so easily!" The premier kowtowed and apologized for their crimes. In a softer tone, Song Jiang further advised them. They thanked him for his kindness and departed.

He put another contingent on the march for home, this one under woman commander Ten Feet of Steel. He directed Xiao Rang to write, and Jin Dajian to inscribe, a stone tablet commemorating the Song victory. The tablet was erected at the foot of Maoshan Mountain, fifteen *li* east of Yongqing County. It is still there today.

His remaining troops he divided into five columns and set a date for the march. But then Sagacious Lu burst into his tent and, clasping both hands together in greeting, addressed him.

"After I killed the Lord of the West, I fled to Yanmen County in Daizhou Prefecture, and Squire Zhao brought me to Mount Wutai, where I took refuge with the abbot and became a monk. Because I twice got drunk, knocked open the gates and rioted in the monastery, the abbot sent me to the Great Xiangguo Monastery in the Eastern Capital, and the abbot there gave me a job looking after their vegetable garden. But Marshal Gao wanted to have me killed because I rescued Lin Chong, and I became an outlaw. I got to know you, brother, and I've been with you for many years.

"I've been thinking of my first teacher, the abbot at Wutai. I haven't been to see him in all this time. I often remember what he told me—Even though it's my nature to kill and burn, I'll eventually be purified and become a saint. Since everything is quiet and peaceful at present, I'd like to ask for a few days off and pay my respects to him. I want to contribute the rewards I've accumulated to the monastery and request him to predict the future. You and the army go on ahead, brother. I'll catch up."

Song Jiang was surprised. He thought a moment, then said: "I had no idea you knew this holy man. Why didn't you say so? We'll go with you and also pay our respects and ask him to foretell the future."

He discussed it with the other chieftains. They all wanted to go, except for Gongsun Sheng who was a Taoist. Song Jiang decided, after talking it over with Military Advisor Wu Yong, to leave Jin Dajian, Huangfu Duan, Xiao Rang and Yue Ho to aid Deputy Vanguard General Lu Junyi in commanding the army, which was to continue returning by contingents to the capital.

"We'll take only a thousand men, and our chieftains," said Song Jiang, "and go with Sagacious Lu to call on his abbot."

Sagacious Lu expressed his willingness. The party prepared gifts of famous incense, fine silks, clothing and money, and set out for Mount Wutai.

Truly, they left aside their armor and weapons to wander through lonely forests. By the Terrace of Rain and Flowers they called on a high-ranking monk of great virtue, at the Hall of Virtue they saw gleaming lamps and ancient Buddhas.

And as a result, a single phrase scorned the search for name and fame, a few brief words kicked aside obsession with life and death.

How did Song Jiang and Sagacious Lu call upon the abbot? Read our next chapter if you would know.

CHAPTER 90

ON MOUNT WUTAI SONG JIANG CONSULTS THE SEER

AT DOUBLE WOODS CROSSING YAN QING SHOOTS A GOOSE

Song Jiang and the chieftains, taking only a thousand men, arrived with Sagacious Lu at the foot of Mount Wutai, and there made camp. A messenger was sent up the mountain to announce their presence. Divesting themselves of their armor, Song Jiang and his brothers started climbing the slope, on foot, wearing their military robes of embroidered silk. As they neared the monastery archway, they heard the pealing of bells and the beating of drums. Monks in large number came out to welcome them. They courteously greeted Song Jiang, Sagacious Lu and the others. Many of them remembered Sagacious. The sight of the hundred or more chieftains, arrayed neatly in ranks behind Song Jiang, filled them with awe and admiration.

"The abbot is meditating and cannot be disturbed," the elder told Song Jiang. "Please don't be offended, General." He invited the visitors to sit a while in the reception room.

Tea was served. An attendant entered and said: "The abbot has just completed his meditations. He invites the general to join him in the Meditation Hall."

Song Jiang and his entourage of over a hundred walked to the hall. The abbot came quickly down the steps and led them inside, where they exchanged courtesies. Song Jiang looked at the prelate. He was a man in his sixties. His hair and eyebrows were completely white. He had fine bones and the air of one who has lived long in remote mountains.

When all the chieftains had entered, Song Jiang requested the abbot to be seated. Then he and the chieftains lit incense and bowed. Sagacious Lu did the same.

"In the years you've been gone you've killed and burned just like before," the abbot berated Sagacious.

The Tattooed Monk remained silent.

Song Jiang stepped forward and said: "I have long known of your virtue, Abbot, but I never was fortunate enough to have the chance to see your noble visage. A campaign against the Liao has brought me to this region, and so I am able to offer homage to a great prelate. It gives me the utmost happiness. Sagacious Lu has been my brother. Although he has killed and set fires, he has never harmed good people, and his heart has been pure. It was he who led us here to pay our respects."

"High-ranking prelates who have called here have spoken at times of mundane affairs," said the abbot. "I have long known of your acting in Heaven's behalf, General, and your loyal heart. I know too how much emphasis your commanders place on chivalrous conduct. Following you, my disciple Sagacious Lu of course could do no wrong."

Song Jiang fulsomely expressed his thanks.

Sagacious Lu presented a packet of gold and silver and silks to his teacher, the abbot.

"Where did you get these things, my pupil? Immoral riches I can never accept."

"These are rewards I've accumulated. They're of no use to me. I've brought them especially for you, Teacher, to use for the benefit of all."

"They would mean little to our monks. I'll use the money to buy a set of sutras. Expiate your sins and you'll reach a state of purity."

Sagacious Lu thanked the abbot. Song Jiang, too, presented money and silks. The prelate adamantly refused to take them.

"If you won't accept our gifts, Teacher," said Song Jiang, "at least you can use them to provide vegetarian meals for the monks."

The callers rested at the monastery on Mount Wutai all that day, and the abbot entertained them at a meatless meal. Of that no more need be said.

After another vegetarian repast the next day, bells pealed and drums pounded in the temple on Mount Wutai. The abbot summoned his monks to hear him discourse and make predictions. Cassocks draped over their shoulders and carrying their cushions, they filed into the temple and sat down. Song Jiang, Sagacious Lu, and the other chieftains stood on either side.

A stone chime sounded, and two red gauze lanterns lighted the abbot to his chair on the dais. Holding a stick of smoldering incense, he offered a prayer.

"With this incense, I humbly wish ten thousand years to the emperor, with the empress at his side, and a thousand autumns to the prince. May the imperial children flourish, and the officials rise constantly in rank. Let there be peace throughout the land, and may the people be happy at their labors."

The prelate took another stick of incense. "May our patrons be at ease in body and mind, live for a thousand circuits of the sun, and their fame last forever."

Taking a third stick, the abbot intoned: "May the country be peaceful and the people serene for years to come, the five grains abundant, the three religions glorious, with calm on all four sides, and everything exactly as wished."

The prelate then seated himself, while the monks rose and stood, palms of their hands together. Song Jiang advanced with a stick, bowed and, palms together, addressed the abbot.

"I have a question. I wonder if I dare ask?"

"What is your proper query?"

"One's life on earth is limited, though suffering is without end. Man's body is weak. His greatest concern is life and death. I've come here to ask my fate."

The abbot's reply was cryptic: "By the six senses bound, by the four elements restricted, several times you've tumbled in the flames of battle. Alas, all living things afloat in this world futilely howl in mire and sand."

Song Jiang bowed and stood in attendance. The chieftains also advanced with incense and bowed.

"We pray only that we may live and die together," they said, "and meet always in future incarnations."

The monks then withdrew and the abbot invited his guests to dine on vegetarian fare in the Hall of Clouds. After the meal, Song Jiang and Sagacious Lu accompanied the abbot to Meditation Hall. They chatted until nightfall.

"Sagacious and I had hoped to spend many days with you, Teacher, dispelling our ignorance," said Song Jiang. "But as leader of a large army, I cannot stay too long. I do not understand your pronouncement. Since we're about to return to the capital, I pray you, Abbot, tell me what the future holds in store."

On a sheet of paper, the prelate wrote four phrases: *When the shadows of the wild geese pass, in the east there is no unity. Cocking an eye he scores his mark, at Double Woods full prosperity.*

The abbot handed the paper to Song Jiang. "Your whole life is here, General. Preserve this prediction well. In time it will come true."

Song Jiang looked at the paper. He couldn't make head or tail of it.

"I'm a stupid person. I don't understand. Please explain. Shall I expect good or ill?"

"These are mystic Buddhist words. Think them over. I cannot tell you clearly, lest I reveal Heaven's secrets."

The prelate then called Sagacious Lu before him and said: "I shall soon be leaving you forever, my pupil, to go to my just reward. You, too, I give a four phrase prediction. Keep it and use it all your life."

And the abbot wrote: *Take Xia when you encounter him. Seize La when you meet. When you hear the tide, round out the circle. When you see the tide, in silence rest.*

Bowing, Sagacious accepted the paper. He read it several times and concealed it on his person. Again he bowed and thanked his teacher.

"Remember these words, my pupil," said the abbot. "Don't forget your original form."

All retired to rest for the night. The following day, Song Jiang and Sagacious Lu, plus Wu Yong and the chieftains, bid the abbot farewell. The abbot and all the monks saw them off as far as the mountain arch of the monastery.

Song Jiang and his entourage hurried through the night and returned to the main army, where they were met by Lu Junyi and Gongsun Sheng. Song Jiang told them what had transpired on Mount Wutai and showed them abbot's prediction. They couldn't decipher it either.

"How could the likes of us hope to understand such secret religious Words," exclaimed Xiao Rang. Everyone sighed regretfully.

Song Jiang ordered the army to march. All three divisions headed for the Eastern Capital. After several days on the road, they reached a place called Double

Woods Crossing. Happening to look up at the sky, Song Jiang saw several lines of wild geese. But they were not in their usual formations. Some flew high, some low, and all were squawking in alarm.

While puzzling over this, he heard cries of admiration further up the line of march, and sent a mounted scout to inquire. The man quickly returned and reported that Yan Qing the Prodigy had been practicing with his bow. Every arrow had hit a goose, bringing down well over a dozen, thus arousing the watchers' acclaim.

Song Jiang directed that Yan Qing come to him immediately. The Prodigy wore a broad-brimmed white felt hat and a parrot-yellow tunic quilted with flaxen floss. Astride a roan desert steed and carrying his bow and arrows, he cantered up to halt before Song Jiang, the dead geese hanging over his horse's rump. He dismounted and stood waiting.

"Was that you, shooting geese just now?"

"I needed practice and saw them flying overhead. I didn't expect every arrow to score a hit. I must have brought down more than a dozen."

"A military man ought to practice his archery, and you're an expert at it. I was just thinking—these geese leave the Tianshan Range in autumn and fly south across the Yangzi with reeds in their beaks to where it's warm and they can find food, and don't return till the following spring. They're the most virtuous of birds. They travel in flocks of up to half a hundred, flying in orderly ranks, with the leader at the head and the inferiors behind. They never leave the flock, and post sentinels when they rest at night. If a gander loses his goose, or a goose her gander, they never mate again. These fowl possess all five attributes—virtue, righteousness, propriety, knowledge and faith.

"If a goose dies in flight, all utter cries of mourning, and none will ever harass a bereaved bird. This is virtue. When a fowl loses its mate, it never pairs again. This is righteousness. They fly in a definite order, each automatically taking its place. This is propriety. They avoid hawks and eagles, silently crossing the passes with reed sticks in their beaks. This is knowledge. They fly south in autumn and north in spring, every year without fail. This is faith.

"How could you have the heart to harm such admirable creatures? Those geese passing in the sky, all helping one another, are very much like our band of brothers. Yet you shoot them down. How would we feel if it were some of our brothers we had lost? You must never hurt these virtuous birds again!"

Yan Qing listened in penitent silence. Emotionally, Song Jiang composed and recited a poem:

> Jagged peaks draped in mist,
> Three lines of geese across the sky.
> Suddenly in flight a mate is lost—
> Cold moon, chill breeze, a mournful cry.

He felt extremely depressed. That night, the army camped at Double Woods Crossing. Song Jiang brooded in his tent. He called for paper and writing brush and composed these lines:

Far from the startled scattered flock
In the vast clear firmament
A wild goose flies.
A lone shadow seeking a sheltering pond
Finding naught but dry grass, sandy wastes,
Open water, endless skies.

No poet,
I can only set down these few thoughts.
Dusk in an empty ravine,
Campfire smoke in an ancient fort,
I'm more dejected than I can say!

Though we've cleared the reeds
We've no place to spend the night.
When, oh when, will we see once more
The Yumen Gate to our homeland!

Drearily, I sob and sigh,
Longing to depart this hateful river.
Would that spring come soon again,
With swallows nesting in the beams.

Song Jiang showed what he had written to Wu Yong and Gongsun Sheng. His sadness and loneliness were quite apparent. He was very unhappy. That night Wu Yong plied him with wine until he was drunk.

The next morning they mounted and continued the southward march. It was early winter, and the desolate landscape deepened Song Jiang's gloom.

After many a day, they finally neared the capital. They made camp at Chen Bridge Station and awaited the emperor's directive.

Marshal Su and Commissioner Zhao, who had reached the city first with the central army, praised Song Jiang's deeds to the sovereign, and reported that he and his forces were already outside the pass in the environs of the capital. Commissioner Zhao related the arduous exploits of Song Jiang and his generals in the border region. The monarch warmly voiced his approbation. He instructed the royal chamberlain to summon them to his presence, and permit them to enter the capital in full armor.

On being notified by the royal chamberlain, Song Jiang and his chieftains—one hundred and eight in all—donned armor and helmets, carried their weapons, hung gold and silver slabs on their silken robes, and filed into the palace through the East Glory Gate. His Majesty received them in the Hall of Culture and Virtue, where they kowtowed and shouted long live the emperor. Their magnificent military apparel impressed the monarch. Only Wu Yong, Sagacious Lu and Wu Song wore the clothes of their religious calling. The sovereign was very pleased.

"I have heard much of your hardships on the expedition and your dedication in the border region. I was greatly concerned over the many casualties you suffered," he aid.

Again kowtowing, Song Jiang replied: "Thanks to the good fortune emanating from Your Majesty, the border region is now at peace. Some of my generals were wounded, but none seriously. The sandy kingdom of the Liao has already capitulated. This, too, is a result of Your Majesty's benevolent teaching." He bowed once more and expressed his gratitude.

The emperor wanted to confer on Song Jiang a rank of nobility, but Premier Cai Jing and Chancellor of Military Affairs Tong Guan advised against it.

"Our borders are still troubled," they said. "He should not be raised. Give him an honorary title of Defender of Righteousness, let him bear imperial arms, and put him in charge of guarding the palace. As to Lu Junyi, he can be called Military Teacher and be permitted to bear imperial weapons; make him head of military training. Wu Yong and the rest of the thirty-six can become full commanders, Zhu Wu and the remainder of the seventy-two can be vice-commanders. We can also spread some money among the soldiers."

The sovereign agreed. He instructed the Council of Military Affairs to grant the appropriate ranks and issue the monetary rewards. Song Jiang and his chieftains kowtowed and thanked the emperor for his benevolence. The monarch ordered the Imperial Caterers to give a banquet in their honor. When it was over, Song Jiang was presented with a silken robe, a set of gold armor, and a fine horse. Lu Junyi and the others were also given gifts drawn from the Treasury. All expressed their thanks. They withdrew from the palace through the West Glory Gate, mounted and returned to camp, there to await further orders from the imperial court.

Gongsun Sheng, the following day, came to Song Jiang's tent. He placed his palms together and bowed in the Taoist fashion to Song and the other chieftains.

"My teacher Luo the Sage instructed me to return to the mountain and continue my studies after escorting you safely to the capital. You agreed to this, brother," he said to Song Jiang. "Now that you have returned, famous and in triumph, I must not linger. I shall say farewell, go back to the mountain, and spend the rest of my days studying the Way and caring for my old mother."

Song Jiang couldn't renege on his promise. With tears in his eyes he said: "Our days together were like opening flowers. Our parting is like flowers that fall. I gave my word, but it breaks my heart to see you go!"

"I would be lacking love and respect if I left you halfway. But you're already famous and a success. This is no place for a poor Taoist. You must give your consent."

When all Song Jiang's urgings proved in vain, he ordered a large farewell banquet. All sighed as they raised their cups. Tears flowed with the wine. Gongsun refused gifts of gold and silks. The chieftains, over his protests, stuffed them in his luggage.

The next day he took his leave. He wore hemp sandals and carried his luggage on his back. Palms together, he bowed his head, then set off towards the north.

For several days Song Jiang grieved. His tears fell like rain.

New Year's Day was fast approaching, and the officials prepared to celebrate. Premier Cai was afraid that if Song Jiang and all his chieftains were present at the court festivities the emperor would see them and be reminded to make important use of them. He therefore persuaded the monarch to limit the invitations to Song Jiang and Lu Junyi, the only two who held imperial posts. The other chieftains who had been on the expedition against the Tartars had no official ranks. They were "excused" from attending lest they "alarm the sovereign."

On New Year's Day the emperor held court, and the officials came to offer their congratulations. Song Jiang and Lu Junyi, both in formal dress, were in the Waiting Room for the morning imperial audience, and kowtowed with the officials. The emperor, in fringed hat and wearing a jade-encrusted girdle, was seated on his throne, attended by his high ministers. But neither Song Jiang and Lu Junyi nor the officials were allowed to enter the imperial hall. They could only observe the jewelled ornaments and fine trappings of the ministers, coming and going as they toasted the sovereign.

This went on from dawn until noon. Only then were those outside given a little imperial wine with which to express their thanks. Then the officials withdrew and the emperor concluded his court.

Song and Lu left the palace, removed their court dress, mounted their horses and returned to camp, their faces dark. Wu Yong and the other chieftains were waiting for them. As they offered congratulations on the holiday, they observed Song Jiang's gloomy expression. The hundred or more of them lined up on either side. Song Jiang sat in silence, his head lowered.

"You've just been congratulating the emperor, brother. Why so dejected?" Wu Yong queried.

Song Jiang sighed. "I must have been both unlucky. We went through so much hardship to smash the Liao, but I've obtained very little for you brothers. I myself have been made only a petty official."

"Though you haven't yet achieved good fortune, why be downcast? All things are pre-ordained. There's no need to worry."

Li Kui the Black Whirlwind spoke. "You still haven't thought this out, brother! When we were in Liangshan Marsh, nobody could push us around. But all you could talk about was amnesty, amnesty! Now that we've got it we have nothing but aggravation. We brothers are all here together. Let's go back to Liangshan Marsh, I say, and be happy!"

"You're talking wild again, black beast," Song Jiang shouted. "All of us have been made officers in the imperial army. You don't understand these things. You're still a rebel at heart!"

"If you don't listen to me, brother," Li Kui insisted, "all you'll get is more abuse!"

Everyone laughed. They raised their cups and congratulated Song Jiang on the New Year. They drank until the second watch before breaking up.

The next day, with a dozen horsemen, Song Jiang entered the city and offered congratulations on the New Year to Marshal Su, Commissioner Zhao, and various ministry officials. Many persons observed this, and one of them reported to Cai Jing. The following day, after obtaining the emperor's approval, Cai had notices posted on every city gate!

They read as follows: *All officers and commanders of expeditionary forces shall remain in camp and wait for orders. They are not to enter the city without specific instructions in writing from higher headquarters. Whoever disobeys shall be punished according to military law.*

One of the notices was posted at Chen Bridge Gate, and a person who saw it told Song Jiang. His depression deepened. The chieftains were furious. Except for Song Jiang, all seethed with rebellion.

Several naval chieftains requested a conference with Wu Yong. Escorted on board a warship, he met Li Jun, Zhang Heng, Zhang Shun and the three Ruan brothers.

"The imperial court doesn't keep its word. Treacherous ministers wield power and block the correct path," they said. "Although Brother Song Jiang has broken the Liao, he's been made only a petty palace functionary. He hasn't been able to obtain any raise in rank or rewards for the rest of us. Now a notice has been posted forbidding us entry into the city. We think those evil ministers are trying to split us up, to transfer us away. We'd like you to support us. If we ask brother, he'll flatly refuse. Our idea is to fight a bloody battle, pillage the city clean, go back to Liangshan Marsh and become brigands again! That would be best!"

"Brother Song Jiang will certainly refuse. You're wasting your time. If the arrow point doesn't leave the bow, the shaft is sure to snap. The headless snake cannot crawl. How can I propose such a thing? We can't do anything until brother is willing. If he doesn't agree and you rebel on your own, you'll never succeed."

It was plain that the military advisor would not be their advocate. The six naval chieftains fell silent.

Returning to camp, Wu Yong chatted with Song Jiang about military affairs. Then he said: "Our brothers usually were free to come and go as they pleased, and they were quite happy with the situation. Yet today, even though we've been amnestied and you've been made an official, they're suddenly been restricted. They can't accept it. They're very angry."

Song Jiang was startled. "Has someone been saying something to you?"

"No one had to say anything. It's common sense. As the old saying goes: 'People want wealth and position, they hate being poor and lowly.' You've only to look at their faces to see their mood."

"The brothers may want to revolt, Military Advisor, but though I die and go to the Nether World I'll never abandon my loyalty to the emperor!"

The next morning Song Jiang summoned all his chieftains for a conference. When they had assembled before his tent, he addressed them.

"After starting in life as a petty functionary in Yuncheng, I committed a major crime. Thanks to your support, brothers, I became your leader and, today, a government official. Since ancient times it has been said: 'A mature man is not without restraint; without restraint one cannot achieve maturity.' The court has its reasons for posting those notices. You're not to go into the city without permission. Many of us in the mountain forests were just rough soldiers. Whoever stirs up trouble will surely be dealt with according to law. Our reputation will be damaged. It's lucky for us we're not allowed into the city. If you feel so hampered that you must revolt, cut off my head first! Otherwise I won't be able to face the world. I'll have to kill myself! The choice is yours!"

At Song Jiang's words, the chieftains wept. They reaffirmed their fealty, and the meeting disbanded.

From then on, unless on official business, none of them went into the city. As the first lunar festival drew near, in the Eastern Capital, as was the annual custom, the streets were festooned with lanterns. In the camp, Yan Qing the Prodigy had a proposal for Yue Ho the Iron Throat.

"The emperor and the people are celebrating the New Year with fireworks and lantern displays. Let's disguise ourselves and go in and have a look."

"If you're going to see the lanterns," someone said, "You'll have to take me."

Yan Qing turned around. It was Li Kui the Black Whirlwind.

"There's no use trying to fool me," said Li Kui. "I heard everything."

"We can take you easily enough," said Yan Qing, "but I'm worried about that temper of yours. You're sure to stir up trouble. The Council of Military Affairs has posted notices forbidding us to enter the city. If you create a row, we'll fall right into their trap."

"I won't cause any fuss. I'll do whatever you say."

"All right, then. Dress up as a traveller tomorrow, and you can come."

Black Whirlwind was delighted.

The next day, in the garb of travellers, the three set out. Yue Ho and Shi Qian, whom they happened to meet, sneaked in first. Yan Qing couldn't get rid of Li Kui and had no choice but to let the Black Whirlwind accompany him. They dared not enter the Chen Bridge Gate. Making a detour around the capital, they went in through Fengqiu Gate.

Hand in hand they strolled towards the amusement center. Li Kui, hearing the sound of music, insisted on going in. He and Yan Qing pushed through the crowds to where a performer was reciting a ballad based on an episode in the novel *The Romance of the Three Kingdoms.* It was about the famous hero of antiquity, Guan Yu, who had been struck in the left arm by an arrow. The poison had seeped into his bone.

"If you want me to cure you," said the doctor, "you'll have to put your arm through iron hoops attached to a bronze rod and let me bind it tight. I'll slice open your flesh and cut out the three tenths of the bone that's been poisoned. After putting growth-promoting medicine inside, I'll sew you up with oiled thread and apply ointment to the outside. In less than half a month you'll be as good as new. But the operation is very painful."

Guan Yu laughed. "Even death doesn't daunt a real man. Would I worry about a mere arm? No need for your rod and hoops. Just slice away!"

He called for his chess-board, and played a game with a friend, while the doctor carved the bone and extracted the poison. Guan Yu never blanched. He chatted and laughed with his friend all the while.

When the ballad reciter reached this point, Li Kui shouted out: "Now that's what I call a brave man!"

The startled audience turned to stare. Yan Qing hastily restrained him.

"How can you be so dumb, brother? An amusement center is no place to make a big disturbance over a little thing!"

"I couldn't help it. I was carried away."

Yan Qing dragged him out. They left the amusement center and walked along a cross-town street. A man was slinging bricks and tiles at another man's house.

"Twice I've loaned you money," cried the person under attack. "Not only do you refuse to pay back but, out of a clear blue sky, you bombard my house!"

Aroused by the injustice, Li Kui wanted immediately to intervene. Yan Qing flung both arms around his waist. Li Kui glared.

"There's a debt question between him and me," said the brick thrower. "What's it to you? I'm going south of the Yangzi any day now in an expedition against the bandits, so you'd better not rile me! It's sure death down there! I'd just as leave fight you and be killed here! I end up in a coffin either way!"

"What's this about going south?" said Black Whirlwind. "We haven't had any mustering of troops or orders to commanders."

Yan Qing calmed the combatants and, with Li Kui, left the cross-town street. Traversing a lane, they saw a small tea-shop, went in and sat down. As they were sipping their beverage, they got into conversation with an old fellow, opposite.

"Can you tell us something, grandpa?" said Yan Qing. "We ran into a brawling soldier just now who said he was leaving soon on an expedition across the Yangzi. Where exactly are they going?"

"Oh, you don't know? A bandit there named Fang La has rebelled. He's occupied eight prefectures from Muzhou to Runzhou and twenty-five counties. He calls this territory a nation. Sooner or later the rebels will attack Yangzhou. The emperor has ordered Military Governor Zhang and District Commander Liu to clean them out."

Yan Qing and Li Kui paid their bill and hurried back to camp, where they reported their conversation to Wu Yong. The military advisor was very pleased. He told Song Jiang about it.

"Being idle here is not right," said Song Jiang. "We should ask Marshal Su to petition the emperor to let us join the expedition."

He discussed the matter with his chieftains. They all liked the idea.

The next day Song Jiang changed his clothes and went into town with Yan Qing. At the residency of Marshal Su they dismounted. They were announced and, on the marshal's instructions, ushered in. Song Jiang bowed in greeting.

"Why are you dressed in civilian garb, General?"

"The Military Affairs Council has forbidden all expeditionary officers to enter the city unless summoned, and I wanted to see Your Excellency privately. I hear that Fang La, south of the Yangzi, has rebelled, occupied several prefectures, and calls himself a king. He's advanced as far as Runzhou. It's expected that, sooner or later, he'll cross the river and attack Yangzhou. My forces are idle, just camped here. It's not right. I'd like to lead them on an expedition against Fang La and demonstrate our loyalty. I pray Your Excellency petition the emperor for us."

Marshal Su was very pleased. "Exactly what I'd been thinking, General. This is of great importance to our country and our people. Why shouldn't I petition the emperor? Go back. I'll do it first thing in the morning. He's sure to give it serious attention."

Song Jiang bid the marshal farewell, returned to camp, and informed his brothers.

When the marshal attended the early court the next day, he found the monarch conferring with his civil and military officials in the Mantled in Incense Hall. The emperor was speaking of how Fang La was ravaging the south, how he had occupied twenty-five counties in eight prefectures, given himself a dynastic title, had rebelled and proclaimed himself king. It was only a question of time until he attacked Yangzhou.

"I have directed Governor Zhang and District Commander Liu to lead an expedition, but so far I haven't seen any results," the emperor said.

"The bandits are a serious menace," Marshal Su agreed. "Why not send, in addition, Song Jiang who defeated the Liao Tartars? The two combined forces can surely wipe out the rebels and win a great victory."

"Your proposal suits my purposes excellently," said the monarch. He ordered that the Chancellor of Military Affairs be summoned to hear his decree.

Governor Zhang and his staff officers Cong and Geng requested that Song Jiang and his troops go as the vanguard of the expedition. When the Chancellor of Military Affairs had received his orders, Song Jiang and Lu Junyi were sent for. They kowtowed before the emperor.

The sovereign proclaimed Song Jiang Commander-in-Chief of the Southern Pacification, and Vanguard of the Expedition Against Fang La. He named Lu Junyi as second in command. To each he awarded a gold belt, a silk robe, golden armor, a fine horse, and good cloth for twenty-five garments. The other generals were given cloth and silver, and a promise of a rise in rank and status upon displays of merit in battle. Silver was given to the various chieftains. All these awards were to be drawn from the official treasury. A time limit was set for the departure of the expeditionary force. Song Jiang and Lu Junyi begged to take leave of the emperor.

"You have a carver of jade seals, Jin Dajian, and an experienced judge of horses, Huangfu Duan," said the monarch. "Leave those two for our use."

Song Jiang and Lu Junyi again kowtowed. They thanked the emperor, left the palace, mounted their steeds and headed for camp. They rode side by side in high spirits.

In a marketplace outside the city they saw a man shaking out a rhythm on a pair of wooden castanets. They clattered with the movements of his hand. Song Jiang had never seen such a contraption.

He had a soldier ask the fellow: "What is that thing?"

"It's called a Foreign Clapper. When you shake your hand, it makes a noise."

Song Jiang composed a poem on the spot:

Now a low sound, now a high,
Clackety-clack into the sky,
Though heroic strength pervades the air,
If not used, it's wasted there.

From his seat in the saddle, he laughed. "That Foreign Clapper is like you and me. Between us, we have heaven-piercing capabilities. But if no one shakes us into action, how can we perform any resounding deeds?"

He told his aides to give the man some silver, and they rode on. Song Jiang continued to chat with Lu Junyi. Again poetic images rose in his mind, and he composed another verse:

Though by the finest craftsmen made,
Feeble chime the hearts of jade.
Only taken well in hand,

Will they ring throughout the land.

"Why do you say that, brother?" Lu protested. "Our talents are equal to those of any general, past or present. If that weren't so, what good would it do to take us in hand?"

"You're wrong, brother. If Marshal Su hadn't petitioned for us, would the emperor have given us such important assignments? A man who gains fame shouldn't forget his benefactors."

Lu felt the reprimand was justified. He had nothing more to say.

Returning to camp, they convened a meeting of the chieftains and directed that as many horses and as much armor as possible be assembled in preparation for an expedition against Fang La. The next day the emperor's awards were drawn from the treasury and distributed, and Jin Dajian and Huangfu Duan were sent off to serve the imperial court.

Song Jiang instructed the armada to leave first, directing the naval chieftains to put the craft in ship-shape condition. They were to sail towards the Yangzi. The cavalry chieftains were told to ready their weapons and armor. When the expedition started, land and water forces would proceed together.

Premier Cai Jing suddenly arrived at the camp. He demanded that Xiao Rang the Master Hand be given into his service. The following day District Commander Wang appeared and asked for Iron Throat Yue Ho. He said he'd heard that Yue Ho was a good singer and he needed such a person in his residency.

Song Jiang had no choice but to consent, and he saw the two of them off. He had now lost five brothers, and he felt very badly. He finished making plans with Lu Junyi and ordered the contingents to get ready to march.

The revolt of Fang La, south of the Yangzi, had commenced some time before. It developed gradually. No one had expected it to turn into such a large affair. Fang La had been a woodcutter in the hills of Shezhou Prefecture. One day, while washing his hands in a stream, he observed his reflection in the water. He seemed to be wearing a crown and a dragon robe. Fang La therefore announced he was destined to be a king, and started his rebellion.

He established a Precious Hall in the Pangyuan Cavern in Qingxi County, and built a Royal Garden and Palace. He set up smaller palaces in Muzhou and Shezhou, and designated civil and military ranks, created ministries, appointed premiers and generals, and a whole panoply of ministers. (When reconquered by the Song Dynasty Muzhou became Yanzhou, Shezhou became Huizhou. Today they are called Jiante and Wuyuan.)

Subsequently, Fang La took Runzhou, present-day Zhenjiang. By then he controlled a total of eight prefectures containing twenty-five counties. The eight prefectures were: Shezhou, Muzhou, Hangzhou, Suzhou, Changzhou, Huzhou, Xuanzhou and Runzhou. Jiaxing, Songjiang, Chongte and Haining at that time were counties, and were among the twenty-five under the eight prefectures. Fang

La proclaimed himself king and appointed provincial, prefectural and departmental officials. This was no small organization. It was infinitely larger than some gang of bandits in the hills.

Fang La fulfilled a heavenly prophecy which read: *Ten thousand plus a dot and the last winter month shall a monarch be. Across the Zheshui River, in Wuxing, proclaim aloud your sovereignty.* A dot above the character for "ten thousand" converts it into "fang." The last winter month is known as "la." Thus "Fang La" the king. Of course his eight prefectures south of the Yangzi were much smaller in area than the kingdom of Liao.

Song Jiang, meanwhile, fixed a date for his march and bid farewell to the various ministers. Marshal Su and Commissioner Zhao saw the army off personally, and rewarded the troops. The naval chieftains had already sailed their boats from the Sishui River into the Huai, and were moving in the direction of the Huai'an Dyke. They would ultimately assemble at Yangzhou.

Taking a respectful leave of the marshal and the commissioner, Song Jiang and Lu Junyi set forth. The army was divided into five columns. Their destination was also Yangzhou. The march was without incident, and the vanguard unit reached Huai'an County and made camp. The Yangzhou prefectural officials provided a banquet for Song Jiang and quarters in the city when he arrived.

"Fang La has a powerful army. You mustn't underestimate him," they said. "Ahead is the Yangzi, which flows 9,300 *li* before emptying into the sea. That's the first dangerous barrier you have to cross. Then you come to Runzhou, which is held by Fang La's Minister of Military Affairs Lu Shinang and twenty-four commanders whose job it is to defend the banks. Unless you can take Runzhou, you'll have a hard time withstanding Fang La."

Song Jiang called Military Advisor Wu Yong into conference. How were they going to cross the Yangzi? Their campaign against the Liao Tartars had been on dry land. It required no contribution from the naval chieftains. But now a navy was indispensable.

"There are two islands in the river near Runzhou—Jinshan Hill and Jiaoshan Hill," said Wu Yong. "Send a few brothers there to spy out the approaches to the city and learn what kind of boats are needed to get across."

Summoning his naval chieftains, Song Jiang said: "Which of you brothers will find out about water approaches and think of a plan for getting our soldiers over?"

Four men stepped forward and proclaimed their willingness.

And because these scouts went forth, corpses were piled as high as Beigu Mountain and the Yangzi River flowed red with blood. The sacked city of Runzhou was left an abode for naught but weeping ghosts and howling demons, and the Jinshan Monastery was turned upside down. A great army soared over Black Dragon Range, an armada swallowed White Goose Shore.

How did Song Jiang's forces proceed against Fang La? Read our next chapter if you would know.

CHAPTER 91

ZHANG SHUN STAGES A NIGHT AMBUSH AT JINSHAN MONASTERY

SONG JIANG CLEVERLY TAKES RUNZHOU CITY

The mighty Yangzi has two large tributaries—the Hanyang River and the Xunyang River. It passes many places in its 9,300 *li* march from Sichuan to the sea. For this reason it is called the Long River of Ten Thousand *Li*. In the Wu and Chu areas there are two islands in the river. One was known as Jinshan Hill, the other Jiaoshan Hill. On Jinshan Hill a monastery wound up the slope into the heights, and so was called the Monastery Embracing a Hill. The monastery on Jiaoshan Hill was hidden in a declivity, and so was called the Hill-Embraced Monastery. The islands were precisely on the dividing line between the Chu and Wu areas. On the north bank was Yangzhou, on the south bank was Runzhou— today called Zhenjiang.

At Runzhou, Fang La's Minister of Military Affairs, Lu Shinang, defended the river banks. Lu was a rich man from Shezhou who obtained his position as a reward for contributing money and grain to Fang La. When he was young he studied books on military strategy. He used a snake lance eighteen feet long with outstanding skill. Under him were twelve commandants, better known as "The Twelve Gods South of the Yangzi." They cooperated in defending the shore in each of the twelve prefectures.

Lu was general of a total of fifty thousand southern soldiers. They held the banks. More than three thousand warcraft rode the waves near Dew Pavilion. It was clear water between there and Guazhou, the ferry point on the opposite north shore.

Meanwhile, Song Jiang's army had reached Huai'an, the last stage before assembling in Yangzhou. Song was conferring with Wu Yong in his tent.

"We're not far from the Yangzi, now," he said. "The enemy hold the southern shore. Who can I send as scouts to find a way of getting across?'

Four chieftains promptly volunteered. Who were they? Chai Jin the Small Whirlwind, Zhang Shun the White Streak in the Waves, Shi Xiu the Rash, and the Devil Incarnate Ruan the Seventh.

"Form two teams—Zhang Shun with Chai Jin, Ruan the Seventh with Shi Xiu," Song Jiang directed. "Go to the islands of Jinshan Hill and Jiaoshan Hill. Find out the strength of the foe in Runzhou and report back to me in Yangzhou."

The four took their leave of Song Jiang, divided into two teams, and proceeded first to Yangzhou, disguised as travellers. They met no one along the road. The local populace, hearing that an expeditionary army against Fang La was on its way, moved and hid themselves in outlying villages. The four split up after reaching Yangzhou. Each took along some dry rations. Shi Xiu and Ruan the Seventh set out for Jiaoshan Hill with two servants.

Chai Jin and Zhang Shun, armed with sharp daggers and halberds, also with two servants, all carrying dry rations, hurried to Guazhou. It was early spring. The sun was warm and the air fragrant with flowers when they arrived at the banks of the Yangzi. From a height, they observed the tumbling misty waves. A magnificent river scene!

On the other side they could see a long stretch of green and white flags at the foot of Beigu Mountain, and a line of many craft flanking the shore. On the north bank where the four stood there wasn't even a wooden spar.

"All the houses on the road to Guazhou were empty," said Chai Jin, "and here at the river there are no boats. How can we learn what's happening over there?"

"Let's find a house to rest in," Zhang Shun suggested. "I'll swim to Jinshan Island and see what I can find out."

Chai Jin agreed, and the four walked along the shore until they came to a thatched shack. The door was locked from the inside. They couldn't push it open. Zhang Shun knocked a hole in the side wall and crawled in. A white-haired old woman rose from beside the stove. "Why didn't you open your door, old mother?"

"We've heard that the emperor is sending an army to fight Fang La, and we're right on the road to the river. A lot of people have moved away and gone into hiding. They've left me to take care of the house."

"Where's your son?"

"He went to the village to look after his wife and children."

"There are four of us, and we want to cross the river. Is there a boat around?"

"Where could anyone find a boat? Lu Shinang, when he heard the army is coming, took all the boats to Runzhou."

"We have our own rations. If you let us live here a day or two, We'll give you some silver as rent. We won't disturb you."

"You can stay. That's no problem. But I don't have any beds."

"We'll manage."

"I'm only afraid that big army will come here pretty soon."

"We'll be able to hide."

Zhang Shun opened the door and Chai Jin and the two servants entered. They rested their halberds, put down their luggage, brought out their dry rations and wheat-cakes, and ate.

Zhang Shun again went down to the river and looked. He saw Jinshan Monastery on an island precisely in the middle of the Yangzi. "Minister of Military Affairs Lu must go to that hill frequently," he said to himself. "I'll slip over tonight and pick up some news."

He returned and told Chai Jin what was on his mind. "There isn't even a small boat around here. How can we find out what's doing on the other side of the river?" he said. "Tonight I'm going to make a bundle of my clothes, wrap in two ingots of silver, put the whole thing on my head, and wade over to Jinshan

Monastery. I'll bribe some monks, get the news, and come back and tell Big Brother. You wait here."

"Go and return quickly," said Chai Jin.

It was a starry evening, with a gentle breeze. The waves were calm, the water and the sky were the same color. Zhang Shun tied his clothes and two silver ingots in a bundle which he bound to his head, tied a sharp dagger at his waist, and entered the river at Guazhou. The water only came up to his chest. It was virtually like walking on dry land.

As he neared the foot of Jinshan Hill, he spotted a small craft moored beside the rocky slope. He crept over to it, removed the bundle from his head, stripped off his soaking garments, rubbed himself dry, changed into the clean clothes, and sat down in the boat. He could hear a watchman's drum in Runzhou striking the third watch.

Concealing himself, he looked around. A small vessel was sculling, downstream in his direction. "Those fellows are up to no good, zigzagging like that," he mused.

He decided to shove off. It was then he discovered that his boat had only a mooring rope, but no oars or poles. Once again he removed his clothes. Pulling out his dagger, he waded towards the approaching craft.

The two men plying the sweep oar were watching the north shore, and didn't see Zhang Shun closing in from the south. He suddenly popped up at the side, grasped the gunwale and slashed with his dagger. The men dropped the oar and toppled into the river. Zhang Shun sprang onto the craft. Two more men emerged from the cabin. Again Zhang Shun stabbed. One collapsed into water, the other, terrified, fell backwards into the cabin.

"Who are you? Whose boat is this?" Zhang Shun shouted. "Tell the truth and I'll spare you!"

"Hear me, good sir. I'm the steward of the Chen Guan family in Dingpu Village outside of Yangzhou City. I've just delivered a gift of grain to Minister Lu in Runzhou. He's accepted it and sent me back with one of his captains to demand fifty thousand bushels of white rice and three hundred boats. That will be my master's entrance fee into Lu's forces."

"What's the captain's name? Where is he?"

"His name is Ye Gui. He's the man you just cut down."

"What's your name? When did you bring the surrender offer to Lu? What's in this boat?"

"I'm called Wu Cheng, sir. We crossed over on the seventh of this month. On Minister Lu's instructions, I went to Suzhou to see the king's younger brother Fang Mao, the Third Great Prince, and drew three hundred unit banners and my master's official appointment document. He's been made prefect of Yangzhou and a Lord of Central Clarity. I have also a thousand uniforms and a letter from Minister Lu."

"How many soldiers does your master command?"

"Several thousand infantry and a hundred or so cavalry. His two sons, Chen Yi and Chen Tai, are both formidable warriors."

Having obtained the information he wanted, Zhang Shun with one stab of his dagger thrust Wu Cheng into the river. Then he took over the sweep oar and rowed back to Guazhou.

Chai Jin hurried out at the sound of the oar and saw Zhang Shun arriving in a boat. Zhang Shun related what had happened in detail. Chai Jin was very pleased. They took from the cabin the document and letter, three hundred unit designation banners of red silk, and a thousand army uniforms of various color. They formed two large loads.

"I'll get my clothes," said Zhang Shun. He rowed back to Jinshan Island, retrieved his clothing, his head kerchief, and the silver ingots. By the time he returned to the Guazhou banks it was almost dawn. A heavy mist blanketed the ground. At the shack they paid the old lady two or three ounces of silver, shouldered the loads, and went back to Yangzhou.

Song Jiang's forces were camped outside the city. The prefectural officials gave a banquet in his honor and invited him to move into the hostel for visiting dignitaries. They wined and dined him several days in a row, and fed his soldiers.

When the feasting was over, Chai Jin and Zhang Shun called on Song Jiang in the hostel. They said: "Chen Guan has tied in with Fang La. He's about to sneak rebel troops across to attack Yangzhou. Luckily, I intercepted Chen's steward in midriver. This is your chance, brother, for a brilliant stroke."

Song Jiang was delighted. He called Wu Yong into conference and asked: "How shall we go about it? What would be our best plan?"

"Under the circumstances, taking Runzhou will be as easy as turning over your hand," said the military advisor. "Once we nab Chen Guan, it will be a sure thing." He spelled out his strategy.

"Excellent," said Song Jiang. He directed Yan Qing the Prodigy to disguise himself as Captain Ye, and Xie Zhen and Xie Bao to dress as two southern soldiers. He gave them specific instructions. The three left the city for the village of Dingpu, the Xie brothers carrying the loads.

Forty *li* or more from Yangzhou, they neared Chen Guan's manor. Twenty or thirty vassals, in ordinary garb, were lined up neatly at the gate. Yan Qing hailed them, assuming a local accent.

"Is the master at home?"

"Where are you from, traveller?"

"Runzhou. Took a wrong turn after crossing the river. We wandered around for hours before reaching here."

The vassals ushered the visitors into the guest-house and told them to rest their loads. Then they led Yan Qing to Chen Guan in the rear of the manse. Yan Qing bowed.

"Ye Gui presents his respects."

"Where are you from, sir?"

"If you'll ask the others to withdraw, I'll venture to tell you."

"These are all trusted associates. You can speak freely."

"My name is Ye Gui. I am a captain under the command of Minister Lu. On the seventh day of the first month he received Wu Cheng with your secret message. He was very pleased. He directed me to escort Wu Cheng to Suzhou to convey Your Excellency's idea to the Third Great Prince, the king's younger brother. The prince petitioned His Majesty and obtained for you the position of prefect of Yangzhou. After you have met with the minister, he will determine ranks for your two sons. Wu Cheng has unfortunately been laid low by the flu. In order not to delay matters, the minister has dispatched me with your certificate of appointment, along with his letter, as well as your seal of office, tablet of authority, three hundred unit banners and a thousand uniforms. He would like Your Excellency's grain vessels to make delivery on the Runzhou river bank at the appointed time."

Yan Qing handed over the official appointment certificate. Chen Guan read it joyfully. He hastily lit incense and, facing south, voiced thanks for this benevolence. He summoned his two sons, Chen Yi and Chen Tai, and presented them to the "captain." Yan Qing instructed the Xie brothers to deliver the banners and uniforms to the rear manse. Chen Guan invited Yan Qing to be seated.

"I'm only a common soldier. How dare I sit in Your Excellency's presence?"

"You come as an emissary of His Majesty with documents of appointment for my humble self, sir. I would not be lacking in courtesy. Please be seated. It's quite proper."

After repeatedly protesting, Yan Qing finally sat down at a distance. Chen Guan called for wine and preferred him a cup. Yan Qing politely refused.

"I never drink," he said. He nevertheless downed two or three cups.

Then the two sons came forward to congratulate their father. With a significant glance, Yan Qing signalled to the Xie brothers. Xie Bao slipped a powerful drug into the wine pot when no one was looking. Yan Qing rose and spoke.

"I have brought no wine with me from across the river, but if I may use Your Excellency's brew, I would like to offer my congratulations."

He poured a goblet to the full and urged Chen to drain it. He also gave a cup each to the two sons and the various close cronies. When all had drunk, Yan Qing pursed his mouth and gestured with his head. Xie Zhen left the building, found a firebrand, took out a small cannon and signal flag concealed on his person, went outside the manor, and fired the cannon. At the sound, chieftains, who had been waiting in concealment to the left and right, came running.

Yan Qing, in the manse, watched man after man collapse. He whipped out his short sword, and he and Xie Bao cut off all the heads. Ten gallant fellows poured in, yelling, through the manor gate. The vassals were unable to stem their rush. Yan Qing and the Xie brothers strode out carrying the heads of Chen Guan and his sons.

By then another six chieftains had arrived, leading a thousand troops. They ringed the manor, rounded up Chen Guan's family, and killed them all. Then, with the vassals in tow, they marched down to the cove. Riding at anchor were three or four hundred craft, laden to the brim with rice. The vessels were counted and a report rushed to Song Jiang.

He conferred with Wu Yong. Then they packed, took their leave of Governor Zhang, and marched with the army to Chen Guan's manor. They selected troops to board the craft, meanwhile dispatching a man to urge the naval vessels to hurry over.

"We'll send three hundred fast boats, first," said Wu Yong, "each flying Fang La's banner. On deck, a thousand men will dress in the uniforms we got from him, and another three or four thousand will wear ordinary garb. An additional twenty thousand troops will be concealed in the cabins. Mu Hong will be disguised as Chen Yi, Li Jun as Chen Tai. They will each captain a large boat. Other chieftains will command the remaining craft."

Mu Hong and Li Jun headed the first fleet. Each was supported by ten chieftains. Zhang Heng and Zhang Shun led the second fleet. They were backed by four chieftains each. Ten chieftains captained the third fleet. That made a total of forty-two chieftains commanding the three hundred vessels.

These were to be followed by Song Jiang and the others in boats carrying the horses, a thousand warcraft like swimming dragons and speeding leviathans, all flying Song Jiang's banner and containing the whole force of infantry and cavalry and commanders. The admirals of this armada would be Ruan the Second and Ruan the Fifth.

Meanwhile, on Beigu Mountain in Runzhou, a lookout observed the three hundred craft setting sail from the cove. Fluttering from their masts was the red banner designating the grain convoy. This was immediately reported to the harbor master. Minister Lu, accompanied by twelve commandants, all in full armor, their bows strung, their swords unsheathed, rode down to the river bank. With them was a unit of crack troops.

A hundred boats were nearing the shore. On the first two vessels were two men who appeared to be leaders. They were surrounded by soldiers in uniforms with a lock designation, stalwart fellows every one.

Minister Lu dismounted and sat down in a silver armchair. The twelve commandants formed two lines along the bank. Mu Hong and Li Jun hailed Lu respectfully. Captains to the left and right shouted for the boats to halt. The hundred craft, in a straight line, dropped anchor.

Sailing with a favorable wind from the north, the next two hundred also arrived. They divided into a hundred to the right and a hundred to the left, so that each of the three groups was equi-distant from the others.

The shipping commissioner approached the near craft.

"Where are you from?"

"My name is Chen Yi," said Mu Hong, "and my brother is called Chen Tai. Our father, Chen Guan, has ordered us to deliver these fifty thousand bushels of white rice, three hundred vessels, and five thousand crack troops, in gratitude to Minister Lu for having petitioned the king on his behalf."

"Minister Lu dispatched a Captain Ye the other day. Where is he?"

"Captain Ye and Wu Cheng both have typhoid fever. They're bedridden and couldn't come. But we've brought our father's seal of office and his appointment document."

The shipping commissioner took them and walked up the bank to Minister Lu. "The sons of Chen Guan of Dingpu Village outside Yangzhou have brought grain and soldiers," he said. "And here is the seal of office and appointment certificate you sent him."

Lu examined them. It was indeed the original document. He ordered that the two sons be allowed ashore. The shipping commissioner shouted for Chen Yi and Chen Tai to be brought before the minister.

Mu Hong and Li Jun mounted the bank, followed by twenty chieftains. "The minister is here," yelled the guards. "Persons with no business, stay away!" The twenty chieftains halted. Mu Hong and Li Jun, each with hands clasped and bodies inclined deferentially, also waited at a distance. After a lengthy pause, the shipping commissioner again conducted the two forward. They knelt before the minister.

"Why hasn't your father Chen Guan come in person?" Lu demanded.

"Our father has heard that Song Jiang of Liangshan Marsh is approaching with a large army," replied Mu Hong. "He's afraid the bandits will disturb the countryside. He's staying at home to deal with them."

"Which of you is the elder?"

"I, Chen Yi, am," said Mu Hong.

"Have you two brothers learned the martial arts?"

"Basking in Your Excellency's propitious emanations, we have had some training."

"This rice you're bringing, how is it stored?"

"Three hundred bushels per large vessel, one hundred bushels per small."

"No doubt there's more to your mission than delivering grain!"

"Father and sons, we're completely loyal. We'd never venture to do anything untoward!"

"Your personal intentions may be all right, but there's something fishy about those troops on your craft. I can't help being suspicious. You two stay here. I'm going to send four commandants with a hundred soldiers to search your boats. It'll go hard with you if we find anything wrong!"

"We came hoping that you would make important use of our services. How can you doubt us!"

Before Lu could issue his order, a mounted scout trotted up and reported. "An order from the king has arrived at the South Gate. Your Excellency is requested to go at once to receive it."

The minister hurriedly mounted. "Hold this bank. Don't let anyone ashore," he instructed his officers. "Chen Yi and Chen Tai are to come with me."

Mu Hong shot Li Jun a significant glance. Lu rode on ahead. Calling their escort of twenty, they followed him into the city. But the guards at the gate barked a command.

"Minister Lu said that only these two are allowed in, no one else!"

Mu Hong and Li Jun were permitted to pass. The twenty chieftains had to wait. Minister Lu proceeded across the city to the South Gate, where he met the royal emissary.

"What's so urgent?" Lu asked.

The messenger was Fang La's royal usher, Feng Xi. He replied in an undertone: "Eunuch Pu Wenying the court astrologer has recently reported that, according to the night sky, many star spirits have entered this Wu area. He says half of them emit no light, a sure sign of serious trouble. The king has handed down this order, instructing you, Minister, to guard the bank well. Any persons coming from the north must be closely questioned. Kill them immediately if they arouse even a shadow of suspicion! They must not be allowed to remain!"

Lu was shocked. "A party of men has just come that I'm very doubtful about, and now this order. Please come into the city and read it to me."

Feng Xi went with Lu to the provincial office, and there the emissary read the directive aloud. Just then, a messenger galloped up with a report.

"An order from the Third Great Prince in Suzhou. He says: 'Your news about the surrender of Chen Guan of Yangzhou is incredible. It's probably invented. At the same time there has been the announcement by the royal astrologer regarding the entry of star spirits into this Wu area. You must hold the river bank firmly. I am sending a man to supervise.'"

"So the Great Prince is also concerned," said the minister. "I've ready received a royal edict."

He ordered his forces to closely guard the river front. No one was to be allowed to disembark. Lu then feasted the two emissaries.

Meanwhile, time was dragging for the men on the three hundred boats, and nothing was stirring. First Zhang Heng, Zhang Shun and the eight chieftains came ashore from the hundred craft on the left, carrying their arms; then another hundred, weapons in hand, from the hundred vessels on the right. The southern soldiers guarding the bank were unable to stop them.

Li Kui the Black Whirlwind and the Xie brothers headed for the city. Officers at the gate hurriedly blocked their path. With a hack and a chop, Li Kui promptly cut two of them down. Yells were heard as Xie Zhen and Xie Bao, each wielding a steel pitchfork, charged into Runzhou. With all this happening at the same time, it was impossible for the guards to close the gate.

As Li Kui bored into the passage, killing everyone he met, the twenty chieftains who had been denied entrance earlier now rushed in and seized the guards' weapons.

The twelve commandants had just received Minister Lu's order to hold the river front when the noise of the fighting at the city gate erupted. Hurriedly, they mustered their forces. But by then Shi Jin and Chai Jin had directed their troops on the decks of the three hundred craft to divest themselves of their southern uniforms and had led them ashore. They were followed by the soldiers who came swarming out of their concealment in the cabins.

Commandants Shen Gang and Pan Wende hastened with two columns to defend the city gate. Shen Gang was cut down from his horse by a single thrust from Shi Jin. Zhang Heng's spear ran Pan through the side. A wild melee followed, during which the remaining ten commandants fled into Runzhou to protect their families.

When Mu Hong and Li Jun heard the news, they took firebrands from a tavern and began setting blazes. Minister Lu sprang into the saddle. Three of the commandants had come to his support. By then the city was burning as if the sky had fallen.

Guazhou, seeing the conflagration, rushed a relief force. Battles raged at all four of the city gates, but on Runzhou's walls the banners of Song Jiang were already flying. The slaughter and confusion on every side were beyond description.

Another hundred and fifty warcraft arrived from the north shore and unloaded two thousand cavalrymen and their mounts, led by ten chieftains in full armor. They charged into the city. Minister Lu was badly defeated. With his broken army he fled to Dantu County.

The expeditionary forces occupied Runzhou. They extinguished the fires and took command of the four gates. At the shore they welcomed Song Jiang's boat, and watched the other vessels, like swimming dragons and speeding leviathans, arriving on favorable winds at the south bank.

Chieftains of high rank and low led Song Jiang into the city. First, he posted notices reassuring the local populace. Then he mustered his military officers and assembled them at central headquarters, where they claimed their awards.

Shi Jin presented the head of Shen Gang, Zhang Heng the head of Pan Wente, Liu Tang the head of Shen Ze. Kong Ming and Kong Liang came forward with their captive Zhuo Wanli, Xiang Chong and Li Jun with their prisoner Ho Tong. Hao Siwen had killed Xu Tong with an arrow from his bow.

The attackers had taken Runzhou, killed four commandants, and captured two others. They had slaughtered southern aides, officers and soldiers without number.

Song Jiang's army had lost three chieftains, either killed by arrows or trampled to death by horses in the confusion of battle. They were Guardian of the

Clouds Song Wan, Jiao Ting the Merciless, and Tao Zongwang the Nine-Tailed Tortoise. Song Jiang was very distressed.

"Life and death come to every man," said Wu Yong. "Although we've lost three of our brothers, we've taken our first prefecture south of the Yangzi and removed a dangerous obstacle. Why upset yourself and injure your health? If we're to serve our country well, we'd better discuss national affairs."

"The hundred and eight of us are inscribed on the stone tablet, we correspond to stars in the sky. First in Liangshan Marsh, and then on Mount Wutai, we vowed to live and die together. Who would have thought that after we returned to the capital Gongsun Sheng would leave us, the emperor would retain Jin Dajian and Huangfu Duan, Premier Cai would take Xiao Rang, and District Commander Wang would demand Yue Ho! And now, when we've just crossed the Yangzi, we've lost three more brothers! Song Wan wasn't very accomplished, but I remember what a great help he was when we first established ourselves on Mount Liangshan. And today he's gone to the Nether World!"

Song Jiang ordered the soldiers to set up a sacrificial altar on the spot where Song Wan died, and to lay out paper silver ingots, a black pig and a white sheep. He personally dedicated the sacrificial wine. Zhuo Wanli and Ho Tong, the commandants who had been taken prisoner, were decapitated, and the blood from their severed heads sprinkled to propitiate the spirits of the three departed heroes.

After revising the prefectural government and the local administrations, Song Jiang issued awards and wrote a report of his victory to Governor Zhang, inviting him to come and inspect. Corpses on the streets were collected, removed from the city, and burned. The bodies of the three slain chieftains were buried outside of Runzhou's East Gate.

Minister Lu had lost half his effectives. He retreated to the county town of Dantu with his six remaining commandants, and dared not venture out again. In a written dispatch to Suzhou, he begged the Third Great Prince to rescue him. Suzhou sent an army under General Xing Zheng. Lu welcomed him gratefully. In county headquarters, Lu told how, in the guise of Chen Guan's surrendering troops, Song Jiang's forces had been able to sneak across the Yangzi.

"But now that you are here, General," Lu concluded, "we shall regain control of Runzhou City."

Xing Zheng replied: "When the Third Great Prince was informed that certain stars were invading this region, he decided to dispatch me with an army to patrol the river front. We didn't expect that you would have already been put at a disadvantage. But with your assistance, Minister, I will avenge you."

The next day, Xing Zheng marched forth with his army to recapture Runzhou.

In Runzhou, meanwhile, after consulting with Wu Yong, Song Jiang sent Tong Wei and Tong Meng with a hundred or more men to Jiaoshan Hill to look for Shi Xiu and Ruan the Seventh. He also dispatched a contingent to take Dantu. Five thousand strong, it was commanded by ten chieftains.

On the way, they encountered Xing Zheng's army. An exchange of arrows caused both forces to halt out of each other's bow range and set up positions. Battle drums thundered, multi-colored embroidered banners fluttered in the breeze.

Xing Zheng rode forward with levelled lance, flanked on either side by the six commandants. From the Song army midst, Guan Sheng, brandishing his crescent halberd embossed with a dragon design, cantered out to meet the foe. The two contenders clashed in a murderous rage, their mounts stirring up clouds of dust. After fourteen or fifteen rounds, one of the men fell from his horse.

Truly, the boldness of heroes is no match for a general's clever plan. Relying on the capture of officers and men, they sought to retake the first prefecture south of the Yangzi.

Of the two contending warriors, who killed whom? Read our next chapter if you would know.

CHAPTER 92

LU JUNYI MARCHES ON XUANZHOU PREFECTURE

SONG JIANG BATTLES AT PILING SHIRE

After only fourteen or fifteen rounds, Guan Sheng swung his halberd and cut Xing Zheng from his saddle. Poor southern hero, his life vanished like a dream! At this, Huyan Zhuo urged his men into the fray. The six commandants fled southwards. Minister Lu abandoned Dantu and led his broken contingents in the direction of Changzhou County.

The ten chieftains occupied Dantu and notified Song Jiang of their victory. He moved a large force into the county and there made camp. After rewarding the troops, he rushed a dispatch to Military Governor Zhang reporting that he now was in control of Runzhou. The following day, staff officers Zong and Geng arrived in Dantu with rewards from the governor. Song Jiang distributed them among his commanders.

Conferring with Lu Junyi, Song Jiang said: "Xuanzhou and Huzhou prefectures are also being held by Fang La's brigands. Let's divide the army into two columns, and each of us lead one. We can draw lots to determine who goes where."

Song Jiang drew Changzhou and Suzhou, Lu drew Xuanzhou and Huzhou. Song directed Ironclad Virtue Pei Xuan to divide the officers and men. With the exception of Yang Zhi who was ill and remained in Dantu, the others were assigned to the different columns.

In Song Jiang's contingent there were thirteen senior commanders, who, apart from Song Jiang himself, were Wu Yong the Wizard, who served as the chief of staff; Li Ying the Heaven-Soaring Eagle; Guan Sheng the Big Halberd; Hua Rong the Lesser Li Guang; Qin Ming the Thunderbolt; Xu Ning the Metal Lancer; Zhu Tong the Beautiful Beard; Sagacious Lu the Tattooed Monk; Wu Song the Pilgrim; Shi Jin the Nine Dragons; Li Kui the Black Whirlwind; and Dai Zong the Marvelous Traveler. And there were twenty-nine lieutenant commanders, who are: Huang Xin the Suppressor of Three Mountains; Sun Li the Sickly General; Hao Siwen the Wild Dog; Xuan Zan the Ugly Son in Law; Han Tao the Ever-Victorious General; Peng Qi the Eyes of Heaven General; Fan Rui the Demon King Who Roils the World; Ma Lin the Elfin Flutist; Yan Shun the Elegant Tiger; Xiang Chong the Eight-Armed Nezha; Li Gun the Flying Divinity; Bao Xu the God of Death; Wang Ying the Stumpy Tiger; Hu Sanniang the Ten Feet of Steel; Yang Lin the Elegant Panther; Shi En the Golden-Eyed Tiger Cub; Du Xing the Demon Face; Kong Ming the Comet; Kong Liang the Flaming Star; Ling Zhen the Heaven-Shaking Thunder; Cai Fu the Iron Arm; Cai Qing the Single Blossom; Duan Jingzhu the Golden Dog; Hou Jian the Long-Armed Ape; Jiang Jing the Magic Calculator; An Daoquan the Skilled Doctor; Yu Baosi the Spirit of the Dangerous Road; Song Qing the Iron Fan and Pei Xuan the Ironclad Virtue.

These senior and lieutenant commanders led a force of thirty thousand crack troops.

In Lu Junyi's contingent there were fourteen senior commanders, who, in addition to Lu Junyi himself, were: Zhu Wu the Miraculous Strategist; Chai Jin the Small Whirlwind; Lin Chong the Panther Head, Dong Ping the General Two Spears; Huyan Zhuo the Two Rods; Suo Chao the Urgent Vanguard; Mu Hong the Unrestrained; Yang Xiong the Pallid; Lei Heng the Winged Tiger; Xie Zhen the Two-Headed Snake; Xie Bao the Twin-Tailed Scorpion; Zhang Qin the Featherless Arrow; Liu Tang the Red-Haired Demon and Yan Qing the Prodigy.

The thirty-three lieutenant commanders were: Shan Tinggui the Water General; Wei Dingguo the Fire General; Lu Fang the Little Duke; Guo Sheng the Second Rengui; Ou Peng the Golden Wings Brushing the Clouds; Deng Fei the Fiery-Eyed Lion; Li Zhong the Tiger-Fighting General; Zhou Tong the Little King; Chen Da the Gorge-Leaping Tiger; Yang Chun the White-Spotted Snake; Xue Yong the Sick Tiger; Du Qian the Skyscraper; Mu Chun the Slightly Restrained; Zou Yuan the Dragon from the Forest; Zou Run the One-Horned Dragon; LiLi the Hell's Summoner; Li Yun the Black-Eyed Tiger; Shi Yong the Stone General; Zhu Gui the Dry-Land Crocodile; Zhu Fu the Smiling Tiger; Sun Xin the Junior General; Mistress Gu the Tigress; Zhang Qing the Vegetable Gardener; Sun Erniang the Witch; Zheng Tianshou the Fair-Faced Gentleman; Tang Long the Gold-Coin Spotted Leopard; Cao Zheng the Demon Carver; Bai Sheng the Daylight Rat; Gong Wang the Flowery-Necked Tiger; Ding Desun the Arrow-Struck Tiger; Wang Dingliu the Lightning and Shi Qian the Flea on the Drum.

This column also contained thirty thousand crack troops. Still another group of chieftains captained the naval units.

Tong Wei and Tong Meng, who had been sent to Jiaoshan Hill to look for Shi Xiu and Ruan the Seventh, returned and said: "They killed a whole family at the river bank, seized a light craft and went over to the monastery on the island. When the abbot heard that they were bold fellows from Liangshan Marsh, he invited them to a vegetarian meal. Later, after learning what Zhang Shun had accomplished, they got a boat at the foot of the hill and captured Maogang. That's a good place for an assault on Jiangyin and Taicang on the sea coast. They've sent a written request for naval chieftains and warcraft."

Song Jiang directed Li Jun and seven other chieftains to join Shi Xiu and Ruan the Seventh with a fleet of a hundred vessels and five thousand men. Reader, please note, when Song Jiang divided his army into two columns at Dantu he had less than a hundred chieftains— ninety-nine, to be exact, including himself. The large boats sailed with the naval chieftains to assault the seaports of Jiangyin and Taicang, the smaller entered the streams around Dantu and went with Song Jiang for the attack on Changzhou.

Meanwhile, Lu Shinang, Fang La's minister of military affairs, withdrew to Piling Shire—major defense sector of Changzhou. The governor of Changzhou was Qian Zhenpeng, and under him were two generals. One was Jin Jie, from Shanghao in Miug County. The other was Qian's trusted associate Xu Ding. Qian originally had been a constable in Qingxi County. But he had helped Fang La capture several cities and had been given charge of governing Changzhou.

When Qian heard that Lu had retreated to Changzhou after having been defeated and losing Runzhou, he went with Jin Jie and Xu Ding, opened the gates, and invited him into the city. He entertained Lu courteously and discussed future measures.

"Set your mind at ease, Minister," said Qian. "I am a man of no talents but, thanks to the emanations of His Majesty's good fortune and Your Excellency's prestige, I shall gladly give my all to drive Song Jiang and his gang back across the Yangzi and recover Runzhou. Those rogues will never dare to so much as look south of the river again!"

Reassured, Lit said: "With you exerting such efforts, Governor, our country has no reason to be alarmed. After you have expelled the foe and restored Runzhou to us, I shall earnestly urge the king to bestow on you the highest honors."

That day Lu gave a feast. Of that we need say no more. In his expedition against Changzhou and Suzhou, Song Jiang now neared Piling Shire with a large force. Under him were eleven commanders headed by Guan Sheng, and three thousand troops. At the outskirts of Changzhou they waved their banners and thundered a challenge on their drums.

"Who dares to drive back the enemy?" queried Lu.

"Permit me to offer my services," said Qian, from the saddle of his charger.

The minister assigned six commandants to assist him. They mustered five thousand men, opened the city gate, lowered the drawbridge, and marched forth. Qian, gale-stirring sword in hand, astride a curly-maned swift roan, rode in the van.

Guan Sheng pulled his men back a short distance and allowed Qian Zhenpeng to deploy in battle position. The six commandants flanked Qian on either side. Guan Sheng reined in his steed and brandished his sword.

"Hear me, bandits," he shouted. "You're aiding a rebel who destroys life and angers the Heavenly Spirits. Our imperial army has arrived, but instead of realizing your deadly danger, you dare to resist! We'll not leave until we've slaughtered every last one of you knaves!"

Qian was furious. "You're just a bunch of scruffy robbers from Liangshan Marsh who don't know the will of Heaven! Instead of supporting a rightful king, you surrender to an immoral moron of a sovereign and come to vie against our great kingdom! We're going to pulverise you till there's nothing left of you or your armor!"

Guan Sheng, raging, charged waving his dragon-engraved halberd. Qian met him, wielding his gale-raising sword. Evenly matched, they clashed in a battle worthy of record in book or painting. Blades flashed icily in an atmosphere heavily lethal. The horses pranced and neighed as the contestants struck and parried. Like a streaking meteor was the gale-stirring sword, like lightning across the plain was the dragon-engraved halberd. Hoofs churned the dust, bridle bells jingled into the clouds. Weapons darted, the murderous intensity terrified the celestial spirits.

More than thirty rounds the warriors fought and Qian gradually was forced on the defensive. Two commandants on the southern side, seeing him weaken, galloped out with levelled lances and attacked Guan Sheng in a pincers. They were Zhao Yi and Fan Chou. This angered two chieftains in the Song army. One brandished a lethal sword, the other clutched a tiger-eyed cudgel, as they raced out on their horses. They were Huang Xin the Suppressor of the Three Mountains and Sun Li the Sickly General. Six warriors, three pairs, fought desperately on the field of combat.

Minister Lu hastily sent generals Xu Ding and Jin Jie from the city to join the fray. Weapons in hand, they rode forth.

Zhao Yi versus Huang Xin, Fan Chou versus Sun Li—they were at first evenly matched. But as the battle intensified, southern commandants Zhao and Fan began gaining the advantage. And now Xu Ding and Jin Jie, each wielding a big halberd, were also in the field. The Song army sent Han Tao and Peng Qi to engage them. It was Jin Jie against Han Tao, Xu Ding against Peng Qi. The five pairs battled in deadly earnest.

Actually, General Jin Jie had secretly made up his mind to surrender to the Song forces. In order to create confusion in his own ranks, he retreated to them after desultorily fighting only a few rounds. Han Tao pursued him. At this, southern commandant Gao Keli quickly fitted an arrow to his bow, pulled it to the full, and let fly. The feathered missile struck Han Tao in the cheek, knocking him from his steed.

Qin Ming hastily clapped his horse and raced to the rescue, flourishing his wolf-toothed cudgel. But southern commandant Zhang Jinren, with one thrust of his lance, pierced Han Tao's throat and killed him. Peng Qi and Han Tao had been first and second in command of the same unit, and close as brothers. Burning to avenge Han, Peng broke off from Xu Ding and rode directly towards Gao. Xu Ding galloped after him, but was intercepted by Qin Ming. Gao levelled his lance and prepared to meet his assailant. But Peng Qi was taken unawares by a thrust of Zhang's lance from the side and tumbled from his saddle.

Infuriated by the loss of two chieftains, Guan Sheng couldn't wait to charge into Changzhou. Concentrating his remarkable strength, he sliced Governor Qian to the ground. He was about to capture the governor's curly-maned roan when his own mount stumbled and tossed him off. Gao and Zhang galloped forward to seize Guan Sheng, but Xu Ning, Xuan Zan and Hao Siwen raced ahead and snatched their fallen brother back to the Song position.

Minister Lu's entire army then came pouring out of the city. Guan Sheng and the chieftains had lost the initiative. They retreated north. The southern contingent pursued them for more than twenty *li* before giving up the chase.

Guan Sheng returned with his beaten forces to Song Jiang and told him of the death of Han Tao and Peng Qi. Song Jiang wept bitterly.

"Who would have thought that after crossing the Yangzi I would lose five brothers? Can I have angered Heaven? Am I not to be allowed to capture Fang La? Am I destined for defeat?"

"You're wrong, Commander-in-Chief," said Wu Yong. "Victory and defeat are common in warfare, and man's birth and death are predestined. They're nothing to wonder about. Today, our two chieftains were fated to die, and that's all there is to it. Please don't upset yourself. Concentrate on our important affairs."

Li Kui came to the tent and said: "Let a few fellows who recognize my brothers' murderers point them out and I'll kill the rogues and avenge them!"

Song Jiang ordered his units to fly white mourning banners on the morrow, and said: "I'll lead you all to the city personally! We'll have a showdown with those bandits!"

The next day Song Jiang and his entire army, on water and on land, in boats and on horse, left camp and set forth. Li Kui the Black Whirlwind, leading chieftains Bao Xu, Xiang Chong, Li Gun and five hundred tough brave infantry, moved up as a vanguard to the walls of Changzhou.

Minister Lu, depressed by the loss of Governor Qian, had dispatched three urgent messages in a row to the Third Great Prince in Suzhou, begging for assistance. He also had sent a plea to the throne. Now, he received a report.

"Five hundred infantry are advancing on the city. Their banner says they are led by Li Kui the Black Whirlwind."

"That lout is the fiercest man in Liangshan Marsh. He's a born killer. Who will take him on?"

Gao Keli and Zhang Jinren, two distinguished commandants, stepped forward.

"If you capture the rascal," said Lu, "I will see to it that the king raises you in rank and rewards you handsomely."

The two took their lances, mounted, and marched from the city with a thousand infantry and cavalry. Li Kui stretched his troops before them in a line. He stood in front, grasping his two battle-axes. By his side was Bao Xu, a broad cutlass in hand. Xiang Chong and Li Gun, nearby, held barbed shields. In their right hands they gripped steel javelins. Chests and backs protected by armor plate, the four chieftains stood in a line at the front.

Southern commandants Gao and Zhang, wildcats who were stronger than tigers, ravens who could bully eagles, deployed their thousand soldiers near the city walls.

A few of Song Jiang's scouts recognized Gao and Zhang as the killers Of Han Tao and Peng Qi. They pointed them out to Black Whirlwind. Dispensing with any challenges, Li Kui charged across the field with his axes. Bao Xu hastily called Xiang Chong and Li Gun, who were waving their barbed shields, and all four swept into the enemy position.

The astonished Gao and Zhang were completely unprepared. They turned their horses to flee, but the barbed shields were already twirling under the animals' muzzles. Gao and Zhang lunged with their lances, but the shields warded off the thrusts. Black Whirlwind hacked the legs of Gao's mount and brought the rider tumbling to the ground.

"Take him alive," cried Xiang Chong. But Li Kui was a killer. He couldn't be stopped. He decapitated Gao with a single blow of his ax. Bao Xu pulled Zhang from the saddle and cut off his head as well.

The four then ripped into the southern troops. Li Kui tied Gao's head to his belt and, with both hands free, swung his axes left and right. A thousand enemy infantry and cavalry ran pell-mell back into the city, but not before Black Whirlwind had mowed down three or four hundred of them.

At the drawbridge Li Kui and Bao Xu wanted to fight their way into Changzhou. They were restrained only by the strenuous efforts of Xiang Chong and Li Gun. Cannon balls pelted down on them from the city walls, and the four withdrew. They found their five hundred men still standing in a line exactly where they had left them. The soldiers had wanted to join in the fighting, but no one dared to get near Li Kui when his blood lust was aroused and he was slaughtering indiscriminately.

By then Song Jiang had come riding up. Li Kui and Bao Xu presented the heads. The other chieftains were amazed.

"How did you do it?" they asked.

"We destroyed many of the foe and intended to take these two alive. But our hands itched. We couldn't control ourselves. So we killed them."

Song Jiang said: "Since we have the heads of the murderers of Han Tao and Peng Qi, we can look up at the sky from under the white mourning banners and offer them as sacrifices."

Again he wept bitterly. Then he had the white banners taken down, rewarded the four raiders and marched with his troops to the walls of Changzhou.

Inside the city, Minister Lu was highly alarmed. He conferred with Jin lie, Xu Ding and the four commandants on how to drive Song Jiang back. They all had seen Li Kui's one-man massacre, and their hearts were chilled. No one would venture out. Again Lu called for volunteers but, like geese whose beaks had been pinned shut by arrows, like fish hooked through the gills, they couldn't utter a sound. Not a man dared to respond.

Sunk in gloom, Lu sent observers up on the walls. Song Jiang's army had surrounded the city. They were pounding drums, waving banners, yelling challenges. Lu ordered all his generals to man the ramparts. They left his headquarters. Alone, he pondered fruitlessly. Finally, he summoned his closest confidants. Their only wish by then was to escape. Of that we'll say no more.

Meanwhile Jin Jie returned home and said to his wife Jade Orchid: "Song Jiang has ringed the city and is pressing from three sides. Changzhou is short of grain. It can't hold out for very long. Once they break in, their blades will turn us all into ghosts!"

"You're loyal to the emperor and want to surrender. When you were a Song official the imperial court treated you well. Since you're willing to abandon evil and return to righteousness, why not capture Minister Lu and turn him over to Song Jiang? That will ensure your welcome."

"Lu has four commandants under him, each with his own troops. That oaf Xu Ding and I have never got along, and he's one of Lu's most trusted associates. A single strand can't spin a thread, a single hand can't clap alone. I'm afraid I couldn't bring it off. It would only end in disaster."

"Write a secret message, bind it to an arrow, and shoot it out of the city tonight. Let Song Jiang know what you're planning. By coordinating from within and without, he'll be able to take Changzhou. Go forth tomorrow and pretend to be defeated. Let the Song forces follow as you retreat into the city. It will be a splendid deed."

"Very clever, my dear wife. I'll do as you say."

The next day Song Jiang stepped up his assaults on the city and Minister Lu called his generals into conference. Jin Jie spoke.

"Changzhou is on high terrain. It's easy to defend but not a good place from which to attack. We should hang on until relief comes from Suzhou. Then we can all go into battle together."

Lu agreed. "Well said." He instructed Ying Ming and Zhao Yi to hold the East Gate, Shen Bian and Fan Chou the North Gate, Jin Jie the West Gate, and Xu Ding the South Gate. The generals and their soldiers took up their respective posts.

That evening Jin Jie wrote a secret letter and attached it to an arrow. In the still of the night he sped it from atop the wall towards an enemy patrol outside the West Gate. The officer in charge hurriedly delivered it to Sagacious Lu the Tattooed Monk and Wu Song the Pilgrim, who commanded the western camp. They had Du Xing rush it to the main camp to the northeast, where Song Jiang and Wu Yong were conferring by candlelight in the headquarters tent. Song Jiang read the letter with joy. He had its contents immediately transmitted to all three camps.

The following day they launched an offensive from three sides. Minister Lu, in the command tower on the wall, heard an earth-shaking explosion in Song Jiang's position, and a fiery cannon ball flew over and struck a corner of the tower. Half of it collapsed with a crash. In mortal fear, Lu hurried down from the wall. He exhorted the generals guarding the four gates to go out and repel the foe.

Three rolls on the battle drums, and the city gates were opened wide and the drawbridges lowered. From the North Gate Shen Bian and Fan Chou marched forth with their men. Guan Sheng the Big Halberd rode out to meet them on Governor Qian's curly-maned roan.

He was just about to engage Fan Chou in combat when Jin Jie and his troops emerged and challenged the enemy to fight. Sun Li cantered forward and took on Jin Jie. Before they had fought three rounds, Jin Jie, feigning defeat, turned and galloped away. Sun Li pursued, closely followed by nine more chieftains. Jin Jie retreated into the city, and the chieftains pushed in after him, capturing the West Gate.

The news that Song Jiang's army was pouring in through the West Gate put Changzhou in a turmoil. Fang La had cruelly oppressed the people, and their hatred knew no bounds. They rushed out in full force to help the Song attackers. Song Jiang's banner was already flying on the city ramparts.

Fan Chou and Shen Bian, seeing that the tide had turned, hastily started back to Changzhou to protect their families. But Wang the Stumpy Tiger and woman warrior Ten Feet of Steel cut in from the left and grabbed Fan Chou. Xuan Zan and Hao Siwen dashed up on the right and knocked Shen Bian from his saddle with their lances. The Song soldiers captured him.

Now the entire army under Song Jiang and Wu Yong surged into the city, seeking out southern troops and killing them in great number. Minister Lu and Xu Ding fled desperately through the South Gate. Pursuing Song troops were unable to catch them, and returned to Changzhou. While awaiting further orders, they discussed the awards they would claim.

Zhao Yi, who had been hiding in the home of one of the local populace, was seized by his host and handed over. Ying Ming had been killed in battle. His head was presented as proof.

Song Jiang, on entering Changzhou, posted notices reassuring the masses. They crowded to the prefectural center, supporting the old and carrying the infants, to express their thanks. Song Jiang comforted them, and promised they would be considered as good, law-abiding citizens. The chieftains also came to claim their awards.

When Jin Jie arrived to pay his respects, Song Jiang descended the steps to greet him personally and invite him into the hall. Kowtowing at the foot of the steps, Jin Jie voiced his gratitude. He said his wife deserved the credit for his return to the Song regime as a loyal official.

Song Jiang directed that Fan Chou, Shen Bian and Zhao Yi be locked in cage-carts and escorted by Jin Jie to Governor Zhang in Runzhou. He wrote a covering document which he gave to Jin Jie. At the same time he instructed Dai Zong the Marvellous Traveller to fly on ahead with a letter vouching for Jin Jie and urging that he be accepted into the main Song army. Song Jiang praised his loyalty so highly that Zhang received him when he arrived at Runzhou. The Governor was very favorably impressed. He presented Jin Jie with gold and silver and silks, a fine horse and ceremonial wine.

Deputy District Commander Liu Guangshi appointed him an expeditionary commander. Later, when they broke the Golden Tartars under Fourth Prince Wushu, Jin Jie distinguished himself many times in battle. He eventually was given his own command, and died while fighting at Zhongshan.

But to get back to that day in Runzhou, Zhang and Liu, after rewarding Jin Jie, had the three rebel commanders killed, their bodies pulverised and their heads hung up on public display. They also sent lavish rewards to Song Jiang and his forces.

After settling his army at Changzhou, Song Jiang dispatched Dai Zong to learn the results of Lu Junyi's campaign against Xuanzhou and Huzhou. Meanwhile, a mounted scout arrived with a report.

"Minister Lu is in Wuxi. He's joined forces with a rescue army from Suzhou, and they're heading this way."

Song Jiang selected ten infantry and cavalry chieftains and ordered them south with ten thousand men to meet the foe. Guan Sheng and other chieftains commanding the advance contingent bid Song Jiang farewell and left the city.

Dai Zong returned with Chai Jin and told Song Jiang: "General Lu Junyi has captured Xuanzhou. He's sent Chai Jin to tell you about it."

Song Jiang was delighted. He greeted Chai Jin with wine and conducted him to the rear hall. Chai Jin handed him a detailed written report which read:

"Fang La's garrison general of Xuanzhou, Jia Yuqing, had under him six commandants, all natives of Shezhou and Muzhou. Jia sent them forth with three columns. Our chieftains killed four in personal combat, and their columns retreated into Xuanzhou. Lu Junyi ordered an all-out assault. When we neared the city gates, enemy soldiers on the walls threw down a grind stone, killing one of our chieftains. Their arrows flew like rain. All were poison-tipped. Two more of our chieftains were hit. Both died when we got them back to camp.

"General Lu, angered, pushed the attack through the night. The East Gate was not very well defended, and so we took Xuanzhou. We killed their fifth commandant during the assault. Garrison General Jia fled with his remnant troops towards Huzhou. We don't know where Cheng Shengzu, the sixth commandant, has gone. The grindstone killed Zheng Tianshou the Fair-Faced Gentleman. Slain by poison arrows were Cao Zheng the Demon Carver and Lightning Wang Dingliu."

On hearing that he had lost three more brothers, Song Jiang wept wildly and collapsed in a faint. His skin was yellow, his lips purple, his finger-nails blue, his eyes lustreless. There was no telling about the state of his five organs, but his four limbs were paralyzed.

Truly, flowers open, only to be blown down by the wind. Can the moonlight withstand dark gathering clouds?

Could Song Jiang recover after falling unconscious? Read our next chapter if you would know.

CHAPTER 93

TURBULENT RIVER DRAGON PLEDGES BROTHERHOOD ON TAIHU LAKE

SONG JIANG CONVENES A LARGE MEETING IN SUZHOU CITY

It was some time before the chieftains were able to revive Song Jiang. When at last he could speak, he said to Wu Yong: "We'll never take Fang La. We've been very unlucky since crossing the river. We've lost eight brothers, one after another!"

"Talking like that will only discourage our forces," said the military advisor. "We returned to the capital intact after defeating the Liao because that was Heaven's will. Some of our brothers' time was up, and we lost them. But we've captured three big prefectures— Runzhou, Changzhou and Xuanzhou, thanks to the emperor's fortunate emanations and your own splendid prestige. What's unlucky about that? You've no reason to be discouraged."

"You're right, of course. I guess I was counting too heavily on the hundred and eight of us being star spirits and our names appearing on the stone tablet. We've all been as close as arms and legs to a single body. I couldn't help feeling grieved by the bad news today."

"Please don't upset yourself. You must preserve your health. Concentrate on the disposition of troops and the Wuxi offensive."

"I'll keep Lord Chai Jin with me. Have Dai Zong notify Lu Junyi to attack Huzhou and meet us in Hangzhou as soon as possible."

Wu Yong had Pei Xuan write the dispatch and sent Dai Zong off with it to Xuanzhou. Of that we'll say no more.

Meanwhile, Minister Lu and Xu Ding, fleeing to Wuxi, met the relief army sent by the Third Great Prince from Suzhou. It was headed by General Wei Zhong, and under him were a dozen or more commanders and ten thousand men. The two contingents joined forces and prepared to defend Wuxi. Lu told how Jin Jie had virtually made a gift of Changzhou to the enemy.

"Don't worry, Minister," said Wei Zhong. "We'll get it back for you."

A cavalry scout reported! "Song Jiang's army is nearly here. Better get ready." Wei Zhong mounted his steed and led his troops out of the North Gate to confront the foe. But when he saw how strong Song Jiang's army was, with Li Kui the Black Whirlwind, followed by Bao Xu, Xiang Chong and Li Jun, charging directly towards him, he knew his army couldn't withstand them, and pulled back in disorder, completely routed. As he hastily retreated into the city, the four chieftains were right behind him. Lu fled through the South Gate. Guan Sheng and his troops by then had captured Wuxi, and the city was in flames. Wei Zhong and Xu Ding also escaped through the South Gate, returning to Suzhou.

Guan Sheng rushed a report of the victory to Song Jiang, who soon arrived with the other chieftains. Notices were posted reassuring the local populace that they would be treated as good citizens. The army made camp in the county, and a request was sent to Governor Zhang and Deputy District Commander Liu that they retain control over Changzhou.

Minister Lu, with Wei Zhong and Xu Ding, leading their defeated forces, hurried to Suzhou city and begged succor from the Third Great Prince. They said they had been unable to hold Wuxi because Song Jiang's army was of overwhelming strength. Infuriated, Fang Mao ordered his guards to execute Minister Lu at once.

"Song Jiang's commanders are experienced warriors, men of remarkable Courage," said Wei Zhong, "and their soldiers are all Liangshan Marsh bandits with plenty of battle experience. They're hard to beat."

"I'll withhold the sword from your neck for the time being," Fang Mao said to the minister. "You can have five thousand more troops. Go out first and patrol. I'll also assign some more generals. We'll make farther plans later."

Lu bowed and thanked him. Dressing in full armor, he took his snake lance, eighteen feet long, mounted and led his soldiers from the city.

Fang Mao summoned eight more generals, each tall and strong and highly skilled with weapons. A sickle-bladed lance in hand, he rode out with them personally to observe the combat. Preceded by the eight generals, and followed by thirty-two commanders in neat ranks, he led fifty thousand soldiers through the city's Changho Gate. Minister Lu, with Wei Zhong and Xu Ding, who had left earlier, by then had passed the Cool Hill Monastery and were advancing towards Wuxi.

Already informed by his scouts, Song Jiang had marched more than ten *li* from Wuxi County with a large contingent under several generals. The two armies sighted each other and deployed into battle positions. Minister Lu angrily cantered forward, lance in hand, and challenged Song Jiang to do combat.

Song Jiang was standing beneath an arch of pennants. He turned his head and called: "Who will capture this knave for me?" Before the words were out of his mouth, Xu Ning the Metal Lancer galloped out with his golden lance and engaged Minister Lu. To the encouraging shouts from their respective sides, they fought more than twenty rounds. Then Lu tried a feint, and Xu ran him through the ribs. The minister fell dead to the ground. Both armies yelled. Li Kui the Black Whirlwind brandishing his axes, and Bao Xu the God of Death flourishing his sword, plus Xiang Chong and Li Gun each twirling his barbed shield, tore across the field. The southern soldiers were thrown into confusion. Poised for a charge, Song Jiang's forces found themselves confronted by Fang Mao's main army. They halted each other's advance with swarms of arrows, and both contingents took up battle positions. The eight southern generals spread out in a straight line. Fang Mao was enraged to learn that Minister Lu had been killed. He rode forth, lance athwart his saddle, and reviled Song Jiang.

"You're only a gang of petty robbers from Liangshan Marsh! The doomed Song court has named you a Vanguard General and sends you to invade our land of Wu! I'll not withdraw my soldiers till we've slaughtered you, every one!"

Song Jiang, also on horseback, retorted: "You're just a bunch of rustics from Muzhou! What chance have you of ever winning sovereignty! Surrender and save your necks. We are the imperial army. How dare you resist us with tricky words? We're not leaving till we've killed you all!"

"Enough of this chatter. I have here eight fierce generals. Dare you select eight to do them battle?"

Song Jiang laughed. "We'd be no true gallants if we pitted two against one. We'll match you eight for eight. But no man knocked from his horse is to be killed. He must be carried back to his own side. There must be no sniping with arrows and no seizure of corpses. If there is no clear victor, no general melee shall be allowed, and the contest must be continued the following day."

Fang Mao agreed. At his order, his eight generals rode forward, weapons in hand. Song Jiang spoke to his own officers. "Let eight cavalry commanders enter the field." Through the arch of pennants, from the left and from the right, eight chieftains moved forward on their steeds in formation. Drums thundered, banners fluttered, each side fired a signal cannon, and shouts rose from the two armies as the sixteen mounted figures lined up against their opposites.

For more than thirty rounds they fought, until a man was downed. And who was the victor? Zhu Tong the Beautiful Beard. His lance had stabbed his opponent from his saddle. Trumpets in both armies sounded the withdrawal. The remaining seven pairs disengaged and returned to their original positions.

Fang Mao the Third Great Prince, due to the loss of his general, felt at a disadvantage. He pulled his forces back into the city of Suzhou. Song Jiang praised his cavalry chieftains and made camp near the Icy Hill Monastery. He raised Zhu Tong in rank. Pei Xuan wrote a report of the matter to Military Governor Zhang. Of that we'll say no more.

The Third Great Prince held the city but wouldn't come out and fight. He posted his generals at the gates, laid a field of barbed branches in depth, lined the walls with bowmen and cannon, prepared to heat molten metal, and piled bottles of lime along the ramparts. He would defend Suzhou stubbornly.

Song went to view the situation with four chieftains and thirty some-odd cavalry. The city was surrounded by water and the walls were strong. "We won't take this place in a hurry," he thought. He returned to camp and conferred with Wu Yong.

Li Jun the naval chieftain was announced. He had just arrived from Jiangyin. Song Jiang directed that he be invited into the headquarters tent. He entered and Song Jiang asked him about the situation along the coast.

"We sailed against Jiangyin and Taicang and they battled us with naval craft," said Li Jun. "Ruan the Second finished one of their commanders with a thrust of his spear, another was killed by our arrows, and we captured both towns. Then Shi Xiu, Zhang Heng and Zhang Shun took Jiading, and the three Ruan brothers occupied Changshu. I've come specially to report."

Delighted, Song Jiang rewarded Li Jun. He sent him on with a dispatch concerning the victories to Governor Zhang and Deputy District Commander Liu in Changzhou. There, the two officials further rewarded Li Jun and instructed him to return to the camp at Icy Hill Monastery.

Realizing that only a naval offensive could crack the watergirt Suzhou, Song Jiang kept Li Jun with him, and directed that he prepare vessels for the assault.

"Better let me go and have a look, so that I'll know what I'm doing."

"Right."

Li Jun was gone two days. When he returned he said: "The southern side of the city is near Taihu Lake. I'll need a boat that will take me into the lake from the Yixing tributary. From there, I'll cross over to Wujiang and see what news I can pick up about the southern end. Then we'll be able to attack from four sides and break in."

"An excellent idea. Just what I've been thinking. But I must get some good assistants to go with you."

Song Jiang appointed four chieftains to aid in capturing more coastal towns and directed the recall of Tong Wei and Tong Meng. Li Jun took the order and the replacements to Jiangyin and returned with Tong Wei and Tong Meng two days later. Song Jiang greeted them, and instructed them to go with Li Jun and spy out the southern end of Suzhou.

The three set sail in a little craft. Two boatmen plied the sweep oars. They followed Tixing Creek around to Taihu Lake, a broad body of water of beautiful emerald green. Crossing the lake, they neared Wujiang and saw in the distance forty or fifty fishing boats.

"We'll pretend we're fish buyers," said Li Jun, "and ask some questions."

They rowed over to the first vessel and Li Jun queried: "Got any carp?"

"If it's carp you want, come home with me and I'll sell you some."

Li Jun's boat accompanied a few of the fishing craft. Before long they sighted a hamlet of twenty or so households in a grove of bent-backed weeping willows. There the fishermen moored their boats and led Li and his party to a compound on the bank.

The moment he set foot inside the compound gate, the first fisherman whistled. Seven or eight big fellows with hooked poles immediately closed in from both sides, snagged Li and his two companions and dragged them further into the compound. They tied each of the three to a big stake without a word.

Li Jun looked around. He saw four bold gallants sitting in a thatched hall. The first of these had a red beard and brown hair and wore a blue quilted silk tunic. The second, a tall thin fellow with a short mustache was dressed in a dark green cotton shirt with a round collar. The third was swarthy and had a long beard. The fourth had a broad bony face, a curly spade-shaped beard and, like the third fellow, was dressed in a blue quilted tunic. All wore broad-brimmed hats of black felt and carried weapons. The leader shouted at Li Jun.

"Where are you rogues from? What are you doing on our lake?"

"We're traders from Yangzhou. We've come to buy fish."

"Don't bother to question him, brother," advised the bony faced man. "He's obviously a spy. Just let me cut his heart out to go with my wine!"

Li Jun said to himself: "I was a smuggler on the Xunyang River for a long time, and for several years a gallant in Liangshan Marsh. Who would have thought I'd end my life here. Well, if I'm finished, I'm finished!" He sighed, looked at Tong Wei and Tong Meng and said: "I got you two into this. We'll all become ghosts together!"

"Don't talk like that," the brothers replied. "Death doesn't matter. It's only a pity that dying here like this will reflect on Big Brother's prestige."

The three gazed at each other. Chests high, they waited for death.

The four bold gallants observed them and heard what they said. They exchanged glances. "That leader of theirs is clearly no lowly person," they remarked.

"Who are you, really?" Red Beard demanded. "What are your names?"

"If you're going to kill us, then kill us," Li Jun retorted. "Though we die, we're not going to tell you, lest we be shamed before the whole gallant fraternity!"

Convinced that the three were bold fellows like himself, Red Beard jumped up, cut their bonds and released them. The four escorted them into the hall and invited them to be seated. The leader kowtowed before them.

"We have been robbers all our lives," he said, "but we never have met such chivalrous men as you. Where are you from, gallant sirs? We would be pleased to learn your names."

"We can see that you four elder brothers must be bold fellows, so we'll tell you. Then you can take us wherever you wish," said Li Jun. "We are chieftains under Song Jiang of Liangshan Marsh. I am Li Jun the Turbulent River Dragon. These two are brothers—Tong Wei the Dragon from the Cave and Tong Meng the River Churning Clam. Our band has been amnestied by the imperial court. After breaking the Liao Tartars we returned to the capital and were ordered to destroy Fang La. If you are his men, you can turn us in and claim your rewards. We won't offer any resistance."

The four gallants promptly kowtowed. Kneeling, they said: "We have eyes but couldn't recognize Mount Taishan! Please forgive our rude blunder. We four have nothing to do with Fang La's bandits. Originally we were robbers in the forest, but now we live here in Willow Hamlet. On all sides are deep coves. No one can get in without a boat. Our fishing is only a pretext. Actually, we grab whatever we can on the lake. Last winter we learned how to swim, and now no one dares to interfere with us. We heard long ago that Song Jiang had gathered some of the boldest gallants under the sky in Liangshan Marsh. His name is well known. We've heard too about Zhang Shun the White Streak in the Waves. We never dreamed we'd meet you here today!"

"Zhang Shun is one of us," said Li Jun. "He also is a naval chieftain. Right now he's chasing bandits around Jiangyin. I'll introduce you to him. May we ask you four your names?"

"Because we were operating in the greenwood, they're kind of odd," said the leader. "Don't laugh! I'm Fei Bao the Red-Beard Dragon. This is Ni Yun the Curly-Haired Tiger, this is Pu Qing the Taihu Python, and that's Di Cheng the Thin-Faced Bear."

Li Jun was very pleased. "Now we need have no doubts about one another." And he explained: "Big Brother Song Jiang is vanguard general of an expedition against Fang La. He wants to take Suzhou but he has no plan. He's sent us three to spy out the terrain. If you four bold fellows will come with us to Song Jiang, I guarantee you'll be made officials. After we've finished Fang La, the emperor will raise you still higher."

"If we wanted positions, we could have become commanders under Fang La long ago," said Fei Bao. "But we seek only a free life, not rank. We'll go through fire and water if you need our help. But if you want to make us officials, we're not interested."

"In that case," said Li Jun, "how about pledging ourselves as blood brothers?"

The four bold fellows gladly agreed. They slaughtered a pig and a sheep, poured cups of wine, and vowed to consider Li Jun their elder brother. Li instructed Tong Wei and Tong Meng to make the same pledge to the others.

Li Jun told of Song Jiang's desire to take Suzhou. "But Fang Mao won't come out and fight," he said, "and the city is surrounded by water. There are no roads we can advance on, and the creeks are narrow and difficult to navigate. How can we break in?"

"Stay here and relax a couple of days, brother," Fei Bao advised. "Functionaries from Fang La in Hangzhou go to Suzhou often on government business. We can use this as a means of getting into the city. I'll send a few fishermen to inquire. If any Fang La people are en route, we can decide what to do next."

Li Jun agreed, Fei Bao sent off the fishermen, and the seven remained in the hamlet, chatting and drinking. Two or three days later, the fishermen returned and reported.

"In Pingwang Town there are about a dozen cargo vessels flying yellow banners from their stern which read *Royal Armor*. They're obviously from Hangzhou. Only six or seven people man each boat."

"This is our chance," said Li Jun. "We hope you brothers will help."

"Let's go," said Fei Bao.

"If just one of those boats get away," warned Li Jun, "our plan will fail."

"Don't worry," said Fei Bao. "We take full responsibility." Sixty or seventy small craft were gathered and set sail. The seven gallants sat in seven boats.

Fishermen manned the others. All were laden with concealed weapons. The little vessels slipped from the creeks into the river, then spread out.

That night the moon and stars filled the sky. The ten government craft were moored neared the Dragon King Temple at the eastern end of the river. Fei Bao's boat got there first. He whistled shrilly, and the sixty-odd fishing craft closed in and affixed themselves to the government vessels.

Startled sailors rushed out of their cabins, only to be hooked by the grappling poles and tied up in batches of four or five. Those who jumped in the water were fished out and hauled on deck. The little craft pulled the big vessels into the lake, and across to Willow Hamlet.

By then it was the fourth watch. The batches of bound prisoners were weighted with big rocks and thrown into the lake and drowned. Questioning of the two leaders revealed that they were store-house keepers of Fang La's eldest son, Fang Tianding the Prince of Southern Peace. On his orders they had been delivering three thousand suits of armor to Fang Mao the Third Great Prince in Suzhou. Li Jun asked the leaders their names, confiscated their documents, then had them killed.

"Before we take any action, I must consult with Big Brother about this," he said.

"I'll have you ferried across," said Fei Bao. "We'd better sneak you through the creeks past the enemy positions." He directed two fishermen to take Li Jun in a fast boat.

"Conceal the captured vessels and armor in the creek behind the hamlet," he instructed Fei Bao and the Tong brothers. "Don't let anyone know about them."

"No problem," said Fei Bao. He went to attend to it personally.

Two fishermen, propelling a little craft through the creeks, conveyed Li Jun past the enemy positions. He disembarked at Icy Hill Monastery and returned to camp. He told Song Jiang what had happened. Wu Yong, also listening, was overjoyed.

"'Capturing Suzhou will be as easy as spitting on your hands. Let Li Kui, Bao Xu, Xiang Chong and Li Gun take two hundred shield bearers and go to the hamlet on Taihu Lake. There they can work out a plan with Fei Bao and his three gallants. Tomorrow, they can go into action."

Li Jun crossed the lake with the two fishermen, got more boats, fetched Li Kui and the others, then proceeded to the hamlet and introduced the four chieftains to Fei Bao, who was somewhat startled by the appearance of the Black Whirlwind. He wined, and dined them, as well as the two hundred shield bearers.

The next day, after conferring, Fei Bao and Ni Yun dressed as the storekeepers of the armor, put on southern official uniforms, and pocketed their documents. The fishermen disguised themselves as sailors on the government boats. Li Kui and the two hundred shield bearers hid in the holds. Pu Qing and Di Cheng captained the rear vessel, which carried incendiary equipment.

They were about to sail when a fisherman came and announced: "A boat out there is zig-zagging across the lake."

"Something's up," exclaimed Li Jun. He hurried to have a look.

Two men were standing on the prow of the vessel—Dai Zong the Marvellous Traveller and Ling Zhen the Heaven-Shaking Thunder. Li Jun whistled sharply, and the boat flew towards the hamlet. The two men came ashore.

"What brings you here? Is there any news?" asked Li Jun.

"In his rash to get Li Kui to you, Big Brother forgot something important," said Dai Zong. "He's dispatched me and Ling Zhen specially with a hundred cannon. We couldn't catch you when you were on the lake, and we didn't dare land on these unknown banks. He wants you to enter the city at dawn. Once you get in, fire the cannon as a signal."

"Perfect!" said Li Jun. He had the cannon barrels and carriages shifted over to his craft and concealed beneath the armor.

When Fei Bao heard that it was Dai Zong, he entertained him with food and wine. Ling Zhen and the ten gunners who had accompanied him hid themselves inside the third boat.

They sailed for Suzhou that night at the fourth watch. They arrived after the fifth. Soldiers on the walls, seeing the southern flags they flew, quickly reported. The official in charge of the gate was General Guo Shiguang the Flying Panther. He mounted the wall, questioned the commanding officer, and demanded the convoy's documents. They were hauled up and examined, then sent to the headquarters of the Third Great Prince for certification. Only after Guo posted observers below did he open the gate. But he also sent men down to inspect the boats. They reported that they were piled high with armor. Guo let them sail in, one by one, but when ten had entered he had the gate closed again.

An observer dispatched by the Third Great Prince arrived—an official accompanied by five hundred soldiers who took positions along the bank and moored the craft. Li Kui, Bao Xu, Xiang Chong and Li Gun emerged from the cabins. Their rough appearance startled the official, and he hastily inquired who they were.

By way of answer, Xiang Chong and Li Gun charged, with twirling shields. A sword flew, cutting the official down from his horse. Li Kui leaped ashore, swinging his axes. He ploughed into the five hundred soldiers, hacking chunks out of a dozen in a row. The others fled.

Two hundred shield bearers poured from the cabins and swarmed upon the shore. They began setting fires. Ling Zhen positioned his gun carriages, mounted the barrels, and loosed a dozen in a volley that rocked the tower on the wall. From four sides, attackers closed in on the city.

Fang Mao the Third Great Prince, planning in his palace, nearly jumped out of his skin at the sound of the signal cannon. Commanders guarding the various gates rushed with their men towards where the salvoes were thundering without cease. From all of the gates came the report: "Snipers' arrows are mowing down our men! Song soldiers are already on the walls!"

Suzhou was thrown into a turmoil. No one knew how many Song troops had got in. Li Kui the Black Whirlwind and Bao Xu were tearing around the city with two shield bearers slaughtering southern soldiers. Ling Zhen, protected by Li Jun, Dai Zong and the four bold rustics, continued to fire his cannons. Song Jiang sent all three columns against Suzhou. As these fought their way in, the southern troops scattered and fled for their lives.

The Third Great Prince hastily donned his armor and mounted his horse. With six or seven hundred armored troops he attempted to break out of the South Gate. But he bumped into Li Kui and his cohorts, who wreaked havoc among them. The Southerners broke and ran, at a moment when Sagacious Lu barged out of a lane, brandishing his iron staff. Fang Mao knew he couldn't resist. He turned his steed and galloped back towards his palace.

But Wu Song suddenly emerged from beneath Raven Bridge, chopped the animal's leg with his sword, and brought the prince tumbling to the ground. Another swing cut off Fang Mao's head.

Wu Song presented his trophy to Song Jiang in his new headquarters in the prince's palace. The order was to destroy the southern army and capture as many of the foe as possible. Only Liu Yun managed to get away. With some remnant troops, he fled towards Xiuzhou.

Seated in the palace, Song Jiang ordered a halt to the killing of civilians and directed his men to put out the fires. He also issued a proclamation reassuring the populace. Then he summoned his chieftains to the palace to claim their rewards.

He already knew that Wu Song had slain Fang Mao, Zhu Tong had caught Xu Fang, Shi Jin had captured Zhen Cheng, Sun Li had killed Zhang Wei with his staff, Li Jun had run Chang Sheng through with his lance, and Fan Rui had destroyed Wu Fu. Xuan Zan and Guo Shiguang had inflicted such grievous wounds on each other that both had died beneath Horse Watering Bridge. Many subordinate enemy officers had been made prisoner, and their captors also came forward, seeking recognition.

Song Jiang directed that Xuan Zan's body be laid in a fine coffin with full mourning decorations and that he be buried at the foot of Tiger Mound Hill. The head of Fang Mao and the prisoners Xu Fang and Zhen Cheng were sent to Changzhou for disposition by Governor Zhang. The governor had the two captives sliced to pieces in the public square. Fang Mao's head was dispatched to the capital. Substantial rewards were sent to Suzhou for distribution among the commanders. Zhang then issued an order that Deputy District Commander Liu take over control of Suzhou and that Song Jiang continue with his expedition against the rebels.

Before long a mounted scout arrived in Suzhou with the news: "Deputy District Commander Liu and staff officer Geng are here to assume command."

Song Jiang and his chieftains went out to greet them and escort them into the city. They were moved into the palace and formally congratulated.

In the prefectural office, Song Jiang conferred with his chieftains. He dispatched scouts to learn what progress his navy was making along the coast. They returned and reported that when the rebel officials in the coastal counties heard that Suzhou had fallen, they had scattered and fled, and that in these counties all was now peaceful. Very pleased, Song Jiang reported the victory in writing to the Central Army and requested the governor to restore all former Song officials to their posts. He then ordered various commanders to take over control of the captured coastal counties and let the naval chieftains who had been holding them return to Suzhou. Within a few days, this was done.

The naval chieftains told Song Jiang that when the three Ruan brothers attacked Changshu, Shi En had been lost. Kong Liang died in the assault on Kunshan. Neither of them knew how to swim, and each had fallen into the water and drowned. Shi Xiu, Li Ying the others had all come back.

Another two chieftains gone. Very unhappy, Song Jiang sighed without end.

Fei Bao and his three gallant companions came to bid him farewell. They were leaving for home. When his pleas that they stay proved in vain, he rewarded them and instructed Li Jun to escort them to Willow Hamlet. With Tong Wei and Tong Meng, Li Jun saw them home, and there the four bold rustics wined and dined the three chieftains. Fei Bao rose and, handing a cup of wine to Li Jun, said a few words.

And as a result, Li Jun's fame spread across the seas, his name was known throughout the world. He became king of a foreign land, but never encroached upon the borders of China. Truly, realizing its fate the toad sloughs off its skin, performing great deeds a fish becomes a dragon.

What were the words Fei Bao spoke to Li Jun? Read our next chapter if you would know.

CHAPTER 94

IN NINGHAI DISTRICT SONG JIANG WEARS MOURNING

AT YONGJIN GATE ZHANG SHUN BECOMES A SPIRIT

Fei Bao said to Li Jun: "I'm a crude stupid fellow, but I've heard clever persons say: 'One must have failures as well as successes, one must have sorrow as well as joy.' You've built a career in Liangshan Marsh in a score or more years, winning every battle, and when you defeated the Liao Tartars you lost none of your brothers. But now you're going against Fang La, and clearly your vitality is crumbling. You won't be able to last much longer.

"Why am I not willing to become an official or general? Because once peace is restored, there would be one person after another trying to take my life. As the old saying goes: 'In order to keep the peace, the general himself can have no peace.' That's very well put. We four and you three have pledged ourselves blood brothers. Why not, while the tide is still with us, find a quiet refuge? Let's put some money together, buy a large boat, hire a few sailors, and search the rivers and seas for a good place to settle down and live out the rest of our lives. What could be sweeter?"

Li Jun bowed and replied: "Your words are most enlightening, brother. What you suggest would indeed be fine. It's just that we still haven't beaten Fang La. I can't cast aside my obligation to Song Jiang. It isn't time yet for me to leave. If I were to go with you today, I'd be violating my chivalrous duties. If you're willing to wait until we've conquered Fang La, I and my two brothers will gladly join you. You can start preparing now. Heaven crush me if I go back on my word! I'll be no real man!"

"We'll make arrangements about the boat," the rustic gallants said. "We'll be looking forward to your arrival, brother. Don't disappoint us!" Li Jun and Fei Bao sealed their pact with wine. All vowed to carry it out scrupulously.

The next day, Li Jun said good-bye to the four, and with the Tong brothers went back to Song Jiang. He told him they had no desire to become officials—they felt they would be happier remaining fisherman. Song Jiang sighed, then went on readying his land and naval forces for the offensive. Wujiang County was already free of rebels, and the Song forces had taken Pingwang Town. They set out now for a drive on Xiuzhou Prefecture.

Duan Kai, the general responsible for its defense, had learned that Fang Mao the Third Great Prince had been killed in Suzhou, and his only thought was to wind things up and leave. When he heard that the main Song army was already not far from the city, and saw in the distance the advancing banners blocking out the sun on land and water in a combined operation of boats and cavalry, he was scared stiff. The vanguard under Guan Sheng and Qin Ming had reached the city walls, and their naval vessels were closing in on the West Gate.

"You needn't attack," he called from the ramparts. "We will surrender." And he ordered that the gates be opened.

He directed that Song Jiang be welcomed with sheep and wine, and conducted him, amid burning incense and flowery lanterns, to the prefectural center. Duan Kai was the first to present himself. Song Jiang promised him that he would be considered a good official, and issued proclamations reassuring the local populace.

"I originally was a law-abiding citizen of Muzhou Prefecture," said Duan Kai. "But I was repeatedly oppressed by Fang La, and was compelled to serve under him. Today the Celestial Army has arrived. I wouldn't dream of not submitting." People like Duan Kai realized the Heavenly destiny of the Song Dynasty.

"Who is defending the city of Hangzhou in the Ninghai Military District?" Song Jiang asked him. "How many effectives has he?"

"Hangzhou covers a wide area, and is densely populated. North and east is dry land, the river is on the south, to the west is the lake. It's held by Fang La's son Fang Tianding the Prince of Southern Peace. He commands an army of more than seventy thousand, and has twenty-four generals and four marshals—a total of twenty-eight.

"Two of them are especially formidable. One is a monk from Shezhou, known as the Buddha of Precious Light. His original name was Deng Yuanjue. He wields an iron Buddhist staff weighing over fifty catties. Everyone calls him 'National Advisor'.

"The other, Shi Bao, comes from Fuzhou. His weapon is a comet hammer, and when he throws it, he never misses. He also has a fine sword called the Wind Splitter. It can cut bronze and iron. Even three layers of armor the Wind Splitter slices right through.

"The remaining twenty-six are all selected generals, all extremely tough and courageous. You mustn't underestimate this foe, Excellency."

Song Jiang rewarded Duan Kai, and ordered him to report these matters to Governor Zhang. Later on, Duan Kai marched with the governor's army and took part in the defense of Suzhou. Deputy District Commander Liu Guangshi was made military governor of Xiuzhou. Now, Song Jiang shifted his troops to the village of Zuili Pavilion and established a base.

After banqueting and rewarding the chieftains, he discussed with them the attack on Hangzhou. Chai Jin the Small Whirlwind rose to speak.

"Ever since you rescued me in Gaotang Prefecture, you have lavished your affection on me and given me undeserved honors," he said to Song Jiang. "So far, due to my own weak fate and personal inadequacies, I have not been able to requite this benevolence. I would like, today, to penetrate into Fang La's lair as a spy. If I can perform with merit I will be of service to the throne and will reflect honor on you, brother, at the same time. I wonder whether you will permit me to try?"

Song Jiang was very pleased. "If you can learn the enemy's internal situation we shall be able to attack and capture the chief bandit Fang La, deliver him to the capital and, for this small achievement, share in the honors. But I'm afraid the task may be too much of a hardship, brother."

"What of it? The possibility of death doesn't daunt me. My only request is that Yan Qing go with me. He knows the local dialects and is quick to seize opportunities."

"Of course, brother. Yan Qing is with Lu Junyi's forces at the moment. I'll dispatch an order for him to come at once."

Just then someone announced: "General Lu's special emissary Yan Qing has arrived to report a victory."

"You're sure to succeed, brother," Song Jiang said happily to Chai Jin. "He's come precisely when we need him. It's a good omen."

Chai Jin, too, was delighted.

Yati Qing entered the tent and respectfully greeted Song Jiang. They welcomed him with food and wine.

"Have you come by land or water, brother?" he was asked.

"By boat," he replied.

"Dai Zong told us you were attacking Huzhou. How is it going?" Song Jiang queried.

"After leaving Xuanzhou, General Lu divided his forces into two," said Yan Qing. "Half went with the vanguard against Huzhou. They killed the puppet garrison head Gong Wen and five of his sub-commanders and took the city. They destroyed and dispersed the enemy troops, reassured the populace, and dispatched a written report to Governor Zhang requesting that he send a prefect to take control for the crown. I was ordered to report the news to you. The other half, under Lin Chong, was ordered to capture Lone Pine Pass, then join us for the Hangzhou offensive. I've heard that they're fighting every day along the road to the pass, but they haven't been able to take it. General Lu and Zhu Wu have gone personally to assume command, leaving General Huyan to hold Huzhou until the governor sends a prefect. Then he is to attack and take Deqing County, before joining the offensive against Hangzhou."

"How many chieftains are involved in these campaigns? Can you tell me the names?"

"Twenty-three have gone for the assault on Long Pine Pass," Yan Qing replied. "They are Lu Junyi, Zhu Wu, Lin Chong, Dong Ping, Zhang Qin, Xie Zhen, Xie Bao, Lu Fang, Guo Sheng, Ou Peng, Deng Fei, Li Zhong, Zhou Tong, Zou Yuan, Zou Run, Sun Xin, Mistress Gu, LiLi, Bai Sheng, Tang Long, Zhu Gui, Zhu Fu and Shi Qian.

"Nineteen, including Huyan Zhuo, are to hold Huzhou the moment and later attack Deqing County. They are Huyan Zhuo, Suo Chao, Mu Hong, Lei Heng, Yang Xiong, Liu Tang, Shan Tinggui, Wei Dingguo, Chen Da, Yang Chun, Xue Yong, Du Qian, Mu Chun, Li Yun, Shi Yong, Gong Wang, Ding Desun, Zhang Qing and Sun Erniang.

"When I left the actions were already being carried out."

"Dividing the force into two, under the circumstances, is obviously the best method. Lord Chai Jin has asked that you go with him into Fang La's territory and gather intelligence. Are you willing?"

"Certainly, if that is your wish, Commander-in-Chief." Pleased, Chai Jin said: "I will dress as a white-robed minor scholar. You disguise yourself as my servant. We'll stroll along carrying a lute, a sword, and a bag of books. Master and man—no one will suspect us. At the coast we'll find a boat and sail past Yuezhou, then follow a small road to Zhuji County. Then we'll cross the hills. It's not far from there to Muzhou."

"Yuezhou is part of our Central Plain," said Song Jiang. "Fang La has no control in that sector. I'll notify the local officials to give you safe conduct."

On the day designated Chai Jin and Yan Qing bid Song Jiang farewell and departed with lute, sword and books. They headed for the coast to find a boat and commence their intelligence operations. Of that we'll say no more.

Meanwhile, Military Advisor Wu Yong, addressing Song Jiang, said: "Along half the southern side of Hangzhou is the Qiantang River. It empties into the sea. A few men in a small boat could sail in around the coast, pass through the Zheshan Gate, and get up near the South Gate of the city. If they fired cannons and raised signal flags, they could cause great alarm in Hangzhou. Which of your naval chieftains could handle this mission?"

"Let us go," cried Zhang Heng and the three Ruan brothers, almost before the words were out of his mouth.

"Hangzhou's west side fronts on the lake. We'll need naval forces to get across there, too," said Song Jiang. "I can't let you all go."

"Zhang Heng and Ruan the Seventh, then," Wu Yong said to the two chieftains. "And you can take Hou Jian and Duan Jingzhu."

The chosen four set off with thirty or so sailors, and took with them a dozen cannons and signal flags. They skirted the coast until they found a craft, then sailed up along the Qiantang River.

Hear me, reader. This is a very diverse tale, handed down to us from the story-tellers of old. We couldn't possibly tell it all at one sitting. But we will sketch the broad outline, as you shall see. Remember it, for only thus will you be able to follow the complications and subtleties of the plot.

Song Jiang returned to Xiuzhou to plan the attack on Hangzhou. Suddenly, he was informed that an emissary was arriving from the Eastern Capital with imperial wine and rewards. Song Jiang and his commanders, high and low, welcomed him into the city, expressed their thanks, and feasted him at a banquet at which the imperial wine was served. During the course of the drinking the emissary said the emperor had a slight illness, and that the Royal Hospital wanted to summon Dr. An Daoquan to treat him. An imperial order had been issued, and the emissary had come to fetch the doctor. Song Jiang dared not refuse. The next day, he and his chieftains saw Dr. An off ten *li* out of the city on his journey back to the capital with the emissary.

After dispensing rewards among the chieftains, he selected a day for dedicating his flags at a sacrificial ceremony and starting his march. Then he bid farewell to Deputy District Commander Liu Guangshi and staff officer Geng, mounted, and set forth, advancing on land and water, navy and cavalry coordinating. When they neared Chongte, the rebel general who was holding the county fled to Hangzhou.

Meanwhile, Fang La's eldest son Prince Fang Tianding was consulting with his generals in his external palace. It was located on the site of where the Soaring Dragon Palace stands today. The twenty-eight senior officers were discussing how to meet the threat of the Song army. Of these, four were marshals: Buddha of Precious Light Deng Yuanjue the National Advisor, Marshal Shi Bao the Great Southerner, General Li Tianrun the National Suppressor, and General Si Xingfang the Defender of the Country. Their military titles had been conferred on them by Fang La.

"Since Song Jiang has crossed the Yangzi as the vanguard of a combined land and naval operation, we've lost to him three large shires," said Prince Fang Tianding. "Only Hangzhou remains as the bulwark of our Southern Country. If we lose that, how will Muzhou stand? Not long ago our Astrologer the eunuch Pu Wenying reported to the throne that stars of earthly fiends would be invading our Wu area, and indeed we have suffered heavy losses there, precisely to those Song forces. You officers all hold high ranks, you owe our nation the utmost loyalty. Let no one be remiss in his duties to the crown."

"Rest assured, Your Highness," the generals replied. "With our crack troops and fierce commanders, we're more than a match for Song Jiang. Although we've lost several prefectures, the officers in charge were all incompetents. That's why they were defeated. We hear that Song Jiang and Lu Junyi are advancing on Hangzhou in three columns. If Your Highness and the National Advisor will hold the district of Ninghai as our eternal base, we generals will go forth and meet the foe."

Very pleased, the prince ordered his army to divide into three columns also to counter the enemy offensive. He retained only National Advisor Teng as defender of the city. The other three marshals each commanded a column. Si Xingfang, with four generals, was ordered to go to the relief of Deqing Prefecture. Li Tianrun, with four generals, was directed to reinforce Lone Pine Pass. Shi Bao as commanding marshal, plus eight generals, were to meet the foe's main contingent.

Each marshal was presented with gold and silks as an encouragement to an early departure. Marshal Si, on the way to Deqing with his column, headed first for Fengkou Town. Marshal Li and his column's first objective on their march to Lone Pine Pass was the prefecture of Yuhang.

Song Jiang and his army, winding forward, arrived at Linping Mountain. They saw on the summit a swath of red flags and considerable activity. Song Jiang sent Hua Rong and Qin Ming ahead as advance pickets, and urged his naval officers to get their boats—which were being transported on wheels—across the Changan Dyke.

Hua Rong and Qin Ming, with a thousand men, rounded the entrance to the mountains and ran directly into Shi Bao and his southern troops.

Two of his generals promptly charged the two chieftains. One was named Wang Ren, the other Feng Yi, and each wielded a long lance. The Song contingent spread out in battle formation. Qin Ming, brandishing his wolf-toothed cudgel, took on Feng Yi. Hua Rong, lance at the level, met Wang Ren. The four steeds dashed together, and their riders fought more than ten rounds, with neither side emerging as victor. The two chieftains observed that the southern army was being reinforced from the rear.

"A brief rest," they called, and all rode back to their respective positions.

"Don't be so impatient for battle," Hua Rong said. "Report the news to Big Brother, quickly. He'll have to discuss this."

A dispatch was rushed to the Central Army. Song Jiang, accompanied by Zhu Tong, Xu Ning, Huang Xin and Sun Li, hurried to the front. Southern generals Wang Ren and Feng Yi rode forward once more.

"We dare you defeated officers to come out and Fight again," they yelled.

Qin Ming, angered, waved his wolf-toothed cudgel and galloped towards Feng Yi. Wang Ren challenged Hua Rong. Before Hua could respond, Xu Ning kicked his mount and raced out with levelled lance. Xu Ning and Hua Rong were first and second in command in their unit—one gold lancer, one silver. Hua Rong now hastened after, fitting an arrow to his bow. When he was close enough, before the two could clash, he shot. The feathered missile hit Wang Ren and knocked him from his saddle.

The southern troops were much disheartened. Feng Yi, startled to see his colleague fall, grew clumsy. A blow on the head from Qin Ming's cudgel felled him to the ground.

The southern soldiers scattered and fled, with the slaughtering Song army hot on their heels. Shi Bao was unable to stem the tide. He retreated to the Gaoting Mountains and made camp near New East Bridge. But the Southerners didn't feel secure. They withdrew into the city that evening.

By the next day, the imperial forces had already crossed the Gaoting Mountains and themselves made camp at New East Bridge. Song Jiang directed that the army divide into three columns and proceed against Hangzhou in a pincers offensive. The first column—an infantry unit —would march from the town of Tangzhen against the city's East Gate. The second column—a naval unit—would go from New North Bridge to take Gutang, cut the western approaches, and assail the city gates facing the lake.

The center column was to consist of infantry, cavalry and naval forces and be divided into three detachments. Their objectives were Hangzhou's Beiguan Gate and Genshan Gate. Behind the advance detachment would come Song Jiang,

Military Advisor Wu Yong and the overall command, followed by the third detachment—which would provide reinforcements and supplies on both land and water.

These dispositions having been agreed upon, the three columns set forth.

We'll speak first of the central column's advance detachment under Guan Sheng. Probing to New East Bridge, they encountered not a single southern soldier. Guan Sheng grew suspicious, pulled back and reported by messenger to Song Jiang, who then replied via Dai Zong.

"We cannot advance carelessly. Let two chieftains go out with pickets every day," was Song Jiang's order.

Hua Rong and Qin Ming went the first day, Xu Ning and Hao Siwen the second. But several days passed without any of the enemy coming forward to do battle.

Then Xu Ning and Hao Siwen, with a few dozen cavalry, roved as far as Hangzhou's Beiguan Gate. It was wide open. They rode up to the drawbridge. Battle drums thundered on the city wall, and out charged a troop of horsemen. The two chieftains hastily wheeled their mounts. Wild shouts rose on the road skirting the west of Hangzhou, and more than a hundred enemy cavalry galloped before them. Xu Ning, fighting desperately, managed to break through, but when he glanced back, there was no sign of Hao Siwen. Then he looked again, and saw scores of enemy officers leading the captured Hao into the city.

As Xu Ning hurriedly turned, and arrow struck him in the neck. He raced off with the missile still imbedded in his flesh, pursued by six southern generals. Luckily, he ran into Guan Sheng and was rescued, but he fainted from loss of blood. The six generals, chased off, returned to the city.

Guan Sheng hastily reported to Song Jiang, who rushed to see Xu Ning. The chieftain was bleeding from every orifice. Weeping, Song Jiang summoned an army doctor. The arrow as extracted and a salve for wounds from metal weapons applied. Song Jiang ordered that Xu Ning be placed on one of the naval vessels to rest, and he personally supervised the transfer. Four times Xu lapsed into unconsciousness. Only then did they realize he had been struck by a poisoned arrow. Song Jiang gazed up at the heavens and sighed.

"Our marvellous Dr. An Daoquan has been called to the capital. We have no talented physician here who can save him. We're going to lose another of our limbs!" Song Jiang was very distraught.

Wu Yong urged him to return to camp, and not let his feelings for a brother distract him from important military problems, to the detriment of the country. Song Jiang had Xu Ning sent to Xiuzhou to recuperate. Half a month of treatment was in vain. The poisoned arrow wound could not be cured, and Xu Ning died. But that was later.

Now, Song Jiang sent an agent into the midst of the foe to inquire about Hao Siwen. The next day he received a report: "On the city wall above the Beiguan Gate, Hao's head is hanging on display from a bamboo pole. We've just heard that Fang Tianding has cut his body to pieces!"

Song Jiang felt very badly. Half a month later, he received news of the death of Xu Ning. The loss of these two chieftains created difficulties for him in deploying his troops. He remained holding the highway.

Li Jun, whose column arrived at New North Bridge, sent a unit ahead to scout out the road to Gutang, deep in the hills. A report was quickly brought back: Hao Siwen had been decapitated and Xu Ning killed by a poisoned arrow.

"It seems to me," Li Jun said to Zhang Shun, "our main objective is the juncture of the roads to Lone Pine Pass and the Huzhou-Deqing sector. Enemy soldiers are in and out of there all the time. But while we're throttling their transport lines, they can be attacking us from two sides. We don't have enough men to meet a double assault. We'd be better off pushing into the western hills and setting up there. Our battlefield will be West Lake. Behind the hills is the road to Zhongxi. It's a good escape route."

He dispatched a junior officer to get Song Jiang's approval, then led his troops over Taoyuan Ridge into the western hills. They made camp at what is known as Lingyin Monastery. He also established a small encampment on the north side of the hills at Xixi Gap, today called Gutang Hollow. His forward pickets were at Tangjiawa.

"The southern soldiers have withdrawn into Hangzhou," Zhang Shun said to Li Jun. "They haven't come out to fight in half a month. If we just hang around in these hills we'll never earn any distinctions. What I'd like to do is swim across the lake, slip in under the water gate and set some fires. That will be your signal to assail the water gate. Once you've taken it, report the seizure to Big Brother, and all three columns can attack Hangzhou together."

"A good idea. But I'm afraid you can't do it alone."

"After all the kindness Big Brother has shown me over the years, it will be a small recompense."

"Wait at least till I've requested him to send us reinforcements."

"We can be doing both at the same time. He'll know by the time you've entered the city."

That evening, Zhang Shun concealed a sharp dagger on his person, ate a good meal replete with wine, and walked to the edge of West Lake. He gazed at the green hills on three sides, at the azure water, and peered across at the distant city, with its four closed gates fronting on the opposite shore. The gates were called Qiantang, Yongjin, Qingbo and Qianhu.

Reader, please note, West Lake was not then what it became subsequent to the southern migration. Only after the Golden Tartars and the Song Empire made peace and ended their warfare, and the emperor moved the capital to Hangzhou, did the area achieve its great prosperity. Dozens of scenic spots were set up along the lake. The green hills on three sides provided a remarkable background. The colorful boats and taverns, the cool pavilions overlooking the water, were indeed a pleasure to behold. As the famous Su Dongpo put it in one of his poems:

Neath Clear skies how charmingly glistens the lake,
Strangely lovely the hills when shrouded in rain.
West Lake may with Xi Zi compare,
Adorned or natural, equally fair.
Another of his verses remarks:

Hill after green tower beyond tower,
Song and dance at West Lake endlessly flow.
Visitors drunk on the heady warm breeze,
Consider Hangzhou another Bianzhou.

Subsequently others also wrote poems and rhymes about the beauties of West Lake—far too many to record.

On Xiling Bridge, Zhang Shun halted and stared for a long time. It was a warm spring day, the lake was a deep blue, the surrounding hills were jade green.

"I grew up on the Xunyang River and encountered many a wind and wave," Zhang Shun mused, "but never have I seen such an enthralling body of water! Whoever died here would be a happy ghost!"

He removed his cloth shirt and put it beneath the bridge. He bound his hair in a topknot with red yarn. He tied a silk skirt round his waist with a sash, and from this hung a dagger. Barefoot, he plunged into the lake and swam across under water. It was around the first watch, and the moon was pale.

When he neared Yongjin Gate, Zhang Shun raised his head above the surface and listened. A drum on the city wall struck the fourth interval of the first watch. The area between the wall and the lakefront was still and deserted. Four or five soldiers were watching from the ramparts. Zhang Shun quickly submerged. After a time, he again poked his head out. There was no one to be seen upon the wall.

He groped in the channel beneath the water gate. It was blocked by an iron lattice, and above that, a heavy drape. The ropes by which the drape was attached were hung with copper bells. Zhang Shun, finding the lattice-work impenetrable, tugged at the drape, setting the bells to jangling. Men shouted on the wall. Zhang Shun, moving swiftly beneath the surface, swam back to the lake.

Soldiers came down and examined the drape, but they couldn't find anyone, and returned to the ramparts. "Some large fish must have bumped into it," they concluded, "and set those bells off." They maintained a lookout for a while, then went back to sleep.

Zhang Shun listened. Soon, the drum on the wall struck the third watch. He waited a long time, till he was sure the soldiers were sleeping soundly. Then he crept ashore. Since he couldn't get in through the water gate, and since he couldn't see anyone on the wall, he decided he would attempt to climb over.

"If there are soldiers up there, I'll be throwing my life away," he said to himself. "Let's see."

He felt around for a clod of earth and tossed it up. Soldiers who weren't asleep raised a clamor. Again they descended and inspected the water gate, and again they found nothing. From the tower on the wall, they peered out at the lake. There wasn't a single boat anywhere. Prince Fang Tianding had ordered all craft to moor outside Qingbo Gate or in Jingci Cove, and no other place.

"Queer," the soldiers exclaimed. "It's surely a ghost. We'll just go to sleep and ignore it."

Although that was what they said, actually they didn't retire, but crouched vigilantly behind the ramparts. Zhang Shun listened for an entire watch. Nothing was stirring. He crept to the foot of the wall. There was no sound from the watchman's drum. Zhang Shun cautiously threw up another clod. Still no response.

"It's the fourth watch already. The sky will soon be light," he thought. "It's now or never!"

He was halfway up the wall when a loud tattoo roused the soldiers. He leaped down into the channel and started to swim. A deluge of arrows, javelins and stones poured into him from the ramparts. Poor heroic Zhang Shun gave his life in the channel at Yongjin Gate!

That same day, Song Jiang received a report from Li Jun: "Zhang Shun is swimming into Hangzhou. He'll set fires as a signal for us to attack." The information was transmitted to the troops outside of East Gate.

Song Jiang conferred in his tent with Wu Yong that night until the fourth watch. Wearily, he dismissed his aides and reclined his head on the table.

A sudden gust of icy wind brought him bolt upright. The lamplight dimmed. It was frightfully cold. When his eyes adjusted to the gloom, he saw a figure that was neither ghost nor human, standing in the chill mist. It was spattered with blood.

"Big Brother has lavished his kindness upon me for many years," said the figure in a low voice. "I offer my dead body as recompense. I was killed today by javelins and arrows at Yongjin Gate. I come to bid you farewell."

"Aren't you brother Zhang Shun?" Song Jiang cried. He turned and saw on the other side of the tent another three or four bloodstained figures. He couldn't make out who they were. He burst into tears and awoke. It had all been a dream.

Aides, hearing the sound of his weeping, rushed into the tent. "How strange," said Song Jiang. He asked the military advisor to interpret the dream for him.

"You were just over-tired," said Wu Yong, "and you had a nightmare."

Song Jiang told exactly what had occurred in his dream. Wu Yong replied soothingly: "Didn't Li Jun say that Zhang Shun was going to cross the lake and set signal fires in the city? It was on your mind and you had a bad dream."

"Zhang Shun was a very clever fellow. If he perished, it surely was a blameless death," Song Jiang avowed.

"That's a very dangerous stretch, from the shore to the city wall. It's quite probable he lost life, and his ghost came in a dream to inform you."

"But who were the other three or four?"

Neither Song Jiang nor Wu Yong could guess. They sat talking until daybreak. Nothing seemed to be happening in the city, and this made them all the more suspicious.

In the afternoon, Li Jun rushed a dispatch to them: "Zhang Shun tried to scale the wall at Yongjin Gate, and was killed in the water by arrows! His head is hanging from a bamboo pole on the wall west of the lake!"

Song Jiang wept and collapsed in a faint. Wu Yong and the other chieftains all felt terrible. Zhang Shun was exceptionally good to people, and was very well liked.

"I feel worse than if I lost my father or mother," cried Song Jiang. "The agony goes to my very heart and marrow!"

"You should concentrate on important national affairs, brother," Wu Yong and the chieftains urged. "Don't let your grief injure your health."

"I must go to the lakeside and mourn him."

"It's too risky. If the enemy finds out, they'll surely attack."

"I know how to deal with that."

Song Jiang sent Li Kui, Bao Xu, Xiang Chong and Li Gun on ahead with five hundred infantry to reconnoitre. He himself followed with Shi Xiu, Dai Zong, Fan Rui and Ma Lin and another five hundred. They proceeded quietly along the paths in the western hills towards Li Jun's camp. On learning that they were coming, Li Jun met them halfway. He led the chieftains into the meditation hall of the Lingyin Monastery for a rest. Song Jiang again wept. He asked the monks to pray that Zhang Shun's ghost be allowed to become a spirit and enter Heaven.

The next evening, he directed a junior officer to erect a white banner on Xiling Bridge by the lake shore, reading: *Soul of Departed Brother and General Zhang Shun,* and lay out many objects for a sacrificial ceremony. He also gave secret instructions to Li Kui. At the start of the road leading to the northern hills he put Fan Rui, Ma Lin and Shi Xiu into ambush on both sides of the bridge. Dai Zong he kept with him.

Shortly before the first watch, Song Jiang donned a white robe and golden helmet bound in mourning silk, and walked with Dai Zong and six or seven monks from Small Stroll Hill to Xiling Bridge. The young officer had already tethered a black pig and a white sheep, laid out sacrificial objects of gold and silver, and lit candles and lanterns and incense.

Song Jiang testified to his friendship with Zhang Shun and, facing the Yongjin Gate, wept. Dai Zong stood by his side. The monks rang their bells and chanted scriptures. They called to the soul of Zhang Shun, beseeching it to descend on the spirit flag. Then Dai Zong read the sacrificial address, and Song Jiang poured the libation wine upon the ground. Weeping, he raised his head to the eastern heavens.

Suddenly, shouts arose on either side of the bridge. Drums thundered in the northern and southern hills, and from each direction a troop of horsemen came tearing down to seize Song Jiang.

Truly, a place of sacrifice to a chivalrous departed comrade became a small battlefield in the service of the sovereign; the slaughter of a few southern officers stirred the waves of West Lake sky high.

How did Song Jiang and Dai Zong meet the foe? Read our next chapter if you would know.

CHAPTER 95

ZHANG SHUN'S GHOST CATCHES FANG TIANDING

SONG JIANG BY A RUSE TAKES NINGHAI DISTRICT

When he went with Dai Zong to sacrifice to the spirit of Zhang Shun at Xiling Bridge, Song Jiang hadn't realized that Prince Fang Tianding knew about it and ordered two columns under ten generals to capture him. Now these burst out of the city and came charging forward, five via the southern hills, five via the northern, leading a total of three thousand soldiers. They had emerged through the Front and Rear Gates around midnight.

The imperial units lying in ambush to the left and right of the bridge, five thousand men in each, saw the torches on the road ahead. They promptly lit their own torches and advanced in two bodies to meet Prince Fang's contingents marching from the northern and southern hills. Finding their foe prepared and waiting, the Southerners beat a hasty retreat, pursued by imperial forces on either flank.

One column, hurrying to go back across the river, was surprised by the Ruan brothers' unit of five thousand. It swarmed out from behind Baoshu Pagoda Hill, cut off the escape route, captured one general and killed another. The other column was intercepted at Dingxiang Bridge by five hundred infantry under Li Kui. Shield twirlers Xiang Chong and Li Gun plunged in among the foe, and their throwing knives quickly dispatched a southern general. Bao Xu hacked another down with his sword, while Li Kui's axes cleaved a third in twain. Most of the southern soldiers were driven into the lake and drowned.

By the time reinforcements rushed from the city Song Jiang's troops had withdrawn into the hills. They reassembled at the Lingyin Monastery, and each hero came forward to claim his reward. Together, the two units had captured more than five hundred good horses.

Song Jiang left Shi Xiu, Fan Rui and Ma Lin to aid Li Jun in guarding the hillside emplacement overlooking West Lake, and ordered them to prepare to assault the city. He returned with Dai Zong and Li Kui to the camp on Mount Gaoting. He met with Wu Yong and other chieftains in his tent.

"By following our plan," he said to the military advisor, "we've already killed four of their generals and captured a fifth. We're sending him to Governor Zhang for execution."

Only the situation in Lone Pine Pass and Deqing was unknown to Song Jiang. He sent Dai Zong to find out. A few days later the Marvellous Traveller returned and reported.

"Lu Junyi has taken Lone Pine Pass and sooner or later will be arriving in this sector."

Pleased but worried, Song Jiang asked: "How are our officers and men?"

"I have the whole story. But you'd better read it in this dispatch. Please don't be upset."

"We must have lost more of our brothers. Don't try and conceal anything. Tell me everything frankly."

"Lone Pine Pass has high mountains on either side, with only a single road running through it. On the heights, controlling the pass is a fort, and beside it is a tree, dozens of meters high, from which a lookout can see far in every direction. Below are groves of pine. Three generals command the fort. The first is called Wu Sheng, the second Jiang Yin, the third Wei Heng. In the beginning they came down every day and battled with Panther Head Lin Chong until he wounded Jiang Yin with his lance. After that, Wu Sheng dared not come out, but remained holding the pass."

"Then Li Tianyou and four other southern generals arrived as reinforcements. They emerged the next day and gave battle. Lu Fang killed Li Tianyou with his lance after nearly sixty rounds. The enemy soldiers retreated into the pass and remained there. Our troops waited in vain for several days. General Lu sent Ou Peng, Deng Fei, Li Zhong and Zhou Tong to find an approach up the sharp and dangerous mountain heights. They were taken by surprise by Li Tianrun, who charged out of the fort to avenge his brother. With one sweep of his sword he killed Zhou Tong, and Li Zhong was wounded. If our rescue force hadn't arrived in time, all four scouts would have been lost. As it was, three were able to return to camp."

"The next day General Two Spears Dong Ping, burning for vengeance, reined his steed at the foot of the pass and loudly reviled the enemy commanders. A cannon ball skimmed him so closely that the concussion injured his left arm. He couldn't use his lance and had to return to camp and have the arm put in splints.

"He wanted to go out again the next day, but Lu Junyi wouldn't let him. Another night passed. The arm was slightly better. Without telling General Lu, Dong Ping conferred secretly with Zhang Qin, and the two set out on foot. Li Tianrun and Zhang Tao came down from the fort to give battle. Dong wanted to take Li alive, and they fought ten rounds. But Dong's skill didn't match his zeal. His left arm had been wounded and he had to fall back. Li drove him out of the pass.

"Zhang Qin then thrust at Li with his lance. Li dodged behind a pine. The point of the weapon sank deep into the tree. While Zhang was frantically trying to pull it out, Li stabbed him through the stomach, and he collapsed to the ground. Dong saw him go down, and he started to rush forward with his two spears. But Zhang Tao, behind him, swung his sword and cleaved him in twain at the waist.

"By the time General Lu learned about the fight, it was too late to go to the rescue, and the enemy soldiers had already withdrawn to their fort. There was nothing he could do about it.

"He sent Sun Xin and Mistress Gu, husband and wife disguised as refugees, deep into the mountains, where they found a path to the fort. They led LiLi, Tang Long, Shi Qian and Bai Sheng up this path in the middle of the night and set the fort on fire. The southern generals realized our forces were already in the pass, so they abandoned the fort and fled. When General Lu took over and made a count of our troops, he discovered that Sun Xin and Mistress Gu had captured southern general Wu Sheng, LiLi and Tang Long had nabbed Jiang Yin, and Shi Qian and Bai Sheng had caught Wei Heng—the original commanders of the fort. All three were delivered to Governor Zhang. The bodies of Dong Ping, Zhang Qin and Zhou Tong were recovered and buried above the pass.

"General Lu chased the enemy soldiers forty-five *li* beyond the pass, caught up and engaged Li Tianrun in battle. They fought more than thirty rounds, and Lu killed Li with his lance. The southern reinforcement troops were in no condition to fight, and they retreated with the three remaining generals. Lu Junyi will be here soon. If you don't believe me, Commander-in-Chief, you can read this dispatch."

Song Jiang read the document, deeply depressed. Tears gushed from his eyes.

"General Lu has won a victory," said Wu Yong. "We can move troops to form the other side of a pincers. We'll surely defeat the Southerners. What we should do now is link up with Huyan Zhuo's column in Huzhou."

"You're absolutely right," said Song Jiang.

He ordered Li Kui, Bao Xu, Xiang Chong and Li Gun to go with three thousand infantry over the hills and make the connection. Black Whirlwind, thanking Heaven and Earth, set forth with the contingent.

For his attack on Hangzhou's East Gate, Song Jiang dispatched Zhu Tong with five thousand infantry and cavalry. They advanced rapidly along the Tangzhen road from the village where they had been camped to a point outside Vegetable Market Gate, as the East Gate was also known. The eastern suburbs along the river were then heavily populated, with more homes and shops than in the city, and many vegetable gardens and orchards. Here, the Song forces spread out, and Sagacious Lu, iron staff in hand, strode to the foot of the walls.

"Come out, you friggin barbarians," he shouted. "I dare you to fight!" The soldiers on the ramparts hurriedly reported to the prince's palace. Monk of Precious Light Deng Yuanjue the National Advisor, learning that it was a monk who was issuing the challenge, addressed himself to the prince.

"I've heard that in Liangshan Marsh there is a monk called Sagacious Lu who wields an iron staff," he said. "If Your Highness will mount the wall at East Gate, you can watch me go a few rounds with him."

Prince Fang Tianding was very pleased. He issued his instructions. Accompanied by Marshal Shi Bao, he went with his eight top generals to Vegetable Market Gate. The gate was opened, the drawbridge lowered, and Deng and five hundred infantry swordsmen sped forth.

"So the southern army has a shaven-pate of its own," Sagacious Lu said to himself. "I'll give the churl a hundred licks of my staff!" Without a word, he charged.

In the shadows of the weeping willows, on the lush green turf, two silvery serpents flew, a pair of jade dragons leaped. The furious Lu had not a bit of cleanliness in his heart. The angry Deng was completely devoid of compassion. When did the first ever respect the Buddhist laws? He murdered people in the dark of the moon! When did the second ever read the scriptures? He set fires when the wind was high!

They fought more than fifty rounds, but neither could vanquish the other. Prince Fang, watching from the wall top, was filled with admiration.

"I've heard of Sagacious Lu the Tattooed Monk of Liangshan Marsh, but I didn't realize he was so formidable! He certainly deserves his reputation," he said to Shi Bao. "Fighting all this time, he hasn't yielded an inch to our Precious Light Monk."

"I'm dazzled myself," said the marshal. "I've never seen such a match!"

Just then, a mounted messenger galloped up and reported: "More enemy troops at Beiguan Gate!" Shi Bao hastily left the prince.

Wu Song the Pilgrim saw that Sagacious could not defeat the Precious Light, and he feared there might be an accident. Brandishing his pair of swords, he charged. The National Advisor knew he couldn't cope with the two of them. He retreated into the city. Wu Song started to pursue, but out through the gate galloped a ferocious commander. He was Bei Yingkui, one of Prince Fang's generals, and he assailed Wu Song with levelled lance.

They clashed on the drawbridge. Wu Song closed in, cast aside one sword, grasped his opponent's lance and, with a yank, pulled man and weapon from the saddle. Slash went his blade, and Bei's head rolled on the ground, Sagacious Lu moved up with reinforcements.

Prince Fang hurriedly ordered his men to raise the drawbridge, and pulled his troops back into the city. Zhu Tong withdrew the Song forces ten *li* and made camp. He dispatched a messenger to Song Jiang reporting the victory.

That day Song Jiang had led his troops to Beiguan Gate and challenged the foe to battle. Southern general Shi Bao took his Comet Hammer and mounted. Carrying his Wind Splitter sword, he had the city gate opened and rode forth. From the Song army, Big Halberd Guan Sheng cantered out to meet him. More than twenty rounds they fought, then Shi Bao turned his steed and withdrew. Guan Sheng quickly checked his horse and returned to his position.

"Why didn't you pursue?" Song Jiang queried.

"His swordsmanship is in no way inferior to mine," said the Big Halberd. "When he retreats like that, he must be up to some trick."

"Duan Kaizeng says the man flings a comet hammer," Wu Yong interjected. "He rides off, feigning defeat, and lures his adversary deep into enemy territory."

"If we go after him, he'll play us dirty," said Song Jiang. "We'll recall our troops and go back to camp." He dispatched a man with a reward for Wu Song.

Meanwhile, Li Kui marched with his infantry to join Lu Junyi. On a mountain road they ran into Zhang Jian and his defeated soldiers, and fiercely attacked, killing southern general Yao Yi in the course of the wild skirmish. Zhang Jian and Zhang Tao fled towards the pass, but were intercepted by General Lu Junyi. After another big clash, the two southern generals fled along a path into the mountains. Their pursuers were hot on their heels. They had no choice but to abandon their mounts and plunge ahead on foot.

But then, from a bamboo thicket, two men suddenly emerged. Each held a steel pitchfork. Before the southerners could defend themselves, they were knocked flat by the two and hauled down the slope. Their captors were none other than Xie Zhen and Xie Bao.

When General Lu saw the two prisoners he was very pleased. Joining forces with Black Whirlwind Li Kui, he proceeded to the main camp on Mount Gaoting. He told Song Jiang of the deaths of Dong Ping, Zhang Qin and Zhou Tong. Both men were deeply grieved. The other chieftains in Lu's army paid their respects to Song Jiang, and the reunited units made camp.

The next day Song Jiang sent Zhang Jian to the Governor in Suzhou to be executed and his head hung up on display. Zhang Tao was disemboweled in front of the camp and his heart raised towards Heaven in a sacrifice to Dong Ping, Zhang Qin and Zhou Tong.

"I'm going to ask General Lu to go with has contingent to the Deqing County road," Song Jiang said to Wu Yong, "connect with Huyan Zhuo's column and come back here together, to join in our attack on Hangzhou City."

Lu accepted the mission, mustered his troops, and marched in the direction of Fengkou Town. Just as they arrived, they ran into the returning defeated forces of Si Xiangfang. A murderous battle ensued. Si fell into the water and drowned. What was left of his soldiers fled. Lu and Huyan combined units and returned to Song Jiang in the camp at Mount Gaoting.

The reassembled chieftains conferred. Now that the two main columns had reached Hangzhou, Song Jiang left control of Xuanzhou, Huzhou and Lone Pine Pass to Governor Zhang and staff officer Cong, who would keep the peace in all captured territory.

He noticed that Lei Heng and Gong Wang were missing from Huyan Zhuo's contingent. Huyan told him what had happened.

"Lei Heng fought Si Xingfang for twenty rounds outside the South Gate of Deqing County Town, and Si hacked him from his steed. Gong battled Huang Ai. Huang drove him into the stream. Horse and rider fell, and the southern soldiers stabbed him to death with their spears. Suo Chao split southern commander Mi Quan open with his ax. We captured Generals Huang Ai and Xu Bai. We drove Si Xingfang into the water and he drowned. Xue Dounan managed to escape in the confusion of battle. We don't know where he's gone."

Song Jiang's tears fell like rain at the news of the death of Lei Heng and Gong Wang. "Zhang Shun appeared to me in a dream the other day," he said to his chieftains, "and I saw to the right of him several bloodstained figures. I know now that they were the ghosts of Dong Ping, Zhang Qin, Zhou Tong, Lei Heng and Gong Wang. If I can take Hangzhou and Ninghai District, I shall ask the monks to conduct a fine service to ensure the passage of our brothers' souls into Heaven."

He had Huang Ai and Xu Bai delivered to Governor Zhang for execution. Of them we'll say no more.

That day he ordered that cattle and horses be slaughtered and gave a banquet for his army. The next day he and Wu Yong planned the division of their forces for the Hangzhou offensive.

Lu Junyi, with twelve senior and lieutenant commanders, would at tack the Houchao Gate. The twelve commanders were Li Chong, Huyan Zhuo, Liu Tang, Xie Zhen, Xie Bao, Shang Tinggui, Wei Dingguo, Chen Da, Yang Chun, Du Qian, Li Yun and Shi Yong.

Hua Rong would strike Genshan Gate with fourteen senior and lieutenant commanders, who were, apart from Hua Rong himself, Qin Ming, Zhu Wu, Huang Xin, Sun Li, Li Zhong, Zou Yuan, Zou Run, LiLi, Bai Sheng, Tang Long, Mu Chun, Zhu Gui and Zhu Fu.

Supported by ten chieftains, Mu Hong would proceed to the camp in the western hills to help Li Jun assault the gates fronting on the West Lake. The eleven commanders were Li Jun, Ruan the Second, Ruan the Fifth, Meng Kang, Shi Xiu, Fan Rui, Ma Lin, Mu Hong, Yang Xiong, Xue Yong and Ding Desun.

Sun Xin and other seven commanders would go to the camp outside East Gate and assist Zhu Tong in attacking Vegetable Market and Jianqiao gates. The seven chieftains were Zhu Tong, Shi Jin, Sagacious Lu, Wu Song, Mistress Gu, Sun Erniang and Zhang Qing.

From the East Gate camp eight chieftains were chosen who would handle intelligence and logistics. They were Li Ying, Kong Ming, Yang Lin, Du Xing, Tong Meng, Tong Wei, Wang Ying and Hu the Ten Feet of Steel.

Song Jiang himself was to lead twenty-one senior and lieutenant commanders to attack along the road to Beiguan Gate. These commanders were Wu Yong, Guan Sheng, Suo Qiao, Dai Zong, Li Kui, Lu Fang, Guo Sheng, Ou Peng, Deng Fei, Yan Shun, Ling Zhen, Bao Xu, Xiang Chong, Li Gun, Song Qing, Pei Xuan, Jiang Jing, Cai Fu, Cai Qing, Shi Qian and Yu Baosi.

Thus, the gates on all four sides of the city would be assailed.

Song Jiang and his contingent pushed right up to the Beiguan Gate and issued their challenge. Drums and gongs sounded on the walls, the gate was opened, the drawbridge lowered, and Shi Bao rode forth to give battle. Suo Chao the Urgent Vanguard, impetuous as always, galloped out, waving his big ax, and engaged him.

After less than ten rounds, Shi Bao executed a feint and withdrew. Suo Chao, ignoring Guan Sheng's shout of warning, pursued. A flying hammer suddenly struck Suo Chao full in the face, knocking him from his saddle. Deng Fei rushed to the rescue, but Shi Bao's horse got there first. Before Deng could defend himself, Shi Bao, with one sweep of the sword, cut him in two.

At this, the monk Precious Light the National Advisor came charging out of the city with a number of fierce commanders. Song Jiang's unit, badly defeated, retreated north. Hua Rong and Qin Ming slashed into the pursuing southerners from the side and drove them off, then escorted Song Jiang back to camp. The victorious Shi Bao returned to Hangzhou in jubilation.

Song Jiang, in his tent in the Mount Gaoting camp, brooded over the loss of Suo Chao and Deng Fei.

"There are some very tough generals in that city," Wu Yong said. "We can only take it by guile, not by direct confrontation."

"We keep losing men. How do you propose to do it?"

"You've already arranged for our army to assault all of the gates. Hit the Beiguan Gate again tomorrow. The foe is sure to come out and fight. We'll pretend to be defeated and lead them far from the city. At the sound of a signal cannon, our other forces will then hit all the gates at once. Whichever one manages to break in will immediately set fires as a signal calling for reinforcements. The enemy soldiers won't know which way to turn, and we'll win a big victory."

Song Jiang directed Dai Zong to transmit the appropriate orders. On his instructions, Guan Sheng went with a small cavalry troop the next day to Beiguan Gate and challenged the foe. Drums pounded on the walls and Shi Bao again rode forth with a contingent. The southern general engaged Guan Sheng. They had fought less than ten rounds when Guan Sheng hastily retreated. Shi Bao and his soldiers gave chase. Ling Zhen Fired a cannon. At this signal, the Song troops shouted and attacked the city gates in simultaneous drives.

We'll tell first of the assault on Houchao Gate by General Lu Junyi with Lin Chong and the others. As they neared the city they saw that the gate was open and the drawbridge down. Liu Tang, eager to win first honors, galloped straight in, sword in hand. The soldiers on the wall cut the rope and dropped the slab gate. Poor Liu Tang. Both he and his horse were quickly killed in the gateway.

When Hangzhou became the capital in the days of King Qian, he built the city gates in three layers. The outermost was a slab gate, next was a two-leafed set of iron doors, and innermost was a large grill gate. As soon as the slab gate dropped behind him, Liu Tang was attacked by soldiers who had been hiding on both sides. How could he not die?

Lin Chong and Huyan Zhuo went back with their men to headquarters and reported to Lu Junyi. None of the Song troops had succeeded in forcing any of the gates, and all withdrew. A messenger raced with the news to Song Jiang in the main camp. He wept bitterly over the death of Liu Tang.

"Another brother gone! From the day we pledged brotherhood in Yuncheng County and went with Chao Gai into Liangshan Marsh, Liu suffered years of tribulation. He never knew any happiness. But he survived hundreds of battles and engagements and never lost his fighting spirit. Who would have thought he'd die in this place today!"

"That plan was no good," Wu Yong admitted. "Not only did it fail, but we lost a brother to the bargain. Call our troops back from the gates. We'll think of something else."

Song Jiang was very upset. He longed for quick vengeance and sighed without end. Black Whirlwind tried to reassure him.

"Don't worry, brother. I'll go out tomorrow with Bao Xu, Xiang Chong and Li Gun. One way or another we'll take that oaf Shi Bao."

"He's a remarkable hero. You won't even get near him."

"I don't believe it. If I don't nab him tomorrow, you'll never see me again!"

"Be very careful. He's no pushover."

Li Kui went to his own tent, poured out a big bowl of wine, piled a platter with sliced beef, and asked Bao Xu, Xiang Chong and Li Gun to join him.

"We four have always fought as a team," he said. "I just bragged to Big Brother that we were going to capture Shi Bao tomorrow. I don't want any of you holding back."

"Big Brother is always letting the cavalry take the lead," said Bao Xu. "We four must vow here and now that we'll show what our infantry can do. When we grab that churl tomorrow we'll be able to hold our heads high."

The following morning the four ate and drank their fill, took up their weapons and prepared to march. "Watch us slaughter them," they said.

Song Jiang saw that they were half drunk. "Don't you go throwing your lives away," he admonished.

"You underestimate us, brother!" Li Kui replied.

"I just hope you keep your word."

Mounting, Song Jiang rode with cavalry commanders Guan Sheng, Ou Peng, Lu Fang and Guo Sheng to Beiguan Gate. They beat drums, waved banners and challenged combat. The fiery Li Kui planted himself before them, brandishing his axes. Bao Xu, holding a big broad cutlass, glared wildly, waiting only for the carnage to start. Xiang Chong and Li Gun grasped their shields, each fitted with twenty-four throwing knives, and stood on either side with levelled spears.

On the wall, drums thundered and gongs crashed, and Shi Bao rode forth on a melon-yellow steed, carrying his Wind Splitter Sword. He was accompanied by two generals named Wu Zhi and Lian Ming. They advanced to meet their adversaries.

Li Kui was a man who feared neither Heaven nor Earth. With a roar, he and his three companions rushed Shi Bao. They were upon him by the time the Wind Splitter was raised. Li Kui swung his ax and broke the leg of Shi's horse. Shi leaped from the saddle and took refuge among his cavalry.

Bao Xu had already hacked Lian Ming from his steed, and the throwing knives of the two shield-wielders were darting everywhere like jade fish and silver needles. Song Jiang sent his cavalry in a charge up to the walls. They were greeted by a deluge of logs and ballista stones from the ramparts. He hurriedly called them back. He saw Bao Xu plunging through the city gate. Song Jiang could only groan.

Shi Bao was hiding within the gate. When Bao Xu came running in, he dealt him a slanting blow from the side that cut him in two. Xiang Chong and Li Gun quickly covered Li Kui and the three retreated. Song Jiang and his contingent returned to camp. His gloom deepened over the death of Bao Xu. Li Kui also wept.

"This plan was no good either," said Wu Yong. "Although we killed one of their generals, we've lost Li Kui's right-hand man."

Everyone was very depressed. Just then the Xie brothers returned with a report. Song Jiang directed that they speak in detail.

"I scouted with Xie Bao twenty or so *li* from Hangzhou's South Gate to a place called Fan Village," said Xie Zhen. "We saw moored along the river bank a line of several dozen boats, and went down for a look. It turned out that they were a convoy of grain vessels commanded by an administrator named Yuan from Fuyang County. We were going to kill him, but he cried and said: 'We're all good citizens of the Great Song Empire, but Fang La is crushing us with levies. If any man refuses to pay, he and his whole family are slaughtered. We've heard that the imperial soldiers have come to remove the blight. We want nothing more than to see peace again. We're sick of all this suffering!'"

"He obviously was honest, so we didn't kill him. We asked: 'What are you doing here?' He said: 'The counties received an order from Prince Fang Tianding to clean out the reserves of all the villages and hand over fifty thousand bushels of white rice. I was put in charge, and was on my way to turn over what's been collected so far—five thousand bushels. Because your great army has surrounded the city and there's fighting, we haven't dared go any closer, and are laying over here temporarily.' That's the whole story, General. We've returned specially to let you know."

Wu Yong was delighted. He said: "This is a Heaven-sent chance. Those grain vessels will serve us well." And he requested Song Jiang to issue the following order: "Let the Xie brothers lead a group of fifteen chieftains, disguised as boatmen and their wives. They are not to say a word, but mix with the crews and sail with them into the city. Once there, let Ling Zhen fire a volley of cannon shots. That will be our signal to move up troops as reinforcements."

The Xie brothers called Administrator Yuan ashore and informed him of Song Jiang's instructions. "As good Song Dynasty citizens you must carry them out," they said. "After it's over, you'll be handsomely rewarded."

Yuan had no choice but to comply. Many army officers boarded the craft and took over as boatmen. The original boatmen were put to other tasks. Wang Ying, Sun Xin and Zhang Qing changed clothes with three of them, and their wives Ten Feet of Steel, Mistress Gu and Sun the Witch disguised themselves as boatwomen. Junior officers manned the sweep oars. Weapons were hidden in the holds. The boats then sailed to the banks outside the city.

The Song forces were not far from Hangzhou's gates. Administrator Yuan went ashore, followed by Xie Zhen, Xie Bao and many of the boatmen. They walked up to the gate and demanded entry. Soldiers on the wall queried them, then informed the palace. Prince Fang Tianding sent Wu Zhi, who went out, counted the vessels, returned and reported. Fang ordered six generals to go forth with ten thousand soldiers and guard the northeast approaches while Yuan sailed in with his convoy. The chieftains and their wives, mingled with the crews, went in together. The five thousand bushels of grain were soon unloaded, and the six southern generals marched back into the city with their troops.

Song Jiang's forces again ringed Hangzhou at a distance of only two or three *li* and spread out in battle deployment. At the second watch, Ling Zhen went with nine cases of Mother and Sons small cannons to the top of Wushan Hill and set them off. The chieftains lit torches and started blazes in many parts of the city. All Hangzhou was thrown into confusion. They had no idea how many Song troops had entered the city.

Prince Fang in his palace was shocked. He hastily donned his armor and mounted. But by then the soldiers on the walls above the gates had fled from their posts. The Song units launched a massive offensive, all eager to gain glory in capturing the city.

Meanwhile in the hills to the west Li Jun, on receiving his orders, led his unit rapidly to Pure Benevolence Cove, obtained boats, and crossed West Lake. They landed near Yongjin Gate and began seizing each of the water gates. Li Jun and Shi Xiu started by climbing over the wall. In the darkness of night they engaged in mixed fracases.

Only South Gate was unbesieged. Through this the defeated southern army fled. Prince Fang, on his horse, couldn't find a single officer. Scurrying like a cur whose master has died, frantic as a fish dodging the net, he left Hangzhou accompanied by only a few infantrymen.

At the foot of Five Clouds Hill, they saw a man, buff naked, emerge from the river, a knife in his teeth, and leap upon the bank. Frightened by this fierce apparition, Prince Fang struck his mount and tried to flee. But no matter how he flailed, the animal refused to budge. It was as if someone was grasping its bridle.

The man ran up, pulled Fang from the saddle and cut off his head with a single sweep of the knife. The head in one hand, the knife in the other, the man then mounted Fang's horse and galloped towards Hangzhou.

Lin Chong and Huyan Zhuo encountered him just as they reached Six Harmonies Pagoda with their troops. They recognized him in astonishment as Zhang Heng the Boat Flame. "Where are you coming from, brother?" Huyan called. Zhang Heng didn't reply, but continued racing towards the city.

Song Jiang and his main force had already entered Hangzhou. He made Prince Fang's palace his headquarters. The chieftains in occupation were startled to see Zhang Heng galloping up. He rode directly to Song Jiang, rolled from the saddle, flung the head and the knife on the ground, kowtowed twice, and burst into tears. Song Jiang embraced him.

"Brother, where have you come from? And where is Ruan the Seventh?"

"I'm not Zhang Heng."

"If you're not Zhang Heng, who are you?"

"I'm Zhang Shun. Because I was killed by spears and arrows in the channel outside Yongjin Gate, a trace of my spirit refused to leave and floated on the water. This moved the Marsh-Shaking Dragon King residing in West Lake. He made me Lord of Jinhua and kept me on in his underwater Dragon Palace as a spirit noble. When you were breaking into Hangzhou today, brother, I dogged the footsteps of Prince Fang and, in the middle of the night, followed him out of the city. I saw brother Zhang Heng on the river, borrowed his body, flew up the bank, hastened to the foot of Five Clouds Hill, killed that scoundrel and hurried back to see you!"

He fainted dead away. Song Jiang raised him up. Zhang Heng opened his eyes. He saw Song Jiang and the chieftains, the bristling swords, the crowds of soldiers.

"Is it in the Nether Regions that I'm seeing you, brother?" he asked.

Song Jiang wept. "You loaned brother Zhang Shun your body and he killed the rogue Prince Fang. You're not dead. We're all very much alive. You're fine."

"That means, then, that my brother is dead!"

"Zhang Shun tried to swim under a water gate on West Lake and get into the city and set fires. But he was discovered and killed outside the gate by spears and arrows."

Zhang Heng wept bitterly. "Brother!" he cried, and collapsed to the ground, unconscious. His limbs were rigid, his eyes closed. His seven souls and three spirits hung in the balance.

Truly, if he hadn't gone with the King of Hell's commanding general, he surely would have been called by Hell's Summoner.

What was the outcome for Zhang Heng, crushed by distress? Read our next chapter if you would know.

CHAPTER 96

LU JUNYI ASSAILS THE SHEZHOU ROAD

SONG JIANG BATTLES ON BLACK DRAGON RIDGE

At last Zhang Heng was revived.

"Help him into a tent," said Song Jiang, "and give him medical treatment. Ask him what happened along the coast."

He instructed Pei Xuan and Jiang Jing to record the valorous deeds of the chieftains in the recent fighting. By then it was morning, and all had gathered in the camp. Li Jun and Shi Xiu had captured southern general Wu Zhi; the three women chieftains had caught Zhang Daoyuan; Lin Chong, with his long serpent lance, had run Leng Gong through; and the Xie brothers had killed Cui Yu. Only five of the southern commanders had escaped.

Song Jiang issued a proclamation reassuring the populace and rewarded his troops. Zhang Daoyuan was sent to Governor Zhang for execution. In a written dispatch, Song Jiang recommended that Administrator Yuan, who had contributed his grain, be appointed magistrate of Fuyang County. The governor issued a certificate of office with the name left blank. Of that we'll say no more.

The chieftains rested in the city. An aide reported: "Ruan the Seventh is here. He's come by way of the river." Song Jiang summoned him to his tent and questioned him. Seventh told his story.

"I set out with Zhang Heng, Hou Jian and Duan Jingzhu and our men, and along the coast we found boats. We sailed off Haiyan, intending to go inland up the Qiantang River. But the winds and tides were against us and we were driven out to sea. When we tried to get back, the gale capsized us, throwing everyone in the water. Hou Jian and Duan Jingzhu couldn't swim and were drowned. Most of the sailors managed to survive, but scattered in all directions. I swam to Haikou and got as far as Ochre Hill Gate, when the tide swept me to Banfan Hill, and I swam ashore there. I saw brother Zhang Heng in the river off Five Clouds Hill. I waited for him to come up the bank, but then he disappeared again. Last night I saw the light of the fires here in Hangzhou, and I heard the cannon. I figured you must be fighting in the city, so I swam here up the river. Has brother Zhang Heng come ashore yet?"

Song Jiang told him about Zhang Heng, then had him rejoin his brothers. He instructed the three Ruans to resume their duties as naval commanders. He also ordered all naval chieftains to gather their boats on the river and get ready to sail against Muzhou.

Because the spirit of Zhang Shun had appeared in human form, he built a temple to him on the banks of West Lake outside Yongjin Gate, calling it Lord of Jinhua and sacrificing there. Later, after defeating Fang La and earning honors, Song Jiang returned to the capital and reported Zhang Shun's feat. The emperor bestowed the posthumous title of General of Jinhua. The temple to Zhang Shun's memory has remained in Hangzhou.

Song Jiang was deeply saddened by the loss of so many chieftains since crossing the Yangzi. In the Pure Benevolence Monastery he had prayer services conducted for seven days and seven nights, dispensed charity, sacrificed to the spirits of the departed, prayed for their smooth passage into Heaven, and set up memorial tablets. After these good deeds were done, he destroyed all of Prince Fang's paraphernalia of rank and office and distributed his valuables among the Song army officers.

Peace was restored to Hangzhou, and the people feasted in celebration. Song Jiang conferred with Military Advisor Wu Yong on a long-range plan for the offensive against Muzhou.

It was by then the end of the fourth lunar month. Suddenly, the report came in: "Deputy District Commander Liu Guangshi has arrived with an emissary from the capital." Song Jiang and his chieftains met them outside Beiguan Gate and welcomed them into the city. At headquarters the imperial decree was read.

Vanguard General Song Jiang: You have attained great merit in the war to wipe out Fang La. We bestow thirty-five bottles of imperial wine and thirty-five sets of silk clothing as rewards to your senior commanders. To the lieutenant commanders we bestow bolts of satin.

The monarch only knew that Gongsun Sheng had not crossed the river with them, but not that they had suffered heavy casualties.

At the sight of the thirty-five sets of clothes and thirty five bottles of imperial wine Song Jiang's heart was stricken, and tears flowed from his eyes. The emissary asked him what was wrong. Song told him of the loss of the chieftains.

"The emperor hasn't heard," cried the emissary. "I shall certainly tell him when I get back."

Song Jiang gave a banquet for the emissary and Liu, attended by all the remaining chieftains, big and small. They drank the imperial wine and expressed thanks to the monarch for his kindness. The wine and clothing intended for the chieftains who had died were kept.

The following day Song Jiang took one bottle and one set of clothes to Zhang Shun's temple. He called his name and sacrificed the wine to him. The clothing he draped on a clay idol. The rest of the clothes he burned in sacrifice to the other departed chieftains.

The emissary stayed a few days, then returned to the capital. Song Jiang saw him off.

Ten or so days quickly passed. Governor Zhang sent a dispatch urging Song Jiang to begin his offensive. Song and Wu Yong invited Lu Junyi to a conference.

"To get to Muzhou, we go directly along the river," said Song Jiang. "To reach Shezhou, we must follow the small road through Yuling Pass. That means we'll have to divide our forces and hit two objectives. Which one would you prefer, brother?"

"The soldier obeys his general. Whatever you order, brother. I wouldn't presume to choose."

"Let's leave it to Heaven's will, then."

Song Jiang decided on the number of men for each column, wrote out two lots, burned incense and prayed for guidance. The two leaders then drew. Song Jiang picked Muzhou, Lu's slip read "Shezhou."

"Fang La's lair is in Bangyuan Cavern in Clear Stream County," said Song. "After you've taken Shezhou, brother, camp there and notify me immediately. We'll fix a date to drive on Bangyuan Cavern together." At Lu's request, Song allocated the chieftains. Thirty-six would accompany Song Jiang in his offensive against Muzhou and Black Dragon Ridge. They were the military advisor Wu Yong, Guan Sheng, Hua Rong, Qin Ming, Li Ying, Dai Zong, Zhu Tong, Li Kui, Sagacious Lu, Wu Song, Xie Zhen, Xie Bao, Lu Fang, Guo Sheng, Fan Rui, Ma Lin, Yan Shun, Song Qing, Xiang Chong, Li Gun, Wang Ying, Hu Sanniang, Ling Zhen, Du Xing, Cai Fu, Cai Qing, Pei Xuan, Jiang Jing and Yu Baosi. Seven senior and lieutenant naval chieftains would command the naval vessels going with the army to Muzhou. They were Li Jun, Ruan the Second, Ruan the Fifth, Ruan the Seventh, Tong Wei, Tong Meng and Meng Kang.

Twenty-eight commanders would support Lu Junyi in his assault on Shezhou and Yuling Pass. They were military advisor Zhu Wu, Lin Chong, Huyan Zhuo, Shi Jin, Yang Xiong, Shi Xiu, Shan Tinggui, Wei Dingguo, Sun Li, Huang Xin, Ou Peng, Du Qian, Chen Da, Yang Chun, Li Zhong, Xue Yong, Zou Yuan, Zou Run, LiLi, Li Yun, Tang Long, Shi Yong, Shi Qian, Ding Desun, Sun Xin, Mistress Gu, Zhang Qing and Sun the Witch. He would have an army of thirty thousand.

Lu departed on the appointed date after bidding farewell to Song Jiang and Deputy District Commander Liu. He and his troops wound through hill country, skirting Linan County.

Song Jiang prepared his boats, Organized his infantry and cavalry and assigned his commanders, on the day selected he dedicated his banners at a sacrificial ceremony, then set forth on land and water, war vessels and horsemen moving in coordination. A plague was rampaging in Hangzhou and six of the chieftains were ill and couldn't march. Two others were looking after them, making a total of eight who had to be left behind. The remaining thirty-seven headed for Muzhou with Song Jiang, following along the river first in the direction of Fuyang County.

We'll talk now of Chai Jin and Yan Qing who had departed from Song Jiang at Xiuzhou. From there they had proceeded to Haiyan County, gone by boat from the seacoast to a point past Yuezhou, then followed a winding road overland to Zhuji County, forded the Yupu and travelled to the border of Muzhou Prefecture. The officer guarding the pass stopped them.

"I am a scholar from the Central Plain," Chai Jin told him. "I know astrology and geomancy, I understand *yin* and *yang,* the wind and clouds, the Three

Astral Glows, the Nine Schools and the Three Religions. There's nothing in which I'm not versed. I've come because I've seen from afar emanations of a new emperor emerging south of the Yangzi. Why do you block my virtuous path?"

Impressed by Chai Jin's high-flown language, the officer asked him his name.

"I am called Ke Yin, and I come alone, except for a single servant, to offer my services to your exalted country. I have no other purpose."

The officer kept Chai Jin at the pass and dispatched a messenger with the news to Muzhou. He reported to Deputy Prime Minister Zu Shiyuan. Advisor Shen Shou, Royal Inspector Huan Yi and Grand Marshal Tan Gao. They had Chai Jin brought before them and greeted him kindly. They were very interested in what he had to say. Since he had such a fine appearance, they were not in the least suspicious.

The prime minister directed the royal inspector to take Chai Jin to the palace in Clear Stream to meet the king. At that time Fang La had palaces both in Muzhou and Shezhou prefectures. The main palace housed the highest civil and military offices. The palace in Bangyuan Cavern in Clear Stream County was also such a headquarters.

Chai Jin and Yan Qing went with Huan Yi to Clear Stream where they were first introduced to Lou Minzhong the prime minister. Chai Jin held forth in elegant language which pleased Lou very much. He insisted on entertaining Chai Jin in his chancellery. He admired Chai Jin's intellectual attainments and propriety. Lou originally had been a teacher in Clear Stream County. Although he had some learning, it wasn't very high. Chai Jin's manner of speaking delighted him.

The following morning they waited in the palace for Fang La to hold court. In the throne room royal concubines and beautiful serving maids were arrayed in attendance. Outside in ranks were high civil and military officials, and before the palace stood the royal guards with their golden melon emblems. The prime minister then addressed the throne.

"I would like to present a worthy gentleman named Ke Yin from the Central Plain, the land of Confucius. Thoroughly conversant with the civil and military arts, he is both learned and courageous. He knows astrology and geomancy, understands the winds and clouds, can read the signs of Heaven and Earth, is expert in the Three Religions and Nine Schools. All philosophies are to him an open book. He has been drawn here by emanations of an imperial emergence. He is now outside the gate awaiting Your Majesty's summons."

"Let the worthy gentleman enter," said Fang La. "He may wear ordinary dress."

Chai Jin was called into the palace. He kowtowed, fervently wished the king long life, then was led before the throne. Fang La was favorably impressed by Chai Jin's noble mien.

"Where are these imperial emanations you've seen, sir?" he asked.

"I am from the kingdom of the Central Plain, Sire. Both of my parents are dead. I am my own sole support, and I live by the occult learning handed down from the ancient sages. Recently the Imperial Star has been very bright, casting its light directly on the eastern part of your Wu region. I therefore had no hesitation to make the long arduous journey. Here, south of the Yangzi I have again seen the five-hued imperial glow, and find that it rises from Muzhou. Today I am privileged to view Your Majesty's holy visage, your imperial carriage, your face like the sun—all manifestations of that glow. I am indeed the most fortunate of men!" Again Chai Jin kowtowed.

"Although I possess a kingdom here in the southeast, my cities have been invaded and captured by Song Jiang's forces." said Fang La. "Now they are heading this way. What should I do?"

"The ancients had a saying: 'Easily obtained, easily lost; arduously obtained, strongly held.' After Your Majesty established your kingdom here in the southeast you conquered many prefectures. Although Song Jiang has invaded some of them, good fortune will soon return to this sacred land. Not only will Your Majesty's territory south of the Yangzi be secure, but in days to come your reign will extend to the Central Plain, restoring the Golden Age of Antiquity, exceeding the past glories of Han and Tang."

Overjoyed, Fang La directed that Chai Jin be seated on a satin cushion. He feted him at a royal banquet and gave him the title of Royal Secretary.

From that day forward, Chai Jin was very close to Fang La, and he deliberately cajoled and flattered him. In less than half a month every official inside and outside the palace was strongly attached to Chai Jin.

Chai Jin's fairness in everything he did before long won him still greater favor in the eyes of the king. Instructing the deputy prime minister to act as intermediary, Fang La gave his daughter the Princess Jinzhi to Chai Jin in marriage, and bestowed on him the title of Duke Consort. Yan Qing, who called himself Yun Bi, was made a royal attendant, and became known as Attendant Yun.

After his marriage to the princess, Chai Jin could go anywhere he pleased in the palace, and he knew all the inside stories. Fang La also consulted him on important military matters.

"Your aura is correct, Sire," Chai Jin often said to him. "It's just that you are being assaulted by certain stars. You'll have no peace for the next half-year. But when Song Jiang is depleted of generals, those stars will retreat and your reign will be restored. You'll roll up the foe far and wide, and you'll control the Central Plain."

"Song Jiang has killed many of my best-loved generals," said Fang La. "What can I do about that?"

"I have examined the night sky. The signs for Your Majesty show that although you have dozens of generals, they are not righteous and soon will perish. But Twenty-eight stars will come to replace them and restore your reign. Moreover, a dozen or more of Song Jiang's generals will surrender and join you.

They too are stars in your destiny, and will be your loyal officials aiding you to expand your borders."

To Fang La these were happy tidings.

Meanwhile, Song Jiang's army, having left Hangzhou, advanced on land and water towards Fuyang County. Deng Yuanjue, the Southerners' National Advisor, with four generals, was holding the pass with remnants of their defeated forces, and sent an urgent plea to Muzhou for support. Deputy Prime Minister Zu dispatched ten thousand troops under two of his most trusted commanders. One was called Bai Qin, the other Jiang De, and both were men of boundless valor. When they reached Fuyang County, they joined forces with National Advisor Deng and, together, occupied the mountain top.

Song Jiang's expedition had already reached Seven *Li* Bay, and pushed on, with the navy leading the cavalry. Learning of this, southern general Shi Bao rode down from the summit with his Comet Hammer and Wind Splitter Sword and headed for the foe. Guan Sheng was about to go forth when Lu Fang stopped him with a shout.

"Wait a bit, brother. Watch me fight a few rounds with the lout!"

While Song Jiang observed from the shadows of the arch of pennants, Lu Fang cantered towards Shi Bao, crescent-bladed halberd in hand. The southern general, grasping his Wind Splitter Sword, met him on the field of combat. They battled fifty rounds and Lu Fang began to weaken. Guo Sheng, also wielding a crescent-bladed halberd, galloped to his assistance. Fighting two against one, Shi Bao never faltered.

It was at this moment that the National Advisor sounded the retreat. He saw from the mountain top that Song Jiang's fleet, sailing the river on a favorable wind, had reached the shore and the men were already landing. Afraid of being caught in a pincers, he ordered a withdrawal.

But Lu Fang and Guo Sheng had no intention of letting Shi Bao escape. After they had fought another four or five rounds, Zhu Tong rode out from the Song Jiang position. Shi Bao couldn't handle three against one. He knocked their weapons aside and fled.

Song Jiang pointed with his whip, and his army charged the ridge. The southerners were unable to withstand them. They pulled back into Tonglu County. Pressing forward through the night, the Song army crossed White Hornet Ridge and made camp. At the same time the Xie brothers, Yan Shun, Stumpy Tiger and Ten Feet of Steel were sent to secure the east road, while Li Kui, Xiang Chong, Li Gun, Fan Rui and Ma Lin were directed to seize the west road. Each contingent commanded a thousand infantry, and their orders were to march on Tonglu County and capture the enemy installation. The armada was to continue its advance upon the river, captained by Li Jun, the three Ruan brothers, the two Tong brothers and Meng Kang.

By the time Xie Zhen and his contingent reached Tonglu County it was nearly midnight. The National Advisor was conferring with Shi Bao when suddenly they heard cannon fire. The southerners hastily mounted.

They saw the torches of three columns approaching at a rapid clip. Shi Bao fled, and the others hurriedly followed. None of them dared stand and fight.

Now the columns were upon them. Southern general Wen, who had been a little slow in getting on his horse, raced along a small path, only to be confronted by Stumpy Tiger and Ten Feet of Steel. The husband and wife team dragged him from his saddle and took him captive. Black Whirlwind Li Kui and his unit slaughtered and set fires. Song Jiang ordered the rest of his troops to break camp and move into the county town of Tonglu. There, Stumpy Tiger and Ten Feet of Steel presented their prisoner Wen Kerang and claimed their reward. Song Jiang directed that the southern general be sent to Governor Zhang for execution. Of that we'll say no more.

The next day Song Jiang moved both his land and naval units up to the foot of Black Dragon Ridge. Beyond the ridge was Muzhou. The National Advisor and his southern generals occupied the pass and stationed their troops all around. Because it was near the Yangzi, the pass was flanked by swift waters on one side and steep cliffs on the other, with fortifications above and a naval fleet below.

After making camp and building palisades, Song Jiang directed Li Kui and his contingent to go out with five hundred shield-bearers and scout the paths. But at the base of the ridge they were greeted by a shower of logs and rocks from above and had to return. Song Jiang then called half the fleet ashore and instructed Ruan the Second to take two assistants and a thousand sailors in a hundred boats and row, beating drums and singing folk songs, to a point near Black Dragon Ridge.

Fang La had a naval base there with five hundred vessels of war and five thousand sailors. They were commanded by four admirals known as the Four Dragons of Zhejiang. The top-ranking admiral was Cheng Gui the Jade-Clawed Dragon. His lieutenants were Zhai Yuan the Satin-Scaled Dragon, Qiao Zheng the Wave-Breasting Dragon, and Xie Fu the Pearl-Playing Dragon. Fang La himself had given them these names. The four originally were boatmen on the Qiantang River. After they joined him, he made them officials of the third degree.

Ruan the Second and his craft, travelling with the swift current, rowed to the shore. The four admirals in the naval base were already informed. They had prepared fifty fire rafts. Built of large pine logs they were piled high with hay under which incendiary fuses were concealed, and lashed together by strips of bamboo. The rafts lay waiting on the beach. As Ruan the Second, Meng Kang and the Tong brothers neared the shore, the four admirals watched for a while, then each waved a pale red signal flag and shoved off in four fast boats. They were dressed in ordinary garb.

The boats drew close quickly. Ruan the Second shouted an order, and his sailors loosed a volley of arrows. The fast boats withdrew. Yuan chased them towards the shore. The four admirals leaped upon the bank and ran, followed by many of their sailors. Ruan saw the naval base further up the beach and did not venture to approach. He and his men returned to their vessels.

Suddenly, a banner waved on Black Dragon Ridge and gongs and drums thundered. The fire rafts were ignited and pushed down into the river, where they advanced rapidly with the wind. Behind the raiding party large boats loomed up. The southern sailors on them yelled. All were equipped with long spears and grappling hooks, and they closed in, thrusting and killing.

The Tong brothers saw that the enemy was too strong. They beached their craft, crawled to the mountainside, then began climbing, seeking a path that would bring them back to their camp.

Ruan the Second and Meng Kang were left to confront the foe, alone. The fire rafts floated nearer. Ruan was about to jump into the water when a southern craft glided up behind and a grappling hook snaked out and nabbed him. Afraid that he would be humiliated if captured, Ruan the Second cut his own throat and died.

Meng Kang also started to dive into the river. Cannons on the fire rafts all fired together. A projectile from one of them crushed his helmet and pulverized his skull.

The four admirals advanced rapidly on fire-spewing vessels. Li Jun, Ruan the Fifth and Ruan the Seventh were in the rear of the raiding party fleet. When they saw that their forward craft were defeated, and that the foe was moving towards them fiercely along the bank, they hastily turned their boats and retreated with the current. Abandoning their attempt to land, they returned to Tonglu.

On Black Dragon Ridge, National Advisor Deng and Marshal Shi Bao followed up the victory of their fleet by sweeping down the mountain. But the water was too deep and the distances from their bases too far for the contending forces to maneuver freely. The Song raiders went back to their Tonglu camp, and the southerners withdrew again to Black Dragon Ridge.

Song Jiang brooded in his tent in Tonglu over the death of Ruan the Second and Meng Kang. He ate and slept badly. Wu Yong and the chieftains could not console him. Ruan the Fifth and Ruan the Seventh, who wore mourning, finally came and spoke to him.

"Our brother gave his life for his country," they said. "That was a lot better than dying in disgrace in Liangshan Marsh. You're our Commander-in-Chief. You mustn't distress yourself. Concentrate on important national affairs. We two will get our own revenge."

On hearing this, Song Jiang cheered up a bit. The following day he mustered his troops and prepared to set forth once more. Wu Yong advised against it.

"Don't be impatient, brother. We must work out a good plan, first. Then it will be time enough to cross the ridge."

Xie Zhen and Xie Bao said: "We brothers were hunters, originally. We're well accustomed to climbing mountains and crossing ridges. Why don't we dress as hunters again, go up the mountain and set a big fire? That will throw a scare into those southern rogues. They'll abandon the pass and run."

"A good idea," said Wu Yong. "But that mountain's a dangerous place. It will be very hard to get up there. One slip and you may lose your lives."

"Since escaping from prison in Dengzhou and joining the band in Liangshan Marsh, thanks to Big Brother's fortunate aura we've enjoyed many years as gallant men. And now the government has pardoned us and we can wear silken clothes. If for the sake of the imperial court and to repay Big Brother we're smashed to bits, it won't be too much for us to give."

"Don't speak such unlucky words," Song Jiang cried. "I only hope we can win a great victory and return to the capital. The emperor will see to it that we're properly rewarded. You two must do your utmost for our country."

The Xie brothers went to prepare. They put on their tiger skin tunics, hung sharp knives at their waists, and took up their steel pitchforks. Bidding Song Jiang farewell, they set out along a path in the direction of Black Dragon Ridge.

It was only about the first watch. They met two junior officers lying in ambush along the road and killed them both. By the time they reached the foot of the ridge it was the second watch. They could hear the watchman's drum striking the hour in the southerners' fort above.

Travel on an open path would have been too dangerous. The Xie brothers ascended the steep side of the mountain, grasping vines and shrubs and hauling themselves laboriously upwards. The moonlight was as bright as day. When they had completed two-thirds of their climb they could see lamps glimmering on the ridge top. They hid themselves in a hollow and listened. The watchman's drum sounded the fourth watch.

"The night is short. It won't be dark much longer," Xie Zhen whispered to his brother. "Let's go on."

They resumed their arduous ascent. Soon they reached a sheer cliff face which required all their attention and the full use of their hands and legs. For this reason, they tied their steel pitchforks to their backs. One of these, caught by a vine, clanged loudly against a rock. Sentries on the top spotted them.

Xie Zhen, who was just crawling into a declivity, heard a voice above shout: "Got you!" A hooked pole reached down and tangled itself in his hair. Zhen hastily reached for his knife. The man above tugged. In an instant, Zhen was dangling free in the air. Panic-stricken, he swung his blade, snapping the pole in two. Poor Xie Zhen, a gallant half his life, plunged from the high cliff a hundred and ten feet to his death, smashed on the jagged rocks below!

Seeing his brother fall, Xie Bao began to climb down hurriedly. He was deluged by shower of rocks, large and small. Crossbow darts bit into him from a bamboo thicket. Poor Xie Bao, a hunter all his life, joined his brother in death near a bamboo grove on the side of Black Dragon Ridge!

At daybreak men were sent down to fetch their bodies. They were left exposed to the elements on the ridge.

A scout reported the news to Song Jiang. He wept so bitterly he fainted several times. He ordered Guan Sheng and Hua Rong to muster soldiers at once, capture Black Dragon Ridge and the pass, and avenge the four chieftains.

"Don't be impatient, brother," Wu Yong cautioned. "They died because it was Heaven's will. Rash actions won't win the pass. We need to work out clever strategy and shrewd tactics. Only then can we deploy troops."

"Already a third of my brothers are gone," Song Jiang cried angrily. "I can't permit those wretches to leave those bodies out in the open. We've got to bring them back, tonight, and give them a proper burial, in coffins!"

"The rascals are leaving them there like that with a purpose. You mustn't be rash, brother."

But Song Jiang refused to listen. He mustered three thousand crack fighters, designated Guan Sheng, Hua Rong, Lu Fang and Guo Sheng as his lieutenants, and arrived at Black Dragon Ridge that very night.

Around the second watch a young officer said: "Can those be the bodies of Xie Zhen and Xie Bao there ahead?"

Song Jiang rode up for a look. Suspended from bamboo poles on two trees were two corpses. A piece of bark had been stripped from one of the trees and on the exposed white of the trunk some words had been written. But they couldn't be distinguished in the dark of the moon. Song Jiang called for a glowing punk used to ignite cannon fuses. Blowing on it, he lit a lantern. He read the inscription: Sooner or later Song Jiang shall end like this.

Furious, he ordered the bodies removed from the trees. Suddenly, on four sides torches glowed, drums thundered, and southern troops closed in. Arrows zinged down from above. Warships in the river were landing men on the bank.

Song Jiang could only groan, completely at a loss. Hastily he retreated, but Shi Bao was blocking his path. He turned, only to find Deng Yuanjue charging his flank. Poor Song Jiang, he'd always been chivalrous, his nobility was as lofty as the eternal sky. Now disaster and death without burial stared him in the face.

Truly, slaughter on a huge scale impended, the situation was fraught with danger.

How did Song Jiang and his forces extricate themselves? Read our next chapter if you would know.

CHAPTER 97

AT MUZHOU AN ARROW STRIKES DENG YUANJUE

ON BLACK DRAGON RIDGE A SPIRIT ASSISTS SONG JIANG

In a stentorian voice Shi Bao shouted: "Song Jiang dismount and surrender! What are you waiting for?"

This greatly angered Guan Sheng. He clapped his horse and charged Shi Bao, brandishing his halberd. But before they could clash, shouts arose in the rear. The four admirals had mounted the bank and now came tearing forward, in conjunction with southern commanders Wang Ji and Chao Zhong who rushed down from the ridge.

To halt this assault, Hua Rong hurriedly engaged Wang Ji. They fought several rounds and Hua Rong retreated, pursued by Wang and Chao. Hua quickly shot two arrows in succession and brought both of them down. The Song forces cheered but dared not advance. Instead, they withdrew.

The quick disposal of Wang and Chao halted the admirals in their tracks. Hua Rong had stemmed the rear assault successfully. But suddenly two more southern units moved up on the Song flank. One was led by Bai Qin, the other by Jing De. Lu Fang and Guo Sheng rode out and engaged them. The four battled fiercely in a fight to the death.

Song Jiang was very worried. But just then yells rang out behind the southern forces, and they broke and ran. Li Kui and the shield bearer Chieftains Xiang Chong and Li Gun and a thousand infantry had smashed into Shi Bao's rear. When National Advisor Deng rushed reinforcements, his own rear was assaulted by Sagacious Lu and Wu Song, their blades hacking and cleaving, the pure iron staff pulverizing all in its path. With them were a thousand foot soldiers. And behind these were eight more chieftains leading a charge of mixed infantry and cavalry. From all sides the Song troops ripped into the contingents of Shi Bao and Deng Yuanjue. After rescuing Song Jiang they escorted him back to Tonglu. Shi Bao withdrew his forces up the ridge. In the camp Song Jiang thanked his chieftains.

"If you brothers hadn't come to my aid, I would have joined Xie Zhen and Xie Bao as ghosts in the Nether Regions!"

"You went despite my advice," Wu Yong reminded him. "I was afraid there would be some mishap, so I sent our chieftains to relieve you."

Song Jiang was profuse in expressions of gratitude.

On Black Dragon Ridge, Shi Bao and National Advisor Deng conferred in their camp. Shi said: "Song's forces are back in Tonglu at the moment. But if they sneak around the rear of the mountain, Muzhou will be in imminent danger. I wish you'd see the king in his palace in Clear Stream, National Advisor, and request him to send us reinforcements. Then we can hold out for a long time."

"You're absolutely right, Marshal," said Deng. "I'll go at once."

He mounted and rode to Muzhou, where he called on the prime minister Zu Shiyuan and said: "Song Jiang's army is strong. It can't be stopped. If they come rolling towards the pass, we'll be in trouble. I've come to request the king for reinforcements."

Zu rode with Deng from Muzhou to Bangyuan Cavern in the county of Clear Stream. There, they saw Lou Minzhong the prime minister and told him of their intention to petition for more troops.

Fang La the king held court the next morning. The prime minister, his deputy, and National Advisor Deng attended. They kowtowed, and Deng came forward and hailed the sovereign respectfully.

"This humble monk, on receiving your royal orders, went with the prince to hold Hangzhou. Song Jiang attacked with strong troops and brave generals. We had great difficulty in withstanding them. Then Administrator Yuan slipped them in on his grain boats and we lost the city. The prince was eager for battle, and he died in the fray. Marshal Shi Bao and I retreated to Black Dragon Ridge, where we are guarding the pass. Recently we've killed four of Song Jiang's generals, and he's rather shaken. He's camped now in Tonglu, but sooner or later he'll sneak along some path into the pass. It will be very hard for us to hold the ridge. We earnestly beg Your Majesty to give us more crack forces so that we may defend the pass, drive back the brigands and regain our cities. This humble monk has come specially to submit this petition."

"We've already allocated all the troops we can spare to our critical points," said Fang La. "We've just sent tens of thousands to the pass at Yuling, another place where the situation is tight. All we have left are the Royal Guards who protect my palace. I can't very well let them go."

"If you don't give us reinforcements, Sire, there's nothing I can do," Deng said. "There will be no way to defend Muzhou if Song Jiang crosses the ridge!"

Prime Minister Lou added his plea: "Black Dragon Ridge is vital. There are thirty thousand Royal Guards. Give the National Advisor ten thousand. I beg Your Majesty to consider."

But Fang La was adamant. He refused to send any of the Royal Guards to the aid of Black Dragon Ridge.

Royal court ended and the participants left the palace. Lou conferred with the officials. It was decided that Deputy Prime Minister Zu would dispatch a general and five thousand troops as reinforcements. Deng and. Zu returned to Muzhou together and selected a crack force of five thousand and a top-ranking general—Xiahou Cheng. Deng went back with these to the ridge, where he told Shi Bao what had transpired.

"Since the king won't give us any of his Royal Guards to repel the invaders, we can only hold the pass, but not go out and give battle," said the marshal. "The four admirals must firmly secure the river banks. If enemy vessels come, they can drive them back. They cannot take any offensive action."

Meanwhile, because his losses in chieftains were heavy, Song Jiang remained camped in Tonglu. For more than twenty days his soldiers did not venture forth. Then a mounted scout arrived with a report.

"Chancellor of Military Affairs Tong has arrived in Hangzhou with rewards from the emperor. He has sent General Wang Bing with rewards also to General Lu's army at Yuling Pass. Chancellor Tong will soon be here to make the presentation."

Song Jiang hastened with Wu Yong and the chieftains twenty *li* outside the town to greet him. When they were back in the county government center, the imperial decree was opened and read, and the gifts distributed among the chieftains. Song Jiang and the others paid their respects to Chancellor Tong and gave a banquet in his honor.

"During my journey here I heard your losses were severe," said Tong.

Song Jiang replied with tears in his eyes. "When I went with Commissioner Zhao on the northern expedition against the Liao Tartars, we were victorious and didn't lose a single commander. But in this campaign against Fang La, even before we departed from the capital Gongsun Sheng left us. The emperor has retained several of our chieftains. After crossing the Yangzi, at each place we attacked we lost a few more. Recently, eight or nine have fallen ill in Hangzhou, and there's no guarantee they'll survive. We fought twice at Black Dragon Ridge, and lost another few. That sector is a combination of dangerous mountains and swift waters, a difficult place in which to battle. We haven't been able to break into the pass no matter how we've tried. How fortunate that your benevolent presence should come among us just when we were most distressed!"

"The emperor knows of your great accomplishments," said Tong. "He's heard also of your losses, and therefore has dispatched me, with Generals Wang Bing and Zhao Tan, to assist you. I've sent Wang to General Lu's camp to distribute part of the rewards there."

He introduced Zhao Tan to Song Jiang. The new-comers made their quarters in Tonglu Town, and were feted by their hosts.

The next day, in preparation for an assault on the ridge and the pass, Chancellor Tong mustered the troops. Wu Yong urged restraint.

"You must be cautious, Excellency. Let us send Yan Shun and Ma Lin along secluded paths to find some villager who can tell us of a route to the other side of the pass. Then we'll be able to launch a pincers' attack. The foe won't be able to cope with two fronts at once. We'll take the pass as easily as spitting on our hands."

"An excellent idea!" Song Jiang agreed.

He dispatched the two chieftains with a few dozen stalwarts to scour the countryside for an informant. In the evening they returned with an old man.

"Who is he?" asked Song Jiang.

"A local person," said Ma Lin. "He knows the mountain paths well."

"Old fellow," said Song Jiang, "if you can lead us past Black Dragon Ridge I'll reward you handsomely.

"My family have been ordinary residents around here for generations," the old man said, "but Fang La is oppressing us cruelly and we have no place to hide.

Fortunately, the emperor's soldiers have come and the people can have peace again, I'll take you beyond the ridge to Dongguan Town. Muzhou isn't far beyond. Near the city's North Gate, you swing around past the West Gate, and there's Black Dragon Ridge."

Song Jiang was delighted. He directed that the old guide be given silver and kept in the camp. He had him served food and wine.

"Hold Tonglu County," Song Jiang requested Chancellor Tong the following day. "I will go out with our troops near Muzhou and hit the ridge and the pass from both sides. We'll take them all right."

On Chancellor Tong's instructions, Song Jiang divided his forces into two columns. With twelve chieftains, he marched off along a path. Tong led the other column openly down the road.

Song Jiang had a contingent of ten thousand. Guided by the old man they moved silently, the bridles of the horses muffled, the men biting stick gags. Halfway up the slope, they were intercepted by enemy soldiers. At Song Jiang's order, Li Kui, Xiang Chong, Li Gun and their man charged. They annihilated all four or five hundred of the foe.

Around the fourth watch the column reached Dongguan Town. Wu Yingxing the garrison commander had only three thousand troops. They couldn't possibly hold out against Song Jiang's overwhelming numbers. They left in a rush and returned to Muzhou. Wu reported to Deputy Prime Minister Zu.

"Song Jiang's army has slipped past Black Dragon Ridge and is already at Dongguan."

Zu was shocked. He hurriedly called his generals into conference.

Meanwhile, on Song Jiang's instructions, cannoneer Ling Zhen fired off a volley, startling Shi Bao in the fort on the ridge. He sent Bai Qin and a detachment out to scout. They saw the banners of Song Jiang carpeting the plains and wooded slopes. They hastily returned to the fort and Bai Qin reported to Shi Bao.

"Since the king won't give us any reinforcements, we can only hold the pass," said Shi Bao. "We can't go to the rescue."

"You're making a mistake, Marshal!" Deng the National Advisor remonstrated. "Whether or not you aid Muzhou is up to you. But if the palace falls, there'll be no guarantee for any of us. Stay here if you like. I'm going to Muzhou!"

Shi Bao's urgings that he remain were useless. Deng mustered five thousand soldiers, took up his Buddhist staff, and departed with General Xiahou down the ridge.

Song Jiang's contingent at Dongguan, instead of driving on Muzhou, went first to assault the ridge and the pass, and ran directly into National Advisor Deng's force. As the two units neared each other, Deng rode forward and challenged individual combat. Hua Rong leaned close and whispered into Song Jiang's ear. Song Jiang nodded his agreement. He summoned Qin Ming and the three conferred. Then Qin Ming cantered out to meet Deng.

Fifty or sixty rounds they fought. Qin Ming turned and fled, and the Song army scattered. Thinking he had defeated Qin Ming, Deng abandoned him and galloped to capture Song Jiang.

Hua Rong was all prepared. Protecting Song Jiang, he waited until the National Advisor came near. Then he drew his bow to the full, aimed, and let fly. The arrow streaked like a comet into Deng's face and knocked him from his horse. The Song soldiers immediately closed in and killed him.

A wild and bloody battle ensued, and the southern troops were badly defeated. General Xiahou couldn't withstand the foe. He fled to Muzhou. Song Jiang's column raced to Black Dragon Ridge. But a rain of logs and ballista stones drove them back. Song Jiang turned his unit abruptly and headed for Muzhou.

Xiahou, in the southern capital, told Deputy Prime Minister Zu: "The Song army has passed Dongguan, killed National Advisor Deng, and will be here today!" Zu immediately deputed a man to go with Xiahou to Clear Stream and tell the prime minister. Lou relayed the information to the king.

"The Song army is already beyond Dongguan and is hurrying to attack Muzhou. We beg Your Majesty to dispatch troops quickly, or all will be lost."

Fang La was astonished. He hastily summoned Marshal Zheng Biao to the palace, gave him fifteen thousand of the Royal Guards, and ordered him to reinforce Muzhou that same night.

"I shall obey your decree, Sire," said Zheng, "But I request that the Royal Astrologer go with us, In that way we shall be able to defeat Song Jiang."

The king agreed and summoned Bao Daoyi the royal astrologer. With palms pressed together, Bao bowed before the throne.

"Song Jiang and his army have invaded our territory and destroyed our cities, our troops and our generals. Even now they are marching on Muzhou," said Fang La. "We hope you will work your magic, save our country and people, and preserve our land."

"Set your mind at ease, Sire." said Bao. "Though I am not talented, I do have a little learning. With the aid of Your Majesty's powerful good fortune, I shall sweep the ground with Song Jiang's army, and they shall lie everywhere dead and unburied."

Very pleased, Fang La feted the astrologer. After the banquet, Bao bid the king farewell. Then he conferred on tactics with Zheng and Xiahou.

This Bao Daoyi hailed from the Jinhua Mountains. He became a priest very young, and studied the unorthodox school of Taoism. Later, he threw his lot in with Fang La, turned schemer and rebel, posed evil for righteousness and, whenever engaged in battle, used his wicked magic to harm others. He had a precious sword called the Occult Universe which could fly a hundred paces and kill a man. As a reward for his help in unvirtuous activities, Fang La named him Able Royal Astrologer.

Zheng Biao had been a constable in Lanxi County, Wuzhou Prefecture, and was a skilled wielder of spear and staff. After joining Fang La he was appointed Marshal of the Royal Guards. Entranced by Taoist magic, he became a disciple of Bao the Royal Astrologer, and learned many spells from him. Because whenever he was fighting to the death he could produce a mystic cloud, everyone called him Zheng the Prince of Demons.

Xiahou also was from the Wuzhou hills. He started life as a hunter, and was good with a steel pitchfork. He was part of the entourage of Deputy Prime Minister Zu ruling Muzhou.

Now, the three were conferring in the headquarters of the Royal Guards. The gate-keeper announced that the eunuch Pu Wenying had come to call on the Royal Astrologer.

Pu entered and said: "I have heard that you are considering how to cope with the Song army. Last night I examined the sky. The stars of the southern generals all are lusterless, while the stars of half of Song Jiang's generals are bright. Although it's good that you march against the foe, Royal Astrologer, I'm afraid you're doomed to failure. It would be better if you petitioned the king to discuss terms of surrender, and save the country from calamity."

Furious, Bao whipped out his Occult Universe sword and, with one blow, cleaved Pu Wenying in two. He hurriedly reported the incident to the king in writing. Of that we'll say no more.

Then, the vanguard under Zheng Biao left Clear Stream. Bao followed with the central unit, Xiahou brought up the rear. They marched to save Muzhou.

Song Jiang's forces assailed Muzhou without any fixed plan. A mounted scout reported that reinforcements from Clear Stream had arrived for the beleaguered southerners. Song Jiang sent Stumpy Tiger Wang and his wife Ten Feet of Steel out with a patrol of three thousand cavalry to confront the foe. They met on the Clear Stream road, and Zheng Biao rode forth to engage Stumpy Tiger. Without exchanging a word they fought eight or nine rounds.

Zheng muttered an incantation under his breath, and shouted: "Speed!" A cloud of black vapor spewed from the top of his helmet. In the cloud stood a Heavenly spirit in golden armor, raising a Demon-Smiting precious cudgel. Panic-stricken, Stumpy Tiger floundered, and Zheng ran him through with his lance.

When Ten Feet of Steel saw her husband fall from the saddle, she charged Zheng brandishing her two steel-blue swords. They fought briefly and Zheng turned and galloped away. Burning for vengeance, the girl raced after him. Zheng put aside his lance and, from a silken pouch, drew out a gold-plated bronze brick. Suddenly he twisted around and flung it at his pursuer's forehead. It struck squarely, and Ten Feet of Steel fell dead to the ground. Poor beautiful female warrior, her life was gone like a dream of spring!

Zheng the Prince of Demons pressed his advantage to drive back the Song patrol. The northerners were badly defeated. They returned and reported to Song

Jiang that Stumpy Tiger and Ten Feet of Steel had been killed by Zheng Biao, and that the patrol had lost more than half its effectives.

Enraged by the death of his two chieftains, Song Jiang mustered five thousand men and rode out to battle, accompanied by Li Kui, Xiang Chong and Li Gun. They soon were within sight of Zheng the Prince of Demons and his contingent. Song Jiang cantered forward and shouted at Zheng angrily.

"Rebellious bandit, how dare you kill two of my chieftains!"

Zheng rode towards him with levelled lance. This infuriated Li Kui. Swinging his axes, Black Whirlwind raced out, covered by Xiang Chong and Li Gun, who also ran at Zheng twirling their shields. The Prince of Demons turned and fled, with the three hotly pursuing him, directly into the southerners' position. Fearful for Li Kui's safety, Song Jiang threw in another five thousand troops. The southerners broke and scattered.

Song Jiang had the trumpeters blow the call to reassemble. The two shield chieftains, escorting Li Kui back, suddenly found themselves enveloped in a black cloud that obscured the sky. They couldn't tell north from south, day from night. Song Jiang's army lost its sense of direction completely. Zheng the Prince of Demons had imposed a spell. The Song forces, unable to see a thing, began floundering about.

Song Jiang raised his face to Heaven and cried: "Am I really doomed to die in this place!"

By then it was already afternoon, and the cloud broke up and the mist dissolved. All around Song Jiang saw huge fellows in golden armor surrounding them in ranks. The Song forces prostrated themselves and waited for death. Song Jiang dismounted and surrendered.

"Kill me quickly," he exclaimed. He crouched on the ground. He heard the sound of wind and rain, but he saw no one.

His officers and men covered their faces and waited for the thrusts that would finish them. But soon the wind and rain passed, and no blades descended.

A hand grasped Song Jiang and a voice said: "Arise, please!"

Song Jiang lifted his head and looked. Standing before him was a scholar. Astonished, Song Jiang scrambled to his feet and bowed.

"Who are you, sir?"

"My name is Shao Jun. I'm a native of these parts. I've come specially to inform you, righteous warrior—Fang La's number is nearly up. In only ten more days he'll be destroyed. I have expended myself several times on your behalf. Although you've suffered some difficulties today, relief will soon be here. Are you aware of that, righteous warrior?"

"When, exactly, can we capture Fang La, sir?"

The scholar gave him a push, and Song Jiang awakened. It had all been a dream. The huge fellows he had seen surrounding them were only pine trees, gilded by the sun.

He shouted for his chieftains to get up and find a road. The cloud and mist were gone, the sky was clear. Beyond the pines, yells were heard. Song Jiang led his men quickly in that direction. There was Sagacious Lu and Wu Song, about to engage Zheng Biao.

Royal Astrologer Bao, watching from his horse, saw Wu Song striding towards Zheng with a pair of swords. He pulled his Occult Universe sword from its scabbard and flung it. The blade bit into Wu Song's arm so deeply he fainted from loss of blood. Sagacious Lu, enraged, barged in with his iron staff. By the time be rescued his companion, Wu Song's arm was dangling inert, but they had captured Zheng's mystic sword. Wu Song regained consciousness. With one slice of his knife, he cut off the useless left limb. Song Jiang ordered that he be carried back to camp to recuperate.

Sagacious Lu, who had barged right through to the rear of the enemy unit, now engaged General Xiahou. The two fought several rounds, and Xiahou left in defeat. Sagacious ploughed into the southern soldiers with his Buddhist staff. They fled in every direction. Xiahou headed for the wooded mountains. Sagacious pursued him tenaciously into their depths. Zheng the Prince of Demons and his troops came hurrying towards the Song contingent, Li Kui, Xiang Chong and Li Gun, with twirling shields, flying knives, swift javelins and mighty axes, rushed to meet them. Unable to stem the assault, Zheng retreated over hills and waterways. The three pursuers, although they were unfamiliar with the terrain, wanted to distinguish themselves before Song Jiang, and gave headlong chase across a stream.

On the west bank, three thousand southern soldiers suddenly blocked their path. Xiang Chong hastily turned to go back, only to find his retreat cut off at the shore by two southern commanders. He called to Black Whirlwind and Li Gun, but they were already well beyond in their pursuit of Zheng Biao.

Li Gun, fording another stream ahead, stepped unexpectedly into a deep hole and fell. He was immediately riddled by arrows and killed. Xiang Chong, as he attempted to plunge down the bank, was tripped up by a rope. Before he could struggle to his feet, southern soldiers swarmed all over him and hacked him to mincemeat.

Poor Li Gun and Xiang Chong, what chance had they to display their heroism! That left only Li Kui, continuing the chase into the mountains.

Meanwhile, the Song unit at the shore pushed across. Before they had gone half a *li* they heard shouts behind them. Hua Rong, Qin Ming and Fan Rui had caught up with reinforcements. Together, they smashed the southerners, drove into mountains and rescued Li Kui. Only Sagacious Lu was nowhere to be seen.

They returned and told Song Jiang what had happened. He wept bitterly. A count of his troops revealed he had lost about half. Sagacious Lu was missing, and Wu Song was minus a left arm.

A mounted scout announced: "Military Advisor Wu Yong has come by water with ten thousand troops."

Wu Yong arrived and explained: "Chancellor of Military Affairs Tong and his column have joined forces with the units under Generals Wang Bing, Zhao Tan and Liu Guangshi, and all are at the foot of Black Dragon Ridge. Only thirteen chieftains have been left behind. The remainder are here with me."

Song Jiang told him of their losses, adding: "Wu Song is a cripple, and nobody knows what's become of Sagacious Lu. Is it any wonder I'm heartsore!"

"Take a broad view, brother," Wu Yong urged. "This is the time to capture Fang La. It's a matter of major national importance. You mustn't let your distress over our brothers ruin your health."

Song Jiang pointed at the surrounding pines and told Wu Yong about his dream.

"There must be a temple near here for you to have had such a remarkable dream," said the Military Advisor. "That spirit who appeared obviously was protecting you."

"You're absolutely right. Let's look around and see if we can find it."

They walked into the wooded mountains. Sure enough, less than half an arrow-flight away, they came upon a temple. On a plaque in gold letters were inscribed the words: *Temple of the Black Dragon Spirit.*

The two men entered and gazed at the idol of the Dragon Spirit at the upper end of the building. Song Jiang was amazed. It was none other than the apparition which appeared to him in his dream! Song Jiang kowtowed and voiced his gratitude.

"I cannot thank you enough, oh Dragon Spirit, for saving me! I beg for your continuing aid. If I conquer Fang La, I shall petition the emperor to build here a magnificent temple, and confer on you an exalted title!"

After kowtowing once more the two left the building and examined the stone tablet in the courtyard. It said that during the Tang Dynasty a scholar named Shao Jun failed in the imperial examinations and drowned himself. The Lord of the Heavens pitied him and made him a Dragon Spirit. Thereafter, when the local people prayed for wind they got wind, when they prayed for rain they got rain. And so they built this temple and sacrificed in each of the four seasons.

Song Jiang called for a black pig and a white sheep and held his own sacrificial ceremony. On leaving the temple, he looked carefully at the surrounding pines, and told Wu Yong how they had marvelously been converted into giant warriors.

To this day there is a Temple of the Black Dragon King outside Yanzhou's North Gate. And the Forest of Ten Thousand Pines still stands.

Returning to headquarters, Song Jiang and Wu Yong sat up half the night discussing how to repel the enemy and attack Muzhou. Song Jiang then wearily laid his head on the table and slept. A voice announced: "Scholar Shao has come." Song Jiang hastily got up and left the tent to greet him.

The Dragon Spirit bowed and said: "If I hadn't protected you yesterday, Bao the Royal Astrologer, who by a magic spell changed the pines into warriors, would have captured you. But I'm grateful for the sacrifices you made to me, and I've come specially to thank you. I want to tell you also that you soon will break into Muzhou, and within ten days capture Fang La."

Song Jiang wanted to invite his visitor into the tent and question him further, when he was awakened by a sudden gust of wind. It had been another dream.

He urgently summoned the Military Advisor and told him what he had dreamt.

"Since the Dragon Spirit has appeared to you again, we definitely can launch our attack on Muzhou," said Wu Yong.

"Perfectly correct," cried Song Jiang.

At daybreak he ordered that the troops be mustered for an offensive against the city. He directed Yan Shun and Ma Lin to hold the Black Dragon Ridge road, and Guan Sheng, Hua Rong, Qin Ming and Zhu Tong to drive towards the North Gate with the vanguard. Ling Zhen was instructed to fire directly into the city nine vollies of Mother and Sons shells.

Their bursts shook the earth and sky, and the hills and mountains trembled. The southern soldiers in Muzhou were scared out of their wits. They were in a panic before the fighting even started.

The rear army contingent of Royal Astrologer Bao and Zheng the Prince of Demons had already been scattered by Sagacious Lu, and Xiahou chased off to parts unknown. The remainder withdrew into the city. Bao and Zheng conferred with Deputy Prime Minister Zu and the other leaders.

"The Song army is upon us," they said. "What can save us?"

"Since ancient times whenever enemy soldiers are at the gates a battle to the death is the only solution," said Zu. "If they break in, we'll surely be captured. The situation is critical. We must go forward."

Zheng the Prince of Demons, seconded by Tan Gao and Wu Yingxing and a dozen or more subordinate officers, opened the gates and led forth ten thousand crack troops. Song-Jiang directed his forces to fall back half an arrow-flight, and permit the foe to emerge completely from the city and deploy in battle positions.

Bao the Royal Astrologer seated himself in an armchair atop the city wall. Deputy Prime Minister Zu, Advisor Shen, and Royal Inspector Huan also took seats and watched from the ramparts.

With levelled lance Zheng cantered forward. Song Jiang sent Guan Sheng the Big Halberd against him. They fought only a few rounds. No match for Guan, Zheng could only parry and dodge.

Seeing this, Bao on the wall worked his magic. He muttered an incantation and shouted: "Speed!" Bao puffed out a breath, and from the top of Zheng's head black vapor billowed. In the cloud a spirit in golden armor appeared, grasping a Demon-Smiting Cudgel which he raised to strike. Another black cloud spread from the southern army.

Song Jiang immediately directed Fan Rui the Demon King Who Roils the World to counter the magic. He himself chanted the secret incantation from the Heavenly Books for dispelling wind and darkness.

From Guan Sheng's helmet rolled a white cloud. In it was a spirit astride a black dragon, an iron hammer in his hand. He charged the golden-armored spirit which had emerged from Zheng's head. The contending armies yelled as the supernatural warriors fought. After only a few rounds, the dragon-riding spirit drove off his opponent.

With one swing of his halberd Guan Sheng cut Zheng from his horse. Bao the Royal Astrologer, shocked by the wind and thunder amid the Song army, hastily started to rise. A flaming ball from Ling Zhen's heaven-shaking cannon smashed his head and body to smithereens.

The southern forces were defeated, and the Song army surged towards Muzhou. Zhu Tong ran Grand Marshal Tan Gao through with his lance, tumbling him from his mount. Li Ying's flying sword killed Garrison Commander Wu.

When the flaming cannon ball disintegrated Bao the Royal Astrologer, the southern soldiers on the wall scrambled down and ran. Song Jiang's troops were by now inside the city. In their massive advance they captured Deputy Prime Minister Zu, Advisor Shen and Royal Inspector Huan.

The subordinate officers were slain, every one, with no one bothering to ask their names.

Song Jiang burned Fang La's palace and distributed his gold and silks among the commanders. He also issued a proclamation reassuring the populace. Even before a count of his soldiers was completed, a mounted messenger raced up with a report.

"On Black Dragon Ridge Ma Lin was knocked from his saddle by Bai Qin's javelin. Shi Bao sped over and cut him in two with his sword. Yan Shun dashed into the fray, but Shi Bao threw his Comet Hammer and killed him. Shi Bao is pressing his advantage to drive this way."

Deeply grieved, Song Jiang wept over the death of yet another two chieftains. He ordered Guan Sheng, Hua Rong, Qin Ming and Zhu Tong to battle Shi Bao and Bai Qin, and capture Black Dragon Ridge and the pass.

And because the chieftains fought at Black Dragon Ridge they annihilated the enemy bandits in Clear Stream County and nabbed the hay-haired king in Bangyuan Cavern. The names of Song Jiang and his chieftains were inscribed in historical annals for a thousand years; the story of their splendid deeds has been passed down through the ages. They demonstrated their courage in Black Ridge Pass; in the cavern at Clear Stream they won their fame.

How did the Song Jiang forces meritoriously meet the foe? Read our next chapter if you would know.

CHAPTER 98

LU JUNYI WAGES A BIG BATTLE AT YULING PASS

SONG JIANG CLEVERLY TAKES CLEAR STREAM CAVERN

Guan Sheng and the other three chieftains led their men rapidly up Black Dragon Ridge. They soon encountered the army of Shi Bao.

"Bandit, how dare you kill my brothers!" Guan Sheng shouted from his horse.

Shi Bao saw it was Guan Sheng, and he lost his eagerness for combat. He withdrew to the top of ridge and ordered Bai Qin to take him on. The two had fought less than ten rounds when, from the summit, gongs hastily sounded the call to retreat. Guan Sheng did not pursue.

The southern soldiers had been thrown into confusion. Shi Bao, repelling the raiders from the east, had neglected the west. Now, a large unit under Chancellor Tong was swarming up this side of the ridge.

Song army general Wang Bing clashed with southern commander Jing De. After something over ten rounds, Wang cut Jing from his saddle. At the same time, chieftains Lu Fang and Guo Sheng raced to capture the top. But before they reached it, a huge boulder came bounding down. Guo Sheng and his steed were crushed to death.

Meanwhile on the east side Guan Sheng, noting the confusion in the southern position above, realized that Song forces must be attacking on the west, and led his men in a charge to the summit. The enemy contingent, assailed from two sides, was quite disorganized.

Lu Fang and Bai Qin met in battle. They hadn't fought three rounds when Bai lunged with his lance. Lu dodged and the thrust slid by his ribs. But Bai grabbed Lu's lance and twisted it completely around. Too close to ply their weapons, they both dropped them of one accord and, still mounted, grappled in hand-to-hand combat. The perilous ridge was a difficult place for horses to keep their footing. The strenuous wrestling of their riders threw the animals off balance. They stumbled over the edge and rolled down the cliff. Both warriors were killed in the fall.

Guan Sheng and his men drove upwards on foot. Shi Bao saw that he was blocked on both sides. He feared humiliation if captured. With his Wind Splitter Sword, he cut his own throat. The Song forces were in control of Black Dragon Ridge and the pass. Guan Sheng dispatched a swift messenger to Song Jiang with the news.

Upstream from Muzhou, another Song unit closed in, so that a squeeze was being exerted from both above and below. The four southern admirals in the naval base on the river saw that Black Dragon Ridge was gone, and that Muzhou had fallen. They abandoned their boats and fled to the opposite shore. There, the local people caught Cheng Gui and Xie Fu and turned them over to the conquerors in Muzhou. Zhai Yuan and Qiao Zheng managed to escape.

The large Song force under Chancellor Tong and Deputy District Commander Liu returned to Muzhou, and Song Jiang went out to welcome them into the city. The armies were installed in camps, and proclamations issued exhorting the people and local soldiers to resume their jobs. Countless southern troops had surrendered. Song Jiang opened the storehouses and distributed grain among the populace. They went back to their original occupations as good citizens.

The hearts of Admirals Cheng Gui and Xie Fu were cut out and offered in sacrifice to Ruan the Second and Meng Kang. Similar ceremonies were held for the chieftains slain on Black Dragon Ridge. Li Jun was ordered to take the captured high southern officials on many vessels and deliver them to Governor Zhang.

Song Jiang was greatly distressed by news of the death of Lu Fang and Guo Sheng. He made no further troop movements, but waited for Lu Junyi and his column. When Lu arrived they would jointly assault Clear Stream.

After the division of forces at Hangzhou, Lu had set forth with twenty-eight chieftains and thirty thousand men. They marched along mountain paths in the direction of Shezhou. Passing through Linan Town, an ancient capital, they neared Yuling Pass.

The pass was held by Pang Wanchun, one of Fang La's leading generals, and the best archer in the southern kingdom. His lieutenant commanders were called Lei Jiong and Ji Ji, each of whom operated an eight-hundred-catty crossbow which had to be cocked by foot pressure, and wielded a big spiny club. Pang had a force of three thousand. He had heard Lu was coming, and was all prepared, just waiting for him to get closer.

Lu sent an advance probe of thee thousand infantry under six mounted chieftains headed by Shi Jin. Winding towards the pass they didn't encounter a single enemy soldier. Shi Jin grew suspicious and conferred with the other chieftains.

At that moment a white banner appeared at the top of the pass, and beneath it stood the crack archer Pang Wanchun. Pang looked at Shi Jin and laughed.

"You should have stayed in Liangshan Marsh, scruffy bandit," he said contemptuously, "where you begged an amnesty from the Song emperor. You've got a nerve coming to my country and playing the bold hero! Of course, you've heard of me, and I know you have among you some scamp called Hua Rong. Let him come out and match archery with me. But first I'll show you one of my marvellous shots."

Before the words were out of his mouth, he whizzed an arrow at Shi Jin, hit him squarely and knocked him from his horse. The other five chieftains rushed forward, helped him back into the saddle, and they all withdrew.

A gong crashed on the mountain top, and from the pine groves on both sides swarms of arrows flew. The chieftains abandoned Shi Jin in their haste to get away. But when they rounded the gap, they saw Lei Jiong on one of the opposite slopes and Ji Ji on the other. The two deluged them with bolts from their crossbows. Not even the nimblest heroes could have avoided those lethal shafts. Poor

Liangshan Marsh chieftains, life passed from them like a dream! Six of them lay below the pass in a heap of corpses.

Of the three thousand infantry only a hundred odd managed to escape. They told Lu what happened. It was a paralyzing blow. For a long time he sat in a dazed silence.

"Taking it so hard will only delay our important mission," Zhu Wu the Miraculous Strategist said. "We can work out another plan, capture the pass, kill their generals and obtain our revenge."

"Brother Song Jiang made a point of giving me many excellent chieftains," said Lu, "but I've already lost six of them without winning the battle. And only a hundred or so of the three thousand infantry remain. How am I going to face him when we get to Shezhou!"

"The ancients had a saying: 'The time isn't as important as the terrain. But the terrain isn't as important as unity with the people.' We're all from Shandong and Hebei on the Central Plain. We're not used to hilly warfare, and so we lost the advantages of terrain. What we now need is one of the local people to serve as our guide, someone who can show us through the twists and turns of the local mountain paths."

"You're quite right. Who can we send to scout the trails?"

"In my humble opinion, Flea on a Drum Shi Qian would be just right. He can fly over eaves and climb walls. He'll find a way if anyone can."

Lu summoned Shi Qian and spoke to him. Flea on a Drum took some dry rations, hung his dagger at his waist, and left the camp.

He travelled half the day. As night began to fall he saw a lamp gleaming in the distance. "Where there's lamplight there must be people," he thought, and groped towards it through the darkness.

The glow was coming from a small monastery. Flea on a Drum slipped in. An old monk was sitting in one of the buildings, chanting scriptures. Shi Qian knocked on the door. The old man told a young acolyte to open it. Flea entered and bowed.

"No need for ceremony, sir traveller," said the monk. "What brings you here in these times of war and slaughter?"

"To tell you the truth, Reverend, I'm a commander under Song Jiang of Liangshan Marsh. My name is Shi Qian. We have been dispatched by imperial decree to destroy Fang La. But last night the bandit generals at Yuling Pass killed six of our chieftains with arrows, and we can't get through. My mission is to find out whether we can bypass it, and I've wandered here deep in the mountains. Can you help us solve the problem, Reverend? If you know of some path that will get us secretly by the pass, we'll reward you handsomely."

"All the local people have been harmed by Fang La. There isn't one who doesn't hate him. The villagers here used to support me, but they've all ran away and scattered. I have no place to go, so I can only stay on and wait to die. Fortunately, the emperor's soldiers have arrived to restore happiness to the people.

Finishing off the bandits will rid us of a scourge. I haven't dared to say much before, for fear the bandits would find out. But since you're a commander from the Imperial Army, I'll speak freely. There isn't any path here, but if you go to the ridge of the west mountain you'll find one that will take you above the pass. I'm only afraid that the bandits have blocked it and you won't be able to get through."

"Do you happen to know whether it goes to the enemy's fort?"

"It goes behind it. Another path goes down from there through the pass. But you may not be able to get through. They've probably built a big stone barricade."

"As long as there's a path I'll get by no matter what they've built! You've given us our opening. I'll report back to my chief and you'll be richly rewarded."

"Please don't tell any outsiders you got the information from me."

"I'm a very careful person, Reverend. I won't give you away."

Shi Qian bid the old monk farewell, returned to camp, and told Lu Junyi about the path. Delighted Lu called his advisor into conference.

"Excellent," said Zhu Wu. "We'll take Yuling Pass as easily as spitting on our hands. We must send another man with Shi Qian so that they can put through our plan."

"What has to be done, Advisor?" asked Flea on a Drum.

"Setting blazes and firing a cannon are the most important. You'll have to carry the cannon, flint and steel, up behind the fort above the pass, and fire a shot as a signal. That's your main task."

"Is that all? Then I don't need anybody else. I can do it myself. No companion can fly over eaves and walls like I do. He'd only slow things down. While I'm doing my part of the job, how will you be capturing the fort?"

"That's easy. The foe are sure to have troops lying in ambush, and we'll have to deal with them. All we have to do is set to the torch every thicket and grove along the way, and they'll have no place to hide."

"Very shrewd, Advisor."

Shi Qian took his fire-making equipment, toted the cannon in a pack upon his back, and bid Lu farewell. Lu gave him twenty ounces of silver and a bushel of rice for the old monk, directing a junior officer to carry the gifts.

In the afternoon of that day they reached the monastery. "Our Vanguard General is deeply grateful," Shi Qian said to the monk. "He sends these small things as a token of his appreciation."

Flea on a Drum handed over the gifts. He instructed the junior officer to go back to camp, then turned again to his host.

"Could I trouble you to tell your young acolyte to lead the way?"

"It would be better to wait till late at night. You might be seen from the fort during daylight."

That evening the monk laid a meal for Shi Qian and, when it was night, said to his acolyte: "Lead this commander over there and come right back. Don't let anybody know."

Shi Qian and the boy left the simple monastery and headed deep into the mountains. Through forests and over ridges, grasping bushes and vines, they laboriously climbed the rugged slopes in the dim light of a pale moon.

At last they came to a steep cliff face. Higher up were traces of a small path which had been cut into the rock. But at the top boulders had been piled and surmounted by a stone wall. How could anyone get past?

"Commander," said the boy, "the fort is on the other side. There's a road leading to it from the wall."

"You can go back, young acolyte. I know the way now."

The boy departed.

Flea on a Drum was a man who could fly over roofs, walk on walls, leap fences and steal horses. Using that ability now, he scaled the barricade easier than twiddling your thumbs.

In the wooded area to the east, half the sky was red. Lu and Zhu had broken camp and marched, setting fires as they advanced towards the fort. A forward unit of four or five hundred cleared the road of corpses, for the fires had left the enemy ambushers no place to hide.

Pang the crack archer in the fort above was informed. "Their method makes our ambushers useless," he said. "But we'll hang on here. Let's see them get through!"

As the Song forces drew near, he rode out with Lei Jiong and Ji Ji to defend the entrance to the pass.

Step by step, Shi Qian crept towards the fort. He climbed a tall tree and concealed himself amid the leafy branches. He saw the three southern commanders, with bows and arrows and big crossbows, lying in wait outside the pass, and the Song column moving up like a trail of fire. Lin Chong and Huyan Zhuo reined in their horses below and shouted at the foe.

"Bandit generals, how dare you resist the emperor's troops!"

The southern commanders, intent on readying their bows, had no idea that Flea on a Drum was already above the pass. He slid down the tree stealthily and crept to the rear of the fort. There he saw two haystacks. He hid between them, took out his fire-making apparatus and placed the cannon on one of the stacks. With sulfur and nitrate, he ignited first one stack, then the other. Lighting the fuse, he climbed swiftly with the cannon to the roof of the fort. It went off with a heaven-shaking boom just as the two haystacks burst into blaze.

Panicked before the fighting even started, the southern soldiers yelled and ran. Who had any stomach for battle? While Pang and his two lieutenants watched flames leaping behind the fort, Shi Qian, on the roof, fired another blast from his cannon. The explosion shook the entire fort, terrifying the southerners so that they dropped their weapons, shed their armor, and fled through the fort's rear.

From his perch on top of the roof, Shi Qian uttered a loud cry: "Ten thousand Song troops are already in the pass! Surrender quickly if you don't all want to die!"

Scared out of his wits, Pang could only stamp in frustration. Lei and Ji were wooden with shock. They couldn't move a muscle.

Lin Chong and Huyan Zhuo were the first up the mountain. The other chieftains rushed beyond the fort and chased the fleeing foe more than thirty *li*. Sun Li caught Lei Jiong, Wei Dingguo captured Ji Ji. Only Pang Wanchun escaped. Over half the southern effectives were rounded up. The Song column camped at the fort.

Lu rewarded Flea on a Drum generously. He cut the hearts from Lei Jiong and Ji Ji and offered them as sacrifices to Shi Jin and Shi Xiu and the other four chieftains who had been slain. Their six bodies were recovered and buried high on the slope. All the other corpses were burned.

The next day Lu and his chieftains donned their armor and mounted. Lu rushed a dispatch to Governor Zhang reporting the capture of the pass. At the same time, the column hastened through and marched directly to the outskirts of Shezhou, where they made camp.

Prince Fang Hou, the Governor of Shezhou, was Fang La's uncle on his father's side. Under him were two generals, and together they ruled Shezhou Prefecture. One was Minister Wang Yin, the other Vice-Minister Gao Yu. They garrisoned Shezhou with twenty thousand troops led by a dozen or more commanders. Wang originally was a stonemason in the Shezhou hills. He wielded a steel lance and rode a fine horse called Around the Mountains Flyer. This steed could climb slopes and ford rivers as if on level land. Gao was also a local man. He came from an old family. His weapon was a segmented lance. Because both were only slightly literate, Fang La, while giving them high administrative posts, actually limited them to military affairs.

After his defeat, Pang Wanchun returned to Shezhou and reported to the prince in the palace. "A native resident gave us away," said Pang. "He guided the Song forces along a secluded path to the pass. Our soldiers were scattered and we were unable to resist."

The prince was furious. "Yuling Pass is the most important barrier before Shezhou! Now that the Song troops have taken it, they'll be here sooner or later! How are we going to repel them?"

"Restrain your anger, Your Highness," urged Minister Wang. "As the ancients have said; 'Failure in battle should not be censured. Heaven gives perfection to no one.' Postpone punishing General Pang. Instead, issue a decree that he must win. Let him lead forth an army to drive back the Song column. If he fails to wrest victory, his crimes can be treated as double."

Fang Hou agreed. He gave Pang five thousand soldiers and ordered them to march, demanding that they return triumphant.

That day Lu Junyi launched his assault on Shezhou. The city gates opened and General Pang emerged with his large contingent. The two armies deployed in battle positions. Pang rode forward and challenged personal combat. From the Song side Ou Peng, carrying an iron lance, cantered out to meet him.

Less than five rounds they fought when Pang withdrew in defeat. Ou Peng, wanting to display his valor, galloped after. Pang turned in the saddle and let fly with an arrow. The skilful warrior Ou Peng caught it in mid-air. He didn't know that the southern general shot his arrows in series. After snatching the first missile, he raced heedless in pursuit of his foe. Pang's bow-string twanged, and a second shaft hit Ou Peng squarely, knocking him to the ground. Ministers Wang and Gao, on the city wall, saw Ou Peng fall and Pang lead his unit in a fierce charge.

The Song forces, defeated, retreated thirty *li* before making camp. A count of their officers and men revealed that Zhang Qing the Vegetable Gardener had been killed in battle. Sun the Witch, with the help of her soldiers, retrieved her husband's body and burned it. She wept distractedly. Lu was distressed at the sight. He felt his tactics were wrong.

"We lost another two chieftains in our attack today," he said to Zhu Wu. "How can we go on like this?"

"Victory and defeat are both usual fare to military men, and times of life and death are all predestined," said Zhu Wu. "The southerners believe they've compelled us to retreat. They're sure to launch a sneak raid against our camp tonight. We can move out and lie in ambush on four sides. In the center of camp we can tether a few sheep and then ..." Zhu Wu whispered the rest of his plan.

Huyan Zhuo hid with one unit to the left of the camp, Lin Chong with another unit to the right, Shan Tinggui and Wei Dingguo with a third unit to the north, and the other chieftains with the remaining forces along the paths all around. When the southerners raided that night, fire in the middle of the camp would be the signal for the ambushers to strike. The Song contingents took up their positions.

Meanwhile, Ministers Wang and Gao, who knew a bit of strategy, conferred with Fang Hou the king's uncle. They said: "We beat the Song forces today and forced them back thirty *li*. Their camp is defenseless, their men and horses exhausted. If we raid them now we can win a complete victory."

"Work it out carefully. If you're sure you can do it, go ahead."

"Pang and I will stage the raid," said Gao. "You and Wang stay here and guard the city."

That night the two generals donned their armor and marched with their troops. The horses' equipage was muffled, the men clamped sticks in their teeth to ensure silence. Nearing the camp, they saw that the stockade gate was open, and were hesitant to advance any further. The sound of the watch drum was clear, but its beat was confused. Gao reined his mount.

"Don't go in."

"Why not, sir Minister?"

"Their watch beat is all wrong. They must be up to something."

"Surely you're mistaken, sir. They're defeated, dispirited and weary. Even the watchman must be half asleep. No wonder his beat is sloppy. It's nothing to worry about. Let's just push on in."

"You're probably right."

They urged their raiders forward. Armed to the teeth, the troops entered the camp. The two southern generals went directly to headquarters, but not a commander was in sight. Suspended a few feet above the ground from some willows were a couple of sheep, drum-sticks tied to their legs. When they kicked about, they struck the drums beneath them. Thus, the erratic beat. The raiders had captured an empty camp.

"We've been tricked!" the two generals cried in alarm. They turned and ran.

Flames had begun to rise in the center of the stockade. On a mountain top a cannon boomed, and a fiery ball hit the camp. On four sides the men who had been lying in ambush now charged fiercely. The two generals, rushing through the stockade gate were met by Huyan Zhuo.

"If you want to live, bandits," he roared, "dismount and surrender!"

Minister Gao fled in panic. He wanted only to escape, he had no heart for battle. Huyan caught up, and brought his twin rods down in a blow that shattered half of Gao's skull.

General Pang fought desperately to break out of the encirclement. Just as he was getting away, a hooked pole snaked out and tripped up his horse. Tang Long, who had been hiding by the side of the road, captured Pang alive.

Song chieftains were slaughtering southern soldiers on all the mountain paths. At daybreak, they returned to camp. Lu Junyi, seated once again in his headquarters, handed out rewards. Of that we'll say no more.

A count of Lu's forces revealed the loss of chieftain Ding Desun. While in the mountains he had been bitten in the foot by a snake. The poison had seeped into his abdomen and killed him. The Song victors cut the heart out of Pang Wanchun and offered it in sacrifice to Ou Peng, Shi Jin and the other slain brothers, and sent Pang's head to Governor Zhang.

The next day, Lu and his column marched to Shezhou. The gate was open, no banners flew on the walls, the ramparts were devoid of soldiers. Shan Tinggui and Wei Dingguo, eager to win first honors, dashed in with a detachment before Lu could stop them. By the time he arrived with his central unit, they were already inside.

Minister Wang had been informed of the losses the southerners had sustained in their abortive raid on the camp. He pretended to have abandoned the city and dug a large concealed hole within the gate. When the two Song chieftains barged in, horses and riders landed in the pit. Southern spearsmen and archers, who had been hiding on either side, riddled them with spears and arrows. Poor mortals, their spirits left them in an earthen hole!

Angered by their loss, Lu ordered his vanguard to attack. Each man carried a clod of earth which he threw into the pit, then went on to join the wild carnage. In the end it was the bodies of southern soldiers and horses which filled the cavity.

On a cavorting steed at the head of his troops, Lu galloped to the center of Shezhou and ran directly into Fang Hou the king's uncle. They fought only a single round when Lu in his terrible fury called on all his might and cut Fang Hou from the saddle with a single thrust of his halberd.

The southern troops opened the West Gate and fled, hotly pursued by the Song forces. Many of the foe were killed or captured.

Meanwhile, the fleeing Minister Wang was stopped by Li Yun. Wang levelled his lance and cantered forward. Li Yun was on foot. Wang's charging steed knocked Li to the ground. Shi Yong, also on foot, ran to the rescue. But he was helpless against the southerner's lance, which darted like demon. After several rounds, it took Shi Yong's life.

From the city Sun Li, Huang Xin, Zhou Yuan and Zhou Run raced out and assailed Wang. He battled all four courageously and without fear. But then the formidable Lin Chong joined the fray. Even if he had three heads and six arms Wang couldn't have withstood five chieftains. In a concerted move, they closed in and stabbed him to death. Poor southern minister, thus ended his aspirations!

They cut off his head and galloped with it to General Lu, who was resting in the Shezhou palace. Order had been restored and proclamations reassuring the populace posted. The troops were already stationed in the city. Lu dispatched a messenger to Governor Zhang with news of the victory, and sent a similar report to Song Jiang.

Song Jiang, waiting with his army in Muzhou, was pleased that the joint offensive against the enemy's lair could now begin. But he was devastated by the loss of thirteen more chieftains, and he wept as though his heart would break. Military Advisor Wu Yong consoled him.

"Life and death are pre-ordained. Don't ruin your health with grieving. You have to deal with matters of major national importance."

"Yes, I know, but I can't help feeling awful. One hundred and eight are listed on the stone tablet in Heavenly script. Who would have thought we'd be cut down so severely. It's like losing my arms and legs!"

Wu Yong begged Song Jiang to calm himself. "Reply to Lu and fix a date for an assault on Clear Stream County," he urged.

Meanwhile, Fang La in his palace in Bangyuan Cavern in Clear Stream County summoned all of his top officials, civil and military, to discuss how to deal with Song Jiang's army. Leaders of defeated troops who had just returned reported: "Shezhou is finished, the Royal Uncle and Ministers Gao and Wang have been killed. The Song army is advancing in two columns to attack Clear Stream."

Startled, Fang La said to his ministers: "You have been appointed to the highest positions and have reaped the benefits of ruling our prefectures, shires and towns. But Song Jiang's army is rolling across the land and all of our cities have fallen, except for Clear Stream and this palace. Now he is coming here as well, in two columns. How shall we repel the foe?"

Prime Minister Lou Minzhong came forward and said: "The Song forces have nearly reached our palace, and it will be difficult to defend. Our soldiers are weak, our generals few. Unless Your Majesty takes personal command I'm afraid they won't do their utmost."

"It is indeed as you say," Fang La agreed, and he issued the order: "Let all officials of every rank prepare to go with me and fight a decisive battle."

"Who will lead the vanguard?" queried Lou.

"The Security General, Governor and Commander-in-Chief, our Royal Nephew Fang Jie. General Du Wei, Marshal of the Infantry and Cavalry, shall be his second in command. Under them will be thirty commanders leading fifteen thousand troops of the Royal Guards. Let them open paths through the mountains, bridge rivers, and advance in an offensive expedition."

Fang Jie, nephew of the king, was also the grandson of Fang Hou who had been killed at Shezhou. He had been about to ask to be sent out to avenge his grandfather, and now he was appointed leader of the vanguard. A diligent person, Fang Jie wielded a crescent-bladed halberd and was utterly fearless.

Du Wei had been a blacksmith in the mountains of Shezhou. He could forge arms and was a trusted confidant of Fang La. In battle he used six throwing knives. He fought on foot.

Fang La appointed Ho Conglong, who was master-instructor of Royal Guards, commander of another ten thousand Royal Guards, and ordered him to march against Lu Junyi in Shezhou.

Song Jiang's army meanwhile was advancing on land and water from Shezhou to Clear Stream. Li Jun was in charge of the naval units proceeding along the river. Wu Yong, riding by Song Jiang's side, had a suggestion.

"Fang La must know we're closing in. If he decides to hide in the mountains he'll be hard to find. To catch him and bring him before the emperor in the capital, we'll have to operate from within and without. Someone who recognizes him has to point him out before we can nab him. We also have to know where he's heading, so he won't escape.

"A false surrender will get our people inside his camp and enable us to cope with his moves. Chai Jin and Yan Qing have already gone as spies, but we haven't heard anything from them. Who should we have to pretend to surrender?"

"Li Jun would be best, in my humble opinion. He can sail in with grain boats and offer them as his entry gift. That will allay their suspicions. Fang La is a petty-minded fellow from a mountain hamlet. When he sees so much grain, he won't be able to turn it down."

"Very clever, Military Advisor," said Song Jiang. He dispatched Dai Zong with secret instructions to Li Jun.

The naval chieftain thereupon directed Ruan the Fifth and Ruan the Seventh to disguise themselves as captains and the Tong brothers to pretend to be sailors. They then set sail from Daxi with sixty vessels laden with grain. All flew banners indicating that they were delivering the cargo as a gift. As they neared

Clear Stream County, they were met by a southern warcraft which showered them with arrows.

From the deck, Li Jun shouted: "Cease fire! I have something to say. We have come to surrender! We present this grain to your great country as a gift to your soldiers. We hope you will accept."

Clearly Li Jun and his men were unarmed. The southerners stopped shooting. They sent a boarding party, which made a careful examination then reported back to Prime Minister Lou.

"Li Jun is surrendering with a gift of grain."

Lou ordered that he be permitted to land. Brought before Lou, Li Jun bowed.

"What are you to Song Jiang?" Lou demanded. "What's your rank? Why have you come with this grain to surrender?"

"My name is Li Jun. Originally I was a bold fellow on the Xunyang River. I snatched Song Jiang from the execution grounds in Jiangzhou and saved his life. But now that he has been amnestied by the emperor and made a Vanguard General, he's forgotten the favor I and my mates have done him. Several times, he's humiliated me. Although he's occupied a number of prefectures in your great country, many of our brothers have been killed. He himself doesn't know whether to advance or retreat, but he's forcing me and my naval forces to go forward. I can't take any more of his insults! So I'm turning his grain vessels over as my personal gift, and surrendering to your great country."

Convinced, Lou conducted Li Jun to Fang La in the palace and told him about it. Li Jun kowtowed and repeated his story. Fang La saw no reason to doubt him. He appointed Li Jun Chief Admiral, and made admirals of Ruan the Fifth, Ruan the Seventh, Tong Wei and Tong Meng. The boats were to be moored in the Clear Stream naval installation.

"After I have driven back Song Jiang and restored my royal rule, I will reward you further," Fang La promised.

Li Jun bowed his thanks and left the palace. He unloaded the grain and delivered it to the granary. Of that we'll say no more.

Meanwhile, Song Jiang sent Guan Sheng, Hua Rong, Qin Ming and Zhu Tong forward with a probing contingent to the border of Clear Stream County. There they met Royal Nephew Fang Jie and his army. The two forces spread out in battle formation.

In the southern position, Fang Jie sat his horse, holding his halberd athwart. To his rear was Du Wei, on foot. Clad in full armor five throwing knives concealed behind his back, Du Wei carried a seven-starred precious sword. The two men proceeded to the front.

Qin Ming rode out from Song Jiang's position. Brandishing his wolf-toothed mace, he cantered directly towards Fang Jie. Without a word from either, they dashed. Fang Jie was young and spirited, and highly skilled with the crescent-bladed halberd. They fought more than thirty rounds, with neither emerging the victor. Both men battled relentlessly, exerting their utmost talent.

Since Fang Jie obviously wasn't making any progress, Du Wei slipped out from behind his horse and threw a knife directly at Qin Ming's face. As the thunderbolt dodged the flying blade, Fang Jie finished him with one thrust of his halberd. Poor Qin Ming the thunderbolt, he died an untimely death!

Fang Jie dared not press his advantage to attack the Song position. Junior officers quickly pulled back their slain leader with hooked poles. When informed of the loss of Qin Ming, Song Jiang blanched. He directed that the body be encoffined and prepared for burial, and again sent forward another contingent.

Emboldened by his triumph, Fang Jie shouted: "If you have any more bold warriors, let them come out and fight!"

Song Jiang hurried to the front. To the rear of Fang Jie he saw Fang La's royal entourage advancing in a body, amid poles topped by golden gourds and row upon row of battle-axes. There were lines of crescent-bladed halberds, corps of flags embroidered with dragon and phoenix, pennants of green and red, jade stirrups, tooled leather saddles, banners encrusted with pearls and sewn with kingfisher-blue thread. On panoplies of dragons rampant were stitched azure clouds and purple mist. On flags of flying tigers were designs of auspicious clouds and smoke. Civil officials stood to the left, military to the right, all in full ranks. The usurper king made a great show of having "ministers." No better than a bandit in the hills, he aspired to sovereign's rule!

And there in the middle, beneath a nine-segment imperial yellow umbrella, seated easily on a steed with a jade-encrusted bridle, was the usurper king himself—Fang La. He wore a high hood of bright gold with turned-up corners and a robe embroidered with nine dragons amid sun, moon, and clouds. A jade belt embossed with gold and precious stones bound his waist. His feet were shod in a pair of royal boots stitched in gold thread with soles of cloud design.

On a silver-white thoroughbred he rode to the front to direct the battle personally. He spotted Song Jiang, opposite on horseback, and ordered Fang Jie to capture him. The Song forces also prepared to fight and catch Fang La. Fang Jie was about to go forth when a mounted messenger galloped up and reported.

"The Song forces under General Lu Junyi captured Ho Conglong when his army went to the rescue of Shezhou. They have scattered our troops and are already at the rear of the mountain!"

Fang La was shocked. He hastily ordered a withdrawal and a defense of the palace. Fang Jie instructed Du Wei to hold the position while the king retreated, then the two commanders followed.

On arriving in Clear Stream, Fang La heard cries and lamentations rising from the palace. Everywhere was the glow of flames. Soldiers and horses milled about in confusion. Li Jun and his four companions had set the city to the torch. Fang La rushed in with his Royal Guards in an attempt to save Clear Stream.

Song Jiang and his army gave chase, fighting and killing. They saw that the city was on fire and knew that Li Jim and the others had performed their mission. They drove on. Just then Lu Junyi and his column rounded the mountain, and they joined forces and attacked together.

The Clear Stream palace was crushed in a vice of Song troops. Everywhere they captured southern soldiers. They broke the defenses of the city completely. Guarded by Fang Jie and his men, the king fled to Bangyuan Cavern.

Song Jiang and his main army entered Clear Stream. They sacked Fang La's palace, destroying his illegal royal paraphernalia and confiscating his valuables. They burned the palace to the ground and cleaned out his treasury and granary.

Reunited, the forces of Song Jiang and Lu Junyi made camp in Clear Stream, and the chieftains came forward to claim their rewards. A count revealed more losses. The tall Yu Baosi and Sun the Witch had died of wounds inflicted by Du Wei's throwing knives. Zou Yuan and Du Qian were trampled to death by horses. LiLi, Tang Long and Cai Fu had all been severely wounded, and medical treatment had been of no avail. Ruan the Fifth had been killed by Prime Minister Lou in Clear Stream County.

The chieftains received awards for the ninety-two southern officials they had caught. Lou and Du Wei had disappeared. Notices were posted reassuring the population, and the captured officials were sent to governor Zhang's headquarters, where they would be decapitated and their heads hung up on display.

A local informant reported: "When your army broke into Clear Stream, Lou hung himself in a pine grove because he killed Ruan the Fifth."

Du Wei hid in the home of the mistress he was keeping, a young singer. Her pander exposed him, and Song Jiang rewarded the man. On Song Jiang's orders Du was decapitated. Cai Qing cut out Du Wei's heart and offered it, dripping blood, in sacrifice to the chieftains who died in the Clear Stream battle. Song Jiang officiated personally at the ceremony.

The next day, he and Lu Junyi marched with their units to Bangyuan Cavern and surrounded the entrance. Fang La sat tight in his cavern, defended only by Fang Jie and his troops. But the southerners would not come out and fight, and the Song contingents had no way of getting in. Although Fang La was on pins and needles, there was nothing else he could do. The stalemate continued for several days.

Fang La was sunk in gloom. Suddenly, a high official in an embroidered silken robe prostrated himself at the foot of the gold dais. "I have no talents, Sire," said the man, "but I have never repaid for the great benevolence Your Majesty has bestowed upon me. I am familiar with all the books of military lore and have devoted my life to weaponry. If you will give me a detachment, Sire, I will drive back the Song army and restore our nation. I hope my proposal meets with Your Majesty's wishes."

Delighted, Fang La mustered the soldiers in the cavern palace and sent the man forth with them to fight Song Jiang. It was impossible to predict who would win, since both sides were strikingly impressive.

And because Fang La dispatched this unit, heads rolled at the foot of the golden dais and hot blood spattered the jade-panelled palace door. Fang La's nest was swept clean and Song Jiang performed a great deed.

Who led forward Fang La's southern soldiers? Read our next chapter if you would know.

CHAPTER 99

SAGACIOUS LU EXPIRES IN ZHEJIANG IN A TRANCE
SONG JIANG GOES HOME IN HIS OFFICIAL FINERY

The official who offered to lead the expedition from the Cavern was none other than Ke Yin the Duke Consort. Fang La was overjoyed.

"We are very fortunate," he said, "that the consort is willing to exercise his might in battle against the brigands. We gladly utilize his genius to regain our national glory."

Ke Yin immediately prepared to set forth with his troops. Yun Bi was his second in command. Fang La presented the consort with his personal golden armor and silken robe and a fine horse. Accompanied by Fang Jie the Royal Nephew and more than twenty generals, Ke Yin marched from Bangyuan Cavern with ten thousand of the Royal guards and spread out in battle position.

The news was reported to Song Jiang and Lu Junyi, who also deployed their forces. They saw Duke Consort Ke Yin riding forward. No one recognized him as Chai Jin. Song Jiang ordered Hua Rong to fight him. Lance at the ready, Hua Rong cantered to the front and shouted derisively at his challenger.

"Who are you, knave, that you dare help rebels against the Imperial Army? Just wait till I get my hands on you! I'll pound you to mincemeat! Dismount and surrender, and I'll spare your life!"

"I'm Ke Yin from Shandong. Everyone knows my fame. A bunch of scruffy robbers like you from Liangshan Marsh are really beneath my notice! We're more than a match for you! I'm determined to wipe you out and recapture our cities!"

Song and Lu, on their horses, listened and thought: "That's Chai Jin's voice. He never in the past said anything which indicated he might betray us. He's changed his name from Chai Jin to Ke Yin, but the names mean virtually the same thing."

"Before Lord Chai became an outlaw he often gave shelter to wanted men and disguised them as merchants," said Wu Yong. "Can he have forgotten his old loyalties?"

"Let's see what happens in his joust with Huan Rong," said Lu Junyi. Hua Rong kicked his steed faster. The horses met, the weapons clashed, and the warriors fought. Gradually they moved into a ravine, battling ever closer to one another.

"Pretend to be defeated, brother," Chai Jin said in a low voice. "I'll explain later."

Hua Rong heard. After three rounds, he turned his mount and withdrew.

"Beaten officer, I won't chase you," Ke Yin shouted. "Is there anyone else who thinks so well of himself? Let him come out and fight!"

Hua Rong galloped back to the position and told Song and Lu what had happened. "Let Guan Sheng do combat," Wu Yong suggested. Waving his halberd, with its blue dragon etched into the steel, Guan Sheng raced to the front.

"Petty officer from Shandong," he yelled, "I dare you to joust with me!"

Fearlessly, they battled less than five rounds when Guan Sheng feigned defeat and returned to the Song lines. Ke Yin did not pursue. Instead, he rode forward and shouted another challenge.

"Is there any strong general among you who dares to fight?"

On Song Jiang's orders, Zhu Tong was the next contender. Back and forth the two battled, deceiving both armies. After only six or seven rounds, Zhu Tong fled. Chai Jin gave chase and lunged in a false thrust with his lance. Zhu Tong leaped from his saddle and ran back to the Song position.

The southern soldiers captured the abandoned horse and the consort waved them forward in a wild charge. Song Jiang and his troops hastily retreated ten *li* before making camp. Ke Yin pursued them for a distance, then returned with his contingent to the cavern.

The news was reported to Fang La: "The heroic duke consort has defeated three enemy generals and driven the Song forces back ten *li.*"

Fang La, delighted, ordered a royal banquet. After the consort had removed his armor he was invited into the rear palace and given a seat of honor at the festive board. The king raised his gold goblet and toasted him personally.

"I knew you were a scholar, but I never realized you had such military skill! Had I known earlier what a hero you are, we wouldn't have lost so many cities. Give full play to your brilliance, slaughter the bandits, and restore our sovereignty, and you shall share with us the glories of peace and enjoy together national restoration."

"Rest assured, Sire," said Ke Yin. "I will do my utmost. I pray Your Majesty will watch tomorrow from the top of the hill while I annihilate Song Jiang and the rest of his crew!"

Fang La consented. He was very pleased. That night they feasted until late, then each retired to his quarters in the palace.

The next morning Fang La held no royal court, but ordered the slaughter of steers and horses to feed his troops to the full. Then all donned armor and mounted. They rode cheering from the cavern, amid waving banners and pounding drums. Accompanied by his retinue and cabinet officials, the king climbed to the top of the hill above the cavern to watch the duke consort do battle.

Song Jiang transmitted this order to all his chieftains: "Today's engagement will be critical. Do your utmost to catch Fang La, but don't kill him. When your soldiers see Chai Jin in the southern position turn his horse, charge after him into the cavern and capture Fang La."

Rubbing their hands in anticipation, the northerners took up their weapons. Every man was eager to plunder the riches of the cavern, and win glory and rewards by seizing Fang La.

The Song forces deployed outside the cavern. On the southern side, Ke Yin sat his horse beneath an arch of pennants, about to ride forth into combat. But Fang Jie the Royal Nephew, his lance held athwart his saddle, intervened.

"Wait until I've killed one of their generals," he urged. "Then you can lead our men against the foe."

The Song units were pleased to see that Yan Qing was standing behind Chai Jin. "This scheme is sure to succeed," they said, and prepared for action.

Fang Jie rode forward and issued his challenge. From the Song position Guan Sheng cantered out, brandishing his halberd. The two warriors had fought only ten rounds or so when Hua Rong joined in the fray. Though assailed by two opponents, Fang Jie battled without fear. They could not subdue him, but gradually he was forced onto the defensive.

Then Li Ying and Zhu Tong rode forth and also attacked. Four against one were too much. Fang Jie turned his mount and started to leave. Ke Yin emerged from the arch of pennants and blocked his way. The consort waved his hand, and the four Song chieftains closed in, while Ke Yin himself charged with levelled lance. Fang Jie jumped from his steed and tried to flee, but Chai Jin pierced him with a single thrust. Yan Qing dashed up from behind and finished Fang Jie off with his sword.

The southern soldiers were stunned. Then they ran for their lives. The "duke consort" raised his voice in a shout.

"I am not Ke Yin but Chai Jin, a chieftain in the army of Song Jiang. The Royal Attendant, with me, is actually Yan Qing the Prodigy. We now know all about everything inside and outside the cavern. Whoever captures Fang La alive will be made a high official and ride a fine horse. Surrender and avoid bloodshed! Resist and be slaughtered with your entire family!"

Chai Jin, Yan Qing and the four chieftains, leading a large contingent, drove into the cavern. Fang La saw it all from the top of the hill. Angrily, he kicked over his golden throne and plunged deep into the hills. When five columns of Song Jiang's army rushed into the cavern, they discovered he was gone, and caught only some of his retinue.

Yan Qing and a few trusted confidants, after removing two loads of gold and jewels from the treasury, set fire to the inner palace. When Chai Jin entered his own consort's residency, he found that his wife the princess had hung herself. He burned the residency down, cremating her inside it. He allowed her attendants to run away.

In the main palace the Song chieftains slaughtered everyone—the king's concubines, his personal guards, his royal relations... and plundered his treasures. Song Jiang urged them to search the palace for Fang La.

Ruan the Seventh discovered in an inner room the trunk in which Fang La kept his crown, his royal robe, his green jade belt, his white jade scepter, his Care-Free boots. He couldn't resist the temptation to try the lavish finery on. In full regal attire, he mounted his steed and trotted to the front of the palace. The soldiers at first thought he was Fang La. But when they crowded around they saw it was Ruan the Seventh, and everyone laughed. Ruan thought it was all a great joke, and rode about the palace grounds watching the looting.

Wang Bing and Zhao Tan, the two generals who had come from the Eastern Capital with Minister Tong, had taken part in the assault on Bangyuan Cavern. They heard the tumult among Song Jiang's troops, and someone said that Fang La had been caught. They hurried to join in the seizure so that they could claim some of the credit. But they saw only Ruan the Seventh, all togged out the royal robe, the crown upon his head, laughing uproariously.

"You've got a nerve dressing up like Fang La and making a spectacle of yourself!" they fumed.

Ruan pointed his finger at them and raged. "Who do you pricks think you are! If it weren't for our brother Song Jiang your donkeys' heads would have been chopped off by Fang La long ago! All you can do is try to cut in on the glory my brother chieftains and I have earned! You'll go back and tell the emperor it couldn't have done without the help of you two big generals!"

Wang and Zhao, infuriated, were ready to fight. Ruan snatched a spear and raced towards them. Huyan Zhuo, who witnessed the quarrel, galloped up and separated the contestants. An officer had notified Song Jiang, and he too hurried to the scene. He and Wu Yong yelled at Ruan to dismount, remove the royal vestments and cast them aside. Song Jiang apologized to the two generals. Although Wang and Zhao had no choice but to accept the placatory words of Song and his chieftains, inwardly they would not forget their hatred.

That day corpses littered the ground in Bangyuan Cavern, and blood flowed in streams. According to *Song Annals* over twenty thousand of Fang La's soldiers were annihilated. On Song Jiang's orders, the palace buildings were put to the torch. The royal halls, the ornate towers, the inner chambers, the bejewelled alcoves—all were reduced to ashes. The Song army made camp at the entrance to Bangyuan Cavern and built a stockade, A check of the prisoners revealed that only Fang La had escaped. Song Jiang ordered a search of the mountains and had the local populace notified: Whoever captured Fang La would be recommended to the emperor for a high official post; whoever supplied information as to his whereabouts would be rewarded.

Meanwhile Fang La scurried through the mountains like a dog whose master just died, like a fish which evaded the net. Discarding his robe of imperial yellow, his golden-flowered hood, his royal court boots, he fled over the heights in grass and hempen sandals. In a single night he crossed five mountains.

He came at last to a hollow. There, nestled against a slope was a rude monastery. Fang La was hungry. He started towards it to ask for something to eat. From behind a pine tree a big fat monk suddenly emerged. He knocked Fang La down with his Buddhist staff and tied him up. The cleric was none other than Sagacious Lu the Tattooed Monk. He took Fang La to the monastery, obtained some food, then started down with him. They met a party of soldiers who had been searching the mountains for the former king. Together, they escorted the captive under guard and brought him before Song Jiang.

When he saw who it was, Song Jiang was delighted. "Where did you find him, Reverend?" he asked Sagacious Lu.

"After the battle in the Grove of Ten Thousand Pines on Black Dragon Ridge, I chased Xiahou Cheng into the mountains and killed him. I pushed on in deeper, looking for more of the southern brigands. But I got lost and was wandering around when I met an old monk on a wild and verdant slope. He led me to his rustic monastery and said: 'We've plenty of fuel and grain and vegetables. Wait here. If you see a big fellow come out of the pine forest, grab him.' I saw fires burning at the foot of the mountains, and kept watch all night. I didn't know where the paths ran in those parts. But this morning I spotted this rogue climbing over the rise. So I knocked him down with my staff and tied him up. I had no idea it was Fang La."

"Where is the old monk now?"

"I don't know."

"He must be a saintly person to be so psychic. When I get back to the capital I'm going to report your great deed to the emperor. You'll be able to return to secular life and become an official. Your future wife and children will be honored, you'll be a credit to your ancestors, you'll recompense your parents for their kindness in raising you."

"I've lost interest in mundane affairs. I don't want to be an official. It will be enough if I can find a quiet place to live out the rest of my life in peace."

"We'll make you abbot of some big monastery. That also is very honorable. Your parents will be proud of you."

Sagacious Lu shook his head. "I don't want any part of it. Having a lot of things is no use. Just this flesh on my frame of bones— nothing could be better than that."

Song Jiang fell silent. Neither he nor Sagacious was happy. The troops were already mustered. Fang La was locked in a cage-cart, to be delivered to the emperor in the Eastern Capital. Song Jiang issued the order and the army left Bangyuan Cavern in Clear Stream County and headed for Muzhou.

In Muzhou Governor Zhang, Deputy District Commander Liu, Chancellor Tong and staff officers Cong and Geng joined forces and made camp. They learned of Song Jiang's great victory, and that he had captured Fang La and brought him to Muzhou. All called to congratulate him. Song Jiang and his chieftains bowed respectfully.

"We've heard that it was an arduous campaign, General, and that brothers have been lost," said Zhang. "But you've been completely victorious. We're extremely happy."

Song Jiang again bowed. Weeping, he replied: "There were a hundred and eight of us when we went to break the Liao Tartars, and we returned to the capital intact. Gongsun Sheng left us, and several more remained in the capital. But since conquering Yangzhou and crossing the Yangzi, we've lost seven out of ten. Although I'm still alive, how can I go back to Shandong and face my old neighbors and relations!"

"Don't talk like that, General. You know the old saying: 'Poverty or wealth, high rank or low, short life or long—all are predestined.' Those fortunate enough to live must send off the unfortunates who have died. You have no reason to be ashamed of your losses. You're successful and famous. The emperor will surely reward you with high honors and rank. When you visit home in your official finery you'll be envy of all. Don't concern yourself with incidentals. Just concentrate Oil returning with your army and reporting to His Majesty."

Bowing his thanks, Song Jiang issued appropriate orders to his chieftains. Governor Zhang directed that, with the exception of Fang La who was to be delivered to the Eastern Capital, all captured southern officials were to be decapitated in Muzhou's public square.

Officials of counties not yet captured, on learning that Fang La had been taken, either fled or came to Muzhou to surrender and pay their respects to Governor Zhang, in about equal number. The capitulators were accepted and treated as good citizens. Notices, posted everywhere, reassured the populace.

As to the remaining adherents of the southern rebels, if they hadn't harmed anyone and were willing to surrender, they were allowed to return to the countryside and their land and property were restored. With all the counties and prefectures now under control, Song officials and garrisons were placed in charge to defend the territory and protect the people. Everyone resumed his original occupation.

Zhang gave a large banquet in Muzhou to celebrate peace, congratulate his officials and generals, and issue awards. He directed that Song Jiang and Lu Junyi return with their Vanguard Army to the capital. The various units assembled their equipment and got ready to march.

Tears fell from Song Jiang's eyes whenever he thought of the chieftains who had died. Then Zhu Fu and Mu Chun went to visit the six chieftains who were ill in Hangzhou, and they too were stricken. Only Yang Lin and Mu Chun survived and were able to join the march. Today, at last, there was peace, after the many hardships they had been through together, but six poor brothers had passed on.

In a quiet spot in a Muzhou temple Song Jiang had a long banner hung, three hundred and sixty scriptures read, and prayers offered so that the deceased might ascend from the Nine Depths into Heaven. The next day he had steers and horses sacrificed at the Black Dragon Temple in ceremonies which he attended with Wu Yong and the other chieftains. They burned paper replicas of gold and silver ingots as thanks to the Black Dragon Prince for his benevolent protection. Returning to camp. Song Jiang collected the bodies of all the chieftains who had died and gave them proper burial.

The expeditionary army prepared to follow Governor Zhang to Hangzhou, there to await the official imperial decree ordering their return. A list of chieftains who had distinguished themselves was sent to the sovereign with a report. Only thirty-six of the original one hundred and eight were left. They were as follows:

Song Jiang the Defender of Chivalry; Lu Junyi the Jade Unicorn; Wu Yong the Wizard; Guan Sheng the Big Halberd; Lin Chong the Panther Head; Huyan Zhuo the Two Rods; Hua Rong the Lesser Li Guang; Chai Jin the Small Whirlwind; Li Ying the Heaven-Soaring Eagle; Zhu Tong the Beautiful Beard; Sagacious Lu the Tattooed Monk; Wu Song the Pilgrim; Da Zong the Marvelous Traveler; Li Kui the Black Whirlwind; Yang Xiong the Pallid; Li Jun the Turbulent River Dragon; Ruan the Seventh the Devil Incarnate; Yan Qing the Prodigy; Zhu Wu the Miraculous Strategist; Huang Xin the Suppressor of Three Mountains; Sun Li the Sickly General; Fan Rui the Demon King Who Roils the World; Ling Zhen the Heaven-Shaking Thunder; Pei Xuan the Ironclad Virtue; Jiang Jing the Magic Calculator; Du Xing the Demon Face; Song Qing the Iron Fan; Zou Run the One-Horned Dragon; Cai Qing the Single Blossom; Yang Lin the Elegant Panther; Mu Chun the Slightly Restrained; Tong Wei the Dragon from the Cave; Tong Meng the River Churning Clam; Shi Qian the Flea on the Drum; Xun Xin the Junior General and Mistress Gu the Tigress. To the mountain-shaking pounding of drums and gongs, their red victory pennants stretching over a distance of ten *li, the* triumphant Vanguard Army left Muzhou. The cavalry rhythmically beat their metal stirrups, the entire force raised their voices in murderous song.

The march to Hangzhou was uneventful. Because Governor Zhang's troops were in the city, Song Jiang camped at Six Harmonies Pagoda. He and his chieftains took quarters in the Six Harmonies Monastery. Song Jiang and Lu Junyi went frequently into Hangzhou while waiting for orders.

Sagacious Lu and Wu Song, quartered in the monastery, relished the beauty of the hills and streams in the outskirts of the city. That night the moon was bright and the breeze cool, the sky and waters an azure blue. The two were asleep in the monastery when, around midnight, they were awakened by the boom of the incoming river tide. Sagacious Lu was from west of the Pass and had never heard this sound before. He thought it was a battle drum, that brigands were again attacking. He leaped from his bed and grabbed his iron staff. With a yell he started to rush outside. The monks were astonished.

"What's wrong, Reverend?" they asked. "Where are you going?"

"I heard a battle drum. I'm going to fight!"

The monks laughed. "You're mistaken, Reverend. That's no battle drum. It's the Old Faithful Tide on our Qiantang River."

Lu was surprised. "Why do you call it that?"

Opening the window, the monks pointed at the great head of water rolling up the river. "The tide comes in once during the day and once at night, always on time. Today is the fifteenth of the eighth month, and it arrives at the third watch. We call it Old Faithful because it's never late."

Sagacious peered at the water, then suddenly he understood. He clapped his hands and laughed.

"The prophesy of my old abbot said: 'Take Xia when you encounter him,' and after the fight in the Forest of Ten Thousand Pines I captured Xiahou Cheng. 'Seize La when you meet,' said the abbot, and I've caught Fang La. Now I must fulfil the rest of the prophesy: 'When you hear the ride, round out the circle. When you see the tide, in silence rest.' Well, I've heard the tide and I've seen it, but how do I do the other part? Can you brothers tell me?"

"You've joined the Buddhist order, how is it you don't understand?" said the monks. "In our religious parlance 'to round out the circle and in silence rest' means to die."

Sagacious laughed. "So that's what it's called. In that case I'll have to round out my circle and rest in silence. Heat a few buckets of water. I must bathe first."

The monks thought he was joking. But they knew he had a violent temper, and dared not refuse. After Lu had cleansed himself and changed into the fresh monk's clothing presented to him by the emperor, he instructed one of his junior officers.

"Notify brother Song Jiang. Ask him to come here and see me."

He went into the interior of the temple and wrote an ode on a slip of paper. In the meditation hall, he pulled a hassock to the center, lit some fragrant incense in a burner, and placed the slip of paper on a meditation couch. Then he seated himself cross-legged on the hassock, with his left foot resting on his right and, quite naturally, transcended into space. By the time Song Jiang received the message and hurried with his chieftains to the temple, Sagacious Lu was already motionless. The ode read as follows:

In life I performed no virtuous deeds, preferring murder and arson.
Suddenly my metal shackles were opened, the jade lock shattered.
Hark! The Old Faithful Tide comes on the Qiantang River, and today I know myself at last.

On reading the ode, Song Jiang and Lu Junyi sighed without cease. The chieftains burned incense to the departed Sagacious Lu and kowtowed. Governor Zhang and Chancellor Tong and the other officials hastened from the city and did the same.

Song Jiang distributed the deceased's Buddhist garments and the rewards given to him by the emperor among the monks, and asked them to conduct memorial services for three days and three nights. The body he had put in a cinnabar red casket and requested the abbot of Jiangshan Monastery to officiate at the cremation. Abbots came also from ten other monasteries to join in the prayers.

Sagacious Lu's remains were cremated behind the Six Harmonies Pagoda. The Jiangshan abbot approached the encoffined body, torch in hand, and pointed at it.

"Sagacious Lu, Sagacious Lu," he intoned, "you began your career in the greenwood. Arson burned in your eyes, murder festered in your heart. Now you have gone with tide to where none can find you. Amazing! Flying white jade flakes shall fill the sky, the earth shall be covered with yellow gold!"

The abbot lit the pyre, the monks prayed, and flames consumed the casket. Then the bones were collected and interred in the pagoda courtyard. All of Sagacious Lu's extra clothing, money and the contributions he had received from various officials were donated to the Six Harmonies Monastery for the common use of whoever resided there.

Wu Song, though he was still alive, now had only one arm.

"I'm a cripple," he said to Song Jiang, "and I don't want to go to the capital to be presented to the emperor. I'm giving all my money and awards to Six Harmonies Monastery so that I'll be clean and unencumbered. When you send in the list of those going to the capital, brother, leave my name off."

"As you wish," said Song Jiang.

Wu Song became a monk in the Six Harmonies Monastery. He lived to the ripe old age of eighty, but that was later.

Song Jiang went daily into Hangzhou to inquire for news. Governor Zhang and his forces departed first, and Song Jiang moved his troops into the city. Half a month went by and an imperial emissary arrived with an order directing Vanguard General Song to return to the capital with his army. By then Governor Zhang, Chancellor Tong, Deputy District Commander Liu, staff officers Cong and Geng, Generals Wang and Zhao, and the central forces had all departed for the capital.

When Song Jiang and his army were about to set forth, Lin Chong was unexpectedly stricken by paralysis, Yang Xiong developed a growth on his spine and died, and Shi Qian expired from appendicitis. Song Jiang felt very badly. Then a dispatch arrived from Dantu County saying that Yang Zhi had died and had been buried there. Since Lin Chong's paralysis could not be cured, they left him in Six Harmonies Monastery under Wu Song's care. He passed away half a year later.

Yan Qing the Prodigy approached his former patron Lu Junyi privately after they left Hangzhou.

"I have been with you since childhood," he said, "and you have been kinder than words can say. Now that we have accomplished our mission, why shouldn't we two give up our official ranks and live out our lives in some secluded place where our fame is unknown?"

"Ever since Liangshan Marsh returned to the fold of the Song Dynasty, we've been going north to subdue the Liao Tartars and south to capture Fang La. They've been bitter costly campaigns in which many of our brothers have been lost. Of my own family, only you and I are left. Now that we shall soon be able to return home in official finery and have honors bestowed on our future wives and children, why should you choose so pointless a course?"

The Prodigy smiled. "You're making a mistake, patron. There is a point to my course. It's your course which probably will turn out badly."

Yan Qing was a very far-sighted young man.

"I haven't the slightest personal ambition," Lu protested. "Are you suggesting the imperial court will consider me dangerous?"

"Many famous and loyal heroes of ancient times who contributed much to the founding of new dynasties were executed by their sovereigns."

"They all committed offenses of one sort or another. I've done nothing wrong. What cause have I for concern?"

"You'll be sorry that you haven't listened to me, but then it will be too late. I was going to bid farewell to General Song Jiang, but he's very strong on fraternity. I'm afraid he wouldn't let me go. So I'll take my leave only of you, patron."

"Where will you go?"

"Either ahead of or behind you!"

Lu Junyi laughed. "All right, have it your way. Let's see where you end up."

Yan Qing kowtowed eight times. That night he gathered some money and valuables and departed for a destination unknown. The next morning a note was delivered to Song Jiang. It read:

I, Yan Qing, greet the Vanguard General with the deepest respect. I am extremely grateful for your benevolent teachings. Even my utmost efforts could never repay you. Because of my feeble destiny and weak talents I am not worthy of official honors. I intend to retire to rustic life. I wanted to bid you farewell, but knowing your strong fraternal sentiments I feared you would not let me go, and slipped away in the night Please forgive me. I would like to leave these four lines by way of respectful farewell:
I gladly relinquish official rank,
For wealth and honors I have no need.
Only the amnesty I retain,
With simple fare my life sustain.

The verse struck a chord of melancholy in Song Jiang's heart. He collected the tablets of office of the chieftains who had died and sent them on to the capital, so that the appointments might be cancelled.

Travelling along a winding road, the troops reached the outskirts of Suzhou. Li Jun the Turbulent River Dragon pretended to be stricken with an ailment and took to his bed. The news was reported to Song Jiang, who came personally with a doctor to see him.

"Don't delay the march on my account, brother," Li Jun pleaded. "The emperor will reproach you. Governor Zhang probably has already been back for some time. Have pity, brother, and leave Tong Wei and Tong Meng to look after me. We'll catch up and attend the imperial court as soon as I am well again. You hurry on to the capital with the army."

Though reluctant, Song Jiang could not procrastinate. Zhang was sending dispatches urging speed. Li Jun and the two Tong brothers were left behind, and Song Jiang and his chieftains rode on.

Li Jun and the Tong brothers then sought out Fei Bao and the three other rustic friends, and the seven conferred in Willow Hamlet. They disposed of their family possessions, built a ship and set sail from the port of Taicang for foreign parts. Li Jun eventually became king of Siam. Tong Wei and Fei Bao also became officials in a foreign land, each occupying coastal territory and doing as he pleased. But that was all in Li Jun's later history.

The march of the Song troops was uneventful. Song Jiang's heart was heavy when they traversed Changzhou and Runzhou, where the had fought costly battles. Only two or three out of ten of his chieftains remained since crossing the Yangzi. The army passed Yangzhou and entered Huai'an. The capital wasn't far away. Song Jiang ordered the chieftains to get ready to be received by the emperor.

They reached the Eastern Capital on the twentieth day of the ninth month. Governor Zhang and his forces entered the city first. Song Jiang's men camped at their old site in the outskirts, Chen Bridge Station, and waited for orders.

A count of the chieftains showed a total of twenty-seven, including Song Jiang. Of these, only twelve were senior officers. He wrote out a list of those who had died for their country to present to the emperor, and instructed his remaining chieftains to prepare suitable attire for attending the imperial court. Three days later, they received the emperor's summons.

That morning at daybreak the twenty-seven rode into the city. This was the third time the capital's populace had seen the chieftains arrive for a reception by the Taoist Sovereign. The first was when they were granted the imperial amnesty. They were garbed in the silks of red and green given to them by the emperor then, and wore tablets of silver and gold. The second time, on their return to the capital after defeating the Liao Tartars, they were dressed in armor. Today, on His Majesty's orders, they wore civilian robes and headgear. The watching crowds sighed in admiration.

At the palace gate, the twenty-seven dismounted and entered. They kowtowed eight times at the foot of the vermilion jade stairs, then retreated and kowtowed another eight times, then advanced to midway between the two positions and kowtowed eight times more. Their twenty-four obeisances raised a cloud of dust, and their cries of "Long live!" shook the air.

Emperor Hui Zong saw how drastically their numbers had been depleted, and his heart was moved. He summoned them into the hall. With Song Jiang and Lu Junyi in the lead they mounted the golden stairs and knelt before the jewel-encrusted curtain. The sovereign instructed them to rise. By then his ministers had rolled up the curtain.

"We have heard of your hardships in the punitive expedition across the Yangzi, and that you have lost more than half your brothers," said the emperor. "We feel very badly about that."

Song Jiang, weeping, remained on his knees. "Because I am only a crude talentless rustic, I can never repay Your Majesty's kindness, though I spill my liver and brains on the battlefield! There were a hundred and eight of us when we pledged brotherhood in the Wutai Mountains. Who would have thought we'd lose eight out of ten! I have a list here, Your Majesty, which I hesitate to present. I pray that in your benevolence, Sire, you will make a suitable disposition."

"We shall honor the graves of those who died for the throne. Their contribution shall not be forgotten."

Song Jiang again bowed and submitted his petition. It read:

Vanguard General and Commander-in-Chief of the Pacification of the South Song Jiang and others respectfully report: Though ignorant and crude and having committed heinous crimes, we have been the recipients of Your Majesty's kindness, for which we can never repay though our bones be ground to powder and our bodies pulverized. We and our brothers, on leaving the Marsh, have done our utmost to eradicate evil. Of one mind, we vowed fraternity on Mount Wutai, and have been defending our country and protecting the people with full loyalty ever since. In Youzhou we defeated the Liao Tartars, near the cavern in Clear Stream we captured Fang La.

In making these modest contributions, we have lost many excellent commanders. For this we grieve night and day. We pray Your Majesty will consider the matter and bestow your benevolence on those who have died and your protection on those who still live.

Our only wish is to return to the countryside and till the land. We beseech you, Sire, to allow us to retire. Earnest and trembling, we await Your Majesty's decision with bowed heads. The following is a list of our commanders...

The itemization showed that fifty-nine had been killed in battle, ten died of illness, one expired in a religious trance, one was crippled and became a monk at Six Harmonies Monastery, another was a Taoist who returned to Qizhou, four had gone off on their own, five had remained in or returned to the capital, and twenty-seven now presented themselves before the throne. The petition was signed by Vanguard General Song Jiang and Vice-Vanguard General Lu Junyi.

"One hundred and eight of you, all stars in the firmament," the emperor sighed, "and only twenty-seven left after another four departed! You literally have lost eight out of ten!"

He bestowed posthumous titles on those who had died. If they had surviving sons, he called them to the capital and gave them official posts. If they had none, he had temples built where sacrifices might be dedicated to their memories. Because Zhang Shun's spirit had performed deeds of conspicuous value, it was named a Golden Glory General. Sagacious Lu, for having captured Fang La and transcending from life in a trance, was named the Chivalrous Illustrious Reverend. Wu Song was made abbot of the Six Harmonies Monastery, where he lived out his days. Ten Feet of Steel and Mother Sun, who had died in battle, were also given honorific posthumous tides.

The ten senior chieftains present at the imperial ceremony were made prefects or prefectural or district military commanders. The fifteen lieutenant chieftains were given command of various army units. All were to await formal certification by the appropriate departments. Mistress Gu was appointed magistrate of Dongyuan County.

Song Jiang was entitled Marshal of Military Virtue and made governor of Chuzhou Prefecture and commander of its armed forces.

Lu Junyi was entitled Marshal of Military Contribution and made governor of Luzhou Prefecture and deputy commander of its armed forces.

His Majesty also presented the fifteen lieutenant chieftains with three hundred ounces of gold and silver and five sets of silken clothing each. For each of the ten senior chieftains the gift was five hundred ounces of gold and silver and eight sets of the silken clothing. Song Jiang and Lu Junyi were each awarded one thousand ounces of gold and silver, ten sets of silken clothing, an imperial court robe, and a fine horse.

All thanked the sovereign.

The spirit of the Black Dragon Prince had twice manifested itself in Muzhou, defended the country and the people, and enabled the army to win complete victory. The emperor bestowed on the Black Prince a long and magniloquent title. He also changed the names of Muzhou to Yanzhou, and Shezhou to Huizhou, because these had been seats of Fang La's rebellion.

Clear Stream County became, for the same reason, Chunan County, and Bangyuan Cavern was split away from the rest of the peninsula to form an island in the river. The prefect of Muzhou was directed to use money from his treasury to erect a temple for the Black Dragon Prince, and the emperor personally sent a name plaque. The building still stands to this day.

South of the Yangzi Fang La's depredations had been severe. His Majesty exempted the people there from all taxes and labor levies for the next three years.

Each of the chieftains thanked the monarch. He invited them to an imperial feast to celebrate the peace and to congratulate them on their achievements. Civil and military officials of the highest rank entered the banquet hall. When it was over, Song Jiang addressed the sovereign.

"Since receiving the amnesty in Liangshan Marsh, we've lost more than half our troops. Some wish to return home. We pray, Sire, that you exercise your benevolence."

The emperor decreed as follows: Those who wished to remain in the army would be given a hundred strings of cash, ten bolts of silk and be assigned to either the Fierce Dragon or the Imposing Tiger Camp, where they would receive monthly stipends of money and grain. Those who wished to leave would be given two hundred strings of cash, ten bolts of silk, and be permitted to return home and be civilians again.

"I was born in Yuncheng County," said Song Jiang, "but since committing my crimes I have not dared to go back. Pray grant me permission, Sire, to sweep my family graves and visit my relatives and neighbors. I will then go to Chuzhou and assume office."

Very pleased, the monarch presented him with ten thousand strings of cash for maintaining his ancestral manor. Song Jiang and the chieftains, again expressing their gratitude, took leave of the sovereign and withdrew.

The next day the Council of Administration gave a banquet to celebrate peace, to which all the chieftains were invited. The day after, the Council of Military Affairs did the same. Governor Zhang, Deputy District Commander Liu, Chancellor Tong, staff officers Cong and Geng, and Generals Wang and Zhao were all raised in rank. But that is not part of our story.

On the recommendation of the Military Procurate, and in accordance with an imperial decree, Fang La was sliced to bits and beheaded in a public square of the Eastern Capital, and the remains placed on display for three days.

Song Jiang and his brother Song Qing left the capital with a company of one or two hundred soldiers who carried their chieftains' luggage and awards. The return to Shandong Province was without incident.

On reaching their native village in Yuncheng County, they were welcomed by neighbors and relations, but when they arrived at the manor they found that their lather, the old squire, had died, and that he was still lying in his coffin. The two brothers wept heartbrokenly. They were deeply grieved. Family and vassals offered condolences.

The old squire had kept the manor's farm and property in excellent condition. Song Jiang was able to concentrate on making funeral arrangements. He hired monks and priests to offer prayers for his departed parents and ancestors. Officials from county and prefecture called without cease.

A propitious day was chosen and, with the brothers serving as pallbearers, the squire's body was carried to a high plateau and laid to rest. Prefectural officials, neighbors and elders, friends and family, all attended. Of that we'll say no more.

Song Jiang thought of the Mystic Queen of Ninth Heaven, and recalled that he had not yet shown his gratitude. He paid artisans fifty thousand strings of cash to build her a temple. Soon it was completed —with two covered walks, a mountain gate, a statue of the Mystic Queen, and painted decorations.

Afraid that if he stayed too long in the countryside the emperor would reproach him, Song Jiang selected a date for the removal of his mourning vestments and again had several days of prayer services conducted. Then he gave a farewell feast for neighbors and village elders. The following day his relations gave him a banquet to congratulate him and demonstrate their affection. Of that we'll say no more.

Song Jiang entrusted the affairs of the manor to his brother. Although Song Qing had also been made an official, Song Jiang instructed him to remain at home, attend to the farm, and maintain the family shrine. What money he still had with him he distributed among the people.

But to put idle chatter aside, after several months at home Song Jiang left his native village and returned to the Eastern Capital. Many of his brother chieftains had fetched their families and settled down. Some had already assumed office. Families of those who had died for the throne went back to their villages with the bonuses the emperor had bestowed upon them.

Song Jiang gradually dispersed his army. Soon the families of the slain had all departed. Those appointed to office bid farewell to the various ministers and left to take up their duties.

Dai Zong the Marvellous Traveller came to see Song Jiang. As they sat and chatted, Dai told him something.

And as a result Song Jiang the hero of Yuncheng County became the ghost of Liao Er Flats. His name was recorded in history for thousands of years, his deeds were inscribed for centuries.

Truly, his splendid spirit pervaded his temple, and his picture was hung in the Imperial Hall of Fame.

What were the words which Dai Zong spoke to Song Jiang? Read our next chapter if you would know.

CHAPTER 100

SONG JIANG'S GHOST HAUNTS LIAO ER FLATS

EMPEROR HUI ZONG DREAMS OF LIANGSHAN MARSH

Dai Zong rose and said to Song Jiang: "The emperor in his benevolence has appointed me prefect of Yanzhou. Today I intend to submit my resignation and leave for the Sacred Mountain Temple in Tai'an Prefecture where I shall become a Taoist priest and live out my life in tranquility."

"Why do you take this course of action, brother?"

"I had a dream that the Summoner to the Nether World was calling me. So I made up my mind."

"You have that marvellous ability to travel quickly, brother. You'll surely become a spirit of the district after you die."

They parted. Dai Zong resigned his post, went to the Sacred Mountain Temple, and became a Taoist priest. Every day he burned incense and diligently prayed for the Emperor of Heaven. Though he was not ill, several months later he bid farewell to his fellow priests and died, smiling cheerfully. His spirit appeared in the temple frequently after that. Worshippers set up a statue of him in the temple, using his original skeleton as the framework.

Ruan the Seventh, when he received his appointment, took leave of Song Jiang and assumed office as commandant of the Gaitian Military District. In the next few months, Generals Wang Bing and Zhao Tang, remembering how he had insulted them at Bangyuan Cavern, frequently complained about him to Chancellor of Military Affairs Tong.

"He put on Fang La's royal garments and jade girdle. Though it was only a joke at the time, it's still on his mind," they said. They wanted to have him killed. "That Gaitian Military District is a secluded place, and the people there are savage," they said. "He's sure raise a rebellion."

Tong told Premier Cai Jing, who reported to the emperor and requested an order canceling Ruan the Seventh's appointment and reducing him to ordinary civilian status.

No one was more pleased than Ruan when the decree was issued. He returned with his old mother to Stone Tablet Village in Liangshan Marsh and became a fisherman again. Ruan supported the old lady for the rest of her days. He himself later died at the age of sixty.

Chai Jin the Small Whirlwind, in the capital, noted that Dai Zong had resigned his post and become a priest. He learned, too, that the imperial court had removed Ruan the Seventh from office and reduced him to an ordinary citizen on the theory that because he had worn Fang La's royal vestments he probably wanted to rebel.

"I was a duke consort under Fang La," Chai Jin said to himself. "If those evil ministers find out and slander me before the emperor, won't I be dismissed and humiliated also? It would be better if I took the initiative and saved myself the trouble."

Claiming that he could not function efficiently because of recurring bouts of rheumatism, he asked to resign and return to his farms. Permission was granted. He bid farewell to the officials and went back to his estate in Henghai District, Cangzhou Prefecture, where he lived a life of ease. One day, though in perfect health, he suddenly passed away.

Li Ying served as commandant of Zhongshan District for half a year, when he heard of Chai Jin's retirement. He too claimed inability to serve due to rheumatism. He resigned and returned to his village of Lone Dragon Mountain. Later he joined up with Du Xiang, and they became rich. Both came to a good end.

Guan Sheng, commandant of the Darning garrison in the Northern Capital, won the respect of his troops and the local populace. One day, returning drunk from military maneuvers, he fell from his horse and took ill and died.

Huyan Zhuo, who had been appointed a commander of the Imperial Guards, drilled his men every day. In later years he led an army against the Fourth Prince of the Golden Tartars. He was killed in battle west of the Huai River.

Zhu Tong performed well as commandant of the garrison at Baoding. Later he fought under General Liu Guangshi against the Golden Tartars, and ended his days as governor of the Taiping Military District.

Hua Rong assumed office as prefect of Yingtian, where he went with his wife and younger sister. Wu Yong, who was unmarried, took charge in the Wusheng Military District, where he arrived accompanied only by a boy servant. Li Kui, also unmarried, had just two servants with him when he assumed office in Runzhou Prefecture.

Why do we tell of these latter three only up until the time they commenced their official duties, but reveal the final fate of the previously mentioned seven? That is because the seven do not appear again in our story. As to the other five senior chieftains—Song Jiang, Lu Junyi, Wu Yong, Hua Rong and Li Kui—we shall be hearing more of them.

Regarding the fifteen lieutenant chieftains, aside from Song Qing who was already at home, Du Xing also returned to the countryside to join Li Ying. Huang Xin assumed office in Qingzhou. Sun Li, with his brother Sun Xin and sister-in-law Mistress Gu, plus his own wife and children, resumed their former jobs in Dengzhou. Zou Run had no desire to become an official and went back to the Mountain in the Clouds.

Cai Qing returned with Guan Sheng to the Northern Capital as an ordinary citizen. Pei Xuan and Yang Lin, after talking it over, returned to Horse Watering Valley and retired. Jiang Jing, missing his old home, went back to Tanzhou as a plain civilian. Zhu Wu had been learning Taoist lore from Fan Rui for some time and, like him, became a Taoist priest. Together, they roamed the land, finally joining the temple of Gongsun Sheng, where they lived out their days.

Mu Chun returned to civilian life in Jieyang Town. Ling Zhen the remarkable cannoneer was appointed to the Imperial Explosives Bureau. Doctor An Daoquan became a senior physician in the capital's Imperial Hospital. Huangfu Duan was given charge of the Imperial Stables. Jin Dajian was already an official of the Imperial Treasury. Xiao Rang was named tutor in the Residence of Premier Cai. Yue Ho remained in the palace of Prince Consort Wang, where he lived out his days in ease and contentment. Of these we'll say no more.

Song Jiang and Lu Junyi, after parting, left to take up their respective posts. Lu Junyi, who had no family, proceeded to Luzhou accompanied by a few travelling companions. Song Jiang bid farewell to the emperor and his ministers and departed for Chuzhou with several family servants.

From then on, each of the chieftains went his separate way. We'll say no more of that either.

When Tai Zong succeeded Tai Zu the first Song emperor he proclaimed his aims, but in the end he couldn't see through the deception being practiced upon him. Hui Zong the present sovereign was clairvoyant and wise, but corrupt ministers managed to gain control under him as well, to the detriment of the virtuous and loyal. It was a great pity. Cai Jing, Tong Guan, Gao Qiu and Yang Jian created wide confusion and harmed the country and the people sorely.

The high honors and substantial rewards given to Song Jiang and his chieftains profoundly disturbed Marshals Gao and Yang. They conferred about it.

"Song Jiang and Lu Junyi are our enemies," said Gao. "Now they've been made high officials and honored by the imperial court. Swinging into the saddle they command armies, dismounting they rule the population. We ministers have become a laughing stock! We must remember the old saying: 'Gentlemen scorn the timid, heroes must be ruthless.'"

"I have a plan," said Yang. "We'll get rid of Lu Junyi first. It will be like cutting off Song's right arm. The man's tremendously brave. If we dealt with Song first and Lu found out he'd surely turn on us and create a very bad situation."

"Let's hear your plan."

"Have a couple of Luzhou military men complain to the ministry that Lu is raising an army and storing up grain and fodder with the intent to revolt. We'll take them to the premier and they'll ask him to report this to the emperor. Premier Cai will carry through the deception and request the emperor to invite Lu to the palace. When His Majesty entertains him at an imperial feast, we'll slip some mercury into his food. It will lodge in his kidneys and he'll be incapacitated. He won't be able to do anything of any importance. Then we can send an emissary to Song Jiang with imperial wine in which we'll have put a slow-working poison. In half a month he'll be beyond saving."

"An excellent idea," said Gao. The two wicked ministers dispatched a confidant to fetch two local men from Luzhou. They wrote out a complaint for them and sent them to the Council of Military Affairs. The complaint alleged that Lu

Junyi was raising an army in Luzhou and storing fodder and grain in preparation for a revolt, also that he was in constant touch with Song Jiang in Chuzhou and kept him informed of his scheme.

Tong Guan the Chancellor of Military Affairs also hated Song Jiang. He accepted the complaint and relayed it to the office of the premier. Cai read it and summoned the others to a conference. Gao and Yang proposed that the accusers be brought directly before the emperor. This was done.

"When Song Jiang and Lu Junyi smashed the Liao Tartars, and later when they captured Fang La, they had hundreds of thousands of soldiers under their command, yet they showed no indication of wicked ideas," said the sovereign. "Now that they have taken the path of virtue, would they leave it and return evil for good, revolt even? I have never wronged them. Why should they rebel against the throne? There's something fishy here. I don't believe it."

"Your Majesty talks of loyal love," said Gao and Yang. "But a man's heart is hard to fathom. Lu Junyi probably considers his rank too low. He's not satisfied and wants to rebel. Fortunately, people have discovered it."

"I shall call him before me and get at the facts personally."

Cai and Tong had a suggestion. "Lu Junyi is a wild beast. He's difficult to control," they said. "If he's startled he'll become suspicious. That will make things very awkward. It won't be easy to catch him. Why not invite him to dine, Sire? In the course of conversation Your Majesty can feel out his real intentions. If there's nothing to it, we can forget the whole thing. He'll think inviting him is just a sign that Your Majesty doesn't forget his meritorious officials."

The emperor agreed. He sent an emissary with a summons to Lu Junyi to appear at the imperial court for an assignment. When the emissary arrived at Luzhou, officials came out of the city to greet him. They escorted him to the prefectural office, where he read the document.

To skip the petty details, Lu immediately rode back to the capital with the emissary. He rested in quarters outside the palace. Early the next morning, he waited at the East Glory Gate for the imperial audience to commence. Premier Cai Jing, Chancellor of Military Affairs Tong Guan, Marshals Gao Qiu and Yang Jian escorted Lu Junyi before the monarch. When obeisances were completed, the sovereign spoke.

"I wished to see you again. Are you comfortable in Luzhou?"

"Thanks to Your Majesty's fortunate emanations, the army and populace are all peaceful."

The emperor chatted with Lu until nearly noon. The Master of the Imperial Chefs announced that lunch for the traveller was ready if the monarch wished him to dine. Gao and Yang had already placed mercury in the food which was set upon the table. The emperor directed the Chef Master to serve Lu Junyi. Lu bowed to the sovereign and ate.

"You must look after our troops in Luzhou well," the emperor admonished. "We don't want anything to happen."

Lu Junyi respectfully expressed his thanks and left for Luzhou. He had no inkling of what the four wicked ministers were plotting.

"We'll soon see important results," Gao and Yang exulted.

Starting the return trip, Lu felt a pain in his back and a general weakness. He couldn't ride a horse, so he took a boat. After several days on the Huai River, they reached Sizhou Prefecture. There, something happened. Lu had been drinking that night, and he insisted on standing on the prow. By then the mercury had seeped not only into his kidneys but into his bones as well. He was unable to stand firmly, and his drunkenness made him stumble. Lu fell into the Huai River and drowned.

Poor Jade Unicorn of Hebei, to become a wronged ghost in the watery kingdom! His body was fished out, encoffined in Sizhou, and buried on high ground. The local officials wrote a report to the imperial ministries.

When the four plotters received the news, they reported to the emperor: "Sizhou notifies us that Lu Junyi fell into the Huai and drowned. Song Jiang is sure to become suspicious. He may start something. We suggest Your Majesty send an emissary with imperial wine as a mark of sympathy and calm him down."

The monarch thought for some time. If he didn't agree, he wasn't sure what Song Jiang's reaction would be. Yet if he did agree, he had a feeling Song Jiang might be harmed. But he could see no other alternative. In the end he let himself be persuaded by the lies and deceptions of the four wicked ministers. He directed an emissary to take two bottles of imperial wine to Chuzhou.

It happened that the man was a trusted crony of Gao and Yang. Fate had determined the day when Song Jiang must die, but who would have thought that the four would be the instrument of his demise! They put a slow-working poison in the wine and directed the emissary to go directly to Chuzhou and deliver it.

After Song Jiang assumed the governorship of Chuzhou and command of the local troops, he was solicitous of the welfare of both the soldiers and the people. The populace loved him like a parent, the troops adored him. He was lenient in his judgments, wise in his administration. The people willingly obeyed him, he had the respect of all.

He enjoyed walking outside the city's South Gate, where there was an area called Liao Er Flats. It was laced with waterways and in the center was a tall beautiful mountain thickly covered with pine and cypress. Its scenic loveliness reminded him of Mount Liangshan and its surrounding marsh. Though smaller, it had the same peaks and winding paths, the same swelling heights like crouching dragons and tigers, the same abrupt cliffs, stairways and terraces, the same streams everywhere, and lakes front and rear.

The place gave him much pleasure, and he said to himself: "When I die, this is where I'd like to be buried." Whenever he was free, it was here he wandered, happy and relaxed.

During the first ten days of summer in the sixth year of Xuan Ho, half a year after he took office, Song Jiang heard that an emissary had arrived from the capital with imperial wine. Accompanied by other officials, he went out of the city to welcome him and escort him in. In the public hall the emissary read the emperor's greeting, presented the wine and urged Song Jiang to drink. When Song Jiang requested the emissary to join him, the man refused, saying he was a teetotaler. Song Jiang ceremoniously drank and the emissary returned to the capital. He would not accept the gift which Song Jiang offered.

Song Jiang's stomach began to pain him soon after, and he suspected something had been added to the wine. He quickly made inquires and learned the emissary had in fact done some drinking while stopping at a hostel for officials along the road. Song Jiang realized he had been tricked. He was positive the wine had been poisoned by the evil ministers. He sighed.

"Since childhood I studied Confucianism, and when I grew up I learned how to be a minor official. Unfortunately I became involved in crime, but I never had the slightest desire to rebel. Now the emperor listens to deceitful ministers and sends me poisoned wine! What have I done to deserve this! It doesn't matter if I die, but Li Kui, who is today the commandant of Runzhou, will certainly take to the hills again when he hears about this dirty trick the imperial court has played. That will ruin the reputation of loyalty to the emperor I have sought so diligently all my life! There's only one thing I can do."

He dispatched a man that same night to Runzhou with a message to Li Kui to come to Chuzhou immediately.

Black Whirlwind Li Kui was morose and depressed ever since becoming commandant of Runzhou. All day long he drank with his companions. That was the only thing he enjoyed. When he received the message from Song Jiang he said to himself: "Big Brother has sent for me. It must be important." He embarked by boat at once with an aide. On reaching Chuzhou he went directly to Song Jiang in the prefecture.

"From the time we broke up I've done nothing but think of you brothers," said Song. "Wu Yong is in the far-off Wusheng Military District. Hua Rong is in Yingtian, but I haven't had any news of him. Only you, brother, are relatively near. So I've asked you to come and discuss a very serious matter."

"What is it, Big Brother?"

"First have some wine."

Song Jiang escorted Black Whirlwind into a rear hall, where wine and a goblet was waiting. Li Kui drank for some time until he was half intoxicated.

"I must tell you, brother," said Song. "I hear the imperial court is sending me poisoned wine. If I die what will you do?"

"Rebel, brother," Li Kui shouted. "Let's rebel!"

"Our army is gone, our brothers are scattered. How can we rebel?"

"I've got three thousand men in Zhenjiang, you have soldiers here in Chuzhou. We'll muster them, and as many of the local people we can get to join us, raise more troops, buy horses, and fight! We'll be happy back in Liangshan

Marsh. At least we won't have to take any more crap from those rascally ministers!"

"Slowly, brother. We must talk this over."

Black Whirlwind of course didn't know that the wine he imbibed contained a slow poison. That night he drank more. The next day Song Jiang saw him off to his boat.

"When will you start your revolt, brother?" Li Kui asked. "I'll come with my troops and reinforce you."

"Brother, don't blame me!" said Song Jiang. "The emperor sent me some poisoned wine the other day, and I drank it. I'm going to die soon. All my life I've tried to adhere to two principles—loyalty and righteousness. I would never practice deceit. Now, though I am innocent, the imperial court is causing my death. But I'd rather the emperor wronged me than wrong the emperor.

"I was afraid that after I died you would rebel and spoil our reputation for loyalty and righteousness, earned while acting in Heaven's behalf in Liangshan Marsh. And so I asked you here and gave you the poisoned wine also. When you return to Runzhou you'll surely die.

"After you've expired, come to Liao Er Flats, outside Chuzhou's South Gate. It's a beautiful place, and looks just like Liangshan Marsh. Our spirits can meet there. That's where I'm going to be buried after I die. I've already decided!" As he spoke, Song Jiang's tears fell like rain.

Li Kui also wept. "Enough, enough, enough!" he cried. "I took care of you in life, Big Brother, and I'll be a minor ghost and serve you after death as well!"

His body felt heavy. Weeping, he bid Song Jiang farewell and boarded his craft. When he reached Runzhou, sure enough, the poison activated.

As Black Whirlwind lay dying, he instructed his attendants: "After I'm gone you absolutely must take my coffin to Liao Er Flats outside Chuzhou's South Gate and bury me beside Big Brother." Later, his orders were carried out.

Song Jiang felt very badly when Li Kui sailed away that day. He thought of Wu Yong and Hua Rong, and sorrowed that he'd never see them again. The poison began to work during the night. On his deathbed he said to his trusted followers: "You must fulfil my request. Bury me on high ground above Liao Er Flats. Your virtuous conduct will certainly be rewarded. Promise that you will." So saying, he died.

His followers prepared to bury him in Chuzhou, according to ceremony. The prefectural officials, informed of his request, agreed to honor it. Together with his intimates, functionaries young and old carried his coffin to a place above Liao Er Flats and buried him there. A few days later, the coffin of Li Kui was brought from Runzhou. His associates kept their word and interred him next to Song Jiang.

Song Qing was ill at home. A member of the family returning from Chuzhou informed him that his brother Song Jiang had passed away there. Qing was too sick to attend the funeral, but he sent a family member to conduct a sacrificial ceremony at Liao Er Flats and arrange for the grave to be kept in order.

As for Wu Yong, he was not happy either after assuming office. He thought constantly of the affection between Song Jiang and himself. Suddenly, one day he felt very depressed and uneasy. That night Song Jiang and Li Kui came to him in a dream and tugged at his clothes.

"We always put loyalty and righteousness above all, acting on Heaven's behalf and never wronging the emperor," they said. "But the imperial court sent us poisoned wine and, though blameless, we died. We're buried in Liao Er Flats outside Chuzhou's South Gate. If you still remember the old days come and visit our graves."

Wu Yong was about to ask questions when he suddenly awakened. It had been only a dream. But his tears fell like rain, and he sat up in bed until daylight.

The next day he packed some belongings and hurried, alone, to Chuzhou. When he got there he learned that Song Jiang indeed was dead. There wasn't a person he spoke to who didn't sigh. He went to Liao Er Hats, swept the graves, and sacrificed to the spirits of Song Jiang and Li Kui. Beating his hand on Song Jiang's grave mound, he wept.

"Your spirit is not yet gone, brother, hear what I say! I was a village school teacher. First I followed Chao Gai, then I met you, brother, and you saved my life. We shared honors together for several decades, all thanks to your virtue. Now you have died for our country and appeared to me in a dream. I still haven't repaid your kindness, brother. I shall be glad to take the dream as an omen and join you in the Nether World."

Wu Yong wept bitterly. He decided to hang himself. Just then Hua Rong, who had arrived in Chuzhou by boat, came rushing to the grave. He was startled to see Wu Yong.

"I thought you were an official in Yingtian," said Wu Yong. "How did you hear about Big Brother's demise?"

"Ever since we broke up I've never felt easy in my mind. I kept thinking of all of our brothers. The other night Song Jiang and Li Kui came to me in a dream and said they had been killed by poisoned imperial wine and were buried above Liao Er Flats. They said if I hadn't forgotten the old days I must visit their graves. I dropped everything and travelled day and night to get here."

"I had the same dream and came for the same reason. Nothing could be better than our meeting here today. I've been thinking—I can never repay brother Song Jiang for all he's done for me, and I can't bear to part with him. I'm going to hang myself here so that our spirits can be together, and as a demonstration of my loyal and righteous heart."

"Since that's how you feel, General, I'll join you," said Hua Rong, "and show my devotion to Big Brother as well."

"I was hoping that after my death you'd bury me here," said Wu Yong. "How is it that you want to do the same thing?"

"I hate to part with Big Brother, and I can't forget his kindness. In Liangshan Marsh we were major criminals, but luckily we survived. We fought in battle after battle as bold gallants together. Then the emperor amnestied us, and we marched on expeditions north and south, distinguishing ourselves by our valor. Today, we're known throughout the land. But the imperial court suspects us. They're bound to be watching us for 'offenses.' If they trump up charges and have us executed, regrets will be too late. I'd rather go with you to the Nether World. I will at least leave a clean name and my body will be given proper burial."

"Listen to me, brother, I'm alone, without any dependants. It doesn't matter if I die. But you have a young son and a sweet wife. What will they do?"

"There won't be any problem. I've left them a bit, enough to feed themselves. Besides, my wife's family will look after them."

The two men wept together, then hung themselves from a tree.

On Hua Rong's boat his attendants became concerned when, after a long time, their master failed to return. They went to the graves and found him and Wu Yong dead. Hastily, they reported to the local officials, obtained coffins, and buried the two beside Song Jiang's grave. The burial mounds were like four hills.

Moved by Song Jiang's virtue and righteous loyalty, the people of Chuzhou erected a shrine to his memory. They offered sacrifices the year round, and none of their prayers were unanswered.

Meanwhile in the Eastern Capital, the Taoist Sovereign had been uneasy ever since sending Song Jiang the imperial wine. Though he had no news, he thought of him frequently. But Gao Qiu and Yang Jian constantly diverted him with talk of pleasurable pursuits. They wanted only to block off the righteous and injure the loyal.

Then, one day, while amusing himself in the palace, the monarch suddenly recalled his mistress Shishi. Accompanied by two young eunuchs, he went through the tunnel to her rear garden and pulled the bell cord.

The girl hurried out and received him. She led him to the bedroom and asked him to be seated. The emperor ordered that all the gates, front and rear, be bolted. The girl adorned herself formally and proffered respectful obeisances.

"I've been slightly unwell lately," said the sovereign, "but Dr. An Daoquan has cured me. It's been months since we've met, beloved, but you've been always on my mind.. Seeing you again makes me very happy."

"I'm unworthy of your affection, Sire." The girl laid out wine and delicacies for the ruler's delectation.

After only a few cups, he felt very sleepy. The lamps flickered and a chill breeze blew through the room. He saw standing before him a figure in a yellow robe.

"Who are you?" asked the startled monarch. "Why are you here?"

"I am Dai Zong the Marvellous Traveller, a lieutenant of Song Jiang of Liangshan Marsh."

"What brings you to this place?"

"Brother Song Jiang is nearby. He requests that Your Majesty come with me."

"Where do you wish to take me?"

"To a place that's pure and fair. Please come, Sire."

The emperor rose and walked with Dai Zong to the rear garden. A horse stood waiting. The monarch mounted and they were off. Travelling through cloud and mist, he could hear the sound of wind and rain. At last they arrived.

All around were misty waters and cloud-obscured heights. Neither the sun nor moon could be seen, the sky and water were of one color. Liao Er Flats was a riot of red smartweed and green reed leaves. Waterfowl gambolled on stony beaches, mandarin ducks and drakes rested in pairs beside ponds of lotus. On the wooded slopes frost had turned the leaves to ten thousand scales of a fiery dragon, dew on the dykes glistened like the golden eyes of countless savage beasts. Gradually, a pale moon and a few scattered stars appeared in the night sky. It was autumn, and the breeze was chill and the dew icy.

The emperor couldn't gaze enough at the beautiful scene. "What is this place?" he queried. "Where are you taking me?"

Dai Zong pointed to a pass on the top of a mountain. "You'll soon know, Sire. There's where we go."

They climbed the slope, passing through three fortified passes. Before the third, more than a hundred men prostrated themselves by the roadside. All were armed, and wore helmets and armor of gold. The monarch was astonished.

"Who are these people?"

The first of them, plumes flying from his golden helmet, stepped forward and said: "I am Song Jiang of Liangshan Marsh."

"I appointed you governor of Chuzhou. What are you doing here?"

"Please come to Loyalty Hall, Your Majesty, and I will tell you all about my wrongful demise."

At the hall the emperor got down from his horse, entered the building and was seated. He saw many people kowtowing in the mist outside.

The monarch couldn't understand. Song Jiang mounted the steps and knelt, tears streaming down his face.

"Why do you weep?" asked the sovereign.

"Although I at one time fought against the imperial troops, I was always loyal to Your Majesty and never had a seditious thought. After the amnesty, I drove back the Liao Tartars in the north and captured Fang La in the south, at the cost of eight out of ten of my brothers, who were like my arms and legs. In keeping with your decree, Sire, I took office in Chuzhou. I never squeezed a penny from the army or the people. Heaven and Earth knew the purity of my heart. Your Majesty sent me poisoned wine and I drank it. I died with no regrets."

"But I was afraid Li Kui would be angry, and rebel. So I summoned him from Runzhou and killed him with the poisoned wine. Wu Yong and Hua Rong visited my grave and hung themselves out of chivalry. We four are buried above

Liao Er Flats outside of Chuzhou's South Gate. Pitying us, the villagers have built a shrine there. But although we are dead, our souls will not depart. We have remained to inform Your Majesty of our unwavering fidelity and to beg you to determine the justice of the matter."

The monarch was amazed. "I sent an emissary with sealed imperial vintage. Who could have substituted poisoned wine?"

"Ask your emissary. Then you'll know which treacherous scoundrels were behind it!"

Gazing around at the magnificent citadel and its three fortified passes, the emperor was impressed. "What is this place?"

"Liangshan Marsh, Sire, where we dwelt in the old days."

"Although you have passed on, you will be reincarnated as men again. Why do you congregate here?"

"The Jade Emperor of Heaven, moved by my righteous loyalty, designated me Deity of Liangshan Marsh. Since this is my domain, my chieftains have joined me. We sent Dai Zong, the Marvellous Traveller to bring you, Emperor of Ten Thousand Carriages, to our marsh, so that we might state our grievances and assure you personally of our devotion."

"But why didn't you appear to me in my inner palace?"

"I am a spirit of the Nether World. How could I appear amid imperial splendor? Today you left your palace, so we were able to invite you."

"I've been sitting a long time. Is it possible for me to look around?"

Song Jiang bowed and conducted him from the building. The sovereign noted the plaque above the entrance. It read, in large letters, *Loyalty Hall.* He nodded and descended the steps. Suddenly, from behind Song Jiang, Li Kui appeared, battle-axes in hand.

"Emperor, emperor!" he cried in a terrible voice. "How could you believe your four deceitful ministers and wrongfully destroy us? Today we've met and I can take vengeance!" Brandishing his axes, he rushed at the monarch.

Startled, the sovereign awoke. It had all been a dream. He was drenched in perspiration. Shishi was sitting alone in the lamplight.

"Where was I just now?" he asked.

"Why, you've been lying on the bed, Sire."

He told her of his strange dream, and she said: "The righteous become saints when they expire. Can it be that Song Jiang really has died and appeared to you in a dream?"

"I'll certainly inquire about this. If it's true, I'll have a temple built in his memory and give him a posthumous title."

"A good idea. It will show that Your Majesty does not forget your meritorious officials."

The emperor sighed much that night.

The next morning he summoned his ministers to the palace. Cai Jing, Tong Guan, Gao Qiu and Yang Jian, afraid he would question them about Song Jiang, left the moment the imperial court was concluded. Only Marshal Su and a few other high officials remained waiting for an audience.

"Have you any news of Song Jiang, Governor of Chuzhou?" the sovereign asked Su.

"No news, Sire, but last night I had a peculiar dream."

"Tell me about it."

"I dreamt that Song Jiang came to my home dressed in his usual armor and helmet. He said he had died from poisoned wine Your Majesty had sent him. Sympathizing with his righteous loyalty, the people of Chuzhou buried him above Liao Er Flats outside the South Gate of the city and built a shrine where they sacrifice to him."

The emperor shook his head. "Very strange. I had the same dream." And he said to the marshal: "Send someone you trust to find out whether this is true, and report back to me immediately."

Su dispatched a man as directed.

The next day, the monarch sat in his Hall of Culture and Virtue. Gao Qiu and Yang Jian were present.

"Have your ministries any news of Song Jiang?" he asked them.

They dared not reply truthfully. Both said they did not know. Suspicious, the emperor had an uncomfortable feeling.

Marshal Su's man returned from Chuzhou. He said that Song Jiang had died of drinking poisoned imperial wine, that the people, respecting his loyalty to the emperor, had buried him on high ground above Liao Er Flats. Moreover, Wu Yong, Hua Rong and Li Kui were interred there with him. Local citizens, out of pity, had built a shrine to his memory. They sincerely worshipped there, and their prayers were always answered.

Su hastily led his emissary before the emperor in the palace. The man repeated his story. The sovereign was stricken with grief.

At his imperial court the next day he was very angry. He berated Gao and Yang in the presence of all his officials.

"Traitorous liars, would you ruin my empire!"

Falling to their knees the two kowtowed and begged forgiveness. Cai and Tong spoke up on their behalf.

"Life and death are pre-ordained. The ministries have received no official notification, so they dared not report. As a matter of fact, they didn't know. A document arrived from Chuzhou only last night. They were intending to report to you this morning, Sire. They were just waiting for you to ask."

Again the monarch was deceived by the four rogues, and their crimes were concealed. He shouted for Gao and Yang to withdraw, and directed that the emissary who delivered the wine be produced. But the fellow had unexpectedly died on the return trip from Chuzhou.

The next day Marshal Su called on the sovereign and related how Song Jiang had become a saint, and how efficaciously he responded to the prayers of the people. The emperor ordered that Song Qing carry on his brother's rank and office. But the younger man was suffering from rheumatism and could not assume the duties. He sent a reply of thanks and regrets, saying he wanted only to remain in Yuncheng and farm the family estate.

Sympathizing with Qing's filial sentiments, the sovereign made him a gift of a hundred thousand strings of cash and three thousand *mu* of land. He decreed that if Qing had a son he would be given an official post. In subsequent years Qing's son Song Anping, after qualifying in the imperial examinations, was appointed a secretary scholar. But that was later.

At Marshal Su's request, the emperor conferred on Song Jiang the posthumous title of Loyal, Chivalrous and Efficacious Duke, and authorized funds for the construction of a temple dedicated to his memory in Liangshan Marsh. In the main building, statues were placed of Song Jiang and the other chieftains who died for the empire. The monarch personally wrote the words for the name plaque—*Loyalty Temple*. On receipt of the imperial funds, Jizhou Prefecture immediately started construction.

Song Jiang's spirit appeared frequently in Liangshan Marsh, and the people sacrificed to him constantly. When they prayed for wind they got wind, when they prayed for rain they got rain.

He appeared too in Liao Er Flats. There the people also built a large temple, with two wings. They petitioned for and received an imperial donation. In the main hall they installed statues of the thirty-six senior chieftains. In the wings they put statues of their seventy-two lieutenants, plus figures of servants. People came from near and far to worship, and their prayers were always answered.

Those who defend their country and protect the people have incense burned to their memories for ten thousand years. Sacrifices are made to them for generation after generation. They bring to their worshippers security and peace. In response to prayers they bestow riches and prosperity.

Remains of these ancient sites still exist to this day.

CPSIA information can be obtained at www.ICGtesting.com
Printed in the USA
LVOW03s1600060814

397843LV00008B/200/A